LOVEJOY AT LARGE AGAIN:

An Omnibus

featuring

THE JUDAS PAIR
GOLD FROM GEMINI
THE GRAIL TREE

Jonathan Gash

ARROW

Published by Arrow Books Limited
20 Vauxhall Bridge Road, London SW1V 2SA

An imprint of Random House UK Limited

London Melbourne Sydney Auckland Johannesburg
and agencies throughout the world

This omnibus first published in 1993 by Arrow Books

© Jonathan Gash 1993

Incorporating
THE JUDAS PAIR
First published by William Collins (The Crime Club) 1977
Hamlyn Paperbacks edition 1980
Arrow edition 1986
© Jonathan Gash 1977

GOLD FROM GEMINI
First published by William Collins & Sons Ltd 1978
Hamlyn Paperbacks edition 1981
Arrow edition 1987
© Jonathan Gash 1978

THE GRAIL TREE
First published by William Collins (The Crime Club) 1979
Hamlyn Paperbacks edition 1981
Arrow edition 1986
© Jonathan Gash 1979

Printed and bound in Great Britain by
Cox & Wyman Ltd, Reading, Berkshire

ISBN 0 09 925451 4

Contents

THE JUDAS PAIR   7

GOLD FROM GEMINI   215

THE GRAIL TREE   405

THE
JUDAS PAIR

A Lovejoy Narrative

CHAPTER I

THIS STORY'S about greed, desire, love and death – in the world of antiques you get them all.

Just when I was in paradise the phone rang. Knowing it would be Tinker Dill I pushed her into the bathroom, turned all the taps on and switched the radio on.

'What the hell's that noise?' Tinker sounded half-sloshed as usual.

'You interrupted again, Tinker,' I said wearily.

'How am I to know you're on the nest?' he said, peeved.

In the White Hart they only had one record that worked and it was notching up the decibels in ι background muddle of voices.

'What is it?'

'Got somebody for you,' he said.

I was all ears. You know that tingling a sexy promise gives? Double it for religion. Treble it for collecting. And for antique dealers like me, hearing of a customer, multiply by infinity to get somewhere near the drive that forces a man over every conceivable boundary of propriety, common sense, reason – oh, and law. I almost forgot law. I'd been on the nest two days with Sheila (was she Sheila, or was that last Thursday? I couldn't remember) and here I was, quivering like a selling-plater at its first race. All because one of my scouts was phoning in with a bite.

Scouts? We call them barkers, in the trade. An antique dealer has scouts, people who will pass information his way. Tinker Dill was one of mine. I have three or four, depending on how rich I'm feeling at the time, paid on commission. Tinker was the best. Not because he was much good, but because he was loyal. And he was loyal because he judged every deal in terms of whisky. Or gin. Or rum.

'Buying or selling?' I said, quite casual. Twenty years

dealing in antiques and my hands sweating because a barker rings in. It's a right game.

'Buying.'

'Big or little?'

'Big.'

'You having me on, Tinker?' That stupid bird was banging on the bathroom door wanting to be let out.

'Straight up, Lovejoy,' he said. All right, all right. I was born with the name. Still, you can't forget Lovejoy Antiques, Inc., can you? The 'Inc.' bit was pure invention, brilliance. It sounds posh, reeks of dollars and high-flying American firms backing that knowledgeable antique wizard Lovejoy.

'Got enough copper in case the bleeps go?' I asked.

'Eh? Oh, sure.'

'Hang on, then.'

I dropped the receiver, crossed to open the bathroom door. There she was, trying to push past me into the room, blazing.

'What the hell do you mean – ?' she was starting to say when I belted her. Down she went on the loo amid the steam.

'Now,' I explained carefully. 'Silence. Si – lence. Got it, luv?'

She rubbed her face; her eyes glazed at the enormity of these events. I pinched her cheek, making the nails bite.

'I'm waiting. I said, Got it, luv?'

'Yes.' Her voice barely made it.

'I've got a deal coming in. So – shut your teeth. Sit there and listen to all my lovely hot water going to waste.'

I slammed the door on her, locked it again and found Tinker hanging on by the skin of his alcohol-soaked teeth.

'Big? How big?' I demanded.

'Well –'

'Come on.'

'S and four D's,' he said shakily.

My scalp, already prickling and crawling, gave up as the magic code homed in.

'Give over, Dill.'

'Honest, Lovejoy. God's truth.'

'In this day and age?'

'Large as life, Lovejoy. Look – this bloke's real. He's here now.'

'Where?'

'White Hart.'

My mind took off. Computers aren't in it. Speed they've got and memory too, so people say. I have both those attributes and a bell. This bell's in my chest. Put me within a hundred feet of a genuine antique and it chimes, only gently at first, then in a clamour as I get nearer the real thing. By the time I'm touching it I can hardly breathe because my bell's clanging like a fire-engine. It's never been wrong yet. Don't misunderstand – I've sold some rubbish in my time. And lies come as natural to me as blinking in a gale. After all, that's life, really, isn't it? A little half-truth here and there, with a faint hint of profit thrown in for good measure, does no harm. And I make a living, mainly from greed. Not my greed, you understand. *Your* greed, his greed, everybody's greed. And I want no criticism from self-righteous members of the indignant honest old public, because they're the biggest school of sharks on this planet. No? Listen : –

Say you're at home, relaxing in your old rocking-chair. In comes a stranger. He's heard of your old – or indeed your *new* – rocking-chair. Could it be, he gasps, that it's the one and only rocking-chair last used by Lord Nelson on his flagship the *Golden Hind*? Good heavens, he cries, clapping his eyes on it in ecstasy. *It is*!

Now, you put your pipe down, astonished. What the hell's going on? you demand. And who the hell is this stranger butting into your house? And what's he babbling about? And – *take your hands off my old rocking-chair!*

With me so far? Good.

The stranger, confronted with your indignation, turns sincere and trusting eyes to you. I've searched all my life, he explains. For what? you demand suspiciously. For Lord

Nelson's famous old rocking-chair, he confides. And here it is, at last. It's beautiful. My life-long search is over.

See what I'm getting at? At everybody's dishonesty. At mine. And at yours. No? *Yes!* Read on.

Now, if I were a trusting soul, I'd leave you to complete the story, give it a proper ending, so to speak. How you smile at the stranger, explain that the chair's only a second-hand mock-up your cousin Harry's lad did at night-school, and how in any case Nelson, who is pretty famous for rocking on the cradle of the deep for years on end, was the last bloke on earth ever to need a rocking-chair, and how you kindly proceed to put the misguided stranger right over a cup of tea with gay amusing chat. But you can't be trusted to end the story the way it really would happen! And why? Because the stranger, with the light of crusading fervour burning in his eyes, reaches for his wallet and says those glorious, magic words . . . *How much?*

Now what's the *real* ending of the story? I'll tell you. You leap off your – *no, Lord Nelson's!* – rocking-chair, brush it down, bring out the Australian sherry left over from Christmas, and cod on you're the hero's last living descendant. And you manage to stifle your poor little innocent daughter as she looks up from her history homework and tries to tell the visitor that Nelson missed sailing on the *Golden Hind* by a good couple of centuries, and send her packing to bed so she won't see her honest old dad shingling this stupid bum of every quid he can.

Convinced? No? *Then why are you thinking of that old chair in your attic?*

Everybody's got a special gift. Some are psychic, some have an extra dress sense, beauty, a musical talent or have green fingers. Some folk are just lucky, or have the knack of throwing a discus. But nobody's been missed out. We've all got one special gift. The only trouble is learning which it is we've got.

I had this pal who knew horses – they used to come to him even when he'd no sugar. He and I once collected a

Chippendale from near a training stables and we paused to watch these nags running about like they do. 'Quid on the big one,' I said, bored. 'The funny little chap,' he said, and blow me if it didn't leave the rest standing. It was called Arkle, a champion, they told us. See what I mean? To me that tiny, gawky, ungainly brute breathing all wrong was horrible. To my pal it was clearly the best of the lot. Now, to him, a Turner painting – screaming genius over every inch of canvas – would look like a nasty spillage. Not to me. I've only to see an 88 bus labelled 'Tate Gallery' and my bell goes like the clappers. Like I say, a gift.

Once, I bought this dirty old monstrosity for ten quid. It looked for all the world like a little doll's house with a couple of round windows stuck on, and a great sloping piece of broken tin fixed to the back. The boys at the auction gave me an ironic cheer making my face red as fire. But my bell was bonging. My find was eventually the only original Congreve clock ever to be exhibited within living memory – a clock worked on a spring controlled by a little ball rolling down a groove cut in an inclined plane, designed and made by the great inventor William Congreve almost two hundred years ago.

If you've got the courage, find out what your own particular knack is, then trust it. Obey your bells, folks. They're telling you about cold stone certainties.

Where was I?

Tinker Dill. S and four D's, and he'd sounded frantic. Ten thousand.

S and D's? Look in any antique shop. Casually, you'll find yourself wanting some lovely little trinket, say a twist-stem drinking glass. The more you look the more you want it. So you search it for the price, and find a little ticket tied on, marked HA/-, or some such.

We use codes, all very simple. One of the most element-ary is that based on a letter-number transposition. Each code has a key word – for example, SUTHERLAND. Note that it has ten letters. For S read 1, for U read 2, and so on to N, which is 9. For D read, not 10 but nought, because you already have a letter to denote 1. So the glass goblet you fancied is priced at forty-eight quid. There are several ten-letter codes. A quick look round tips you off.

One further point. X is often used to denote the pound sign, £, or zero. That way, the customer thinks the ticket is something mysterious to do with book-keeping or identification. Not on your life. When in doubt, it's money. The code-price marked is often what the dealer paid for the glass in the first place, so naturally he'll stick about fifty per cent on, if not more. And remember you may actually look a mug. In antiques you pay for appearances – yours, the antiques themselves, and the antique dealer's wife's fur coat. So my tip is : argue. Even though it goes against the grain in polite old Britain, never pay the marked price, not even if the dealer offers an immediate discount. Hum and ha, take your time, look doubtful. Spin it out and then, as gently and sincerely as you possibly can, barter.

Listen to me, giving away my next year's profit.

'Look, Tinker,' I said, not daring to believe him.

'I know what you're going to say, Lovejoy,' he said, desperate now.

'You do?'

'Trade's bad. Profits are bad. Finds are bad. Everything's bad.'

Like I said, some are psychic.

'Who's got ten thousand these days?' I snapped.

'It's right up your street, Lovejoy.'

'Where's the mark?'

'In the saloon bar.'

Yet something was not quite right. It was too good to be true.

'How did he know you?'

'Came in looking for barkers and dealers. Somebody in the Lane told him we used this pub. He's done a few pubs at the Lane and on the Belly.'

Petticoat Lane and Portobello Road, the London street markets. To ask after reliable dealers – and I'm the most reliable of all known dealers, honest – was reasonable and sounded open enough.

'He spoke to you first?'

'No.' Tinker was obviously proud from the way his voice rose eagerly. 'I was at the bar. I heard him ask Ted.' Ted is the barman. 'He asked if any antique dealers were in the bar. I chipped in.' He paused. 'I was in like a flash, Lovejoy,' he added, pained.

'Good lad, Tinker,' I said. 'Well done.'

'I told him I was your runner. He wants to see you. He'd got your name in a notebook.'

'Look, Tinker,' I said, suddenly uneasy, but he protested.

'No, no, he's not Old Bill. Honest. He's straight.' Old Bill was the law, police. I had licences to worry about. And taxes, paid and unpaid. And account books. And some account books I hadn't got at all.'

'What's he after?'

'Locks. Right up your street.'

My heart almost stopped.

'Locks locks, or just locks?' I stuttered.

'Locks,' Tinker said happily. 'Flinters.'

'If you're kaylied,' I threatened.

'Sober as ever was,' the phone said. That'll be the day, I thought. I'd never seen Tinker Dill vertical in twenty years. Horizontal or listing, yes.

'Any particular ones?'

'See him first, Lovejoy. I'll keep him here.'

'All right.' I suddenly decided. A chance was a chance. And buyers were what it was all about. 'Hang on to him, Tinker. Can you hear a car?'

He thought for a second.

'Yes. One just pulling into the car park,' he said, sounding surprised. 'Why?'

'It's me,' I said, and shut off, grinning.

To my surprise the bath-taps were running and the bathroom door was shut. I opened up and there was this blonde, somewhat sodden, sulking in steam.

'What on earth – ?' I began, having forgotten.

'You pig,' she said, cutting loose with the language.

'Oh. I remember.' She'd been making a racket while I was on the phone. 'You're Sheila.'

She retorted, 'You pig.'

'I'm sorry,' I told her, 'but I have to go out. Can I drop you somewhere?'

'You already have,' she snapped, flouncing past and snatching up her things.

'It's just that there's a buyer turned up.'

She took a swing at me. I retreated.

'Have you seen my car keys?'

'Have I hell!' she screamed, rummaging under the divan for her shoes.

'Keep your hair on.'

I tried to reason with her, but women can be very insensitive to the real problems of existence. She gave me a burst of tears, a few more flashes of temper and finally, the way women will, began an illogical assault on my perfectly logical reasons for making her go.

'Who is she?'

'That "she" is a hairy bloke,' I told her. 'A buyer.'

'And you prefer a buyer to me. Is that it?' she blazed.

'Yes,' I said, puzzled at her extraordinary mentality. She went for me, firing handbag, a shoe, and a pillow as she came, claws at the ready. I gave her a backhander to calm the issue somewhat, at which she settled weeping while I found a coat. I'm all for sex equality.

'Look, help me to find my keys,' I said. 'If I don't find them I'll be late.' Women seem to have no sense sometimes.

'You hit me,' she sobbed.

'He's been recommended to me by London dealers,' I said proudly, ransacking the bureau where my sales-and-purchases records are kept – occasionally and partly, that is.

'All you think of is antiques,' she whimpered.

'It isn't!' I said indignantly. 'I asked you about your holidays yesterday.'

'In bed,' she cut back viciously. 'When you wanted me.'

'Look for the keys. They were here the day before, when I brought you back.'

I found them at last under a Thai temple woodcut and rushed her outside the cottage, remembering to leave a light on and the door alarm switched over to our one vigilant hawkeye at the village constabulary station, in case the British Museum decided to come on a marauding break-in for my latest aquisition, a broken Meissen white I'd have a hard time giving away to a church jumble.

My elderly Armstrong-Siddeley waited, rusting audibly in the Essex night air between the untidy trees. It started first push to my delight and we were off.

'Antiques are a sickness with you, Lovejoy,' she sniffed. I turned on the gravel, and the old banger – I mean the car – coughed out on to the dark tree-lined road.

'Nothing but,' I replied happily.

'I think you're mad. What are antiques for, anyway? What's the point?'

That's women for you. Anything except themselves is a waste of time. Very self-centred, women are.

'Let me explain, honey.'

'You're like a child playing games.'

She sat back in the seat, staring poutishly at the nearing village lights. I pushed the accelerator pedal down hard. The speedometer needle crept up to the thirty mark as the engine pulsed into maximum thrust. With a following southwesterly I'd once notched forty on the Cambridge Road.

'He might be a collector,' I said. She snorted in an unladylike manner.

'Collector,' she said scornfully.

'The collector's the world's greatest and only remaining fanatic,' I preached fervently. 'Who else would sell his wife, wreck his marriage, lose his job, go broke, gamble, rob and cheat, mortgage himself to the hilt a dozen times, throw all security out of the window, for a scattering of objects as diverse as matchboxes, teacups, postcards of music-hall comedians, old bicycles, steam engines, pens,

old fans, railway-station lanterns, Japanese sword-decor-
ations, and seventeenth-century corsets? Who else but
collectors?' I looked rapturously into her eyes. 'It's greater
than sex, Sheila —'

'Nonsense,' she snapped, the wind from the car's speed
almost ruffling her hair.

'It's greater than religion. Greater love hath no man,'
I said piously, 'than that he gives up his life for his collection.'

I wish now I hadn't said that.

'And *you* make money out of them. You prey on them.'

'I serve them.' There were almost tears in my eyes. 'I
need to make the odd copper from them, of course I do.
But not for profit's sake. Only so I can keep going, sort of
make money to maintain the service.'

'Liar,' she said, and slapped my face. As I was driving
I couldn't clock her one by way of return so I resorted to
persuasion.

'Nobody regrets us having to split more than me,' was
the best I could manage, but she stayed mad.

She kept up a steady flow of recrimination, the way
women will, as I drove into the village. It must have been
nine o'clock when I reached the White Hart. The Armstrong was wheezing badly by then. Its back wheels were
smoking again. I wish I knew what made it do that. I
pulled into the forecourt and pushed a couple of quid into
her hand.

'Look, darling,' I said hastily. 'See you soon.'

'What am I to do now?' she complained, coming after
me.

'Ring for a taxi, there's a good girl,' I told her. 'To the
station.'

'You pig, Lovejoy,' she wailed.

'There's a train soon — probably.'

'When will I see you?' she called after me as I trotted
towards the pub.

'I'll give you a ring,' I said over my shoulder.

'Promise?'

'Honestly.'

I heard her shout something else after me, but by then I was through the door and into the saloon bar.

Women have no sense of priorities. Ever noticed that?

CHAPTER II

THE SALOON BAR was crowded. I labelled everybody in there with one swift glance. A dozen locals, including this bird of about thirty-six, sitting stylishly on a barstool and showing thighs to the assembled multitude. We had been friends once – twice, to be truthful. Now I just lusted across the heads of her admirers and grinned a lazaroid greeting, to which she returned a cool smoke-laden stare. Three dealers were already in: Jimmo, stout, balding, and Staffordshire pottery; Jane Felsham, thirtyish, shapely, would have been desirable if she hadn't been an antique dealer, blonde, Georgian silver and early watercolours; and finally Adrian, sex unknown, elegant, pricey and mainly Regency furniture and household wares. Four strangers, thinly distributed, and a barker or two chatting them up and trying to interest them in antique Scandinavian brass plaques made last April. Well, you can only try. They can always say no.

Tinker Dill was in the far corner by the fireplace with this middle-aged chap. I forged my way over.

'Oh,' Tinker said, acting like the ninth-rate Olivier he is. 'Oh. And here's my friend Lovejoy I was telling you about.'

'Evening, Tinker.' I nodded at the stranger and we shook hands.

He seemed fairly ordinary, neat, nothing new about his clothes but not tatty. He could have saved up ten thousand all right. But a genuine collector . . . ? Not really.

'Mr Field, meet Lovejoy.' Tinker was really overdoing it, almost wagging like a dog. We said how do and sat.

'My turn, Tinker, from last time,' I said, giving him a note to shut him up. He was off to the bar like a rocket.

'Mr Dill said you are a specialist dealer, Mr Lovejoy.' Field's accent was anonymous southern.

'Yes,' I admitted.

'Very specialized, I believe?'

'Yes. Of course,' I hedged as casually as I could manage, 'from the way the trade has progressed in the past few years I maintain a pretty active interest in several other aspects.'

'Naturally,' he said, all serious.

'But I expect Dill's told you where my principal interest lies.'

'Yes.'

This guy was no dealer. In fact, if he knew a Regency snuffbox from a Rolls-Royce it was lucky guesswork.

Barkers like Tinker are creatures of form. They have to be, if you think about it. They find possible buyers who are interested, say, in picking up a William IV dining-set. Now, a barker's job is to get clients : buyers or sellers but preferably the former. He's no right to go saying, Oh, sorry, sir, but my particular dealer's only interested in buying or selling oil paintings of the Flemish School, so you've had it from me. If a barker did that he'd get the push smartish. So, whatever the mark — sorry, buyer — wants, a barker will agree his particular dealer's got it, and not only that, but he will also swear blind that his dealer's certainly the world's most expert expert on William IV dining-sets or whatever, and throw in a few choice remarks about how crooked other dealers are, just for good measure.

Now a dealer, coming strolling in at this point only showing interest in penny-farthing bicycles, would ruin all the careful groundwork. The customer will realize he's been sadly misled, and departs in a huff for the National Gallery or some other inexperienced amateur outfit. Also, and just as bad, the barker (if he's any good) pushes off to serve another dealer, because clearly the dealer's going to starve to death, and barkers don't find loyalty the most indispensable of all virtues. The dealer then starves, goes out of business, and those of us remaining say a brief prayer for the repose of his soul – while racing after the customer as fast as we can go because we all know where we can get a mint William IV dining-set at very short notice.

'He has a very high opinion of your qualities,' Field informed me.

'That's very kind.' If Field got the irony it didn't show.

'You made a collection for the Victoria and Albert Museum, I understand, Mr Lovejoy.'

'Oh, well.' I winced inwardly, trying to seem all modest. I determined to throttle Tinker – even innocent customers know how to check this sort of tale.

'Wasn't it last year?'

'You must understand,' I said hesitantly, putting on as much embarrassment as I dared.

'Understand?'

'I'm not saying I have, and I'm not saying I haven't,' I went on. 'It's a client's business, not mine. Even if South Kensington *did* ask me to build up their terracotta Roman statuary, it's not for Dill nor myself to disclose their interests.' May I be forgiven.

'Ah. Confidentiality.' His brow cleared.

'It's a matter of proper business, Mr Field,' I said with innocent seriousness.

'I do see,' he said earnestly, lapping it up. 'A most responsible attitude.'

'There are standards.' I shrugged to show I was positively weighed down with conscience. 'Ordinary fair play,' I said. Maybe I was overdoing it, because he went all broody. He was coming to the main decision when Tinker came back with a rum for me and a pale ale for Field.

I gave Tinker the bent eye and he instantly pushed off.

'Are you an . . . individual dealer, Mr Lovejoy?' he asked, taking the plunge.

'If you mean do I work alone, yes.'

'No partners?'

'None.' I thought a bit, then decided I should be straight

– almost – with this chap. He looked as innocent as a new policeman. I don't know where they keep them till they're grown up, honest I don't. 'I ought to qualify that, Mr Field.'

'Yes?' He came alert over his glass.

'There are occasions when an outlay, or a risk, is so large, that for a particular antique it becomes necessary to take an . . . extra dealer, pair up so to speak, in order to complete a sale.' I'd almost said 'accomplice'. You know what I mean.

'In what way?' he said guardedly.

'Supposing somebody offered me the Elgin Marbles for a million,' I said, observing his expression ease at the light banter. 'I'd have to get another dealer to make up the other half million before I could buy them.'

'I see.' He was smiling.

'For that sale, we would be equal partners.'

'But not after?'

'No. As I said, Mr Field,' I said, all pious, 'I work alone because, well, my own standards may not be those of other dealers.'

'Of course, of course.'

For some reason he was relieved I was a loner.

'Any arrangements between us – supposing we came to one – would concern . . . ?' he waited.

'Just us,' I confirmed.

'And Dill?'

'He's freelance. He wouldn't know anything, unless you said.'

'And other employees?'

'I hire as the needs arise.'

'So it *is* possible,' he mused.

'What is, Mr Field?'

'You can have a confidential agreement with an antique dealer.'

'Certainly.' I should have told him that money can buy silence nearly as effectively as it can buy talk. Note the 'nearly', please.

'Then I would like to talk to you – in a confidential place, if that can be arranged.'

'Now?' I asked.

'Please.'

I glanced around the bar. There were two people I had business with.

'I have a cottage not far away. We can chat there.'

'Fine.'

I crossed to Jimmo and briefly quizzed him about his Chinese porcelain *blanc de Chine* lions – white pot dogs to the uninitiated. He told me in glowing terms of his miraculous find.

'Cost mé the earth,' he said fervently. 'Both identical. Even the balls are identically matched.'

For the sake of politeness (and in case I needed to do business with him fairly soon) I kept my end up, but I'd lost interest. The 'lions' are in fact the Dogs of Fo. The point is that even if they are K'ang-hsi period, as Jimmo said, and 1720 AD would do fine, they should *not* match exactly to be a real matched pair. The male Dog rests one paw on a sphere, the female on a pup. Jimmo had somehow got hold of two halves of two distinct pairs. I eased away as best I could.

Adrian, handbag, curls and all, was next. He and Jane Felsham were bickering amiably over a percentage cut over some crummy 'patch-and-comfit' boxes. 'Real Bilston enamel,' Adrian was telling her. 'Pinks genuine as that. Oh.' He saw me at his elbow and stamped his foot in temper. 'Why won't the silly bitch listen, Lovejoy? *Tell* her.'

'How many?' I asked.

'He's got six,' Jane said evenly. 'Hello, Lovejoy.'

'Hi. It sounds a good collection.'

'There you are, dearie!' Adrian screamed.

'Only two are named.' Jane shook her head. 'Place names are all the go.'

These little boxes, often only an inch across, were used in the eighteenth century for holding those minute artificial

black beauty-patches fashionable gentry of the time stuck
on their faces to contrast with the powdered pallor of their
skins. Filthy habit.

'Any blues?'

'One,' Adrian squeaked. 'I keep begging her to take
them. She can't see a bargain, Lovejoy.'

'Any mirrors in the lids?'

'Two.'

'Four hundred's still no bargain, Adrian dear,' Jane said
firmly.

'Show us,' I said, wanting to get away. Field was still
patient by the fireplace.

Adrian brought out six small enamelled boxes on his
palm. One was lumpy, less shiny than the rest. I felt odd
for a second. My bell.

'I agree with Jane,' I lied, shrugging. 'But they are nice.'

'Three-eighty, then,' Adrian offered, sensing my reaction.

'Done.' I lifted the little boxes from his hand and fought
my way free, saying, 'Come round tomorrow.'

Adrian swung round to the surprised Jane. 'See? Serves
you right, silly cow!' I left them to fight it out and found
Field.

'My car's just outside.'

I gave the nod to Tinker that he'd finished on a good
note. He beamed and toasted me over a treble gin.

The cottage was in a hell of a mess. I have this downstairs
divan for, so to speak, communal use. It looked almost as
if somebody had been shacked up there for a couple of
days with a bird. I smiled weakly at my customer.

'Sorry about this – I had a, er, cousin staying for a while.'

He made polite noises as I hid a few of Sheila's under-
clothes under cushions and folded the divan aside. With
only the tablelamp the room didn't look too much of a
shambles. I pulled the kitchen door to in case he thought
a hurricane was coming his way and sat him by my one-bar
fire.

'A very pleasant cottage, Mr Lovejoy,' he said.

'Thanks,' I could see he was wondering at the absence of antiques in an antique dealer's home. 'I keep my stock of antiques dispersed in safe places,' I explained. 'After all, I'm in the phone book, and robbery's not unknown nowadays.'

Stock. That's a laugh. I had six enamelled boxes I'd not properly examined, for which I owed a mint payable by dawn.

'True, true,' he agreed, and I knew I had again struck oil.

In his estimation I was now careful, safe, trustworthy, reliable, an expert, and the very soul of discretion. I drove home my advantage by apologizing for not having too much booze.

'I don't drink much myself,' I confessed. 'Will coffee do you?'

'Please.'

'Everybody just calls me Lovejoy, Mr Field,' I informed him. 'My trademark.'

'Right,' he smiled. 'I'll remember.'

I brewed up, quite liking him and wondering how to approach his money – I mean, requirements. So far he hadn't mentioned flinters. On the drive back in my jet-propelled Armstrong-Siddeley we had made social chitchat that got us no nearer. He seemed a simple chap, unaware of the somewhat horrible niceties of my trade. Yet he appeared, from what Tinker had said, to have gone to a lot of trouble to find a dealer known to have a prime interest in flinters.

'How long have you lived here?'

'Since I started dealing. I got it from a friend.'

She was a widow, thirty-seven. I'd lived with her for two years, then she'd gone unreasonable like they do and off she pushed. She wrote later from Sienna, married to an Italian. I replied in a flash saying how I longed for her, but she'd replied saying her husband hadn't an antique in the place, preferring new Danish planks of yellow wood to furniture, so I didn't write again except to ask for the cottage deeds.

'Instead of London?'

'Oh, I go up to the Smoke maybe once a week on average.' And do the rest of the Kingdom, as well, inch by bloody inch, once every quarter. On my knees, mostly, sniffing and listening for my bell. I didn't tell him that, seeing I was supposed to be temporarily the big wheeler-dealer.

'To the markets?' he persisted.

'Yes. And some, er, private dealers that I know.'

He nodded and drew breath. Here it comes, I thought. And it did.

'I'm interested in a certain collector's item,' he said, as if he'd saved the words for a rainy day. 'I'm starting a collection.'

'Hmmm.' The Lovejoy gambit.

'I want to know if you can help.'

He sipped and waited. And I sipped and waited. Like a couple of those drinking ostriches we dipped in silence.

'Er, can you?' he asked.

'If I can,' I countered cagily. For an innocent novice he wasn't doing too badly, and I was becoming distinctly edgy.

'Do you mean Dill didn't explain?'

'He explained you were interested in purchasing flint-locks,' I said.

'Nothing else?'

'And that you had, er, sufficient funds.'

'But not what it is I'm seeking?'

'No.' I put down my cup because my hands were quivering slightly. If it turned dud I'd wring Tinker's neck. 'Perhaps,' I said evenly, 'you'd better tell me.'

'Duelling pistols.'

'I guessed that.' Flintlock duellers are the P and O Line of weaponsmen.

'A very special pair.'

'That too.' I cleared my throat. 'Which pair, Mr Field?'

He stared at me across the darkened room.

'I want the Judas pair,' he said.

My heart sank. With luck, I could catch Tinker before Ted called 'Time' at the pub, and annihilate him on the spot for sending me a dummy. No wonder he'd been evasive when I asked him on the phone.

I gazed at the poor misguided customer.

'Did you say, the Judas pair?' I said, still hoping I'd misheard.

'The Judas pair,' he affirmed.

Digression time, folks.

Flintlocks are sprung iron gadgets which flip a piece of flint on to a steel so as to create a spark. This spark, at its most innocent, can be used to ignite a piece of old rope or other tinder and set it smouldering to be blown into a flame for lighting the fire, candles, your pipe. This is the standard tinder-lighter of history. You'd be surprised how many sorts of tinder-lighters there are, many incredibly ingenious. But those instruments are the humdrum end of the trade, interesting and desirable though they are. You see, mankind, being mankind, made this pleasant little system into the business bit of weapons for killing each other.

About the time of our Civil War, the posh firing weapon was a wheel-lock. This delectable weaponry consisted of a sprung wheel, spinning at the touch of a trigger and rubbing on a flint as it did so. (The very same mechanism is used in a petrol-fuelled cigarette lighter of today, believe it or not.) They were beautiful things, mostly made in Germany where there were clock-and-lock makers aplenty. A ball-butted German wheel-lock costs the earth nowadays. And remember, the less marked the better – none of this stupid business of boring holes and chipping the walnut stock to prove it's old. Never try to improve *any* antique. Leave well alone – Sheraton and Constable knew what they were doing, and chances are that you are as ignorant as I am. Stick to wiping your antiques with a dry duster.

Better still, don't even do that.

These wheel-locks were rifled for accuracy. Prince Rupert, leader of his uncle's Cavaliers, had a destructive habit of shooting weathercocks off steeples as he rode through captured towns. However, they were somewhat slow, clumsy, heavy and took time to fire. The reason was the spark. It plopped into a little pan where you had thoughtfully sprinkled black gunpowder. This ignited, and burned through a small hole into *your* end of the barrel, where you'd placed a larger quantity of gunpowder, a small lead bullet about the size of a marble, and a piece of old wadding to keep it all in. Bang! If you knew the delay to a millisec, the shift of the wind, could control your horse, pointed it right and kept everything crossed for luck, you were one more weathercock short. It asked to be improved.

The culmination in weapons was the true flintlock, faster, and quicker to fire again should you miss. This may not be important – but only if your enemies are all weather-cocks. Once the idea caught on, the wheel-lock was re-placed and the true flintlock came on to the historical scene.

The French had a crack at making them, and wonderful attempts they were. Some superb examples exist. I've had many with knobs on, gold inlay, silver escutcheons, damas-cus-barrelled beauties with delicate carving on precision locks that would melt your heart. And some beautiful Spanish miquelet pistols – a Mediterranean fancy of a strangely bulky style – are decorated to perfection. I admit that tears come to my eyes writing this, mostly because everybody else has them, not me. And Dutch too, though their taste for carving ugly ivory heads and figurines on the grips gives me the willies. All nations did their stuff on the flintlock, from the early snaphaunces and English doglocks to the final great explosions of exquisite functional murder-ous perfection in – you've guessed it – dear old peaceful Britain.

Came the Industrial boom days and an outburst of in-ventive genius which was to catapult these islands into

wealth, prominence and power. Don't think our armies
won by unaided valour, though they had it in plenty. They
used an improved flintlock, standardized by a thoughtful
young English squire, Oliver Cromwell by name. And it
fired faster, surer and noisier than anyone else's, which
was a blessing in war.

From then the flintlock didn't look back. Inventors
added devices you would hardly believe : flintlocks that
fired under water (work it out), flintlock repeating rifles,
flintlock revolvers, flintlock machine guns, ingenious safety
catches that actually worked even if you forgot to slip them
on, breechloading flintlocks by the score all the time edging
towards a shorter firing time between pulling the trigger
and sending regrets to your opponent's widow. And ladies
were at it too – no more than you'd expect – in subtle little
ways having a charm all their own. Muff-pistols, made for
folding away in their hot little hands, were their scene but
they also liked tiny collapsible guns built into their prayer-
books – presumably in the *Exodus* bit. Church was more
exciting in those days.

By the 1770s duelling was in, and here comes the Judas
pair. Or, rather, here they don't come.

Be careful, O ye innocent purchaser of these valuable
– I mean, and repeat, *valuable* – weapons. They should
be damascus-barrelled (ie : wiggly-patterned surfaces) and,
at their best, *brown* because of a skilful veneer of faint
rust applied to the metal by skilled makers of genius. They
should have walnut stocks, and usually be rifle-grooved.
But, if the barrel measures less than nine inches, utter a
loud derisory snort and mentally divide the asking price
by three, if not four, because you are being had by some
dealer who is trying to pass off a pair of officer's holster
pistols as genuine duellers. A sneer is useful at this stage.
On the other hand, if, say, they have ten-inch barrels, try
to keep cool and go on to the next step, which is to look
for decoration. Almost *any* metallic decoration on the
barrels or on the locks disqualifies, because duelling, remember, was naughty, and silver squiggles and gold inlays

tended to catch the first gleam of light on Wandsworth
Common and reflect it unerringly into the eagle eyes of
London's annoyed watchmen. You are allowed one silver
escutcheon plate on the butt. And even this displeases you,
because the real flintlock geniuses of Regency London knew
their onions. Sombre perfection was their aim. They
achieved it.

Pick up a genuine Regency dueller. Hold it with your
arm straight down. Now lift as if about to aim. Its weight
makes it wobble in the strongest fist as it rises. Up it
comes, wobbling and waggling, and you begin to wonder
how they managed to hit anything with the long barrel
waving in the breeze. Then, just about on a level with your
bottom rib, something so remarkable happens you won't
believe me, but it's the truth – a genuine flintlock dueller
begins to lift itself! Honestly. Try it. The weight evaporates.
The wobble disappears. Up it goes, seemingly of its own
accord, and all you need to do is point it right. Its perfect
balance, its meticulous design and the love and joy expended in its making have achieved the seemingly impossible. That's the genuine dueller – grim, sombre, almost
dull of appearance, lying with its identically-matched
partner in a wooden case with powder-flask, bullet moulds,
flints, separate ramrod and screwdrivers. It reeks of class. It
screams of perfection.

A pair of mint – that is, perfectly-preserved – cased flintlock duellers would buy you a couple of new cars nowadays,
minimum. A mint pair of them with a pedigree – belonging, say, to some hero, a famous dandy of the time, or
perhaps some pal of Beau Brummell's or a member of the
then royalty – will virtually buy you anything. If you discover such a pair of old pistols in a dirty old box upstairs,
rush to the nearest church and light a candle in thanks to
your Maker, Bate, Monlong, Murdoch, Pauly, whoever
it turns out to be. *Then retire for life in affluence.*

Finally, one point more. Just like Queen Anne silver,
each weapon is, or should be, named on the lock. Don't

throw value away. Your famous silversmith's monogram can double or treble the value of your fruit bowl. So your famous maker's engraved name can send your find ever upwards in value. The names are too many to give here, but Joseph Manton, John Manton, Wogden who gave his name as a nickname to duelling (a 'Wogden affair'), the brilliant Joseph Egg, Henry Nock the Great and his younger relative Sam that he had a terrible row with, Mortimer, Tatham who blew himself to pieces on a cannon for reasons best not gone into, Freeman, the fashionable Rigby, the Reverend Alexander Forsyth – who invented the percussion system which did away with flintlocks altogether and doubled the killing speed – are some you should not lose on your way home.

And last but not least, one Durs (nearly as bad as Lovejoy) Egg, flintlock maker to kings and princes, genius extraordinaire, maker – so they say – of the one and only Judas pair of flintlock duellers. Well.

This young man came to London about 1770 to seek his fortune. With another Swiss, Pauly, he became interested in the science of pneumatics and air propulsion and between them they produced a variety of odd but lethal airguns. In later years he lost a fortune by inventing a flying machine, the Flying Dolphin, which he kept in a hangar down Knightsbridge way, to London society's huge delight and derision. A genius whose habit was to pattern the walnut stocks of his flintlocks with a curiously-stippled star design, to aid in the grip. He signed himself always by his nickname, Durs.

The legend is that he made twelve – only twelve – pairs of duelling pistols. The legend goes on to say that he privately made a thirteenth pair, when something terrible happened. What it was the legend fails to explain.

That thirteenth pair, sinister weapons of ill-omen, were his last. They were never found nor heard of except as obscure rumours. Any antique dealer worth his salt will laugh till he falls down if you ask after them. They don't exist, and everybody knows it.

That thirteenth pair of flintlock duellers is the Judas pair.

I drew breath.

'I've bad news, Mr Field,' I managed to get out.

'Bad news?'

'The Judas pair. They don't exist,' I said firmly, and rose to get my emergency beer. 'They're a myth, a legend. The antique trade's riddled with myths.'

'Is it really?' He was oddly calm for somebody who'd just been put down.

'Really,' I told him. No use mucking about.

He watched me splash the ale as I drove the truth savagely home. 'Michelangelo's *Goliath* to match his *David*. Turner's mysterious set of portraits and industrial paintings. Napoleon's woodcuts done by his very own lily-white hands. Sir Francis Drake's poetry in two breathtaking volumes. Bill Shakespeare's latest play *King Penda*. Robin Hood's diary. Czar Alexander's secret will. The Grail. Excalibur. Prince John's necklace from The Wash. Friar Bacon's perpetual clock. Leonardo's jewelled casket of secrets. Cleopatra's ruby ring. The Koh-i-noor's partner diamond, even bigger and better. Nazi treasure chests in those tiresome bloody lakes. Rembrandt's French land-scapes. Chippendale's missing design books. All myths. Like,' I added harshly, 'the Judas pair.'

'Did Dill tell you how much I was willing to pay?' he asked.

'Ten thousand,' I said bitterly. 'Just my luck.'

'Now I believe you, Lovejoy,' he said, calm as you please.

'Look,' I said slowly. 'Maybe I'm not getting through to you. Can't you understand what I'm saying? Ten thousand's too little. So is ten million. You can't get some-thing if it doesn't exist.'

'Before,' he continued evenly, 'I thought you were lead-ing me on, perhaps pretending to be more honest than you really were. That is a common deception in all forms of business.' I took a mouthful of ale to stop myself gaping too obviously. 'Now I believe you are an honest man. A dishonest dealer, seeing I know little about the subject, would have exploited my ignorance.'

'It happens,' I admitted weakly.

'I accepted that risk when I came to you.' Field stared thoughtfully at me.

'So you knew about the Judas pair being legendary?'

'From various sources.'

'And it was a try on, then.'

'Yes.'

'Well, Mr Field.' I rose. 'You've had your fun. Now, before you leave, is it worth your while to tell me what you *do* want?' I stood over him. To my surprise he remained unabashed. In fact, he seemed more cool as the chat wore on.

'Certainly.'

'Right. Give.' I sat, still exuding aggression.

'I want you to do a job.'

'Legal?'

'Legal. Right up your street, as Dill would say.' So he'd listened in on Tinker's call as I'd guessed. 'You'll accept? It will be very lucrative.'

'What is it?'

'Find me,' he said carefully, 'the Judas pair.'

I sighed wearily. The guy was a nutter.

'Haven't I just explained – ?'

'Wrongly.' Field leaned forward. 'Lovejoy, the Judas pair exist. They killed my brother.'

It was becoming one of those days. I should have stayed on the nest with Sheila, somewhere safe and warm.

CHAPTER III

ELIZABETHAN LADIES – the First, I hasten to add – had fleas. And lice. And gentlemen suitors, who came courting, also suffered. If these heroes were especially favoured, they were allowed indoors to chat up the object of their desire. If they were really fancied, though, matters progressed to poetry, music, even handclasps and sighs. And eventually the great flea-picking ceremony. You've seen baboons do it on those unspeakable nature programmes. Yes, our ancestors did the same, uttering rapturous sighs at all that contact.

What I am getting at is this : if you see a little (one and a half inches maximum) antique box, dirty as hell, that *should* be neat and enamelled to be a proper patch-and-comfit box and somehow isn't quite right, it can be only one of two things. The first is a battered nineteenth-century trinket or snuff box, in which case you can generally forget it. The second – oh, dear, the second – is an Elizabethan flea- and louse-box. Don't shudder. Don't boil it to kill any remaining creepy-crawlies. Lock it carefully in the biggest, safest safe you can find, swallow the key, and then scream with ecstasy. These little jewelled boxes were used by lovers, for holding fleas and lice that they captured on their paramounts' lovely chalk-powdered skin. It was an exquisitely charming pastime of those days. We don't advertise them as such, these boxes. We call them anything : 'Early antique, sixteenth-century lady's minute toiletry box, heavily inlaid, made by . . .' and so on.

Remember Adrian? I spent part of the night cleaning the lumpy box – it was a genuine flea-box. I kissed it reverently, drew all the curtains, doused my lamp and rolled up the carpet. Underneath was the hinged paving stone. Down I went, eight wooden steps underground into my secret cave. Eight feet by eight, cold as charity, dry as a tinderbox, safer than any bank vault on earth. I laid the box on a shelf and climbed out, replacing the stone flag and making sure the iron ring lay in its groove – it wouldn't do to have a visitor tripping up over an unexpected bump in a carpet, would it? I smoked a Dutch cigar to celebrate, though they make me sleep badly, and went to bed. It was four o'clock.

Field's brother was a collector, apparently. One of the indiscriminate kind. To his wife's dismay he filled the house with assorted antiques and semi-antiques and modern junk, a mixture of rubbish and desirable stuff. In short, a collector after my own heart.

Somewhere, somehow, Field's brother found the Judas pair, so Field told me, not realizing they were anything more special than a pair of supreme antique flintlock duellers made by any old passing genius. He seems to have mentioned to all and sundry about his luck and I dare say let interested callers click the triggers – knocking guineas off their value at every click. Tender-hearted as I am, by this point in Field's narrative I was getting the feeling his brother might have got the same fate from me, but I suppressed it.

Anyway, one night several months ago Field had a phone call from his brother, who told him very excitedly that the flintlocks were very special, unique in fact, if not world-shattering. He would bring them over next day, it being Saturday, and show him.

'He never came, Lovejoy,' Field told me.

He was found by Field himself, at noon. Field drove over to see why he hadn't turned up. He was in his living-room among all his clutter. Blood seemed to be everywhere. He seemed to have been shot through his eye but the bullet was never found, not even at the post-mortem.

'Sorry about this,' I said, 'but did the pathologist say what bore?'

'About twelve, but he wasn't sure.'

'Could be.'

Take a pound of lead. Divide it into twelve equal balls. They are then twelve-bore bullets for flintlock or percussion weapons. No cartridges, remember, for the period we're talking about. The impetus comes from your dollop of gunpowder and the spark. Flintlock weapons range from two-bore or even one-bore monsters which throw a bullet as big as a carrot, to narrow efforts like the eighteen-bore or less. Duellers went with fashions, but twelve-bore were not unusual.

'Where did he buy them?'

'He never said.' Wise man.

'Nor how much he paid?'

'No.' Wiser still.

'Were they cased?'

'Cased?'

'In a special box, the size of a small cutlery box, maybe up to two feet by one, maybe four inches deep.'

'There *was* a box that went with them.'

I stirred from desire.

'And the accessories?'

'As far as I remember, there were some small screwdrivers and a couple of metal bottles, and pliers,' he said slowly, 'but that's as much as I can recall.' He meant a flask and mould.

'So you actually saw them?'

He looked surprised. 'Oh yes.'

'And . . . you didn't notice if they were of any extra quality?'

'To me they were just, well, antiques.' I eyed him coldly. You can go off people.

'Did you notice the maker?'

'Eric – my brother – told me. It's such an unusual name, isn't it? Durs. And Egg. I remarked on it.' He grinned. 'I said, I'll bet his mates pulled his leg at school.'

'Quite,' I said, knowing the feeling well. 'And of course you searched for them?'

'The police did.'

'No luck?'

'Not only that. They didn't believe me about them.'

No good looking for a gun – of any sort – if there's no
bullet.

'They said he'd been stabbed with a metal object.'

'Through the eye?' It sounded unlikely.

'It's hopeless, as you no doubt see.'

'What theories did they have?'

'Very few – they're still searching for the weapon.'

'Without knowing what sort of weapon it was?' I snorted
in derision.

He leaned forward, pulling out an envelope.

'Here's five hundred,' he said. 'It's on account.'

'For . . . ?' I tried to keep my eyes on his, but they kept
wandering towards the money in his hand.

'For finding that weapon.' He chucked the envelope and
I caught it, so the notes inside wouldn't bruise. Not to
keep, you understand. 'My brother was shot by one of the
Judas weapons.'

'The Judas pair don't exist.' My voice sounds weak
sometimes.

'They do.' For somebody so hopeless at pretending to be
a collector he was persistent. 'I've seen them.'

'They don't,' I squeaked at the third try. It's funny how
heavy a few pound notes can be.

'Then give me the money back,' he said calmly, 'and tell
me to go.'

'I could get you a reasonable pair for this,' I said weakly.
'Maybe no great shakes, not cased, and certainly not mint,
but . . .'

'Yes or no?' he asked. Some of these quiet little chaps
are the worst. Never give up no matter how straight you
are. Ever noticed that?

'Well,' I said gamely, feeling all noble, 'if you really
insist . . .'

'If you've got a pen and paper,' he said, smiling
in a rather disagreeable way, 'I'll give you all available
details . . .'

I'd tried, hadn't I?

Adrian brought Jane Felsham along. I handed him a cheque.

'You're flush,' he exclaimed. 'Come across a Barraud?' Barraud, a London watchmaker, about 1815, made some delicious flat-looking watches. Only the central sun decoration and the astounding nineteen-line movement and the sexy gold and enamel surface and the beady surround (pearls) tell you it's somewhat above average. The highest artistic imagination crystallized in a luscious context of brilliant science. I smiled, I think. People shouldn't make jokes. I'd once missed a Barraud by five minutes, late for an auction.

'Steady progress,' I replied.

'Will it bounce?' He draped himself elegantly across a chair. Both he and Jane couldn't help glancing sharply round in case any of my recent finds were on display.

'Don't you want it?' I brewed up to show we were still friends.

'I must confess little Janesy and I were discussing whether you'd have the wherewithal, dear boy.'

'It was touch and go.'

'Business going a bit slow, Lovejoy?' Jane lit one of her long cigarettes and rotated her fagholder. 'Not much about for the casual visitor to see.'

'I have these two warehouses . . .

They laughed.

'That chap last night,' Jane pressed. 'A client?'

'Trying to be,' I said casually.

'After anything we could help with?' from Adrian.

'I doubt it.' I rattled a few pieces of crockery to show I was being offhand.

'A furniture man, I suppose.' Jane waggled her fagholder again. A psychiatrist I sold a warming-pan once told me something odd about women who habitually sucked fagholders. For the life of me I can't remember what it was.

'Asking the impossible as usual.' I hoped that would

shut them up. 'Wanting something for nothing.'

'Don't they all?' Adrian groaned.

'Did you risk him in your car?' Jane was smiling.

'Of course. Why not? I gave him a lift to the station.'

'Did he survive?' She's always pulling my leg about my old bus.

'He said it was unusual.'

'A death-trap,' Adrian interposed. 'All those switches for nothing. Trade it in for a little Morris.'

This sort of talk offends me, not that I'm sentimental about a heap of old iron. After all, though it's a common enough banger, it does give off a low-level bell or two.

'He didn't buy, then?'

'Not even place an order.' I carried in their cups and offered sugar. 'I got a faint tickle, though. Bring in any tassies you find. We'll split.'

'I might have a few,' Jane said, and they were satisfied.

Tassies – intaglios, really – are the dealers' nickname for an incarved stone, usually a semi-precious one. You know a cameo brooch? The figure – a bust silhouette or whatever – stands in relief above the brooch's main surface. Imagine the same figure carved inwards, grooving out the design. That's an intaglio. Mostly oval, about the size of a pea and as high, with a shallow carving. Watch for copies, modern ones you can't even give away except to some mug who can't tell bottle-glass from the Star of India, though the way things are going, by the time you read this . . .

'Harry Bateman phoned in,' Adrian said, pulling a face at my foul coffee.

'On the cadge?'

'Offering.'

'Good?'

'Wordsworth's stuff. Genuine.'

'Really?' I was interested, but Harry Bateman didn't know his bum from his elbow, which when you think of it is pretty vital information.

'His original chair and a shaving case given to him by

his daughter Dora, 1839.'

'Oh.'

Jane looked up sharply. It must have been how I said it.

'Chair's a straight Chippendale –' Adrian was starting off, but I took pity.

'– And he's even got the date wrong as well. Trust Harry.'

'No good?'

'How come he doesn't starve?' I demanded. 'He'll catch it one day. For heaven's sake tell him before he gets picked up – Wordsworth's chair was always a diamond-seater because of his habit of sitting with a hand in his jacket, Napoleon-style. And the National Trust will be narked if he's really got Dora's case – it should still be at Dove Cottage, on show with the rest of his clobber.'

'That's what I like about Lovejoy,' Adrian said to Jane. 'He's abusive without actually giving offence.'

'I'm pretty good value,' I retorted.

We had a few similar rapier-like exchanges of witty repartee and then they left in Adrian's new Jaguar. A shower of gravel clattered the Armstrong-Siddeley as he spun down my path. I could hear the stones pattering into my bushes all the way through the copse on to the road. Jane had blown me an apologetic kiss.

I phoned Tinker to come over.

I had all the Wallis and Wallis auction catalogues out, Knight Frank and Rutley's, Christie's, Sotheby's and Weller and Dufty's of Birmingham, plus every reference book just as a check. My real filing-system was below in the priest-hole. There wasn't time to open up before Tinker showed, and he wasn't that close a confidant. Nobody was, not even Sheila.

'Watcha, Lovejoy.'

'Come in, Tinker.'

He was grinning. 'Did a deal?'

'Not so's you'd notice,' I said, narked.

'He told me to be sure and mention the money.'

'All right, all right.'

'Did he cough up?' He brought out the Black Label from where I hid it and poured a glug.

'No. All we've got is promises.'

'Ah well.' He smacked his lips. 'You can't have everything.'

'I thought he was a nutter at first.' I gave him a glare. 'Especially as you hadn't tipped me off what he was after.'

'Do you blame me? Would you have come if I had?'

'No,' I admitted. 'Anyway, I talked him out of it. I ask you – the Judas pair. At my age.'

'What's the job then?'

'He's decided to become the big collector,' I improvised. 'So he casts about for a real bingo, and hears of the Judas guns. He decides that's what he'll start with. I've told him I'll get going after a pedigree pair that'll be just as good. He bought it.'

'What'll we give him?' Tinker asked. Already I could see his ferret mind sniffing out possibilities.

'The best named pedigree ones we can get.'

'Same name?'

'Yeah – Durs.'

'Some good Mantons might be on the move soon, word is.'

'From where?'

'Suffolk, so people are saying.'

'Well . . .' I pretended indecision. 'Keep it in mind, but Durs for preference. I was just pinning them down.'

'Three in Germany. Four in the States. Four here, and that Aussie.' He ticked his fingers. 'Twelve. That's the lot.'

I nodded agreement. 'I'll make sure none's come through the auctions lately.'

'You'd have noticed, Lovejoy.'

'It'll save you legwork.'

'Right.'

He sat and swilled my hooch while I sussed the auctions. In a dozen auctions three sets of Durs guns had been sold, two pairs of holster weapons, one by Joseph of Piccadilly and one by Durs, and one blunderbuss by Durs.

'Run-of-the-mill stuff,' I said, forcing back the tears. 'Where do we go from here?'

'Out into the wide world.' I watched his face cloud with misery. 'I go to work writing and whizzing round the collectors. You get down among the dealers and listen. You don't ask anything, got it? You just listen.'

'Right, Lovejoy. Only . . .'

I gave him some notes.

'This comes out of your commission,' I warned. He would expect that.

'I'll go careful.'

'Do,' I warned. 'If you go shouting the odds –'

'I know better than go putting the price up.' He winked. 'Cheerio, Lovejoy.'

'See you, Tinker.'

I'd had to do it. If Tinker – who looked as if he hadn't two coppers to rub together – suddenly appeared, asking after high-priced stuff, it would be the talking-point of the antique world within minutes and any trace of the Judas pair would vanish.

I caught myself in time. I should have to remember they didn't exist. What I was really going after was a pair of unusual *real* weapons, which *did* exist.

I put the catalogues away and sat outside the front door on my stone alcove-seat. The day was fine, dry. Birds were knocking around in the haphazard way they do. A squirrel raced up a tree, stopping now and again for nothing. It was all pretty average. I could hear a few cars on the road. When I was settled enough I let my mind flow towards the job.

A pair of guns existed. They had been bought by Eric Field, who'd got excited. They were certainly by the great Regency maker, and therefore not cheap. Said to be flint duellers, but were possibly not. The other possibility was that the weapons had been mere holster pistols, and Eric Field, not knowing much for all his collecting enthusiasm, mistook them as valuable duellers.

Yet – if they *were* only officer's guns, who killed Eric that Friday night, just to get hold of them? Nobody would murder for a couple of antiques you could buy at open auction, however expensive.

But a hell of a lot of people would murder over and over again for the Judas Pair – if they existed. The day took on a sudden chill.

I shook myself and planned action. First, locate for certain all sets over the past twelve months. Assuming they were all where they ought to be, I would have to think again.

I went indoors to warm up a cheese-and-onion pie. That, two slices of bread and a pint of tea, and I would start.

CHAPTER IV

IT WAS ABOUT three that afternoon. I had walked down to my gate, a hundred yards, and latched it as an added precaution. To come in you had to lift the latch and push hard. It screeched and groaned and rattled like the Tower dungeons. Better than any watchdog. My doors were locked, all my curtains were drawn, and I was in my priest-hole.

Every weekend, while other dealers ginned it up at the local and eyed the talent, I cross-indexed sales. Newspapers, auctions, gossip, cheap adverts I'd seen on postcards in village shop-windows, anything and everything to do with antiques. Those little cards and two hard-backed books may be no match for IBM but my skills are second to none, powered as they are by the most human of all mixtures – greed and love. Let a computer get those.

As I checked mechanically back for Durs items in my records I occasionally glanced at the shelves about me, wondering if there was *anything* the Fields could have mistaken for the Judases. I had a pair of lovely mint double-barrelled percussion Barratts cased and complete with all accessories. No goon could mistake percussion for flints, which narrowed the field considerably. There were other relatives of Joseph and Durs, one being Charles, but he came later and in any case was only a pale shadow of the two older craftsmen. Then came Augustus Leopold, no less. Only, to see his masterpieces you have to go to the London art galleries, for he was the famous oil painter pal of Charles Dickens and Wilkie Collins. To read the scathing comments these writers left about him, he'd have run a mile on even seeing a pistol, flintlock or otherwise. No. It all pointed to Durs weapons. My own Durs flinters were holsters. The duellers I owned were a late large-bore pair by Henry Nock. All the rest, carefully wrapped and laid on dry sponges, were unmistakably non-Durs.

The more I thought about it, the more unlikely it was that Eric had got it wrong. His pair probably were duellers, and perhaps even Durs. If a master craftsman can make a dozen pairs, what's to stop him making one more set? Nothing.

But what made them so special that Eric would babble eagerly over the phone about them to his bored brother?

There was no other alternative. I would have to make the assumption that the Judas pair had been found and bought by Eric Field, that they were used to kill him by some unknown person, and that the motive for Eric's death was possession of the unique antiques. How they'd managed to kill Eric without bullets was a problem only possession of the weapons themselves could solve. I put my cards away, switched off the light and climbed out.

It took only a couple of minutes to have the living-room carpet back in place. I opened the curtains and phoned Field.

'Lovejoy,' I told him. 'Tell me one thing. How long before his death did Eric have them?'

'I'm not sure. Maybe a few months.'

'Months?'

'Why, yes,' he said, surprised. 'I'm almost certain he mentioned he'd found a pair of good-quality flintlocks quite some time ago.'

'Who would know for certain?'

'Well, nobody.' He cleared his throat. 'You *could* try his wife Muriel, my sister-in-law.'

'Same address?'

'She still lives in the house. Only, Lovejoy.' He was warning me.

'Yes?'

'Please go carefully. She's not very . . . strong.'

'I will,' I assured him, and hung up.

So Eric had bought them, and only months later had he discovered their unique nature. I was justified, then, in searching for duellers which looked like most other flints.

This was a clear case for Dandy Jack over at the antique mart, the world's best gossip and worst antique dealer. I could do him a favour, as he'd recently bought a small Chinese collection and would be in a state about it. He always needed help.

I locked up and examined the weather. It would stay fine, with hardly a breeze. The nearby town was about ten miles with only one shallow hill to go up. My monster motor would make it. I patted the Armstrong-Siddeley's bonnet.

'Let's risk it, love,' I said, set it rolling with the outside handbrake dropped forward, and jumped in.

Mercifully, it coughed into action just as it reached the gate. The engine kept grinding away while I swung the gate open, and we trundled grandly out on to the metalled road, all its remaining arthritic 20 cc's throbbing with power. I pushed the throttle flat, and the speedo sailed majestically upwards from walking pace into double figures. The jet age.

Practically every town nowadays has an antique market, mart, arcade, call it what you will. Our town has an arcade of maybe ten antique shops. Imagine Billy Bunter's idea of the Sun King's palace, built by our town council who'd run out of money before finishing the foyer, and you've got our shopping arcade. It's given to seasonal fluctuations, because people from holiday resorts along the coast push up summer sales, and the dearth of winter visitors whittles the arcade's shops – stalls included – down to five or six. They throw in a café to entice the unwary. Dandy Jack never closes.

I parked the Armstrong illegally, sticking the card on the windscreen saying 'Delivering', which could be anything from a doctor to a florist. It often worked. The café had a handful of customers swilling tea and grappling with Chorley cakes. I got the cleanest cake and a plastic cup. Within five minutes they were popping in.

'Hello, Lovejoy. Slumming?' Harry Bateman, no less, of Wordsworth fame.

'Hiya, Harry.'

'Hear about my – ?'

'Remember the Trades Description Act, that's all.' He gave me a grin and shrugged.

'I thought I'd done me homework that time. Bloody encyclopedia you are, Lovejoy. See you later.'

'It's Lovejoy – going straight yet?' came a second later.

Margaret Dainty was perhaps a useful thirty-five, tinted hair, plump and prematurely matronly of figure. She was cool, usually reasonably griffed up on her wares, and tended to be highly-priced. There was a husband lurking somewhere in her background but he never materialized. An unfortunate childhood injury gave her a slight limp, well disguised.

'Hiya, Margaret. How's business?'

'Not good.' This means anything from bad to splendid.

'Same all round.'

'Interested in anything – besides Jane Felsham?' She sat opposite and brushed crumbs away for her elbows. I raised eyebrows.

'What's she done wrong?'

'One of your late-night visitors, I hear.'

'Word gets round – wrong as usual. Daytime. Accompanied.'

'I'm glad to hear it, Lovejoy,' she said, smiling.

We had been good friends, once and briefly. I'd assumed that was to be it and that she'd developed other interests.

'Now, now, young Dainty,' I chided. 'You don't want an ageing, dishevelled, poverty-stricken bum like me cramping your style.'

'You *are* hard work,' she agreed coolly. 'But never dull.'

'Poor's dull,' I corrected her. 'Failure's dull. That's me.'

'You're determined not to risk another Cissie.' Cissie, my erstwhile lady wife.

'There couldn't be another. It's one per galaxy.'

'You're safe, then.' She eyed me as I finished that terrible tea. 'Coming to see my stock?'

I rose, bringing my unfinished Chorley cake with me. Frankly, I could have gone for Margaret badly, too deeply for my own good. But women are funny, you know. They keep changing, ever so slightly, from the time you first meet them. There's a gradual hardening and tightening, until finally they're behaving all about you, unmasked and vigilant, not a little fierce. It's all made worse by the crippling need for them that one has. There's an absolute demand, and women have the only supply. I prefer them before their shutters and masks come down. Not, you understand, at a distance.

She had a *bonheur de jour* – lady's writing desk – eighteenth-century.

'Sheraton?' Margaret asked.

'No. His style, though.'

'Why not?'

I shrugged in answer. I couldn't tell her about my bell's condemnatory silence. 'Doesn't seem quite right.'

Tip: look for neat firegilt handles, that lovely satinwood, tulipwood and ebony, and never buy until you've had out the wooden runners which support the hinged writing surface. You'll be lucky if the baize is original – look at it edge on to see if it's standing high or not. High=modern replacement. Low=possibly original. Forget whether it's faded or not because we can do that on a clothes-line, washing and sun-drying repeatedly, day in, day out for a week.

It's only stuck on.

'Good or not?' she pressed.

'Pretty good,' which satisfied her.

She showed me two pottery birds, all bright colours and asked if I liked them.

'Horrible.'

'Genuine?' They looked like Chelsea. I touched one. Ding-dong.

'As ever was.'

'You haven't looked for the gold anchor mark underneath yet,' she said, vexed.

'It'll be there,' I said.

'Seeing you're on form,' she asked, 'what are these?'

There were four of them, shell-cases of various sizes, cut and decorated. A small cross, also brass, had been drilled into each. I picked one up. The crosspiece of each was loose and came free.

'Table bells,' I told her. 'Prisoners of war, probably Boer War. You signalled for the next course by combinations of these four bells. Not valuable.'

'Thanks.'

I cast my eye for flinters, but they weren't in Margaret's line.

In he tore, alcoholic and worried, eagerly trying to judge if we were just browsing or up to something, stained of teeth, unshaven of chin, bleary of eye, shoddy of gear, Dandy Jack.

'Come and see my jades, Lovejoy,' he said.

I tried to grin while backing from his evil breath. A customer was showing interest so Margaret stayed put, making a smiling gesture for me to look in before I left.

I let Dandy tell me how clever he'd been to do the deal. A retired colonel's widow, Far East wars and all that. I would have to be careful asking about flinters, but so far my approach had been casual in the extreme. Out came the jade collection. I sat on his visiting-stool while he showed me. By hook or by crook I would have to do him a good turn.

Jades are odd things. There are all sorts of daft ideas
in people's minds about antiques of all kinds – that *all*
antiques if genuine are priceless, for example, a clear piece
of lunacy. Nothing is truly beyond price if you think about
it. All you can say is that prices vary. Everything's always
for sale. Another daftness is that anything is an antique,
even if it's as little as five years old. Remember the golden
date, 1836. This side equals modern. That side equals
antique. The most extreme of all daftnesses, though, is the
idea that if something looks mint and beautifully preserved,
it shouldn't, and therefore needs false wood-worm holes
bored into it, scratches and dents made in unscathed surfaces, and splinters worked from corners. Wrong. Moral :
the better preserved, the costlier. *Keep things mint.*

Jades attract more daftness than any other antiques. And
Dandy Jack had every possible misconception, displaying
them all to anyone who called.

'It's a pity some aren't proper green,' he was saying,
fetching the small carved pieces out. 'They must be some
sort of stone. But here are some deep green ones . . .' and
so on. I tell you, it's bloody painful. You'd think these
people can't read a reference book between them. 'I played
it cool,' he kept on. 'Maybe I'll let them go for auction.
Do you think Christie's would – ?'

I picked one up – a black-and-white dragonfly, beautifully carved. Not painted, but pure jade through and
through. To tell real jade – though not its age, however
– from anything else, feel it. *Never leave jade untouched.*
Hold it, stroke it, touch it – that's what it's for, and what
it loves. But never touch it with freshly-washed hands. If
you've just washed your hands clean, come back in an
hour when your natural oils have returned to your fingers.
Then pick up and feel the jade's surface. You know how
oil gets when it's been rubbed partly dry, like, say, linseed
oil on a wooden surround? Faintly tacky and slightly stiff?
If the object you hold gives that *immediate* impression,
it's jade all right. To confirm it, look at the object in direct
light, *not* hooded like posh lamps. The surface mustn't

gleam with a brilliant reflection. It must appear slightly matt. Remember what the early experts used to say of jade : 'Soapy to look at, soapy to feel.' It's not too far out.

Now, there are many sorts of jade. Green jades are fairly common, but less so than you might think. 'Orange-peel' is one of my favourites, a brilliant orange with white, not a fleck of green. Then there's 'black-ink' jade, in fact perhaps nearer blue-black, usually mixed with white streaks, as in the dragonfly I was holding. One of the most valuable is 'mutton-fat' jade, a fat-white jade of virtually no trans-lucency despite its nickname.

Of course, nowadays the common green jade comes from damn near anywhere except China – Burma, New Zea-land, you name it. And it's blasted out of hills, in a new and unweathered state, which gives a massive yield but of a weak, scratchable quality. Most of these wretched carv-ings of fishes or horses you see now are done in China, of jade imported there. Green, fresh, soapy, mechanical travesties they are too. Get one (they should be *very* cheap) to teach yourself the feel, texture and appearance of the stuff, but if your favourite little nephew shatters it to pieces one day, don't lose any sleep. China's exporting them by the shipload. 'New-Mountain Jade' they call it in Canton, Kwantung, China.

But. That only goes for the new, modern, mine-blasted green jade. The ancients were much more discriminating. To satisfy them, a piece of jade had to be weathered. The new pieces were found exposed on hillsides, and were taken to a craftsman carver, an artist who loved such a rare material. With adulation he would observe where the flaws ran, what colours were hidden beneath the surface. And then, after maybe a whole year of feeling, stroking the magic stone and imagining the core of beauty within, he would begin to carve. New-Mountain Jade (i.e. modern) is soft. The antique stuff is hard, *hard*, and to carve it took time. This means that a dragonfly such as I was holding took about six months. The craftsman had left the dragon-fly's wings, head and body in black, and the underbelly had been skilfully carved through so it was mutton-fat jade, white like the spindly legs. The dragonfly was on a white mutton-fat jade lotus leaf – all less than two inches long, the detail exquisite, all from one piece of antique hard jade. And not a trace of green. Lovely. An artistic miracle.

I did my own private test – put it down a minute, my hands stretched out to cool, then picked it up again. Yes, cold as ice, even after being held in a hot, greedy hand. That's jade for you. The miracle stone. The ancient Chinese mandarins had one for each hand, a 'finger-jade' just for fiddling with, to comfort themselves. It was regarded as a very human need and not at all unmanly to want dispassionate solace as well as human comfort in that civilization, and what's wrong with either?

Dandy Jack had fetched out about thirty pieces. About half were agate, and of the rest some six were modern ugly deep leaf-green new jade pieces, carved with one eye on the clock and some productivity man whining about output. I found nine, including an orange-peel piece, of old jade, exquisitely carved foxes, hearts, lotus plants, bats, the dragonfly, fungi. It really was a desirable cluster.

'You've got good stuff here, Dandy,' I said. It hurt to tell the truth.

'You having me on, Lovejoy?' He had the sense to be suspicious.

'Those over there aren't jade at all. Agate.'

'The bastard!' he exclaimed. 'You mean I've been done?'

'No. You've got some stuff here worth half your business, Dandy.'

'Straight up?'

'Yes. Those dark things are modern – for heaven's sake don't scratch them. It's a dead give-away and you'll never sell them. These though are rare. Price them high.'

I gave him the inky dragonfly, though my hand tried to cling hold and lies sprang to my lips screaming to be let out so as to make Dandy give it me back for nothing. I

hate truth. Honest. I'm partial to a good old lie now and
again, especially if it's well done and serves a good honest
purpose. Being in antiques, I can't go about telling un-
sophisticated, inexpert lies. They have to be nudges, hints,
clever oblique untruths that sow the seed of deception,
rather than naïve blunt efforts. Done well, a lie can be an
attractive, even beautiful, thing. A good clever lie doesn't
go against truth – it just bends it a little round awkward
corners.

'You having me on?'

'Price them high, Dandy. My life.' The enormity hit
him.

'Do you think they're worth what I paid?'

'Whatever it was, it was too little.' I rose to go. He
caught my arm.

'Will you date and price them for me, Lovejoy?'

'Look,' I told him, 'if I do, promise me one thing.'

'What?'

'You won't sell *me* that bloody inky dragonfly. It's worth
its weight in gold four times over. If I put a price of two
hundred quid on it then offer to buy it from you, don't
sell.'

'You're a pal, Lovejoy,' he said, grinning all over his
bleary face.

I pulled off my coat and set to work. I saw Margaret
make a thumbs-up sign across the arcade to Dandy, who
had to rush across and give her the news. Morosely, I
blamed Field's mad search. If I hadn't needed Dandy's
gossip, I could have tricked most of the old jades out of
him for less than twenty quid and scored maybe a thousand.
Bloody charity, that's me, I thought. I slapped a higher
price on the dragonfly than even I'd intended. Give it
another month, I said sardonically to myself, the way things
are going and it would be cheap at the price.

I eventually had three leads from Dandy Jack, casual as
you like. I think I was reasonably casual, and he was keen
to tell me anything he knew. Lead one was a sale in York-

shire. Jack told me a small group – about seven items is a small group – of weapons was going there. The next was a sale the previous week I'd missed hearing of, in Suffolk.

I loaded up with petrol at Henry's garage.

'Still running, is it?' he said, grinning. 'I'll trade you.'

'For one that'll last till Thursday?' I snarled, thinking of the cost of petrol. 'You can't afford it.'

'Beats me how it runs,' he said, shaking his head. 'Never seen a crate like it.'

'Don't,' I said, paying enough to cancel the national debt. 'It does six – gallons to the mile, that is.'

I drove over to the estuary, maybe ten miles. Less than a hundred houses sloped down to the mud flats where those snooty birds rummage at low water and get all mucky. A colony of artists making pots live in converted boat-houses along the quayside and hang about the three pubs there groaning about lack of government money. Money for what, I'm unsure.

Brad was cleaning an Adams, a dragoon revolver of style and grace.

'Not buying, Brad,' I announced. He laughed, knowing I was joking.

'Thank heaven for that,' he came back. 'I'm not selling.'

We chatted over the latest turns. He knew all about Dandy's jades and guessed I'd been there.

'He has the devil's luck,' he said. I don't like to give too much away, but I wanted Dandy to learn from Brad how impressed I'd been, just in case he'd missed the message and felt less indebted. So I dwelled lovingly on some of the jades until Brad changed the subject.

'Who's this geezer on about Durs guns?'

You must realize that antique collecting is a lifetime religion. And dealing is that, plus a love-affair plus a job. Dealers know who is buying what at any time of day or night, even though we may seem to live a relatively sheltered and innocent life. And where, and when, and how.

This makes us sound a nasty, crummy, suspicious lot. Nothing of the kind. We are dedicated, and don't snigger at that either. Who else can be trusted, but those with absolute convictions? We want antiques, genuine lustrous perfection as objects of worship, and nothing else. All other events come second. In my book, that makes us trust-worthy, with everything on earth – except antiques. So Brad had heard.

'Oh, some bloke starting up,' I said.

'Oh?'

I thought a second, then accepted. 'An innocent. No idea. I took him on.'

'They're saying flinters.'

'Yes.'

'Difficult.'

I told him part of the tale I'd selected for public con-sumption.

'I thought maybe duellers, a flash cased set.'

'I'll let you have a few pair he can choose from.'

I grinned at the joke. 'I'm hardly flush,' I said. 'That's why I was round Dandy's, on the prod. He said you might have word of a pair. Have to be mint.'

He looked up from replacing the Adams in its case.

'I'm in the Midlands next Monday. I'm on to five pieces, but they might turn out relics.'

I whistled. Five possible miracles. A relic is any antique defaced and worn beyond virtual recognition, but you never think of that. The desire for the wonderment of a sensational discovery is always your first hope. Some people say it's ridiculous to hope that way, but doesn't everyone in one way or another? A man always hopes to meet a luscious, seductive woman; a woman always hopes to meet a handsome, passionate man. They don't go round hoping for less, do they? We dealers are just more specialized.

'Keep me in mind,' I said, swallowing. 'The cash is there.'

'Where, exactly?' he rejoined smoothly, and we laughed.

We chatted a bit more, then I throbbed away in my fiery racer. I made a holiday-maker curse by swinging out into the main road without stopping, but my asthmatic old scrap-heap just can't start on a hill whereas his brand-new

Austin can start any time, even after an emergency stop. People ought to learn they have obligations.

Muriel's house turned out to be my sort of house. Set back from the road, not because it never quite made it like my cottage, but from an obvious snooty choice not to mob with the hoi-polloi. I imagined banisters gleaming with dark satin-brown depths, candelabras glittering on mahogany tables long as football pitches and dusty paintings clamouring on the walls. My sort of house, with a frail old widow lady wanting a kindly generous soul like myself to bowl in, and help her to sell up. My throat was dry. I eagerly coaxed the banger to a slow turn and it cranked to a standstill, coughing explosively. I knocked with the door's early nineteenth-century insurance company knocker. (They come expensive now, as emblems of a defunct habit of marking houses with these insignia of private fire insurance companies.) It had shiny new screws holding it firmly on to the door, though the thought honestly never crossed my mind. The door opened. The frail old widow lady appeared.

She was timid, hesitant, and not yet thirty.

'Good day,' I said, wishing I was less shabby.

I've never quite made it, the way some men do. I always look shabby about the feet, my trousers seem less than sharp, my coats go bulbous as soon as they're bought. I have a great shock of hair that won't lie down. I'm really a mess.

'Yes?' She stared from round the door. I could hear somebody else clattering cooking things in the background.

'Look, I'll be frank,' I said, feeling out of my depth. 'My name is Lovejoy. I've called about . . . about your late husband, Mr Field.'

'Oh.'

'Er, I'm sorry if it seems inopportune, Mrs Field . . .' I paused for a denial, but no. 'I'm an antique collector, and . . .' Never say dealer except to another dealer.

'I'm sorry, Mr Lovejoy,' she said, getting a glow of

animosity from somewhere. 'I don't discuss –'

'No,' I said, fishing for some good useful lie. 'I'm not after buying anything, please.' The door stayed where it was. I watched it for the first sign of closing. 'It's . . . it's the matter of Mr Field's purchases.'

'Purchases?' She went cautious, the way they do. 'Did my husband buy things from you?'

'Well, not exactly.'

'Then what?'

'Well,' I said desperately, 'I don't really know how to put it.'

She eyed me doubtfully for a moment, then pulled back the door.

'Perhaps you should come in.'

In the large hall she stood tall, elegant, the sort of woman who always seems warm. Cissie spent her time hunting draughts to extinction. This woman would be immune. She looked deeply at you, not simply in your direction the way some of them will, and you could tell she was listening and sensing. In addition she had style.

Now, every woman has some style, as far as I'm concerned. They are fetchingly shaped to start with, pleasant to look at and desirable to, er, encounter, so to speak. And all women have that attraction. Any man that says he can remain celibate for yonks on end is not quite telling the truth. It's physically impossible. What astonishes me is that very few women seem to see this obvious terrifying fact, that we are completely dependent on their favours. Ah, well.

I had no plan of action, trusting simply to my innate instinct for deception and falsehood. Mrs Field dithered a bit then asked me into a lounge, where we sank into nasty new leather armchairs. There was a rosewood desk, eastern, modern, and one tatty cavalry sabre on the wall. On the desk I could see a chatelaine which looked like Louis XIV from where I was sitting but I couldn't be sure.

'You mentioned you and my husband were fellow-collectors, Mr Lovejoy.'

A chatelaine is a small (six to eight inches or so) case, often shaped in outline like a rounded crucifix. It opens to show scissors, tooth pick, manicure set and sometimes small pendants for powders and pills, that sort of thing, for people to carry about. Quite desirable, increasing in value –

'Mr Lovejoy?' she said.

'Eh? Oh yes. Mr Field.' I dragged my mind back.

'You mentioned . . .'

In the better light she was quite striking. Pale hair, pale features, lovely mouth and stylish arms. She fidgeted with her hands. The whole impression was of somebody lost, certainly not in her own territory.

'Poor Mr Field,' I hedged. 'I heard of the . . . accident, but didn't like to call sooner.'

'That was kind of you. It was really the most terrible thing.'

'I'm so sorry.'

'Did you know my husband?'

'Er, no. I have . . . other business associates, and I collect antiques in partnership with, er, a friend.' It was going to be hard.

'And your friend . . . ?' she filled in for me.

I nodded. 'We were about to discuss some furniture with Mr Field.' I was sweating, wondering how long I could keep this up. If she knew anything at all about her husband's collecting, I was done for.

'Was it a grandfather clock?' she asked, suddenly recalling.

I smiled gratefully, forgiving her the use of that dreadful incorrect term.

'Yes. William Porthouse, Penrith, made it. A lovely, beautiful example of a longcase clock, Mrs Field. It's dated on the dial, 1738, and even though the –'

'Well,' she interrupted firmly, 'I wouldn't really know what my husband was about to buy, but in the circumstances . . .'

I was being given the heave-ho. I swallowed my impulse

to preach on about longcase clocks, but she was too stony-hearted and unwound her legs. Marvellous how women can twist them round each other.

'Of course,' I exclaimed, as if surprised. 'We certainly wouldn't wish to raise the matter, quite, quite.'

'Oh, then . . . ?'

'It's just —' I smiled as meekly as I could as I brought out the golden words — 'er, it's just the matter of the two pistols.'

'Pistols?' She looked quite blank.

'Mr Field said something about a case with two little pistols in.' I shrugged, obviously hardly able to bother about this little detail I'd been forced to bring up. 'It's not really important, but my friend said he and Mr Field had . . . er . . .'

'Come to some arrangement?'

I blessed her feminine impulse to fill the gaps.

'Well, nothing quite changed hands, you understand,' I said reluctantly. 'But we were led to believe that Mr Field was anxious for us to buy a small selection of items, including these pistol things.' I shrugged again as best I could but was losing impetus fast. If any smattering of what Field had told me was remotely true, a pair of Durs flinters had actually resided under this very roof, been in this very room, even. I raised my head, which had bowed reverently at the thought. I felt as if I'd just happened on St Peter's, Rome.

'As part exchange, I suppose?'

'Well, I suppose so. Something like that.'

'I heard about them,' she said, gradually fading into memory. Her eyes stared past me. 'He showed me a couple of pistols, in a box. The police asked me about them, when George —'

'George?'

'My brother-in-law. Eric, my husband, phoned him the night before he . . . He was going to go over and show George the next morning. Then this terrible thing happened.'

'Were you here, when . . . ?'

'No. I was in hospital.'

'Oh. I'm sorry.'

'We'd been abroad, Eric and I, a year ago. I'd been off colour ever since, so I went in to have it cleared up. Eric insisted.'

'So you knew nothing at all about it?'

'Until George came. I was convalescent by then. George and Patricia were marvellous. They arranged everything.'

'Did you say the police asked about the pistols?'

'Yes. George thought whoever did it . . . used them to . . . to . . .'

'I suppose the police found them?' I said innocently. 'They can trace guns these days.'

'Hardly.' Her face was almost wistful. 'They were so old, only antiques, and they don't think he was . . . shot.'

'What were they like?' I swallowed. The words were like sandpaper grating.

'Oh, about this long,' she said absently, measuring about fifteen inches with hands suddenly beautiful with motion. 'Dark, not at all pretty.'

'My friend said something about gold decoration,' I croaked in falsetto.

'Oh, that's all right, then,' she said, relieved. 'They must be different ones. These had nothing like that. Blackish and brown, really nothing special, except that little circle.'

'Circles?' I shrilled. At least I wasn't screaming, but my jacket was drenched with sweat. She smiled at her hands.

'I remember Eric pulling my leg,' she said. 'I thought they were ugly and a shiny circle stuck on them made them look even worse. Eric laughed. Apparently they were pieces of platinum.'

I realized I should be smiling, so I forced my face into a gruesome ha-ha shape as near as I could. She smiled back.

'You see, Mr Lovejoy, I never really . . . well, took to my husband's collecting. It seemed such a waste of time and money.'

I gave my famous shrug, smiling understandingly.

'I suppose one can overdo it,' I lied. As if one could overdo collecting.

'Eric certainly did.'

'Where did he get his items from, Mrs Field? Of course, I know many of the places, but my friend didn't see very much of him.'

'Through the post, mostly. I was always having to send down to the village post office. I think the case came from Norfolk.'

'What?' I must have stared because she recoiled.

'The box. Weren't you asking about them?'

'Oh, *those*,' I said, laughing lightly. 'When you said "case" I thought you meant the *cased* clock I mentioned.' I forced another light chuckle. Stupid Lovejoy.

'The shiny pistols. I remember that because they were so heavy and the woman at the post office said she'd been there.'

You have to pay for the pleasure of watching a beautiful woman. In kind, of course. Like struggling to understand her train of thought.

'Er, been where, Mrs Field?'

'To the place in Norfolk. She said, Oh, that's where the bird sanctuary is, on the coast. She'd been there with her family, you see. I tried to remember the name for the police, but they said it didn't really matter.'

'Ah, yes. Well, I never get quite that far, so perhaps . . . er, one thing more.' I was almost giddy with what she'd told me.

'Yes?'

'What, er, happened to them? Only,' I added hastily, 'in case my friend asks.'

'Well, I don't know.' Any more questions would make her suspicious. 'George asked, and the police asked, but that's the point. When I returned from hospital they were gone.'

'And the rest of the antiques . . . ?'

'Oh, they were sold. I wasn't really interested, you see, and Eric had always said to send them off to a respectable auction if anything happened. He was a very meticulous man,' she informed me primly.

I nodded. He was also a very lucky man, I thought. For a while.

She was waiting for me to go. I racked my exhausted brain. How did the police and these detectives know what questions to ask, I wondered irritably. I knew that as soon as the door closed a hundred points would occur to me. I'm like that.

'Well, thank you, Mrs Field,' I said, rising. 'I shouldn't really have called, but my friend was on at me about it.'

'Not at all. I'm glad you did. It's always best to have these things sorted out, isn't it?'

'That's what my friend said.'

She came with me to the door, and watched me away down the drive. A priest was walking up as I screeched away from the house, probably on some ghoulish errand. They're never far away from widows, I thought unkindly, but I was feeling somehow let down. I gave him a nod and got a glance back, free of charge. I had an impression of middle age, a keen, thin face and eyes of an interrogator. Interesting, because I'd thought fire-and-brimstone weren't policy any more, though fashions do change. I didn't see his cash-register.

She gave me a wave in the driving-mirror. I waved back, wondering even as I accelerated out of the landscaped gardens and back among the riff-raff whether I could ask her out on some pretext. But I'd now blotted my copybook with all the pretending I'd done. Women don't like that sort of thing, being unreasonable from birth. Very few of them have any natural trust.

It's a terrible way to be.

CHAPTER V

BACK AT THE cottage I summed things up, getting madder every minute at those slick so-and-so's on TV that make short work of any crime. I worked out a list in my mind of possible events as I made my tea, two eggs fried in margarine, baked beans with the tin standing in a pan of boiling water, and two of those yoghurt things for afters. I always like a lot of bread and marge and make sandwiches of everything when I've not got company. A pint of tea, no sugar on alternate days because the quacks keep scaring the wits out of you about eating things you like, and I was off.

I sat down at the door to watch the birds fool around while I ate.

I'd learned the pistols were something vital, probably a really good pair, almost certainly Durs, as George said. Shiny, the lovely Muriel had said, and black. No decoration, but a platinum plug for the touch-hole. And she'd indicated about fifteen inches long, not too far out. Shiny might mean not cross- or star-hatched, as Durs did his, but some of his early pieces were known unhatched, so that was still all right. Black, shiny, ugly . . . well, the poor lady was still probably slightly deranged after her shock. Cased. And Brother George had said there were accessories in it. And bought by post from Norfolk, near a coastal bird resort.

All Eric's stuff had been sold, but George was certain the flinters weren't there when he discovered his brother. And if they'd been hidden anywhere in the house, presumably Muriel would have come across them by now.

I finished my meal and sat drinking tea. It was afternoon, and the sun threw oblique shadows across the grass. The birds, a fairly ragged lot with not much to do, trotted about the path and milled around after crumbs. My robin,

an aggressive little charmer who seemed to dislike the rest,
came on my arm and gave its sweet whistle. It was blowing
a cool breeze, rising from the east. With the east coast so
near, afternoons could take on a chill.

'Do people go to bird sanctuaries to look at things like
you?' I asked the robin. He looked back, disgusted. 'Well,'
I explained to him, 'some people must. Know where it is?'

He dropped off and shooed some brownish things off
his patch. You'd think robins were soft and angelic from
all the free publicity they get around Christmas, but they're
tough as nails. I've seen this one of mine take on rabbits
as well as those big black birds that goose-step about after
you've cut the grass. Tough, but means well. I'm just the
opposite, weak and bad-intentioned.

'Margaret?'

'Lovejoy!' She sounded honestly pleased. 'At last! Where
are we to meet?'

'Cool it, babe,' I said. 'I'm after information.'

'I'd hoped you were lusting Force Five at least.' She
heaved a sigh. 'I suppose it's still that tart from London.'

'Which tart?' I asked, all innocent.

'You know. The one you sent walking to the station on
her own.'

'OK, Hawkeyes-of-the-East,' I said sardonically.

'I just happened to notice,' she said sweetly, 'seeing as I
was dangling out of the pub window when you arrived.'

I hadn't seen her. The thought crossed my mind that
she might have overheard Tinker and George Field, but I
hadn't time to hang about if a real genuine pair of flinters
were in all this.

'She'd just been for a short . . . er . . . visit,' I explained.

'How long's long, if three days is short?'

'Two,' I snapped back, and could have bitten my tongue.

'Oh, two, was it,' she cooed. 'You must be tired, sweetie,
after all that entertaining.'

See what I mean? They don't like each other really. I
honestly believe that's what all that dressing up's all about.

It doesn't matter what the bloke thinks, as long as they out-do any other birds in the vicinity. I often wonder how nuns get on, and whether they vie with each other for God in the convent. All the rest are fencing and machin-ating and circling warily, all for nothing. Frightening, if you let yourself dwell on it.

I once had this bird – the one I got the cottage from – and she found that I'd visited this other woman in the village. Honestly, it was quite innocent, really, but I'd had to stay away from the cottage for a night or two, only because I'd got pressing business, you see. My resident bird hit the roof – gave me hell, but was more eager to cripple this other woman for life than she was to tell me off.

I think they just like fighting each other, and I'd just given my bird an excuse for a scrap. How she found out I'll never know. They always assume the worst, don't they? Trust is not their strong point.

'I rang up to ask,' I said with dignity, 'about birds.'

'How many do you want, sweetie?' she said coyly, putting barbs in.

'Birds that fly about,' I reprimanded. 'In the air.'

'Oh, I beg your pardon, Lovejoy,' she said, needling still. 'I misunderstood. I thought –'

'Never mind what you thought.'

'Stuffed?' she drooled.

'Now, look, Margaret –' I snapped, and she relented.

'Sorry, old thing. What is it?'

'I have the offer of some glassed animals,' I improvised. 'Ten.'

'Quite a collection.'

'Well, the thing is, I haven't an idea.'

'Want me to look at them for you?'

This was a blow, because Margaret was something of our local expert on such horrid monstrosities. Stuffed animals might be valuable antiques, rare as hens' teeth, but they still dampen my ardour.

'Er, well, you see . . .' I let it wait.

'All right, Lovejoy, I understand.' She was smiling from

her voice. 'You don't trust me.'

'Of course I do, Margaret,' I said, fervour oozing down the phone. 'It's just that I thought I'd rather learn a bit about suchlike myself . . . anyway, I believe there are some bird sanctuaries further along the coast which are pretty well-known, so I thought – '

'Look, Lovejoy,' she said, serious now. 'I don't know what you plan to do, but if you're aiming to cart a load of stuffed birds into a bird sanctuary and ask them to help you identify them, you're going to be unpopular.'

'Oh. Well, they might have some literature . . .' I said weakly.

'I'll get the details. My nephew's in a club that comes out this way. Hang on.' She left the phone a moment and gave me a list of three bird sanctuaries, of which two were in Norfolk. I didn't say which one I was interested in, but said I'd probably go to the nearest.

Before she rang off, she asked if I was all right.

'Of course I am. Why?' She hesitated.

'Oh, nothing. It's just . . . Look, can I come and see you for a second?'

'Oh, Margaret.' It was a bit transparent, after all, so I can be forgiven for being exasperated.

'Suit yourself, Lovejoy,' she snapped angrily, and slammed the phone down. Women don't like to give up, you see. Seen them with knitting? Yards, hours and hours, years even. And still they're there, soldiering on. Something pretty daunting about women sometimes, I often think. Anyway, it's change I like, and that's exactly what they resent.

While I went again through my records – locking up carefully as usual – there were two further phone calls. One was Sheila, who complained I hadn't rung. I said so what else is new, and she rang off telling me I was in a mood. Tinker interrupted me an hour later saying he'd had four possible tickles. Three were the same as I'd got from Dandy Jack and included the Yorkshire auction, plus one further whisper of a man in Fulham who'd brought

a load of stuff down from the north and had two cased
sets among the items. That could have meant anything
including percussion, so I took the address and said I'd
speed off there in my speedster some time.

There were numerous antique enthusiasts in Norfolk.
Only a hundred lived near the coast. From the bird sanctuaries Margaret had given me I selected some five or six
collectors varying the narrow radius.

Cross-checking with the auction records I had, none of
the six had bought within two years anything remotely
resembling a Durs gun. Indeed, most of them seemed to
be either furniture or porcelain people, though one particular chap, a clergyman called Lagrange, had purchased
a revolving percussion longarm from a local auction not
far from the Blakeney Point sanctuary. Adverts didn't help,
except for a run of them from two Norfolk addresses in
the *Exchange and Mart* some two years ago, wanting
rather than offering flinters.

I emerged from my priest-hole three hours later fairly
satisfied that if Durs duellers had changed hands within
the two years before Eric Field's death, it had been done
so quietly nobody had known. Therefore the ones which
came so innocently by post from Norfolk were a major
find, something newly discovered to this century's cruel
gaze.

My hands were shaking again so I had my emergency
beer. If it wasn't women it was antiques, or vice versa. I
put the telly on and watched some little rag-dolls talking
to each other on a children's programme. That did nothing
for my disturbed state of mind.

I was getting close to believing in the Judas Pair.

Look about. That's all I have to say. Look about. Because
antique discoveries happen. If in doubt read any book on
local history. It'll set you thinking.

I've come across Minden *faïence jardinières* – posh pots
for garden plants – being used as garage toolboxes. I've

seen a set of Swiss miniature gold dominoes making up
an infant's set of wooden building bricks, in the original
gold case. I've seen a beautiful octagonal ruby-glass hall-
marked silver-ended double scentbottle used as a doll's
rolling-pin. I can go on all night.

I've seen a Spencer and Perkins striking watch used as
a weight on a plumb-line. You still don't believe me?
Don't, then. Go and ask the Colchester labourers who dug
out an old bucket a couple of years ago – and found in it
the lost Colchester hoard of thousands of medieval silver
coins. Or go and ask the farmer who four years ago got
so fed up with the old coffin-handles he kept ploughing
up in his field that he took them to the authorities. They're
the famous solid gold Celtic torcs that museums the world
over now beg to be allowed to *copy*. And while you're
about it you can also ask where the most valuable pot in
the world was found – no, not in some sacred tomb. It was
in somebody's porch *being used as an umbrella stand*. Well,
a Charles I silver communion cup is my own principal
claim to fame. I bought it as an old tin shaving-cup years
ago. *And* kept the profits. None of this rubbish about 'fair
play', giving part of the proceeds up as conscience-money.
A sale is a sale is a sale.

My mind was edging further towards an uneasy belief.

I let the evening come nearer the cottage by having a
small cigar. The darkness swung in, inch by inch. I swept
the living-room and got out some sausages for my supper.
Those and chips, with a custard thing from our village
shop to follow.

Though the cottage seemed cosy enough, this Judas
business had taken the steam out of me for the moment.
Perhaps it was just my turn to feel a bit down. I get that
way.

As I listlessly tidied up I realized how really isolated
the cottage was. Solitude is precious to me, but only when
I want it.

I phoned Margaret, intending to say I'd perhaps been rather short with her on the blower. It rang and rang without answer.

While my grub was frying I stood at the darkening window and watched the road lights come on across the valley edge a mile away. The White Hart would be starting up. Harry, possibly Jane Felsham, Adrian, probably Tinker and for absolute certain Dandy Jack – they'd all be there. Later would come the nightlies, the knocker dealers who touted door to door leaving cards or hoping housewives bored to torture would fall for their blue eyes enough to search their attics.

Then the pub dealing would start, cuts, rings, groups, fractional slices of profit, marginal gains, the entire lovely exhilarating game of nudges and nods. I pulled the curtains to.

Suppose I did find the thirteenth pair. What then? I hadn't asked Field. Whoever had them murdered Eric Field. I was to tell George Field, probably, who would accuse the owner, whoever it was, to the police. So the police would then arrest the owner. QED.

I poked the sausages and chips on to a cold plate and margarined some slices of bread. The tea. I'd forgotten tea. I put the kettle on, but before sitting down tried to phone Margaret again. No luck. By then the kettle boiled. By the time the tea brewed the food was cold. I sighed and sat down to supper.

Having the telly on helped, but I keep wondering what they really do for a living during the day.

CHAPTER VI

NEXT MORNING was just my sort, greyish but dry and promising a bit of sun. I had two eggs on bread, lashings of sauce to smother any taste that might linger on after my cooking, and a couple of *Weetabix* and powdered milk.

Two apples and a pear for the journey, and the world was my oyster. My uneasy mood had vanished.

I rang George Field to summarize my progress, not mentioning my clue from Muriel, but saying I was following a couple of leads within the trade. He seemed disappointed, which was only to be expected. He was probably reared on Chandler's slick heroes.

The Armstrong didn't share my enthusiasm. Maybe it knew how far we had to go. I fed the robin, waiting for the engine to recover from an attempt to start it before half past nine. It usually functioned best about dinner-time. Oddly enough, it was also seasonal, preferring winters to summers and rain to sun.

I'm not a sentimental person. You can't be about a mere scrap-heap, can you? But I have a liking for the old banger simply because it's the only time my bell's been wrong. I took the motor in part exchange for a group of four small animal bronzes from a Carmarthen chap who, poor misguided soul, was interested in bronzes. Some people love them, heaven knows why, as very few are attractive. Incidentally, always look underneath a bronze figure first. If it has a four-figure number, it may well be a 'liberated' piece which arrived here after the war. 'DEPOSE GES-CHUTZT' or some such stamped in front of this number can lend weight to your suppositions. The value of most bronzes has increased eight times in the last couple of years among dealers alone.

I was on about my Armstrong. It is an open tourer with big squarish headlamps sticking out and a hood that you pull over by hand. Nothing's automatic. The starter's a handle at the front, and you have to work a fingerpump from the front seat before it will fire. The brake's outside, and a noisy exhaust runs like a portable tunnel from both sides of the long bonnet which is held down by straps. It looks badly old-fashioned and clumsy, but it's strong as hell and safe as houses which is the main thing. As I say, the fuel consumption is terrible. All along where the dash-board would be in a new car, there are switches, handles and a couple of mysterious gauges I've always been too scared to touch in case it stopped altogether. For such a huge car it is weak as a kitten, but once you get it going it is usually fine. The trouble is it seems to have only one gear because there's no gear handle. Other motorists often blow their horns as they pass in annoyance at my slow speed. I only have a rubber bulb-type honker I never use.

It made a successful running start eventually. As I drove at maximum speed I worked my journey out. Margaret had given me the names of three places, Minsmere in Suffolk, Blakeney Point and Cley in Norfolk. I would say I'd been to Minsmere if anyone asked, and, engine willing, would look at the other two places in one go. I would reach home before opening time. I had the six significant addresses with me to consider one by one.

I was frankly disappointed with the bird sanctuaries, not that I knew what to expect. Quite a few cars were around when I drove up to Cley. A few folks, rommellized by great binoculars and businesslike weatherproof hats, stood all forlorn in attitudes of endeavour staring towards acres of desolate muddy stuff where nothing was happening. Occasionally they murmured to each other and peered eastwards. Perhaps they placed bets among themselves to make it interesting. As well as being disappointed I was puzzled. I've nothing against birds, feathered or not, but once you've seen one sparrow you've seen the lot, haven't you? Occasionally, one particular one might become sort of family just by sheer persistence, like some around the cottage. That's different. Unless you know them specially it's a waste of time, like people. I asked one bloke what they were all looking at.

'Oyster-catchers,' he said. I stared about but there wasn't a boat in sight.

'Oh,' I replied, and honestly that was it.

There were no stalls, cafés, not even a fish-and-chip shop. As a resort it was a dead duck, if you'll pardon the expression. I talked the Armstrong into life and we creaked away on ye olde greate mysterie trail. I had more birds in my garden than they had on all that mud. I was frozen stiff.

Now, brilliant Lovejoy had made a plan. Muriel's memory being what it was, I was down to guesswork – scintillating cunning brainwork of Sherlock type.

To post a case you need a post office, right? Sniggering at my shrewdness, I drove around trying to find one, lurching along country lanes where hedges waved in the gales and animals stooged about fields being patient as ever.

I eventually gave up and some time later drove through Wells into Blakeney, where there was a post office. I was dismayed. What do private eyes do now? I couldn't just bowl in and say, 'What ho! Who posted a heavy box about a year ago, give or take six months?' My plan hadn't got this far. I inspected it from a distance and then drove to the Point. More desolation with some different-shaped birds bumming around aimlessly, all watched eagerly by enthusiasts. No shops, no stalls, no real scene. I departed shivering.

All this countryside was damping my earlier high spirits. It's nice from a distance. A few trees and a sparrow or two can be quite pleasant sometimes as a diversion. But you can't beat a good old town crammed full of people milling about on hard pavements, street after street of houses, shops, antique merchants, cinemas, pubs, the odd theatre and lots of man-made electricity. Bird sanctuaries are all very well, but why can't they share them with people?

I drove around Blakeney. In case you come from there I'm not knocking it. Charming little joint, with the odd tasty antique shop and a place I had dinner near a tavern. But it's not a metropolis, is it? And it has no coastal holiday resorts nearby, either. From the way Muriel's postmistress had spoken I wanted something like Clacton. That cold wind started up again. I decided there were no clues in bird sanctuaries and drove south. What dumps those places are, I thought, feeling a witticism coming. Those places, I sniggered to myself, are for the birds.

I like antique dealers. We may not be much to look at,

but scratch us and we're nothing but pure unadulterated antique dealer all the way through. Everything else comes second. This means you've only to put us, blindfolded, anywhere on earth, and we home instinctively on the nearest fellow-dealer. When I'm driving, I swear my banger guides itself along a route that has the highest number of dealers along it.

Trusting the Armstrong, I was at my ninth antique shop asking for nothing in particular, when the name 'Lagrange' accidentally caught my eye. The shop owner, a doctor's wife, Mrs Ellison, full of painting chat, had gone into the back to find a painting I'd heard of, alleged Norwich School, and to fill in time I was leafing through her invoice file. Lagrange had bought a pistol flask from her about a year before, and paid in groats from what I saw.

I was safely near the door hovering over a box of copper tokens when she returned with the painting. It was a water-colour, not an oil, which was a measure of her knowledge. David Cox had signed it, so the name said. I held it. Good stuff, but not a single chime. I showed a carefully-judged disappointment and turned to other things. David Cox taught a lot of pupils water-colour painting, and had an annoying habit of helping them with little bits of their work, a daub here, a leaf there. If their final painting pleased him *he* would sign it, thereby messing up the whole antique business. Worse, his signature's dead easy to forge – so they say. Beware.

I bought a score of her copper tokens, to pay for my journey's expenses. They are cheap, rather like small coins. Merchants in the seventeenth and eighteenth centuries, times when copper change was in short supply owing to incompetence at the Mint among other causes, made their own 'coins' as tokens in copper. These were given for change, and you could spend them when you needed to go shopping again. It must have been a nightmare because some shops would refuse all except their own tokens, so you might finish up with perhaps thirty *different* sets of copper 'coinage' of this kind in your pocket, and still not be able to buy what you wanted from the thirty-first shop. The early seventeenth-century ones are about half the size of those from the next century – an important fact as many are undated. I bought the 'cleanest', that is those least worn, no matter how dirty. 'Buy the best, *then* buy old,' as we say. Of any two antiques, go for the one best preserved and remember that repairs or any sort of restoration doesn't mean well-preserved. Then consider the degree of rarity. *Then,* and only then, consider the degree of age. This is Lovejoy's Law for Collectors of Limited Means. Of course, if you have bags of money, head straight for a Turner seascape, a silver piece made by that astonishing old lady silversmith Hester Bateman, or a Clementi (the London maker) square piano of about 1840, and two fingers to the rest of us. But for other poorer wayfarers, my advice is to have only these three general rules.

I paid up painfully and turned to go.

'Oh, one thing.' I paused as if remembering. 'You've not such a thing as a powder flask?'

'Powder – ? Oh, for *gun*powder?'

I nodded.

'No,' she said. 'I had one a while ago, but it went very quickly.' She'd probably had it on her hands for years.

'I'm trying to make one of those wretched sets up,' I explained.

She was all sympathy. 'Isn't it hard?'

I hesitated still. 'No chance of you managing to pick one up, is there? I don't have much chance of getting one myself.'

'Well . . .'

I was obviously treading upon that sacred confidentiality. 'I'd be glad to pay a percentage on purchase,' I offered, which made it less holy.

'I know,' she said. 'When you have money locked up in stock, trying to move stuff can be so difficult.'

We commiserated for a minute in this style. She told me she'd sold the flask to a local collector. She gave me Lagrange's address, the one I already had. I expressed surprise and gratitude and handed her my card.

'He's a very pleasant padre,' she informed me, smiling. 'A real enthusiastic collector. I'm sure he'll be glad to see you.'

'I'll either call back or phone,' I promised, and set about finding the Reverend Lagrange, collector.

Mrs Ellison had given me the usual obscure directions which I translated by a vintage RAC roadmap. He lived about fifteen miles off the trunk road, say thirty miles. I patted my speedster and swung the handle. I'd be there in an hour and a half with luck.

The trouble was I'd not had any feminine companionship for a couple of days. It blunts any shrewdness you might possess. Your brain goes astray. It's no state to be in.

I drove towards Reverend Lagrange's place thinking of Sheila as a possible source of urgent companionship. No grand mansion here, my cerebral cortex registered at the sight of the grubby little semi-detached house with its apron-sized plot of grass set among sixty others on a dull estate. Such trees as people had planted stood sparse and young, two thin branches and hardly a leaf to bless themselves with. I parked on the newly-made road where there was a slope, a hundred yards away, and walked back among the houses. A curtain twitched along the estate, which pleased me as a sign that women hadn't changed even here in this desolation. But where was the Reverend's church? Maybe he was still only an apprentice and hadn't got one. I knocked.

Ever run into a patch of mistakes? My expectations were beginning to ruin my basic optimism. Just as Muriel had turned out to be half the age I'd anticipated, here was this padre who I'd supposed couldn't be more than twenty-two. He was middle-aged. Worse still – much more upsetting – I'd seen him before, walking up Muriel Field's drive as I had left. All this might not matter to you, but to an antique dealer it's his life-blood. First approaches are everything. I suppressed my flash of annoyance and gave my I'm-innocent-but-keen grin.

'Reverend Lagrange?'

'Yes?' He was a calm and judging sort, in clerical black and dog-collar, not too tidy.

'I hope I'm not intruding.' The thought occurred that it might be a feast-day or Lent or something. Worse, he might be fasting. I eyed him cautiously. He seemed well nourished.

'Not at all. Can I help?'

'Er – I only called on the offchance.'

'Do come in.' He stood aside and in one stride I was in his living-room. There was a cheap rolltop desk and a scatter of Co-operative furniture. He had a one-bar electric fire for the chill winter evenings. My heart went out for him.

'It isn't anything to do with . . . er . . . the soul,' I faltered. 'I'm interested in antiques, Reverend. I was at a shop – '

His eyes lit up and he put his black Bible inside his desk, sliding the lid closed.

'Do sit down, Mr . . . ?'

'Lovejoy.'

'Splendid name,' he said, smiling. I was beginning to quite like him. 'The shop was – ?'

I told him and he raised his eyes heavenward.

'Ah, yes. I bought a pistol flask there, quite expensive it was,' he said.

May heaven forgive you for *that,* I thought nastily. It was a steal. I would have asked five times what he paid.

'Er,' I began, weighing out those grains of truth which gospel fables, 'don't I know you from somewhere?'

'Do you?' He seemed as careful as I was.

'You couldn't by any chance know the Fields?'

'Ah, yes.' We unbent, full of reassuring noises. 'My poor friend.'

'I visited Mrs Field. I *thought* I saw you arriving.'

' – And you're the gentleman in the long car. Of course. I *thought* I recognized you. Did you manage to get it seen to? I'm no mechanic myself, but I could tell from the noise and all that smoke – '

I wasn't taking that from any bloke.

'You're a friend of Eric Field's?' I interrupted, peeved. My speedster might stutter a bit, but so did Caesar.

'An old friend.' He went all pious like they do. 'I try to visit Muriel – Mrs Field, that is – as often as I can, to lend solace.' He sighed. 'It's been a very difficult time for her, seeking readjustments.'

'I do appreciate that, Reverend,' I said, considerably moved for a second or so.

It's pleasant being holy, but isn't it boring? Holy duty done with, I got down to business.

'I know you'll think it a bit of a cheek, Reverend,' I began apologetically. 'But I'm trying to complete a set of accessories for a pistol I have, in a case.'

'Oh.' His eyes glinted. I was on to a real collector here, no mistake. 'Any special variety?'

'Very expensive,' I said with the famous Lovejoy mixture of pride and regret. 'A pocket Adams revolver.'

'Oh.' His fire damped. 'Percussion.'

'Yes, but almost mint.' I let myself become eager. 'There's one nipple replaced, and a trace of repair – '

His lip curled into an ill-concealed sneer. 'Well, Mr Lovejoy,' he said, still polite. 'I'm afraid percussion's not my first choice.'

'Flinters?' I breathed in admiration.

'It so happens . . .' He controlled himself and said carefully, 'I am interested. If you ever do hear of any flintlocks, I would be most happy to come to some arrangement . . .'

'They're pretty hard to find these days, Reverend,' I told him sadly. 'And the prices are going mad. Never seen anything like it.'

'You're a dealer, Mr Lovejoy?' he asked, as if he hadn't guessed.

'Yes, but only in a small way.' He would check up with the shop lady as soon as I was gone. Always admit what's going to be found out anyway. 'I'm mainly interested in porcelains.'

I got another smile for that. 'I'm glad we're not flintlock rivals.'

'I only wish I had the money to compete,' I confessed. 'What I came about —'

'The flask?'

'If you still have it,' I said, carefully measuring my words in case this all turned into a real sale, 'I'd like to make you an offer.'

To my surprise he hesitated.

'They're fairly expensive,' he said, working out private sums.

I groaned and nodded. 'Don't I know it?'

'And you'll require a flask more appropriate to a percussion —'

'Oh, that's a detail,' I interrupted casually. 'It doesn't matter too much. Anything goes these days.'

I sank out of sight in his estimation. As far as he was concerned, I would forever be a tenth-rate dealer of the cheapest, nastiest and most destructive kind. Even so, he still hung on, hesitating about selling me his flask. It was only after a visible effort he steeled himself to go on further, and courteously refused. I tried pushing him, offering a good market price, though it hurt. By then he was resolved.

We said nothing more. I didn't enlighten him about my visit to Muriel Field's. He'd be on to her soon enough. But, I wondered, had Eric told him about the Judas pair? Very unlikely. Collectors collect to keep, not to brag.

I went down the new road. This little estate miles from anywhere probably hadn't an antique from one end to the other. On the other hand, there were a few shapely birds here and there, but the sense of desolation was very real. I would phone Sheila and ask her to come back to Lovejoy's waiting arms in time for me to meet her off the London train in the romantic dusk. As I trotted round the

corner I planned a superb meal for the luscious lady who
would bring a little – maybe much – happiness into my
humdrum existence. I would get three of those pork pies
in transparent wrapping, a packet of frozen peas-and-
carrots mixed, one of those gravy sachets, and two custard
pies for afters. Lovely. How could any woman resist that?

I leapt into my chronic old speedster and started it by
releasing the handbrake to set it rolling on the slope, wondering as I did so if I had any candles to make my supper
party a really romantic seduction scene. I didn't give the
sad new dwellings another glance. Give me bird sanctuaries
any time.

CHAPTER VII

I SHOULD OWN up about women.

It's a rough old world despite its odd flashes of sophisti-
cation. Women make it acceptable the same way antiques
do. They bring pleasure and an element of wonderment,
when oftener than not you'd only be thinking of the next
struggle. There's nothing wrong in it all. It's just the way
things are. Morality's no help. Keep cool, hang on to your
common sense and accept whatever's offered. Take what
you can get from any woman that is willing to give it.

And before you even start to argue – no! I won't listen
to all that junk about waiting for spontaneous out-of-the-
blue 'true-love'. Love is *made*. It is the product of many
makings. A man and woman just don't fall in love at a
glance, sighing and longing and whatever. They have to
make love, build it up month after month, having sex and
becoming loving towards each other. When they've made
enough love and built it around themselves brick on brick,
then they can be said to be in a state of love. Read those
old religious characters. They knew all about love as a
spiritual event. It didn't come to them by a casual notion
as a sudden idea that sounds not too bad or from a weekly

magazine. Love, that mystical magic stuff of a lifetime, came from working at the very idea of it, grieving and straining and suffering the making of it. Then, in possession of it, comes the joy and the ecstasy of knowledge in the substance of love.

Well, sorry about that.

I make it when and where I can. Any honest man will tell you that the main problem is where the next woman's coming from. Women often decry this truth. Cissie used to. For some reason women find it necessary to deny the obvious. Never noticed how many phrases they have for that very purpose? 'That's all you think about.' 'Men are like children.' And so on, all wrong. I can't understand why women aren't more understanding.

Sheila was coming close to it. I'd known her a year, meeting her at one of those traction-engine rallies. She was there with her chap, a dedicated man who was so busy oiling things he didn't even notice when she left with me.

That isn't to say Sheila should go down as a cheap tart. These terms are as irrelevant as differences of racial colour, engine pattern, weight, any non-essential of human behaviour. Women like men, and men like women. It's only natural they tend to bump into each other now and again, sometimes accidentally, sometimes not. And if both parties wish to pretend it's more socially acceptable meeting properly introduced at the vicar's tea-party drinking tea with little finger poised crookedly in the air, big deal. What difference does it make as long as the chance of making love emerges from the great masquerade?

I take love seriously. It's a serious business and doesn't deserve to be left to the tender mercies of penny-paper romances and demented Russian novelists griping at one set of commissars after another.

Her family keep a shop in Islington, clothes and that. She has a younger sister at school. She opted out of typing suddenly. 'I read,' she explained once, 'they'd done experiments on a chimpanzee. It had learned to type. I ask you.' That did it. She hitched up with this traction-engine chap, helping in his garage and generally doing paperwork while he played with plugs and valves.

I collected her at the station.

'Hello, Lovejoy,' she said evenly.

'Hello, Sheila.' I was standing there like a spare tool, holding these flowers.

'Pig.'

She stood unmoving in the station foyer. It was the scene from 'When did you last see your father?' all over again. I felt like the kid on the cushion.

'You know, love,' I said lamely. 'I was busy.'

There were few people around. This was the last train in or out. She'd have to stay the night with me. Alf the porter used to stand and grin at these scenes years ago. Now all he wants to do is to clear up, lock up and push off before the White Hart shuts. We stood under the solitary lamp.

'You're not as thick as you pretend, you know that?'

I nodded. In this sort of mood you have to go along with them. She was wearing one of those fawn swingback coats that seem slightly unfashionable even when they're in, but never seem less than elegant. I'd never noticed before. Her clothes never quite matched the latest trends. She stood in a pool of light, smooth and blonde. My heart melted.

'I'm not very nice, love,' I admitted before I caught myself for a fool.

'I know.'

'I rang because . . .'

'I know why.'

'It was just that . . .' I petered out, holding the flowers towards her instead of explanation. She gazed at me, making no move to take them.

'It's just that you were taken short again.'

'Beautifully expressed,' I tried my clumsy jocularity act, which sometimes worked on the low graders. She evaded my attempt to thrust the bunch into her arms. I'd never seen her in this particular mood before.

'Lovejoy.' Her voice was quite dispassionate.

'Yes, darling?'

'Stop that. I want to ask you something.'

'Go on.' The passengers were all gone. Two cars started up outside and purred away. I could hear Alf clattering buckets encouraging us to leave.

'If I don't stay with you tonight,' she said in that calm voice, 'what will you do?'

'Have two suppers, hot bath and bed,' I lied.

She gave me that new calm look she'd learned during the last two days. I didn't care for it.

'Liar.'

I almost staggered. 'Eh?'

'I said, liar.'

'That's what I thought you said.' Stalemate.

The platform lights suddenly plunged out behind her. The single overhead bulb gave her an uncanny radiance I'd never seen. Maybe it was just that I was wanting her so badly.

'You'll be out picking up some middle-aged tart,' she said serenely.

'What, me?' I never can sound stern, though I tried. It came out weak as a bluster.

'You, Lovejoy.' She reached out and took the flowers. 'And you'll lay her after three pink gins.'

'Look, Sheila,' I said, worried sick by all this.

'You'll give her the eye and come the hi-baby act. I know you.'

'Nothing's further –'

'From your mind? Perhaps not, because I'm dope enough to come.' She sighed and scrutinized my shabby frame. 'You'll get any flabby amateur tart from the nearest taproom and make love to her wherever she says, in the car, your cottage, her place if her husband's out.'

'What's it all about?' I pleaded. 'What did I do?'

'You can't help it, Lovejoy, can you?' she said.

I gave in, shrugging.

'Sometimes it's not easy,' I said.

She smiled and took my arm.

'Come on, you poor fool,' she said. 'I'm famished.' She climbed into the car and started to push the fingerpump. As I said, she'd known me for a year. The motor responded. I saw Alf the porter thankfully closing up as we left the darkened station forecourt. We clanked through the silent village, my spirits on the mend.

'Not to worry, angel,' I reassured her. 'I've a repast fit for the Queen. One of my specials.'

'I suppose that means your sawdust pies.'

'Pork,' I replied, narked.

'Custard tart for afters?'

'Of course.'

'Beautiful.'

I turned to say something and noticed she was laughing. 'What's the joke?' I snapped.

'Nothing.' She was helpless with laughter.

'Look,' I said roughly. 'Don't you like my grub? Because if so you can bloody well – '

'N – no, Lovejoy,' she gasped, still laughing.

'I've gone to a lot of trouble,' I informed her with dignity. 'I always do.'

'I know, love,' she managed to say, and held my arm as I drove. 'It was just me. Don't take offence.'

'All right, then.'

She gave me a peck on the cheek.

'Friends again?' she asked.

'Pals,' I promised fervently, relieved her odd mood was over.

We held hands all the way home.

Next morning.

I was itching to have my priest-hole open to enter up a few oddments of information I'd gathered on my journey the previous day, but with Sheila there I contented myself with cataloguing my tokens. One or two were quite good. I'd advertise those, priced high. The rest I'd sell through local dealers when the big tourist rush began.

She was watching me, turned on her side on the fold-out bed.

'You love them,' she said.

I sighed theatrically. 'Don't come that soul stuff.'

'It's obvious you do.'

'It's also obvious that going all misty-eyed because we had it off is pretty corny.'

She laughed again when she ought to have been put out.

'Have you had breakfast, Lovejoy?'

'Yes, thanks.'

'What time were you up?'

'Seven.'

'Did you notice the bruise?'

'What bruise?' I felt guilty.

'When you belted me in the bathroom the other day.'

'Oh. About that, love.' I didn't look at her. 'I've been meaning to say sorry. It was important, you see.'

'A phone call?'

'Well, yes.' I forced justification into my voice. 'It turned out to be vital. I admit I was a wee bit on the hasty side –'

'Come here, Lovejoy,' she said. I could tell she was smiling.

'No,' I said, concentrating.

'Come here,' she said again, so I did.

See what I mean about women, never giving up?

Muriel answered the door, still jumpy and drawn but as stylish as before.

'I'm sorry to bother you again so soon,' I apologized.

'Why, Mr Lovejoy.'

'I just called –'

'Come in, please.'

'No, thank you.' There was no sound of cutlery in the background this time. A gardener was shifting little plants from pots into a flowerbed. 'I thought they only did that on Easter Monday,' I said. She looked and I saw her smile for the first time. It was enough to unsettle an honest dealer.

'Wait. I'll get my coat.'

She emerged, putting a headscarf on over her coat collar.

'You'll remember me for ruining your day if nothing else.' I shut the door behind her and we strolled to watch the gardener at work.

'These days I welcome an interruption,' she said.

'Mrs Field –'

'Muriel.' She put her arm through mine. 'Come this way and I'll show you the pond.' We left the house path and went between a setting of shrubberies.

'I wish I could return the compliment.' A woman's arm linked with yours does wonders for your ego. I felt like the local squire.

'Compliment?'

'Nobody calls me anything but Lovejoy.'

She smiled and seemed glad to do it. 'Me too?'

'You too. Oh, one thing more.'

She looked at me, worried. 'Yes?'

'Cheer up, love. Nothing's the end of the world.'

'I suppose not.' She was about to say more, but we came upon another elderly gardener tying those mysterious strings around plant stems. I must have looked exasperated because she asked me what was wrong.

'Beats me why they do it,' I said in an undertone.

'Do you mean the gardener?' she whispered back.

'Yes,' I muttered. 'Why can't they leave the blinking plants alone?' I was glad I'd said it because it gave her a laugh.

The pond was a small lake, complete with steps and a boat. A heron, grey and contemplative, stood in the distance. I shivered.

'Cold?' she asked.

'No. Those things.' I nodded to where the heron waited. 'It's fishing, isn't it?'

'Why, yes.' She seemed surprised.

'Can't you give it some bread instead?' I suggested,

which made her laugh again and pull me round to see my face.

'Aren't you . . . soft!' she exclaimed.

'I'd like the countryside, but it's so bloody . . . *vicious*.'

'Don't you like my garden, Lovejoy?'

I stared around accusingly. 'It's a county, not a garden.' I flapped my hand but the heron wouldn't go. 'Does it all belong to the house?'

'Of course. Eighty acres.'

'It's lovely,' I agreed. 'But everything in it's hunting everything else. Either that or trying to escape.'

She shivered this time and raised her headscarf. 'You mustn't talk like that.'

'It's true.'

I watched her hands tidy her hair beneath the scarf's edge. They have a natural grace to set off their own gestures, doing hair, pulling on stockings or smoking a cigarette. She saw me gaping at her. I looked back at the water.

'Lovejoy, what do you really do?'

'Oh, very little. I'm an antique dealer, really.' I paused to let her load. Where the hell was all this kindness coming from? I wondered irritably. She said nothing. 'I'm your actual scavenger. Nobody's sacred. I even winkled out your priestly collector friend, and he lives miles away.'

'Reverend Lagrange?'

'Yes.'

'He's been a good friend. He and Eric met years ago. I don't think he collects the same things Eric did.'

Nobody else does, either, I thought enviously. We moved along a flowered walk with those trellises against a wall.

'I wasn't telling the truth the other day.' Own up, Lovejoy. Never be only half-stupid. Go broke. 'You probably guessed.'

'Yes.'

I eyed her carefully. 'Aren't you mad at me?'

'No.' She pulled a leaf from some thorny plant that

hadn't done her any harm. 'You're not the first to have tried the same . . . thing.'

'Trick,' I said. 'Be honest. We call it the box gambit in the trade.'

'Box gambit?'

'I wish I hadn't started this,' I said.

She put the leaf idly between her teeth and saw me wince.

'What's the matter?'

'You wouldn't like it if you were that leaf.' She looked at it, and dropped it on the path. 'It's not dead.'

'But how on earth do you eat, Lovejoy?' she asked me.

'Like us all, but that's an essential.'

'What's the box gambit?'

I told her, feeling rotten. Box as in coffin. Anybody dying leaves a house and antiques, if he's wealthy enough to get his name reported in the papers. Those who are missed by our ever-vigilant press are listed in the deceased column by sorrowing relatives anxious to do the local antique dealers a favour. We read up the facts of the case. Within seconds, usually, and before the poor deceased is cold in his grave, we kindly dealers are round visiting the bereaved, claiming whatever we think we can get away with. And you'd be surprised how much that is.

'And do . . . widows fall for it?' She stopped, fascinated.

'More often than not.'

'Do you really mean that?'

'Of course,' I snapped harshly. 'Over ninety per cent of the time you come away with a snip, nothing less than useful information.'

She seemed intrigued by the idea, part-horrified and partly drawn to it.

'But that's like . . . being . . .' she hesitated and looked back. The heron was still there. I said it for her.

'Predators.'

'Well . . .'

'You mean yes,' I said. 'Which is what we are.'

'But why do the wives give you – ?'

'*Sell*. Not give. Never leave a box gambit unpaid.' I quoted the trade's unwritten rule. 'It's what makes it legal.'

'And what if you're caught?'

She drew me to a bench-seat and we sat. From there we faced the house beyond the water, trailing trees and sweeping grass studded with bushes. It was as charming as any scene on earth and made me draw breath.

'You think it's lovely,' she said.

'Wonderful. They had a sense of elegance we've lost,' I said. 'It all comes down to judgement. They had it. Whatever shape or design or pattern was exactly right, they recognized it. You have to love it, don't you?'

'I know what you mean, Lovejoy.' Her tone was cold. 'I used to feel the same until Eric died.'

'Will you stay here?'

'No, not now.'

'Where will you go, Muriel?'

'Oh.' She shrugged.

The heron stabbed, was erect and still before the drops fell from his beak.

'What if you *are* caught in the box gambit?' She shook my arm until I relaxed.

'You lie,' I said. The ripples were extending towards us. 'Lie like a trooper. You say that you, in all innocence, called at her house. The widow asks you in to see some heirloom because you'd asked particularly about antiques. You say she bargained like an old hand, and anyway you'd given her money for the object, hadn't you? She won't deny it.'

'How do you know?'

I gazed into her eyes. 'They never do.'

'Have you done it, Lovejoy?' she asked as the first ripple lapped on the bank below us. I nodded.

'I don't believe you,' she said candidly.

'You must.'

'Why must I?'

'Because . . . because, that's all.'

'Why, Lovejoy?'

'Look, Muriel.' I rose and tipped earth with my shoe into the water, staring down. It seemed pretty deep. You could see a few pebbles, then a dark brown murkiness. 'I don't know much about you, your family, who there is to give you a hand now . . . after your husband. But that mansion over there. These grounds. It's enough to bring every dealer and scrounger running from miles around.'

'Are you trying to warn me?'

'Just listen.' I tried to stop myself, but like a fool I talked on. 'We dealers are pretty slick. Some are all right, but some are not. We're good and bad, mixed. There are grafters, crooks, conners, lifters, zangers, edgers, pullers, professional dummyers, clippers – every variety of bloke on the make. Some pretty boys, smart, handsome, looking wealthy. Cleverer than any artists, better than any actor. They'll pick your house clean any way they can and brag about it in the pub afterwards.'

'Are you warning me, Lovejoy?' Woman-like she stuck to her question.

I felt like shaking her. 'Never mind what I'm doing,' I cried, exasperated. 'Just be careful, that's all. Be suspicious and sharp, and don't let in everybody who comes knocking.'

'I let you in, Lovejoy,' she reminded, smiling.

I pulled her on to the seat. 'Can't you see the obvious?'

'What do you mean?'

I drew breath and tried to glare into her innocent eyes. 'You're too damned trusting, Muriel. You should never have let me in the other day. It's too risky. Look,' I said, maddened by her smile. 'Look. In that house, that great mansion you live in, your husband Eric lost his life.'

'I don't need reminding.'

'You do.' I was almost shouting, not knowing why I was so worked up. 'Has it not dawned on you?'

'What?'

'Who killed him?'

She paled instantly. I could see the skin over her cheeks tauten. 'Why . . . why are you asking me?' she said.

'Because somebody must have,' I said. 'Do the police

know who? No. Does anyone else know? No. And not only that. Does anyone know *why* he was killed? Do you? No. The police? No.'

'They . . . they said it must have been an attempted robbery,' she said faintly.

'So they think,' I said. 'But is that reasonable? What was stolen?'

'Why, nothing,' she faltered.

'Not even one or two of your husband's antiques?'

'No. At least, I don't think so.'

'Did the police think so?'

'Practically everything was there, according to Eric's lists. They weren't complete, of course. He never did keep very tidy records.'

'Think,' I urged. 'Was nothing at all missing?'

'The only thing is that my brother-in-law said a pair of pistols were gone. The ones you asked about. The police *did* go over the inventory when all Eric's antiques went to Seddon's afterwards, though. George had rather an argument with them about it, I recall. He seemed to blame them for not being concerned enough.'

'That doesn't alter the fact,' I put in, 'that you're in this house, rich and with plenty of valuable stuff about, I guess.'

She nodded. 'There's the —'

God help me if she wasn't going to give me a run-down of her valuables. I clamped my hands over my ears.

'Don't,' I begged. 'For heaven's sake, you're doing what I told you not to. Keep quiet about your things. Chain everything down. Change the locks. Treble the burglar alarms. Quadruple the dogs.'

'I'll be all right, Lovejoy,' she said, smiling. She pulled down my hands and kissed me. 'I think you're sweet.'

'How can I be sweet when I'm a hard nut?' I said angrily, pulling away. 'You don't realize how versatile dealers, collectors can be. We'll do anything — any*thing* — to get what we want. It may only be a couple of old matchboxes, but if we collect matchboxes we'll do anything to get them.'

Her face was back in its previous solemn, worried expression.

'But that can't be true.'

'It *is* true.'

'It can't be,' she said doggedly.

'It is.'

'But, Lovejoy,' she said, almost pleading, 'that's so unreasonable.'

'Of course it's unreasonable. All collecting's unreasonable. But it's real.' I shrugged and beckoned her to her feet. We strolled on. 'You're not really taking notice of me, are you?'

I could see I had upset her.

'You aren't telling me *all* collectors are like that, are you?' she said, hesitating beside a white-flowered bush set between large rocks.

'I am.'

'All?'

'All,' I said firmly. 'That's what makes a collector special. Unique. Your husband must have been like that too.'

'Well, yes,' she said, 'but he was . . .'

'Eccentric?'

The sardonic note struck. She swung on me.

'How did you know I used to – ?' she blazed, looking momentarily more frightened than angry. I kissed her lightly.

'All wives call their husbands that, Muriel, love,' I said, smiling.

'Oh.'

'Beware collectors,' I warned again.

She glanced obliquely at me as we walked. 'And what about you, Lovejoy?'

I gave her my frankest avaricious leer. 'I'm the worst dealer there ever was, as far as you're concerned,' I said hoarsely.

'I doubt that.'

'The greediest, the cleverest, and the randiest,' I admitted, thinking, what am I doing? 'So don't trust me, especially me.'

'I don't believe that, either,' she said. 'But I'll do as you say.'

'Right,' I said with finality, disengaging my arm. 'That's it, then. Madam, before I rape you under this elm tree, show me the door.'

'I like you, Lovejoy,' she said.

'Don't push your luck, Muriel.' I watched the heron stab and crook in a swallow again. 'You've only been safe so far.'

She tried to laugh again but something had gone from the day. We waited for the next ripple to reach the steps then set off back towards the house as the boat slowly began to tug at its mooring.

Seddon's, I was thinking. They sent his antiques to Seddon's for auction.

CHAPTER VIII

SHEILA SAID DANDY Jack had phoned but left no message, that Margaret had too but said not to bother.

'And a strange gentleman who seemed annoyed,' she added.

'Pansy?'

'He had that ... mannerism.'

'Adrian.'

'Will you call, please. And that's the lot.' She made coffee better than I did, but only Yanks do it properly in my opinion. I drank it for appearances' sake. 'What's she like?'

'Who?' On guard, Lovejoy.

Sheila curled on the divan. 'Whoever it was you've been to see.'

'Oh.' A measure of truth was called for, I thought.

Always dangerous stuff to handle. You know where you are with a good old fable, so much more adaptable.

'Pretty?'

'Yes. Her husband died in odd circumstances some time back.'

'Was it a box gambit?'

'Sort of.' I eyed her unkindly. 'You're learning too much for your own good.'

She blew a kiss. 'I won't split.'

Dated slang, I noticed. Pity there's no market for it.

'Finish up,' I told her. 'We're going to the arcade, then Adrian's.'

Instantly she was all about getting ready. Now, there's a difference for you. I knew a dealer in Manchester once who said that the only real difference between us and women was that they strike matches in an away direction while men did it in a cupped hand towards themselves. But you can list a million things. Say to a chap, 'Come on, I'll give you a lift. It's time to go,' and he'll say, 'Fine. Thanks,' but not move for a while. A woman's immediately all bustle, hardly bothering to listen to the destination. Funny, that.

We pulled up near the arcade, doing the 'delivery' bit. I was proud of Sheila. She looked good enough to eat, as some of our local Romeos perceived. I went straight to Dandy Jack's. He was tilting a bottle.

'For my chest,' he explained, grinning. 'Hello, Lovejoy. Sit down, love.'

His tiny shop was a ruin as usual. Everything lay under a coating of dust. He had two firescreens which would have been superb except that filth made them look like pieces of cladding, all that splendid granular colouring obscured.

'Why don't you spruce your place up, Dandy?' I couldn't help asking.

'Oh.' He grinned. 'Well, I would, but it takes time, doesn't it?'

Sheila sat gingerly on a Victorian piano stool, knees

together and heels off the ground, with the air of a quack in an epidemic through no fault of his own.

'Bonny girl you got there, Lovejoy,' he said.

'Thanks.'

'Dandy Jack and Randy Lovejoy.' He gave out a cackle and swigged again, wiping the bottle neck on his tattered sleeve.

'And they say wit is dead.'

'No harm intended, love,' he confided to Sheila, his hand on her shoulder.

'None taken,' she said bravely without recoiling.

'You phoned,' I reminded him. 'But before you tell me why, have you still got those jades?'

'Of course.' He delved into a pile of open trays and pulled one out. A jade tumbled off. He picked it up, rubbing it on his tatty pullover.

I snatched them all off him irritably and took them towards the light. It was still there, an unreal lustrous netsuke masquerading among jade and agate. I pulled off the ticket I'd written for it. A netsuke is a little carved figure of ivory, jade or other decorative material. The Japanese made them for embellishing sword-handles. We, of course, rip them out and ruin the entire setting.

'I've had second thoughts, Dandy.' I tried not to feel guilty and avoided Sheila's eye.

He crowded close, stinking of rum. 'It's not duff, is it, Lovejoy?' he asked anxiously.

'No. It's superb.' The bitterness in my growl made him cackle with glee.

'You're too bloody soft for this game,' he croaked.

'Don't keep saying that,' I snapped. I wrote out a new ticket upping the price five hundred per cent. 'Here. Now,' I said ferociously, 'move them, Dandy. Move them! They should be treated with velvet gloves, not rattled around this cesspit of yours, and sold fast.'

He cackled again and offered me a swig which I declined. He glanced towards Sheila as a caution but I nodded.

'Well,' he said, reassured. 'Some geezer phones me early.
He'd heard I was putting the whisper out for flinters and
rings to ask what sort. Wouldn't leave a name.'

'That's useless, Dandy.'

'Wait – he asks after a Mr Lovejoy, did I know if he'd
anything for sale in that line.'

'Eh? Are you serious?'

'Straight up.'

There was nothing more. Now, this smacked of some
amateur sleuthing on somebody's part. No dealer would
tackle A about B's intentions so directly. I cast about for
Margaret on the way out of the arcade but didn't see her.
Her small den across the shopping arcade was unlit and
carried its closed sign. I don't know what I'd done wrong.

We pushed down the High Street among buses and cars
towards Adrian's. It's a cut above the arcade. He has a
spruce display, tickets on everything. Today's offerings
included a series of Adam style chairs, good copies, a lush
mahogany Pembroke table by Gillows – a great name –
of Lancaster about 1820, and a run of Byzantine ikons on
the walls among English watercolours. Incidentally, remember that the watercolour game is a characteristically
English art. Continental light is too brilliant. It's the
curious shifting lights in our countryside that imparted a
spontaneity and skill to the art that made it a feature of
this land as opposed to others. Praise where it's due. Adrian
had a Rowbotham (moderate value, great skill), a Samuel
Palmer (much value, brilliant skill) and a minute Turner
that must have taken less than a minute to do. I touched
the frame just to say I'd done so, not kneeling; and recoiled
stunned by bells. Huge value plus the skill of genius.

'Now, dear boy,' Adrian was saying when I could concentrate. 'You're not going to tell me it's phoney. Don't
you dare.'

'It's perfect, Adrian.'

'Isn't he sweet?' he cooed at Sheila. She concurred while
I looked daggers.

'You wouldn't by any chance have popped into one of

the local auctions, Adrian?'

I waited, but he stayed cool.

'All the time, sweetie.'

'Seddon's.'

Still not a flicker.

'Fortnightly.' He smiled. 'To remind myself how low one can sink, dear boy. They have rubbish and rubbishy rubbish, just those two sorts.'

'You wouldn't have bought some gadgets about maybe a year ago? A collection of card cases, early nineteenth-century . . . ?' My lies flowed with their usual serenity.

'No luck, love.' He sat and thought. 'Not heard of them either.'

'Started out from a box job, so word is.'

'Not even a whisper.' He was sympathetic. 'Ask Jane Felsham. It's more in her line. Got a buyer for them?'

I gave a rueful shrug. 'I would have if I could find them.'

'How many?'

'Ten – some mother of pearl, black lacquer, engraved silver, one silver filigree and a couple chatelained.'

He whistled. 'I can understand your concern. Shall I ask about?'

'If you would, Adrian. Many thanks.'

He cooed a farewell waving a spotted cravat from his doorway as we went back to the car. I'd got a ticket from a cheerful traffic warden and grumbled at Sheila for not having reminded me about putting up my infallible 'delivering' notice.

Seddon's is one of those barn-like ground-floor places full of old furniture, mangles, mattresses, rotting wardrobes and chairs. The public come to see these priceless articles auctioned. Dealers and collectors come to buy the odd Staffordshire piece, an occasional Bingham pot or set of old soldier's medals. The trouble is, the trade's non-seasonal at this level. To spot the public's deliberate mistake, as it were, you must go every week and never let up. Sooner or later, there it'll be – a small precious item going for a song. It's not easy. To see how difficult it is, go to the auction near where you live. Go several times and you'll see what dross is offered for sale and *gets bought*! Now, in your half-dozen visits by the law of averages you could have bought for a few coppers at least one item worth a hundred times its auctioned price. The people who actually *did* buy it weren't simply lucky. They study, read, record, assemble information and a store of knowledge. It's that which pays off eventually. That, and flair – if you have any.

I stress 'non-seasonal' because almost all of the antique business at the posher end is seasonal. It's too complex and full of idiosyncrasies to give it my full rip here, but in case you ever want to buy or sell anything even vaguely resembling an antique, follow Lovejoy's Law: All things being adjusted equally, sell in October or November to get the best auction price; buy between May and early September for the lowest prices.

It was viewing day, when you go round the day before the auction and moan at how terrible the junk is, and how there's cheaper and better stuff in the local market. That way, innocents hear your despair and go away never to return. Result: one less potential buyer. Also, it provides the auctioneer's assistants with an opportunity for lifting choice items out of the sale and flogging them in secret for a private undisclosed fee. We call it 'melting down', and deplore it – unless *we* can get our hands on the stuff, in which case we keep quiet.

I took Sheila in and we milled around with a dozen housewives on the prowl and a handful of barkers. Tinker was there and came over.

'Any luck?'

'Yes, Lovejoy. Hello, miss.'

Sheila said hello. We left her leafing through a shelf of drossy books and went among the furniture where nobody could listen in.

'I've got a cracker, Lovejoy,' Tinker said. 'You won't believe this, honest.'

'You're having quite a run,' I commented.

He got the barb and shook it off.

'I know what you're thinking,' he said, 'but it's a whizzer. Listen. You're after a mint pair for that Field I put on to you – right?' I nodded. 'I've found a cased set going.'

'Where?' My mouth dried.

'Part-exchange, though.' This was Tinker creating tension. 'Not a straight sale.'

'What the hell does that matter?' I snarled. 'Who the hell does a straight sale for the good stuff these days anyway? Get on with it.'

'Keep your hair on.'

We chatted airily about mutual friends while an innocent housewife racked herself over a chest of drawers before marking it carefully on a list and pushed off, steeling herself for tomorrow's auction.

Tinker drew me close. 'You know that boatbuilder?'

'Used to buy off Brad down the creek?'

'Him. Going to sell a pair of Mortimers, cased.'

'I don't believe it, Tinker.'

'Cross my heart,' he swore. 'But he wants a revolving rifle in part-exchange. Must be English.'

I cursed in fury. Tinker maintained a respectful silence till I was worn out.

'Where the hell can I get one of those?' I muttered. 'I've not seen one for years.'

I actually happened to have one in my priest's hole, by Adams of London Bridge, a five-chambered percussion longarm. There's bother with a spring I've never dared touch but otherwise it's perfect. I cursed the boatbuilder and his parents and any possible offspring he might hope to have. Why can't people take the feelings of antique dealers into account before they indulge in their stupid bloody whimsies? Isn't that what all these useless sociologists are for? I came manfully out of my sulk. Tinker was waiting patiently.

'All right, Lovejoy?'

'Yes. Thanks, Tinker.' I gave him a couple of notes. 'When?'

'Any time,' he answered. 'It'll be first come first served,
Lovejoy, so get your skates on. They say Brad's going
down the waterside early tomorrow. Does he know – ?'

'The whole bloody world knows it's me that's after
flinters,' I said with anguish.

When a punter puts money on a horse at 2-1 odds, as
you will know, nothing happens at first. Then, as more
and more punters back it, the odds will fall to maybe evens,
which means you must risk two quid to win only two,
instead of risking two to win four as formerly. In practically
the same way, the more people want to buy a thing, the
dearer it becomes. Naturally, merchants will explain that
costs and heaven-knows-what factors have pushed the price
up, but in fact that's a load of cobblers. Their prices go up
because more people want a thing. They are simply more
certain of selling, and who blames them for wanting to
make a fortune?

Gambling is a massive industry. Selling spuds is, too.
Buying flintlocks or Geneva-cased chain-transmission Wikel-
man watches is not a great spectator sport, so the field is
smaller. A whisper at one end therefore reverberates
through the entire collecting world in a couple of weeks,
with the effect that those already in possession of the
desired item quickly learn they are in a position to call
the tune. They can more or less name their terms. Hence
the indispensable need of a cunning barker.

'I'll go and see him,' I said. Nothing makes humanity
more morose than an opportunity coming closer and closer
as the risks of failure simultaneously grow larger.

A toddler gripped my calf crying, 'Dadda! Dadda!'
delightedly. I tried unsuccessfully to shake the little psycho-
path off and had to wait red-faced until its breathless
mother arrived all apologetic to rescue me. The little maniac
complained bitterly at having lost its new find as it was
dragged back to its pushchair. Sheila was helpless with
laughter at the scene. The fact that I was embarrassed
as hell of course proved even more highly diverting.

'Oh, Lovejoy!' she said, falling about.

'You can go off people, you know,' I snarled. 'Very funny. A spiffing jape.'

'Oh, Lovejoy!'

'Mind that apothecary box!' I pushed her away just before she knocked it off a side table.

This gave her the opportunity to ask about it. I saw through her placatory manoeuvre, but for the life of me I couldn't resist. It gave me an excuse to fondle the box, a poor example it was true, but they are becoming fairly uncommon and you have to keep on the look-out.

Watch your words – not an 'apothecary's' box. It wasn't his, in the sense that he carried it about full of rectangular bottles and lovely nooky felt-lined compartments for pills and Galenical 'simples', as his preparations were called. It belonged usually to a household, and was made to stand on a bureau, a medicine-cabinet if you like. You dosed yourself from it, or else hired an apothecary, forerunner of the general practitioner, to give advice on what to use from it. The current cheapness of these elegant little cabinets never ceases to amaze me. I wish they would really soar to a hundred times their present give-away price, then maybe the morons who buy them and convert them into mini-cocktail cabinets would leave well alone and get lost.

You find all sorts of junk put in by unscrupulous dealers and auctioneers besides the bottles. This one had a deformed old hatched screwdriver thing with a flanged blade and a pair of old guinea-scales imitating the original physick balance. I dropped them back in, snorting scornfully. Sheila heard my opinion with synthetic attention and nodded in all the right places.

'If I catch somebody doing it, darling, I'll smash it on his head,' she promised as we strolled round.

'You'll do no such thing.'

'No?'

'Smash a *brick* on his head, and bring the apothecary box to me.'

'For you, Lovejoy, anything.'

After an hour Sheila was protesting. Inspecting stuff's best done by osmosis. Don't rush, stroll. Be casual. Saunter, wander, learn.

'We keep going round and round, Lovejoy,' she complained, sitting to take off a shoe to rub her foot like they do.

'Shut up,' I said, wandering off. Jim, one of the elderly attendants, guffawed.

'Chivalrous as ever, eh, Lovejoy?' he said, and I was in with an excuse.

'This junk's enough to make a saint swear,' I groused. 'Never seen so much rubbish since Field's stuff came through.' He was aggrieved at that. Nobody likes their own stuff being recognized for the rubbish it is.

'We sold some good stuff that day,' he said, quick as a flash. 'If you hadn't gone to Cumberland you'd know better.'

That explained why I'd missed it. I was beginning to feel better as things clicked into place.

'Nothing still around from it, is there?' I asked casually.

He grinned. 'Do leave orf, Lovejoy. It was donkeys' years back.'

'Oh, you never know,' I said, hinting like mad.

He shook his head. 'No – we played that one straight,' he admitted ruefully. 'Practically all of it went the same week as we got it.'

'Just a thought, Jim. Some things do get left behind occasionally.'

'Pigs might fly,' he said.

I played casual another minute then collected Sheila and we made it back to the car.

We pulled out, rolling against protesting traffic to get started.

'We have one more call to make before home,' I told her. 'Game?'

She sighed. 'These places always make me feel so grubby. I need a bath.'

'Same here,' I shrugged. The motor coughed into

emphysematous life and we were under power. 'What's that to do with anything?'

'Where are we going?'

'Down the creek.'

'Is it a tip from Tinker?'

'You guessed, eh?'

'It was pathetically obvious, Lovejoy.'

'You're making me uneasy.'

And she was. Tinker was loyal, wasn't he? I paid him well by comparison with other dealers' barkers. I never disclosed a confidence. Twice I'd bailed him out. Once I'd rescued him from Old Bill, and once saved him getting done over by the Brighton lads. But you could never tell. Was it this suspicion that was worrying me? Something niggled in my memory, something I had seen.

We were out of town and down on the estuary in no time. It's not much of a place, four small boatbuilders in corrugated iron sheds, the usual paraphernalia of the pleasure-boating fraternity and a few boats hauled up on the mud by the wharf. Those big Essex barges used to ply between here and Harwich in the old days, crossing to the Blackwater and even London, but the two that are left are only used for showing tourists the Colne estuary and racing once a year, a put-up job.

I found Barton planing wood. The lights were on inside his boathouse, though outside was still broad daylight. You could see the town hall clock in the distance some five miles off. I waited until he stopped. Well, what he was making could be a valuable antique in years to come. Never interrupt a craftsman.

'Hello, Lovejoy.' He stopped eventually and nodded to Sheila as we sat on planks.

'When are you going to give this boat lark up, Dick?' I said. 'You could go straight.'

It gave him a grin as he lit his pipe.

'Dealing in antiques?'

'Maybe,' I offered. 'I'd take you on as a sub-standard junior partner for a year's salary.'

'I like a proper job,' he countered, winking at Sheila. She was quite taken with him.

'On second thoughts, I couldn't see you standing the pace.'

'Of course,' he yakked on, 'I can see the attraction. Nothing really matters in antiques, does it? Right or wrong, you get along.'

'It's time for his tablet,' I apologized to Sheila. 'This feverish air down on the waterside, you understand. His blood's thin.'

'I turn into a man after dark,' he said solemnly to Sheila. 'If ever you're thinking of ditching this goon, give me a tinkle –'

'Flinters, Dick,' I said gently. There was silence. A water-bird made a racket outside and something splashed with horrid brevity.

'Ah, well,' he said.

These pipe-smokers are one up on the rest of us. It might be worth taking up just for the social advantages. If you want a few moments' peace, out it comes and you can spin out the whole ritual for as long as you feel inclined. The universe waited breathlessly until his pipe was chugging to his satisfaction.

'Launched?' I asked. 'Better now?'

'Flinters,' he said. 'They're a problem, now, aren't they?'

'*You* are telling *me*?'

'And rare.'

'And desirable. Go on, Dick. And costly.'

'Ah, yes.' He stared down the short slipway. 'About a month ago I decided which pair I'd keep. I have two Sandwells and the Mortimers. The Mortimers can go, but I want exchange. A revolving rifle, English.' Sandwell was an early brass-barrel specialist, lovely stuff.

'And cash adjustment.'

'Something of the sort.'

'And the Mortimers?' I could feel that old delicious greed swelling in my chest. Magic.

'Mint,' he said.

'Really mint?'

'Not a blemish.' He'd let his pipe doze. 'Cased. Case-hardening. I don't think,' he said, winking at Sheila, 'you'll be disappointed.' The understatement of all time. Case-hardening. Something scratched again at my memory, worrying me.

If you keep any metallic object in an unopened case for long enough, it acquires a curious characteristic. If the surface was originally made an acid-protected rust brown, it simply becomes shinier, almost oily in appearance. If previously made a fire-protected shiny blue ('gunmetal' blue), the surface develops an odd mother-of-pearl effect very like the sheen of petrol on water. This case-hardening is an especially desirable feature of anything metal having a protected surface, from coins to weapons. *On no account clean it off*; you will be doing posterity a cultural favour and yourself a financial one by leaving it intact.

'Look, Dick.' I drew breath and launched. 'I can lay my hands on one.'

'Good?'

'A faulty spring I've not touched. Otherwise mint.'

'Cased?'

'Come off it.'

'Who by?'

'Adams, London Bridge. Five-chambered.' I photographed it in my mind's eye. 'It's beautiful.'

He thought a second in a cloud of smoke. 'How would we adjust?'

'Because you're a close relative,' I said, in agony, 'I'll pay the difference.'

'Let's settle it tomorrow,' he said, and we shook hands. Sheila rose. 'Is that all that happens?' She seemed peeved.

'What do you want, blood?' I demanded. I was drenched with sweat, as always. The excitement of the forthcoming deal was brewing in me. Tomorrow, with luck and good judgement and money, I would be in possession of a pair of case-hardened flinters made by the most aristocratic and expensive of all the great London makers, Henry Walklate Mortimer.

'Thanks for coming, Lovejoy.' Dick came to the door of his boatshed to see us out. 'Still got your steamer, I see.'

'Any more jokes about my motor and the deal's off,' I shot back. 'At least I've got a licence for it – have you, for that thing?' I pointed to his pipe.

'Bring your lovely lady again, Lovejoy,' he called, and I replied with rudeness.

He was able to get his own back because my wretched banger refused to start despite all the cranking I could manage. Dick borrowed a trio of amused boatmen to push us off, to a chorus of catcalls and derision.

'Why don't you put an engine in, Lovejoy?' was Dick's final bellow as we pulled off the wharfside and escaped on to the road up from the village. I didn't reply because I was white-faced and my teeth were chattering.

'Love?' Sheila asked. 'Are you ill?'

'Shut up,' I hissed, foot flat on the accelerator. The needle flickered up to twenty and we pottered slowly upwards past the church. It was almost time for lights.

'What is it?' She tried to pull me round but I swore and jerked my face away.

'I've just remembered something.'

'For God's sake, darling –'

'This bloody stupid car!' I almost screamed the words. 'Why the hell don't I get a new one? What's the matter with it.'

'Darling, pull over to the side and I'll –'

'Shut up, you stupid –' My hands were ice-cold and my scalp prickled with fear.

'Please, love. I'm frightened. What is it?'

'That frigging box!'

'What box?'

'That apothecary box! There's something in it – a – a –' the words wouldn't come.

'The bottles? Drugs?' I shook my head and strove to overtake the village bus to the driver's annoyance. He hooted and pulled in as we crawled past towards the town. We were up to thirty. 'Those little scales?'

'That other thing.'

'You said it was junk the auctioneers put in to make it look complete. Wasn't it a screwdriver?'

'It was case-hardened!' I snarled. 'Who the hell puts a screwdriver away in a felt-lined case to preserve it for a whole bloody century?' I was practically demented, kicking and blaspheming at the decrepit motor, begging it for greater speed. 'And its handle was hatched – *hatched like a Durs gun.* Oh, God Almighty, please let them still be open. Please, please, please.'

Sheila grabbed my arm. 'Lovejoy, if we see a taxi, flag it down.'

'Yes, yes, yes,' I whimpered. 'Please send a taxi. Please, please.'

'What time do they close?'

'Half five.'

'It's twenty past.'

'The swine will go early. They always do, those bloody attendants, the idle sods.'

We reached the trunk road roundabout by the river bridge at twenty-five past five, and swung left away from the Ipswich road. East Hill was well into lighting-up time as we screeched to a graceful stop outside Seddon's. It was closed and dark.

'Knock,' Sheila said, climbing out.

'They've gone.' I was lost, defeated by the calamity.

She remained resolute and banged on the main door. I stepped down to join her just as one of the stewards opened the partition. My relief almost made me faint.

'What the hell – ?'

'Jim,' I said weakly. 'It's me. Lovejoy.'

'Closed till tomorrow.'

'Not for me you're not.' I pulled out a note. 'A single question, Jim. Just one.'

He eyed it and nodded. I gave it him and asked, 'The question is, will you let me find my nail-file? I dropped it in the showroom an hour or so back.'

'Gawd.' He hesitated. 'Mr St John has the keys.'

'And so have you, Jim.'

'Well –' he was saying, when Sheila came to the rescue.

'It's actually *my* nail-file,' she broke in. 'I was really careless. It's one of a set, you see, in a case.'

'Well, miss, dealers aren't allowed –'

'I know exactly where it is, Jim,' I said, calmer now. 'I'll bet you five of those notes I could put my hand on it in three seconds flat.' That was a mistake and scared him.

'Here, Lovejoy,' he began, starting to close the door, 'I don't want none of your fiddling –'

'You stay here, Lovejoy,' Sheila said chidingly. She stepped into the doorway and turned to push me back. 'You're always so abrupt. The gentleman said that dealers weren't allowed in after fixed hours so you'll have to wait here, that's all.' On a tide of feminine assurance she swept past Jim, who humbly put the door to. I heard their footsteps recede along the passageway and keys rattle in the showroom door.

I hung about the pavement getting in people's way and generally prowling around for quite five minutes before Sheila reappeared. I was up with her in a flash.

'Thank you so much,' she was saying to old Jim, who was smirking at all his extra gallantry. 'I'm so sorry we delayed you. You've been so kind. Good night.'

I honestly tried to grin at Jim, but he wasn't having any from me and banged the door. Sheila walked to the car.

'I've got it in my handbag,' she said, swinging the strap to her shoulder. 'Don't grab, or Jim will see.'

She was really quite smart at that. Old Jim would no doubt be lusting after her as we left. You could see virtually the whole hill from the office. With quivering fingers I set the handle and cranked. We rumbled up the hill and I pulled in by the park railings in town.

The cars pouring from the car park got in the way of this manoeuvre. I'm sure they didn't really mind having to stop suddenly. Muriel Field was at the wheel of a grey Rover, with Lagrange beside her, but I'd no time for light chit-chat. After all, she had no antiques any more. Not like Sheila, who had the device out. I carried it into the lights of the lamps on the war memorial. It was a Durs screw-mechanism, the weirdest I'd ever seen, but authentic, star cross-hatched on the handle and case-hardened, maybe in all five inches long.

'I'm afraid I have a confession, Lovejoy,' Sheila said, beside me.

'Eh?'

'I'm afraid I . . . I stole it.' She pulled away as I tried to embrace her, laughing. 'Promise me.'

'What? Anything.'

'You'll pay for it tomorrow.'

'You're off your head.'

'Promise, Lovejoy.'

I sighed at all this whimsy. 'I promise.' I gave her a rubbery kiss under the memorial's lamp despite the pedestrians. A car's horn sounded. Adrian and Jane sailed past signalling applause. He'd have some witticism ready next time. 'Here. You can have the honour of carrying the find home.'

'Is it important, Lovejoy?' I gave it her and she slipped it into her handbag.

'Somewhat,' I said, beginning to realize. 'Somewhat.'

A hurrying mother pulled her gawping child along the pavement to stop it openly inspecting the couple kissing in the main street. I kept my eye on her as Sheila and I stepped apart to drive home, and sure enough she gave a swift glance back to see how we were managing. Aren't women sly?

CHAPTER IX

I DROPPED SHEILA at the station. She had to go to work, poor lady, on some crummy newspaper. We had a small scene outside.

'I'll be here Sunday,' she told me, and I nodded. She waited. 'Well?'

'Well what?'

'Aren't you going to come on to the platform and see me off?'

'I daren't take my foot off this pedal or she'll never start again today,' I explained. 'Otherwise I'd come in with you like a shot.'

She came round to my side and kissed me.

'You know, Lovejoy,' she said, 'for the world's greatest antique dealer you're an awful dope.'

'I keep telling you your slang's dated.'

'No use trying to needle me,' she said, cool as ever I'd seen her. 'You're falling for me, Lovejoy.'

'Look,' I said testily, 'this accelerator's down to the floor. It's costing the earth in petrol just sitting here while you babble – '

She put her arms round me and hugged me tight. This, note, was about ten in broad daylight with the paperman grinning and the kiosk lady enjoying the show.

'I have a secret to tell you, Lovejoy.'

'You're not – ?'

'Certainly not!' She reached under the dashboard in front of me. 'Take your foot off the accelerator.'

'I can't. The engine'll cut out.'

'Please.'

I did as she said. Just before the engine coughed to silence she twisted something near the steering-rod. The engine muted instantly into a deep, steady thrum. She stood back and dusted her hands.

'There!'

I sat mesmerized.

'Now,' she said casually, 'care for a spin?'

'Er –'

'Push over.' She came into the driver's seat and nudged me across. 'Let the expert do it, honey,' she said kindly, flicked a switch somewhere and yanked on an angled rod-thing near her knee.

We took off. My spine nearly slipped from the force. The old Armstrong boomed easily round the station round-about and Sheila put it on to the hill near the hospital at fifty. We zoomed on to the main A12 about three minutes later and Sheila crashed her slickly up into the seventies. Fields and trees flicked by. Wind pulled at my face and her hair streamed out flat against her temples. In a couple of breaths the signs to Kelvedon darted past. I sat in frozen disorientation while all this happened round me. Sheila pulled out into the middle lane and did her mystery with the levers. We hummed alongside a column of slower cars and as she overtook back into the inside the needle wobbled down to seventy. There was hardly a shudder. A couple more millisecs and we were at Witham. She brought us into the station and switched off. The motor breathed a sigh, quieting into silence.

'Tea, guvnor?'

There was a tea-stall within reach. I nodded and climbed shakily down. Let Sheila pay, I thought angrily. We stood in silence slurping tea from cracked cups. Sheila had this strange feminine knack of being able to drink scalding fluids without losing her oesophagus. I was quite ten minutes finishing mine. I stared at the Armstrong while I sipped, thought and wondered. I handed my cup on to the counter with a nod of thanks. The chap on the stall must have thought we'd had a row because he studiously busied himself picking the losers at Cheltenham and left the cup there.

'Is that what you were doing last night?' I managed to say finally.

'Yes, love. I'm so sorry.' She held my hand.

'Was it . . . really obvious?'

'It was rather, Lovejoy,' she said sadly. 'A massive car like this, so old, supposedly only one gear, fantastic fuel consumption, no speed to speak of, weak as a kitten, all these gadgets within reach.'

'When did you suspect?'

'Yesterday, when we were trying to hurry to Seddon's before it closed.' She smiled. 'It was ridiculous. And everywhere we go other motorists hoot at it, even when you're driving quite well. So, while you got our usual fantastic supper –'

'What's wrong with my suppers?' I said angrily.

'Nothing, love,' she said quickly. 'Nothing at all. Those pies are lovely, and I really look forward to those shop custards. But I had to do something while you, er, got it ready, didn't I?'

'I thought you were cleaning it,' I said bitterly.

'It wasn't me, really,' she pacified. 'It was you. I remember you once told me the car was the only time your wretched bell proved itself wrong. That set me thinking. So I turned a few switches and –'

'Did you know all the time it was special?'

'No, love. Honestly.'

I looked askance at her. Sometimes women aren't quite truthful.

'I think you're lying in your teeth,' I said.

She smiled. 'I quite like a lie now and again,' she said demurely, and I had to laugh.

'You know what?' I asked.

She shook her head.

'I think I'm starting to fall for you.'

She inspected me for a few minutes.

'About time, Lovejoy,' she said. 'We're both suffering from malnutrition with those corny dinners you insist on serving up. I'll bring my things on Sunday to stay for as long as we last.'

'I'll meet you at the station, seeing I'll be able to start the car now.'

'There's a switch near the starting-pump. Push it down, and she'll start with first crank of the handle.' She pulled me into the driver's seat and showed me an exotic circular gear-wheel, five gears and one reverse. I sat like a beginner as she explained the controls.

'The London train, lady.' The tea-man knocked on his window to attract our attention.

'That's it, then, Lovejoy.' She brushed her hair back and got her case out.

'I love you.' I embraced her. 'Give us a kiss, love.'

The train came and took her away.

'Go easy in that monster,' she called, her very last words to me. Go easy in that monster. Some exit line.

'I will. See you Sunday.'

The tea-man was out of his booth and examining the Armstrong as I came up.

'You've a right bit of gorgeous stuff there,' he said.

'Yes. I thought it was an Armstrong.' I kicked a tyre.

'Eh? Oh no. I meant your young lady.'

'Oh yes. Her too.'

I did the necessary and notched an intrepid forty-five on the trunk road back. The Armstrong – was it still an Armstrong? – didn't cough once and went like a bird.

I rolled up to George Field's house in style.

I was beginning to realize there was a lopsided distribution of wealth in the Field family. On the one hand was Eric, evidently wealthy, complete with mansion, eighty acres of manicured grass and gardeners touching forelocks to the boss and his lady as they strolled out for a morning row on the two-acre pond. On the other was George, here in a two-bedroom farce on a small estate, with bicycles and wrecks of lawn-mowers and old bits of wood bulging the garage. His little Ford, clean as a new pin, was parked in a drive barely long enough for it. Despite all this, he had dashed out a handful of notes, hired me as a would-be-sleuth because of my knack of sniffing out antiques, and promised all those lovely D's for what could be a pipe dream.

He came to the door agog for news. It was obviously a major disappointment to him when I told him I'd only called to give him a progress report. We went into the living-room and he asked his wife, a dumpier female version of himself, to bring some coffee. I told him some of the events but was careful when I said I'd visited Muriel.

'I'm so glad she's better now,' Mrs Field said. 'She went through a very bad patch.'

'She's still rather nervous,' I agreed, setting her clucking at the tribulations all about. 'Was she always?'

It seemed she was, but much worse since poor Eric's sudden end. I told George of my find in the apothecary box, mentally absolving myself of the payment I'd promised Sheila the day before.

'Do you recognize it?' I handed it over and he put on glasses.

'I wouldn't,' he said. 'I never touched the weapons, nor the screwdrivers. I wasn't much interested, as I said before.'

I ran down the main events of the past couple of days for him and remembered to ask him if he had any details about the sale of Eric's stuff at the auctioneers, but without luck.

'It seems the cased weapons might have come from near a bird sanctuary near a coastal resort.'

'There's a nice holiday place near Fellows Nab,' Mrs Field said. 'Too many caravans there now though. That's in Norfolk.' Mrs Ellison's antique shop was a few miles from Fellows Nab. I'd seen the sign.

'You never saw the wrapping?' I asked George.

'No. You have to realize I only saw him and Muriel once a week on average, and he was always showing me this and that.'

'You should have taken more notice, George,' his wife said.

'Yes, dear,' he said with infinite patience. I'd have to watch myself with Sheila, I thought uneasily, if this was marriage.

'I'm making a systematic study of every possible flinter transaction during the past two years.' I was eager to show I was really trying. 'It'll take a little time, though.'

'But if you found out where they did come from, what then?' He was a shrewd nut.

'I don't honestly know,' I said as calmly as I could. 'But what else is there? They've vanished. The police are —'

'They've given it up,' Mrs Field said, lips thinned with disapproval. 'I always said they would, didn't I, George — ?'

'I suppose what I'll do is find whoever sold them to your brother and ask who else knew where they were.'

'Well, you know best of course,' he said, worried. 'But poor Eric was a real talker. He wasn't the sort of person to conceal any of his finds in the antique world. He loved company and used to have his friends in.'

'Friends?' I interrupted. 'Collectors?'

'Oh yes. And dealers.'

'And dealers,' Mrs Field echoed. 'Ever so many people thought highly of Eric's opinion. Very knowledgeable, he was, about practically everything. Old furniture as well.'

'So it's probable a lot of people may have seen the Durs?'

'For certain.'

I rose and thanked them. George came with me to the door.

'Look,' I began hesitantly. 'Please don't think I'm rude, Mr Field, but —'

'Yes?'

'Well —' Understanding began to dawn in his eyes.

'You're wondering where I can get so much money from, Lovejoy,' he observed with a smile.

'It's a lot of money,' I said in embarrassment.

'Oh, I'm a careful man. Only thing I've ever done is run a shoe-shop, and I didn't make good like Eric did in the property business.' He was quite unabashed at my rudeness. 'I have some savings, insurance. And the mortgage on the house is almost paid. I could take out a new one. You needn't be afraid the money wouldn't be forthcoming. After all, the Judas guns are the only real evidence, aren't they? If we can buy them back from whoever the . . . murderer . . . sold them to, they'll be proof, won't they?'

I listened as he rambled on about them for a moment, and chose my words with care.

'Mr Field –' I cleared my throat – 'do you mean to say that now, when you're comfortably settled and solvent at last, you'll chuck it all up and start working and paying all over again, just to – ?'

'Don't say it, Lovejoy,' he said gently. 'Of course I would. And don't go looking at Eric's wealth for a reason, either. That just doesn't come into it. I approached you because somebody did Eric wrong. It shouldn't be allowed. It's wrong. It always was. Even these days, robbery and killing is still wrong.'

I mumbled something I hoped sounded humble.

'You see, Lovejoy,' he finished, 'if you take away people, there's nothing else left, is there?'

I drove away. Ever feel you're beginning to lose your faith in human nature?

There was something wrong with the cottage. You get feelings like that, even though there's nothing in particular you can detect consciously. I hadn't switched the alarm on that morning because I had planned only to run Sheila to the station, pop back to the cottage to collect my Adams revolving percussion gun, then drive to Dick Barton's boatshed and complete the deal, all this before going to George Field's. If Sheila hadn't been so knowledgeable about the car I'd have been back in time to prevent the robbery, for robbery it was. You can smell it.

Naturally I'd been done over before – show me the antique dealer who hasn't. It's a hazard of the trade. Like injuries in motor car racing, it comes with the job. Hence my usually meticulous concern for security. And the bloody alarm which had cost me the earth wasn't even switched on. Serves me right, I was thinking as I prowled about to make sure he'd gone. The place wasn't a complete shambles, but had suffered. Somebody in a hurry, obviously.

There were a couple of letters addressed to Sheila care of me on the doormat, so the post girl had called on time. Maybe her arrival had scared him off, I hoped, as nothing seemed out of place at first. The carpet hadn't been disturbed over my clever little priest-hole, thank heavens, but I realized pretty quickly that my walnut-cased so-called carriage-clock had gone.

I gave vent to every expletive I'd ever learned, ranting and fuming. I'd got the clock for a quid from a starving old widow – one of my kinder moments this, because if I'd been true to myself I'd have beaten her down to a few pence. The sheer effrontery of somebody having the gall to come in, finger anything of mine he wanted, then take a rare priceless antique was sickening. Literally, I felt physically sick. I phoned our ever-vigilant constable Geoffrey, who was mercifully in, probably still having his morning nap. He was ever so sympathetic.

'When you've stopped laughing,' I snarled, 'get my clock back.'

'Estimate of value, please, Lovejoy.'

'Six hundred,' I said firmly. He was silent for once.

'Did – did you say – ?' And he laughed again, louder this time.

'Well, maybe three hundred.'

'You mean about eighty.'

'Ninety.'

'As a friend, Lovejoy,' he said sadly, 'I can only make it eighty-five.'

'But that's robbery – '

He agreed. 'You can argue it out with the insurance people, Lovejoy,' he said. 'Incidentally, how'd he get in?'

'I'll look. Hang on.'

There was a cut round the window near its catch. The

window looked right down the back garden and could be reached by anyone standing on the grass which grows right up to the cottage. I told Geoffrey and he said it was typical, but how about my alarm system connected at great expense to a noisy little flashing light in his office? I explained I'd been in a rush that morning.

'Thanks, Lovejoy,' he said cynically. 'We love a bit of help from the public.'

'Are you going to come and look for clues or aren't you?' I snapped and crashed the receiver.

I made some tea while I waited. Apart from scratches on the window-sill there was nothing. I moved about straightening things. The trouble is that you know where to look for antiques – guns must be locked in an enclosed space, says the Firearms Act; porcelain will be in a fastened case, portabilia locked in a safe or drawer. He knew his stuff. Whoever had done this was neat, slick and an opportunist dedicated to walnut carriage-clocks. Now, two things worried me far more than the loss of the clock. One was that Geoffrey's guess about the clock's value wasn't too far out, which was important because nobody robs for very little. The second thing stared back at me from the opposite wall as I lounged on the divan swilling tea. It was my Chien-Lung plate, a lovely disc of hand-painted light pastel colours stencilled by a neat blue running-edge design. It stood in prominence on my desk on a three-leaved ebony hinge support of the sort the Chinese do so cleverly. Neither plate nor clock were unique, but of the two the plate was infinitely – well, ten times – more desirable in anybody's book, as well as being more valuable. So why pass it up?

That left two possibilities. Either my burglar was well-informed enough to know that I had a carriage-clock to suit him, or he hadn't come for the carriage-clock at all. Which raised the question, why take it if he didn't want it? Answer: to cause his intrusion to be written off as a simple uncomplicated robbery by a burglar who happened to have a casual eye for antiques.

It was starting to look as though I'd established contact

with the owner of a very special pair of flinters.

The rest of the day's happenings I don't really want to talk about.

Geoffrey came on his bicycle and took notes. He examined the earth outside, searched patiently for heaven-knows-what sort of clues, and later went round the village asking who'd noticed what and when, with conspicuous failure. Left to my own devices I retrieved my Adams from the priest-hole before driving to Barton's on the estuary and settling with him for too much in part-exchange, and bringing the cased Mortimers back home to gloat over despite the fact that I'd have to pay out to settle it before the month ended. I had my usual supper bought from the Bungalow Shop in the village, read a lot and went to bed, not knowing that by then Sheila was dead.

She had got on the London train, and apparently went home before reporting to work that same day. It was on the way home that evening that she was said to have stumbled and fallen beneath the wheels of an oncoming train.

The platform was crowded. In the friendly reliable way we all have nobody came forward to say who was even standing near her. To hear the witnesses at the inquest the three thousand people must have clustered awkwardly along the platform leaving an open space for several yards all around Sheila as she waited for the train to come and kill her. Don't go trying to say people may not have noticed somebody pushing a woman off a platform because of the crowd. There's no excuse. Women notice a pretty woman because they're practically compelled to, and men notice because they're compelled to in a different way. People simply look away when they want to, and *they've no right*.

Later, a couple of days on, I remembered what George Field had said: if you take away people, there's nothing left. One can't be answerable for all mankind, no. But you can sure as hell stick up for the little chunks of mankind that are linked with you, no matter how that link came about – birth, relations, by adoption, love, it all counts. Podgy old George and his dumpy little wife knew the game of living while I was just a beginner.

I learned about Sheila from Geoffrey the day after the burglary. I just said thank you and shut the door.

No jokes from now on, folks.

CHAPTER X

SOMEBODY ONCE said you get no choice in life, and none in memory either. Judging by what the Victorians left in the way of knick-knacks, they made a valiant attempt to control memory by means of lockets for engravings, 'likenesses' in all manner of materials ranging from hairs from the head of the beloved to diamonds, and a strange celebration of death through the oddest mixture of jubilation and grief. Their memory, they seemed to think, should be neatly ordered to provide the maximum nostalgia centred on the loved one. If it needed extra emotional work to achieve that reassuring state, then the labour would just have to be endured. You can't say the Victorians were scared of hard slogging.

I would have liked to have been as firm as they. You know what I mean, pick out especially fond moments from my friendship with Sheila and build up a satisfying mosaic of memories which would comfort me in my loss by giving assurance that all was really not wasted. Nice, but all really was wasted as far as Sheila was concerned. Finished. Done for. And for me, Sheila was gone. Anyway, I'm not resolute enough to look inward for the purpose of emotional construction. Gone's gone.

So that terrible day I sat and sat and did nothing to my records, left letters unanswered, didn't pick up the phone. For some reason I made a coal fire, a dirty habit I thought I'd given up. I shifted my electric fire, put newspaper in a heap in the grate, chopped wood and got it going first time. There was a residue of coal in the old coalbin by the back door so I set to burning that. The cottage became warm, snug, and the day wore on. I had no control over my memories of Sheila as I watched the flames gleam and flash in the fire.

She had this habit of watching me, not just glancing now and again to check I was still around and not up to no good, but actively and purposely inspecting me. I might be doing nothing; still she'd watch, smiling as if engaged in a private humorous conversation at my foibles. It made me mad with her at first, but you get used to a particular woman, don't you?

Another trick she had was reaching out and absently rubbing my neck for nothing while she was reading or watching TV in the cottage. I'd be searching probably through price data of antiques and she'd just put her hand on my neck. It distracted me at first and I'd shrug her off, but moments later back she would come caressing me. There was nothing to it, not her way of starting sex play or anything. It was just her preference. She used to do it for hours.

Then there was the business with the cheese. While I was studying she would suddenly put down her book, go across to the little kitchen and bring back a piece of cheese so small it didn't matter, and push it in my mouth. Never said anything, never had any herself. It would happen maybe twice or three times in an evening. Often she'd not even stop reading, simply carried her book with her, reading as she went. As well, she was tidy and neat, unlike most birds. They have this great reputation, don't they, but most of them get fed up with the tidiness legend and chuck it in during their late teens. Sheila was really tidy by nature almost to the point of being a bit too careful. Nothing of hers ever got in my way. I never fell over her shoes, for instance, because they were tidied out of sight, not like some I could mention.

And the fights. We scrapped a lot, sometimes because of sex, other times because stress is part of life and you let off steam. She was irritable sometimes. She'd announce it from the doorway on arrival, standing there : 'I'm angry, Lovejoy,' she'd say, blazing. 'With me or without?' I'd say, and every time she'd fling back : 'With you, Lovejoy, who else?' and we'd argue for hours. I've chucked her out before now because of her temper. Once women get their dander up all you can do is send them packing because there's no point in everybody getting in a rage to suit their need for a barney, is there? I've sloshed her, too, sometimes when she'd got me mad, and other times making love, but that's only the love sort of coming out, isn't it? Once I bruised her and got worried afterwards, which made her laugh and call me silly. I don't follow their arguments, really, mostly because they make allowances for all sorts of wrong things yet go berserk over little matters you'd hardly notice.

The fire was hot on my face from staring at it. I needed one of Dandy Jack's embroidered firescreens but wanted to see the fire. Of course, a hundred years ago people had firescreens to protect their complexions from the heat, and to shield their eyes from the firelight while reading or sewing in a poorly-lit room. A bright fire was a source of light. The complexion bit was the important thing, though. Only peasants and country-women had ruddy complexions. Elegant ladies wanted lovely pale faces on the unmistakably correct assumption that though ruddy's only healthy, pale's interesting.

Natural light – fires, candles, oil-lanterns – confers a special feeling in a room. One day a month when I feel like it I switch all electricity off and live by natural light. You'd be surprised at the effect it induces. Try it. Natural lights have sounds, small poppings and hissings betokening they have a life of their own. And that's another thing – notice that word I just used, betokening? By natural light, words you'd never even think of come back as it were from times before. Who uses words like that? See what even thinking of natural light can do for you. It teaches you a lot about times gone by, too. Your eyes begin to sting sometimes if you use too many oil lamps in a room, so three is a maximum or you become uncomfortable.

One odd thing is that rooms which you'd think unduly cluttered become much more acceptable by natural light. You've seen mock-ups of Victorian drawing-rooms in museums beautifully lit by bright inert-gas strip lights, and probably been dismayed by seeing practically every inch of wall space covered by pictures, every surface littered by ornaments and clocks, and the furniture draped with hangings so you wonder how they could stand it. The reason you're put off by all that congestion is that the museum's got the lighting wrong. Tell them to switch everything off and put a single oil-lamp on the bureau and draw the curtains. *What a difference*! Those ornaments which *should* glow by natural light do so, while the rest merely set each other off in an easy, comfortable pattern of cosy acquaintanceship. Beautiful, really beautiful. The clutter becomes friendly and spaced out. Don't ridicule the Victorians when it's us that's being stupid and insensitive.

Sheila wouldn't rub my neck any more. No cheese would suddenly be pushed absent-mindedly into my mouth. No more fights. No more sex with her. No more being watched by her smile.

The fire kept in till dawn. Twice I put the radio on. A stupid woman was trying to be crisply incisive about domestic problems that really needed a kick up the backside instead of a psychiatrist. I told her my opinion in no uncertain terms and switched her off. Later I heard the television news about some Middle East catastrophe and switched that off as well. I managed half a cup of tea about midnight. My coal ran out about five-ish the next morning.

I cut a piece of bread and some Wensleydale cheese to feed the robin. It was down to me within seconds, shooing competitors away from the door. You can't help waiting to see if they do different things from what you expect, or if they'll do exactly the same as they've done for years. In either case you're never disappointed.

'Sheila used to say I was too soft with you Rob,' I said to the robin. He came on my arm for his cheese. 'You'll forget how to go marauding, she says – said.' But that can't be bad, was my standard reply to her when she said that. If that's the worst we get up to the world wouldn't be in such a mess. She'd insist the robin ought to go hunting worms to mangle them in the most unspeakable way because it was naturally what they did in searching for food. My cheese-feeding policy must pay off eventually, though, if you think about it. If you're crammed full of cake and cheese you can't fancy too many worms for at least an hour or two, can you? 'Anyway, cheese is good for teeth and bones,' I said to her. 'You're foolish, Lovejoy,' she used to say, falling about laughing. 'Robins don't have a tooth between them.' I used to say, So what, they'd got bones. It was a stupid argument but she would never see sense.

Any sort of hunting is only very rarely necessary, it's always seemed to me. When the robin had surely eaten enough I scattered the remainder about on the path near the Armstrong for the sparrows and the big browny-black birds to share. Even so the robin wouldn't have any peace. He flew at them making stabs with his beak and generally defending the crumbs against all comers. You can't help admiring a bird like that. I wondered if he was more of a hunter than I thought, but decided to stick to my pacification policy anyway. You have to stand by your theories because they're for that, otherwise there's no sense in making them up.

I left them all to it and rang Geoffrey.

'For God's sake,' he said dozily. 'Look at the time.'

'Did Sheila's handbag turn up?' I asked him as he strove to orient himself. He didn't know. I said to find out and let me know or I'd pester the life out of him. It took twenty minutes for him to ring back.

'She didn't have a handbag with her, your young lady,' he reported.

'Then how,' I asked evenly, 'did they know to get in touch with me?'

'The station police. They asked . . . other passengers to try to recognize . . .'

I suppressed the terrible desire to imagine rush-hour queues being invited to file past.

'I suppose one of her workmates — '

'Eventually.' Geoffrey was not enjoying this. 'They went to her home. Your address was on the back of your photograph.'

'Ta.'

I rang off but he was back on the blower instantly.

'Lovejoy — anything up as well as this?'

'Clever old bobbies should mind their own business,' I said, clicking him off.

I knew exactly what he would do. He'd sniff about the village uneasily for a day then come round to pop the question what was I up to and warning me not to do anything silly. The answer he'd get would be a sort of mystified innocence : 'But what on earth do you mean, Constable?' straight out of amateur rep which would gall him still further.

You can't trust the law. Anybody in business will tell you that. As for me, the law is a consideration to be strictly avoided. Never mingle with it. If it's there in force, bow your head, agree like you meant it and scarper. Then when it's gone for the moment, carry on as normal. It's not for people. I wonder where it all comes from sometimes. Think of it like weather, keep an eye on it and take sensible precautions when it proves intrusive.

The dawn had come. I stood at the door smoking a cigar. Red sky, streaks of crimson against blue and white. It was really average. You get the same shallow blue-on-cream in those Portuguese vases, quite nice. I couldn't finish my smoke. The robin was singing, rolling up his feathery sleeves for the day's battles.

Indoors I ran a bath, thinking, this is where I clouted Sheila that time Tinker rang up about Field. I would do my favourite breakfast, fried cheese in margarine and an apple cut into three and fried in the same pan. Three slices of bread. Tea. Heaven knows how but I managed to eat it all, with the radio going on about politics and me trying to sing with the interlude music like a fool. I banged on the dishes with a spoon pretending I was a drummer in a band. Don't people do daft things?

I'd never forget my alarm again. The doors locked, I repaired the window. Outside I ran some meshwire around the edge and put new bolts on the inside of all the windows. The day promised fine with a watery sun.

The bath water had cooled enough by the time that job was done. I soaked, working out my chain of suppositions.

Suppose somebody had killed Eric Field for the Judas pair. Suppose then he had learned that I'd managed to pick up the one possible gadget missing from the most costly unique set of flinters the antique world could ever dream of – a small case-hardened instrument with all the features of a Durs accessory. It had after all probably been chucked into the apothecary box from ignorance to up that particular crummy article's price, so it was definitely a hang-over from Seddon's sale of Eric Field's effects. Continuing the idea, suppose then he'd seen me come from Seddon's, followed me here to the cottage – he'd have seen me give Sheila the instrument by the war memorial, seen her put it in her handbag. And the town war memorial's as private as Eros in Piccadilly. Adrian and Jane had passed, Muriel and her tame priest were there. It could be anybody, he or she, seen or unseen.

Maybe he'd waited outside all night.

Then, seeing us depart, he'd broken in, searching, failed to find the Durs instrument, taken the carriage-clock as a blind, and, seeing Sheila's letters, guessed wrongly that she still had the instrument in her handbag. Perhaps he'd assumed I realized its importance and was too worried to have it about. So he'd sprinted off to London after her and pushed her under the train when perhaps she'd suddenly realized he was stealing her handbag. Or he'd just pushed her, and in the subsequent uproar picked up her handbag, escaping because of our splendid public's tradiition of keeping out of trouble. Now, she was dead, I had to say it, dead.

It was heavy in my hand, bulbous in my palm. It could have been a straight screwdriver except that it bent at right-angles about the middle of the shaft. Two additional flanges served to catch on some projection, perhaps near a sear-spring in the flintlock. I got the impression it slotted into rather than on to something, but it was like nothing I'd ever seen before. Despite my ignorance I was certain it was the object for which Sheila had been killed.

I was dried and in my priest-hole by nine o'clock. I was nervous, because I was going to kill somebody.

Who, I didn't know. Nor where, nor when, nor in what circumstances.

But I knew how.

He would get nothing but the best, the very best Lovejoy could manage. Price no object.

I had a small amount of black powder – smoky gun-powder – in a pistol flask belonging to the Barratt guns. They wouldn't do. Percussion, after all. Let's do it properly. I began to go over the contents of the shelves.

Now, Lovejoy's no killer. I love these flinters the way I love Bilston enamels and jades, as examples of supreme craftsmanship. I don't like weapons because they're wea-pons. Only maniacs love them because they kill. During one of these tiresome wars we used to have I was conscripted and put into uniform. We were stationed on a snowy hillside in the East and given some field guns to shoot. The trouble was, an army on the opposite hillside had guns of their own and kept trying to kill us by shooting back. For me, I'd just as soon we all kept quiet, but the general feeling was that we ought to keep firing. I couldn't see what it was all about. Our hillside had nothing but a few trees, and from what little I could see of their hillside they were just as badly off. It was a waste of time, in addition to which I was frightened to death. But now I began to wish I'd taken more notice of the bare essentials during training.

The Barratts wouldn't do, so could the Nocks? Samuel Nock had made special holster and pocket flinters swan-necked in the French manner, but occasionally deviated into singles made in a special utilitarian style. I had a pair of double-barrelled side-by-side flinters of his making. They really were precious to me, so I included them as possibles. A Brown Bess, heavy as hell, wouldn't do. The space might be too confined when I came to it and forty-odd inches of massive barrel might prove cumbersome. Also, he was going to die slowly if the opportunity offered a choice; the Land Pattern might help him on his way too precipitately. We had matters to discuss. Reluctantly I put it aside.

The Adams revolving longarm was gone to Dick. That left me with two eastern jezail guns, flintlock of course, the Adams pocket weapon, an elegant gold-inlaid La Chaumette pinfire weapon with a folding trigger, a Durs airgun you have to pump up, a Cooper blunderbuss, an early Barbar flintlock brass-barrelled blunderbuss good enough to eat, a lonely Henry Nock dueller I'd been trying to match with its missing partner for twelve years, and last but not least the beautiful Mortimer weapons acquired that terrible day from Dick's boatyard. The Mortimers it was.

I melted a piece of lead bar over a spirit-lamp and poured it from the pan into the bullet-mould, crushing the brass handles firmly to avoid pocking the bullet surface with bubbles. Twelve attempts it took before I got two perfect spheres of dulled lead. After cooling them, I polished both in a leather cloth until they were almost shiny.

The black powder I poured into the pistol flask. It was set correctly on the dispensing nozzle, so I cleaned inside the barrel with a swab of cloth screwed on to the wrong end of the ramrods. All this is easier said than done with white linen gloves on, but you must never leave fingerprints on a flinter – it ruins the browning after some years, and actually precipitates real rust even on the best damascus barrel. The barrels cleaned, I poured the dose of powder into each, and forced the bullets in after tamping the powder down. It was hard work getting them to the bottom of the breech but I managed it. After that, a soft wad of cloth torn from a handkerchief down each barrel to keep the bullets in. Then a squirt of powder into each flashpan, bringing back the cocks to half-cock position where the triggers wouldn't work them and clapping the steel closed, and all was lovely.

I replaced them in their mahogany case, pulling the safety-catch into the halt position and dusting them off. They looked priceless, stylish, graceful, wondrous in their red-felted boxwood recesses among the accessories. Every item fitted snugly. Even the case itself was brilliantly designed, a product of an age of skilled thinkers.

There was one more thing they looked – lethal, maybe even murderous.

And that really pleased me, because I was going to blow some fucking bastard's brains out.

CHAPTER XI

I'LL BE FRANK.

Before this the business had been a bit unreal-like, you know the sort of thing, income tax rebates or these insurance benefits you get if ever you reach ninety. My attitude, I suppose, was one of blissful pretence. Sheila always said I pretended too much, romancing she called it. The Judas affair had previously been somehow at a distance even though I'd been involved in setting up a search for the pistols through the trade. I suppose there was some excuse since you can't believe in a Martian in Bloomsbury in quite the same way you might believe in the Yeti or Nessie. I'd paid lip-service of sorts to the Judas pair idea. If they were mythical, well, OK – I would spend time chasing a myth. If the bloke that had killed two people for those precious things believed in their existence, so would I.

Funny, but my mind began to work clearer now I believed.

If he had searched and followed and then killed for a small accessory like my turnkey, it followed for certain that there could be no possible doubt about where the Judas pair were – *he had them.* I knew as sure as I breathed.

And I understood his anguish. Imagine the distress of scientists as they search for that one missing link creature whose existence will finally prove a million theories. Imagine the shepherd's grief as he finds his prize sheep's gone absent. Double all those sorrows, and it comes somewhere near the anguish of a collector with a stupendous possession one vital component short. I would have felt compassion in other circumstances, even shared part of his grief. Now I cackled with evil laughter as I emerged from my priest-hole and went about letting the light into the cottage and unlocking doors and windows. Let him suffer. He'd come again, somehow and some time he'd come because I had the instrument he wanted.

From now on I would have to be ready every minute of every day. I therefore checked the garden from behind the curtains and decided to play the game to its fullest.

I telephoned George Field. His wife answered. George was out.

'I want a list from him, Mrs Field,' I explained. 'Tell him I need urgently – within the day – the names of all those people his brother was friendly with, known collectors or not. Dealers included.'

She was all set to chat but I cut it short and then rang Geoffrey.

'Look, Lovejoy,' he began wearily, but I wasn't being told off by any village bobby. I was going to do his job for him and he was getting paid from taxes I provided.

'Silence, Geoffrey old pal, and listen.' He listened in astonishment while I said my piece. 'I want the names, ranks and stations of the people in charge of Sheila's . . . accident.' Straight away he began his spiel about not having the authority to divulge and all that. 'Listen,

Geoffrey – I'll say this once. You give me the names now, or I'll take your refusal as obfuscation and ring the Chief Constable, Scotland Yard and my local MP. I'll also ring the local newspaper, three London dailies and the Prime Minister.' I didn't know what obfuscation was but it sounded good.

'What if I don't have the information you want?' he asked, a guarded police gambit.

'There you go again, obfuscating,' I said pleasantly. 'Goodbye, Geoffrey. You'll be hearing from the communications media and the politicians very shortly, if not sooner.'

'Hang on.'

They can be very helpful, these servants of our civic organizations, when they're persuaded in the right way. He gave me a number to ring and an address of a police station.

'What's got into you, Lovejoy?' he said, very uneasy.

'A rush of civic duty to the head,' I explained.

'I don't like all this, I'll tell you straight.'

'Meaning what?'

'Meaning I want to know what you're up to, Lovejoy.'

'Geoffrey,' I said sweetly.

'Yes?'

'Get stuffed, comrade,' I cooed. 'Go back to sleep.'

I felt better now I was on the move.

Faith is a great prime mover. No wonder the distance to Jerusalem didn't daunt the early crusaders. With all that faith, the fact that they'd have to walk every inch of the way would have appeared a mere incidental. Faith gives a clarity of vision as well as thought and I was reaping the benefit of the new believer. It gave me freedom. Apart from Old Bill I could tell anybody the truth, what I was after and even say why. I could show my Durs turnkey to every collector or dealer I'd ever met, knowing sooner or later I'd strike oil. Word would spread like fat in a hot pan. Then, one fine day, my visitor would arrive at the cottage for his big farewell scene. He wouldn't be able to help it. He'd come back again.

I spent an hour on the blower. First Adrian, explaining a friend of mine, Eric Field, deceased, had had a pair of Durs flinters now untraceable, and would he please keep an ear open for any whisper. I got derision back down the receiver but persevered. In the way of his kind he sensed swiftly there was something seriously wrong and went along with me saying he'd put the word out. No reply from Margaret Dainty though I tried her number three times, and none from Dandy Jack's either. He was probably sloshed still from last night, while Margaret was possibly up in the Smoke doing the street markets. Jane Felsham was in, coughing with the rasping breath of the morning smoker and saying what was the matter with me. She thought I was drunk.

'It's on, Jane,' I said. 'Don't muck me about, love, because I'm tough and nasty today. Just take the essentials down and spread it about. Tell anyone, bring anyone to see me any time. And I'll travel. There's a bonus in it — keep thinking of all those pots you could buy with a bit of taxfree.'

Harry was out too, also probably down on the market stalls the same as Margaret. I left a message at the White Hart for Tinker and Dandy Jack to contact me urgently. The barman was out on the village green with the pub's football team training for the Sunday League but his wife Jenny was reliable.

I wrapped the turnkey in white tissue-paper hankies (always the best for carrying small antiques, even storing them for years) and put it into my jacket pocket, using a safety-pin to fasten down the flap. That way, if he wanted it he'd have to get me first. Before locking up and leaving, I phoned Dick Barton and asked him to sell me some black powder as I wanted to try the Mortimers later on. He was surprised, knowing my antipathy to flinters as actual weapons, but promised me three-quarters of a pound. I would collect it on the way back from Jim's, in case Geoffrey decided to finger my parked Armstrong to learn what I was up to. The sale of the black powder in this cavalier fashion is highly illegal, you see, and the law is especially vigilant in this matter. Terrible what some people will do. I chucked a handful of crumbs to the robin to keep it going and drove to Seddon's. On the way over I decided to park outside the showrooms, in accordance with my new plan of inviting my unknown enemy's attention. Old Jim lived in a neighbouring street some four hundred yards down East Hill.

The town was almost empty of pedestrians and cars. One of those quiet days. Driving through in the dilute sun made a very pleasant change from the untidy scramble of the bad week. I parked, confidently facing uphill, and walked down to the street where Jim lived. Apart from a few folk pottering innocently off to shops and others strolling towards the riverside nursery gardens there wasn't a soul about. The terraced houses seemed cheerful and at ease.

I knocked. Jim came to the door, frowning when he saw my happy smiling face.

'Top of the morning, Jim.'

'Morning.' We stayed in an attitude of congenial distrust for a second. 'No use coming here, Lovejoy,' he said sourly. 'All business must go through the firm, you know that.'

'So I believe,' I said, optimism all over.

'What you want then?'

'Now, Jim, you know me.' I honestly felt benign towards him. 'All for a quiet life.' I let it sink in, then added, 'You must be, too.'

'Aren't we all?'

'Some, only some, Jim.'

He was being careful. 'What's this about?'

'Your new job.'

'Eh?'

'You start now.' He started to close the door but my foot was in the way. 'No, Jim, leave the door open and don't go inside. Stay and listen.'

'I want no trouble.'

'And you'll get none, old pal.' I beamed at him. 'Remember the Field sale? Eric Field, deceased?'

'I *thought* you hinted a bit too much,' he said. 'Nothing wrong, was there?'

'Nothing,' I said easily. 'Your new job's trying to re-member everything about it, sales lists, who the auctioneer was, who was there, who bought what, and how much they paid – '

'Confidential.' Remarkable how self-important these pipsqueak clerks are. I went all concerned.

'What about your arm?' I asked anxiously.

'What about it? Nothing wrong with my arm.'

I beamed into his eyes and winked. 'There will be, Jim. It'll be broken in several places.'

'Eh? You're mad – '

'Left or right, Jim?' I was really enjoying myself. No wonder people change when they get religion if this is what faith does for you. Faith's supposed to cancel doubt, isn't it? Marvellous how much calm conviction can bring. If Jim's four brothers had called about then I'd have said the same thing. Numbers are a detail when principle's the prime mover.

'Get the message?' I was so contented. 'Don't get in my way when I'm moving. Now, you've got three seconds to agree, and by six tonight I'll have the invoices, the lists, the sales notes, and all essential details of the Field sale. You bring them round to my cottage, and wait there until I come.'

'You're off your bleeding head, Lovejoy,' he moaned. 'I've no car.'

'Don't miss the bus from the station, then. Remember it's a rotten bus service.'

'Get stuffed,' he said, kicking at my foot.

My forehead felt white-hot. For a moment I struggled for control, then moved up into the doorway, pushing him back. I kneed him in the crotch and butted his nose with my head. When he was down in an easier position on the carpet I stove a rib in with a neat kick. Heaven knows where I learned it. I honestly am a peaceable chap. He tried to scramble away in terror and found an upright modern Jameson piano, only teak and 1930, to lean against. His face showed white above his 'two-day' stubble.

'For Christ's sake –'

'Peace be unto you too, Jim,' I said. 'Now, be a good lad and get me the details.'

'You've broken me ribs,' he wailed. I nodded patiently. Some people just can't be hurried. Others must learn.

'And I'll break your arm at ten past six if you don't get me the answers, Jim.'

'I've got to get to a doctor –' I kicked him down to his knees again and knuckled his face so blood came.

'No doctors, Jim. No hospitals. You've a job to do, right?' He nodded through pain and fear. 'Another word, Jim. I'm on the move. It's not a pretty sight. Now, you can call the law like any decent citizen and turn me in. I won't deny your allegations. But as God's my judge I'll come back and maim you for life if you do. You just do my little job like I ask and I'll leave you alone ever afterwards.'

I turned to go while he was sick all over his Afghanistan – he'd have said Persian – carpet, flower-fruit design with that rather displeasing russet margin they adopt far too often for my liking. I paused at the door.

'Oh, and Jim.'

'What?'

'Miss nothing out. All details complete, or you'll have to suffer the consequences. I must know everything about the Field sale. Understand?'

He managed a nod and I departed thinking of at least one task well done for a starter.

There wasn't a soul on East Hill except for a queue at the baker's and the car was quite untouched.

Black day. Traipsing from one cop shop to another making bother till they gave in. An inspector went over reports of Sheila's death word for word in the manner of his sort. Ever noticed how many people talk like union officials nowadays? Anonymous speech is everywhere – politicians, lawyers, priests in pulpits, auctioneers, the lot. Too many maybes. Listen to a political speech. I'll bet you a quid everything definite he says is cancelled out by something else he says a moment later. Daft. As I sifted through the details I wondered where all the common sense has gone. It vanished about fifteen years ago, about the time those bone ships made by our French prisoners from the Napoleonic scraps vanished. You don't get either any more.

From Old Bill I went to Camden Town where Sheila's pal lived. Betty, fabulous for multicoloured lipsticks, cleavage and a legendary succession of loves, all with wealthy city men. Her husband, twice her age, kept model trains. I leched away as she gave her tale. She'd missed Sheila at home-time that day. Betty, all nineteen years of her, explained she'd had to work late. I pretended to believe her from politeness.

Seeing her old man was playing trains outside, I gave her my deep dark Lovejoy smoulder. I only wished she'd been a customer. I swear I could have got rid of that tarty Dutch cutlery at last. You get no tax allowance for stock. Bloody Chancellor.

I held Betty's hand at the door. They measure you with their eyes, don't they? I said how I felt biological towards her. She liked biological and gave me the address of a little executive cottage she visited at certain times. These places can be a mine of antiques. What more pleasant than searching for antiques, up and down stairs with the help of a huge cleavage? Two birds per stone and that.

But no clues. Maybe the steam was going out of my crusade. It depressed me. I knocked about, saw the Bond Street arcade, did time in Fairclough's, did a few deals. The 4.30 train was on time from Liverpool Street.

I reached home at ten to six. Jim was waiting, grey-faced, hurting, obedient. I drove up with the now-familiar knot of tension in my belly at the sight of him. It pleased me. My crusading zeal had only momentarily tired because of so many false leads. Here was one I relied on to give me a few more details.

He gave me a photocopied list of the Field sale and every single invoice to do with it. In his own clumsy handwriting was a list of everybody who'd attended, the auctioneers, clerk and his two mates who assisted.

'There's a good lad.' I patted his head. 'Look, Jim –'

'Yes?' He stood mournfully on the gravel.

'I don't want to hurry you, but the doctor's surgery closes at seven. You'll just make it on the bus.'

'Aren't you going to give me a lift?' His spirits were on the mend. There was a faint hint of the old truculence.

I smiled. 'Good night, Jim,' I said, and closed the door.

CHAPTER XII

SOME PEOPLE kill me. You can invent a name for anything and it will be believed. Say anything and somebody'll cheer fit to burst. I'll give you an example. There was Dandy Jack looking for cracks on this piece of 'cracked' porcelain – and him a dealer old enough to be my great-grandad. Of course, Dandy Jack was as indisposed as a newt, as one politician cleverly said of that minister who got sloshed and shot his mouth off on telly.

'Give it here, Dandy.' I took it off him, exasperated. 'Crack porcelain doesn't mean it's got cracks all over it.' His bloodshot eyes gazed vaguely in my direction while I gave him the gory details.

'Kraak', not 'Cracked' porcelain (note that 's'). Once upon a time, the Portuguese ship *Catherine* was sailing along in the Malacca Straits when up came a Dutch ship and captured it, there being no holds barred in 1603. Imagine the Dutchmen's astonishment when they found they'd bagged, not treasure, but a cargo of ceramics of a funny blue-white colour. The *Catherine* was a carrack, or 'Kraak'. The nickname stuck. It looks rubbish but folk scramble for it. I priced it for him and said I'd be back.

The town was jumping. I felt on top of the world without knowing why. A bad memory of something evil having happened recently was suppressed successfully in a wave of sun and crowds. No dull weather, kids well-behaved, trees waggling and people smiling, you know how pleasant things can look sometimes. And the little arcade was thronged. Margaret waved from her diminutive glass-fronted shop, Dandy with his incredible luck was swilling down the profits. Harry Bateman was there with a good, really good, model compound steam engine of brass and deep red copper, Robert Atkinson about 1864 or there-abouts, and shouting the odds about part-exchange for a John Nash painting, modern of course, all those greens and lavender watercolour shades. It would be close.

Several real collectors had turned up in the café and sat about saying their antiques were honest. We were all in brilliant humour, exchanging stories and gossip. Such a cheerful scene, everybody entering into the act and taking risks in deals. It was one of those marvellous times.

I told you I'm a believer in the gifts people have, and luck. Luck is partly made by oneself. Go out feeling lucky, make yourself behave lucky and you will probably become lucky. Let yourself slip into the opposite frame of mind and you'll lose your shirt.

There'd been two flint collectors and one flint dealer in Jim's papers, and both collectors were in my files. The dealer Froude, a pal of Harry's, wasn't bad, just cheap and useless, so I could forget him. The collectors were different mettle. One, a retired major called Lister, was a knowledgeable Rutland man who ran a smallholding in that delectable county. He knew what he was about. The second spelled even more trouble, had an enviable record in my card system as a dedicated and lucky collector given to sudden spurts of buying often without relevance to the seasonal state of the market. Brian Watson was by all accounts one of those quietly-spoken northerners who seem quite untypical of the usual image people have of cheerful, noisy extroverts laughing and singing round pints in telly serials. I had almost all Watson's purchases documented but though I'd never actually met him at sales I'd heard he was hesitant, not given to confidences but gravitating with a true collector's instinct towards the quality stuff. A good collector, Watson, who'd spend what seemed about two years' salary in an hour then vanish for up to a year back to his native Walkden. Also on Jim's list were Harry, Adrian and Jane together, Margaret, good old Dandy Jack, Muriel's Holy Joe Lagrange, Brad, Dick from the boatyard and Tinker Dill, among the dross. And Muriel.

Now, of all these people, Brian Watson was significant because he already had one of the pairs of Durs duellers, and so was Major Lister of Rutland because he'd been making offers to Watson for them ever since Eve dressed. The field was getting pretty big, but I was cock-a-hoop. The pace was quickening. And as I talked in the arcade I smiled to myself at my secret. At the finishing-post lay my beautiful unpaid-for Mortimers – loaded. I left the café and wandered through the arcade.

Tinker Dill was at my elbow full of news. We pretended to examine a phoney Persian astrolabe. It was described by Harry Bateman as 'medieval' and priced accordingly. My sneer must have been practically audible. Don't over-estimate their value, incidentally – eighteenth-century Con-tinental ones are usually more pricey, though they're all in vogue, and certain firms in Italy make excellent copies.

'You're getting busy, aren't you, Lovejoy?'

'Whatever can you mean?' I was all innocent.

'Bending Jim like that.' He enjoyed the thought of Jim's injuries almost as much as a sale.

'I'm quite unrepentant.' I put the astrolabe down, feel-ing it unclean, and took Tinker back into the nosh bar where we could talk.

I told him of my developing interest in Watson and Lister.

He whistled. 'They're First Division, Lovejoy.'

'And Froude.'

'He's rubbish.'

'I have this about the Field sale.'

'Eh?'

Over tea I showed him Jim's lists.

He slurped in his cup. 'They're nicked!'

'On loan. Jim's good-hearted.' I let him recover. 'Heard anything special about any of those names?'

He flipped slowly through the lot, shaking his head each time. 'Except the two big ones – that sale was a right load of heave-ho.'

'You buy anything, Tinker?'

It hurt him. 'You know me, Lovejoy. Antiques aren't my business.'

I grinned in great good humour. 'Neither of these bought anything? Try to remember, Tinker.' He would. It's like being a football fan. Just as they can recall incidents from games seen twenty years past, so we can tick off auctions as if they'd been yesterday. You might wonder why I didn't just look at the purchasers' names on the invoices.

Well. Invoices, however complete, never tell it all. I wish I had time to tell you what goes on in an auction. For every ten lots sold by the auctioneer, another ten are sold among dealers. We buy a lot from the auctioneer sometimes, and even before he's moved on we've sold it to a fellow-dealer. All the time it goes on. 'Ringing' you already know about I'm sure, where dealers get together and do not bid for a choice item, say a lovely French commode. When it goes to Dealer A for a paltry sum – i.e. when it's been successfully 'ringed' – he'll collect his cronies and they'll auction it again privately in a pub nearby, only on this occasion Dealer A's the auctioneer and his mates are the congregation, so to speak.

You'll probably think this is against the law. Correct, it is. And you may be feeling all smug thinking it is rightly so because whoever's selling her old auntie's precious French antique is being diddled out of the fair auction she's entitled to. Well, I for one disagree – nobody actually *stops* the public from bidding, do they? It comes back again to greed, your greed. And why? Answer: you want that valuable commode for a couple of quid, and not a penny

more. If you were really honest you'd bid honestly for it.
But you won't. How do I know? Because you never do.
You go stamping out of auctions grumbling at the price
fetched by whatever it was you were after and failed to
get. So don't blame the dealer – he's willing to risk his
every penny for a bit of gain while you want medieval
Florentine silver caskets for the price of a bus-ride. *You
ring items by your greed*. We do it by arrangement. Why
your hideous but dead obvious greed should be quite legal
and our honesty illegal beats me.

'That Bible pistol,' Tinker remembered. 'Not too bad –
I did drop a note in at your cottage, Lovejoy.'

'I passed it up.'

'Watson bought it.'

'In his usual style?'

Tinker's eyes glowed with religious fervour. 'You bet.'
He rolled a damp fag and struggled to set it afire. 'It was
in one of his buying sprees. You know him, quiet and
hurrying. I reckon he should have been a cop. Busy, busy,
busy.' I wrote a mental tick against Watson's name. He'd
attended six auctions that week, and the date matched
no fewer than eight postal purchases, all after a ten-month
gap. Phenomenal.

'Major Lister buy, did he?'

'Yes, a set of masonic jewels for some museum.'

I knew about those and the Stevens silk prints he'd
bought as well.

'All in all,' I asked, 'a quiet, busy little auction with
more than the average mixture of good stuff?'

'Sure. And not a bad word uttered,' Tinker said, puffing
triumphantly.

I let his little quip pass impatiently. 'Is that list of
people complete? Think.'

He thought. 'As ever was.' He shrugged. 'The odd housewife, perhaps.'

'Thanks, Tinker. Anything else?'

He told me of the Edwardian postcards from Clacton,
the Regency furniture at Bishop's Stortford, that crummy

load of silver being unloaded up in the Smoke, and the Admiralty autograph letters being put on offer in Sussex. I knew them all but slipped him a note.

'You got them Mortimers, then,' he said as we parted.

'A hundred quid,' I replied modestly. He was still laughing at the joke as I left to see Margaret's collection of English lace christening gowns.

'Sorry about everything, Lovejoy.' She pecked my face and brewed up. There were a couple of customers hanging around, one after pottery, one after forgeries. (Don't laugh – collectors of forgeries will walk past a genuine Leonardo cartoon to go crazy over a forged Braque squiggle.) As they drifted out she hooked her 'Closed' notice on the door.

'I've had a drink, Margaret, thanks.'

'I saw you.'

'Tinker reporting in,' I explained, looking round. Her lace christening gowns were beautiful but I always sneeze looking them over. 'I can never understand why these things are so cheap. A few quid for such work, years of it in each one.'

She smiled. 'Keep plugging that attitude. Genuine?'

'Does it matter?' I said. 'Any forger who does something so intricate deserves every groat he gets.' I felt them. 'Yes, all good.'

'I thought you'd been neglecting me till I heard, Lovejoy.' She brought tea over despite my refusal.

'No matter now.' I took the Victorian Derby cup as a mark of friendship because her tea's notorious. 'All over.'

She sat facing. People outside in the arcade must have thought we were a set of large bookends for sale.

'Give, Lovejoy.'

'Eh?'

'I've one thing you've not got, darling,' she said in a way I didn't like. 'Patience. What are you up to?'

'I'm going to find the bastard. And I'm going to finish him.'

'You can't, Lovejoy.' God help me, she was crying. There she sat, sipping her rotten tea with tears rolling on to her cheeks. 'It'll be the end of you, too.'

'Cheap at the price, love.'

'Leave it to the police.'

'They're quite content with matters as they are.' My bitterness began to show. 'It's much more dramatic to rush about with sirens wailing than slogging quietly after the chap on foot.'

'They know what to do –'

'But they don't do it.' I pulled away as she reached a hand towards me. 'I've no grouse with anybody, love. I just want help.'

Two people staring in turned quickly away at the sight of our tense faces.

'Supposing you *do* find him – why not just turn him in?'

I had to laugh, almost. 'And endure months or years of questions while he wheedles his way out?'

'But that's what law is for,' she cried.

'I don't want law, nor justice,' I said. 'From me he'll get his just deserts, like in the books. I want what's fair.'

'Please, Lovejoy.'

'Please, Lovejoy,' I mimicked in savage falsetto. 'You're asking me to let him off with seven years in a cushy gaol thoughtfully provided by the ratepayers? No. I'm going to spread his head on the nearest wall and giggle when it splashes.'

She flapped her hands on her lap. 'We used to be so . . .'

'Things have changed.'

'You'll get yourself killed. Whoever it is must have heard you're spreading word about fancy Durs duellers. It's the talk of the trade. Half of them already think you're off your head.' Good news.

'There's one person who knows I'm serious, love.' I was actually grinning. 'I'm going to needle and nudge till he has to come for me.' I rose and replaced her cup safely.

'All right, Lovejoy.' She was resigned. 'Anything I can do?'

'Spread the word yourself. Tell people. Make promises. Invent. Tell people how strange I've become.' I kissed her forehead. 'And your tea's still lousy.'

I phoned George Field from the kiosk. He agreed to send an advert to the trade journal whose address I gave him:

REWARD

A substantial reward will be paid by the undermentioned for information leading to the specific location (not necessarily the successful purchase) of the Durs flintlock weapons known to the antique trade as the Judas Pair.

I thought, let's all come clean. He gasped at the sum mentioned but agreed when I said I'd waive any costs. I insisted he put his name and address to the notice, not mine because he was in all day and I wasn't.

I called in at the cottage and then drove to see Major Lister, happy as a pig in muck. By the weekend the murderer would know I was raising stink and getting close, and he'd start sweating. Don't believe that revenge isn't sweet. It's beautiful, pure unflawed pleasure. He was losing sleep already because I had the little Durs gadget. I slept the sleep of the just. My revenge had begun.

Major Lister turned out to be a fussy disappointment, a stocky, balding, talkative, twinkly chap who wouldn't hurt a fly. His vast house was full of miscellaneous children. Everybody there, including three women who seemed to be permanent residents, was smiling.

'I'll bet you're Lovejoy,' were his first words to me. 'Come and see my fuchsias.' He drew me away from the front door towards a greenhouse, calling back into the house, 'We'll have rum and ginger with the fuchsias.'

'I like your system,' I said. The nearest child, a toddler licking a dopey hedgehog clean in the hallway, cried out the rum message hardly missing a lick. The cry was taken up like on the Alps throughout the house until it faded into silence. A moment later a return cry approached and the hedgehog aficionado shouted after us, 'Rum on its way, Dad.'

'*They* like the system, not I.' He twinkled again and began talking to his plants, saying hello and so on. A right nutter here, I thought. He chattered to each plant, nodding away and generally giving out encouragement.

Well, it's not really my scene, a load of sticks in dirt in pots. He evidently thought they were marvellous, but there wasn't an antique anything from one end of the greenhouse to the other that I could see. A waste of time. His sticks had different names.

'Same as birds, eh?' I said, getting to the point. 'Identical, but each one's supposed to be distinct, is that the idea?'

'I see you're no gardener.'

'Of course I am.'

'What do you grow?'

'Grass, trees and bushes.'

'What sorts?'

'Oh, green,' I told him. 'Leaves and all that.'

'Yes,' he twinkled as a little girl entered carrying two glasses of rum yellowed by ginger. 'Yes, you're Lovejoy all right.'

'Seen me at auctions, I expect, eh?'

'No. Heard about your famous Braithwaite car.'

'Braithwaite?'

He saw the shock in my eyes and sat me on a trestle. The little girl wanted to stay and sat on the trestle with me.

'Herbert Braithwaite, maker of experimental petrol engines early this century. Some ohv cycles. Yours must be the only one extant. Didn't you know?'

'No. Well, almost.'

'Drink up, lad.' He settled himself and let me get breath. 'Now, Lovejoy, what's all this word about a pair of Durs guns?'

I told him part of the story but omitted Sheila's death and the turnkey.

'And you came here, why?'

'You were at the Field sale.'

'And Watson got the Bible pistol. Yes, I recollect.' He took the little girl on his lap and gave her a sip of his rum. 'Fierce man is Watson. One of those collectors you can't avoid.'

'The Field sale,' I persisted.

'Nothing very special for me, I'm afraid. Naturally,' he added candidly, 'if you're trying me for size as a suspect, ask yourself if I would dare risk this orphanage.'

'Orphanage?' It hadn't struck me.

'I don't breed quite this effectively,' he chided, laughing so much the little girl laughed too, and finally so did I.

'You saw Watson there?'

'Certainly. He'll be not far from here now, if indeed he's on one of his whirlwind buying sprees.'

My heart caught. I put the glass down. 'Near here?'

'Why, yes. Aren't you on your way there too? The Medway showrooms at Maltan Lees. It's about eleven miles –'

I left as politely and casually as I could. Nice chap, Major Lister. I mentally filed him away as I moved towards the village of Maltan Lees : –

Major Lister (retd): collector flck dllrs; orphanage; plants; clean hedgehogs.

Then I remembered I'd not finished my rum. Never mind, that little girl could have it when she'd finished his.

Four o'clock, Maltan Lees, and the auctioneer in the plywood hall gasping for his tea. I had no difficulty finding the place, from the cars nearby. They were slogging through the remaining lots with fifty to go. The end of an auction is always the best, excitement coming with value. By then the main mob of bidders has gone and only the dealers and die-hard collectors are left to ogle the valuables. Medway's seemed to have sold miscellaneous furniture including bicycles, mangles, a piano and household sundries, leaving a few carpets, some pottery, a collection of books and some paintings, one of which, a genuine Fielding watercolour, gave me a chime or two.

I milled about near the back peering at odd bits of junk. The auctioneer, a florid glassy sort, was trying unsuccessfully to increase bids by 'accidentally' jumping increments, a common trick you shouldn't let them get away with at a charity shout. Among this load of cynics he didn't stand a chance. Twice he was stopped and fetched back, miserably compelled to start again and once having to withdraw an item, to my amusement. Another trick they have is inventing a non-existent bidder, nodding as if they've been signalled a bid then looking keenly to where the genuine bidder's bravely soldiering away. Of course, they can only get away with it if the bidder's really involved, all worked up. Therefore in an auction *keep calm*, keep *looking*, keep *listening* and above all keep as *still* as you can. You don't want anybody else knowing who's bidding, do you? If you can do it with a flick of an eyebrow, use just that. Don't worry, the chap on the podium'll see you — a single muscle twitch is like a flag day when money's involved. Where was I?

You've only to stay mum and patterns emerge in a crowd. The old firms were there, Jane, Adrian, Brad, Harry, and Dandy Jack, and some collectors I knew — Reverend Lagrange, the Mrs Ellison from the antique shop where I'd bought the coin tokens while returning from the bird sanctuary, Dick Barton among others.

A handful of travelling dealers had descended on lucky Maltan Lees. They smoked and talked noisily, moving about to disturb the general calm and occasionally calling across to each other, full of apparent good humour but in reality creating confusion. It's called 'circusing', and is done to intimidate locals like us. They move from town to town, a happy band of brothers.

I watched a while. One of the travelling dealers paused near me.

"'Ere,' he growled. 'Are you 'ere for the paintings or not?' I gave him my two-watt beam free of charge. 'I said,' he repeated ferociously, 'are you 'ere for the paintings?'

'Piss off, comrade.' I raised my smile a watt. He rocked back and stared in astonishment at me before he recovered.

'You what?'

'Where I come from,' I informed him loudly, 'you circus chaps'd starve.'

'Clever dick.'

He barged past me, tripping over my foot and ending up among assorted chairs. His pals silenced. I laughed aloud, nodding genially in their direction, and stepped towards their fallen companion.

'Sorry,' I apologized because my foot had accidentally alighted on his hand. He cursed and tried to rise, but my knee had accidentally jerked into his groin so he stayed down politely while my knuckles injured his eye. I get annoyed with people sometimes, but I think I'd been a bit worse lately. I bent down and whispered. 'Me and my mates got done for manslaughter in Liverpool – twice – so go gently with us, whacker. We're fragile.'

'No harm meant, mate,' he said.

As I say, a lie works wonders. I stepped away, embarrassed because people were watching. The auctioneer had kept going to keep the peace and some fortunate chap got his missus a wardrobe for a song. It's an ill wind.

I settled down near the bookcases and all went gaily on. I fancy the auctioneer was rather pleased with my little diversion. I saw Adrian applaud silently and Jane nod approval. I noticed Brian Watson after another twenty minutes and knew instantly who he was.

Some blokes have this chameleon-like ability, don't they? My mate in the army was typical of the sort. The rest of us had only to breathe in deep for all the grenades on earth to come hurtling our way, but Tom, a great Cheshire bloke the size of a tram, could walk on stilts for all the notice the enemy took of him. It was the same everywhere. I've even seen blokes come into pubs, stand next to Tom and say, 'Anybody seen Tom?'

Brian Watson was standing a few feet away, virtually unseen. He stood there watching, quiet, listening, and I knew instantly he was as fully aware of me as I was of him. A careful chap, the sort you had to be careful of. I instinctively felt his capabilities. A real collector. If he starved to death he'd still collect. You know the sort. No matter what setbacks come they weather them and plough on. I honestly admire their resilience. It's a bit unnerving if you ask me, too straightforward for my liking.

I bought a catalogue. Now, Harry and the rest were quite explicable in terms of attendance at any auction virtually no matter what was on offer. But Watson? Every piece he had was known to me, apart from some I only suspected, bought by concealed postal bid but quite in the Watson pattern. A buyer, not a seller. He very rarely sold anything, and when he did it was only to buy bigger still. A cool resilient man. Moreover, one who was now observing me with his collector's antennae.

All of which, I thought as the auctioneer chattered on, raised one central question – if everybody else was here with good reason, what good reason did Brian Watson have? There was nothing to interest him. I scanned the remaining lots but failed to find an answer. He was a pure flint man, never deviating into the mundaner fields of prints, pottery and portabilia, which to my dismay seemed all that was left. There was no choice but to wait and see.

It came to lot 239, the small collection of portabilia. Watson was in character, waiting with the skill of an old hand until the bidding showed signs of ending, then he nodded gently and off we went. We, because I was in, too, all common sense to the winds. People gradually became aware of the contest. You could have heard a pin drop.

While the bidding rose I racked my brains wondering what the hell could be in the portabilia that could be so vital to Watson. On and on we went, him against me. Everyone else dropped out. Portabilia are small instruments made especially for carrying about. They included in this instance a 'sovereign-balance for testing gold coins, a common folding flintlock pistol by Lacy of Regency London's Royal Exchange, a tin box with a tiny candle, a collapsible pipe, a folding compass, a folding sundial, a diminutive snuff horn and other minutiae. It wasn't bad, but you couldn't pay twice their value in open auction and keep sane. I saw Adrian hide his face in his hands as we forged inexorably on and Jane, cool Jane, shook her head in my direction with a rueful smile. Many people crossed to the cabinet to see what they'd missed. Still we drove the price upwards until my calculations caught up with me and I stopped abruptly, white-hot and practically blind from impotent rage at missing them.

'Going . . . going . . . gone. Watson. Now to lot two-forty,' the pleased auctioneer intoned.

I went outside to wait for Watson and partly to avoid the others.

Jane followed me out. 'Better now, Lovejoy?' She had style, this woman with the smile that meant all sorts of business.

'No.'

'What's it all about?'

'I don't know what you mean.'

We crossed the road and sat near the window in the café opposite the auction room. She ordered tea and faced me across the daffodils.

'Aren't you making a fool of yourself?'

'No.'

'You're like a child without its toffee-apple.' She irritated me with her bloody calm dispassionate air and I said so. 'I heard about Sheila,' she went on. 'Do you think it's what she'd want you to be doing, going to pieces like this?'

'I'm not going to pieces.' I wouldn't give in to this smarmy woman who couldn't mind her own business.

'You look like it, Lovejoy.' She should have been a teacher. 'We're all worried about you, everybody. Your business'll go downhill next. Look at you. You haven't shaved, you're . . . soiled-looking.'

That really hurt because I'm not like that. I looked

away in a temper because she was right.

'Somebody killed her – the same character who killed Eric Field.'

Another of her famous appraisals came my way. 'Are you serious?'

I gave her an appraisal back. 'You know I am.'

'By God, Lovejoy,' she breathed, 'what are you up to? You're not seriously thinking –'

'I am.'

'You don't think Watson – ?'

'I'm not sure.' The tea came. 'He's a Durs collector, a clever one. I've eliminated most of the rest one way and another. It could be a dealer of course, or somebody I don't know about, but I must try to follow the leads I've got.'

'Was he at the Field sale you've been on about?'

'Yes.'

'He may have nothing to do with it.'

'And again,' I said coldly, 'he may.'

For the next few minutes Jane quizzed me. I told her the whole story including the turnkey bit while she listened intently.

'Have you anything practical to go on?' she demanded. 'So you found a posh screwdriver – big deal.'

'Yes,' I said after a minute. 'There is something.'

'What?'

'God knows.' A few people drifted out of the doors across the way. It would end in five minutes. 'I couldn't sleep last night for worrying – the answer's been given me, here in my mind, and for the life of me I can't think what makes me think so. I'd know who it is, but the bits of my mind won't connect.'

'From Seddon's?'

'I feel helpless. I just can't think.'

'Give it up, Lovejoy.' She was less forbidding than I remembered. 'It'll ruin you.'

'I might.' And I almost believed me, except that Watson came out of the auctioneer's that instant. I was up and out into the road darting between cars before I knew where I was.

He waited, casually looking through the window at a set of old seaside lantern slides that had gone dirt cheap — there's quite a market for them nowadays. It was decimalization that did it.

'Mr Watson.' We stood together, me somewhat breathless and aggressive, him a little reserved.

'Mr Lovejoy.'

'Right.'

He smiled hesitantly. 'I admired your, er, act with the circus crowd.'

'Thanks.'

'Could I ask — ?' I nodded and he went on, 'Er, if you, er, were very keen to have that group of portabilia?'

'No,' I snapped.

'I thought not. May I ask then why you bid?'

'Never mind *me*, comrade,' I said roughly. 'Why did you?'

He was astonished. 'Me? They belonged to my father.'

'Eh?' I was saying as Jane strolled up.

'My brother put them up for sale,' he explained, 'somewhat against my wishes. Why do you want to know?'

'Well done, Lovejoy,' Jane said sarcastically.

'Keep out of it,' I said. 'Why did you go to the Field sale?'

His memory clicked away for a moment, then his brow cleared. 'After that collector was killed, you mean? Oh, the odd item.'

'Never mind what you actually bought. What attracted you there?'

He glanced from Jane to me, but it was no use messing about at this stage.

'He gets like this periodically.' Jane's casual excuse didn't calm me.

'It's my habit,' Watson replied with dignity, 'to do so. It's also my right.'

'I couldn't agree more,' Jane chipped in.

I looked about. People had gathered round. The windows of the auction rooms were full of faces, staring. Cars were slowing to see what the rumpus was about. My old aunts would have called it a 'pavement scene'.

'You're among friends, Lovejoy,' Jane said kindly, and explained to Watson, 'He's not like this normally. He's been under a strain lately, a bereavement, you know.' Murmurs of sympathy arose from a couple of old dears in the throng who quickly transmuted compassion into reminiscences of similar events in their own past. 'Just like our Nelly's cousin when her Harry was took,' etc, etc.

'Will he be all right?' Watson was asking anxiously of Jane. That more than anything shook me – when people talk over you as if you're not really there, you really might have vanished.

'His car's near here somewhere. Over there.'

Watson and Jane frog-marched me to the Braithwaite. Rage shook me into a sweat, rage at Jane's smooth assumption of power and Watson's obvious concern. If I'd cast him in the role of murderer, why didn't the bastard behave like one?

'You'd better come to my sister's – it's a few miles.' They discussed me while I trembled like a startled horse. My face was in my hands. I could hear their voices but not what was said, so sick did I feel from the stink of the leather upholstery and the extraordinary vertigo which took hold. Jane took my keys and we drove out of Maltan Lees in the wake of Watson's old white Traveller.

There's nothing much to say about the rest of that day except that I stayed at Watson's sister's house in a room the size of a matchbox full of toys. Children came to stare at me as I was given aspirin tablets and milk to swallow – heaven knows why – and finally I dozed until dawn. Watson, my erstwhile villain, slept on a settee, Jane drove home in my old crate saying she'd come back for me in the morning. When I woke I found one of the children had laid a toy rabbit on my bed for company, a nasty sight in the sunrise of a nervous breakdown. Still, thank God it wasn't a hedgehog.

I can't remember much except Watson's kindness, his sister's concern and Jane smiling too quickly at everything that was said as we departed.

'I feel a bloody fool,' were my parting words, epitaph for a crusader. Amid a chorus of denials and invitations to return soon Jane ferried me away. I couldn't even remember what the house was like.

On the way back Jane, a smart, alert driver, told me she'd been summoned into Geoffrey's police station to explain what she'd done with me because the cottage was raided again during the night. Our vigilant bobby, understandably narked by his ruined sleep, told her in aggrieved tones how he'd wakened to the sound of the alarm and arrived before entry was effected. The would-be intruder fled unseen.

I received the news with utter calm and stared at the ceiling.

CHAPTER XIII

WEEKS OF FEEDING my robin and watching weather, occasionally getting the odd visitor. Twice I found myself embarking on gardening expeditions armed with rusty shears and suchlike, but my heart's never in it. After all, grass does no harm growing and birds and bushes don't need mowing anyway so there's not a lot you can do in a garden. Somewhere I'd cleared a patch for growing vegetables years ago but it had reverted to jungle like the herbaceous border did and I couldn't find exactly where it was. I abandoned the attempt, taking the wise view that if vegetables had wanted to grow there they'd have done so whatever assistance they'd been given by me. There's a chap Brownlow in a bungalow not far from me who's never out of his garden. It beats me what he finds to do. Maybe he's got a blonde in the shrubbery.

Ever been stuck at home? You get up and make breakfast, put the radio on and wash up. Then you mill about doing odd jobs like cleaning and washing, and that's the end of it. What housewives keep moaning about heaven only knows, because I was up at seven-thirty and finished easily by ten after which the rest of the day was waiting there – in my case, for nothing. Margaret called at first with provisions, and Jane dropped in with Adrian. The itinerant dealer Jimmo called. Tinker came after the first day, but within a week all the visits had dwindled. I was pretty glad because I was in no mood to talk and they were embarrassed. People are, where a nervous breakdown's concerned. It's posh and gallant to break your leg, and brave to have appendicitis, but a nervous breakdown's a plain embarrassment best avoided. You're better off with the plague. Maybe people think a breakdown's a sign of lack of moral fibre, that you ought to be pulling yourself together, putting your shoulder to that wheel, etcetera. It taught me one lesson at least, that any form of 'weakness' is highly suspect. I wish I knew why.

I'd heard of breakdowns before, of course. Half my difficulty was that I didn't know what they actually were or where they came from, let alone what went on, yet there I was with all my anxieties gone, all my worries vanished, all interests evaporated. It would have been rather disturbing, if I'd been capable of being disturbed, that is. As it was, I was utterly serene – dirty, unwashed, filthy, unshaven, unfed and unkempt, but serene. Calm as a pond I was, uncaring. Worst of all, grief about Sheila had disappeared. Margaret came on a second then a third visit and discreetly left money on the mantelpiece, saying I was to be sure to remember to pay it back when I had the chance. I mumbled vacantly. Finally everyone had stopped coming. The letters lay in a heap by the door.

As days went into weeks I found myself stirring, not physically but something inside me. It really was an awakening. Instinctively my switched-off mind must have realized there was no point in trying to hurry things along, and had stayed resting. My recovery was under way before I realized. The first event I can really recall is making myself some food, sausages and stale bread. Then I started feeding the birds again, sitting with them for a short while as usual although I'd earlier automatically shunned their company as too intrusive, making too many demands on me.

About three days after starting eating I took conscious positive steps. I shaved. The next day I shaved and washed, then after that I bathed and got fresh clothes out. It was about sixteen days before I was presentable. The cottage was reasonable, and I started going down to the launderette. For some reason it was important to set myself a mental limit and stick rigidly to it, no matter how gormless that scheme actually was. Therefore for four consecutive days I walked the garden's borders ten times every afternoon and counted all my trees and bushes assiduously after doing the washing-up about nine o'clock, and for those four days I took my clothes, clean and soiled alike, to the launderette and washed them. Naturally I ran into practical difficulties such as coins for the slots, not knowing when the wretched machines were going to start or stop, what to do with that cup of powder and other details like losing socks. By the fourth day I was becoming quite intrigued at the system – you put in eight socks with your things and get out only five socks and one you've never seen before. Next day's the same. Unless you're careful you can finish up with an entirely different set of miscellaneous gear and all your own socks presumably transmuted into energy. I cut my losses on the fifth day and merely watched other sockless people's machines on the go.

My interest in antiques like everything else had suddenly vanished. Auctions had presumably taken place, the phone had carried on unanswered and Lovejoy was temporarily indisposed. Now, as I mended and consciousness returned, I took up a catalogue and read it in small stages during the course of an entire evening while the telly was on. It was an odd sensation, reading at a distance, as it were, with details registering in the right places yet my own self somehow observing the whole process with caution and not a little distrust. Anyhow, I acted it out, feeling a flicker of interest here and there but suppressing it in case it got out of hand. It must have been the right thing to do because the very next day I was answering letters and making decisions, about half-speed. Injured animals go and lie quiet, don't they? Maybe that's what my mind had done.

The fourth week I faced the world again.

I began life by attending a sale in Colchester and after two more days another, this time in Bury St Edmunds. As a starter, the tokens I'd bought in darkest East Anglia – easy material whose value you can always gauge by an hour's careful checking – were launched out in a coin mart we have not far away, and they went for a good profit. I was pleased, and pleased *because* I was pleased. The cottage hadn't been assaulted while I was out. Cheered and feeling full of emotions that were no longer lying dormant, I whistled and sang and forayed into the garden for some flowers to put in a vase. I was unsuccessful, though, not because there weren't any but because you can't really go hacking plants' heads off just because you feel a bit bouncy. I seriously thought of planting one into a pot and bringing it inside the cottage but decided against that as well. There's no breeze inside a house like there is in a garden, is there, and plants might really depend on being pushed about by the wind, not being able to stretch themselves like we can. Also, you have to think of the proper sunshine outside instead of no real light indoors. And rain. And company. I don't know much about them, not like Major Lister would, for instance, but it stands to reason you're best not trying to dabble in what you don't understand. People do damage when they want things. If people didn't want things hardly anything would go wrong with anybody's life. All bad's desire.

I temporarily shelved the notion that, if it was true that all bad came from desire, then maybe all desire was bad too. Calm but feeling alive again now I gently worked my way back to a proper behaviour.

Six whole weeks after I'd gone up to Maltan Lees and met Watson I was well again.

Not that I was yet in the full circle of my usual life. I kept out of friends' way, didn't phone any of them and only spoke when I was directly addressed if ever I ran into anyone I knew. Business picked up from nil and a trickle of post came again. The phone calls started. It was a pleasure to be active and doing something useful but I had to keep myself from regretting the lost opportunities during my holiday. There'd been an undeniable upsurge of deals in the antiques world during the previous weeks. I just had to accept that I'd done my business no good by chasing all over England looking for a needle in a haystack.

Finally, when I was really well and having to restrain myself hourly, I shook out the reins of my mind and took off.

I rang Field. He was very relieved.

'I'm sorry about your illness. What was it?'

'Oh, you know,' I parried, 'some virus, I expect.'

'Terrible, terrible things, those.' After passing on some amateur therapy he told me of the replies to the advertisement.

'Were there many?'

'You've no idea!' He drew breath. 'The wife nearly went off me – a mountain of letters, some really rather odd. I'd no idea people could be so extraordinary.'

'Are they mostly cranks?'

'Some, but some I would say are worth your attention. You'd better come and have a look.'

'I shall.'

We fixed a time and I rang off. Feeling strong I rang Tinker Dill at the White Hart.

'Tinker? Lovejoy,' I greeted him. 'What's new?'

'Christ!' he exclaimed in the background hubbub from the bar. 'Am I glad to hear you!'

'I want ten buyers tomorrow, first thing.' It was the best joke I could manage, feeling so embarrassed at his pleasure.

'Will do,' he replied cheerfully. 'I heard you was about again. OK?'

'Not bad, ta.'

'When you coming into town again?'

'Oh, maybe tomorrow. I think I'll come into the arcade.' I wasn't too keen on going, but I could always ring later and postpone it if I wanted.

'Everybody asks about you.'

I'll bet, I thought. 'Much stuff around?'

'Some,' he said with sorrow in his voice. 'You've missed quite a bit of rubbish, but there's been some interesting stock whizzing about.'

'Ah, well.'

'Tough, really, Lovejoy. A set of fairings went for nothing last week . . .' He resumed his job, pouring out details of everything important he could think of. It sounded lovely and I relished every word, stopping him only when his voice was becoming hoarse.

'Thanks, Tinker. Probably see you tomorrow, then.'

'Right, Lovejoy. See you.'

It was enough excitement for one day. I drew the curtains and gathered an armful of the sale lists that had arrived while I was ill. There was a lot of catching up to do.

As I read and lolled, lists began forming in my mind, of faces and where I'd seen them. I don't mean I stopped work, just studied on and let faces come as they wished. Tinker Dill seemed everywhere I'd ever been, practically, since the Judas Pair business began. And Jane. And Adrian. Dandy Jack. And Watson, of course. And, oddly, the Reverend Lagrange, which for somebody who lived many miles north in darkest East Anglia was rather enterprising. But he said he went to Muriel Field's house, being such a close family friend and all that. Did priests get time off? Maybe he'd struck a patch of moveable feasts and it was all coincidence. And then there was Margaret, Brad, Dick Barton who'd sold me the Mortimers. Plus a few incidental faces who appeared less frequently, so you barely noticed them at all.

But that's what murderers are supposed to be good at, isn't it?

That same afternoon I had a cup of tea ready for the post-girl, a pleasant tubby lass who worked the village with her brother. He kept a smallholding and sold plants from a stall on the London road by-pass.

'I brewed up, Rose. Come in.'

'Whatever do you do with all these magazines, Lovejoy?' She propped her bicycle against the door and brought a handful of catalogues and two letters. She was a plain girl, long-haired and young. They seem so active these days and full of talk. 'I've just had a terrible row with the Brownlows — oh, you should have heard them going on at me! As if I have anything to do with how much stamps cost.' She sank on to the divan thankfully.

'Been busy?' I knew she had two spoonfuls of sugar.

'Don't ask!' She grinned.

'What time do you start your round?'

'Five, but then there's the sorting.'

'Do you do that as well?'

'Sort of — get it?'

'Super pun,' I agreed, stony-faced.

She grinned and settled back. There's this shed in the middle of the village where the post comes.

'I was worried in case you had one of your birds in with you.'

'You're too young to know about such matters.'

'You're a hoot, Lovejoy, you really are.' I tell you, youngsters nowadays must learn it from the day they're born.

'What's funny?'

'The whole village can hear you making . . . er, contact with your lady visitors some nights. And some mornings.'

'They can?' That startled me.

'Of course.' She giggled. 'We're all terribly embarrassed, especially those of us who are still in our tender years and likely to be influenced by wicked designs of evil men.' A laugh.

'Well, the village shouldn't be listening.'

'Face it, Lovejoy—' she began to look around—'you've something of a reputation.'

'That's news to me.' And it was.

'Is it really?'

'Yes.'

She turned to eye me. 'You're our most exotic resident.'

'Pretty dull place.'

'Pretty exotic character,' she countered.

'I can't be more exotic than our musician.' We have a man who makes an extraordinary musical instrument of a hitherto unknown pattern. Needless to add, it cannot be played—which for a musical instrument is some handicap.

'Compared with you he's a bore.'

'Then there's the preacher.' This is a chap who preaches somewhat spontaneously at odd hours of night and day. Very praiseworthy, you might say, to have deep religious convictions in this immoral world. Well, yes, but to preach to trees, fence-posts and assorted bus-stops is hardly the best way of setting a good example.

'Even the preacher.'

'What's special about me?' I was fascinated. Rose seemed surprised at my astonishment.

'You collecting old pots.'

'Thanks,' I said ironically. So much for years of study.

'And that crazy old car. It's hilarious!'

'Go on.'

'And your . . . lady visitors.'

'Well,' I said hesitantly. 'They've diminished of late, apart from the odd dealer. I was ill, in a way. I expect you noticed.'

'Yes.' She poured herself another cup and stirred sugar in. 'You had one special bird, didn't you?'

'Sheila.'

'Better than that blowzy brunette with all those teeth.'

'Which was she?'

'About four months ago. You remember – she shared you with that unpleasant married lady with the nasty manners.'

'You keep my score?'

She grinned. 'Hard not to, when I'm coming here every day.'

'I suppose so.'

'Did she give you the sailor's farewell?' she asked sympathetically.

'Who?'

'Sheila.'

'No, love.' I drew a slow breath. 'She . . . died, unfortunately.'

'Oh.'

'It's all right.'

'I'm sorry. Was that why you . . . ?'

'Lost control, my grandma would have called it,' I said to help her out. 'Yes, it must have been.'

'Was it over her you – ?' she hesitated.

'I what?'

'You were going to kill somebody?' Word had spread, then. Not really surprising, the way I'd behaved.

'How did you hear that?'

She leaned forward excitedly. 'You mean you are?'

'Do I look in a fit state to go on the prowl?' She looked me up and down.

'Yes, probably.'

'Well, you can think again.' I offered biscuits while I got myself another cup.

'The whole village was talking about you –'

'Even more than usual?'

My sarcasm hardly touched her. 'We were all agog.'

'Well, you can de-gog then. I'm better.'

'Oh.' Her disappointment should have been a bright moral glow of relief at salvation from dastardly sin.

'Sometimes I wonder about you women.'

She beamed roguishly. 'Only sometimes?'

'I mean, you're all interested when you think I'm going to go ape and axe some poor unsuspecting innocent – ' the word nearly choked me – 'yet when I'm going straight again' you're all let down.'

'You must admit, Lovejoy,' she was reprimanding, so help me, 'it's more, well, thrilling.'

'You read too many books for your own good. Or letters.'

She accepted the jibe unabashed. 'No need to read letters the way some people carry on. You found quick consolation, Lovejoy.'

'What do you mean?'

'I nearly saw her the other night, and her natty little blue pop-pop.' She poked her tongue out at me.

I gave a special sheepish grin but shook my head. 'I don't know what you mean.'

'Oh no,' she mocked. 'Just good friends, I suppose.'

'It must have been the district nurse.'

'Like heck it was. Nurse Patmore doesn't go shoving her bike in the hedge – it's been here twice. I saw it.'

'One of the forestry men,' I suggested easily.

'On a *woman's* bike?' She fell about laughing. 'You're either kidding or you've some funny friends, Lovejoy. It's an old-fashioned scooter bike, no crossbar.'

'You're mistaken.' Keeping up my smile was getting very hard.

'Can't she afford a car, Lovejoy? Or is it just that it's quieter in the dark and easier to hide?' She snorted in derision. 'You must think we're dim round here.'

I surrendered, grinning with her.

'A little of what you fancy,' I absolved myself.

'They run a book on you down at the pub.'

'In what race?'

'The Marriage Stakes.'

'Out!' I said threateningly, and she went, giggling.

'You're probably being raped, according to that lot of nosey parkers.'

'That an offer?'

'Don't be cheeky to your elders!'

'Any particular cheeks in mind?'

I waved her off, both of us laughing. She pedalled down the path and was gone. I went in to clear up.

Now, Rose actually starts her work about five, but her actual round only begins once the sorting is ended. That could take up to an hour. So she was round my place no later than six-fifteen in the morning. Her afternoon round was much more variable on account of the number of chats she had to have between the sorting-shed and our lane. She must have glimpsed the woman's – if it was a woman – bike at the 'ungodly hour' of six a.m. or so. How much light was there at that time? I couldn't remember whether the clocks had been put on an hour or whether we still had that to do.

Rose would be out of our lane by now. I locked up, chucked the robin some bread and cheese and walked down to the lane. It's a curving road no more than twelve feet across with high hedges of hawthorn and sloe on either side. My own length is two hundred feet, dipping slightly to the right as you look at it from the cottage. A house is opposite, set a fair way back from the lane like mine. I hardly ever see him, an ascetic chap interested in boats and lawn-mowers while she's a devotee of amateur opera. As I said, it takes all sorts. They have two grown-up children who periodically arrive with their respective families. Down the lane is a copse, if that's the right word, a little wood joining my garden. For some reason old people once built a gate into the copse, perhaps to let pigs in to rummage for berries or acorns. Now it's derelict and falling apart. Up the lane but beyond another strip of hazels and birch is a cluster of a dozen houses centred on a well, then the lane gradually widens and levels off to join the main road at the chapel. Since the lane leads down to a splash-ford going to Fordleigh, the next village, not much traffic

comes along it except for the milk-float, sometimes a car
risking the ford in exchange for rural scenic delights, and
genuine visitors or people out for a walk or cycling. You
can get to the village road again that way, but only with a
bike or on foot. There's no way through for cars except
by continuing on over the river.

Which sets you thinking.

The lane was empty as usual. You can hear cars
approaching a couple of miles away. Nothing was coming,
and with it being schooltime still the children weren't yet
out to raise a hubbub at the chapel crossroads. Whoever
intended to watch the cottage from a hidden position would
have been wise to either come through the Fordleigh splash
and appear in the lane at the copse, or pretend to be out
for a quiet country stroll and walk down from the chapel
towards the river. Whichever way they – she? – came, she
could always duck into the copse and work her way near
to the cottage among the trees. There was little likelihood
of being seen so early anyway.

Yet there was one important proviso in all this. Does
any *reasonable* morning stroller need a bike, and a motorized one at that? Answer: No. But my visitor did. And
why? Because she was a stranger to the village, that's
why. You don't go to a village miles away for a morning
stroll.

All of which meant that my watcher was not a villager,
and had come towards my place by crossing the river. She
had used a motorized cycle of some sort to ride within
walking distance of the copse and pushed the pop-pop into
cover while slinking closer to the cottage. Then she'd
watched me, presumably to nip in and steal the instrument
when it was safe. *She*? But a forester or a farm labourer
would never ride a bike without a reinforced crossbar.

I came to the open gate. I'd not looked at it for years.
You don't scrutinize what's familiar, though I must have
passed it a hundred times. My hedge was only thick enough
for concealment in two places and they were undisturbed.
It had to be here.

My scalp prickled. The gate seemed untouched, but behind the rotting post brambles and hawthorns were crushed. A few twigs were broken and one sloe twig was quite dead, hanging by a slip of bark. Deeper inside the ground was grooved and clods of dried mud still showed above the vegetation. Some scooters have quite wide tyres. Those of the more orthodox ˙bicycle shape have tyres thicker than for ordinary bikes but thinner than the tyres of, say, a Mini-sized car.

I entered the copse with as much care as I could and knelt to examine the ground. It must be a motorized pedal-cycle or something very similar, I thought. The grooves were of a type fairly thin but of a probable radius about bike size.

There's something rather nasty about being spied on. I once knew this woman friend of mine. We'd been out for an evening and on reaching her home for a light chat and a drink – her husband was abroad – found the place had been ransacked by burglars, whereupon she'd been violently sick. It had seemed odd to me at the time, but now I felt nausea rise at the image of a silent watcher here among the trees near the cottage. The intrusion was literally sickening. There wasn't exactly a beaten path through the undergrowth but the path the watcher had taken was pretty obvious if one assumed the purpose was to get near to the cottage. It took me about an hour of careful search-ing to find out where she'd waited.

The ground was dry and had that beaten look it gets from being covered by trees. One edge of my garden runs adjacent to the copse and it was about midway along it that the watcher had established herself, having a broken stump to lean on. There was adequate protection from being seen. I leaned on the stump myself. You could just about see my front door and the near half of the gravel path. The car was in full view, plus a side window looking into my kitchenette and an oblique sight of the front two windows. They're only small so the chances of actually watching me move about inside were practically nil, especially as I'm not a lover of too much light. And, considering how it's my usual practice to draw the curtains as soon as I switched on, that must make it more difficult. What really displeased me was the horrid sensation – I was having it now on the back of my neck as I imitated my silent watcher – of having somebody peering in. I actually shivered.

Moving further through the copse I found that the nearest the ground cover approached the cottage was about a hundred feet, maybe a little more. The trouble was you could see both front and back entrances from the copse. I could neither leave nor enter without being in full view unless she allowed her attention to lapse, which seeing the trouble she'd taken wasn't at all likely. That was the most worrying feature of the whole business.

Taking care not to displace the brambles, I stepped out of the thicket. One pace and I was on my grass in full view of the cottage window. There had been a fence in the old days, long since rotten. I couldn't help looking back, seeing the copse and hedge completely in a new way. Before, everything had been almost innocent and protective if not exactly neat. Now, even the odd bush in my lawn was somehow too near the cottage for comfort. And as if that wasn't enough no sooner was I indoors than I began imagining odd noises, actually hearing them, which is most unlike me. The number of creaking sounds in an old cottage is really very few, but there I was like an apprehensive child full of imagination left alone for the night.

I examined the entire place minutely. The walls were wattle-and-daub, a common construction in East Anglia. These dwellings have been standing hundreds of years. In this ancient method you put sticks in wattle fashion as your main wall structure, and slap mud between, adding more and more until it's a wall. Then a bit of plaster and you're home, providing you've a few beams and thatch for a roof. It's cool in summer, dry in winter, and offers the best environment for the preservation of antiques known. Not all the best preservation happens in museums and centrally-heated splendour – in fact that environment's a hell-of-a-sight worse for the really good stuff.

Like a fool I found myself peering at the copse from every conceivable angle. What I'd seen of the cottage from the murderer's stump told me it would be impossible, without the help of artificial light, for him/her to see much of me unless I was actually close to the window. The trouble was, whoever stood inside the cottage was equally blind because the copse formed a dark opaque barrier at the edge of the grass. Worse, there were two sides of the cottage I couldn't look out from.

I couldn't grumble, though I felt peeved at the mess I was in. I'd told Geoffrey the constable to get lost, alienated all my acquaintances, found myself discredited and scorned and regarded as a mentally-sick buffoon without sense or judgement. To undo this would be the work of a lifetime. And it was no good grumbling that the cottage was an awkward shape, remote and rather vulnerable, because what I now regarded as its defects I'd always thought of as marvellous attributes, exactly the sort I needed for my antiques. And my hidden priest-hole – now seeming so useless because it could have been made into a lovely airy cellar with a cellar-door I could get out of – had seemed in my palmy days a perfect boon. It was private, hidden, and ventilated. Whoever had built the cottage had been wise in the way of country crafts. Two small ventilation shafts, each about six inches wide, ran from the priest-hole to a point about a foot from the outside of the wall, ending in an earthenware grid set in the grass and partly overgrown. I kept the grids clear of too many weeds so the air could circulate. That way there was no risk of undue humidity, the great destroyer of antiques of all kinds.

The chiming clock struck four-thirty, which meant the village shop was still open. Suddenly in a hurry I collected some money and rushed out to the car, remembering and cursing the locks and alarms for holding me up. I made it with about five minutes to spare. Mrs Weddell judged me with an expert eye to list any grim details about me suggesting further decadence, but I wasn't having any. Knowing the dour insistence of the Essex villager upon gossip of the most doom-ridden kind, I gave her a ten-watt beam of exuberance and demanded information about her health. That put her off her stride. She was rather sad I wasn't at death's door and became quite miserable when I kept smiling. Added to that I bought enough provisions to feed a battalion and managed to find the right change with many a quip and merry jest, which was one more in her eye. 'I've decided that a plump man's a happy one, Mrs Weddell,' I told her. 'I'm going to put a stone on.' Exit laughing.

One of the hardest things I've ever done was to drive up to the cottage and not search the copse for the intruder. Whistling flat and nonchalantly I unloaded the three carrier bags, making myself do it one bag at a time and deliberately controlling the urge to sneak a glance.

The night fell quicker than I'd realized that evening. I couldn't help leaving the curtains alone just to get a good look in the direction of the thicket without risk to myself, but finally had to draw them to keep things seeming normal. I sat with the telly and radio silent all evening, listening, and made a supper by the quietest possible means though I usually had a noisy fry-up. A million times I heard something outside. It reminded me of the student's hostel where a studious lad had complained of his neighbour who entertained a girl-friend in the next room – 'It's not the noise, it's the silences I can't stand!'

The distance across the grass grew shorter in my imagination. You could shoot somebody with fair ease from the cover provided by the bushes, especially if killing was getting to be a habit and you had the unique advantage of possessing a priceless flintlock that could kill without leaving the slightest trace of evidence. Still, no matter what else he tried I was fairly secure. I had enough food, milk and water to last well over a week, and there was always the phone.

And the loaded Mortimers, waiting patiently and still

motionless beneath the flagstone floor.

The phone suddenly rang, making me jump a mile. It was Margaret. She'd heard I was on the mend and chatted a full minute about antiques real and imaginary. It was kind of her and I urged her to ring again when finally we'd run out of things to say.

'I miss you round the arcade,' she said. 'Are you really better, Lovejoy?'

'Yes, love,' I said. 'Thanks. I appreciate the phone call.'

'Pop round here whenever you want.' She lives at Ford-leigh. I promised I would, but I wanted friends checking up on *me* to make sure I was in the pink, not invitations to go visiting. I invented a couple of false promises to entice Adrian, Tinker and Harry to phone in, knowing Margaret would pass the messages on.

The rest of the evening was quite uneventful.

I only wish I'd rested and harboured my strength.

CHAPTER XIV

I DIDN'T SLEEP a wink. Long before dawn I was up being brave in daylight. Today was going to be my round of people. Today the old debonair impeccable Lovejoy would hit the road like politicians do to show how young and thrusting they actually are behind that comfortable rotund shape. It's really something of a confidence trick but I was going through with it anyway. The night had taught me how alone I was.

Further reflection had increased my nervousness. Despite having the phone and living so near other people, there was one major problem. Whereas I didn't know who'd killed Sheila, the murderer knew who I was. Collecting's a small world. Sooner or later I would come across him, and whether I recognized him or not was irrelevant. The risk I represented was still there.

I drove to George Field's house and collected the replies
to his advertisement, some twenty replies with one catalogue from an overseas dealer casting bread hopefully on
distant waters. The ones Field thought most likely turned
out dud. Disappointed, I promised to read them with
enthusiasm and left.

Muriel Field was next. I enjoyed the drive, but exactly
how many times I caught myself looking carefully into
the driving-mirror I'll never know. The one blue scooter
I did see turned out to be ridden by a district nurse. She's
probably wondering yet why a complete stranger gave her
a glare for nothing when she was in the opposite lane. I
didn't recover for miles.

Muriel was glad to see me. I honestly mean that, really
pleased. That whole morning was brilliant, every cloud
seemed effervescent and the sky a deeper blue than it had
ever been. She was radiant, dressed maybe somewhat
younger than her age and looked as though the party was
soon to begin. The difference between the anxious, hesitant
woman she'd been some weeks before and the scintillating
beauty I now saw was remarkable. I was coerced into drinking coffee.

'If that heron keeps its distance,' I warned.

She laughed. 'I promise I'll protect you.'

We sat on the patio and made small talk while a crone
fetched coffee, Sheffield plate of some distinction and
Spode. The sugar bowl's fluted design didn't quite match
but could be passed off as the right thing with luck in a
nooky antique shop. My pleasure made me careless.

'I'll remember you above everything else for elegance,'
I said playfully, and saw her face change.

'Don't talk like that.'

'It was a compliment.'

'It sounded . . . so final.'

'A joke,' I said.

She wouldn't be appeased and set about pouring for us
both. 'Everything needn't be bad or sad.' I felt out of my
depth and said so. 'I just don't like it when people talk

about going away or changing things,' she said. 'It happens too often without anyone wanting it.'

'I was only admiring your coffee-set. It would have been terrible if you'd spoilt the effect with a spoon made out of Georgian silver coins.' I took my cup and stirred. 'Have I put my foot in it?'

'No.' She shook her hair, head back and face towards the air like they do.

'I'll be careful in future.' That was better. She raised her cup to toast me.

I asked about her upbringing. As she talked I absorbed security and ease all around. No chance of being spied on here, with the two loyal gardeners busy interrupting plants and keeping an eye on the mistress. Inside the house stalwart ancient ladies – infinitely more formidable than any gardeners – creaked and bustled vigilantly. So many things came down to money. Wealth is safety. Muriel chatted on about her father, her many aunts, her mother's concern with spiritualism (. . . 'but then it was all the fashion in her day, wasn't it?') and her inherited wealth. Husband Eric had been as wealthy as she, it appeared, when they met.

'Will you stay on here, Muriel?' I asked.

She glanced away. 'It depends.'

'On . . . ?'

'Oh, just things.' Her vagueness was deliberate, yet there was a hint of a reflective smile in her expression. Oh-ho. I began to ask about Eric.

Society's cynicism clouds our minds sometimes. When a younger woman marries or cohabits with a much older man, it's supposed to be only for money. Conversely, when an old woman takes up with a much younger man, she's blamed for wanting physical gratification and is condemned on those grounds. This is one of the few occasions women come off worst – society says they're cheap chisellers or sex-crazed. On the other hand, the old chap's regarded as a sly old dog and the young chap's seen simply as having just struck lucky getting steady sex and a steady income together in one parcel, as it were. So as Muriel chatted

happily on about her elderly husband I found my treacherous mind wondering what possible motive she'd dreamed
up for marrying Eric Field in the first place. Naturally
under the influence of Muriel's undoubted attractiveness
and charm I was stern with myself and forced these un-
becoming suspicions out as best I could.

'He had a real sense of fun,' she was saying, smiling.

'I suppose it's a lot quieter now,' I put in.

'Oh . . .' For some reason she was hesitant.

'I mean, fewer visitors,' I hurried to explain. She seemed
to become upset at the slightest thing. 'You won't have
dealers and collectors bothering you quite so much, seeing
we only go for antiques.'

'No.' She saw my cup was empty and rose a little too
quickly. 'You haven't really seen the house, have you?'

'Er . . . no, but –' I was taken a little by surprise.

'Come on. I'll show you.' Mystified by these sudden
changes of course, I followed her in from the terrace.

The house wasn't quite the age I'd expected. Despite
that, it was only just beginning to feel lived-in. Muriel had
taste. Flowers matched the house colours and weren't too
obtrusive the way some people have them, though you
couldn't help thinking what a terrible fate it was to be
scythed off in your prime and stuck in a pot to decay.

'Could I please – ?'

'Yes?' We were on the stairs, apparently about to tour
upstairs.

'Would you mind very much if I asked to see where Eric
was found?'

To my surprise she was unperturbed. 'Not at all.' We
descended together. 'I thought you might.'

The room led off the marble-floored hall and was beautifully oak-panelled, done about 1860 or so at a quick guess.
Muriel's unfaltering taste had enabled it to be exposed to
more daylight than others could have allowed. She'd used
long heavy velvet curtains drawn well back from the tall
windows to draw attention to their height.

'I like it.'

'Eric used it for a collecting-room and his study. I never came in much when he was alive.' She wandered about touching things rather absently, a book, the desk, adjusting a reading-lamp. The carpet was Afghan but pleasing for all that. A small Wilson oil, the right size for that missing Italian waterfall painting he did, hung facing the desk, setting my chest clanging. However, care was needed so I filed the facts and said nothing.

'I warned you about interlopers,' I said.

'I know what you collectors are like. All Eric's things have gone, as I said, so I've no reason to fear.'

'Do you see any of Eric's acquaintances still?'

'No,' she said firmly.

'No collectors?' She paused at that, then again told me no. I shrugged mentally. It was none of my business. 'If one does turn up,' I said, chancing my arm, 'tell him I'd rather like to see him.'

We gazed at the lawns and admired the sweeping landscaped gardens. Muriel was eager to explain her plans for the coming flower show. I let her prattle on and adopting an idiot smile stared towards the flower beds.

In the window was the reflection of a small occasional table, mahogany drop-leaf with a single stem-leg, quite good but Victorian. I couldn't see the top surface because it was covered with a neat new table-cloth. On it were mats and the essentials for starting the inevitable tea ceremony. *I never came in much when Eric was alive* were her words. Therefore she did use it now, and fairly frequently from the way she had spoken. And whoever the visitor was must be a fairly regular customer. He rated the cosy intimacy of a sophisticated room from which all sour memories had been happily erased. I only rated the terrace. Hey ho.

That would account for her reflective smile when I'd asked if she would keep the house on. It depended on *just things,* she'd said. Maybe it would also explain her displeasure when my miscued remark had suggested that collectors were hardly interested in people. *Was he there-*

fore a collector? I wondered about her holy friend. Older, but age doesn't really matter. Never mind what people say.

Still, where was the harm? It was quite some time ago since her husband had died. Sooner or later she was going to meet somebody new, as the song says. You couldn't blame her – or him, come to that. I honestly felt a twinge of jealousy. I couldn't help starting to work out how much I could buy with Muriel's wealth. I'd start with a group of Wedgwood jaspers. Then I'd – no good, Lovejoy.

'Come and see me off,' I asked.

She agreed. 'I'll get my coat and ride with you to the gate.'

I strolled out on to the drive. The gardeners were grumbling with the endurance of their kind. As I approached I heard one saying, 'That swine never grew those leeks himself. The bastard bought them, I'll bet,' and grinned inwardly at the politics of village competitions. At that moment his companion, detecting the presence of an observer, made a cautionary gesture, at which both turned to greet me with rearranged faces. Seeing my slipshod frame they relaxed and grinned. I nodded affably and strolled on. They'd thought perhaps I was Muriel. Or Lagrange?

She was in the car when I returned. I'd get no kiss today. You can tell a woman enraptured by someone else. The delight isn't delight with you. Her vivacity's pleasure at what's to come, and in case you miss the point it's you that's departing. The minute it took to drive her to the gate I used to good effect, being as secure and companionable as other characters of the landscape. She blew me a kiss from the gate.

A child, I thought, just a child. Everything must be kind and happy for her. And in her protective shell of opulence she would instinctively make the whole world appear so. Lucky bloke, whoever he was.

The White Hart quietened a bit as I entered, but when a raving nut goes anywhere people behave circumspectly no matter how hard they try to look normal. Tinker bravely came along the bar for a chat, but Jimmo and Harry Bateman were obviously preoccupied and couldn't manage a nod. I was calm, easily innocent and merely eager to talk about antiques. Jane, cautious on her stool, was relaxed enough to offer me a couple of rare book bindings – though I wouldn't normally touch them with a barge-pole and she knew it – and Adrian gave me a welcome only a little less effusive than usual.

Tinker had a source of antique violins – no, don't laugh, they're not the trick they used to be – for me, owned by a costermonger of all things. He had found as well a collector of old bicycles who was in the market for price-adjusted swaps, wanting assorted domestic Victoriana, poor misguided soul, and his third offer was some collector after old barrows, you know, the sort you use in gardens. At a pinch this last character would buy antique shovels if the antique wheelbarrow market was a little weak.

'An exotic crew, Tinker,' I commented over my pale ale.

'It's the way it's happening, Lovejoy,' he said. 'I don't know whether I'm coming or going these days, honest. No two alike.'

'Good.'

'I wish it was.' Drummers like Tinker are notorious moaners, worse than farmers.

'Better for business when tastes vary,' I said, nodding to Dick, who'd just come in with traces of the boatyard still on him. Dick waved and gave me the thumbs-up sign.

'I like things tidy,' said Tinker, except for Dandy Jack the untidiest man I knew.

'I like collectors,' I answered just to goad him and get a mouthful of invective for my trouble.

A couple of new dealers were in from the West Country and, unaware of my recent history, latched affably on to me and we did a couple of provisional deals after a while. I earmarked for them a small folio of antiquary data, drawings of excavations in Asia Minor and suchlike, done by an industrious clergyman from York about 1820. It was supported by abstracts from the modern literature, photographs and articles, plus the diary of a late-Victorian lady who'd spent a lengthy sojourn near the excavations and described them in detail. All good desirable script. They in their turn came up with a Forsyth scent-bottle lock which they showed me there and then, an early set of theodolites they'd bring to the pub next day and what sounded a weird collection of early sports equipment I'd have to travel to see. Knowing nothing about early sports gear, I fell back on my thoughtful introverted expression and said I was definitely interested but I'd have to think about it. They asked after a Pauly airgun, but I said how difficult it was to find such rarities and I'd see what I could do. I might let them have a Durs airgun in part-exchange.

Ted the barman, pleased at my appearance of complete normality, was only too glad to serve me when I asked for pie, pickle and cheese.

'Nice to see you up and about again, Lovejoy,' he beamed.

'Thanks, Ted.'

'Completely well now, eh?'

'A bit shaky on my pins now and again,' I said.

With transparent relief he said it was understandable.

'The wife had one of these viruses too,' he said. 'She was off work a month. Time them researchers got on to things like that and left smoking alone.'

So my collapse had to be down-graded (or up?) to a virus. Ah well, if that was the party line I'd stick to it.

Back in my old surroundings with Dandy Jack and the rest popping in and out for the odd deal, I passed the time in utter contentment. I honestly admire antique dealers, like me. They are the last cavaliers, surviving as an extraordinary clone against fantastic odds by a mixture of devotion, philosophy and greed. The enemy, it practically goes without saying, is the succession of malevolent governments who urbanely introduce prohibitive measures aimed at first controlling and then finally exterminating us. We don't bow to them. We don't fit neatly into their lunatic schemes for controlling even the air everyone breathes. The inevitable result is hatred, of us and of our freedom. It includes the freedom to starve, and this we do gladly when it's necessary. But we are still free, to be interested in what we do, to love what we practise and to work as and when we choose. And we work on average a good twelve hours a day every day, our every possession totally at risk every minute we live. And these poor duck eggs in the civil service actually believe they can bring us to heel! It's pathetic, honestly. Our ingenuity will always be too profound for a gaggle of twerps – I hope.

Listening to the banter going on hour after hour in the bar, my troubles receded and my fears vanished. We ranged over subjects as far apart as Venetian gondoliers' Renaissance clothing to Kikuyu carvings, from eighteenth-century Esquimaux gaming counters to relics from the early days of the American wild west. It was lovely, warm and comfortable.

Then I noticed it was dark outside.

CHAPTER XV

I ROSE AND left amid a chorus of good nights, quite like old times. The two strangers promised they'd be back about noon the next day, same place, and I promised I'd fetch my stuff.

The road to the cottage seemed endless. Worse still, it was quiet to a degree I'd never before experienced. My old car seemed noisy. Its engine throbbed a beat out into the dark either side of the road only to have it pulsed back to reintensify the next chug. In the centre of a growing nucleus of contained deep pulsation the motor moved on between high hedges behind its great rods of beamed headlight. A moon ducked its one eye in and out of static cloud at me. It was one of those nights where moon shadows either gather in disquieting clusters or spread across moonbright lanes making sinister pools where the ground you have to tread is invisible.

The probing lights turned across the hedges down by the chapel. Unfortunately nobody was about or I could have bolstered my courage by giving them a lift. With a sinking heart I swung into the path and curved to a stop outside my door. The silence, no longer held back by the throb of the great engine, rushed close and paused nearby in the darkness. I switched my door alarm off using the key and went in.

Even the cottage seemed worried. The electric light had a wan air about it as if it too was affected by concern. I examined the miniature hallway for marks but found no signs of intrusion. My unease persisted. I pulled the curtains to and flicked on the living-room lamps to make it seem cosier. Putting the TV on seemed a wise move until I realized that I would be deaf to the sound of anyone approaching as well as blinded by the darkness. Easy meat for whoever was watching out there.

To encourage what resolution I had left I made a rough meal I didn't want. I hit on the idea of putting the radio on for a few moments. That way, when I eventually switched it off it might seem as though I had begun preparations for bed. With another stroke of genius I turned the hall-light out and cautiously opened the front door a chink, just enough to get my arm out and insert the alarm key in the raised box on the door alcove. I usually didn't bother to set the alarm when I was indoors but it might prove one more thing to lessen my many disadvantages. With the door safely closed and barred again I felt pleased at my inventiveness. Nobody could now pierce my perimeter, so to speak, without Geoffrey being roused at his police house. It would admittedly take some while for him to come hurtling over on his pedal-cycle, but I could hold the chap until he came.

A braver man would have decided to be bold, perhaps take a weapon and stalk the blighter out there in all that darkness. I'm not that courageous, nor that daft. Whoever was outside would see me leave from either door, while I would be treading into the unknown. Let the cops pinch him if he tried any funny stuff, I thought. They get paid for looking after us. Geoffrey had had my break-in and two chickens with fowl-pest and that had been his lot since Michaelmas. Big deal.

I've never really believed very much in all this subliminal learning stuff they talk about nowadays. You know the sort of thing, showing a one-second glimpse of a complex map in semi-darkness and getting psychiatrists to see if you can remember its details twenty years later. Nor do I go in for this extrasensory perception and/or psychomotive force, spoon-bending and thought-transference. Yet as I forced my food down and swilled tea my discomfiture began to grow from an energy outside myself. It was almost as if the cottage had been reluctantly forced into the role of unwelcome spectator to a crime about to be committed. That energy was, I became certain, generated by the watcher in the copse. Either I was acting as a sort of receiver of hate-impulses, or I was imagining the whole thing and he was at home laughing his head off knowing I was bound to be getting hysterical. My plan to flush him out by the advertisement and my enquiries had backfired. He was now forewarned, and I was set up for reprisal.

Humming an octave shriller than usual I went about my chores, finished the food and washed up. It was important not to vary my routine. I got my bed ready in the adjoining room, leaving the bedside lamp on for about half an hour to simulate my usual reading-time. Then I switched it off together with the radio and the whole place was in darkness.

Living so far from other people – a few hundred yards seemed miles now – the cottage always had alternative lighting about, candles, a torch, two or three oil-lamps. It would be safe to use the torch only if I hooded it well, say with a handkerchief or a dish-cloth, and was careful to keep the beam directed downwards. There was no need of it indoors because I knew every inch of every room, but there might come an opportunity to catch him in its illumination like a plane in a searchlight. I'd get a good glimpse of him and just phone the police. Notice that my erstwhile determination and rage had now been transmuted through fear into a desire for an army of policemen to show up and enforce the established law – another instance of Lovejoy's iron will.

The curtains were pale cream, a bad mistake. Anything pale is picked out by the moon's special radiance, even a stone paler than its fellows being visible at a considerable distance. Were I to pull them back from the kitchen window the movement would be seen by even the most idle watcher. Still, it had to be risked.

I got the torch ready in my right hand and moved stealthily towards the window. Do everything slowly if you want your movements to be unnoticed, was what they used to tell us in the Forces. Not fast and slick, but silent and slow. Feeling a fool I tiptoed towards the sink. By reaching across I could pull the curtain aside. There was no way to step to one side close against the wall because of the clutter in the corner. A derelict ironing-board stood there with other useless impedimenta. The slightest nudge would raise the roof.

Holding my breath I gently edged the curtain aside. The copse, set jet-black above a milky sheen of grass, seemed uncomfortably close. I hadn't realized it was so short a gap, not even pacing it out the previous day. Nothing moved. *But I knew he was there.* Exactly in the way I was peering out at him, so he was staring at me. Could he see the curtain? I'd moved it without squeaking its noisy runners but there was the danger of the moonlight exposing a dark slit between pale material. I let the edges meet and exhaled noiselessly.

To my surprise I was damp with sweat. Peering eyeball-to-eyeball with a murderer was no job for a growing lad. Maybe the best course would be to telephone Old Bill. Then what if Scotland Yard arrived in force only to discover an empty copse without any trace of a lurking murderer? Imagine their annoyance when discovering they'd been summoned by a nervous idiot with a recent history of a nervous breakdown. That would be crying wolf with a vengeance. I'd have to wait until I had proof he was there. Probably it would be up to me.

The view from the other windows was the same quiet, too quiet scene. No breeze moved the trees, and shadows stayed put. I began to feel somewhat better, a little more certain of myself. No matter what he tried I was certainly a match for him. He was only one bloke. If he had a gun along with him, well, I had a few too. On the other hand, if he was waiting for me to make another mistake, such as going out for a nocturnal car-ride without remembering to set the alarm or something making another burglary easier, he was going to be sadly disappointed.

I waited another thirty minutes. Let him think I was sound asleep. My one bonus was my conviction he was out there. He, on the contrary, knew I was in the cottage but he had no way of knowing I was certain he was sitting on the tree stump and waiting. Sweat broke over me like a wave. What the hell *was* he waiting for? What point was there in watching a silent cottage when I was supposed to have retired for the night? Nothing could possibly happen until dawn when I awoke – or could it? My increasing nervousness took hold. It was ridiculous to let it but I could not withstand the rush of adrenalin.

Shading the torch I read the time on the wall clock. Ten minutes to twelve. A plan evolved in my mind. I would wait until dawn when he was probably dozing, then rush outside, down the path to the lane, sprint across into my neighbour's drive and hide deep in the laurel hedge. Of course I'd have a gun with me, maybe my Durs air-weapon which could shoot three, possibly four, spherical bullets without needing a further pumping up. With that relatively silent weapon I could prevent him leaving the copse from the far side. His bike would be useless.

This cunning plan had an undoubted risk, but there were two advantages. One was that it postponed any action at all, true Lovejoy-style, so I needn't do anything dangerous just yet and maybe by dawn he would be gone. The second advantage was that, in rushing out, I'd set off the police alarm. He'd be trapped. All I'd have to do would be to sit tight and threaten him with the air-weapon. He'd recognize it, collector that he was, with its great bulbous copper ball dangling beneath the stock. No mistake about that. Unfortunately, though, he might guess I would try a morning sprint and simply move towards my path. I wouldn't care to meet him face to face with him sitting ready and me disarrayed and running.

The front-door bell rang.

I dropped the torch from cold shock. A strange echo emitted from the walls about me, taking some seconds to die away. Fumbling along the carpet I found the torch again and dithered, really dithered. Holding it in fear now, I peered out of the dark living-room towards the door. The moon was shading the front of the cottage. Anyone could be there. My heart seemed to boom at every beat. Why does sweat come when you are cold from terror? The shelling I'd endured years ago had been nothing to this. It was somehow worse because whoever waited now at my door was in a sense unknown.

It could be Margaret. She might have sensed my fright and come to make sure I was all right. Why not telephone instead? Surely she'd do that, a far more sensible approach. Maybe she'd wanted to see for herself. I was on my way down the hall towards the door when the obvious flaw came to my mind – the cottage had been still as death. I'd been listening for the slightest sound for nearly an hour now, and had not heard a thing. And the path outside was gravel. You could even hear a rabbit cross it. But not a clever, oh-so-clever, murderer. Nobody creeps up to a door then rings the bell.

Sweat trickled from my armpits. It dripped from my forehead and stung the corners of my eyes. Should I call out, asking who was there? Not if he had the Judas guns with him, which might be used to shoot me down as soon as he located me.

I didn't dare creep closer to the door in case he fired through. And if I crept back to the telephone for the police he'd hear the receiver go and me dialling. Would he honestly dare to break in? Panicking now, I slithered out of the hall and pulled the carpet back from over the priest-hole. I needed no light to find the iron ring in its recess. Astride the flag I hauled it upwards and rested it against the armchair as I usually did. Cursing myself for a stupid unthinking fool I clambered down the steps into the chamber. By feel alone I found the Mortimer case and extracted the duellers. The Durs air-weapon might have been more useful, but I'd relied too much on having the upper hand. Positions were bitterly reversed now.

The slab lowered in place, I covered it with the carpet. Where was he now? Would he still be there at the front door, or was that a mere bluff to draw attention while he crept round the side and gained entrance there? I stood, armed but irresolute, in the living-room. Waves of male-volence washed through me – all from the external source he represented. He was there outside, watching and wait-ing. It was all part of his game. His hate emanated towards me through the walls. I could practically touch it, feel it as a live, squirming tangible thing. The pathetic unpre-paredness of my position was apparent to him as well as to me.

Something drew me towards the kitchen window. Had he given up lurking by the front door and gone back to his place in the copse? I tried turning myself this way and that, stupidly hoping my mental receivers would act like a direction-finder and tell me exactly where he was. Per-haps my fear was blunting the effect. If he was in process of moving through the copse I might see his form. It seemed worth a try. If only it wasn't so utterly dark in the shadows from that treacherous moon.

The difficulty was holding the torch and the Mortimers. I finally settled for gripping one dueller beneath my arm and holding the torch with my left hand. Leaning across the sink I slowly pulled the curtain aside.

For one instant I stood there, stunned by sudden activity. The glass exploded before my eyes. A horrendous crackling sound from glass splinters all about held me frozen. Behind me inside the living-room a terrible thump sounded which made even the floor shudder. The curtain was snapped aside and upwards, flicked as if it had been whipped by some huge force. I stared for quite three or four seconds aghast at the immensity of this abrupt destruction before my early training pulled me to the floor. There was blood on my face, warm and salty.

Something dripped from my chin on to my hands as I crawled on all fours back to the living-room. I had lost one of the Mortimers but still held the torch. Broken glass shredded my hands and knees as I moved, a small incidental compared to the noise I was making. I rolled on to the divan to get my breath and see how much damage I'd sustained.

My face was bleeding from cuts, presumably due to the glass. They'd prove a handicap because they might dampen the black powder if I had to reload, but for the moment they were a detail. My handkerchief I tied round my left hand which seemed in the gloom to look the darker of the two and was therefore probably bleeding more profusely. To my astonishment I was becoming calmer every second. The situation was not in hand, but was at least clearly defined. Even a dullard like me could tell black from white. The issue couldn't be clearer. He was outside shooting at me, and there was to be no quarter. Simple.

I crawled messily towards the telephone. Even as I jerked the receiver into my bandaged hand I knew it would be dead. The sod had somehow cut the wire. OK, I told myself glibly, I'd wait until morning when the post-girl would happen by and bring help. She came every day, rain, snow, hail or blow.

Except Sunday, Lovejoy.

And tomorrow was Sunday. And my neighbours opposite drove to Walton-on-Sea every Saturday for the weekend.

Depressed by that, I set to working out the trajectory

of his missile. Naturally, in my misconceived confidence I'd not drawn a plan showing the position of his stump relative to the windows. That would have helped. Knowing it roughly, however, I peered through the gloom at the corner farthest from the kitchen alcove and finally found it, sticking half-buried in the wall. A bolt, from an arbalest.

Bows and arrows are sophisticated engines, not the simple little toys we like to imagine. An arrow from a long-bow can pierce armour at short distances, and Lovejoy at any distance you care to mention. But for real unsophis-ticated piercing power at short range you want that horrid weapon called the arbalest, the cross-bow. Often wood, they were as often made of stone, complete with trigger beneath the stock. Their only drawback was comparative slowness of reloading. By now though he'd have it ready for a second go.

He was a bright lad. No flashes, no noise, no explosions even if they'd been audible to any neighbouring houses. And I was still no nearer guessing where he might be. My assets were that I was still alive, was armed and had enough food to last out the weekend and more. But I'd need to keep awake whereas he could doze with impunity. I felt like shouting out that he could have the wretched turnkey.

At that moment I knew I was defeated. He had me trapped. And as far as I was concerned he could move about with impunity, even go home for a bath knowing I would be too scared to make a run for it in case he was still at his post. How the hell had I got into this mess? I questioned myself savagely.

Half-twelve, maybe something like five hours till day-light. Then what? I still wouldn't be able to see into the copse. And I would be that much more at risk.

I sat upright on the divan in the living-room. The side window was paler than the rest, showing the moon was shining from that direction. I opened the hall-door wide and, keeping my head down, pulled back the kitchen alcove's curtains as far as they would go. That way I'd be as central as I could possibly be and he'd get the Mortimer first twitch if he tried to break in.

My spirits were starting to rise when I heard a faint noise. It was practically constant, a shushing sound like a wind in trees, not at all resembling someone moving across a gravel path or wading through tall grass. Maybe, I thought hopefully, a breeze was springing up. If it started to rain he might just go home and leave me alone.

The noise increased, hooshing like a distant crowd. Perhaps the villagers had somehow become alarmed and were coming in a group to investigate. Even as the idea came I rejected it – people were not that concerned. Worried, I forgot caution and crept towards each of the windows to listen. The sound was as loud at each. I even risked approaching the front door, then the side door, but learned nothing except that the noise was ever so slightly intensifying as moments passed.

It was several puzzling minutes before I noticed the odd appearance of the side window. Shadows from it seemed to move in an odd way I hadn't seen before. The other window, illuminated blandly by moonlight diffusing through the curtains, cast stationary shadows within the room. My sense of unknowing returned again to frighten me. I couldn't even risk trying to glance out with that arbalest outside waiting to send another bolt trying for my brain.

Then I smelled smoke.

The shushing sound was the pooled noise of a million crackles. My thatched roof had been fired, probably by means of a lighted arrow. A kid could have done it. A hundred ways to have prevented all this rose to mind, all of them now useless. I was stuck in the cottage which was burning. Thatch and wattle-and-daub.

Madness came over me for a second. I actually ran about yelling, and dashed to the kitchen window. Recklessly I pulled the curtain aside and fired into the darkness through the broken pane. I shouted derision and abuse. The copse, vaguely lit by a strangely erratic rose-coloured glow, remained silent. I heard the slap of the lead ball on its way

among the leaves. Maddened, I tried filling a pan with
water and throwing it upwards. It left a patch on the
ceiling. Hopeless.

I had to think. Smoke was beginning to drift in ominous
columns vertically downwards. Reflected firelight from
each window showed me more of the living-room than I'd
seen for some time. I was going to choke to death before
finally the flames got me. The beams would set alight, the
walls would catch fire and the fire would extend downwards until the entire cottage was ablaze. I'd heard glass
exploded in fires. There would be a cascade of glass fragments from every possible direction ricocheting about the
place. Those, and the flames, but first the asphyxiating
smoke, would do for me.

It would have to be the door. I'd make a dash for it.
He'd be there, knowing my plight. He'd let me have it as
soon as I opened the door to step outside. And it would
have to be the front. Going out of the side door I'd just
have further to run to get out of my blind garden. Unless
I ran towards the copse – but once in there, assuming I
reached it, what then? He knew it intimately. Maybe he
would even stay there, confident of his marksmanship and
having me silhouetted against the fire. You couldn't ask
for an easier target.

The smoke intensified. I started to cough. The walls
began creaking as if anticipating their engulfment. Above,
a beam crackled unpleasantly and a few flakes of ash began
to drift downwards. So far I couldn't see the flames but
their din was beginning to shake the cottage. Faint tremors
ran through the solid paving beneath my feet. You die
from asphyxiation in a fire, I'd heard somewhere, probably
in pub talk. Then, dead and at the mercy of the encroaching fire, your body becomes charred and immutably fixed
in the terrible 'boxer's stance' of the cindered corpse. I'd
seen enough of the sickening war pictures to know. Tears
were in my eyes from the smoke.

'You bastard,' I howled at the side door. 'Murderer!'

If I was to dash towards possible safety with all guns

blazing, I would need guns to blaze. Spluttering and now hardly able to see as the cottage began to fill with curling belches of smoke, I dragged the carpet aside and lifted the flag of the priest-hole. As I did the idea hit me.

For certain I was practically as good as dead. No matter which way I jumped he'd kill me. I had enough proof of his intentions to know he was going to leave me dead. There was no escape. So what if I hid in the priest-hole?

I dashed back for my torch, finding it easily in the flickering window-glow. The shaded light showed the cavity at which I looked anew. Could fire ever penetrate paving-stones? Maybe heat could. On the other hand, how long would a cottage like mine burn? And how long would the heat take to cook me alive in there?

The sink. I raced back, filled two pans full of water at the tap and hurried back. The smoke was making it practically impossible to see. I was coughing constantly. The carpet had to be soaked to keep the flags as cool as possible. If they were damp, though they might eventually burn, they would perhaps act as a heat-barrier for a while. I poured the water over the carpet and dashed into the kitchen alcove again.

By plugging the sink and turning both taps on at full blast I might eventually manage to flood the cottage floor. I'd actually done it once by accident. I wedged a dish-cloth into the overflow at the back of the sink, which was the best I could do. It broke my heart to leave the Mortimers, but since he knew I'd fired at him they were going to be evidence of my doom. Quickly filling two milk bottles with water, I grabbed a loaf and a big piece of cheese which would have to last me. I remembered the torch at the last minute.

The idea was to have the flag in place covering the priest-hole with me in it and the wet carpet covering that neatly. Under a mound of ash and fallen debris there'd be little sense in searching the ground unless they knew of my priest-hole, and nobody else did. But how to do it? I stood on the steps with my shoulders bracing back the flag while my fingers inched the carpet forward until it touched the floor. Then I lowered the flag by edging my way down step by step. The last step was done with the heavy paving-stone actually supported by my head. Twice I had to repeat the manoeuvre because the carpet somehow folded inside and wedged the stone open a fraction. I couldn't risk that. I stepped down inch by inch. The stone finally clicked into place without a hitch. Now it was covered by the carpet, and above me the cottage was roaring like a furnace.

And I was entombed. Ovened.

The vents showed a hazy glimpse of orange redness to either side. Fine, but there was smoke starting to drift in from the direction of the back garden. My water and food I placed on the lowest shelf for safety where I couldn't possibly knock them over. I swiftly took stock of what I had to fight with. First, his ignorance of my priest-hole. Secondly, the weapons I had available.

There were the powder guns, but black powder is notor-iously unstable. Even the modern versions such as I had got from Dick Barton could not be completely free from capricious behaviour. Weapons already loaded could easily explode in heat. I'd heard of it happening. Still, if I loaded a couple of pistols and left them cased and carefully point-ing along one of the vents there might not be too much risk, and they'd be cooler. I stuffed my shirt into a vent and shielded the other with my body. I switched on the torch.

I decided on the Barratt pair although they were per-cussion. The sight of my bloodstained hands frightened me almost to death. I was glad I hadn't got a mirror be-cause my face was probably in a worse state still. Sh'akily, taking twice as long as usual, I loaded the pair of twin barrels and slipped valuable original Eley percussion caps over the four nipples. Half-cock. Then I loaded the Samuel Nock pair. They were more of a danger in this growing heat, being flintlock, as the powder in the flashpan was external to the breech and so more easily ignited. For what it was worth I laid them flashpan downwards in one of the vents.

The heat was greater now. Smoke was still drifting from one vent. I must find some means of creating an increased draught from one vent to the other, perhaps bringing in cooler fresh air from outside to dilute this hot dry air inside the priest-hole.

Barrels. Barrels are tubes. The longest barrels I had were on the Brown Bess and the Arab jezails. Perhaps, I reasoned, if I drew in a deep breath facing one vent and blew it out down a barrel lying along the other vent, I would be all right with the faint draught it was bound to create. But I'd need to take the breech-plugs out. The tools were handy, which was one blessing.

As I worked I stripped naked. The heat was almost intolerable now. I used up a whole bottle of water wetting my shirt and using it to cover my head. The barrels together would reach about halfway down one vent, so they'd have to be bound in sequence. I did this with an old duster soaked in my urine, binding the rag round the junction of the two barrels to make it as air-tight as possible. Because the priest-hole was so narrow I had to complete the job standing on the steps with one barrel already poked inside the vent's shaft and the other sticking out past my face. By the time it was done I was quivering from exhaustion.

I tried my idea of blowing but the heat was beginning to defeat me. The air entering my lungs was already searingly hot. From above my head came frantic gushing sounds, creakings and occasional ponderous crashes which terrified me more than anything. The walls would be burning now, and the beams would be tumbling through the living-room ceiling. Twice I heard loud reports as the glass windows went. It must be an inferno. I was worn out and dying from heat. Too clever by far, I'd got myself into the reverse of the usual position. I was safe from smoke and being cooked in an oven. If only I could bring air in.

I forced myself to think as the blaze above my head reached a crescendo. What could make air move? Pro-

pellers, windmills, waterwheels? A fan. A jet engine. A
ship's screw. A paddle-device. What had they used in
prisoner-of-war camps when digging those tunnels? Bellows,
conveyors of buckets, paddle-engine? Bellows.

Below me, on the shelf near my precious bottle of water,
was the air-gun. I had a pump for it, but what rate did it
actually pump air? It usually needed about four minutes to
fill the gun's copper globe going full-pelt, and that was
tiring enough. I took the implement and gave a couple of
trial puffs. The force was considerable, as it indeed would
need to be, seeing the eventual ball-pressure was enough
to propel a fourteen-bore lead sphere some thousand yards
or so. I clasped it to me and put the screw-nozzle against
the open gun-breech projecting from the vent. With some
difficulty I began pumping. Almost immediately I felt a
marvellous gentle breeze against my back from the opposite
vent, but there came an unpleasant inrush of smoke with it.
I would need to blow out air in the opposite direction.
There might be less smoke that side.

The barrels were easy to swap over as the vents were
of a height. I simply slotted them in, having to mend the
junction on the way across. That way round, it was easier
to use the pump because I found I could use the wall as a
support and one of the shelves as a fulcrum for my elbow.
This time I was rewarded by the cool air on my shoulders
without very much smoke. I guessed that a faint breeze
must be blowing the fire and smoke in the direction I was
facing.

There was a certain amount of squeaking from the air
pump and its leather bellows flapped noisily, but in the
cacophony from the fire above nothing I was doing could
possibly be distinguished from the other noise. My only
worry was if he saw a steady current of air somehow piercing the slanting smoke from somewhere in the grass. The
shifting firelight would help.

As minutes went by I improved on the system. Once it
became obvious the system was working I started settling
down to a less frantic rate. I might, I reasoned, have to

do this for ever. You see fires still burning days after they've started, don't you? I counted my rate at about twenty pumps a minute. By stuffing my shirt into the vent round the jezail barrel I improved the motion still further by preventing any back-draught. All incoming air was from the opposite side. Occasional gusts of smoke frightened me now and again but they weren't too bad.

I tried pausing for two consecutive beats to listen. Was there shouting from above? I dreamed – was it a dream? – I heard a big vehicle revving, followed crazily by a sound of splashing water. But the bastard might be trying to pretend the firemen had arrived. Twice I was near screaming for help. Drenched and demented I resisted and pumped on, haunted by the memory of the stables which had burned down behind the old rectory. Submerged by the low evening mist, horses and stables were found as just ashes a full day later. And worse still I had no way out, whether it was friends or foe on the other side, except through the flames. For some daft reason it seemed vital to suppress hopes of people like Margaret and Tinker Dill, those smug bastards in comfort somewhere who were believing I wasn't dying. The smarmy pigs, all of them. I sobbed and sobbed, pumping crazily on amid the lunatic noise.

One really monumental crash interrupted me about an hour or two after my life-supporting system had been started. That would be the central longitudinal beam, I thought. The whole cottage was down now, with the exception of maybe part of a wall here and there.

After that, nothing but the faint shushing roar, the ponderous crumblings and tremors all about me, and the steady slap-click-pat-hiss of the ancient bellow-pump wafting beautiful cool air over my shoulders and out through the old barrels.

Nothing but my arms moving, the pump-handle slippery from sweat and spurts of blood as a cut re-opened briefly. Nothing but leaning one way for a hundred pumps and another way for another hundred to ease my tiredness, nothing but the hiss of outgoing and the gentle coolness of

incoming air. The question of survival receded. I became
an automaton.

There was nothing in my mind, no thought, no reasoning, no plans, virtually no consciousness, nothing but to
continue pumping for ever and ever and ever.

CHAPTER XVI

IT MUST HAVE rained about ten o'clock that Sunday morning as far as I was able to tell. All that did was make the
wretched ashes cool a little faster than they'd otherwise
have done.

As time went on the noise above lessened somewhat,
though the intolerable heat reached a peak some hours
after the sounds of the fire had faded. The first improvement I noticed was that smoke wasn't coming in anything
like as frequently as it had. My breathing was difficult
from the heat though, and once I cried out in pain when,
shifting my cramped position on the steps, I inadvertently
touched the flag-stone above my head. It burnt my arm
and stinging blisters rose swiftly in my skin. As I resumed
my pumping they burst and serum washed warm patches
down my arm and on to my knee. I'd been going some
eight hours at a guess when I finally decided to chance a
minute's rest.

Numbly, I forced myself to work out the time by counting. The vent was showing that daylight glow. I could
actually hear the cracklings of the settling ash mixed incongruously with faint twitters of the birds. No sound of
revving engines now, no faint shouts either real or imaginary. If the firemen had come at all, they were gone now.
And a wise murderer returns to see his job's properly done.
Maybe he was already sifting through the embers for the
turnkey. I know I would have done just that. God knows,
I thought wearily, what the robin thinks of all this. I drank
about a third of my water and endured the discomfort as

the heat rose while I sat down. The ache was almost pleasurable. Sitting and eating dry bread and cheese seemed bliss after the horrible efforts I'd expended at the old bellows. Within two or three minutes, however, the heat rose again and I had to resume my action with the air-pump to cool the cell down and allow me to breathe properly.

Throughout the morning I drove myself into forming a scheme. I would pump for about five minutes, then rest for as long as I could tolerate the heat, upon which I'd resume pumping. Limping along in this fashion for a while I soon realized I'd overestimated the rate at which the incoming air cooled my prison. I reluctantly had to increase pumping time to about half an hour or so, which gave me sufficient coolth for about five minutes. There was an additional danger here, in that I was tempted to fall asleep while resting. I had to prevent this by standing up.

With time to think I became bitter. Where the hell were the fire people? And the police? And my lazy smarmy self-satisfied bloody friends? Why weren't they calling frantic-ally for me, digging through the ash with their bare hands? I would. For them. But Lovejoy's nearest and dearest let him have a private bloody holocaust. The swine had all assumed I was shacked up elsewhere with some crummy bird. Could life be so outrageous that I'd been trapped by an armed maniac and so-say roasted alive by him in my own bloody home, and the entire country was just not caring enough? I wept from frustrated anger at the insult. All life in that moment seemed utterly mad. No wonder people just set out determined to simply get what they could. Who could blame them? The proof was here, in ashes above me. And I, honest God-fearing Lovejoy, finished up buried underneath the smoking ruins of my own bloody house, cut, filthy, bleeding, weary, and as naked as the day I was born.

My elbows were like balloons full of fluid, swollen and soggy. My wrists were more painful still but not so swollen. Despite them and the blisters I had to resume at the bellows.

As time wore wearily on I became aware of lessening temperature. In rest periods I could hear rain on grass and a faint drumming. Could it be rain on the old Armstrong? My rest periods were becoming longer and safer and the need of cool air was not so absolute. I was able to risk sitting down and having a rough meal.

Eventually there came a time when I felt it would not be risking total extinction to fall asleep. I lodged myself upright on the steps and was into oblivion within seconds.

You'd never seen such a sight. The cottage was a pile of smoking cinders and ash. In the dusk the garden seemed so small without the cottage to make the plot seem a little more imposing. The whole scene seemed pathetic. Where the kitchen alcove had been the ash was knee-deep, perhaps the result of my water-trap. Water was seeping from below, there, probably from a damaged rising main.

The rain had ceased. Smoke still rose from the debris in places. You can't help wondering at the curious consequences of physical events, almost as much as at biological goings-on. Why, I wondered, had that particular crossbeam, lying half-charred among the ruins, not burned all the way through as the rest appeared to have done? And why was part of the wattle-and-daub wall still standing to a height of about three feet close to where the front door stood, with the rest in ashes?

It had taken me a full hour to extricate myself from the hole. The weight of smouldering debris had made the slab difficult to lift. Still, I thought grimly, the murderer can't push even his phenomenal luck too far – quick-to-burn stuff makes light ash.

I placed the time at about nine o'clock Sunday night. The grass was wet from the rain. I had the sense to kick ashes back on to the paving over the priest-hole to obscure signs of my escape, and skipped swiftly on to the damp grass because my trousers were smouldering. With the same facility of the previous night I knew he'd gone. I had the Nock with me and slipped it to half-cock for safety.

The motor was a wreck, the tyres shreds of charred rubber, the paint gone, the metal twisted and the trimmings burnt to blazes. I hadn't a bean. Except for the few items down in the priest-hole I was bust. Dizziness forced me to rest a few minutes. I sat in the darkness beneath the hedge to recover and bathed my face with wet grass. There was nothing for it but to ask for help, but from whom?

My neighbours didn't get back until Monday as a rule, so they weren't about yet, assuming I'd guessed right about it being Sunday evening. Other people up the lane couldn't be approached. I knew hardly any of them and anyway would send them into screaming fits by heaving out of the darkness like a charred scarecrow. I would have to phone somebody – Muriel? Margaret? Jane? Tinker? Dick or Brad? Who was safe?

There were signs people had come. Great marks were gouged in the gravel path. Several bushes were crushed. A fire-engine, probably. Foot-hollows in the grass were filled with rainwater already. A small crowd of well-wishers, half disappointed at not seeing Lovejoy crisped, the rest busy speculating which bird it was that had luckily seduced me away from danger. Friendship's a great restorative.

The idea of a telephone seemed bizarre. You just pick up the receiver, dial and have a perfectly normal conversation with whoever's at the other end. After a night such as I'd spent? I'd heard somewhere that people rescued from bizarre episodes full of danger – like sailors on a raft for days – weren't allowed back to normal life immediately, but were put into solitude until the idea of rescue became a tangible reality. Maybe human brains can't accept too much relief all at one go. Not knowing if I was doing right or not, I compelled myself to sit there beneath the darkening hedge watching the ruins smoulder, trying to keep my relief from dominating my thoughts.

The proper thing to do would be to walk through the gathering dusk to the policeman's house. It was only about a half-mile. Nobody would see what a state I was in. He might lend me some clothes. I was wearing socks, shoes, trousers and a shirt, all filthy and torn. Caked as I was with grime, ashes and dried blood I couldn't be a pretty sight, cut and blistered. Or perhaps the telephone box? Our one public phone was always lit and stood by the village pond in front of the White Hart. We have no street lamps but the place was too prominent.

After some two hours or so tasting fresh damp air, I rose creakily, holding on to the hedge to keep myself upright. It proved difficult even to walk, to my surprise. I kept to the verge of the gravel path so as to make no noise and examined the lane before limping quickly across, carrying the two-barrelled pistol now at full-cock should my premonitions let me down.

My neighbour has two cottages knocked into one and extended to the rear. Like me he has a curving gravel path up to the front. I ignored this and crept slowly through his garden to the rear of the house. To help in harvesting his apple trees he has two extending ladders in an open shed there. I laboriously carried one to the house and climbed to an upstairs window. Anybody can get in modern catch windows. Within minutes I was blundering about downstairs in the darkness and on the phone.

I dialled Margaret. Mercifully she was in.

'Thank God!'

'What's He done to earn gratitude?' I snapped. 'Look. Have you your car?'

'Yes. Did you know . . . ?' she began.

'I know. I'm still in it.'

'*What?*'

'Come and get me, please.' I rang off.

I'd cleared away any trace of my trespass in the house as best I could and was back in the shelter of my own hedge by the time her Morris approached. Funny how bright the headlights seemed.

'Lovejoy?' Her voice was almost a scream as she slithered to a halt on the gravel. The cottage really did look like something from a nightmare.

'Here.'

I stepped from the hedge and she really did scream before I could calm her.

'It's only me, Margaret.'

'My God! Are you – ?'

'Sorry about the fancy dress,' I said wearily. 'Calm down.'

'What's happened to you? The police phoned me. I came round. We've looked everywhere. The fire brigade was here. It was terrible. Somebody said you'd gone off with – '

'Turn the headlights off, there's a good girl.'

With her help I got in and leaned back feeling almost safe. She slid behind the wheel. I could see her white face in the dashboard's glow.

'Shouldn't I phone Geoffrey, or – ?'

'Disturb him at this hour?' She didn't miss the bitterness.

'I'll take you round to the doctor's – '

'No,' I snapped. 'Are you on your own at home?' She nodded. 'Then can I come there, to clean up?'

'Yes.' She started the engine and backed us down to the lane. 'Did you manage to save anything?'

'One thing,' I said, lying back, eyes closed. 'Me.'

Bathed and in some clothes Margaret happened to have handy – perhaps from the estranged husband – I examined myself in the bathroom mirror. I'd have been wiser to stay filthy. My face was cut in a dozen places. An enormous bruise protruded from my temple. My left eye was black, a beautiful shiner. I'd lost a tooth. My hands were blistered balloons.

She gave me a razor to shave with, a messy job with more blood than whiskers.

'Your husband's?' I asked.

'Mind your own business,' she said.

She made a light meal and I went to sleep on her couch with the television on. I couldn't get enough normality. She sat in an armchair close by to watch the play.

'Let me take that.'

I hugged the Nock close and refused to give it to her.
'I'm trying to make the pair,' I said, a standard antique
dealer's joke.

She didn't smile.

CHAPTER XVII

THE DAY DAWNED bright and brittle. For an hour I could
hardly move a joint and tottered about Margaret's house
like a kitten. A bath loosened me up. I felt relatively fresh
after that. Just as well, I thought, as it was going to be a
hard week.

The telephone rang about eleven, Tinker Dill asking if
I'd been located. I told Margaret to say I'd gone to London
for a couple of days with a friend. She didn't like this but
went along with it. The story was the post-girl had seen
the cottage afire. She'd called the police, the fire brigade
and an ambulance, a thorough girl. I made Margaret ring
Dandy Jack to say she wouldn't be in to the arcade for a
few days and to let prospective customers know she'd be
back soon.

I also got her to ring Muriel and say there'd been an
accident of some description. She told her about the cottage
and what she'd heard over the phone. Muriel seemed dismayed, Margaret reported to me. Real tears, as far as one
could judge.

'Well, some people love me anyway,' I cracked, leering
with my gappy grin.

'God knows why,' she said.

They gave me a column and a picture – of the burnt
cottage, not me – in the local paper on Tuesday morning.
Police, it said, were making enquiries. Arson could not be
ruled out. My own whereabouts were not known but specu-
lation was that, in the throes of a depressive illness, I had
accidentally started a fire and died, or else I was staying
with friends. It was made to sound fifty-fifty, and who

cared anyway. Too bloody casual by far. The ruins were being searched for clues. It was widely known that I was mentally disturbed after the unfortunate accidental death of a close friend. By Thursday I was written off from public awareness, which suited me. The local paper went back to the more important foot-and-mouth disease.

On Friday I asked Margaret to take me for an evening drive.

I felt absolutely calm. The Nock just fitted the glove compartment, wrapped in a dry duster to prevent scratches. All anxieties and fears vanished in the calm that certainty brings.

Margaret had been marvellous during the week. We'd chatted about antiques and I'd been pleasantly surprised at how stable my thoughts were, and how I enjoyed her company. She'd taken the full account of my escapades at the cottage quite well. The only point where I differed from the truth was the invention of a hidden tunnel beneath the sink out to the back of the copse. After all, the honour among dealers is bendable and my remaining stuff was still down there. I'd partly paid my keep by authenticating some musical seals of about 1790 for her, lovely they were, too.

'You're not going to do anything silly, Lovejoy?' she asked as she drove.

'People keep asking me that.'

'And what do you answer?'

'Women do keep on, don't they?' I grumbled.

'I'm waiting, Lovejoy.'

'Of course I won't do anything silly.'

'Then why the gun?'

'Because he'll have two, and a crossbow.'

The car slowed and she pulled in, angry as hell. 'Who?'

'The murderer.'

'Is that where we're going?'

'Yes.'

There was a prolonged silence. For a moment I thought

she was going to make me get out and walk.

'Does she know?' she asked after a while.

'No.'

'Certain?'

'No.' I paused. 'But she might have guessed – you know how people guess the truth sometimes.'

We resumed the journey.

'Aren't you going to tell me?' she said.

'Lagrange, the Reverend Gentleman from near the wrong bird sanctuary.'

'So that's what all those lies were about stuffed birds?'

'Well, the odd white lie . . .' I mumbled.

'You mean it was him? The shooting? The . . . Sheila's accident? Everything?'

'And poor Eric Field.'

'And you?'

'And *nearly* me,' I corrected.

'But he's a . . . a reverend.'

'Borgia was a pope.'

I told her how my suspicions gradually rose about Lagrange. Who had the best opportunity of learning of Eric Field's find? Who couldn't afford a car yet would need a small putt-putt for frequent local visits in a rural community? And what was more natural than a woman's bike for somebody who occasionally had to wear priestly garb? An authentic collector-friend of Eric Field's, he'd started revisiting Muriel's house. Collectors, like all addicts, need money. He was with Muriel in her posh grey Rover when Sheila gave me the turnkey at the war memorial. Muriel had blossomed with his feet under her table, and he'd started watching me from then on, using Muriel's place as a base. Not a lot of trouble with a small motorized bike, and only a narrow valley to cross.

I'd stirred things up and reaped the consequences.

It fitted together.

'Are you . . . fond of this Muriel?' Margaret wanted to know.

'I suppose so.'

'More than that?'

'I'm always more than that where women are concerned,' I said starchily, then added, 'She's just a child, gormless and bright.'

'Poor Lovejoy,' Margaret commented in a way that told me I'd had my lot. You can tell from how they say things, can't you?

She asked if Lagrange would be at Muriel's. I said I couldn't be sure.

'He's her boy-friend, though,' I said sardonically. 'The gardeners set me off thinking the other day, by being embarrassed at the odd innocent cussword – thought I was him for a moment. He's a cool customer, insists on having tea in the same room where he killed poor Eric Field stone dead. A right nutter.'

'Couldn't we get the police – ?'

'Not just yet.'

After that I got a dose of the thick silence they give you as corrective when you've transgressed. Nothing short of a miracle would make her smile on me again.

There was a small blue motorized bike to one side of the Field drive, no surprise. We rolled to a stop.

'Lovejoy?'

I paused, already at the door.

'Is there no . . . jealousy in this?'

'Jealousy?'

'You. Of him.'

'No.' Nothing had ever seemed so true. She accepted it and came with me.

'Good heavens!' Muriel, open-mouthed, was in the doorway. Her reaction was a disappointment to me. They are supposed to faint or at least go white, but then she hadn't felt quite so gone over me when I was alive so I couldn't really expect too much.

'You remember me, Muriel?' I'd planned a much cuter entrance line and forgotten it like a fool.

'Why of course, Lovejoy!' She drew me in. 'We heard the most dreadful things about you – the papers said you'd had a frightful accident! Do come in.'

'I'm Margaret.'

'I'm Muriel Field – oh, you telephoned. I remember. Please come in. What a perfect nuisance the newspapers are!'

'Aren't they!'

The bastard would be in the study glugging tea from the Spode. Hearing my name would have made him slurp.

'What's happened to your face?'

'The old crossbolt,' I said airily. 'Nothing much.'

'Look, Mrs Field,' Margaret started to say, but I cut in sharply.

'Where's Lagrange?'

Muriel looked blank. 'How did you know he was here?'

'His scooter, and a good guess.'

'Hello, Lovejoy.'

He was standing in the doorway to the study, pale but polite as ever. For some strange reason he was actually glad to see me.

'You bastard,' I said. 'You killed Sheila.'

'Have you brought the police?'

'No. They'll have to wait their turn.'

'Just one witness.' He nodded at Margaret.

'Don't fret,' I snapped.

'This is the man, Lovejoy,' Margaret said to me quietly.

'Eh? What man?'

'He came to the arcade asking about you some time ago. I tried to tell you but didn't see you for days.' The phone message to ring Margaret I'd not followed up.

'Darling, what is this?' Muriel went to stand by Lagrange. He shook her from his arm impatiently.

'Nothing of any importance, my dear.' He was even beginning to talk like a squire.

'He killed your husband, Muriel,' I said. 'He used the Judas guns your Eric had found. Some "accident" while Eric was showing them to him, probably. Then he stole them for himself, only he couldn't quite make up the set. The turnkey was missing. I got it from the auctioneers. He saw me and Sheila. You remember coming out of the car park and seeing us by the war memorial. Then he killed her and tried to do the same for me.'

'That set of sharks – incompetent sharks !'

I understood his anguish and rejoiced. 'You'll never get it now, Lagrange.'

His eyes blazed. 'Won't I ?'

'Lovejoy – what do you mean?' Muriel glanced from me to Lagrange. 'What does he mean?'

'He killed Eric,' I explained. 'Then he realized your brother-in-law had asked me to find the Judas pair. He assumed Sheila'd kept the turnkey in her handbag for safety when his burglary at my cottage proved fruitless. So he pushed her under the train.'

'*No!*' Muriel stood facing me practically spitting defiance. No compassion for Sheila now, I observed.

'Yes,' I said calmly.

The pig was smiling. 'Well, yes,' he admitted, shrugging.

'You must recognize the truth, love,' I told Muriel gently. 'He's mad, a killer. He tried to kill me with a crossbow, and burned my cottage down.'

'I knew you'd get out,' he said regretfully. 'There wasn't a trace of you. I had a suspicion you were still around, an odd feeling you were *there*. Know what I mean?'

'Oh yes,' I said bitterly. 'I know.'

'Lovejoy,' Muriel said.

'What?'

'*He* is my husband.'

'Eh?'

'We were married three days ago.'

I swallowed but it was too late to change things.

'Don't be tiresome, my dear,' Lagrange said to her. 'You'd all better come into the study. No use standing in the hall.'

I uncovered the Nock and brought both flints to full-cock. 'Stay where you are.'

He gave me an amused glance. 'Don't you be tiresome, either,' he said, and walked ahead of us all into the study.

That's the trouble with conviction – it can be crackpot as anything, like the great political capers throughout history, but if it's utterly complete even sane people become meek in its presence. We three followed obediently. He paused at the desk and gestured to us to be seated. I remained standing as an act of defiance. The swine actually smiled at that. 'Now, Lovejoy,' he said conversationally, 'what to do about all these goings-on, eh?'

'Police,' I said.

'Rubbish. Act your age.'

'I'm going for them now. And I'd advise Muriel to come with us for her own safety.'

'You're getting more fantastical every minute.' He put his fingertips together, a thin burning little guy intense as hate, certain of success. How the hell had he got Muriel under his thumb? 'I shall simply deny everything. And you, Lovejoy, aren't exactly the most convincing witness, are you?'

'You'll never get away with it.'

He snorted with disgust. 'That the best you can do, Lovejoy – a line from a third-rate play?' He grinned. 'I already *have*, you see.'

'I . . . I don't understand.' Child Muriel was at it again.

'I'll explain everything ·to you later,' he said calmly. 'Well, Lovejoy?'

'Margaret,' I said desperately. 'We're both witnesses. We heard you admit it.'

'Certainly,' he said. 'A man forces himself into my house carrying a loaded gun and accuses me of murders, burnings, robberies I'd never heard of – wouldn't anyone try to humour him into reasonable behaviour? Especially as he's known to be . . . mentally unstable?'

'Lovejoy,' Margaret said gently. 'Come on home. He's right.'

'Then I'd better kill you now,' I said.

'Alternatively . . .' Lagrange said, and pulled out from his desk a case. He placed it on the leather writing-surface with pure love shining from his eyes. 'Alternatively, Lovejoy, there's a means here to settle your obsessions once and for all.'

'Is that . . . ?' My voice choked and my chest clanged and clanged.

'Oh.' He feigned surprise. 'Would you care to see them?' He turned the case so the keyhole faced the room and gently opened the lid.

Never in all my life. I mean it, never, never. They lay dark and low, glowing with strength. Their sheer lines were hymnal, the red felt imparting to their solemn shading a ruby quality setting them off to perfection. I practically reeled at the class, the dour elegance of the pair of flintlocks embedded in the shaped recesses. Not an atom of embellishment or decoration marred their design, not a hatch on either butt, yet there was the great maker's name engraved in the flickering luminescence of the case-hardened locks. A silver escutcheon plate was set into each stock, but no monogram had been engraved on either. The only jarring feature was the empty recess for the turnkey. Murderer or no murderer, I thought, reverently taking out the missing item from my handkerchief and passing it over. For once he lost his composure.

'Thank you, Lovejoy,' he said, moved. 'Thank you. I'll remember that.'

The set was complete.

'What are you going to do?' Muriel was shaking me. I emerged irritably from my reverie to hear Lagrange say, 'Do, my dear? Why, we're going to resolve poor Lovejoy's delusions permanently.'

'How?' I asked, knowing already.

'Duel,' he replied. 'We have the perfect means here already to hand. And the motivation.'

'You can't!' It hurt me to hear Muriel's cry for him. 'You might be —'

'Not I,' he said calmly. 'Impossible.'

'Is it really?' my voice asked from a distance away.

'Oh yes. I'm afraid so.'

'Lovejoy, come away!' Margaret dragged at me but I

couldn't take my eyes off the Judas pair.

'He won't, my dear,' Lagrange said gently. 'He has to know, you see. Don't you, Lovejoy? Also, let's all four contemplate the benefits of a duel – no loose ends for a start. Either way, I'll gain by knowing Lovejoy won't one day lose his composure and come to kill me with that rather splendid Samuel Nock he's waving, and should matters inexplicably go right for him he'll have the satisfaction of knowing justice was done. And nobody can be blamed afterwards, can they? I'll explain to the police I was made to fight a duel by this maniac here, and alternatively Lovejoy will have the proof of the means of poor Eric's death.'

'Please, Lovejoy.'

'No, Margaret.' That was me speaking, wanting to duel with a monster. I could hardly stand from fear at what I was doing.

'There's no choice,' Lagrange said kindly to her.

'But –'

'No, Muriel.' He pointed to a chair and she crossed meekly to sit down. 'There's absolutely no danger. It will all come right. Now –' he shut the case and carefully lifted it – 'if you will excuse me.'

'Where are you going with that?' I demanded.

He looked pained. 'For black powder,' he said. 'I have it in another room. Surely you don't expect me to leave these in your tender care?'

'You might . . .' I tried, not knowing what he might.

He smiled. 'I'll bring the powder back, dear boy,' he said. 'You can load them any way you like, I promise.'

His bloody certainty dehydrated my tongue and throat. I could feel my forehead dampen with sweat.

The door closed.

'Muriel, you have to stop this –' Margaret shook her shoulder roughly.

'Will he be all right?' was all she could say.

'You stupid woman!' Margaret cried. 'Don't you care that he killed your husband? And Sheila? He's going to do the same to *him*!'

Even paralytic with fear I felt a twinge of resentment that everybody was speaking of me as if I was an odd chair. I spent the few minutes waiting, while Margaret went on at Muriel and me alternately, trying to think and failing hopelessly. The terrible idea emerged that it would happen too quickly for me to understand. I might – would – never know.

'Everyone all agog?' He came in smiling as though to one of his little tea-parties. 'You'll find everything in order, Lovejoy. Oh, and I thought we shouldn't put too many fingermarks on such lovely surfaces. Here's two pair of white gloves.'

'I know.'

'I'm phoning the police.' Margaret rose but Lagrange stepped between her and the door.

'No, my dear. Lovejoy?'

'Er, no,' I managed to croak.

'Lovejoy!' she pleaded once, but I already had the gloves on. He offered me a piece of green velvet to rest the flinters on as I loaded.

I became engrossed. Their sensual balance, vigorous and gentle, almost brought them to life. Their quality sent tremors up my fingers as I poured black powder from the spring-loaded flask. Tamp down. Then bullet, then wadding. Test the vicious Suffolk flints for secure holding in the screwed jaws of each weapon, flick the steel over the powder-filled pan only after ensuring the touch-holes were completely patent. Interestingly, I noticed one had gold stock-pins and the other silver. I'd never even heard of that before.

Ready. Lagrange was waiting at the desk. Throughout the loading he had watched intently. I'd been stupid – only now it dawned on me that I'd fallen for every gambit he'd played. Being so distrustful of him fetching the powder I'd been tricked into loading. Now here I was with the obligation of having to offer both to him for his choice under the rules. No wonder the bastard kept smiling.

'Ready, Lovejoy?' If only he didn't sound so bloody compassionate.

I nodded.

'No!'

'Get away with you!' I snarled at Margaret, and offered both weapons to Lagrange after making a clumsy effort to swap them from hand to hand to confuse him.

'Thank you. This one, I think.' He took one and weighed it in his hand. 'The study's not quite sixty feet, Lovejoy, I'm afraid.'

'That's all right.'

All this stuff about ten paces is rubbish. It was usually ten yards each way, carefully measured, making twenty yards in all.

'Where would you like to stand?' he asked pleasantly.

'I want both of us to sit at the desk.'

His eyebrows raised.

'Isn't that a trifle unusual?'

'There are precedents.'

'So there are.' He wasn't disconcerted in the least.

I brought a chair and sat as close as I could, opening my legs wide for balance. He sat opposite.

'Closer, please.'

'As you wish.' He hitched forward until his chest touched the rosewood. We leaned elbows on the top and waited.

'We need your assistance, Muriel,' he said calmly. 'Over here, please, with your handkerchief.'

She came and stood by the desk.

'Hold your handkerchief up above us,' he told her, watching me. 'When Lovejoy tells you, let it fall.'

'But –'

'Do as you're told, my dear,' he said patiently. 'It won't take a moment. You'll be quite safe. Do you understand?'

'Yes,' she quavered.

It was now. No matter what I did, how fast I was, how good my aim, I would die the instant I pulled the trigger. He needn't fire at all. Yet I'd loaded both meticulously. There couldn't possibly be any trick.

I pointed the beautiful damascus barrel. His gaped back at me. Behind the cavernous muzzle his calm, smiling face gazed into my eyes. We held position, brains and barrels inches apart, me sweating in terror and him enjoying the last few moments of my life. In a blur I saw the single line of awareness – his eyes, his barrel, the black muzzle, then my own ribbed barrel and, in a blur nearest me, the blank silver escutcheon plate just showing above my hand gripping the stock. The silver plate set in the stock. All in a line, from his mad hating brain to my terror-stricken consciousness. Eye to eye, in a line. And, nearest of all to my eye, the silver escutcheon plate. In line with my eye.

'Now,' I said.

The handkerchief fluttered down. I turned my flinter round as the handkerchief fell, *pointed the muzzle of my own gun against my forehead and pulled the trigger.*

There was no explosion but the recoil snapped the barrel *forwards* against my skull and nearly stunned me from the force of the blow. As if in a dream I saw Lagrange's eye splash red and gelatinous over his face. His head jerked back. He uttered a small sound like a cough as he died and the flinter in his hand clumped heavily down on to the desk, firing off as the hair-trigger was hauled back by his convulsing hand. The ball sent glass flying from a shattered window. I was missed by a foot or so.

It seemed an hour before the echoes died away and the screaming began. My senses slowly came creeping back.

It was logical. Your eye's in line with the barrel. So if it's your own gun that shoots you through your right eye, aiming it frontwards at your own right eye will shoot your opponent. But how?

Amid the moanings and the tears, as poor Muriel wailed and screamed on Lagrange and Margaret tried some hopeless first aid, I examined the pistol I held. It was the one with the silver stock-pins – that was probably how to tell them apart. Lagrange had picked the gold-pinned one. Yet mine was still loaded.

I got the green velvet and the case and set to work while somebody phoned the police. It's always important to unload a gun first, no matter how old it is. This I did safely, then dismantled the lock. Any flinter enthusiast lifts the lock out to look. It does the piece no harm and the mechanism's everything.

It was exquisite, delicate as a lady's hand. There were not two lock mechanisms inside as I'd guessed – the standard firing mechanism was actually unworkable. The trigger activated a small air-chamber which worked by propelling a missile along a reverse concealed barrel towards the eye of the person holding the weapon. The missile pushed up the silver escutcheon plate on a minute hinge unlocked by the trigger. Highly ingenious. The better your aim the more likely you were to shoot your eye out.

But what was the missile? What had exploded into his eye with such force? Clutching the parts I went out into the hall. An old crone – the one I'd been so unhappy about on my previous visit – was sobbing information into the telephone.

'Excuse me,' I said politely, taking the phone from her to calm her down. 'When the Reverend came out of the study a few minutes ago, where did he go?'

'Into the kitchen for some ice,' she said, red-eyed, and at last I knew.

You crushed a piece of ice into a sphere in the bullet-mould, inserted it into the concealed chamber and made sure your opponent got the silver-pinned pistol. No wonder the pathologist had never found the bullet. The ice had pierced Eric Field's eye, penetrated his brain from there and instantly melted away from his body heat, just as the ice-ball was now doing in Lagrange's silent skull.

Yet . . . I sat at the hall table examining the weapon further. Who on earth had had the gall, not to mention the authority, to compel the world's greatest gunsmith to make a treacherous pair of weapons like this so long ago? Duelling was crackers, but it *was* supposed to be an affair of honour. Somebody had wanted to be bold and dashing around the Regency clubs, but was unwilling to run any actual risk while going about it. I inserted the turnkey and rotated gently against the spring's weight.

The locks came out and showed their secret beneath the recess. There, engraved in gold, was my revelation: REX ME FECIT. *The King made me.*

It brought tears to my eyes. I had a vision of the old gunsmith in his darkened workshop, all his assistants and apprentices sent away for the night, as in obedience to royal command he fashioned the brilliant device alone. Yet he was determined his complaint should be recorded for others to realize in later years. The old genius *had* made the Judas pair – they bore all the characteristic features of his consummate skills. But he cleverly recorded the customary Latin inscription to tell the despairing truth *why* he had: the King had made him. That deranged sick man George the Third, or the Prince Regent, wencher and gambler? Probably the latter.

Before the police arrived I'd substituted a pair of officer's pistols, Joseph Heylin of London, quite well-preserved in an altered cutlery box, for the Judas pair. Lagrange's small collection in the morning-room cabinet was easy to find and he'd left the key in. I whisked the Heylin pair outside where I burned a little black powder in one and loaded the other. Amid the general alarms and excursions nobody took much notice of me wandering about. I swapped both pairs. Going out to wait for the police to arrive, I tucked the Durs case on top of the engine of Margaret's Morris beneath the bonnet – carefully wrapped, of course, and wedged in good and proper.

And when the pathologist couldn't find the bullet? I was suddenly unutterably weary. I decided to let them all guess till they got tired, just like they did of old Eric Field and Sheila. When the Old Bill came hurtling up I was back in the study wringing my hands with the others. I was clearly very upset.

Three weeks later Margaret was quizzing me again. I was

just back from George Field's.

'What did he say when you told him you'd found the Judas guns?'

There'd been no mention of Margaret's husband. We'd just taken up together, going into her arcade shop daily and scratching a living. Naturally, the inevitable had happened, as it always does when a man and woman live in one dwelling, but that was all to the good and it was long overdue anyway as we both knew.

The trouble was this conversion gimmick they have. That I was quite content to drop in to my old garden and still hadn't started clearing away the cottage's ruins obviously niggled her. She'd let several hints drop, asking what plans I had for rebuilding and suchlike. You have to watch it.

'Lovejoy!' she complained. 'You're dreaming again.'

'Oh. He said he didn't want anything to do with them – said it was poetic justice.'

'And then?' she pressed.

'He shut the door.'

'I don't think he likes your instincts very much, Lovejoy.'

'I'm surprised,' I said. 'I'm really quite lovable.'

'Won't you offer them back to Muriel?' was her next gem. Sometimes I think women have no sense at all.

'Of course,' I said, thinking, That's not poetic justice. 'When?'

'Well,' I said after a long, long pause. 'Well, maybe later.'

'*Lovejoy!*'

'No, look, honestly,' I began, searching desperately for some way out. 'It's honestly a question of time and personal values.'

'Lovejoy! How *could* you! It's stealing!'

'Honestly, love – judgement comes into it,' I said. 'I'd take them back this very minute, but – '

'You've absolutely no excuse!' She started banging things about.

'Maybe in time, honestly,' I said. 'I'm only thinking of her – '

Women have no tact, no tact at all. Never noticed that?

GOLD FROM
GEMINI

Note

The opinion of History is that the Romans did not garrison the Isle of Man, and certainly major finds have not been made. Current belief is that Suetonius did not occupy the Isle, but instead stormed Anglesey.

The author chooses not to trust History on this point, believing like Lovejoy that faith is sometimes preferable to evidence.

CHAPTER I

ANTIQUES is a lovely but murderous game.

Some bits of this story you won't like. I'm telling you now just in case, but that's the way it is in the world of antiques. It's crammed with love, fear, greed, death, hate and ecstasy. I should know – I'm an antique dealer. And don't chuck this book away in disgust just because I've owned up and told you the truth.

I'm the only person in it you can trust.

I was with Brenda on her sofa.

For nearly a month I'd been scouring the surrounding villages without even a sniff of an antique except for a ninth-rate copy of a Norwich School painting, and a Bingham – imagine a blue glaze on the daftest exotic porcelain dreamed up in a nightmare – and I'd had to sweat blood for those. Both were left for collecting later. Both were still unpaid for. The knack is to look fresh and casual when the woman (ten to one it's a woman) opens the door. I've only one suit I try to jazz up with a splash of red, a plastic flower. Then I knock and give them my patter, smiling like an ape.

On the day this story begins I had staggered my way from knocker to knocker, sofa to sofa, my bladder awash with coffee, my mouth sore from snogging, my pockets crammed with phone numbers and dates, but life undeniably grim on this torturing day. Antiques seemed to have vanished from the earth. And they are everything. Everything.

Women and antiques are very similar – they come either in epidemics or not at all. Where all this starts I was in the middle of an epidemic of women, and an antiques drought. The situation was really serious.

When you think of it, making love is rather like picking blackberries from a dense and tangly hedge. You need both hands and a lot of skill to do it properly and get away

unscathed, yet your mind can be miles away. As long as
you're up to the job in hand, as it were, you need not really
concentrate very much. And none of this how-about-her-
tenderest-emotions jazz. All the blackberry knows is it's
being picked. If it's being picked properly, that is. Preferably by me. And as for me, well, I can only think yippee.

This particular blackberry's name was Brenda, a real
goer. Her husband was out – wonderful what a taste of
treachery does for the appetite. And it was beautiful,
heavenly, ecstasy.

It was even better than that, because from where we
were . . . er . . . positioned, I had a perfect close-up view of
the antique painting on her wall.

I could hardly keep my eyes off it.

We were downstairs in her living-room. Only lovers get
the bedroom, and only idiots go up there unless there's a
good reason, such as a granny nodding off in the kitchen or a
baby somewhere which mustn't be disturbed. Wandering
antique dealers like me get gratification at ground level as a
reminder that the affair is temporary. That doesn't mean
temporary's bad or even brief. It can be marvellous, like on
Brenda's sofa.

But this picture.

If the picture hadn't been clearly visible from her front
door I would already have been halfway up the next street.
I was just beginning to fear I was losing my touch when she'd
hauled me in and started ravishing. She shyly drew the
curtains, really quaint.

A glimpse (I mean the picture, folks, the picture) set my
heart pounding. It seemed really genuine late Carolean. A
dark, splendid canvas. Original, too, but somehow . . . A
smiling woman was presenting a little boy to his father in
'cavalier' dress while adoring yokels grovelled in the background. The painting's composition was right. The dresses
were accurate. Most dealers would have leapt at it. Not me.

'Oh, God,' Brenda moaned, eyes closed and brow damp.
It was a superb forgery. Quality. The canvas I knew

would be authentic, not just modern and aged by alternately oven-heating and fan-drying. (A penniless young Austrian painter perfected this particular method when forging pathetically bad copies of Old Masters. Name: Adolf Hitler. He eventually packed it in and turned to other interests.) I guessed the stretcher would be seventeenth century, though naturally pinched. After all you don't spoil the ship for a ha'porth of tar. Brenda lurched and shuddered. Puzzled, I loved on.

It was in our climax that it hit me, maybe from the exploding colours in my mind. The lady's dress had a graceful crenellated peplum of citrus *yellow*, a clear yet quite witty give-away. Yellows have always been in since Roman days, but citrus yellow's essentially a modern colour. I'm quite fond of yellows. While Brenda and I geared down to that quiescent afterglow in which the woman murmurs and the man dreams, I couldn't help wondering what genius had executed a brilliant forgery and then betrayed his work with such knowing elegance. Talent like that doesn't get a whole colour wrong. So it was wit, but expensive wit. He could have bought a new yacht with the proceeds. Honesty can be very inconvenient. Still, I liked him whoever he was. Certainly I couldn't have done a better forgery. I know because I've tried.

She made us coffee afterwards, working steadily towards getting my name the way they do. She laughed at Lovejoy (not the first) but you can't forget Lovejoy Antiques, Inc., can you? It sounds huge and expensive American. It's actually only me and three sets of different phoney visiting cards saying respectively that I'm from Christie's, Sotheby's and the National Gallery. People will believe anything. Never mind what the man said. You *can* fool all of the people all of the time. It's practically my job.

'You have good taste,' I told her.

'Really?' She blossomed. 'I got the curtains from – '

'In antiques,' I said firmly, refusing to be sidetracked. 'That lovely picture, for instance.' Casually I crossed to see it. I'd earned the right.

'Are you married, Lovejoy?'

The brushwork was perfect. He'd even got a good original frame, just that wrong screaming yellow

'Lovejoy? I asked if you're married.' I dragged my eyes away.

'Do I look it?'

She tilted her head, smiling, finally said no.

'I suppose my frayed drip-dry shirt gave me away.'

She laughed at that. I was beginning to like her but shook the feeling off. No dawdling allowed in the antiques game, Lovejoy. When times are especially bad, physical love – and everything else – comes a long second. Lovejoy Antiques, Inc., were fighting for survival, and this in a trade where Genghis Khan wouldn't last a week.

'You have an eye for style,' I flattered, still determined at the picture.

'A present to Peter, my husband. It isn't actually old at all. A friend did it, poor old Mr Bexon. Isn't it good?'

'Great.' I went to sit close beside her, suddenly very bleak. *Poor old* Mr Bexon? I didn't like the sound of that. Poor's okay and old's okay, but *poor old* sounds a goner.

'It's very similar to the Castle's paintings, isn't it?' the dear little innocent said.

'*Very* similar,' I agreed. Just how similar she would probably never realize. I avoided telling her anything about it, though.

The reason people are bitter about us dealers is that they believe us to be openly on the make (true) and un-erringly skilful at recognizing genuine antiques (on the whole, hopelessly wrong. Most of us couldn't tell a Ch'ien Lung vase from a jamjar under a laser beam. I'm an exception).

'Divorced?'

'Eh?'

'I said are you divorced?' Brenda repeated.

'Yes. Her name was Cissie.' Best to be honest when they are doing their intuition thing. 'It was my fault, really.' It had been like living with Torquemada.

She nodded, but women don't really agree with this sort

of manly admission. Shrewd to the last, they *know* everything's always the woman's fault. I just go along with the majority view.

'Too wrapped up in art,' I explained. 'It was just after I'd joined Christie's.'

'Sotheby's,' she corrected. I'd given her the wrong card. She'd actually read it, the pest. I wish women were more reliable.

'Ah,' I said, quick as a flash, 'I was with both of them at that time. Spreading the genius around,' I added, smiling to show I was still modest deep down. 'Is Mr Bexon a neighbour?' Poverty makes you very single-minded.

'He lived here in the village. So wonderful with children.' Oh dear, that past tense again.

'Was?' I managed to get out.

'He died a few weeks ago. Of course he was very old.' People annoy me saying that. Is death not supposed to count just because you're getting on? She put her arms around me and moved closer. 'It was fantastic with you Lovejoy.'

'Yes, great,' I said, now thoroughly depressed. Another empty.

'I don't ... you know, for every man who comes knocking.'

'No, love.' They always go through this.

'You're special.'

'Did he work with your husband?'

'With Peter? Yes, once. Engineering.'

I shrugged and gave in. We were just becoming active again when she said these precious words which ruined all chance of really closer acquaintance.

'I'm glad you liked the painting. If Peter hadn't called to collect it one weekend it would have gone with the rest of his things in the sale.'

'*Sale?*' I dragged my hands from her blouse and withdrew swiftly along the sofa fumbling for my shoes.

'Why, yes.'

'Where?' I broke into a sweat. 'Quick. *Where?*'

'In town. That auction place, Gimbert's. What's the matter, Lovejoy?'

'When?'

'Good gracious!' she exclaimed. 'You look as if you've seen a – '

'*When?*'

'Last week.' She couldn't miss the chance of criticizing another woman. 'There was some . . . bother. So I heard. His nieces had a terrible row. Nichole's quite nice but Kate – '

'Was there much stuff?' I snapped, but saw her pout and had to slow up. 'I have to ask, love, or I get in trouble,' I said, desperate. 'You do understand.'

'It's all right,' she said bravely. 'It was really quite pitiful. I happened to be, well, passing when the van arrived. It was so sad. He only had a few old things.'

It was so bloody sad all right. A few pitiful *old things*? Belonging to an old genius who could forge Restoration with such class? Moaning softly I was off the sofa like a selling-plater.

'Goodness!' I yelped over my shoulder. 'Look at the time!'

She trotted dolefully after me towards the door. 'Do you have to go? Will you come again, Lovejoy?' she said.

'Yes, yes! Thursday. Is a town bus due?' I babbled.

'Not for two hours. Better Monday,' she cried. 'Safer on Monday. Peter's golfing then. Like today.'

'Right, Brenda. See you Monday.'

'I'm Mary,' she said, all hurt.

'Mary, then.' I could have sworn she'd said Brenda.

I was out of the street and running in a sweat through the village towards the main road. Women are born quibblers. Ever noticed that?

CHAPTER II

NOTHING on the main road. Never a bus when you want one. We used to have Nathan's Fliers, three crackpot single deckers which ran fast and on time between the villages, operated by a corrupt old lecher called Nathan.

Then we were amalgamated with the nearby big towns, since which all buses have become either late or extinct. I stood there, cursing.

I tried thumbing a couple of cars but no luck. That's the trouble with East Anglia, too much countryside. Nothing but undulating countryside, mile after mile of rivers, lush fields and woods dotted with small villages. Merrie England. I sometimes feel as if Lovejoy Antiques, Inc.'s the only outfit keeping this particular bit Merrie, especially after a week on the knocker. When I'm reduced to going on the sound (that's banging at doors and asking if people have anything old for sale, the surest sign of impending failure in the antique business), I stick to towns if I can. Country-side gives me the willies. Everything in it seems to eat everything else, preferably alive. It can get you down.

You'll have guessed I'm a real townie. As things get worse, though, you have to go further afield. Villages are best for antiques. They're antique themselves. So there I was in Great Hawkham, two villages from home. Stuck. Bexon's forgery the only good link I'd had for months and no chance of a lift. The situation called for desperate remedies. The pub called.

I knew it a little, the Goat and Compasses, built in King Stephen's reign while his mob were scrapping with the volatile and exotic Empress Matilda. Paid for, I shouldn't wonder, in those ugly hammered silver coins of his – now so rare and prized it's no good even dreaming about them. I sprinted over. Maybe I'd get one in my change.

I entered briskly, hoping to create an impression of a dealer who had just come from doing a deal for everything the National Gallery wanted this year. A dozen or so people were de-stressing from the village's hectic social whirl, including Lennie. He's Victoriana, bygones, glass, crystalware and clueless. I swiftly borrowed a coin off him, partly because I had no change and partly because it's cheaper. I rushed through to the phone and dialled like a maniac.

'Hello?' I put my voice on. 'Is that Mrs Markham's residence?'

'Yes. Who is it, please?'

'This is Doctor Chenies of the hospital,' I said, sounding really good. 'Could I speak to Mrs Markham? It's urgent. About her friend, Mrs Witherspoon.'

'Oh, right.' He sounded suspicious. People who don't trust people get me really mad. Why is there no trust these days? Where has it all gone?

'Hello, Doctor?' Janie's voice, thank God. 'I'm afraid you must have the wrong – '

'It's me. Lovejoy.' I heard her stifle a laugh. 'Come and get me.'

'Is it really urgent, Doctor?' she said, doing her hesitant friend act. 'My husband has guests – '

'Stuff his guests,' I snarled. 'I'm stuck out in the bloody wilds here. The pub at Great Hawkham crossroads. I'm in a hurry.'

'Very well, Doctor. I'll try to come – '

'Be sharp.' I slammed the blower down. I honestly don't know what women think they're playing at sometimes. Full of wrong priorities.

I readjusted my face to a casual smile and strolled back to the saloon bar where Lennie waited. I told him about a wonderful deal I'd just made, buying a Georgian embroidery frame and an early Sheffie. He was all ears and plunged further into his natural gloom. Not that there's such a thing as really very early Sheffield plate. The term's relative. It was only invented in the 1740s by Thomas Bolsover (please don't spell his name with a 'u' stuck in there – he hated it). Elkington finished off the boom in fused sheets of copper and silver by inventing electroplating in 1840.

My eyes wandered while Lennie grumbled on about some Caffieri cast bronzes he'd missed. Dottie Quant was on a barstool, straining half a mile of stylish leg to reach the ground and making sure we all noticed. She's ceramics and silver, in the local antiques arcade. Her legs bring in a lot of deals, they say. I believe it. I waved over, nodding affably, and got a sneer in return. That's better than my average. Distaste from Dottie's like a knighthood. She was

talking to a fair-haired thickset man, maybe a stray golfer or
a buyer? Her balding husband grovelled about trying to
coax his noonday sneer from his alluring wife. A domestic
rural scene.

I promised to sell Lennie my mythical embroidery frame.
I offered to buy Lennie a drink, and escaped before he could
draw breath and say yes please. I blew Dottie a noisy kiss
to get her mad and left, my mind dazzled by old Bexon's
wonderful faked painting which might mean so much.

What messes people get themselves in, I was thinking as I
crossed the road. I stood waiting for Janie under the trees
for coolth. There's Lennie, in his wealthy mother-in-law's
clutches more ways than somewhat. And there's Dottie
having to rub at least shoulders with the riff-raff, and her
with carriage trade aspirations and a whining hubby.

Still, I'd my own problems. Where the hell could I find
a late Georgian embroidery frame by Saturday? The
problem was worsened by not having any money to buy,
even if I found one.

A week ago I'd missed a rosewood table – you won't
believe this – actually signed by Timothy Walford, about
1810, complete with fringed base-edge carving on triple
scrolls. If this page is wet it's because I'm sobbing. Good
class furniture with a provincial maker's name is so rare. It
was sold an hour before I reached the Arcade. What with
taxes and an unbelievably greedy public, life's hard.

You may be developing a low opinion of my most endearing qualities. Don't. My qualities are yours, folks, same as
everyone else's. I would have been as fascinated and excited
by old Bexon's lovely forgery if I'd just made a million in
gold minutes before, instead of being broke and getting
desperate. I tell you all this now because the behaviour you
actually see around antiques is only the tip of the dealer's
iceberg. From there it sinks on and on, down and down to
include the thousands of fearsome emotions sociologists do
not know. And if at the end of this you think I'm lascivious,
crude, sexist and selfish, do you know anybody who isn't?

Janie drew up, calling gaily, 'Hello, sailor!' Her joke.

'Where've you been?' I said coldly. 'I've been here an hour.'

'I've been exactly ten minutes,' she said, calmly eyeing me. I climbed into her Lagonda. 'Where've *you* been?'

'Working.' And how hard, I thought.

'You look exhausted, Lovejoy.'

'I am.'

'Was she worth it?' she asked sweetly, pulling out.

'If you're going to nag – '

'And where were you last night?'

'Ah,' I said, thinking quickly. 'I got stuck.'

'In . . .?' she prompted, all bright innocence.

'Cut it out, Janie.' I tried to seem annoyed. 'With a deal.'

'Anything really good?'

'No.' True, true.

'Where are we going?'

'Woody's.'

'That filthy place gives me fleas, Lovejoy.'

'It gives me a living. Or rather,' I added bitterly, 'it should do.'

'Let me, Lovejoy.' A pause while hedges and fields swished by. 'Give you a living,' she added.

I turned to watch her drive. The Lagonda didn't even purr. Janie's beautiful, twenty-six, wealthy in her own right. Her husband's wealthy too. He often goes abroad to mend companies sick of the palsy. Crackpot. They have a mansion in Little Hawkham, the next village to the one I'd just been working. Great Hawkham has two houses more, hence the adjective.

'I'm good value,' she said, smiling. 'Worth a quid or two. Good legs. Teeth my own. Socially trained, convent-educated. I could buy an antiques auction firm for you to play with. Think, Lovejoy. And take your hand off my knee when I'm driving.'

'And your husband?'

'Who?' She gave me a 1920 stare, trying to make me

laugh. They only do that when they're serious. 'Spell it.'

'Look, love,' I said wearily. 'Am I loyal?' You can't muck about. You have to tell them outright.

'No.'

'Kind?'

'Never.'

'Considerate?'

'Hopeless.'

I went down the list of virtues getting a denial every time.

'Then what's the use?'

'You're worth it, Lovejoy,' she said after a think. 'You understand what love is. If only you weren't an escapist.'

'Flight has a long tradition of success,' I got back.

She wouldn't let go, though. 'Besides,' she said, 'something's always happening around you.'

'I wish it bloody well was,' I groused.

Now I wish I hadn't said that. Not that I'm superstitious, but you can't be sure, can you?

CHAPTER III

JANIE DROPPED ME at the corner post office among prams and shoppers. I told her twenty minutes. Woody's Bar tries to hide itself in an alley between a pub and a jeweller's but gives itself away by gushing out steamy blue fumes swamping the pavement. Wise pedestrians cross over. The alley's partly covered, and is known as the Arcade to locals. It looks like a beginner's cardboard cut-out Camelot joined together wrong. Bloody town council planners. The beauty is that it's crammed with antique dealers'. shops.

I pushed into Woody's Bar and peered through the opaque air. There he was. Tinker Dill, my barker, among the crammed tables. He was lashing into one of Woody's specials and hastily trying to sober up before the pubs got under way again. It's not a pretty sight. A dozen other dealers were about, wolfing mounds of chips, sausages and mashed triffid greasily concealed under slithering mounds of ketchup. I tell you this trade needs nerve.

'Tea, Woody,' I called into the blue haze towards the back. He'd be there, smoking ash into some poor soul's charring haddock.

'Hello, Lovejoy,' a few voices called. I waved, a picture of the successful antique dealer. Cheerful adversity is vaguely entertaining, but even friends steer clear of doom.

I sat and watched Tinker Dill eat. All this yap about civilization really is utter cock. Civilization isn't art, religion and all that. It's two things: paving and cutlery. Without paving everything's jungle. Without cutlery eating's a clumsy dissection which ends by stuffing pieces of dead animals and plants between your jaws. Tinker does it without a net.

'Tinker.'

No reply.

'Tinker,' I tried again, louder. Not a sign. 'Money,' I said softly. The place stilled with utter reverence. I watched Tinker begin to respond to therapy.

I've known him years but it's still gruesome. Bloodshot eyes swivelled as if searching for the next planet. Stubble, corrugated black teeth, skeletal limbs shuffled into human shape. He's thin as a lath. His lazaroid knuckles are always concealed under ketchup-stained woollen mittens, his frame lost somewhere in an overcoat straight from the Crimea. At the magic word even Woody's clattering pans had silenced. Tinker's brain fidgeted painfully into action. His eyes focused, two raw balls wobbling in gin-soaked aspic. He saw me.

'Hello, Lovejoy.'

'Did you pin the scrambler?' I asked.

'Yeh.' He was coming round.

'Settle later, okay?'

'Yeh.' (Translation: Tinker Dill reports he has successfully found a Georgian hurdy-gurdy for me, complete with animated French figurines. He would get it, and I'd pay him enough commission to get sloshed out of his mind again. To continue:)

'Great,' I praised.

Tinker crumpled a grin. The tension all about eased and noise began again. Woody's giant waitress Lisa loomed in the fog with my tea like the *Bismark* through its last smokescreen.

'How's Lovejoy?' She ruffled my thatch.

'Poor. Lonely.' Disbelieving snickers rose from nearby tables. 'No money, but good company.' She surged away, smiling.

'You're always after crumpet, Lovejoy,' Tinker criticized piously. He goes to chapel, but I hear the wine's free.

I waited while he shovelled his huge meal away like a smelter frantically raising steam. All around muttered deals were being made, messages muttered through mouthfuls of grease and tea just too weak to plough. The door tinkled. A tourist peered briefly in and reeled away at the sight of huddled, feeding, smoking, belching humanity still stinking of last night's booze.

To me Woody's permanent fry-up is like a church – holy, something to venerate. Blasphemy? Come down one day and see for yourself. There'll be a Woody's in your town, full of antique collectors and dealers. If you stick it for more than two days you'll be hooked for life on antiques because there's no mistaking that sense of religious devotion. Antiques are everything, even the reason for living. Nothing else exists. It's the feeling that makes crusades. I know because I have it, have for years. Dealers are dealers down to the marrow and out to the skin again, no variation or treachery. And more money passes across Woody's unwashed grease-smeared tables in one week than our town councillors fiddle in a whole year, and that's enough to refloat the franc. Woody's is beautiful.

'Better, Tinker?'

'Yeh.' Tinker finished elegantly as ever, settling like a tattered combine harvester coming to rest. He wiped his mouth on a stained mitten and emitted three rhythmic belches. I got Lisa to bring him a pint of tea. He lit a cigarette, in paradise. Hangover gone, smoking, tea in hand, having survived Woody's breakfast, the auction coming up tomorrow, pulling off a find and almost sober enough to start getting stoned again. To business.

'Bexon,' I began. 'Old bloke, died. Some stuff got into Gimbert's auction last week.'

'What was it?'

'I don't know.'

'Hang on.'

He slurped from his cup to fuel up for cerebral activity. His eyes hazed. I swear his brain becomes audible. He took a deep drag of carcinogens. Blast off.

'Bexon. An old geezer? Great Hawkham?' he remembered finally. I nodded. 'Only rubbish.'

'No paintings?'

'None. Rough old furniture, ordinary modern junk. Couple of carpets.'

'Find out about Bexon, Tinker.' My heart was in my boots.

'Is it urgent, Lovejoy?'

'You just don't know.' I gave him one of my stares and he nodded. It's his job to be concerned about whatever I'm concerned about. It's more than his job – it's his life. Barkers are scouts for antique dealers, the foragers, the pilot fishes questing ahead of the predatory shark . . . er, sorry, that last analogy's unfortunate. Skirmishers, perhaps. 'And try for an antique embroidery frame, Tinker.' A few quid from Lennie wouldn't come amiss.

'Very hard, Lovejoy.'

'Nothing from the robbery up for sale?' I asked helplessly, really scraping the barrel.

Yobbos had hit our Castle museum a couple of weeks before, nicked some ancient British-Roman gold coins and used most of them in slot machines for cigarettes. This is akin to using a Kakeimon bowl for afters or clicking a La Chaumette flintlock from curiosity. The intellects our local lads have. Hopeless. If you stood them outside St Paul's

Cathedral they'd see nothing but a big stone bubble. I'm not being cruel. Most can't tell a gold-mounted glass Vachette snuffbox from a box of aspirins. I mean it. The only gold-and-glass snuffbox ever discovered in our town made by that brilliant Napoleonic goldsmith was being used for aspirins at some old dear's bedside. Two years ago a marine barometer made with delicacy and love by André-Charles Boule of Louis XIV fame was cheerfully nailed in place to span a gap in a shelf in a local farm cottage.

You just have no idea. East Anglia drives you mad sometimes. It's paradise to a good, honest dealer like me, but I thank heavens da Vinci wasn't local. His silly old scribbles would have been used for wallpaper in a flash.

'No.'

'Any news of the coins?' He shook his head.

About three of the tiny – but oh, so precious – gold coins were still missing, according to the papers. Of course, I was only interested because I wanted to see them returned to their rightful community ownership in the museum for future generations to enjoy. Nothing was further from my mind than hoping they'd turn up by chance so a poor vigilant dealer like me could snaffle them and gloat over those delicious precious ancient gold discs positively glinting with . . . er, sorry. I get carried away.

'Hang on, Lovejoy.'

I paused in the act of rising to go. Tinker was quite literally steaming. The pong was indescribable, stale beer and no washing, but he's the best barker in the business. I respect his legwork if nothing else. And he stays loyal, even with things this bad. I let him fester a moment more, looking about.

Helen was in, a surprise. She should have been viewing for tomorrow's auction this late in the day. One of our careful dealers, Helen is, tall, reserved, hooked on fairings, oriental art and African ethnology. I'd been a friend of Helen's when she arrived four years before, without ever having felt close to her – mentally, that is. Self-made and self-preserved. She usually eats yoghurts and crusts in her sterile home near our ruined abbey, St John's. Odd to see her in Woody's grime.

'Slumming?' I called over cheerily to pass the time. She turned cool blue eyes on me, breathing cigarette smoke with effect like they can.

'Yes,' she said evenly and went back to stirring coffee amid a chorus of chuckles. Lovejoy silenced.

'Lovejoy' Tinker Dill was back from outer space. 'What sort of stuff did you want from Bexon?'

'Paintings.'

He thought and his face cleared.

'Dandy Jack.'

'He picked up something of Bexon's?' I kept my voice down. Friends may be friends, but dealers are listeners.

'Yeh. A little drawing and some dross.'

'Where is he?' Dandy's shop was across the main street.

'On a pick-up.'

Just my luck. Dandy was given to these sudden magpie jaunts around the country. He always returned loaded with crud, but occasionally fetched the odd desirable home.

'Back tomorrow,' Tinker added.

'On to something, Lovejoy?' Beck's voice, next table. Beck's a florrid flabby predator from Cornwall. We call his sort of dealers trawlies, perhaps after trawler-fishing. They go wherever tourists flock, usually one step ahead of the main drove. You make your precarious living as a trawlie by guessing the tourists' mood. For example, if you can guess that this year's east coast visitors will go berserk over pottery souvenirs, plastic gnomes or fancy hats you can make a fortune. If you guess wrong you don't. A rough game. Beck fancies himself as an antiques trawlie. I don't like him, mainly because he doesn't care what he handles – or how. He always seems to be sneering. A criminal in search of a crime. We've had a few brushes in the past.

'Is that you, Beck, old pal?' I asked delightedly into the fumes of Woody's frying cholesterol.

'Who's Bexon?' he growled across at us.

'Naughty old eavesdropping Big-Ears,' I said playfully. Not that I was feeling particularly chirpy, but happiness gets his sort down.

'Chop the deal with me, Lovejoy?' To chop is to share. There's nothing more offensive than a trawlie trying to wheedle.

'Perhaps on another occasion,' I declined politely. I could see he was getting mad. The dealers around us were beginning to take an interest in our light social banter. You know the way friends do.

'Make it soon,' he said. 'I hear you're bust.'

'Tell the Chancellor,' I got back. 'Maybe he'll cut my tax.'

'Put that in your begging-bowl.' He flicked a penny on to our table as he rose to go. There was general hilarity at my expense.

'Thanks, Beck.' I put it in my jacket pocket. 'You can give me the rest later.' A few laughs on my side.

We all watched him go. Local dealers don't care for trawlies. They tend to arrive in a 'circus', as we call it, a small group viciously bent on rapid and extortionate profit. They're galling enough to make you mix metaphors. Take my tip: never buy antiques from a travelling dealer. And if there are two or more dealers on the hoof together, then especially don't.

'Watch Beck, Lovejoy,' Tinker warned in an undertone. 'A right lad. His circus'll be around all month.'

'Find me Dandy Jack, Tinker.'

'Right.' He wheezed stale beer fumes at me.

I rose, giddy. A few other dealers emitted the odd parting jeer. I waved to my public and slid out. I was well into the Arcade before I realized I'd forgotten to pay Lisa for my tea. Tut-tut. Still, you can't think of everything.

As I emerged, Janie signalled at me from near the post office, tapping her watch helplessly. Duty obviously called. I must have been longer than I thought. Through the traffic I signalled okay, I'd stay. I'd phone later. She signalled back not before seven. I signalled eight, then, I watched her go,

and crossed back to the Arcade. Now I'd drawn a blank over
Bexon, poverty weighed me down. I meant to go but you
can't avoid just looking at antiques, can you? Especially not
in the Arcade. Patrick yoo-hooed me over to his place before
I'd gone a few windows. I forced my way across the stream
of people. He always embarrasses me. Not because he's, well,
odd, but because he shows off and everybody stares.

'Just the little *mannikin* I've prayed for!' he screeched,
false eyelashes and fingers all aflutter. 'Lovejoy! Come
here this *very* instant!' Heads were turning and people
gaped at the apparition posturing in his shop doorway.
'This way, Lovejoy, dearie!' he trilled. I was a yard away
by then.

'Shut your row, Patrick.' I entered the shop's dusk. 'And
must you wear a blue frock?'

'Ultramarine, you great buffoon!' he snapped. 'Everybody
pay attention!' He did a pivot and pointed at me in tableau.
'Lovejoy's in one of his moods.' The trouble is I always go
red and shuffle. I can only think of cutting remarks on the
way home.

'Don't mind Patrick, Lovejoy.' I might have known Lily
would be there. I don't have time to tell you everything that
goes on, but Lily (married) loves and desires Patrick (single
and bent). Lily insists – in the long tradition of women hooked
on sacrificial martyrdom – that she's just the bird to straighten
Patrick. As if that's not enough, both are antique dealers.
You see the problem. 'He tried to get a museum expert
over,' Lily explained, 'but he's gone to Norfolk.' She spoke
as if Norfolk's in Ursa Major. Our locals are very clannish.

'This way, Dear Heart!' Patrick sailed to the rear followed
by the adoring Lily. Three or four customers hastily got out
of the way of someone so obviously and flamboyantly an
expert as Patrick. I trailed along. '*Regardez!*'

It was a stoneware bottle. A large fish swam lazily in
brushed iron design under the celadon glaze. I reached out
reverently, chest tight and breath dry. My mind was clanging
with greed and love as I turned the little table round to see
better.

'Pick it up, Lovejoy,' Patrick offered.

'Shut up.'

'Oh!' he snapped petulantly. 'Isn't he absolutely *vulgar*.'

I sat and let the beauty wash from the brilliant work of art into the shop. The master had coated the bottle's body with a luscious white slip. It was lovely, a lovely miracle. The ninth-century Korean pots are very different – those imprinted with hundreds of those tiny whorled designs in vertical rows tend to get me down a bit. This was from a much later period.

'It's genuine, Patrick,' I said brokenly. 'Superb.'

'You perfect *dear*, Lovejoy!' he whooped ecstatically.

'Korean, about latish fifteenth century.'

Excited, he dragged me away and showed me a few other items – a phoney Meissen, a modern Hong Kong copy of a Persian-influenced Russian silver gilt tea and coffee service, supposedly 1840 (it's surprising, but modern eastern copies always give themselves away by too rigid a design) and suchlike. We had a final row about a William and Mary commemorative plate. He was furious, wanting everything he showed me to be genuine now.

'It's a genuine blue-and-yellow, Lovejoy!' he protested.

'I'm sure it is, Lovejoy.' That from the anxious Lily, unbiased as ever.

'It's modern,' I said. I touched it. Not a single beat of life in the poor thing. 'They always get the weight and colours wrong. The yellow should be mustard. The blue should be very blue.' The dazzling loveliness of that Korean bottle was making me irritable. I added, 'You know, Patrick. Blue. Like your frock.'

He wailed into tears at that. I left, feeling poorer than ever and a swine. For all I knew ultramarine might have been his colour.

Still two hours to wait for a bus home. And still all blank. I strolled towards the Castle museum. It was time I saw what sort of antique coins had been stolen, in case.

The town museum is in the Castle. Its curator's a small

tidy man called Popplewell. I got to him by telling a succession of uniformed opponents I wanted to make a donation to the museum. One even tried to charge me admission, the cheek of it. People take my breath away sometimes.

'Donation?' I told Popplewell, puzzled at the mistake. 'I'm afraid one of your assistants got it wrong. I said nothing about any donation. I'm here about the robbery.'

'Ah,' he said dismally. 'Insurance?'

Now, to digress one split second. Insurance and I – and I strongly urge this to include you as well – do not mix. As far as antiques are concerned, forget insurance. Concentrate what money you have on the antique's protection in the first place. Don't go throwing good money away.

'No,' I said, rapidly going off him. 'I'm an antique dealer.'

'Really,' he said in that drawl which means, I've met your sort before.

'I want to know what was nicked in case it gets offered me.'

'Is that so?' He eyed me suspiciously, reclassifying me as a lout.

'Yes. They'll start looking for a fence,' I explained. 'They may take the goods to one of us respectable dealers.'

'I see.' He came to a decision. 'Very well. I'll show you. This way please.'

I didn't tell him Lovejoy's Law for the detection of stolen antiques, which runs: any genuine antique offered to you at a third of its known price has been stolen. Blokes like this curator chap are just out of this world. You need somebody like me to amass a collection, not a dozen committees.

We puffed on to the Roman landing. Popplewell halted at a sloping case. He removed a board and its covering beige cloth. The glass beneath was shattered and the display cards all awry. The legend card read 'Gold Coins of the Roman Period: Britain.' Popplewell took my stricken expression for criticism.

'We haven't had time to establish a substitute display,'

he said. 'And the police have taken scrapings and photos for prints.'

'Could you be more specific about the items?'

'A set of Roman staters. Gold. Claudius. And some silver.' He saw me reading the cards scattered in the case. It had been a rough smash-and-grab. 'Those are Mr Bexon's own labels.'

'Er, Bexon?' I sounded hoarse all of a sudden.

'Top right-hand corner.' He pointed. 'The donor wanted his own labels retained. Quite incorrect, of course, but . . .' he shrugged.

I read them through the broken glass, careful not to touch because police can be very funny about fingerprints. The cards all said the same: 'Gold coins, Roman period.' Then a curious sentence on each: 'Found by the donor, Roman Province of IOM.' I read this aloud.

'Was he serious? Isle of Man? But the Romans – '

Popplewell shrugged again. 'He was a somewhat eccentric old gentleman. He insisted that we adhere to that wording exactly, though we all know that the Isle of Man never was colonized.' He covered the scene of the crime. 'We have the most amazing conditions appended to our gifts sometimes. I could tell you – '

'Thank you,' I interrupted hastily. 'One thing. Were they genuine?'

'Of course.' He got nasty. 'If you mean to imply this museum doesn't examine properly and in detail all – '

'Er, fine, fine,' I said, and moved off. 'If I hear anything I'll let you know.'

'Good. You have the phone number?'

The Castle galleries run three sides of the square, leaving a huge central well crowded with visitors at this time of year. Helen saw me looking and waved upwards quite calmly from where she was inspecting one of the coaches on display there. I waved back. Helen wasn't thinking of going in for Queen Anne coaches, that was for sure. When I'd climbed down she'd gone.

I walked thoughtfully across the drawbridge among tourists and children, and found I was worried sick. Bexon isn't all that common a name. I decided to look in at Margaret's. I still had time before the bus.

Hers is the only shop with a good dose of sunshine. She looked up and came limping to welcome me with a smile. I'm too fond of Margaret. There's a husband somewhere in the background but I've never had the courage to ask, though I do know she has a good range of some man's suitings in her bedroom wardrobe. We know each other fairly well. I like Margaret more than I ought, but you get days, don't you? I slouched in like a refugee.

'Stop that,' I told her irritably.

Margaret was twisting a pewter burette. On a good day it turns my stomach. You can imagine what it does to me on a bad one.

'Hello, Lovejoy.' She hesitated. 'I'm seeing if it's genuine.'

'Trust its appearance,' I growled. 'Why torture it just because you're ignorant?'

'Charming,' she said, but she had no right to get nettled.

Dealers get me sometimes. We're all as bad. Pewter's the most maligned, crippled and assaulted of all antiques. Dealers who reckon to show they know a thing or two twist pewter, actually grab hold and twist it hard. When you do it hard enough it screams, screams from its poor little soul. Well, wouldn't you? Really tears you apart. It's a terrible, wailing scream like a child in intractable pain. Only pewter does it. Dealers, the bums, think it's clever. People do similar sorts of things to jade. Ignorant collectors say that if you can scratch it with a key it isn't genuine, which is rubbish. Any reasonable jewellers will give you (free) a card showing Mohs' Scale of hardness for semi-precious stones, which tells you all you need to know about what can scratch what. There's no excuse for simple ignorance. Never be cruel to antiques, folks. They've done nothing to you, so don't go about massacring them. And pewter's got a fascinating history. Of course, it can be very difficult to collect, though you can still buy good pre-Conquest specimens. It was actually forbidden in churches at the Council of Westminster after 1175 AD, but the French allowed it by their Council of Nîmes, 1252, so there's plenty around, and eventually our lot saw the light again. More sense in those days.

I took the little wine vessel from Margaret. It looked like the mark of Richard Marbor, 1706 – a Yeoman and therefore fairly well recorded. Good old Henry VIII took a little time off from attending to Anne of Cleeves in 1540 to encourage the York pewterers to record their touch-marks on their wares, so a lot is known. I told her all this, and added that there's no reason to go throttling these delicate antiques when you can learn twice as much by reading and just looking.

'Tea?' Margaret offered by way of thanks.

'Er, no, thanks.' Margaret's tea's a legend among survivors. 'Who's best with Roman coins round here, beside Cooney?'

Cooney's a mad half-Spanish dog-breeder who lives down on the marshes. He's been divorced six times and he's only twenty-eight.

'There's him,' she said, 'and Pilsen. And that magistrate.' She counted on her fingers. 'And that overcoat man.'

We have a few eccentrics hereabouts. The man with the overcoats is a local living legend. Like Charles Peace he's rumoured to have a fatal attraction for women, which of course may just be him boxing clever, it being well known that women are oddly attracted by such stories. He collects overcoats and Stuart coins. The magistrate is an elderly man who fought at Jutland or somewhere. He's hammered Edward I silver coins. Pilsen's a dealer with a one-room lock-up shop on the Lexton village road. He makes kites and has religion.

'Thanks, love.' I rose to go.

'Lovejoy.' Here it came. I'd watched her working up to it inch by inch. 'What's it about? You aren't usually uneasy.'

'I'm not uneasy,' I said.

'Anything I can do?'

'Look. If I wanted to find out how somebody died,' I asked, taking the plunge, 'how would I go about it?'

'The doctor, I suppose. But he won't tell unless you're

the next of kin.'

'What about Somerset House?'

'Better the local registration office. That's nearer.'

I gave her a kiss and departed.

The woman at the registration office was helpful. Poor old Bexon's death certificate showed he'd passed away without causing the slightest bother or suspicion. Nothing out of the ordinary to hold up wills or bequests. She was pleased at how tidy everything was.

I stood at the bus stop thinking so hard I almost forgot to get on when it finally came.

CHAPTER IV

I LIVE in this cottage, often alone, on the edge of a village a few miles from our main town. There's a garden, a copse, blackthorn hedges good for purple sloe gin at Michaelmas, and a muddy path I keep meaning to macadam over. The village lane begins at my gate. Further down there's just a path to the river's shallow watersplash at Fordleigh. I always set my break-in alarm because we dealers are forever being burgled. It has to be flicked before unlocking the door or Police Constable Geoffrey, our village Sherlock, gets hauled out of his tomato-ridden greenhouse to pedal over and tell me off again for causing false alarms.

Once in the cottage I was at a loose end. I just couldn't get going. Everybody has a blue patch now and then, I suppose. I'm normally a buoyant sort, but I couldn't settle down to anything. It rained for an hour or two about four, so I washed this week's socks and swept up. The vacuum was on the blink so I did without. The village's one shop had pasties in. I got two for supper and some tomatoes.

Normally I read over a meal. This evening I found myself staring at the same page, reading a paragraph of Dean Inge's essays over and over. Poor old Bexon kept coming into my mind. A forger, but apparently an honest one. Why else that

revealing yellow? So he was honest, the poor innocent. But
those Roman golds. Popplewell said they were genuine. The
labels said mostly Nero's reign. There were even one or two
showing the babes being suckled by the wild she-wolf,
Romulus and Remus. Rome's originals. And the famous
arched 'DE BRITANN' gold of Claudius the God. Well,
all right, but there never was such a thing as a Roman province of the Isle of Man. Everybody knows that. They simply
never got there. Even if they'd heard of it they'd ignored it.

A wrong label's the sort of odd mistake you pass off in
any museum. A million like it happen every day. But the
picture in Mary's house was done with love and almost
incredible skill. And gold's gold. And, far more to the point, a
Roman antique's a Roman antique. I thought on, guiltily
knowing I should have been bringing my notes up to date.

At the finish I gave up and got a map. You can see why
they didn't occupy it of course, way out in the middle of the
Irish Sea. Not wealthy, not very populous, probably poor
weather much of the year. No wonder. I locked the front
door, drew the curtains and rolled back the living-room
carpet.

The easy way to lift the giant flagstone would have been
to use a beam winch rigged to a two-horse-power motor
connected to the iron ring set in the floor. That would have
been a bit obvious, though, so I lift it with my own lilywhites. There's a switch by the steps leading down into the
priest-hole. Nothing had been disturbed. It was probably an
old vegetable store, but you'll have noticed by now I'm
incurably romantic, if a bit cynical with it. There are a few
tea-chests down there for storing my vast stock of priceless
antiques (temporarily sold to buy a luxury called food).
It's ideal for storing antiques. The old folk had their heads
screwed on. Nowadays it's all builders can do to stick houses
down straight, let alone include anything useful for the
occupants.

I drew out the folding Regency table and opened my card-
index. Penniless or not, antiques impose their own demand on
any dealer worth a light. I meet it by keeping notes. Paper

clippings, book abstracts, catalogued details from sales, hints picked up at auctions, eavesdroppings, museum listings – many horribly wrong, by the way – and advertisements, all get stored away. I searched frantically for any suggestion of a brilliant forger operating locally. Plenty of duds, and one or two not so bad. But brilliant? Not a sign. I looked up names.

I found two Bexons. One's a collector in Norwich. He's hooked on Victorian mechanicals. Three years before he triumphed by snapping up a beautiful late model of Thomas Newcomen's engine. He must still be paying, but I'd bet he was smiling through his tears. Mechanicals are worth their weight in gold, plus ten per cent of course. The second (braver) Bexon was a regular buyer of *découpage* – paper cutouts varnished on to surfaces for decoration of furniture, ornaments, firescreens, tableware and such. In itself it's a small antique field, but you can say the same about Leonardo da Vinci's stuff, can't you?

More worried than ever that I'd somehow missed a really golden opportunity, I closed up.

I went out to check my two budgerigars as soon as it stopped raining. The garden was drenched, the grass squelching underfoot. A sea wind had sprung up. As darkness falls my cottage seems to move silently away from the two other houses nearby. One had lights in the window. I was pleased about this, though it was only old Mrs Tewson and her dog. I checked the budgies' flight with a torch and said goodnight. They fluffed and chirped.

The budgerigars, Manton and Wilkinson, were how I'd met Janie. I'd done over one of the stallholders on our Saturday market. He'd had the birds in an old shoe box covered by a piece of glass, no food or water. Practically accidentally, I'd stumbled against him, breaking his shoulder, poor man, after buying them from him. Worse, I'd accidentally broken his fingers by standing on his hand. The police had come along and tried to make a case out of it, but luckily Janie saw it all and explained it was an accident. They'd let me go suspiciously, which only goes to show how they're completely lacking in trust these days. I'd taken one look at Janie, smiling and wealthy, and that was that. She'd given me a lift back, helped me to buy the cage and seed, and matters took their own course, as folks say. Janie says I'm soft about them, but I'm not. At the moment I could only think of Bexon. Forger or not, he was my lifeline back into the antique business.

Inside the cottage I fidgeted and then cleared up and fidgeted again. I even wished I hadn't had to pawn the telly. Isn't it funny how you get feelings. I decided to use my one remaining asset and phone the names Margaret'd given me. Cooney's always in because of his dog kennels. I told him I was interested in the stolen coins.

'You and the rest of us, Lovejoy,' he said, laughing.

'From the Isle of Man,' I explained innocently.

He snorted disbelievingly. 'There's no such thing,' he told me. 'Oh, they've had the odd stray Roman denarius show up, but no hoards or anything like that. The old chap who donated them went about saying he'd found them there.'

'Where?'

'On Man. Wouldn't say exactly. There was a row about the labels, I remember. He insisted on writing his own.'

'Thanks, Cooney.'

I got Pilsen next, the only religious antique dealer-cum-kite-collector in the universe. He blessed me down the phone and intoned a short prayer for my success but couldn't help. He tried to sell me a kite but forgave me when I said some other time. The old magistrate barked that the robbers should be horsewhipped, and slammed the receiver down when I admitted I had no Edward I coinage for sale. The overcoat man after a chat gave me a commission to bid for him at a local auction for an officer's greatcoat of the Essex Regiment, but otherwise nothing.

No use phoning Janie when I had the blues, though she'd be blazing tomorrow. You can't help being on edge sometimes.

Imagine suddenly meeting somebody who believed they could prove there'd been a hitherto unidentified King of England whose existence nobody else had ever suspected.

Or an extra American President. Or an extra moon for Earth.
I felt just like that.

It probably didn't matter, I decided. The wrongest
guess I ever made..

I decided to sleep on it but tossed and turned all night.

CHAPTER V

NEXT MORNING Janie was waiting, illegally parked, pretending to look at the cutler's wares in Head Street. I'd caught
her by phone just as she was going out for a hair-do. We
agreed to make up over coffee. She took one look at my face.

'Oh, dear.'

We went to a place near Gimbert's auction rooms on East
Hill. I could see them unloading the antique furniture from
the window table. Janie paid, pretending to do it absent-
mindedly so I wouldn't take it bad.

I told her the tale of Patrick's wonderful find, the Korean
vase. She said I should have tried to learn where he'd got
it, but that's something dealers never do. She listened about
Bexon, Popplewell, the Roman golds. I told her that Dandy
Jack had got hold of the remnants of old Bexon's belongings.

'What's the mystery?'

'There never was a Roman Province of the Isle of Man,
Janie. Caesar never bothered.'

'Then where did the coins come from?'

'Exactly.' I stirred uncomfortably. The nasty feeling was
still there. Earlier I'd found Mary's surname from the
register and telephoned. Her husband had been golfing
since dawn, obviously a nutter. 'Take me to the golf club,
Janie.'

'My God, Lovejoy! How can I?' She shook her head.
'My neighbour's a golfer. I'd better drop you beyond the
station bridge. Can I come round later if I can get away?'

'No,' I said too quickly. 'Er, I've a deal on.' I do a special
job at home some afternoons which Janie doesn't know

about. Tell you about it in a minute.

'If I find you haven't, Lovejoy,' she said sweetly, 'I'll
murder you. I hope you understand that.'

'Don't start,' I pleaded, but she put her lips thin the
way they do and wouldn't answer. Women never trust people.
Ever noticed that? Sometimes I wish they would. It'd make
my arrangements so much easier.

Janie ran me to the railway, periodically telling me to
take my hand off her knee when she was driving, but it
was honestly accidental. It's a mile uphill from the station
bridge. The golf club stands back from the narrow road
among trees, quite a fetching low building. You never pass
it without seeing a score of cars.

I asked for Peter Chape in the bar. He was out on the
course. I waited, watching golfers from the bar window. I
have no interest. To me golf's a good walk spoiled. Behind
me people entered the bar, had a drink, smoked. I listened
to the talk of birdies, eagles, five irons and rough chipping.
It was another language to me, like Swahili. The great thing,
it seems, is to ask everybody else what their handicap is.
Mine's women.

I was being pointed out to a tall newcomer by the barman.
He started across the room. Peter, Mary's husband.

Peter Chape was a thin, rather casual man, disappointed
that I wasn't a golfer. I explained I was a dealer searching
for Bexon's paintings and told innocently how I had been
directed to his house earlier in the week by some anonymous
wellwisher. He confirmed what Mary had said about old
Mr Bexon. They worked as engineers together only for a
short period before the old chap retired.

'He lived with his two girls,' he said. 'Nieces by adoption,
really. Kept house and so on. A quiet, clever old chap.'

'I believe they're easy to get along with,' I fished cleverly.
'Maybe I should call around.'

'Well . . . Nichole, yes. Katie . . . maybe not so easy.'
Clearly the gentlemanly sort. I thanked him and went.

It's a long walk out to the village. Not one antique shop
for ten miles in any direction. A short cut runs across fields

into our village but I never take it. There's too much countryside about already without going looking for the rotten stuff.
As I walked I kept wondering if mashie niblick was in the
dictionary.

It was coming on to rain as I trudged eventually into my
lane. A familiar motor-cycle was propped against the cottage.
I groaned. I'd forgotten Algernon, a trainee would-be dealer
lumbered on me by a kindly crucifixioneer. I was struggling
to educate him in antiques. Talk about a sow's ear.

It was becoming one of those days again.

'Lovejoy!' He was beaming at me through his goggles
coming round the garden. Toothy, specs, motor-cycle
leathers. He's mad on bikes.

'Hiyer, Algernon. You'll frighten the budgies in that gear.'

'I've read it.' He dragged from among his leathers a book
and held it up, proud as a peacock. 'Like you said.'

'Not in the rain, Algernon.' I took the precious volume
and put it inside my jacket.

'Fascinating! Such an amazing group of people!'

I squinted at him. The burke was serious. If I ever
strangled him I'd have to get Janie for an alibi. He was
wagging like a gleeful dog fetching its stick.

'An absolutely marvellous read,' he was saying when his
voice cut out. That was on account of my hand scrunging
his windpipe. I pinned him against the wall.

'*Goon!*'

He was puce. I took my hand away and watched the cyano-
sis go.

'But, Lovejoy!' he gasped. 'What's wrong?'

Algernon is a typical member of the public. That is to say,
piteously ignorant of practically everything, but mainly and
most painful of all entirely ignorant of antiques. Trying to
teach a twenty-two-year-old Neanderthal the trade was the
result of my habit of going broke. Algernon was steadily
breaking my heart.

'What book,' I asked gently, 'did I give you?'

Algernon backed away. He was beginning to realize all was not well.

'*Biographical Memoirs of Extraordinary Painters.*'

'By?'

'William Beckford. 1780.'

'And you took it seriously?' I yelled.

'B . . . b . . . but you said study it.' He fell over his bike, backing off.

I leaned over him. They say Beckett put his face to the wall when asked about his plays. Sometimes I know exactly how he felt.

'Algernon,' I said. 'Beckford's showing us the stupidity of the fashionable artistic judgement of his times.' I watched light dawn in his thin, spotty countenance. 'Are you receiving me, Algernon?'

'I *see*! A literary joke!' He scrambled to his feet, all excited. 'How clever!' I just don't believe in people like Algernon. I've stood him next to a Turner oil and he's not even trembled in ecstasy. 'I'll read it again!' he exclaimed. 'I will keep that new satirical aspect uppermost in mind!' He really talks like this, the Piltdowner. No wonder he's thick.

'Tomorrow, Algernon,' I said slowly, carefully not battering his brain to pulp, 'you come here – '

'Thank you, Lovejoy! I accept your kind invitation –

I struggled to keep control, my voice level gravel. 'By tomorrow make sure you've read Wills on Victorian glass and Baines on brass instruments.'

'But tomorrow's only a day away,' he said brightly.

'It always is, Algernon,' I cut in. 'But it's still the deadline. And you'll get your next test on miscellaneous antiques.'

'Yes, Lovejoy.' His face fell. He hates tests. I gave him the Beckford again and stood in the porch to wave him off. He fired his bike and boomed away, waving and grinning through the hedge's thin bits.

'You're too hard on Algernon,' Janie's always saying, but she's wrong. I just worry about him. As a dealer Algernon wouldn't last a month. Where I come from he'd starve. I switched the alarm key and went in.

I made some soup from one of those crinkly packets, three sandwiches – fish-paste and tomato – and brewed up. No sugar in case it made me feel guilty. I had one egg left which I was saving because Henry was due at teatime. He's ten months old and my second visible means of support. Henry's the special job I mentioned earlier. Well, it's not my fault.

When you're broke a number of quite interesting things happen. You see at first a whole new set of people you otherwise would have missed, milkmen, children, housewives, shopkeepers. You get to recognize bus conductors because you've no car. Cyclists come and ride talkatively alongside as you bike into town. The second thing's that old demon gelt – one clink and you prick up your ears like a warhorse at a bugle. The money problem intrudes. It gets everywhere, like soot. Everything reminds you of it – women, the garden, posting a letter, wondering if you can afford a newspaper. You become a sort of accountant. It's really rather unpleasing. The third thing is that people start agreeing with what you say and even with what you think. It's very odd. Like if you buy a lettuce and you're thinking, that's a hell of a lot of money just for one measly lettuce, ten to one a horde of other shoppers will be at your elbow in a flash, all saying, 'It *is* a lot, love. For one lettuce! Isn't it terrible?' and things like that. The point is, nobody would have said a thing before you got broke. See what I mean?

I'd been destitute some three weeks before the local village housewives understood. Gradually they began pausing at the gate if they were down my lane. We started exchanging the odd word in our one street. It was pretty pleasant. There are even hidden fringe benefits but I'd better not go into that because people gossip so. I kept up a front for a week or two ('Well, I've a lot of work to do at home, so I've not gone in today . . .') but it was only politeness. They realized. After that I found myself winkled into their problems, women being born winklers. Before long I was going errands into town for medicines and then doing the shopping for them. From there I was walking dogs and holding keys to let the oil people deliver. They paid me in change, odd tips. My final graduation in social acceptance was Henry.

I asked Eleanor – his mother, twenty-five, wife of a publisher – what to do with him but got no straight answers. She said Henry eats most things, by which she meant everything, including light furniture and curtains. He never seems to do much, just lies about and mutters. Once you actually get to know him he's a ball of fire. At first I was worried when it was his hometime because Eleanor never used to check him over. I wanted to show her he wasn't at death's dark door on return of goods, even thinking of making her sign a receipt in case he was sick in the night and I got blamed. He lasted out the first week though and after that I stopped bothering. I was daft to worry because Henry's as hard as nails. Eleanor gives me tips for helping her, a quid here and there. I know it's not very dignified, in case that's what you're thinking, but it keeps me in the antiques game during these bad patches. That's what matters.

I finished my grub, chucked the remains to the robin and thought about the old genius with his two ratty nieces. I was getting a permanent feeling about it, but maybe it was the fish-paste.

I've got to tell you about Henry's revolting habits here, because without them I'd never have got any further with the Bexon problem. In fact, in a way Henry lit on my first clue.

Eleanor came racing up the lane five minutes early, out of breath as usual. Henry was strapped in his push-chair, jerking as she ran.

'I'm late, Lovejoy!' she gasped. She always says this. 'Hurry!'

'I don't have to,' I pointed out. 'I'm staying here. It's you that's going somewhere.'

'And I'm late! Goodbye, Henry darling. Be good!' We go through this rigmarole every time, saying the same things.

I don't mind, though it's unproductive.

She streaks off to collect her two children from our village
school, which is why I lodge Henry.

I wheeled Henry in and unfixed him. He got ready to
laugh. We have this joke. I opened his coat and peered.

'Nope. Still no hairs on your chest yet, Henry,' I said
sadly. He roared at that, his favourite and most hilarious
quip. He was still falling about when I carried him to the
divan. They never look heavy, do they? Henry's a crippling
welterweight.

'Let's see what she's put in for you today, sunbeam.' I
opened his bag. It comes fastened on his pram thing. We
looked at his teatime offering distastefully. 'Fancy it?' A
tin of baby food, a really neffie powdery stuff. We'd tried it
a couple of times at first but I think I made it wrong He
went off it after one spoonful. Two rusks and a little tin of
some tarry stuff were the rest of his ration, which he eyed
with hatred. You can't blame him because his food looks so
utterly boring. 'Then there's nothing for it, Cisco,' I told
him. 'Chips, sardines and . . . an *egg*!' I held it up to excited
applause.

I carry Henry about while I make his tea. It's not easy.
Women have hips and can simply hold spherical offspring
on their ledge. They've also got the fascinating knack of
somehow walking slanted. Men, being basically cylindrical,
have no ledge to speak of. It's tough, needing continuous
muscular effort. I natter about my day's work while I get
going.

'Another list of dazzling failures, Henry,' I told him. 'No
luck. But I saw a picture . . .' I explained what a clever
forgery Bexon had made. 'Some old geezer from Great
Hawkham.' Henry watched me open the tin of sardines, a
drool of saliva bouncing from his chin. 'What do you reckon?'
He said nothing, just pistoned his legs and ogled the grub.
'If I'd done a lovely forgery job like that I'd have found some
swine like Beck and sold it to him.'

Henry chuckled, clearly pleased at the idea of doing a
trawlie like Beck in the eye. Maybe he had an antique dealer's

chromosomes surging about in his little marrow. I peeled
two spuds and hotted the oil.

'Instead,' I went on, 'he paints in a wrong colour. Give-
away. And don't try telling me – ' I shook the peeler at
Henry warningly – 'that it was a simple mistake. It was
deliberate.' Saying it straight out made it seem even weirder.
I gave him the whole tale. At least Henry listens. Algernon's
not got half his sense. 'The more you think about it, Henry,'
I said seriously, 'the odder it becomes. Odderer and odderer.
Right?'

I put him down and gave him a ruler to chew while I fried
up. I told him about the golds. He tends to follow you round
the room with his eyes. I leave the kitchen alcove uncurtained
while I cook so I can keep an eye on my one and only ruler.
They're expensive.

I was prattling on, saying how I was hoping to pick up the
rest of Bexon's stuff from Dandy Jack, when the bell rang.
It's an old puller, 1814. (Incidentally, household wrought-
ironwork of even late Victorian vintage is one of the few
kinds of desirables you can still afford. It's becoming a serious
collectors' field. Decorative industrial ironwork will be the
next most sought-after. Don't say I haven't warned you.) I
wiped my hands and went into the hall. Janie's silhouette
at the frosted glass. Great. All I needed.

I rushed about hiding Henry's stuff and cursing under my
breath. The bloody push-chair wouldn't fold so I dragged it
into the main room and rammed it behind a curtain.

'This is all your fault,' I hissed at Henry. He was rolling
in the aisles again, thinking it another game. 'Look.' I
pushed my fist threateningly at his face. 'One sound out of
you, that's all. Just one sound.' It didn't do much good.
He was convulsed, cackling and kicking. I told him bitterly
he was no help but anything I say only sends him off into
belly laughs. He never believes I'm serious. Nothing else
for it. I went to the door.

'Hello, love.' My casual Lovejoy-at-ease image. A mild
but pleased surprise lit my countenance at seeing Janie
again so soon.

'You've been an age answering.' Janie gave me a kiss and tried to push past. I stood my ground. She halted, her smile dying. 'What's the matter, Lovejoy?'

'Matter? Nothing,' I said, debonair. I leant casually on the doorjamb all ready for a friendly chat.

Her eyes hardened. 'Have I called at the wrong time?' There was that sugary voice again.

'Er, no. Of course not.'

She stared stonily over my shoulder. 'Who've you got in there, Lovejoy?'

'In . . .?' I managed a gay light-hearted chuckle. 'Why, nobody. What on earth makes you think – ?'

'I go to all this trouble to get this box of rubbish from that filthy old man,' she blazed. 'And all the time you're –'

'Jack?' I yelped. 'Dandy Jack?'

'You horrid –'

'You found Dandy?' She was carrying an old cardboard shoe box. I took it reverently and carried it into the hall. I didn't notice Janie storm past.

I removed the lid carefully. There was the inevitable jam-jarful of old buttons (why the hell do people store buttons? Everybody's at it), a rusty tin of assorted campaign medals – expression of an entire nation's undying gratitude for four years of shelling in blood-soaked trenches – and a loose pack of old photographs held together by a rubber band. At the bottom were two worn but modern exercise books, cheap and pathetic. It really did look rubbish as Tinker Dill said. My heart plunged.

'Is that all, Janie?'

She was standing in the hall behind me, desperately trying to hold back a smile.

'I trust,' she said with pretended iciness, 'you've some perfectly reasonable explanation for your little friend in there?'

'I asked if this is everything,' I said sharply. Now she'd rumbled Henry it had to be first things first.

'There's a sketch,' she said. 'Dandy wouldn't sell it me. What's he called?'

'What did it look like?' I led her into the room. She picked Henry up to fawn on him. He gazed dispassionately back, probably wondering if the changed arrangements meant less grub all round.

'He wouldn't show me.'

I put the box down dejectedly. Disappointments come in waves. While I went back to doing Henry's tea she told me how she'd phoned Tinker Dill at the White Hart. He'd found where Dandy Jack was by then, somewhere over Ipswich way. She'd scooted along the main A12 coast road and cornered Dandy at a little antiques fair – the sort I had the money to go to. Once.

'I thought you'd got some woman in here,' she said.

'I see.' I went all hurt, obviously cut to the quick at such mistrust.

'Don't be offended, Lovejoy.' She came over and put her arms round me. 'I know I shouldn't be so suspicious.'

One up, I relented and explained about Henry. She thought he was delightful but was up in arms about his food.

'You're not giving him *that*!'

'What's wrong with it?' It looked all right to me. I poured the sardine oil on the egg to save waste.

'I thought it was yours, Lovejoy!'

'I've had mine.' I shook sauce on. Henry was all on the go.

'Dear God!' she exclaimed faintly. 'Does his mother know?'

'Well, actually,' I confessed, 'I chuck his powder away so she won't worry.' In fact I sometimes eat it to fill odd corners. Well, Henry's a gannet. I can't afford to feed us both properly and his own food tastes horrible. He's not so dumb.

Janie watched in horror as I fed him. All this mystique about feeding babies is rubbish. It's not difficult. You prop them up in some convenient spot and push bits towards their mouth. It opens. Slide it in lengthwise but remember to snatch your fingers back for further use. The inside looks soft and gummy but it works like a car cruncher. You have to concentrate. I mean, for example, it's not the sort of thing you can do while reading.

'His face gets some too,' I told Janie.

'So I noticed.' She looked stunned.

'It's all right. There's no waste. I scrape it off and put it in afterwards. It's his big finish.'

'My God. I feel ill.'

I was rather put out by Janie's reaction. Secretly I'd expected her to be full of admiration at my domestic skills. Admittedly he was beginning to get a bit smudged but that always happens. 'Try it. You can tell when he's finished,' I added. 'He starts spitting out.'

'What a mess. How does the poor little mite survive, Lovejoy?'

I ignored this. No meal's ever pretty, is it?

'Mind your manners.' Women are great critics, mainly when they see other people doing all right. It's mostly jealousy. 'I think he's full.' He was bulging but still moving impatiently. 'Time for pudding.'

'There's *more*?'

I'd got Henry two pieces of nougat, which would have to do for today's afters. I was embarrassed, Janie being there to see it wasn't done as properly as it should be. Puddings should be on a plate and everything with custard.

'Here. Unwrap it.' She took the nougat carefully. 'Hold it by one end and push a corner in his mouth,' I told her. 'Blot the dribbles as you go.'

Once she got going I took Bexon's pathetic belongings and began to rummage.

'Dandy said he'd give you the sketch if you'd scan for him,' Janie said, intent on Henry.

We were all sprawled on the divan.

'Dandy would,' I said bitterly. Scanning means examining supposed antiques to separate genius items from the junk. I hate doing it for others. It's something I never do normally, only when I'm broke. Dealers are always on at me to scan for them because I'm a divvie.

'Where does this infant put it all, for heaven's sake?' Janie exclaimed. She glanced across and saw I was flicking through one of the exercise books. 'You're wasting your time with that rubbish. I've looked.'

'Keep your mind on your job,' I said. I hate being interrupted.

It *was* rubbish. The old exercise books were just scribbled boredom, perhaps some fragments of a diary of the sort one always means to start but never quite gets round to. Dejected, I decided on the spur of the moment to teach Henry to read, which of course made Janie split her sides. I've tried before but Henry ate the highly-educational alphabetic book I got him. I showed him a line and said to concentrate. He seemed to be amused, but obligingly gaped at the pages while he noshed the nougat.

'I then caught the train back to Groundle Glen,' I intoned, pointing to the words as I read.

'They start learning on single letters, Lovejoy,' Janie criticized.

I reached obligingly for the other booklet. Maybe there was a set of capitals.

'I then caught the train back . . .' caught my eye. 'Hello. What have we here?' It was the ninth page about halfway down. 'That's the same sentence.'

I flipped the pages over. The sentence was identical, ninth page about halfway down.

'What is it, Lovejoy?'

'They say the same things.' And they did, both dog-eared exercise books. 'One's a copy of the other.'

The pages were ruled, obviously for school use. About twelve pages were filled with meticulous writing, ballpoint. I examined both books swiftly. The words were identical, word by word. Even the blot on page ten was carefully copied into the other book's tenth page. Each written sheet was signed 'James R. Bexon.' I picked a page at random. Page six. The other book's page six was identical, sentence for sentence, down to the last comma. Crazy.

'If you ask me he's a madman,' Janie said. 'Who writes a diary, then copies it out all over again?'

Maybe the old man *was* a maniac. The Restoration forgery

and its clever give-away leapt into my mind. Then again, I
thought carefully, maybe he wasn't.

'Bexon was no nutter. I've seen a painting he did.' I
checked Henry over. 'He'll need changing in a few minutes.'

While Henry whittled his way through the rest of his
nougat I read one of Bexon's exercise books. Absent replies
from me kept Janie going while she prattled away, how she'd
buy a town house for us and I could keep the cottage on if I
really wished. I was absorbed.

The diary was twelve pages, each page one day. A simple
sentimental old chap's account of how he had a holiday on the
Isle of Man. The dates were those of a couple of years
previously. It was all pretty dreary stuff. Well, almost all.

He'd rented a bungalow, walked about, visited places he'd
known once years before. He'd gone to the cinema and hadn't
thought much of it. Pub on a few occasions at night. He
complained about prices. Chats with taxi-drivers, boats
arriving and the harbour scenes. He'd gone about, seen a few
Viking tumuli and Celtic-British remains, watched the sea,
ridden on an excursion. Television shows, weather. It was
dead average and inordinately dull. Home on the Liverpool
ferryboat. Argument with a man over a suitcase. Train to
London, then bus out to Great Hawkham. That was it.

But there was this odd paragraph about the coffin. The
same in both books, in Bexon's careful handwriting:

I eventually decided to leave them all in the lead
coffin, exactly where I would remember best. I can't face
the publicity at my age – TV interviewers are such
barbarians. That is to say, some three hundred yards
from where I first dug down on to the mosaic terracing.
I may give a mixed few to the Castle. Let the blighters
guess.

Both diaries continued with chitchat, how the streets of
Douglas had altered after all these years and what changes
Millicent would have noticed. That was his wife. Apparently
they'd honeymooned on the Isle years before.

'It sounds so normal there,' Janie said into my ear. 'Even sensible.' She'd been reading over my shoulder. Careless old Lovejoy.

'Very normal,' I agreed. Then why did it feel so odd?

'What do you think he gave to the Castle?' she asked. Henry gave a flute-like belch about C-sharp.

'Heaven knows,' I said as casually as possible. Popplewell's face floated back. The cracked glass, the cards in disarray under the cloth. 'It could have been anything. Henry needs changing. The clean nappy's in his sponge-bag.'

I half filled a plastic bucket with water and undid him. It's easy as long as you stick to the routine. Unpin him on a newspaper, wash off what you can in the lavatory, chuck the dirty nappy in the bucket and wash him in a bowl. Then dry and dust. Five minutes.

'Eleanor takes the dirty one,' I explained.

I set about making some coffee. I keep meaning to buy filter-papers and a pot thing but so far I've never managed to get beyond that instant stuff.

'Lovejoy. Mine's different after all.' She'd been showing Henry how the pages turned. 'At the back.'

I came over.

'There's a drawing of a lady in mine. Yours hasn't.'

On the inside cover Bexon – or somebody – had painstakingly drawn a snotty crinolined lady riding in a crazy one-wheeled carriage, splashing mud and water as it went. A carriage with one wheel? It looked mad, quite crazy. The drawing was entitled 'Lady Isabella.' Pencil, Bexon's hand.

'There's no horse pulling it,' Janie pointed out. 'And only one wheel, silly old man.'

'Unless . . . Janie.' I fetched coffee over. Henry likes his strong. 'You said Dandy Jack has a separate sketch?'

'Yes. He said he'll see you tomorrow.'

We all thought hard.

'So if there's a message,' I reasoned aloud, 'it's in the words, not the sketch. The drawing's only a guide.'

'Oh, Lovejoy!' This made her collapse laughing. 'You're like a child! Are you sure it isn't a coded message from the

Black Hand Gang?'

'Cut that out,' I said coldly, but she was helpless laughing.

'Anyway, who in their right minds would make a coffin out of lead?' she gasped.

'You're right.' I gave in sheepishly and we were friends again.

But the Romans did.

You know, sometimes events gang up on you. Even if you decide against doing a thing, circumstances can force you to do it in the end. Ever had that sensation? The last time I'd had the same feeling somebody'd got themselves killed and the blood had splashed on me. For the rest of Henry's time we played on the divan. I'd invented this game where I make my hands into hollow shapes and Henry tries to find the way in.

I shivered. Janie looked at me a bit oddly. She switched the fire on, saying it was getting chilly. Henry began to snore, about an octave deeper than his belches.

'He sleeps for an hour now, till Eleanor comes,' I said. 'You'd better go just before she calls.' I didn't want my women customers believing the cottage was a den of vice.

I lay back and watched the ceiling.

I've been assuming up to now you know the facts, but maybe I'd better slip them in here. If you're a bag of nerves you should skip this bit. It gives me nightmares even yet, and I read it first as a lad at school.

Once upon a time our peaceful old land was still and quiet. All was tranquil. Farmers farmed. Cattle hung about the way they do. Folk didn't fight much. Fields, little towns, neat forests and houses, Thursday markets. Your actual average peace. Then one day an anchor splashed in the Medway, to the surprise of all.

The Romans had landed.

The legions, with Claudius the God Emperor bored stiff on his best war elephant, paraded down our High Street after dusting over the Trinovantes, boss tribe in those days. Our

town was called Colonia, capital of the new colony of Britain
under Governor-General Gaius Suetonius Paulinus.

It would have all gone smoothly, if only the Druids had
not got up his Roman nose. They skulked over to Anglesey,
off the coast of Wales, almost as if Rome could be ignored.
Well, you can imagine. Suetonius was peeved and set off
after them, leaving (here it comes) Britain in the hands of
tax gatherers. Usual, but unwise, because Claudius was a
real big spender and had left millions for the tribal kings as
a gesture of goodwill. The politicians showed up and pinched
the money. Sound familiar? They had a ball – especially the
night they raped the daughters of a certain lady called
Boadicea.

Now Boadicea was no local barmaid. She happened to be
the Queen of the Iceni, a tough mob. Breasts seethed in the
Iceni kingdom. And, remember, Suetonius was away in
Anglesey with his legions, a detail the arrogant conquerors
forgot.

It was all suddenly too much for the bewildered British
tribes. One dark day the terrible Iceni rose. The whole of
eastern England smouldered as the Roman settlements were
annihilated crunch by savage crunch. The famous Ninth
Legion strolled out from Lincoln innocently intending to
chastise the local rabble, a shovel to stop an avalanche. The
thousands of legionaries died in a macabre lunatic battle in
the dank forests. St Albans was obliterated in a single
evening's holocaust. The outposts and the river stations were
snuffed as Boadicea's grim blue-painted hordes churned
southwards, until only the brand new Roman city of Colonia
was left. Catus the Procurator skipped to Gaul in a flash,
promising legions which never came. Politicians.

There was nothing left but the smouldering forests, the
waiting city, and silence. Then the spooks began. The
statue of Victory tumbling to the ground and swivelling its
sightless stone eyes ominously away from Rome. Omens
multiplied. Rivers ran red. Air burned. Statues wailed in
temples. I won't go on if you don't mind. You get the
picture.

Finally, one gruesome dark wet dawn Boadicea's warmen erupted from the forests, coming at a low fast run in their tens of thousands. The Temple of Jupiter, with the Roman populace crammed inside, was burned. The rest were slaughtered in the streets. The city was razed. Boadicea jauntily crucified seventy thousand people, Roman and Briton alike, and nobody survived. It's called patriotism.

In the nick of time Suetonius miraculously returned to evacuate London, shoving everybody south of the Thames while Boadicea burned London and everywhere else she could think of. See what I mean, about women never giving up. Naturally, Rome being Rome, Suetonius made a come-back and the British Queen took poison after her great defeat, woman to the last.

I'd always accepted the story at its face value, but now I couldn't help wondering about something which had never struck me before.

Hadn't Suetonius been a long time coming back?

Nowadays our locals say to newcomers, 'Don't dig below the ash, will you? The ash is so good for the roses. And there's bits of bone, too. Calcium and phosphorus. We're quite famous for our roses hereabouts.' It's such good advice to gardeners.

I don't do any gardening.

Janie went in the nick of time. Eleanor collected Henry, now awake and singing with his foot in his mouth. I'm really proud of that trick, but Janie said they all do it. I waved from the front door.

I cleared up and got the map. The Isle of Anglesey is about half a mile from the Welsh coast. Thomas Telford even flung a bridge over the narrow Menai Straits. (Incidentally, Telford's engraved designs are worth far more nowadays than the paper they're printed on. They're hardly impressionistic but give me first choice of any you get.) One old historian, Polydore Vergil, always said Suetonius invaded the Isle of Man, but he was an erratic Italian everybody said was a nut anyway. There is ever. a belief that Suetonius had with him the famous Gemini Legion, but that must be wrong as well.

Augustus Caesar once received a delegation from a far country and is reputed to have whispered behind his hand to an aide: 'Are they worth conquering?' The country happened to be Ceylon, Sri Lanka, which for size could dwarf Rome any day of the week. The point is that the ancient Romans were distinctly cool. And one of the coolest was Suetonius, that dour, unsmiling, decisive and superb soldier whose tactical judgement, however grim, was unswervingly accurate.

As the evening drew on I tried to light a fire but the bloody wood was wet. I switched on the electric again instead. The birds outside had shut up. Only the robin was left on a low apple branch. My hedgehogs were milling about for nothing, rolling from side to side like fat brown shoppers.

Had the might of Rome been paralysed by a stretch of water you can spit over? Was Suetonius held up by a few Druids booing on the other side? History says yes. This old chap Bexon was telling me no.

I gazed at the garden till it was too dark to see.

CHAPTER VI

NEXT MORNING I shaved before seven. I had some cereal in powdered milk and fed the robin my last bit of cheese. I went to have a word with Manton and Wilkinson, gave them their groundsel.

'Now, Manton,' I demanded as it noshed its greenery sitting on my arm, 'what's all this Roman jazz?'

It wisely said nothing, knowing there was more to come. 'The old man leaves two diaries. But why two?'

Wilkinson flew on me for his share.

'If he was crackers, let's forget it, eh?' They hesitated suspiciously. 'On the other hand, curators may be duckeggs but Popplewell can tell genuine Roman antiques, coins or otherwise. Right?' They closed up along my arm, interested now. 'Bexon's coins being genuine, pals, what can there possibly be, I wonder, stuck in an old lead coffin in some well-remembered spot in the Isle of Man?'

We thought hard.

'And who should benefit better,' I demanded, 'than Lovejoy Antiques, Inc.?'

Wilkinson fluffed out, pleased. Manton looked sceptical.

'Don't be so bloody miserable,' I told Manton angrily, 'just because I haven't the fare to get there. You're always critical.'

I shoved them on to a branch and shut their flight door. Both were looking sceptical now.

'I can get some money,' I snapped. 'Don't you worry. I'll have the sketch *and* the fare from Dandy. I'll be back. You see.'

By my front door the robin was cackling with fury. He was quite full but battling to keep the sparrows from the cheese he didn't want. Very feminine, robins.

The bus was on time. In my innocence I thought it a good omen.

Dandy Jack's is a typical lock-up, a shop front and two rooms. The clutter held miscellaneous modern tarted up as old, a brass 1890 bedstead (worth more than you'd think, incidentally), pottery, wooden furniture and some ornamentals plus a small gaggle of portabilia in a glass-fronted cabinet.

A few people milled about inside, mostly grockles (dealers' slang: tourists, not necessarily foreign, derogatory) and the odd dealer. Big Frank Wilson from Suffolk was there. He gave me a nod which said, nothing worth a groat. I shrugged. He's a Regency silver by desire, William IV furniture by obligation, and undetected bigamist by the skin of his teeth, as if scratching a quid in the antiques game isn't enough nightmare to be going on with. Jenny from the coast (she's

tapestries and Georgian household items) was painstakingly
examining a crate of porcelain. She and Harry Bateman were
desperately trying to stock up their new shop on East Hill.
They'd badly overspent lately to catch the tourist wave, but
their stuff was too 'thin' (dealer's slang again: much low
quality spiced with only rare desirable items).

I pushed among the driftwood – not being unkind, but I
really had seen better antiques on Mersea beach.

'Hello, Lovejoy.'

'What's new, Dandy?'

'Bloody near everything,' he grinned. I had to laugh.
'Message for you from Bill Fairdale. He says to call in.'

Bill was from my village, rare manuscripts and antique
musical instruments. The only trouble was that his rare
illuminated manuscripts are a bit too good to be true. The
sheepskin parchments pegged out drying in his garden do
very little to restore a buyer's confidence. He's even been
known to ask a visitor's help in mixing 'mediaeval' monks'
egg-tempera pigments with an unfinished carpet page of
Lindisfarne design in clear view, only to offer the same visitor
the completed 'antique' next day. He's very forgetful.

'Has his handwriting improved any?'

Dandy Jack fell about at my merry quip. Once, Bill
actually acquired a genuine love-letter from Horatio to his
dearest Emma Hamilton. Nobody else dared believe Bill. I
bought it for a song. That's the danger of forging too much
and not doing it well enough. A happy memory.

'He's got something right up your street.'

It was probably that bone flute, cased, sold in Bury the
previous week. I'd heard Bill had gone up. Potter, the great
old London maker, if Tinker was right. Very desirable. I
said nothing, nodding that I'd pop in.

'I want a favour, Dandy. A certain sketch.'

His eyes gleamed. 'Come back here.' We withdrew into
his inner sanctum. He offered to brew up but my stomach
turned. That left him free to slosh out a gill of gin. Dandy was
permanently kaylied. He perched on a stool opposite his

crammed sink, shoddy and cheerful, a very rum mixture.
Where I think in terms of mark-up, Dandy thinks booze.
I've never seen him sober in n years, where n is a very large
finite integer. He has a good eye, sadly wasted. For some
reason he believes there's no way of actually learning of the
beautiful objects we handle, but then you don't get libraries
in pubs.

'An old chap called Bexon. You got his stuff at Gimbert's
auction.'

'Your young lady spoke to me yesterday. I gave her the
box.'

'That's only rubbish, but he was an old friend and –'

'Yeah, yeah,' he said. 'Never mind all that, Lovejoy.'

I said, desperate now, 'She said you had a sketch he did.'

'That sketch'll cost you.'

'How much?'

'Do me a scan and you can have it free.'

'Get lost,' I groaned. It always came down to this, from
fellow dealers too useless to do their own work.

'Go on, Lovejoy. You're a divvie. Help me out.'

I had enough trouble without feeling sympathy. 'Commission?' I tried hopelessly, but the wretch was grinning.
He knew he had me and shook his head.

'Scan my stuff or you don't even get to see Bexon's
picture.'

'All right,' I gave in bitterly. 'Anyhow, your commission
wouldn't keep me in pobs.'

'My stuff's in that crate. I'll fetch it.'

He dragged in a tea-chest of miscellaneous porcelain,
followed by Jenny Bateman protesting she'd not finished
looking.

'Hard luck,' Dandy told her, pushing her out. All heart.

'Is this it?' I hate scanning junk.

'A job lot. There's a ton of valuable stuff in there, Lovejoy.'
The eternal cry of mankind since Adam dressed.

I sat wearily, waiting for the mystic mood to come over
my mind. A divvie always suffers. Having friends irritates
me sometimes. I closed my eyes and stilled. Sounds receded.

The world slipped into silence and all feeling fell gradually into the distance.

Divvie? Maybe from the old word 'diviner', as in water, but who knows? It's slang for anybody who can guess right about a thing without actually knowing. Some people have it for gems or paintings, others for racehorses, thoroughbred dogs or scenic design, a precious knack that goes separate from any learning. I'm an antiques divvie. And, incidentally, I'm the very best there is.

I've tried asking other divvies how they know, what actually happens. Some say they are 'told', others say it's a feeling. Water diviners say it's a foot-tingle or a twisting stick. To me it's a kind of bell, and it rings in my chest. My knowledge, on the other hand, only tells me what an antique is. But my bell just rings for truth. And look, folks – good news. *Every*body alive has this knack for *some*thing. Maybe not for antiques or diamonds, but for *some*thing. Nobody's been left out. It's superb news really, because you're included too. You. All you need to find is what your particular gift is for. You might actually be the most original and creative porcelain or furniture expert without knowing it. If you don't already know you're being dreadfully wasted.

The way I do it's to get close as possible, look and then maybe a light touch if that's not damaging to the antique. Always remember to leave antiques alone. Never fondle, clean, wipe, polish or brush. And I don't mean 'hardly ever', like in the song. Never is never. Leave antiques alone. *Never* scrape, improve, smooth, fill in or dissect. Remember that all antiques really are Goya, Chippendale, Sheraton or Michelangelo until proved otherwise. If you say that yours aren't, I'd like to know what makes you so sure.

Dandy Jack was very considerate as I worked, tiptoeing in like a steamhammer for another pint of *White Horse* and having a hell of a row with a customer over the price of a modern vase he swore was Ming. Honestly, my head was throbbing by the time I finished. I was finished.

'Dandy,' I called. 'Done.' He dropped a pile of books with a crash and reeled in.

'Prime stuff, eh, Lovejoy?'

'Not bad.'

He grinned at the three objects on the table and nodded wisely.

'Bloody rubbish,' he agreed. 'I knew it was all valuable except for them.'

'*They're* the good stuff, Dandy.' I rose, stretching. 'Chuck the rest.'

'Eh?' He glared into the heaped chest. 'All this? Duff?'

'Duff,' I nodded. 'Have you any grub?'

'Margaret fetched these over for you. She'll call back.' He held out a brown paper bag towards me, two whist pies and an Eccles cake.

I sat and ate, recovering, while I explained the three pieces to him. He listened quite mystified.

'Candle snuffer, Worcester.' I nodded at the smallest item, a tiny bust of a hooded Victorian woman. 'It's 1864, give or take a year.' I hate them. Collectors don't.

'Pity it's not earlier.' He peered blearily in my direction. Good old Dandy. Always wrong, not even just usually.

There was a shaving mug shaped like a white monkey, grotesque with an exquisite glaze. I honestly don't know what the Victorians were thinking about, some of the things they made. The bowl was the precious item, though Dandy Jack could see nothing special about it. Like I say, some people can hear fish squeak. Others wouldn't hear a train in a tunnel. He said it looked like Spode, when it was clear Daniel, early 1830s. I tried not to stare at the lovely thing, but the elevated tooled bird motifs in gold, with curves resting on feet of bright blossoms, dragged my eyes. Blues screamed at pinks, greens and shimmering maroons in a cascade of colour. It sounds garish, but it really is class, and incredibly *under*priced at today's prices, though that only means for a second or two. Dandy was more than a little narked that the rest was mostly junk.

'Bexon's sketch, Dandy,' I reminded him. Scanning stuff really takes it out of me, why I don't know. After all, it's only sitting and looking.

'Here.'

I took the drawing from Dandy's grimy hands. Bong went my chest. Simple, stylish, very real, a tiny pencil caricature with some colour. It was her again. The artist had pencilled her name in, Lady Isabella. She was the same snooty lass, doubtless made to look starchier than in real life, riding in a high absurd one-wheeled carriage with idiotically long shafts and no horse. The wheel splashed water as it rolled through the streets. It was probably one of those crazy skits they got very worked up about before steam radio and television blunted pens and sense.

'Is that all?'

'Yes. Straight up, Lovejoy. What is it?'

'Looks like a caricature. Genuine Burne-Jones.'

'Genuine?' A long pause, during which Greed crept ominously in. 'I'll give you the rubbish for nothing, Lovejoy,' Dandy said. Oh-ho, I thought. Here we go.

'You said – '

He crouched into his whining position. 'Look, Lovejoy – '

'Bastard.' I should have known he'd let me down, though Dandy Jack's no worse than the rest of us.

'No, honestly, Lovejoy. I didn't mean I'd give you the drawing as well.'

'Sure, sure,' I said bitterly. I was unable to resist one final glance at the Burne-Jones. He was a Victorian painter, a bit of a lad who did a few dozen caricatures to amuse Maria Zambaco, a gorgeous Greek bird he shacked up with for three years before 1870. Maybe Maria put him up to sketching one of her bosom friends.

Dandy offered me a drink but I staggered out into the oxygen layer, as broke as when I'd arrived. That's typical of some days in this trade.

There was a blue Lagonda occupying two-thirds of the High Street.

'At last, Lovejoy.'

'Oh. Hello.' I really was pleased to see her. It's the way it gets.

'Well?' She nodded at Dandy Jack's window. 'Did you get the picture?'

'Er, no,' I said lamely. 'He, er, he wanted to hang on to it – '

'You mean he won't give it to you?' she fired back. She stepped out angrily. 'You look drained. Have you scanned for him?'

'Yes, but – '

'Right. Wait here.' I caught hold of her.

'No, love. I'm not up to a battle today – '

'You're a *fool*, Lovejoy,' she stormed. 'No wonder you're penniless. You let everybody take advantage – '

I turned away, meaning to walk off because people were beginning to stare. And this lovely blonde was standing beside me, breathless and pretty.

'Excuse me, please,' she said. A picture, her lovely face anxious and her deep eyes troubled. 'Are you Lovejoy? Can I have a word, please?' There she stood, nice, worried, determined. Her smile was brilliant, full of allure. Women really have it. I decided I needn't walk off after all.

'Yes, dear?' Janie cooed. She drummed her fingers on her elbows, smiling.

Now, women don't like each other. Ever noticed that? If two meet, you can see them both instantly thinking (a) what's this bitch *really* up to? (b) thank God her clothes are a mess, and, following on pretty smartly, (c) isn't it time this ghastly female was leaving?

'I heard you're trying to find an old picture, sold at Gimbert's auction, belonging to a Mr Bexon?'

I gaped. You just don't ask that sort of thing in this trade. It's like asking a Great Power which other nations it really hates at a peace conference. I suddenly caught sight of Beck stepping inside Dandy Jack's. I instantly realized why Dandy hadn't kept his promise about the sketch. Beck had heard me talking to Tinker Dill and was now arriving to buy the worthwhile stuff.

'Eh?' I responded cautiously.

'I want it,' she explained. 'I'm Nichole Bexon.' She took hold of my arm confidingly, better and better. 'I'm trying to find my uncle's things. A sketch, mainly. And two diaries. I was . . . away, you see, when his things were . . . taken to a sale. My sister cleared the house. It's so unfortunate. I heard you were trying to find them as well. A neighbour.'

Good old Mary. That's the trouble. In these remote little East Anglian villages rumour does a faster job than the new electric telegraph.

'Ah, sorry, love,' I said, smiling. 'You'll have to try Dandy Jack.' I nodded at his emporium. And, innocently thinking to get one back on poor old Dandy for changing our agreed deal in mid-scratch, I added malevolently, 'He has the things you want. He won't let them go, I'm afraid. I've offered him the earth.'

'Oh, *dear*.' She looked almost in tears.

'Is there no way at all?' this chap asked. He'd been listening. I dragged my eyes from the lovely Nichole and noticed him.

Nichole seemed to have brought her tame male along, a real weed in Savile Row gear. The fool wore a city titfer. Honestly, some people. A hat in the Arcade's like wearing a coronet at football. You know how some couples are just not suited? Well, here was the archetypal mismatch. Her: lovely, cool, gleaming, luscious, a pure swinger. And him: neat, precise, waistcoat complete with gold watch-chain (not antique, the pathetic slob), rimless specs, glittering black shoes, and a Rolls the size of a tram. A worrier, accountant if ever I saw one. How a pill like him ever got her . . .

'No,' I said. Luckily Janie had reached (c) by now.

'Mr Lovejoy is a well-known art expert,' she cut in crisply, 'and even he hasn't been successful. Sorry we can't help.'

She slipped into the Lagonda. It was sneering at the Rolls, nose to nose. The Rolls wasn't really up to noticing riffraff for the moment and gazed into the distance. She gunned the engine. They got the message.

'Then what shall I do?' the beautiful Nichole said. 'I must have Uncle's things back. They're nothing much. But he'd have wanted me to have them.' She actually twiddled a button, one of the remaining few, on my coat.

I cleared my throat. 'Er, well . . .'

'Please?' Flutter, flutter.

Women intrigue me. No, they really do. Say a woman wants ten yards of lovely Thai silk. She'd expect to have to pay for it, right? Same as a bloke wanting tobacco. Everybody knows it – you have to pay. But mention antiques and suddenly everyone wants something for nothing. Or, at the very least, a Constable or Rembrandt for a quid or two. And make no mistake, women are the worst. A man will laugh ruefully, say no hard feelings. But a woman won't. You get the whole bit, the smoulder, the come-on, derision, the wheedle, and finally everything they've got thrown into the fray. Born dealers, women. You have to be careful.

'Can you not help, please?' Her chap tried to smile ingratiatingly. 'You've been highly recommended to us, Lovejoy, as an antiques dealer. I would make it particularly worth your while. If it's a question of money . . .' he said.

The town stilled. The universe hesitated. The High Street froze. Nobody in the known world breathed for a few lifetimes as that delightful scent of money hung in the air.

He really seemed quite pleasant after all. Charming in fact. Then Janie hauled me, literally yanking me off balance so I tumbled back into the Lagonda.

'So sorry,' she called out brightly, swinging me round and slamming the door. I grappled to lower the window.

'My card,' the chap said. 'Phone me. Edward Rink.' We were off like a Brands Hatch start. I sulked most of the way home holding his engraved card.

It'd soon be time for Algernon's test. What a bloody day. Diddled by Dandy Jack, frogged by Beck and no nearer understanding the Bexon business, and now Algernon.

I'd reluctantly cleared away by the time Algernon arrived.

In he came, cheerful and gormless. In his own way he's an entire miracle. A trainee dealer for six long months and still thinks Fabergé eggs are crusty chocolate.

'Good evening, Lovejoy!'

'How do.' I stared morosely into his beaming face. Why was somebody who gets me so mad so bloody pleased to see me every time?

'Let us anticipate that my efforts will meet with your approval this evening!' the nerk said. He reached out and actually wrung my hand. He stripped a layer of motor-cycle leathers and left them heaped in the hallway. 'I am all keyed up!' he exclaimed.

'Did you read Wills?'

'Certainly, Lovejoy! And the brass instrument book. And – ' he blushed – 'the jokey book all over again. I appear to have been quite taken in!'

He laughed merrily as I led the way into the main room without a word. You can see why Algernon gets me down. He's always like this.

'On the table, Algernon,' I cut in sourly, 'are several objects.'

'Right! Right!' He sprang at them, oily fingers at the ready. I caught him in mid-air and put him back.

'I shall cover all but one with a dark cloth, Algernon. You have to identify and price whichever's exposed. Okay?'

'Ah!' He raised a finger delightedly. 'Your identification game!'

I fetched the carriage clock across.

'You're allowed one minute. Remember?'

'Of course, Lovejoy! How absolutely right to be so precise – !'

I lifted him out of his chair by the throat, struggling for iron control.

'Algernon,' I hissed. 'Silence. Clam. Shut up.'

'Very well! I follow exactly!' He frowned and glared intently. Then he closed his eyes to concentrate, heaven knows what with. Your modern intellectual at bay. I watched this performance wearily. I suppose it's meant to be like I do when I'm scanning, the idiot. He opened his eyes, thrilled. 'Right! Ready, Lovejoy!'

'No,' I said.

He concentrated hard. 'Ah! The lights!'

'Good, good, Algernon.'

We lit two candles and the oil lantern before switching the electric off. I suppose there's no point in rubbing these details in too much or you'll not read on but I have to say it. You'll all have made this mistake. What's the point in looking at Old Master paintings by neon or tungsten-filament glare? Dolphins don't do well in pasture land. Stick them in an ocean and you'll never see any living thing so full of beautiful motion. Give antiques the kind of light they're used to and you're halfway there. And for heaven's sake space the flames about the room. Never cluster natural flamelight. It's no wonder people get antiques wrong.

I sat myself down and took the time. I uncovered one small silver object. He prowled about, peering at and over it, for all the world like an amateur sleuth. I observed this weird performance with heartbreak.

'Time's up.' I covered it. This is the nightmarish bit.

We sat in silence broken only by my drumming fingers, the tick of the clock and the squeaks Algernon's pores made as sweat started on his fevered brow.

'Go on, Algernon,' I encouraged. 'Any ideas?'

'Erm.' He glanced to judge the distance to the door. 'Erm. It looks . . . sort of . . . well, a *spoon*, Lovejoy.'

'Precious metal? Plastic? Wood? Gilt?'

'Erm . . . silver?' he guessed desperately. 'Caddy spoon?'

'Certainly.' He beamed with relief. Examine antique silver in the correct light and even Algernon can spot it. 'Yes.' I even smiled. 'By . . ?' He didn't know. 'Three giant steps back, Algernon.' His face fell a mile while I rose and uncovered all the little silvers.

He missed Hester Bateman, whizz-kid of 1785. He missed the stylish Sam Massey, 1790, and the appealing work of Charles Haugham, 1781. He had omitted to learn a table of hallmarks, and thought that a superb artistic piece of brilliant silverwork from Matthew Linwood's gnarled hands was plastic.

'Compare this lovely silver shellfish,' I ended brokenly, 'with the three in the museum tomorrow. His best work's 1808 to 1820. Look up the history of tea drinking. I'll ask you tomorrow why they never drank tea with milk or even sugar in the seventeenth century, and suchlike background gems.'

'Yes, Lovejoy,' he said dejectedly.

'And go round the shops that sell modern spoons. Right?' He opened his mouth. 'Never mind why,' I said irritably. 'Just do it.' I keep telling him there's no other way to learn how to spot crap, gunge and dross. I saw his blank face and wearily began to explain for the hundredth time.

You teach a beginner about antiques by seeing if he has any feeling for craftsmanship. It's everything. Antiques aren't alien, you see. They're extensions of mankind through time. It may seem odd that love instilled into solid materials by loving craftsmanship is the only creation of Mankind to defeat Time, but it's true. In holding antiques you reach across centuries and touch the very hands of genius. I don't count plastic cups or ball-point pens stamped out by a machine. Fair's fair. Man is needed.

First you look round the local furniture stores to see new furniture. Then lampshades. Then shoes. Then modern mail-order catalogues. Then mass-produced prints and paintings. Then books. Then tools. Then carpets. Then . . . It's a terrible, frightening experience. Why do you think most modern furniture's so ghastly? And why's so much art mere dross? And fashions abysmal? And sculpture grotty? Because of Lovejoy's Law of Loving – a tin can is a tin can is a tin can, but a tin can made with loving hands glows like the Holy Grail. It deserves to be adored because the love shines through. QED, fans. Most of today's stuff could last a thousand years and never become antique simply because love's missing. They've not got it. The poor things were made without delight, human delight.

Therefore, folks, into your modern shopping precincts
for a three-day penance of observation. And at every single
item stop and ask yourself the only question which ever
mattered: 'Does that look as though it was made with love,
from love, to express love?' Your first day will be bad. Day
Two'll be ruinous. Your third day will be the worst day of
your life because you will have probably seen nothing which
gets a Yes. Score zero. Nothing you see will have been made
with love. It is grim – unbelievably, horrendously and
frighteningly grim.

Now comes Day Four. Go, downhearted and dismal by
now, into your local museum. Stand still quite a while.
Then drift about and ask yourself the same question as you
wander. *Now* what's the score? You already know the
answer.

It's the only way to learn the antique trade. Look at
rubbish, any cheap modern crud on sale now. You'll finish
up hooked for life on what other people call antiques, but
what I call love. Laugh if you like, but antiques are just
things made full of love. The hands that produced them, in
factories like flues from Hell, by some stupendous miracle of
human response and feeling managed to instil in every
antique a deep hallmark of love and pride in that very act of
loving.

That's why I'm an antique dealer. What I can't understand is why everybody else isn't.

I ended my explanation. Algernon was goggling. He's
heard it umpteen times.

Algernon failed that whole evening miserably. He failed
on the precious early Antoine Gaudin photograph I'd
borrowed. He failed on a rare and valuable 'Peacock's New
Double Dissection and History of England and Wales', 1850,
by Gall and Inglis of Paternoster Square ('What a tatty old
jigsaw, Lovejoy!'), and a child's George IV complete teaset,
almost microscopically small – the teapot's a quarter of an
inch long – brilliantly carved from hardwood and very, very

costly. Of this last Algernon soared to his giddiest height yet, asking brightly, 'What kind of plastic is it, Lovejoy?'

I slung him out after that, unable to go on. I'd not laid a finger on him. Willpower.

The world would have to wait with bated breath for Algernon's judgement of paired water ewers, Wedgwood and Bentley polished black basalt, which I'd borrowed to include in his test. But I was especially keen not to hear him on the film transparency of a tortuously elaborate weapon by that genius Minamoto Tauguhiro. I couldn't bear hearing him say it was a fancy dagger for slicing bread.

He donned his motor-bike leathers. I pushed him forcibly into the dark garden.

'I expect you're letting me off early because I was doing so well,' he said merrily. He believes every word.

'Sure, sure.'

'Will you please inform Uncle how successful I was with those sugar ladles?' he asked at the door. 'He will be so hugely delighted.' His uncle pays me for teaching the goon.

I wonder where all my patience comes from, honestly. 'I'll tell him you're making your usual progress, Algernon.'

'*Thank* you, Lovejoy!' he exclaimed joyously. 'You know, eventually I anticipate to be almost as swift as your good self – '

I shut the door. There's a limit.

Normally I'd stroll up to the pub to wash all that Algernon-induced trauma out of my mind. This particular night I was too late to escape. There was a knock at my door.

'Nichole. What – ?'

'Kate,' she said. Her smile made it the coldest night of the year. 'The wicked sister.'

'Oh, come in.' She was slightly taller than Nichole but the same colouring.

'No, thank you. You're Lovejoy?' I nodded. You feel so daft just standing holding a door open, don't you? You can't shut it and you can't go out or back in. 'I want to

ask you not to help my sister,' she said carefully. 'She . . .
her judgement is sometimes, well, not too reliable, you
understand.'

'I haven't helped her,' I explained. 'She wanted a sketch
and some –'

'Some rubbish,' Kate cut in. 'Uncle was a kindly man,
but given to making up fanciful tales. I don't want my sister
influenced.'

'About his other belongings,' I began hopefully.

'Very ordinary furniture, very cheap, very modern,' she
stated, cold as ever. 'And now all sold. You do understand
about Nichole?'

'Sure,' I said. She said goodnight and drove into the
darkness in an elderly Mini. I sighed and locked up. I
seemed to be alienating the universe.

I've told you all this the way I have because it was the last
quiet time there was in the whole business. I realized during
the rest of that evening that something was rapidly going
wrong in my humdrum normal life. Looking back, I don't
see to this day what else I could have done.

The murder honestly wasn't my fault, and I don't think
the other deaths were, either. Honest.

CHAPTER VII

JANIE HURTLED IN early next morning. Her husband had
been called away to the city for the day, the early train.
It wasn't any good, though. The feeling was still on me.
I sent her packing. She was wild and refused to go but I
picked her up and chucked her outside in the porch. She
even tried scratching my eyes as I slammed the door. To be
fair, I hinted I'd work to do, quite politely. She even rushed
round to the back. I reached the bolt first, pulled the
curtains and with Janie banging on the door hauled up my
paving. She'd be mad for days. She'd brought a picnic

basket, as if there's time for that sort of thing.

Down in the priest's hole the cardboard box's contents
seemed even more pathetic. I unfolded the small ledged
Regency table, a godsend in these days of wobbling warping
junk, and poured the buttons out. I started on them with a
lens and prism. It takes time. The photos were 1930s, old
churches, a beach, a boarding-house. An hour later I reached
the first medal, the old 'ration gong' of the War. Ordinary.
There seemed not a single hint among the lot.

I have twenty shoeboxes full of what history got up to,
but I couldn't find a trace of any Lady Isabella. The books
showed nothing special under the microscope, no microdots,
no secret inks, no oiled-in watermarks. I cleared up and got
ready to leave. The box was better left in the hidden cellar.
When I came out into the garden I found Janie had driven off
in a huff. Now I'd have to walk up into the village and wait
for our single market bus about noon. Why have women no
patience? I had no more cheese for the robin. I borrowed
some budgie seed and told them I owed it.

'The message is in the words,' I told the robin. 'And
they're only a list of places, right? All you need to do is
visit each place and you'd find where he's put the Roman
stuff. It should be obvious. Easy.'

Easy. Even if they were in the Isle of Man, and me only
with the bus fare to town. I'd walk back. Still, things were
definitely looking up for Lovejoy Antiques, Inc. At least I'd
a ray of hope now.

'I'll go and do a bit to the painting,' I told the robin.

Inevitably the phone rang.

'Lovejoy. I hope you don't mind?' Nichole.

'No. Glad to hear you.'

We held the pause. There's a sudden affinity between two
people sometimes when nothing really needs saying.

'I . . . I was ringing to ask your help. The sketch and the
rubbish from Uncle James.'

'Dandy Jack has them,' I told her carefully. 'I did some
work for him but he wouldn't part with the sketch.'

'I see,' she said icily. 'Are you sure your girl-friend

hasn't bought them for you?'

'No, look, love,' I was saying when she slammed the phone down.

I went out to work on my painting, whistling. She'd come round.

In the back garden near where Manton and Wilkinson fly I have this workshop. The big work of the moment was transferring a genuine 1774 Wilson painting to a new canvas. I goggled up, apron, mask and all. Janie laughs at my garb, but what's wrong with being not stupid?

When your superb antique painting's rotting to hell you must act. If you're a beginner, take it to an expert for advice. This painting's Richard Wilson, possibly the most underrated grand master. I'd found it being used to pad the back seat of an old Austin Ruby. The bloke thought I was off my head. He was the sort who would chuck away a First Folio and keep the string.

If a painting's canvas is literally falling to bits you've a choice, of simply (figure of speech, that – it's really very complicated) rebacking with a new canvas, or of lifting the old delicate work of art *off* the canvas and putting it on a new one. This isn't fraud. It saves a precious thing for another three centuries. It's therefore essential. My method is to stretch small-grain gauze until it's even, then stick it carefully to the painting's face. (My glue's secret. Find your own.) Several layers of paper tissue stuck to the gauze, and you now remove the painting, still on its decrepit canvas, from the wood stretcher. After days of drying, tissue-gauze surface downwards, and, on an absolutely even bench, in the right wooden frame to hold it still, you gently caress the old canvas away. It takes maybe three months to a year's sparetime caressing. It's not much. For a beautiful luscious – or even an ugly – antique oil painting it's worth every second. You need to remove the debris as you go. Some use pumice stone, others special flat-face drills. I use me and a special powder I make up myself. Then stick a new canvas on any way you like. Tip: if you ever do it, be careful to announce the painting's been re-canvassed or you'll not get a

bean for it. You can't blame the honest old public for being
worried if they see yesterday's date stamped on the canvas
of a genuine Constable. They're a very shrewd and suspicious
mob.

I was caressing away when somebody coughed at my elbow.

'There's a bell at the gate,' I said angrily, not looking
up.

'So sorry.' Great. Nichole's bloke, your actual Edward
Rink.

Eventually I rose, stepped carefully back from the bench
and turned. He was there, hesitant but determined. He must
have left his car in the lane.

'I called in Dandy Jack's early this morning.'

'Survive, did he?'

'He says he sold the sketch.'

'That's life,' I said, wondering if Dandy actually had.

He pulled out a gold case and did the fire ritual. No
kind offer of a fag to one of the world's workers.

'To a young lady.' His bottled eyes quivered indignantly.
'I think it was your young lady, Lovejoy.' Two little discs
of red glowed on his cheeks.

'Oh?' Typical of Dandy. I bet he'd really sold it to Beck.
Dealers are rarely truthful about these innocent details.
I decided not to say this, and to mention nothing about
Nichole's phone call.

'And the diaries Nichole's uncle wrote. I understand from
Dandy Jack you have them.'

'You do?' I was thinking, what the hell's going on?

'Now, Lovejoy.' He was trying so hard. I watched
curiously. 'I'm willing to pay for them. You – you have no
car, I believe.'

'True.'

'Nichole treasures her uncle's things.' He swallowed
shakily. There were beads of sweat on his forehead. 'I'm
willing to buy you a popular car. In exchange.'

'What's so precious about them, Rink?'

'Nichole's sister. She . . .' his voice hardened. 'They
don't see quite eye to eye. Kate's often . . . unpleasant to

Nichole. It happens in some families. I heard she called on you last night, Lovejoy.'

I eyed him. How did he know that?

'Yes. And practically told me to get stuffed. Anyway, it's a lot of money for two old scrap-books, isn't it?'

'Lovejoy,' he said, whitening round his lips. 'You *will* let me have them. And obtain your girl-friend's co-operation. Or else.'

'Eh?' I couldn't believe my ears.

'You heard, Lovejoy.' The pillock mistook my amazement for awe.

'Are you trying to – ?'

'Threaten?' His little eyes flicked round the garden, the shed. 'Yes.'

'You? *Me?*' I asked fascinated. I'd seen some rum customers in my time, but this . . .

'You.' He flung his cigarette down and stood on it – note, not stamped or ground it in with his heel. Simply stood. I should have been thinking at the time. I'd have seen what sort of a swine he was. 'You have a choice, Lovejoy. Money plus physical well-being. Or poverty and . . .'

'And?' I prompted hilariously.

'And pain, Lovejoy,' he said gravely.

'Look,' I tried to say, but this wart actually tapped my chest to shut me up.

'You look, Lovejoy.' Worse, his breath was unfortunate. 'I'm a businessman. I can play rough. I have the money to get things done. By others. Tougher than you. And you are strapped, practically in the soup queue.'

Well, I laughed. Honestly, I was helpless. Here was this nerk threatening a bloke like me. I've been in more dust-ups than dances, so maybe you can't blame me for the hilarity. I had to sit down on the orange-box. He stood there, ashen.

'Listen, mate,' I managed to gasp at last. 'Dandy Jack's having you on. If it was a bird bought it, she wasn't mine. And,' I finished, sobering, 'if you'd asked more politely I'd have sold you the diaries for a couple of quid. As it is, get lost.'

'So Dandy Jack was lying?'

'How the hell should I know?'

He looked me over, a really cold fish.

'The next time we meet you'll beg me to accept them as a gift, Lovejoy,' he said portentously. 'You've been adequately warned.'

'Sure, sure.'

He turned and stalked off.

I was still laughing when I caught the noon bus.

On the way to town I found myself thinking about an old chap possibly finding a coffin full of antiques.

You may believe that expecting to find (as opposed to buying) is something of a pipedream. Long may you so believe, because that lessens the chances of you doing any finding. The odds for me then get better. From the bottom of my atherosclerotic heart take my tip: keep looking. And above all keep expecting. When all's said and done, those London bankers who found that stache of Lord Byron's poems in their cellars weren't out for a casual stroll, were they? They were tidying up old deed boxes. Hence the now legendary discovery of documents and poems from 1820, the Scrope Davies find (of 'inaccurate memory', as Byron called this celebrated Dandy – note the capital letter; they were very particular). So when I hear of 'lucky' finds I always think to myself, what were they doing looking in the first place? And I mean them all. The nine-year-old Yorkshire lad who found that priceless Saxon longsword in the silt of the stream at Gilling West. The two Colchester children who dug down on to the Romano-British temple in Lexden. The East Anglian farmer who noticed a large circle of wheat standing tall and perfect during a recent wilting drought and had the sense to measure the circle carefully with his hobnails for thinking about after the harvest was gathered in – and discovered the burial tomb circle of one of King Tasciovanus's tributary kings. And me: I once bought an 'old' Victorian knitting needle found locally from Wilkie's shop (he's navigation and naval instruments of the eighteenth century) and 'an

iron Georgian drinking cup' from Harry's in our High
Street on the selfsame day – because I can smell a Roman
legion's doctor's instruments at a thousand leagues. So
look with courageous expectation, folks. You may have a
king buried in your own back yard.

I wistfully remembered the story of the lovely, mystic
Beaworth Box, holding a good ten thousand dazzling coins
from AD 1087. It was a small lead box, very like a coffin.
Like the Cuerdale Chest, complete with its precious silver
ornaments. Like the Flaxton Box. I can't go on. It's too
painful. And really delicious hoards have been found on the
Isle of Man, like the two at Andreas.

See how you can talk yourself round?

'This is as far as we go, mate,' the conductor was saying,
giving me a nudge.

'Then I'll get off,' I said, and I did.

In town I phoned Janie. Luckily she herself answered.
I asked her if she'd gone to Dandy's and bought the Burne-
Jones sketch. She said no, still mad at me. That made
Nichole, Janie, Nichole's private nutter Edward Rink,
Mary the housewife, Kate, and eighteen debtors all blazing
at me, just within two days. I honestly do try but sometimes
nobody else bothers. There are times like that.

CHAPTER VIII

EARLY AFTERNOON. I was in Margaret's shop in the Arcade.
She and I had been good friends when Janie'd happened,
which was a bit tough. There were a score of customers
drifting along the covered pavement, a few in and out of
Margaret's. I jokingly accuse her of showing herself off to
get customers in. Like all women she has attraction, but I
like Margaret especially. No bitterness and a lot of compassion. She could teach a million things to a lot of younger
women.

Margaret had picked up a job lot of eighteenth-century household stuff I'd promised to price. We sat in her glass-fronted area as I sorted through. It was interesting enough but low grade. Best was a collection of Regency pipe stubbers in the form of gloved hands, erotic figurines, tiny pipe racks, people, tennis racquets, rings, shapely legs, wine bottles. You get them in silver, brass, ivory, pewter, even hardwood and glass. She'd got twenty, by some miracle. Incidentally, always go for collections rather than items. I also liked a box of braided matches, R. Bell & Co., the elegant braid still on every single match – quaint Victorian elegance if you like, but fascinating.

'Not bad, Margaret.'

'I was lucky.' She eyed me. 'Anything you like?'

'Everything.' I couldn't keep the bitterness out.

Her hand touched my arm.

'It's a spell of bad luck, that's all, Lovejoy.' She paused. 'Anything I can do?'

I pulled a scarey face to show I couldn't care less. Women who offer help need watching. Just then Patrick hurtled in with a fit of vapours and flung himself down on a William IV diamond seat, a nice pale oak with very few markings.

'Lovejoy!' he screamed, holding out his handbag to me.

'Yes?' I gazed apprehensively at his gilt plastic accessory.

'Well?' he screeched. 'Get my smelling salts out, you great fool!'

'No. You.' I never go along with his hysterics. Tantrums are personal things.

'Whatever's the matter, Patrick?' Margaret did it and set about restoring him.

'Not too close with the little bottle, dear,' he snapped. 'I need reviving, not gassing.'

'What is it?'

'Dandy Jack.' Patrick swooned backwards. 'He's been run over. Outside. I just can't *tell* you.' But he did, emphasizing his own reactions most of all. It seemed Dandy was sprinting to the Red Lion as usual when he was knocked down by a car. It didn't stop.

'Am I pale as absolute death?' Patrick asked fearfully
of all and sundry. He peeped into his handbag mirror.

'You *are* pale, dear,' from Margaret.

He leaned back and closed his eyes. 'I'm positively
drained to my ankle-straps.'

'Did somebody take the number?'

'Hardly, dear.' Patrick patted his cheeks. 'We were
fainting like flitted flies.'

'Bloody idiot,' I said.

He glared. 'Shut your face, you great oaf, Lovejoy,' he
spat. 'If you'd been through what I've just undergone – '

'You only watched,' I pointed out. 'Dandy got done.'

'How do you *bear* him?' Patrick cooed to Margaret.
'Uncouth ape.'

Lily came trotting after, as always typical of sacrificial
desire. Hope beats eternal in the human breast but I honestly
wonder what the hell for sometimes. She was more precise
than Patrick had been.

'They've taken Dandy to hospital,' she said breathlessly.
'He looked really awful, blood everywhere.'

'Don't!' Patrick moaned, doing his swoon.

'Are you all right, lovie?' Lily rallied round him frantically.

'Sod him,' I said. 'The point is will Dandy be all right?'

'Charming!' Patrick instantly recovered enough to glare
daggers at me.

'I don't know, Lovejoy.' Lily dabbed anxiously with a
tissue at Patrick, who irritably jerked away.

'Mind my mascara!' he screeched. 'Silly cow!'

'Sorry, dear,' Lily was saying when I pecked Margaret's
cheek and moved off.

'If Patrick wants to do the entire scene,' I said, 'lend him
an asp.'

'May your ceramics turn to sand, Lovejoy!' he screeched
spitefully after me.

'Shush, lovie! Try to rest!' from Lily.

'Why does everybody *hate* me so?' he was wailing as I left
the Arcade. I suppose it takes all sorts.

The hospital is a few streets away. You cut alongside

the ancient steps through the remains of the Roman wall.
As I hurried among the crowds I couldn't help thinking that
too many things were happening too quickly all of a sudden.
In spite of my hurry I couldn't help pausing at Dig Mason's,
the poshest of the Arcade's antiques windows. Pride of place
was given to a delightful veneered drop-sided portmanteau.
It contained an entire set of dining cutlery, china service,
glass tableware down to cruets and serviette rings. Everything was slightly smaller sized than normal. My heart
melted. Perfect. Dig beamed out at me through the window
miming an invitation to make an offer. I gave him the thumbs
down and hurried away. He'd labelled it 'Lady's travelling
dining case. Complete. Victorian.' All wrong. I'd have
labelled it 'Officer's mess dining portmanteau. Complete.
1914–15. World War I' and been correct. The poor sods
were made to provide complete mess gear and often their
own china and cutlery in the Royal Flying Corps. As I
hurried along I prayed Dig wouldn't realize his mistake
before I got some money from somewhere. He'd underpriced it a whole hundred per cent.

I looked among the cars but there was no sign of Janie.
She must have decided to stay away in a temper. Typical.
Just as you need women they get aggro. They make me mad.
They lack organization

Helen was at the hospital. She came over as soon as I
entered the foyer. Funny what impressions hospitals leave.
All I can remember is a lot of prams, some children and an
afternoon footballer being wheeled along with his leg in
plaster.

'He's not too good, Lovejoy,' Helen said.

'I'm glad you came.'

She shot a look at me and together we climbed to the
second floor. I never know who's boss nurse any more.
Once it was easy – dark blue were sisters, pale blue stripes
nurses and doctors in white. Now they seem as lost as the rest
of us. Helen accosted a matron who turned out to be a
washer-up. We made three mistakes before we stood at the

foot of Dandy Jack's bed.

He appeared drained, newly and spectacularly clean and utterly defenceless. Drips dripped. Tubes tubed into and out of more orifices than God ever made. Bottles collected or dispensed automatically. It seemed nothing more than one colossal act, a tableau without purpose or message. Dandy Jack was never a divvie, but even boozy dealers deserve to live.

'Did you see the accident?' a tired young house doctor asked. I said no.

'I did. From a distance.' Helen linked her arm with mine. I think we both felt under scrutiny, somehow allowed in under sufferance.

'Did he go unconscious instantly?'

'Yes. The car pushed him along quite several yards,' Helen told him. 'It wasn't going all that fast.'

'Did Dandy see it?' I asked her. She shook her head.

The doctor moved us out of the ward with a head wag.

'Are you next of kin?'

We stared, hesitated before answering.

'Well, he has none, Doctor,' Helen said at last. 'As far as we know.'

'He's . . . seriously injured, you see.' He asked us to leave a phone number.

We finished up giving Margaret's. Helen meant, but didn't say, that she'd know to reach me through Janie somehow. On the way back to High Street we carefully disengaged arms just in case. Helen told me the car was a big old Rover.

'I could have sworn, Lovejoy . . .' Helen paused. 'I had an idea the driver might have been . . . that chap you were talking to outside Dandy's.'

'The one with the blonde?' Rink.

'Yes, but a different car.'

'Well,' I said carefully, 'one doesn't use one's very best for dealing with the vulgar mob, does one?'

'I could be wrong, I suppose.'

'You could.' I left it at that.

'I'll tell Margaret we gave her home number,' Helen said.

She paused as we made to part. 'Lovejoy.'
   'What?'
   'Ring me.' She met my eyes. 'Whenever.'
   'If I come into money,' I quipped.
   'Have you eaten?' she examined my face. 'You're gaunt.'
   'It's the ascetic life I lead.' We looked at each other
another moment. 'See you, Helen.'
   'Yes.'

I was wondering, can a duckegg like Rink be so savage?
Then I thought, aren't we all?

CHAPTER IX

THAT AFTERNOON I'd never been so famished. Hunger's all
right but bad for morale. I combed the cottage for provisions
and ended up with a quarter-full tin of powdered milk, a tiny
piece of cheese I'd overlooked, one small cooking apple, some
limp celery, a bottle of sauce and five grotty teabags. Hardly
nosh on the Elizabethan scale. Just as well Henry wasn't
due today. He'd have started on the divan. I glanced at my
non-edible walnut carriage clock and decided to call on
Squaddie. He's always good for a calorie.
   First I would cerebrate for a minute or two. This Bexon
business was starting to niggle. I strolled into the garden.
On the face of it, you couldn't call it much of a problem. I
sat on the garden steps near the budgies' flight, whistling to
think better.
   An old geezer dies leaving behind a scrawled tale telling
how he'd had a holiday and found some ruins or other. A
mosaic. And a gold or two, Lovejoy. Don't forget them. Then
he leaves his story in duplicate. Well, big deal. Two nieces
explained that. Clearly one booklet each and a funny drawing
of Lady Isabella chucked in for luck. From the way Nichole's
henchman Rink had behaved none of us knew any more
than that. I chuckled at the memory of his absurd threat,

making Manton and Wilkinson look round irritably at my whistling's sudden halt. Then I thought of Dandy Jack.

'Sorry, lads,' I told them. 'Just thinking.'

We all resumed, me sitting on the cold stones and the birds trilling on their enclosed branches. Singing makes their chests bulge so they rock about. Ever noticed that? It's a miracle they don't fall off. I expect their feet keep tighter hold on the twigs than you'd think from a casual look.

The problem lay of course in what we were all busy guessing. Nichole's wealthy hero obviously guessed an enormous crock of gold somewhere. Greedy sod. He was already at least a two-Rolls man. Janie guessed I was wasting my time again when I should have been seducing her away from her posh hubby. Dandy Jack was guessing that his Burne-Jones drawing would settle his boozing bills for some time to come, and he was right. Always assuming he got better and those bouncy nurses let him loose.

'Manton.' He looked at me in silence. 'What,' I asked, 'am I guessing? That's the real problem, isn't it?'

They glanced at each other, then back at me. We all thought hard.

'You're right,' I said, got out my rusty old bike and hit the road. I had to pump its front tyre up first, this being the space age.

About three miles from my cottage tidal creeks begin. Low-lying estuaries, woods, sloping green fields, orchards and beautiful undulating countryside blending with the mighty blue ocean and getting on my wick, though not everybody sees sense like I do. Even though it was quite early a couple of anglers were ruminating on the Infinite along the Goldhammer inlet, and some nut was trying to get the total boredom of the scene on canvas – tomorrow's antique. Or even today's? I pedalled past with a cheery greeting. The artist was pleased and shouted a good day, but the anglers were mad because a bicycle bell warns the fish away. I gave it a couple of extra rings.

Cheered by my day's good turn, I rode out on to the strood.

That's a road sticking out from the shore across a short reach of sea to an island. You can easily pass over when the sea's out but have to wade chest-deep when the tide's in. People who live on these low windswept islands have the times of the tides written out and stuck inside their car doors. Always assuming you have a car, I thought nastily. There's a lifebelt hung on the wooden railing so you get the message. The North Sea's no pond.

This particular strood's about half a mile long. Three or four boats lay sprawled close to the roadway on the exposed mudflats among reed wisps. A couple of fishing ketches were standing out to sea in the cold light. But the boat I was heading for would never sail again. It came into view halfway across, a blue lifeboat converted for house-boat living and sensibly rammed as far as possible on the highest inlet out of the sea marshes.

Squaddie was in and cooking. I could tell from the grey smoke pouring from the iron stack. I whistled through my fingers. He likes a good warning.

'After some grub, Lovejoy?' his voice quavered from the weatherbeaten cabin. He's getting on.

'Yes. Get it ready,' I yelled back and slung my bicycle among the hawthorns.

He has a double plank with railings sloping from the old towpath to his deck. How lucky I'd called at mealtime. Frying bacon and eggs. He gives me that and some of those malt flakes and powdered milk, my usual once a week.

'Hiyer, Squaddie.'

'Hello, Lovejoy.'

An old geezer can get about a lot even if he's blind. Squaddie used to be our best antique dealer (me excepted) till his eyes gave in. A curious old chap, wise enough for more than me to use as an oracle.

'You're a day early.'

'Not brewed up yet, Squaddie? I'm gasping.'

Squaddie scratched his stubble and listened acutely to the momentary silence between us His sightless rheumy eyes could still move. It was a bit disconcerting in the small

cabin, to catch a sudden flash of white sclera from a face
sightless five years and more. I slewed across the tilted floor
and sat where I could see to seaward.

'You on to something, Lovejoy?'

I shrugged evasively, remembered in time he couldn't see
shrugs and said I wasn't sure.

'Good or bad?'

'Neither.'

He cackled at that and mixed powdered milk.

'It's got to be one or the other,' he corrected, shuffling
dextrously from galley to table and laying for me as well.
'Antiques are either lovely and real or imitation and useless.'

'It can be neither,' I said. 'It can be funny.'

'Oh. Like that, eh?'

While we started to nosh I told him about Bexon, the
forgery, the lovely Nichole and her pal, Dandy Jack's
accident and the diaries. You can't blame me for missing out
Janie and the leading details of old Bexon's holiday trip
because Squaddie still does the occasional deal. Nothing
wrong with being careful.

'How does it sound?' I asked him.

'Rum. Where's the picture?'

'Dandy Jack kept it – after I'd sorted for him.'

He laughed, exposing a row of rotten old teeth.

'Typical. That Dandy.'

'Did you ever hear of Bexon?'

'Aye. Knew him.' He stirred his egg cleverly into a
puddle with a bread stick. You couldn't help staring. How
does a blind man know exactly where the yolk is? 'Tried to
get him to copy a Wright canvas for me. Seascape. He
wouldn't.'

'Money?'

'Not on your life.' Squaddie did his odd eye-rolling trick
again. Maybe it eases them. 'Bexon was honest.'

'Was he off his rocker?'

'Him? A northern panel bowler?'

That said all. Panel bowlers are nerveless team players
on crown bowling greens. They never gamble themselves, but

they carry immense sums wagered on them by spectators at every match. You can't do that and be demented.

'When did you see him last, Squaddie?' I could have kicked myself even if it is only a figure of speech. Squaddie didn't seem to notice.

'I forget.' He scraped the waste together and handed it to me to chuck out of the cabin window. 'He was just off somewhere on holiday. Isle of Man, I think.'

'What was he?'

'Trade? Engineer, draughtsman and all that. Local firm.'

'Go on digs?' We suffer a lot from epidemics of amateur archaeologists hereabouts. And professional ones who are much, much worse.

'He wasn't one for hunting Camelot at weekends, if that's what you mean, Lovejoy.' He was laughing as he poured, thick and tarry. Lovely. 'Nieces wouldn't let him. Real firebrands, they are.'

I caught myself thinking, Maybe that explains why Bexon found his hoard on the Isle of Man and not locally. Almost as if I was actually coming to believe his little diaries were a perfectly true record. You have to watch yourself in this game. Persuasion's all very well for others.

We chatted then about antiques in general. He asked after friends, Jimmo, the elegant Patrick, Jenny and Harry Bateman, Big Frank. We talked of prices and who were today's rascals (plenty) and who weren't (very few).

'How's Algernon?' he finally asked me, chuckling evilly. Well he might.

'Bloody horrible.'

'He'll improve, Lovejoy.'

I forgot to tell you Algernon is Squaddie's nephew.

'He won't. Green as the proverbial with the brains of a rocking-horse.'

'He's your bread and butter for the moment, Lovejoy.' It was Squaddie who'd foisted him on to me as soon as I went bust, to make him the world's greatest antique dealer for a few quid a month. Your actual Cro-Magnon. I'd never have taken a trainee in a million years if Squaddie hadn't taken the liberty. It's called friendship. I visit Squaddie weekly to report our complete lack of progress.

'What's he on?'

'Glass. Musical instruments. He doesn't know the difference.'

'You cruel devil, Lovejoy. He'll learn.' That's what blood does for you. You can't spot your own duds.

'He's a right lemon. Should be out earning his keep like a growing lad, van-driving.'

'One day he'll surprise you.'

'Only surprise?' I growled. 'He frightens the frigging daylights out of me.'

'Not need the money any more, Lovejoy?' Squaddie cackled slyly.

I swallowed. 'I'll keep on with him,' I conceded at last. He passed my notes over. I earn every farthing.

'He's got the gift,' Squaddie said determinedly. 'He'll be a divvie like you.'

I sighed heavily and thanked him for the nosh. Before I left I arranged to skip tomorrow's visit. 'Unless,' I added cruelly as a parting salvo, 'Algernon's skills mushroom overnight.'

'They will,' he promised. 'Anyway, good luck with the Roman stuff, Lovejoy.'

'Cheers, Squaddie.' I paused on the gangplank, thinking hard. 'Did you say Roman?' I called back. No answer. I called louder. 'Who said anything about Roman stuff?'

'Didn't you?' he quavered from the cabin. He'd already started washing up.

'Not a word.'

'You mentioned digging, archaeology, Lovejoy. That's Roman.'

'So it is,' I said. Well, it is, isn't it?

But I'd said nothing to young Algernon at the cottage. Nothing could have got back to Squaddie through him. Maybe it was an inspired guess. There are such things, aren't there? We said our farewells all over again, ever so polite.

I got my bicycle. My picture of Bexon was building up: a highly skilled painter, known among a select few old friends in the antiques trade. A good quiet family man. Cool under stress. And honest with it, to boot. Still, I thought, pedalling down the marshes to the strood again in the cutting east wind, nobody's perfect. I started ringing my bicycle bell to warn the fish those two anglers were still bent on murder. The artist waved, grinning. The anglers didn't. Perhaps they thought me unsporting.

I pedalled off the strood on to the mainland. The only difference between cycling and being in Janie's Lagonda is that she's not there to keep saying take your hand off my knee.

Now I had money. Not much, but any at all is more than twice nothing. The trouble is people have to *see* money, or they start jumping to all sorts of conclusions. This trade's very funny. Reputations matter.

The White Hart was fairly full, everybody talking all at once as usual. I paused for a second, rapturously inhaling the boozeladen smoke and gazing round. Jenny and Harry were huddled close, uptight. I'd heard Jenny was seeing some wealthy bloke on the sly. Maybe Harry had tumbled, or maybe they'd bounced a deal wrong. Well, antiques occasionally caused difficulties, I snickered to myself. Tinker Dill was there, holding forth against the bar to a cluster of other grubby barkers. I still wonder who'd bought that round. Helen was resting, long of leg and full of curves, on a stool like women with good legs do and gave me a half-smile and a nod. She's always exhaling smoke. She even smokes in bed. (Er, I mean, I *suppose* she probably does.) Margaret was in, too. I waved. Big Frank wasn't in yet. Patrick was showing off to anyone who cared. Lily gave me a wave. She'd been to a silver sale in Lavenham that day.

'What'll you have, Lily?'

Only Ted the barman didn't eye the money in my hand. He assimilates feelings about solvency by osmosis.

'No. My turn.'

'I insist.' I had a pint, Lily a mysterious rum thing. I asked if she'd visited Dandy in hospital.

'I went,' she said. 'Patrick would have, but he's not very ... strong.'

'That plump nurse'll hose Dandy down a bit, eh?' I chuckled.

'Lovejoy,' Lily said carefully. 'I don't know if Dandy's going to be, well, all right.'

'Not get better? Dandy Jack?' I smiled at that. 'He's tough as old boots. He'll make it. Did the Old Bill catch the maniac?'

'Not yet.' Her voice lowered. 'They're saying in the Arcade it looked like –'

'If it was Rink he'll have a hundred alibis.'

The interlude done with, Lily turned to her own greatest problem, who was now lecturing Ted on lipstick. ('That *orange* range is such a poxy risk, Teddie dear!')

'What am I doing to go, Lovejoy?'

'Give him the sailor's elbow,' I advised.

She gazed at Patrick's blue rinse with endearment. Patrick glanced over, saw us and coo-eed extravagantly.

'Do you like it, Lovejoy?' he shrieked, waggling his fingers.

'Er . . .?'

'The new nail varnish, dear! Mauve!' He emitted an outraged yelp and turned away. 'Oh, isn't he positively moronic?'

'Would you speak to him, Lovejoy?' Lily begged. She'd made sure nobody was in earshot. 'He treats me like dirt.'

'Chuck him, love.'

'He admires you. He'd listen. He says you're the only proper dealer we've got.'

'That's a laugh.'

'It's true,' she said earnestly. 'He's even been trying to help you. He's been making enquiries about Bexon all afternoon.'

'Eh?'

'For you, Lovejoy.' Lily smiled fondly in Patrick's

direction. 'Even though there's nothing in it for him. He went down to Gimbert's.' The auction rooms where Bexon's belongings went. 'One day he'll realize I love him – '

'Does your husband know?' I asked, thinking, since when. does an antique dealer do anything for nothing? Even one like Patrick. He used to deal in goldsmithy till that gold price business ten years ago, antique gold.

'Not yet,' she admitted. 'When I'm sure of Patrick I'll explain. He'll understand.'

'It's more than I do,' I said. 'Look, love. Can't you see that Patrick's – er – ?'

'It's a phase,' she countered. 'Only a phase.'

Jill Jenkins made her entrance, a nimble fortyish. She's mediaeval, early mechanicals, toys, manuscripts and dress items. I like her because she's good, really as expert as any dealer we have locally. Not a divvie, just an expert. I'd never seen her boy-friend before, but then I'd never seen any of Jill's boy-friends before. They all look the same to me. Only the names change, about once every twelve hours. Tinker Dill once told me he can tell the new ones by their ear lobes. Jill picks them up on the harbour wharf. Our port can just about keep pace with Jill's appetite as long as one of our estuary fogs doesn't hold the ships up. Her husband has this farm in Stirling, very big on agriculture. Well, whatever turns you on, but there are some rum marital arrangements about these days.

'Lovejoy! My poppet!' I got a yard of rubberoid lips and a waft of expensive perfume. 'And Lily too! How nice!' she added absently, glancing round with the occasional yoo-hoo and finger flutter.

'Hiyer, Jill.'

'This is . . .' she started an introduction. 'What is it, darling?'

'Richard,' the lad said. 'Rum and blackcurrant.'

'Richard,' Jill said, pleased somebody had remembered. 'That's it. He's left his boat down in the water.'

'How very wise,' Lily said sweetly, moving away. 'Now he'll know where to find it, won't he?'

'Ship,' Richard said sourly. 'Not boat. Ship.'

'I hear,' Jill said, taking my arm and coming too close, 'Lovejoy's roamin' after Roman.' She has a beautiful Egyptian scarab brooch, genuine. My bell clamoured.

'Roman stuff?' I said calmly. 'Whoever told you that?'

'Big Frank,' she admitted, not batting any one of her false eyelashes. 'And that whore Jenny Bateman.' She caught Jenny's eye the same instant and trilled a greeting through the saloon. The Batemans waved.

Ted fetched Richard's drink. Jill always has ginger wine. They allow Jill's drinks on the slate. For some reason they don't trust the rest of us.

'Lily just said that,' I said. 'Funny how things get about.'

'Any special Roman stuff, dear?'

'Must have been a misunderstanding, Jill,' I replied. I was distinctly uncomfortable.

'Did Popplewell help you clear it up?' she asked roguishly.

'I was only doing a routine call at the Castle,' I said.

'If you've the money,' she said, suddenly businesslike, 'I've some Roman bronze statuary. No gold coins, though. What time're you due back, William?'

'Couple of hours. And it's Richard.'

'That'll give us just long enough. Then I'll run you back to your boat.'

'Ship,' I said for him, got another moist plonk from Jill's mouth and escaped.

CHAPTER X

ON THE WAY BACK I called in at Ruffler's bakery, four meat-and-potato pasties and two flour cakes. It's very interesting being poor at this level. You'd think that you'd start buying foods again in exactly the reverse order you gave them up. It's not true. For example, I'd not tasted butter or margarine for four months at the cottage. And here I was with a few quid, splashing out on a quarter of marge and a pot of honey.

Big spender. For sheer erg value I bought a dozen eggs, a tin
of powdered milk and a slab of Lancashire cheese the size
of a Queen Anne *escritoire*. Manton and Wilkinson had seed
forever so I got two loaves, a cob and a farmhouse. That made
a hell of a hole in Squaddie's few quid. I dithered about a tin
of corned beef and a custard but decided not to go mad.
My belly would be shocked enough as it was. I bought tinned
sausages and salad cream for Henry.

I felt so proud having a proper tea. You do, don't you?
Even got my tablecloth out and laid it. It's Victorian
embroidered white linen, lovely. White-on-white's stylish
needlework, but hell to iron. (Tip: use an old non-electric
flat-iron. Don't think that electric's always right just because
it's easy.) I washed the cutlery and found a napkin from
somewhere. My Indian bone-and-rosewood inlaid teatray
made everything look really sophisticated. If anyone had
come in they'd have thought how homely it all was. Funny
how a person's mind works. I put the margarine and honey
in a prominent position so they could be seen clearly by
unexpected visitors. They'd think it was routine. To reinforce the image I put both loaves and the flour cakes on
show. The message for the casual observer: that Lovejoy
lives really well, always a choice of bread. I had two pasties,
hotted up. The others went away for the morrow.

As I stoked up even my old table manners returned. No
elbows on the table, knife and fork demurely parallel. I was
charming, and not a little narked nobody came to witness
the exhibition.

That done, I went to see Manton and Wilkinson. Darkness
was about to fall on the valley. From the cottage you can
see the lights along the Lexton village road some four miles
away. There's a cluster of cottages, the river and the railway
about a mile closer. At dusk it's quite pretty, but coolish and
always misty. A faint foggish air drifts in from the estuary,
slow and rather ominous sometimes. That makes the lights
gleam prettily for a few minutes. Then you notice the cold
dankness hanging to cut off the last of the valley's dusk, and
the day has ended. The night is a swamp through which

sounds fail to carry. Trees loom wider and hedges crowd
close. And my phone was dead of non-payment from today.

I told Manton and Wilkinson goodnight. They were locked
in well. Odd, but I distinctly remember wishing for once
that I'd a dog. One of the villagers has two geese. He says
they're better than any watchdog.

Algernon was due soon for his test. I'd have to get ready.
I went in and shut the cottage door.

Outside the lights of all the world must have seemed to
dowse with a slam.

It was late. I'd given Algernon his quiz. Results: dreadful.
I'd been teaching him the difference between jet, black
jadeite and black pigmented acrylate resins. (Today's hint:
go for nineteenth-century Whitby jet brooches if you're
wanting the very best. They're worth the premium. And
genuine jet's practically impossible to copy.) He'd suggested
the easiest way's burning – jet burns, you see. I'd explained
that keeping the jewellery intact's preferable to a heap of
ash. I'd shown him how I measure specific gravity (jet's
not more than 1.40, which is peanuts to jadeite's 3.30 or
even more; acrylate resin's never far from 1.18.) It's not
foolproof, but you're a lot nearer the truth knowing details
like this. I sent Algernon home after he'd made me lose my
temper.

I was wondering whether to slip over to the White Hart.
Even with only a few quid staving the wolf from the door a
body has a right to drown his sorrows, after Algernon. There
was a knock at the door. Funny how you get the feeling. It
was Algernon again.

'Forgotten something?' I snapped. I hadn't heard his
bike go.

'Er . . . Lovejoy.' No stammer, no cheery grin, no move to
barge in and start dropping the nearest valuable.

'What is it?'

'Something's wrong,' he said quietly. 'Your budgies.'

I was out and round the side of the cottage before I could
think, blundering blindly into my precious camellia. Like a

fool I'd not pulled back the curtains for light. I couldn't
see a damned thing.

'Fetch a light, Algernon, for Christ's sake!'

'Coming!'

'Manton?' I said softly towards the flight pen. 'Wilkie?
Are you – ?'

The click behind me trapped the garden in light. Algernon's
headlamp.

'Mantie?' For a second I could see nothing wrong. I
fumbled for the key, thinking perhaps to undo the padlock.
Then I noticed the lock's iron loop was wrenched free.
The flight's door was aslant and pulled away.

'What is it, Algernon?' I asked, puzzled, stepping forward.
Near my face a small breath sounded. I looked at the door
jamb.

Wilkinson was crucified on the wood. Nails were projecting
through his blue wings. There was some blood. His feet were
drawn upwards tight clenched, as if a groping search for a
twig on which to rest had been too hopeless anyway.

'A hammer,' I babbled. 'Pincers. For Christ's *sake* – '

I pushed Algernon aside and crashed through the garden
to my shed, scattering tools and cutting myself in a demented
crazy grope along shelves. Things went flying. I tore back,
smashing plants and blundering into the cottage wall as I
went.

I'd got a claw hammer. It was too short, but it's the only
one I have.

'There's not the leverage,' I sobbed in a blind rage,
trying to get purchase of the claw on the nail. The distance
from the nail to the door jamb was too great. I needed some
sort of support, some bloody thing to rest the sodding
hammer on. Why do I never have the proper fucking tools?
I daren't press on his wing. Wilkinson tried to turn his head.
I couldn't lodge the hammer against his frail body or it'd
crush him.

'Coming, Wilkie,' I blubbered. 'Coming.'

There was nothing for it. I put my thumb under the
hammer to protect him and yanked the claw up. My thumb

spurted blood. The pain flashed me backwards like a blow
but the nail was out. Thank Christ. I got up. Wilkinson
was hanging by one wing, trying to flap with his bloodstained wing. I held him in my palm to take his weight. I'd
forgotten. And I call other people Neanderthal.

'Come here, Algernon.' I was suddenly pouring sweat but
calm at last. I gave him the hammer in the mad silent glare
and nodded at the second nail. My bad hand cupped Wilkinson's body for his own weight. I put my good one over
Wilkinson's impaled wing.

'Do it.'

'But your hand will – '

'*Do it!*'

He shoved upwards. The hammerhead grated smoothly
into my knuckles. I heard two bones go. Oddly the pain was
less this time though the blood poured in a great stream down
my forearm. Wilkinson came free. As he did, he arched his
little back. Then he bowed his beak and bit my bloodied
thumb as he died. I felt the life go out of him like, well, like
a flying bird. It was his last gesture to the world he had
known. All that he was or ever had been culminated in one
futile bite.

'Hold him, please.'

Algernon cupped his gauntlets to receive Wilkinson.

'He's dead, Lovejoy.'

'Shut your stupid face,' I snarled. 'Did you see Manton?'

'No. Maybe he's escaped.'

Please God, please. I moved quietly about the flight.
'Mantie? Mantie?' Maybe he'd ducked inside his covered
house. There was a lot of space where a budgie could hide.
Or even get out. I edged towards it, calling softly.

Algernon spotted Manton first. He was hunched on the
ground in the corner of the flight, squatted down in the
grotesque shadows.

'There!'

'He's safe!' I said. 'Manton!' I went over. He didn't
move, just stayed facing the flight's open space in that
crouching attitude. He'd normally have edged over but was

probably stunned at the shock. 'Mantie!' I sat on the ground beside him feeling the relief. I was suddenly giddy. I think I'd lost a lot of blood. It seemed everywhere. My hands pulsed pain.

'Lovejoy.'

'Yes?'

'I'm afraid I think your other budgie's . . .'

'Algernon,' I whispered softly from my position on the grass. 'Come here.'

He stepped over, still cupping Wilkinson, for all the world like a weird lunar being blocking the headlight's shine.

'Yes?'

'What were you going to say, Algernon?' I asked, still ever so soft and gentle.

I saw his eyes wander nervously behind his specs.

'Er . . . nothing, Lovejoy. Nothing.'

'That's good,' I whispered. 'Now put Wilkinson on his ledge inside.'

He moved carefully past, carrying Wilkinson in his hands like a priestly offering. A moment later he emerged and stood fidgeting. Everything some people do drives you mad sometimes. Algernon's that kind.

'I've done it.'

'Not so loud!' I hissed.

'What will you do now, Lovejoy?' he whispered.

'I'll stay here. He's frightened.'

'But he hasn't moved,' he said.

'Of course he hasn't,' I shot back furiously as loudly as I dared. 'He's in a state of shock. Wouldn't you be?' Bloody fool.

'Yes. Of course.'

'Then shut your teeth.'

'Certainly.' He dithered in the oblique light. 'What do you want me to do? You're all bleeding.'

I was, too, both hands. My left thumb was a pulp. I couldn't move my right hand which was swelling rapidly. It looked huge, but things always look worse badly lit.

'Shall I get a vet, Lovejoy?'

I peered at him suspiciously. 'What would you get a vet for?'

'Er, to tell you . . .' He ground to a halt.

'To tell me what, Algernon?' I whispered savagely.

'Nothing.'

'Go home, Algernon.' I was suddenly finished.

'Home?'

'Home,' I nodded. 'Now.' I watched him back away towards his motor-cycle. It was tilted crazily on the grass. I remember feeling surprised. He's mad about his pop-pop, yet he must have just rushed the machine across the garden and flung it down with the headlamp on.

He pushed it on to the gravel and started up. I heard him call something but that's typical of Algernon, start up a motor-bike and assume it's inaudible. Stupid. He slithered down the driveway and out on to the metalled road. Gravel everywhere, of course. Manton and I watched the lights swathe the hedgerows. Finally only the sound remained, faintly humming through the village. We heard him change up, sudden as ever, on the Bercolta road. Then he faded and we were left alone, sitting on the grass in the wretched flight.

The lights of Lexton were shining in the distance, an unpleasing orange. The sky picks up the illuminance and casts a faint tinge on the starglow. I talked to Manton, trying to make him feel that maybe the nightmare was over now and things were at least moving towards normal.

'It's my fault, Mantie,' I told him. No use trying to shelve the blame.

He'd normally have chirped there, but it's sensible to harbour your strength if you've had a bad shock, isn't it? You know how it is when you've been ill, how conversation takes it out of you. It's best to stay quiet.

'There's a sensible bird!' I praised, still in a whisper. 'Keep warm, Mantie.'

No good getting one place warm and moving to another, is it? That would be stupid. They know what to do when they're off colour. Not like people. We're daft as brushes. Animals are practical. They have an innate sense, haven't they?

I don't remember much of the rest. I remember feeling a cold wind springing up, but maybe that was just the effect of the blood loss. I saw blackish gobs and strings of blood on the ground, and all over my leg, and wondered how the hell that had happened. I fell over a few times, mercifully avoiding where Manton huddled. Janie came. I cursed her from habit, and told her to shut the light off.

I remember arguing with her and calling her a stupid obstinate bitch. She tried bringing an umbrella from the car to shield us from the driving rain which started up. Good old Algernon had telephoned her. It must have been some conversation.

About dawn I vaguely remember hearing a man's voice asking if this was the one, something like that, and Janie's defiance. I had to pee *in situ*, which can't have improved my appearances much. The blood on the mud was like those Victorian oil-layered flyleaf bindings. I told Janie to get his seed for him, as he was probably hungry.

I woke in the early light. The rain had ended. No wind. No noise. The robin was looking down at me. I came abruptly out of the nightmare. The robin flew, suddenly sticking like glue to the twig as they do in midflight. I made myself turn and look at Manton. He was crouched because he was impaled on a stake driven into the ground through his little back. Janie was there, a blanket over her dress and almost concealing her mink coat. Stiletto shoes and all. I remembered her husband's voice saying, 'And people in our position, Janie,' and asking, 'What are you thinking of?'

After a bit I told her to help me up. I leaned on her like a drunken matelot, quite unable to see much that wasn't swivelling round and round. She fetched a spade and I dug a hole, alternately yelping and fainting from the excruciating pain and bleeding all down the handle. I wouldn't let her do it. I buried them between the lovely Anne Cocker rose and a pink grandiflora. Then Janie got me stripped indoors and on the divan for a wash. I was all filth and blood.

'You're in a worse state than China, Lovejoy,' Janie
called from the alcove.

'Your slang's dated,' I gave back. 'Gives your age away.'

'The doctor will go mad.'

'Oh, him,' I said.

I wasn't up to repartee. For the first time in the entire
business I was aware of the slightly disturbing fact that I
was up against a madman. Nichole might be the sweetest
woman on earth, but she sure as hell had no control over her
tame lunatic.

It was beginning to look as if old Bexon's find was as
precious as he'd thought it was.

CHAPTER XI

ONCE UPON A TIME I was a virgin. No, honestly. A bit sweaty
and newly hairy, but the real thing. You may remember
how it was yourself. I exchanged it for a fob watch. A kindly
lady pressed it on me (I mean the watch, folks, the watch)
as I left her doorstep, fifteen years old but aged inexpressibly
in an hour. She was thirty or so. I couldn't help wondering
at the time how someone so obviously senile (over *twenty*
whole years of age!) was still managing to get about without
a wheelchair, let alone sprint into my big seduction scene
with such breathtaking relish. It was a fascinating business
and preoccupied me for several hours, after which time I
went back for a further lesson. I soon learned her moans
were not exactly grief.

Other points also obsessed me. Despite having endured
years of teaching to the contrary, I realized that women might
actually like males. And I was one of that category. I began
watching the sorts of things they did, to see what they
really wanted as opposed to what they were supposed to
want. I caught on. Women need to be used, to help. I was up
against an arch villain in the form of Edward Rink. I needed

help. I looked fondly at Janie as she pottered about, and began to think clearly. It was about time I did.

As Janie got us both ready for bed I watched her every movement. She knew it. They always know when something's on the boil.

Conviction came upon me like an avenging angel. Manton, Wilkinson and Dandy Jack couldn't do anything about Rink. I could. The police would be all puzzled questions and no help. Therefore Bexon's find had to be rediscovered. Not by Edward Rink, but by Lovejoy. That would put the boot into Rink like nothing else on earth. I needed help urgently, until I got my hands back. And I needed money.

'Janie?' I said as she came in beside me that night.

'Yes, love?'

'Look, Janie . . .'

Ever noticed how time goes sometimes? You might think it's all the same stuff, day in, day out. It's not. It really does vary. Some minutes leave centuries of wear on you. Others don't age you a second. I'll bet you know the feeling.

That next week was a few aeons long. Janie got me the two latest *Time* editions. I usually read that when I can afford it because its punctuation cares. Incidentally, correct grammar's a must for antique manuscripted letters and diaries, some of today's soaring valuables. You can allow for spelling mistakes by the milliard, but grammar has to be impeccable. And grammar isn't just using semicolons. If you suspect the genuine old letter which your best friend offers you ('. . . actually signed by *her*! On real old-type paper!') could be a forgery, try this test: even if you have no special knowledge of vegetable inks, papers, literary styles or script characteristics, just sit a moment and bother to read it. No cheating, start to finish. Bad grammar or really neffie punctuation should make you think twice, modern education being what it is. This test has saved me more than once. Another tip's the length of sentences. I'm not telling you any more or I'll lose the thread.

Janie got me a recent biography – Queen Mary. I read it,

not to see if they mentioned her fabulous collection of jade
snuff bottles, but to see if it mentioned how she acquired it.
It didn't. They never do, which really tickles me. Word is
that round the British Museum an impending visit from the
great lady acted like a tocsin warning of the Visigoths landing.
She's rumoured to have admired any particular jade piece
with such fixed (not to say immovable) admiration that, just
to get off the hook, squirming administrators felt compelled
to offer her the object. Graciously accepted, of course. I
really admire her for that, a collector after my own heart.
An example for us all to follow. Of course, it's taking
advantage of one's position. But do you know anyone who
doesn't? Even God does that.

Janie had the phone reconnected in one day, which must
be a record.

'Did you resort to bribery?' I demanded suspiciously.

'They're above that sort of thing,' she replied airily,
almost as if people ever are. She rang the news round I'd
got 'flu. Our local quack came and did his nut. People phoned
with mediocre deals, all out of my reach. Big Frank nearly
infarcted because I was late getting his silvers back. Janie
ran them over to the Arcade the first morning to leave them
with Margaret.

'We had a little chat,' Janie reported back, smug as any
woman is after a scrap. I sighed on my sickbed. As if I'd
not enough trouble.

Algernon came tiptoeing breathlessly in. The stupid burke
brought an enormous bunch of lilies.

'I'm not dead yet, Algernon,' I said angrily.

Janie whisked them away diplomatically.

Algernon was cheerfully unabashed. 'I've brought you
some grapes,' he said, 'for restorative nourishment.'

Janie swiftly bundled him outside. I heard him being full
of solace in the porch.

'How very sad to witness poor Lovejoy's indefatigable
high-spirited pleasantries dampened by such tragic in-
firmities.'

'Quite, Algernon,' Janie said firmly. 'I'm sorry I can't

otfer you some coffee, but in the circumstances . . .'

'Absolutely!' he prattled. 'On behalf of all of us antiques experts, Janie, may I express gratitude for your *undying* charity in so devotedly sticking to the task of restoring his poor battered physique!'

'Oh, er, well.'

One thing. No matter what goes wrong you can always depend on Algernon. I liked the antiques experts bit, may heaven forgive him.

Janie bought food from our village shop, setting tongues wagging. She said nothing to me about there being very little grub in the cottage, but her back had that critical look. I made her write down what she spent and told her I owed it.

Doc Lancaster injected me with some rubbish or other that first day. Janie drove me to the local hospital and they trussed my hands. God, they did hurt.

Janie stayed the first night, jumping a mile at every stray noise. She was terrified and kept asking what sort of maniac would do a thing like that and why.

'We ought to report it,' she said more than once.

In the circumstances it was brave of her to stay. The evening of the second night she reported back home in wifely obedience, to check that none of her servants had pinched any of the nineteen bedrooms in her centrally heated mansion. Her husband was throwing a dinner-party for business friends and Janie had to baste the carrots.

'Can't stand the pace, eh?' I accused.

'I promised, Lovejoy.'

'Remember to crook your little finger over sherry, like posh folks.'

She pulled a face and left. Everything I needed was in reach, drinks with straws and all that.

The second day Janie showed me the letter. It had arrived without a stamp. Somebody'd shoved it under the door early.

'I kept it,' Janie told me, 'because you weren't well enough.'

It was mid-morning. I was listening to the radio. One of those staid 'experts' was talking about mother-of-pearl decorations – incidentally coming back fast into fashion – and never said the only important thing about it. Keep it covered. Keep it dark. Never *ever* put mother-of-pearl under a strong light or on a sunny windowsill. If you do it'll fade, become dull and lifeless. It's practically the only shine we cunning dealers can't ever restore, imitate properly, or forge. Once it's gone it's gone for good.

This letter.

'I think it's something to do with . . . you know.' She opened it for me.

Dear Lovejoy,

Are you any nearer to handing over the diaries? I sincerely hope that recent events have persuaded you to a wiser course of action than hitherto.

Do not hesitate to contact me should you see sense and wish to sell. Those scribbles can only bring you trouble.

Yours sincerely,
Edward Rink.

I looked at Janie, marvelling. 'He's mad,' I said. 'And bloody cool.'

'Is he the one that . . .?' She shivered.

I turned the radio off.

'It's evidence,' I said, puzzled. 'I'll give it to the police. They'll pick him up.' Geoffrey, our local bobby, is rumoured to wake soon after Easter. Time he did something.

We read the letter again. Janie disagreed with me. 'He could mean practically anything.'

'He says "recent events",' I countered. 'It's in his own handwriting.'

'That could be anything from the weather to a new offer. You once told me there are a thousand auctions a week. He could say he was talking about a commission.'

She was right.

'I'm going to phone him.'

'Now, Lovejoy,' Janie warned, but I got her to dial the number from his card. We got him third go, a telecommunications miracle.

'Lovejoy? I'm so pleased you rang,' the swine said urbanely. 'How sensible!'

I tried to hold the receiver lightly but my hand took no notice and hurt itself tightening up.

'Cut it, Rink,' I said. 'Did you do it?'

'Now, Lovejoy,' he purred. 'No silliness. I merely want you to be aware your movements are being observed. If you suddenly take it into your head to go anywhere, you'll be spotted. Day or night. More sensible to sell me the diaries and have done.'

'What if I've got this conversation on tape?' I asked suddenly.

'You'd be wasting the magistrate's time, Lovejoy.' He was laughing, the pig. 'I hope you'll see reason. Nichole's desperate.'

'No.'

He sighed down his end of the blower. 'You have one other choice. To become my agent. I would pay you well. And a percentage.'

'Why me?' He was off his rocker.

'Because you have the diaries. And the sketch. And I believe you have a peculiar skill where antiques are concerned.' He paused. 'And that other thing. Poverty.'

'I haven't got the sketch.'

'Tut tut, Lovejoy. Lies.' There was a pause. He cleared his throat, coming to a decision. 'Incidentally,' he said at last, 'I'm so sorry about your friend.'

'Friend?'

'Dandy Jack.' I'd forgotten about him and his accident. 'Such a shame. Still, if he lied to Nichole, he deserved – '

I rang off. My hands seemed made of wood. Janie was making coffee. I made my way shakily back to the divan. Curious, but my head seemed cold and the scalp tight. I let her get on with it for a while before I managed to speak.

'Janie.' I saw her back stiffen. 'How's Dandy?'

'Mmmm?' She was ever so busy.

'That smelly old geezer from the Arcade. Remember?'

We shared the long horrid silence.

'I couldn't tell you yesterday,' she said.

We both watched her assemble my tin coffee gadget. Only Yanks can make coffee properly. They have this knack. I wonder what our women do wrong. I try, but I'm even worse at it than Janie and that's not far from horrendous. It might come out right, we were both thinking, because you never know your luck. The fuse went in the electric plug. She had a high old time unscrewing it and putting it right. We got mixed up over the wires. Well, morons keep changing the colours of the bloody wires. It's a wonder we aren't all electrocuted.

'He died early yesterday morning, love. I'm so sorry.'

Everything seemed falling to pieces. 'Police say anything?'

'Nobody really saw,' Janie said. 'No witnesses came forward.'

I thought a lot. Dandy suddenly seemed very close. And Manton and Wilkinson. Then fat Henry, and Eleanor. I looked across at Janie. She smiled up, feeling my eyes. We'd a real fire because I'd asked. It was raining. Outside in darkness my robin was probably nodding off. And Crispin my hedgehog was probably roaming, his snuffly infants behind him on the prowl in the muddy grass, filthy beasts. And Tinker Dill, three sheets sloshed in the White Hart by now. And Helen. And Margaret. And Nichole. If you ever bothered to list your responsibilities you'd go spare. I got a pen. Janie saw what I was up to and started us both on separate sheets, copying the diaries. My slowness almost made me bellow with frustration. She was twice as fast. I couldn't do the drawing. Janie had to do that.

It was gone midnight when I phoned Edward Rink to surrender. I wouldn't let him call at the cottage. He gave me a different postal address.

'I give you all I've got of Bexon's,' I told him. 'You leave my friends alone. Okay?'

'With pleasure,' he replied. I swear he was smiling.

We made the diaries into an envelope ready for posting, though it was a homemade job and looked botched.

Janie took it up the lane to our post office as soon as it opened in the morning. By then we'd copied the lot, word for word.

For the rest of the day I let my mind rest. I suppose Janie had slipped me a Micky on Doc Lancaster's orders. Or maybe it was her brew, the western world's most soporific stimulant. Anyway, I dozed a lot.

By evening I was alert enough to feel certain. Edward Rink was a maniac. He'd killed Dandy Jack. He was determined that, if old Bexon had left a clue about a Roman find, nobody else would get it but him. But what the hell did a beauty like Nichole see in a nerk like that? Doesn't it make you wonder, all those old sayings about women and rich men? Rink must have burgled the Castle to get Bexon's coins from the display case. To check they were genuine Romans, not crummy electrotypes people are always trying to sell you these days. It was as simple as that. A cool swine. We're never ashamed of our crimes, not really, but being thought inadequate in some way's the absolute humiliation. Aren't people a funny lot?

About eight o'clock our vicar, Reverend Woking, came to ask if I'd sufficiently recovered from my mythical 'flu to sing in the choir for Dandy Jack. The service would be at ten in a couple of days. They would do the Nelson Mass, though he's not supposed to have papist leanings. I said okay.

'I don't think Lovejoy will be well enough, Reverend,' Janie said. 'He's had an, er, accident in his workshop.'

'Yes, I will,' I said. 'I'm fine.'

'Good, good!' He hesitated, wondering whether to chance his arm and preach to us about Janie's status, but wisely decided to cut his losses.

'Before you start,' I put in as Janie prepared to go for me, 'you've never heard our tenors. Without me the *Sanctus* is doomed.' We bickered this way all evening.

CHAPTER XII

HALF THE CHURCH was crowded. Half was bone bare. We were all there. Helen holy without a cigarette. Jimmo with his asbestos cough. Ted the barman from the White Hart. Jill Jenkins with her poodle and a bewildered young uniformed navigator she'd somehow got off a coaster new in harbour that day. Harry Bateman and Jenny lighting candles for all they were worth because their new place opened in the morning. Patrick sobbing into a nasturtium hankie, Lily trying to comfort him and weeping worse. Big Frank from Suffolk trying to look as if he wasn't reading a Sotheby's catalogue of seventeenth-century German and French jewellery. Tinker Dill giving everybody a nasty turn having no cloth cap on and shaming us all to death by stubbing out his fag in our church's exquisite thirteenth-century baptismal font ('Well, what's the bleeding water in it for, then?' he whispered in an indignant stage bellow when Lily glared). A miscellany of shuffling barkers unrecognizable with washed heads and clean fingernails – one had even pressed his trousers. Margaret, the only one of us all who knows when to kneel down and which book has the right hymns – we all followed her example. Gimbert's auctioneers had sent a ghoul or two by way of unmitigated grief. And Dig Mason in a morning suit for God's sake, gear so posh we all knew the Rolls outside was waiting for him and not the coffin. And Algernon falling over twice moving along the pew. He'd brought his uncle, Blind Squaddie from the houseboat, who felt the hand-embroidered kneelers a little too long. I'd have to count them after he'd gone. And a few villagers on a day trip from across the road to get a kick out of life.

Oh, and Dandy Jack.

We'd got some flowers in wreaths, one lot shaped like a cross. I'd sold Big Frank my single display Spode plate, cracked and just about in one piece, and bought a lot of

flowers. I could tell Janie thought they were the wrong
colours but they were bright. Dandy Jack liked bright
colours. By then I'd spent up. I got three lengths of wire
from a neighbour's lad and threaded the flower stems in and
out with green stuff I'd taken from my hedge. It's hard to
make a circle. Try it. You don't realize how much skill goes
into making things till you do it yourself. It looked just like a
real wreath when it was finished. Making it didn't do my
hands any good, but I was proud of it. Janie went off somewhere and came back with one of those cards. We wrote
'In Remembrance' and our names on it and tied it on with
black cotton.

'It looks great, doesn't it?' I asked Janie.

'It's beautiful,' she said, which was a relief because Janie
can be very critical sometimes. The trouble is I knew she'd
have said the same if it hadn't been right. Still.

The coffin was on a bier. I wasn't to carry Dandy because
of my hands. Patrick nobly volunteered, but broke down.
Trust Patrick. A barker stood in at the last minute. Our
church has this small orchestra, five players, counting the
organ. Reverend Woking arranging the choir stuck me
behind Mary Preston, our plump and attractive 'cellist.
('You like being here, Lovejoy, don't you?' he said brightly
while I avoided Janie's eyes, large in the congregation.)

We didn't sing badly for Dandy Jack. Owd Henry's
probably our best bass. He's an eccentric filthy old farmer
whose legendary battles with the government over farm
subsidies will be sung of by future generations of ecstatic
minstrels. It's better than *Beowulf*. He wears an outlandish
stovepipe hat for posh, which is hard luck on our altos
because as a result they haven't seen a choirmaster's baton
beat time since before the war.

Helen never looked up once. She seemed really upset. We
listened gravely to Reverend Woking's sermon on Dandy
Jack's virtues. It was fifty minutes long, practically par for
the course. As far as I could make out it dealt mainly with
problems of translating Greek non-deistic pronouns from
the Aramaic in the synoptic gospels. Gripping. We'd just got

going again when in the middle of it all your friend and mine
Edward Rink pottered in, taking my breath away. It was
lucky we weren't at the risky bit in the *Agnus Dei*, which is
nobody's plaything. Nichole, pale and elegantly fragile,
slipped along the pew after him. Algernon kindly passed
Rink a hymnal, acknowledged by a curt nod. I'd have to
speak to Algernon. Politeness is all very well.

During the service Rink's eyes only met mine once. It was
during the *Dies Irae*. That instant any doubts left me. He
wouldn't give up, not him. The swine was as cold as any
reptile. It was as if I'd gazed into the eyes of the stone
crusader on his plinth in our nave. Stone, solid stone. I was
so calm I lost concentration for a moment and felt our
blacksmith tenor Jim Large's surprised glance along the row.
There and then I made my first and last original *De Profundis*.
Rink's head was reverently bowed as I prayed, aiming at the
middle of his balding spot. That tonsure would have to go.
And the scalp as well. I know that a funeral isn't exactly the
place to pray for a successful execution, but matters were out
of my hands now.

I prayed: Dear Lord, Sorry about this, but Somebody's
got to finish Darlin' Edward. And if Somebody doesn't get a
move on pretty sharpish, I suppose it'll be up to me. Don't
say I didn't warn Somebody in good time. Okay?

The whole lot of us sang a beautiful Amen.

Reverend Woking shook me by suddenly announcing that
I would stand and utter a short homily on Dandy Jack. He's a
forgetful old sod. He should have said. I could have worked
out what to say.

I rose and gazed about. Silence hung. Everybody but
Helen was looking.

Dandy Jack's known as Dandy because he's so tatty. He
was always cheerful. I remember once he passed over a job
lot of two exquisite model railway pieces at an auction. One
was a brass miniature of the famous *Columbine* made about
1850 (the one drive-wheel looks a bit big, but don't be dis-
couraged because it always tends to on models). The second
was a lovely model of Queen Adelaide's bed coach, No. 2. I've

only ever seen their kind once before so they're hardly penny a dozen. When I'd groaned and cursed Dandy for missing a real find, he looked rueful for a second and said, peeved, 'I thought they were just bloody toys. What the hell did grown engineers want to make little things like that for?' Then he'd laughed and laughed at his own idiocy, so much that I'd found myself grinning too. Finally, I gave up being mad and laughed as well. We were in Woody's over egg and chips at the time. Lisa thought us barmy and Woody shouted from the back what the hell was going on in there and if people couldn't behave in a restaurant they'd have to piss off. That only made us worse. The place finished in uproar. Finally we'd gasped our way over to the Marquis of Granby and got paralytic drunk. It's a right game, this.

I looked about. Big Frank was reading his catalogue. Rink was piously bowed. I'm normally quite a good speaker, even with no notice, but it was a bit hard this time. I think I had a cold coming. I tried to start a couple of times but it didn't work. Dandy was almost in arm's reach. The coffin was covered beneath its heaps of flowers by a delicious purple embroidered pall, the precious and delicate *Opus Anglicanum* gold under-couching glittering against the rich colour. It's murder trying to copy. You just try. I recognized it as the one I'd tried to buy off Helen a year before. She'd sent me off with a flea in my ear: 'It's for millionaires and the crowned heads of Europe only, Lovejoy.' Dandy was neither.

I found myself just looking at the floor in silence. Some woman coughed to fill in, helping out.

'Dandy,' I managed at last. 'Whatever you find there, be a pal and save some for the rest of us.' I paused, thinking of me and Dandy getting ourselves chucked out of Woody's for laughing. It took another minute to get going. Bloody churches are full of draughts. 'It's not much help now, Dandy,' I said, 'but I'll do for the bastard that killed you whoever he was, so help me.' There was a lot of sudden shuffling. I heard Reverend Woking rise suddenly and then sit, aghast. 'Goodnight, Dandy,' I said. We all fidgeted a bit, coughed ourselves back into action.

That was it. It doesn't seem very much for a whole person.
I'd tell you the rest of the service but there's not much
point. Afterwards we all went round saying we were sorry.
Daft, really. It does no good. It's just what people do, I
suppose.

Outside the Reverend Woking was worried sick. He had
the harrowed look of a vicar burdened by a debt in search of a
debtor.

'Er, Lovejoy – ' he said.

'Don't worry. I'll pay for the funeral and the service,'
I said.

'Oh, fine, fine!' He went back to beaming goodbyes. Isn't
religion a wonderful thing?

The rest were already stampeding back to town. Nichole
tried to speak to me but her eyes filled up and she turned
aside, poor kid. Rink gave me a blank specky stare as they
drove past. Yes, I thought, I mean you, you bastard.

Janie stayed with me while they buried Dandy Jack. I told
the vicar to get a posh stone for the grave. I'd pay, I said
again. Not that it mattered. I'd no money for that either.

'Lovejoy,' Reverend Woking intoned in farewell. 'Remember that God works in mysterious ways.'

I nodded. I accept all that. It's just that I wish the Almighty
had a better record in social reform.

I walked home.

Janie told me there was a man watching the cottage. I'd
seen him on the wooden seat outside the chapel when I
went to the village shop.

'He comes sometimes and sits on the ruined gate by the
copse,' she reported.

'Any special time?'

'Morning and evening.'

I went up the lane and accosted him late on the third day.
He was rather apologetic about it all, a pleasant bloke,
about twenty-five.

'I hope you don't mind,' he said, embarrassed.

'Are you from Janie's husband?' I tried to snarl like I do

at Algernon but couldn't.

'No. I've tried to keep – ' he thought a moment, then brought out with pride – 'a *low profile*.' He smiled anxiously.

'Are you supposed to be a . . . private eye?' We were both using words nicked from those corny detective series on telly.

'I *am* one,' he said defiantly, actually believing it.

I looked at him with interest. He was the first I'd ever seen.

'We never get them hereabouts.' We were as embarrassed as each other. 'Who employs you?'

'I can't tell.' He was going to die at the stake for his profession. What a pathetic mess.

'Rink?' I said, and he quickly looked away. 'Thank you. That's what I want to know. Don't catch cold.'

So it was Rink. That gave me time. I must have read both diaries a hundred times that week but I'd learned nothing. Rink must be in the same boat as I was. Reading them over and over would have been as dull as ditchwater if it hadn't been for Dandy Jack and that other business in my garden.

'He's just an ordinary bloke,' I reported to Janie. 'I thought they were all hard as nails, as in Chandler.'

'How horrid. What will he do?'

'Oh, wait till I set off for the Isle of Man and phone Rink.' I shrugged. 'Then they'll follow me, I suppose.'

'Are you going after all?' she asked.

I gave her my very best and purest stare.

'Of *course* I'm not,' I said. 'I only meant if.'

CHAPTER XIII

THE THIRD DAY I burned the flight. I know how the Vikings felt. An end, a beginning. I used paraffin to get it going and stood back. My cherry tree got a branch singed, but then living's just one risk after another, isn't it? A neighbour came running down the lane to see if the sky was falling. He

breeds those long flat dogs which bark on middle F. I
reassured him. He left after giving my wrapped hands a
prolonged stare.

I waited for Janie. She arrived about teatime.

'Can I . . . have some money, Janie?' I watched her turn
from hanging her coat up. I've only three pegs behind the
hall door. I'd sold the mahogany stand that morning through
Tinker Dill. That's Janie's best character point – never asks
where things have suddenly gone. She may not care for my
behaviour very much, but she accepts that it goes on. I
think she tolerates me like a sort of personal bad weather,
changeable and just having to be endured.

'Yes, love.'

'I'll pay it back. Soon.'

'How much?' She fumbled in her handbag. 'Will a cheque
do?'

'Yes, please. Just enough for a couple of weeks.' I had to
say sorry, after refusing all this time, but she said men
were stupid sometimes and what were bits of paper. I'd have
agreed if she meant compared with antiques.

'Keep it,' she said.

'No, no,' I said. 'A thousand times, no.' You have to be
patient. She called me silly and got all exasperated. I think
women have very simple minds.

I looked at the cheque. Funny that a small strip of marked
paper can mean so many antiques. When you think.

'It's beautiful.' That must have been me speaking. I took
it reverently off the table. 'What are you laughing for?'

'Oh, shut up, Lovejoy.' She turned away. It didn't sound
like laughing.

'I love you,' I said to her.

She laughed and faced me, wobbling. Her cheeks were a
bit wet.

'Lovejoy, you're preposterous!'

'Eh?'

'You get everything wrong,' she said, subsiding somewhat
and smiling out of character. 'It's the other way round. *I*
love *you*.'

'That's what I said.' I was puzzled. Just when things seemed on the mend between us. Women surprise me sometimes.

'Come here to me,' she said, smiling properly now.

'Just a minute.' I found a pen and paper to make a list, but Janie took the paper away. My hands were too clumsy to argue.

'Shut up, Lovejoy,' she said, 'for heaven's sake.' So I did.

An hour later I woke from the post-loving doze. My mind instantly thought of what I should do.

Friend Rink had money. He could afford a watcher. All he had to do was wait. And if I ever made a dash for the Isle of Man he could either fly ahead or send his watcher to keep track. But nobody can move without money, and my income from Squaddie barely kept me alive. Janie's money was only for starters. I'd need more. I didn't know how long the search would take. Suddenly Janie was watching me, worried. She cheered up when I said I needed her help.

'With some antiques?'

'Yes. Cleaning and improving them.'

'For selling?'

'You're learning.'

A mischievous smile lit her face.

'Lovejoy. You . . . really need *my* help? Not Algernon's?'

'Especially not Algernon's.'

'Nor Margaret's?'

'Good heavens, no.' I wanted no dealers.

'But I know nothing about antiques.'

Careless old Lovejoy almost said that was the point, but I covered up quickly by telling her I trusted her.

'More than your friends?' she pressed. 'More even than Helen?' Typical.

'Much more,' I said. Honesty was everywhere. I felt quite moved myself.

'Then I will. On one condition.'

'Eh?'

'That you pay me, Lovejoy.'

'Pay?' I yelped, starting upright in the bed. 'What the hell with?'

'Give me one day – of your time.' She was adamant. I'd have to go carefully. What a dirty trick.

'One day?' I countered uneasily. 'You can have tomorrow. That do?'

She shook her head prettily. She's always especially attractive when she's up to no good. Sometimes I think women play on our feelings.

'No. When I say. For *me* to decide what we do for a change.'

'But what if – ?'

'No deal if you're going to make excuses, Lovejoy. Get somebody else.' I thought hard and with cunning but there seemed no way out.

'Well, it's a bit unfair,' I said reluctantly. 'Will you give me some notice?'

She hugged me, delighted.

'Possibly, Lovejoy,' she said. 'And possibly not.' I tried wheedling but got no further. She told me, smiling sweetly, 'All we have is time.' She fluttered her eyelashes exaggeratedly. I thought of the forthcoming death of Edward Rink, Esq., and smiled, in control.

Now here comes the bit I said you wouldn't like. Same as your grandma's beef tea it won't be pleasant but it will do you good. If you're poor it will save you a few quid. If you're one of the struggling rich it may save you millions.

All I've said so far about antiques is right *for antiques*. But think a second. What exactly is 'an antique'? Look about at the articles round you. We can agree on many items, for a start. Your teacup made last week in good old Stoke-on-Trent isn't antique, for example. And that ball-point pen made last year isn't either. Right. But those three decorative Coronation mugs on your mantelpiece, how about them? Well, Liz II hardly qualifies. And that George VI cup? Not really. That George V mug, then? Sorry, no. Notice how difficult it's getting. None of these is 'an antique', not truly. Some people define 'antique' as being one hundred years from today. Others claim twenty-five years is plenty. And there's some logic in that, I suppose. After all, jubilees begin at twenty-five years, and a century's the magic hundred, isn't it? But the actual honest truth's sadly different. Anything from now to twenty-five years ago is *modern*. Going back from then to a century ago's *bygone*. Then there's a bit of a twilight zone. *Then* come antiques.

Antiques begin, fans, in the shoulder of that lovely blissful Year of Grace 1836. No matter what dealer groups do with fanciful definitions, keep that magic date in mind. But please don't think I'm advising you to sprint out and hurl your Coronation souvenirs into the nearest jumble sale. That would be foolish, because three other factors besides age come into it. They're *rarity*, *nature*, and *condition*.

And here it comes, pals, the end of our beautiful friendship. What I've just told you is okay for antiques as such. It's known by any dealer worth a light, and by most collectors with any sense.

But nobody knows it like forgers do.

You reach antiques by standing on piles of money. So my mind went:

One, I have no antiques of my own.

Two, I need money.

Three, I therefore need to sell antiques, *but I've got none*.

Four, I therefore need to sell some things that resemble antiques but which aren't the real thing. Hey ho.

CHAPTER XIV

BEFORE I GO ON, don't knock forgery. It's a respectable trade and has done a lot of good for mankind. Anyway, what's wrong with a good honest forgery? People only hate the idea because it means they can't afford to be lazy when buying.

Michelangelo started out as the most expert forger of the
Renaissance, copying an ancient sketch so well even his
teacher Ghirlandaio was misled, mainly because Michelangelo had cleverly aged it. And even then he didn't own up,
only being caught out by being overheard bragging about it
in the boozer. And he went from strength to strength. It's a
sobering thought that he would never have got himself
launched, had it not been for his famous Sleeping Cupid
forgery – he buried the statue where it would be found, and
saw it actually sold to the famous collector Cardinal Riario.
He'd the sense to include a 'straightener' (a give-away) so he
could claim his just deserts later on.

So, folks, an expert may *do* the actual forging, but it's us
that make it something it never was in the first place.

Ever since I can remember I've been making. As a kid
I'd only to hear how William Blake revived and modified
Castiglione's monotype engraving for me to go thieving
copper sheet and working dementedly till all hours to see
how it could have been done. It might sound odd behaviour,
but it's taught me more about antiques than any other
experience – and I include reading. I've tried everything:
casting bronzes, silver-smithing, hammering coins, early
'chemical' photogravure, wood-block printing, making flintlocks, copying early German clocks, making parchment like
St Cuthbert's monks in his Lindisfarne outfit, ironwork,
Chinese glazes, making chain armour, anything.

I often think of Fabergé, that great (permit me to repeat
that, folks: great) designer. He didn't actually make his
brilliant masterpieces: that beavering was all done by subterranean troglodytic minions in his workshop such as
Durofeev, the self-taught mechanic of St Petersburg who
made the fabulous gold peacock which still trots out of
Fabergé's exquisite rock crystal Easter egg he gave to the
Czar. When the new bureaucracy poured into his Moscow
business at the Revolution's takeover, Fabergé simply begged
leave to be allowed to don his coat and hat and politely faded
out of this modern era. The coming of the Admin. Man was
just too much. Understandable, perhaps. My reaction's

different. I fight. The opponent is barbarism.

Being an antiques man and not having much else to fight with, I fight with antiques. And now I had a fight on my hands.

I explained to Janie I had work to do.

'More of that mysterious business in the cottage you won't let me see?' she complained.

'That's it.'

'If I find it turns out to be a secret cupboard containing a dumb blonde, Lovejoy – '

'Very funny,' I got back, not wanting her to think of hiding places. 'Your husband's back today anyhow. Time for your homework.'

'There's an alternative course of action.' Janie never smiles in this sort of conversation.

'Tell any dealers you see I'm still contagious and they're not to call.' I pushed her out. I could tell that pleased her. She didn't even say 'Including Margaret?' which I expected.

'Phone me,' she said.

'Yes,' I promised. She'd written the best times down in case some stray serf picked up the blower and summoned her better half to take me to task. I stood at the door watching her drive off in the Lagonda. Like a mobile Stately Home.

My workshop's only a shed. As much as possible I like the scene to be set correctly. No electricity. No gas. No lasers or power drills, just candles and an oil lamp. I have one wooden bench, a marble slab for special work and an old dental drill, foot-pedalled to a horizontal spindle for grinding and polishing. At the back of the garage there's a small brick kiln I've built and some leather foot-bellows I made. That's really it.

The law on forgery's a bit funny, as on everything else. Anyone's allowed to make likenesses without infringing copyright law. But if you pass one off as somebody else's work for gain, the magistrates get cross and you're for it. So, sign any fake you've made *with your own name*, however skilfully hidden, and you're in the clear. I decided that Beck was the mark. For him I decided to make a special effort. I would skate very close to the edge. Beck unsuspectingly would provide the money. I would knowingly provide the forgeries, and I'd stay legal.

I'd already tried copying Roman and Egyptian glass. One heats the glass – pick modern glass tubing because it's so easy to melt and get going. The idea is to get a blob of glass on the blowpipe, fairly centrally. Then push it into a mould you've made ready, of earthenware, sand or whatever. Blow like hell and keep the pressure up until you're practically on your knees. Then simply cut the glass off with big shears. Whatever impressions or patterns you've made to decorate the mould's inner surface, that's the pattern you'll have on your little glass bottle. Okay?

Well, no, not really. The weight and density of the glass will give you away – ancient glass seems so light. And the colours (green, yellowish, blue). So add some colour from mineral compounds when the glass is in the molten state. Trial and error's the only thing here, I'm afraid.

It took me a day to make three. One was a bowl, another a small jug and the last a small bottle. I did one extra by the lost-sand process because it was probably the first-ever of all processes mankind found. My own method is to sink a weighted earthenware bowl into a crucible and let the crucible cool, probably how it was done in Phoenician times.

I engraved LOVEJOY FECIT, my address and the day's date in minute stippled lettering as deep inside as I could reach. A buyer wouldn't look with a hand lens. I was really proud. They looked more Roman than the Roman stuff. Or did I mean Egyptian?

I next did a découpage, from an old – last year's – Christmas card. This was for speed, though my hands made it a painfully slow business. Profits are not enormous, but you can knock out a few quid by forging your first 'antique' as follows: find a ruined wardrobe, table, anything on its last legs, say your auntie's worm-pocked cupboard. Make sure it's not antique. Take the back off. Old, dried, wrinkled,

warped wood, right? Cut a piece about thirteen inches by
nine. Now go to that heap of Christmas cards you keep
meaning to chuck out. Find one picture print you think looks
oldish. Peel the design – perhaps flowers and grasses – off
the thick card, and glue it to the wood which you'll have by
now sandpapered smooth and wiped clean. Leave it a day.
Scrape some burnt umber from your nephew's paint set
on to your finger, and rub it into the *edges* of the stuck design.
Not too much. Warm it all in a fireplace. Then varnish the
lot, several coats. Use the new synthetic varnishes if you
like, with maybe a scratch of chrome yellow to the final
coat. Rose madder does quite well, too, but you'll need to be
very careful with that. And there's your genuine William IV,
or even late Georgian, decorated place-mat ('from the house
of a local country squire' as we dealers would say). Never
mind that Georgian country squires practically never used
table mats. You have the money for your next meal.

   Then I did a lovely tiling job. A tiler is a low quality
forged painting, a sort of beginner's forgery, though with an
impressive record of giddy success. It's done like this: take a
modern book showing the paintings by, say, Samuel Palmer.
You take one area of a picture (say, a mid-ground forest) and
trace its outline on to a paper. Then you trace a barn from a
second painting, the mountain from a third, sky from a
fourth and so on. If you don't care about the book you cut
the pictures out, and assemble the paper bits, very like a
jigsaw or tiling on a wall, until all the area of your blank
paper's area is filled. Then, with any old watercolour paint-
box, you assemble the painting. Tip: do it fast. You'd be
astonished at the speed real forgers work. I suspect the
original masters worked just as fast. Think for example of
the contemporary descriptions of Turner. He always had
his skates on.

   For Beck's 'Palmer' I used the heaviest paper I could
find, which was about one hundred and twenty poundage.
Heavy paper always helps. It took about an hour. Then,
ensuring I'd a lovely straightener – my name in pencil, done
minutely in a crease folded into the area to be covered by the

frame – I blew a faint gust of soot and heated soil-dust over
it. *Never* use soot alone. I fronted it with faintly brown-
tinted glass. (Well, actually, I couldn't afford that, so I
inserted a sheet of thin plastic over which I'd washed a
mixture of Vandyke brown and chrome yellow.) Any trick
for age's sake, forgers say.

Next was a copy of a letter, copied from a famous book of
Peninsular War letters, ostensibly from one of Wellington's
soldiers at Salamanca. I used ordinary typing paper, two
sheets glued together to get that crackle and frayed with a
wire brush. I wrote using a real quill and some ink made
from crushed oakgalls out of the garden. Two or three very
warm warmings in the oven, and my own name in a grand
convoluted signature so complex even I had to trace the
scrolled lines to read it.

I invented my own antique musical instrument next.
Vaseline smeared over an old bike inner tube, cut and
clipped to be one long inflated rubber. Two inner cardboards
from lavatory rolls, also Vaselined, and a handful of four-
inch glue-soaked bandages rolled round the tube and the
cardboards and waggled into a double-S shape. Once they'd
set, I pricked the inner tube and pulled it out as it deflated.
The rigid S-shaped piece was now solid enough to wind
more glue-soaked bandages around. When it hardens you can
cut oval holes at various distances along it. I drilled a piece
of horn into a mouthpiece shape and stuck it in the thin
end. The trouble is that bandages are white so I stained the
thing with teabags crammed into a jamjar with a little burnt
umber and saffron powder before varnishing. I engraved
my signature, the date and my address round the inner rim
of the mouthpiece and the belled rim. LOVEJOY FECIT again.
Ten to one Beck would call it a crumhorn without knowing
a crumhorn from a foghorn. A million to one he'd never
look for the maker's name. I baked it gently in a low oven.

They looked really good. I'll have to be careful what I
buy in future, I thought. I lined them up on my bench for a
last look. Good. Or, rather, bad. I normally only do things

properly to teach myself. But this was different. Once people
start going about killing people, people have to take very
special measures against certain people, don't people? Even
if it means people taking frightful risks.

I was ready.

That evening I took out my one precious piece, very dear to
me. A jade coin, apparently from the Ch'ien Lung period.
I had it in my priest-hole. Now the cupboard was bare.

I phoned Tinker Dill at the White Hart. He called at the
cottage for the jade. I told him to enter it at Gimbert's
auction by a devious route and under a fictitious name. He
was going to ask what it was all about but looked at my face.

'Will you be there, Lovejoy?' he asked.

'Oh yes,' I said. 'Wouldn't miss an auction for the world.'
I gave him the bus fare back to town. 'I'll be in action again
soon, Tinker.'

'See you, then.'

'Oh, Tinker,' I called after him. 'See that Beck's there,
can you?'

He grinned. 'Thought as much.' He waved from the drive.
I saw him hitch a lift from the milk float further up the lane.

Ready, steady, go.

CHAPTER XV

THE DAY of the auction dawned blue and clear. By six o'clock
I was up and sweating like a dog, nervous and on edge. I go
about trembling and singing, clattering the pots and getting
ready twice. I'm always like this. Janie was due to come for
me at nine-fifteen. By then I was a wreck. The wildlife
got their breakfast three times over and I lost pounds. I
couldn't eat any breakfast though I'd got some of those
flaky things out and made some toast.

'There must be easier ways to earn a living, Lovejoy.'
Janie pulled the Lagonda in and sat staring at me.

'Why are you so bloody late?' I couldn't unlock the car
door for fumbling.

'I'd like to point out that I'm early,' she said sweetly.
'And good morning, world.'

'Well, then,' I said lamely.

'And it isn't locked.'

Two down. I got in sheepishly and we left the village
sedately, a visiting lady and her agent respectably bound for
an ordinary sale. I always feel so sick at this stage. The
first sight of town by the nursery gardens makes me retch.
That's the trouble with ordinary sales – there's no such thing.
Every single one's a matter of life and death.

'Are you all right, darling?' Janie slowed at the station.
'Shall I stop?'

'No.' I'd only have to get out and run.

'If I see something I like in the auction, can I get it?'

'Tell me.' It took me three tries to speak. My mouth was
sand. 'And I'll tell you what to do.'

'Oh, I can bid,' she said, poor little innocent. 'I know how.'
The eternal cry.

'Everybody knows *how* about everything,' I said. 'Only
Caesars and Wellingtons know *when.*'

She shrugged. 'Anyway, there may be nothing nice there,'
she countered. 'And keep your hand off my knee when I'm
driving, Lovejoy.'

'Oh, sorry.' My hand had actually fallen on her knee again.
My mind was on other things.

No matter what the auction is, somewhere deep in that
crush of old mangles, derelict bikes and discarded trinkets
is a gem, a real trophy going for a song.

I've never yet been to an auction where every single thing's
rubbish. I don't deny that on viewing day you'll hear
plenty of people all about you saying disgustedly, 'Did you
ever see such rubbish?' Have you ever wondered why? If
you'd spotted, say, the missing chunk of the Cullinan
Diamond thinly disguised as a paperweight between a
battered radio and a heap of gardening tools, what else

would you do but go about pretending everything was a waste of time? I mean, you don't want all Hatton Garden clattering in. So naturally you go about saying it's all a heap of dross. Loudly. Often. We call it 'shading' the stock. It puts honest people (me, maybe you) off. You'd be surprised how effective it is. You'd also be astonished at seeing how many of these doom-gospellers actually turn up on sale days all eager to bid for the same rubbish they've previously decried.

Janie put the Lagonda in Gimbert's yard with the dealers' old bangers. We left it looking like a cathedral among kennels. We walked down the hill, Janie primly keeping her distance from me and smiling good mornings to one and all. We were all assembling. Barkers tend to huddle in doorways, smoking and nodding. A housewife who will be bidding usually stands waiting vigilantly in one spot, presumably in case Sotheby's suddenly send a dozen experts to bid for the ashtray she fancies.

It's a saying round here that the best trees are found in forests, and they're very hard to tell from all the rest. When you go bidding just remember that people aren't what they say or think or seem. We're all what we *do*.

There were already eighty or so people in. Everybody was on tenterhooks, hearts thumping and fingers itching. I had to tell Janie about her coat. She had unconsciously adopted the old shoplifter's trick of carrying her coat over her arm.

'Do you mean they'd think me a . . . thief?' She was outraged.

'No, love. Er,' I invented, 'you *remind* them, that's all.' It had to do, though she was deeply riled. The dealers relaxed as she slipped the coat over her shoulders.

This morning Gimbert's auction warehouse was offering several hundred items of assorted junk ranging from battered old tables to tatty trinkets in those pathetic little boxes signifying recent bereavements and relatives desperate to clear out. Some people say all life's only must, dust and rust. People wandered about among the bicycles and lawnmowers,

mostly without any idea. From the entrance it was ugly,
dowdy, pretty rough. To me, exquisite. Somewhere in all
that rubbish was that missing Leonardo. I would find it or
get damned close. To some that single bargain would be
nothing more than a ring, a worn Edwardian matchbox, a
Victorian maid's mob cap. To me, a delight as spectacular
as the Crown Jewels.

There's a technique. You *drift*. Don't tear in thinking to
see it all and race on to the next auction. Don't search. Idle
about. After an hour or so a gradual change takes place.
Objects begin to move like swallows shuffling on a wire. I
swear it. You can feel it, even see it. Dusty old items you
wouldn't look at twice shift into prominence as if they
somehow grow taller and beckon stealthily. But take no
notice yet, just carry on drifting. In time one will be practically shrieking for your attention. That grotty old desk
covered with rubbish will have grown to twice its size and be
throbbing like an old cinema organ. Everything else will
fade into the background. And of course it will turn out to
be a genuine early New England block-fronted desk, so
ugly yet so much desired today. On a good day maybe two
or even three items call you. Once I even had to mortgage
my cottage again to pay for the seven delicious items I'd
bought.

Smiling with anticipation, I drifted in.

Gimbert's is two enormous galleries half-roofed in glass
so the shadows confuse the innocent. Light's the auctioneer's
worst enemy. It isn't bad as auction halls go but you have to
watch it. Ringers turn up once a month. They're easy to
spot, shuffling about looking at customers and nowhere else
the way they do. They *have* to, in case a serious collector
turns up. If one does he spells trouble – the collector may be
willing to pay an antique's true worth and ringers aren't.
They pretend to ignore the desired object, except for one
ringer who bids. After the auction they'll meet in some bar
and auction the antique among themselves, sharing the net
gain.

It's illegal.

'Morning, Lovejoy.' Dear old Beck. Fancy that.

'Morning.'

'On the borrow?' he asked, grinning. 'Or selling that Isen?'
He'd fished me more than once, knowing I can't help
going after antiques. You fish friends – or, indeed, enemies –
by telling them, say, a genuine painting by Isen (Kano
Eishin) is somewhere or other, making it up. Well, who in
their right mind can resist Isen's luscious white highlighted
robes and his gusting winds driving those painted ships?
Naturally one hares off after it. For somebody like Beck it's a
joke. For somebody like me, going without grub to raise the
fare on a wild goose chase, it's no giggle.

'Sold it,' I said back coolly. He stared. 'Thanks for the
tip, Beckie.' That shut him up.

I drifted on, nodding and passing the occasional word.
A mote spoon donged for attention from among a mass of
crud in a crammed cutlery drawer. I'm always astonished
people's heads don't swivel at the sudden clanging. The
trouble is that genuine antiques make your breathing funny. I
went over casually and pretended to examine the kitchen
cabinet. Mote spoons are often forged, but this was true 1752
or so. No maker's mark. Odd long pointed handle and a
fenestrated bowl.

Lily and Patrick arrived to look at the phoney tapestries
and Big Frank lumbered in to maul the silver. Delmer came
flashily in, staggering under the weight of his gold rings.
Even before he was through the door those of us who knew
him glanced about to see where the books were heaped and
stepped out of the way because he's a fast mover. I like
dealers like Delmer. Only books. He'd walk past a Rubens
crucifixion painting to bid for a paperback. Sure enough he
streaked for the corner, slamming a nice pair of Suffolk
chairs aside on the way. I sighed. It takes all sorts, but God
alone knows why.

'Anything, Lovejoy?' Tinker Dill, an unnerving sight this
early, obediently emerging from the mob on time. This was
my cue. I hoped Tinker could remember his lines.

'Not really, Tinker.' I made sure I said it wrong enough

for alert friends to notice.

'I'll slide off, then.'

'Er, no, Tinker.' A lot of ears pricked. 'Hang about.'

'Lovejoy wants you to bid for that drawerful of old knives and forks, Tinker.' Beck again.

'Right,' I said angrily. I didn't have to act. Beck really does rile me. 'Get it, Tinker.'

'It looks a right load of rubbish, Lovejoy – ' Tinker, badly overacting.

'*Get it*, Tinker.'

'Lost your wool?' Beck said innocently. 'Just because I got that Burne-Jones sketch? Sold it yesterday, incidentally. To your friend, businessman with the blonde.' So Rink had traced it successfully after all. I hadn't time to worry about the implications for the minute.

'Look, Lovejoy – '

'Do as you're bloody well told, Tinker.'

I pushed off through the crowd, pretending to be blazing.

'Easy, Lovejoy.' Lennie offering me a fag. I shook my head irritably. I deserved an Oscar.

'Those bloody trawlies get to me, Lennie.'

'Jill said she'd be in with that opal photo.'

'Thanks.' I'd dated it for her, about 1800. Photographs were once done on opal glass and coloured by watercolours. She was asking the earth, naturally.

I drifted. Delmer had found a copy of *The History of Little Goody Two-Shoes* and looked as pleased as Punch. Don't laugh. The public's soaked up over two hundred editions since 1765.

'Is it one of Newberry's?' I couldn't help muttering the vital question as I drifted past. He dropped it casually back into the job lot and sauntered off, shaking his head absently. A good dealer's a careful one. I touched it for the clang and drifted in the opposite direction. The unique copy's in the British Museum, but Newberry turned them out for donkey's years in St Paul's Churchyard during Georgian times so they're still knocking about. I had a brief look at the rest. Delmer would have spotted the first edition of Ransome's

Swallows and Amazons which lay among a pile of gramophone records, so no chance there.

I drifted some more. The crowd collected. Ringers were there, trimmers, hailers, tackers, lifters, nobbers, screwers, backers and sharpers, a real tribe of hunters if ever there was one. I can't help smiling. I actually honestly like us all. At least we're predictable and therefore reliable, which makes us a great deal more preferable than the good old innocent public. Some people were gazing in the window at us. Well, if you stay out of the water at least the sharks can't get you.

The jade coin was in the corner case, numbered seventy. By the time the auctioneer banged us to the starting gate practically everybody in the room was pretending to ignore it.

'Lot One,' he piped, a callow youth on his tenth auction. 'A very desirable clean modern birdcage complete with stand. Who'll bid?'

'Dad send you to feed the crocodiles, sonny?' one of the Aldgate circus called. Laughter.

A woman near me tutted. 'How rude!' she exclaimed.

I nodded sadly. 'Modern manners,' I said. She approved of my sentiments and I was glad. I'd seen her inspecting the kitchen cabinet, and Tinker Dill was on to it, with my money.

Sharks and cut-throats, we all settled and paid rapt attention to the sale of a birdcage.

I watched it come. Ten, twenty. At thirty-two Margaret bid for and got a pair of small Lowestoft soft-paste porcelain animal figures, a swan and a dog. I don't like them much because of the enamelling but I was glad for Margaret. Delmer got his *Goody Two-Shoes* and a pile of others for a few pence at thirty-eight. At forty Tinker Dill got the cabinet, though Beck had a few laughs at my expense and threatened loudly to compete in the bidding. One of the Birmingham lads wandered over curiously during the bidding to look at the cabinet, but by then Tinker had guessed right and was standing idly by, leaning against the

drawer where the mote spoon was. *My* mote spoon now.
The Brummie stared across at me carefully. I smiled
benevolently back. I saw him start edging across to the
others of the Brummie circus. Well, they're not all daft.

Harry Bateman tried a few bids for a Victorian copy of an
anonymous Flemish school oil and failed. Why first-class
nineteenth-century artists wasted their talents making copies
of tenth-rate seventeenth-century paintings I'll never know,
but you couldn't say this to Harry.

'Lot Seventy,' the auctioneer intoned.

This was it. My jade piece, a dark lustrous green with
brown flacks and one oblique growth fault, was carved in the
form of an ancient Chinese cash coin. Jade is the wonder
stone, matt and oily and soft to look at yet incredibly hard.
It can resist shock blows time after time. (Remember that
those large but thin uninteresting jade rectangles you see are
most probably nothing less than temple *bells*, to be struck
when tuning string instruments. Very desirable. A complete
set is worth . . . well, a year's holiday. Give me first offer.)
I saw Beck glance around. The bidding started. I went in
quick, too quick for some. Jimmo was prominent in the early
stages. Then Jonas came in, raising in double steps to the
auctioneer's ecstasy. Jonas is a youngish retired officer with
money, no knowledge and determination. This combination's
usually at least fatal, but Jonas has survived in the business
simply by refusing to give up. From an initial dislike his
fellow dealers, me included, switched to neutrality and
finally with reluctance to a sort of grudging acceptance. He's
silver and pre-Victorian book bindings with occasional
manuscripts thrown in for luck. Lily was there but left the
bidding when I started up. Patrick looked peevish when she
stalled – there'd be trouble over her tea and crumpets when
he got her home. Four others showed early and chucked up.
That left me, Jonas, a Brummie and Beck. I bid by nodding.
Some people bid by waving programmes or raising eyebrows. Remember there's no need to wave and tell everybody
who's bidding. Don't be afraid your bid will be missed. A

creased forehead is like a flag day to an auctioneer. He gets a percentage.

On we went, me sweating as always. I was beaten when Beck upped. Jonas must have sensed something wasn't quite right because he hung on only briefly, then folded. I saw that the Brummie bidder was the one who'd crossed to look at the kitchen cabinet. He finally stopped when Beck showed the first sign of wavering, clever lad. The jade was knocked down to Beck.

Beck glanced triumphantly in my direction through the throng. I glared back. He would brag all year how he picked up this rare ancient Chinese jade coin in the face of organized local opposition.

'He had us, Lovejoy,' Jonas said, pushing past at the break. I followed him muttering to the tea bar.

'Hard luck, Lovejoy,' from Jimmo. 'Hell of a price.'

'Outsider!' I heard Patrick snapping at Beck.

'Things are getting worse every day,' I agreed.

Janie had our teas waiting in the brawl. We had to fight our way into a corner to breathe. Tinker kept Janie a part of a bench. I kissed her.

'Watch out, Lovejoy,' she said, smiling brightly to show eagle-eyed watchers we were only good friends. 'One of my neighbours is here.' She flashed a brilliant grimace towards a vigilant fat lady steaming past. 'I'm sorry, love,' she added, moving primly away from my hand which had accidentally alighted on her knee.

'What about?'

'The old jade.' She reproved me under her breath, 'I'd have given you some money. Nobody need have noticed.'

'Why?'

'Then *you* could have got the jade instead.'

'Oh. Thanks, love,' I said bravely. 'You get these disappointments.'

She eyed me shrewdly. 'Didn't you want it, Lovejoy?'

'Of course I did,' I lied evenly. 'I always want ancient Chinese jade, don't I?'

She kept her eyes on me. 'Then why are you so pleased, Lovejoy?'

'Oh, just life in general.'

'Was there something wrong with it?'

'Certainly not!' I said indignantly.

I ought to know. It had taken me nine weeks to make, nine weeks of pure downright slavery over my old pedalled spindle. It was absolutely perfect. Authentic in every detail, except for the small point that it was a forgery.

Now calm down, gentle reader. Can I be held responsible if some goon buys a piece of jade – it really was jade, which is mined nowadays in Burma, New Zealand and Guatemala – without examining it? And if you're still wondering why I bid for a forgery I'd made and put up for auction myself, take my tip: please feel free to read on, but don't ever go into the antiques game. My name and address I'd scratched in minute letters around the margins of the inside hole, date included. If customers don't look with a handlens, it's just tough luck, and the more fools they. I couldn't exactly put my name in neon lights on a thing the size of a dollar, could I? It would spoil the effect.

'Lovejoy.' She had that odd look.

'I didn't touch your knee,' I said indignantly.

'What are you up to?'

I was narked with Janie. Right in the middle of a chattering mob of customers in an ordinary small-town auction she starts suspecting me of being up to some trickery. Women can be very suspicious of fundamentally good honest motives. It's not very nice. I really do believe they have rather sinister minds. Where there's no reason to be suspicious they suddenly assume you can't be trusted. I find it very unsettling. They're the ones who're always on about trust, then they go and show they've got none themselves. It's basically a sign of poor character.

At Lot Two-Eighty I crossed to Tinker. The crowd had thinned. In the smoke the substitute auctioneer, a hoary old veteran who wasn't letting us get away with anything, droned cynically on. We had space to pretend interest.

Tinker made a great show of pulling out the drawer and complaining about the uselessness of the buy I'd made. The auctioneer called for quiet, please, during the bidding. I slipped the mote spoon into my pocket and relaxed.

'Put the rest back in next week's auction, Lovejoy?' Tinker asked. This is all quite legal.

'Yes.' I made sure we weren't overheard. 'Grumble a lot while you do.'

'I'll try.'

I had to stop myself from a wide grin at Tinker's crack. Barkers can out-grumble the most miserable farmer.

Janie went to have her hair done. We eventually met at a coffee garden near the river walk, a short distance away. I'd tried to get her to come to Woody's but she wouldn't. I said I could return her the money she'd lent me. She said don't be silly.

We talked on the way back to Gimbert's, where the auction was practically over. I caught sight of Beck and said so-long to Janie. They were in the auction yard among starting cars and people hauling various lots out of the covered part. A woman was asking how to get an enormous cupboard home. Time to haul in the net.

'Look, Beck,' I said. He stopped bragging to his mates. 'About that jade.'

'Want it, Lovejoy? It's for sale.' There was a roar of laughter, my expense.

'I've a couple of things you might swap.'

'Good stuff?'

'Two are.'

'What kind of stuff?'

'Good stuff,' I said cagily.

'Where?'

'My place.'

He thought a moment. Finally he trod his cigarette.

'I'll come.'

I got a taxi. In the ride out to the village he showed me the jade.

'Lovely piece of work, eh?'

I could hardly disagree. At the cottage he insisted the taxi waited.

I had the pieces distributed around the living-room. It wouldn't do to show him the workshop.

'This glass jug,' I told him. He reached out for it. 'I've this bowl as well.'

'Both yours?' he asked warily. I nodded. 'Honestly? Roman or Egyptian?'

His eyes were everywhere while I busied myself getting a glass of beer. I had to steady my hands, back turned towards him, while I poured in case the glass clinked and gave away my anxiety. It's a right bloody game this. When I gave him the drink I could see he'd noticed my tiler, hung prettily on the wall. And my non-musical instrument casually placed over the fireplace.

'You've one or two things here, Lovejoy,' he said.

'I don't want to sell.'

'No?' He looked shrewdly about. 'This place looks pretty bare. And where's your car? You used to have one.'

'Well, I had to sell it.'

'I see.' He sat examining the glass bowl and jug I'd made. 'Good Roman,' he pronounced. I said nothing. 'Cash adjustment, Lovejoy?'

'No,' I said. 'One for one.'

'No deal.'

'Well, then,' I hesitated. 'I'm not really in the jade field any more, but . . .'

'No?' He actually laughed. 'Then what are we arguing about?'

We began dealing. It's done by mental palpation, not actual utterances. You talk all round the subject, how difficult things are, what clients want nowadays, how troublesome barkers are. We ended with Beck accepting the glass bowl and the jug, plus the painting, in exchange for the jade coin. He took the instrument as well and paid a few notes to make up the difference.

He carried his trophies into the waiting taxi.

'Here, Lovejoy,' he said from the window as the car

turned in the lane.

'Yes?'

'I don't see why I should pay the driver.'

I paid up with ill grace and watched the taxi dwindle uphill towards the chapel. He'd paid anyway. He'd be jubilant, until he found out.

Still, I'd not been untruthful. 'That Palmer looks wrong to me, somehow,' I'd said. And I'd told him of the instrument, 'I'm not sure what you'd call it.'

I stood in the garden tying my jade on to a string to wear round my neck under my shirt. Contact with living human skin really does restore life and glow to jade. *Never* leave jade untouched if you can help it. It's the only antique of which this can be said. Jade is the exception which proves my no-touch rule. Even the funeral pieces from ancient China recover their life and lustre by being fondled. Love, folks, as I said, is making it. Jade tells you that.

I totted up. I'd sell the mote spoon to Helen. That would pay Janie back and, with what I'd got extra from Beck just now, give me the fare to the Isle of Man. As for the rest, I'd just swapped one set of forgeries for another. Right?

Yes, right. But there was a balance, the money Beck had just given for the jade at Gimbert's. He had successfully bid for it against fierce opposition. I was proud of him.

I'd promised to ring Janie and say what I'd decided to do, but then I thought it over. It'd be better just me against Edward Rink.

I went in to pack.

Early morning and I was on the train to Liverpool.

CHAPTER XVI

THE TRAIN's the easy bit.

I like the sea. It's natural, somehow never fraudulent. From the ferry wharf I gazed down the Mersey out to sea.

If Bexon was right, Suetonius had probably sailed from
Chester. The more I thought about it the more it fitted. The
Roman Second Legion had been stationed in Chester when
Boadicea vented her spleen. That's known nearly for
absolute certain. The wily Roman had left his harbour base
firmly held in strength, the most orthodox of all military
moves. He'd hardly have needed it protected this way if he'd
sailed from Wales because the powerful Queen Cartimandua,
as nasty a piece of work as ever trod land, was too busy
ravishing successions of stalwart standard-bearers in Manchester to notice if the political weather outside changed much
from day to day.

The ferry was two-thirds full with passengers. I must have
expected a few logs loosely lashed together because I gaped
at this huge ocean-going boat. It had a funnel and round
windows and everything. Cars were streaming aboard, even
lorries.

You can get a meal or snacks and there's a bar. The
general impression's a bit grubby but a few hours is not for
ever. I like wandering about on ships. It being latish September holidaymakers weren't too plentiful, only a few clusters
of diehards catching the cheaper rates of early autumn. We
were a mixed bunch. There were the usual tribes of business-
men discussing screws and valves over pale ales, hysterical
crises over lost infants finally miraculously found again
where they'd been left in the first place, and couples snogging
uninterruptedly on the side decks. They're my favourite. If
Janie had been with me she'd have said not to look at them,
then looked herself when we'd gone past. Women do that.

Liverpool began to slide away. I looked everywhere on the
ferry for my watcher. Twice I went round the lower decks,
strolling among the cars and pretending boredom. No sign.
He wasn't on board. I must admit I was rather put out. You
eventually feel quite proud, being shadowed. After all, not
everybody gets trailed, if that's the right word. Maybe he'd
been laid off. I already knew that good old Edward was of an
economic turn of mind. That meant Rink would be flying
first class, of course. I just hoped he'd have sense enough to

leave Nichole behind. If there was going to be any rough stuff I didn't want her involved.

Seagulls cawed and squawked for nothing. They went and sat floating in our wake a lot. Somebody once told me they can actually drink seawater. They have this gland for handling the sodium or something. We had over a hundred following us out of the Mersey estuary into the open sea. You'd think they'd get tired because they've only got to find their way home again.

Ships are noisy, not just the people but the engines, the sea, the floor, the walls as well. Even the funnels make a racket. Somebody always seems to be ringing bells in the downstairs rooms. I went up into the air though the wind was cutting. A sheepdog came and sat near me by the railings.

'Are you lost?' I asked it. It smiled like they do and edged closer to lean on my leg. We looked at the sea rushing past below us. 'If you're lost, mate, there's not much hope for the rest of us, is there?'

It said nothing back. I bent down and peered. It had nodded off, probably fed up. I knew how it felt. Me without antiques, the dog without a single sheep. I pulled it away from the railings for safety and hauled it next to me on a wooden seat. When you lift dogs up they seem to have so many ribs.

'Some bloody watchdog you are,' I told it. 'What if we were sheep?'

I nodded off too. It's the sea air.

Ships docking unsettle me. I'm not scared but they seem to head towards the walls so fast. Then the whole thing shakes for all it's worth and stops. Some men threw ropes from our front end. Two chaps on land pulled them round a big iron peg set in the stone road, a queer business. Some others did the same at the back end. We all marched up a flat ladder thing and crocodiled up the stone steps to the town of Douglas, Isle of Man.

'Do you all live on that thing?' I asked the uniformed chap

who was seeing us off.

He seemed surprised. 'Where else?' he said.

It's a rum world.

I humped my case along a glass cloister affair and crossed over to the taxis. I spent a few minutes describing Bexon's abode, carefully using the same descriptive terms in Bexon's diary. One taxi-driver nodded finally and took my case.

'Only one place that can be,' he announced. 'Groundle Glen.' I was pleased. Bexon had used that name, though somewhat ambiguously.

The main Douglas beach is rimmed by a wide promenade and a curved road. Houses, shops and hotels gathered parallel for a dense mile or so. Then the hillside begins, suddenly rising to high green fells.

'What's a railway line on the main road for?' I asked him as the north road started to lift out of Douglas town. It had been on my mind.

'For that.' He was laughing.

A tiny train, engine and all, was chugging uphill on our left, beside us on the road. One carriage carried the sign *Groundle Glen.*

Ask a silly question.

About a mile out the road ran above a small bay cleft in the rock. A cluster of newly built bungalows shone in the late sun. Ships hung about on the sea.

'This is it.'

We turned right down a sharp incline towards the sea. There were maybe thirty or forty dwellings ribbed on the hillside, mainly greys and browns. New flower-beds surmounted bank walls by the winding road.

'Do they have an office?'

'It's only one of the bungalows. A lassie sees to you, Betty Springer.'

The taxi-driver carried my suitcase to my door. I was becoming edgy with all this courtesy. He praised the view and I tried to do the same, but all you could see was the

green hillside and woods on the opposite side of the valley
and the blue sea rustling the shingle below. A stream in its
autumn spate ran below. There was a bridge leading to the
trees.

'Don't you like the view?' my driver asked happily as I
paid him off. I strained to see the town we'd left down by the
harbour but couldn't. It was hidden by the projecting
hillside. Bloody countryside everywhere again.

'Lovely,' I said.

The girl came to see I got the gas working all right as I
explored the bungalow.

'The end bungalow's a shop too,' she told me. 'Papers
and groceries. Nothing out of the ordinary, but useful.'

'Great.'

'Are you a friend of the other gentleman?' she asked
merrily, putting on the kettle. She showed me how to drop
the ironing-board, clearly a born optimist.

'Er, who?'

'From East Anglia too,' she said. 'Mr Throop. Just
arrived this very minute.'

'What a coincidence,' I observed uneasily. My private
eye?

'I put him next door. You'll have a lot to talk about.'

'How do I get a car, love?'

'Hire.' She fetched out some teabags. 'I'll do it if you tell
me what kind. Have some tea first. I know what the ferry's
like.'

'And I need a good map.'

'In the living-room bookcase. Please don't lose any if
you can help it. What are you?' She faced me frankly.

'Eh?' I countered cunningly.

'Well, are you a walker, or an archaeologist after the Viking
burials, or a tape-recorder man who wants me to speak
Manx, or what? Sugar and milk?'

'I'm . . .' I had a brainwave and said, 'I'm an engineer.
Like my old friend Bexon who used to come here.'

'You know him? How nice!' She poured for us both while

I rejoiced inwardly at my opportunism. 'Such a lovely old
man. He'd been to Douglas on his honeymoon years ago.
How is he?'

She'd obviously taken to the old chap. I said he was fine
and invented bits of news about him.

'He was so proud!' she exclaimed. 'He'd helped to build a
lot of things on Man. Of course, that was years ago. Are
you here to mend the railway? It seems so noisy lately.'

We chatted, me all excited and trying to look casual and
tired. Betty finally departed, promising to get a car. We
settled for first thing in the morning.

So I'd hit the exact place Bexon had stayed. Now, then.
Businesslike, I went to suss out the scenery.

The bay window overlooked the valley. Over a row of
roofs the light was beginning to fade. Something was
rankling, slightly odd. If Bexon was an ailing man, why ever
stay at Groundle Glen? Betty Springer had told me the little
train stopped near the crossroads up on the main road,
maybe four hundred yards away. And an old man walking
slowly up to the tiny roadside station could get wet through
if it rained. So he was here for a purpose.

The bungalows were too recently built to be of any
romantic significance to the old man. There seemed to be
only one reason left. I peered down towards the river.

Tally-ho?

I went out to buy some eggs, cheese and bread. They had
some lovely Auckland butter which I felt like. I bought a
miserable pound of margarine instead because the quacks are
forever on at you these days. They had no pasties or cream
sponges. I found I'd accidentally bought a cabbage when I
got home. What the hell do people do with cabbage? I
suppose you fry it some way. I opened the windows and
looked about for some ducks but saw none. But do ducks
like cabbage? I gave up and put it in a drawer.

I fried myself an omelet. That, a ton of bread and
marge, a pint of tea and I was fit enough to switch on the
news to see who we were at war with. Outside hillside
creatures stalked and cackled. The sea shushed. The sun

sank. Lights came on in the bungalows here and there. A ship's green lamp showed a mile or two off shore.

It seemed a fearful long way to town. When you're in countryside it always does.

I got the fright of my life that evening.

It was about midnight. The lights were on in the next bungalow. It was the man who'd followed me. I knew that. Throop. My lights were off. The telly was doing its stuff but I'd turned the sound down.

This figure moved in silhouette. My kitchen door was glass so he was easily visible. Probably thought I was out. I got the poker and crept to the little passageway. The stupid man was fumbling noisily with the latch. Some sleuth.

I hid in the loo doorway, trembling. My mouth was dry. In he blundered. His glasses gleamed in the part light as I leapt and grabbed him.

'Right, Throop, you bastard!' He was too astonished to struggle. I clicked on the light.

'Greetings, Lovejoy!' It was Algernon, pleased we'd met up.

'You stupid . . .' I let him go. 'You frightened me to death.'

'Did you not realize?' He went all modest. 'I'm being your . . . *undercover agent*!'

'Brew up,' I told him, trying to keep the quaver out of my voice and trying to hide the poker. I felt like braining him.

'Certainly!' He breezed into the kitchen, falling over a stool. 'How perfectly marvellous that someone so per-spicacious failed to penetrate my *subterfuge*!' he nattered, chuckling. He pulled a kitchen drawer out all the way. The crash of the cutlery as it spread over the tiled floor made me jump a mile. Unabashed, he wagged a finger playfully while he grabbed the kettle. 'You should have realized, Lovejoy! Algernon sort of goes with Throop!'

'What else?' I put my head in my hands. A spray of water wet me through, just Algernon trying to fill the kettle.

It was rapidly becoming a bad dream. Here I was trying to

slip about quietly, a difficult, risky business with that sinister nut Rink on my tail. I'd thought I was doing reasonably well. Now, thanks to Algernon, following me would be like shadowing a carnival. I had to get clear.

'And I have another surprise for you!' he crowed, plugging the flex in with a blue flash.

'Please, Algernon.' I couldn't take any more. My heart was still thumping.

'No, Lovejoy!' he cried roguishly, spilling tea round his feet and skilfully nudging a cup into the sink as he turned. I heard it break on the stainless steel. 'I won't tell you! It's a *surprise!*'

Somehow he'd managed to pour hot water into the teapot though it was touch and go and a lot of luck went into it. To save breakages I got the cups. He broke the fridge door looking for the milk which I'd got prominently displayed on the table anyway. He prattled on about his journey, hugging himself with glee about the mysterious surprise he'd lined up for me. I had a headache.

'Push off, Algernon,' I said.

'Very well, Lovejoy!' he cried. 'Your tea's all ready! See you in tomorrow's fair dawning! And when you wake . . .' He went all red and bashful and tripped head over heels down the passage. The door crashed. I could have sworn something splintered. I listened, wincing. No tinkle of glass, thank God. Another crash. He'd made it home, the next bungalow. I took a sip of tea and spat it out. He'd forgotten the bloody teabags.

I sighed and looked for a bottle of beer. A secret with Algernon's like a salvo. I'd have to get some sleep. Algernon's secret would be on the night boat. Always assuming her car wasn't too long to fit on the deck.

Somebody was in the kitchen again. Light tottered through curtains, still drawn. I vaguely remembered making love when it was dark. I forget to wind watches so there's no point in having one, and those new digital efforts are always trying to prove themselves. I could tell it was about after

seven o'clock. I went to the bedroom window and peered out.
Sure enough, a Lagonda by the shop.

I climbed back into bed, sitting up. In she came, lovely
and floury from baking.

'Morning, Lovejoy, darling.'

'I'm supposed to be here alone,' I said bitterly.

She set the tray right and got back in with cold feet.

'You can't possibly manage without me, Lovejoy.'

'It'll be like a Bedouin caravan with you lot. How did
you know I was here?'

'Algernon,' she said brightly. 'I persuaded him your
welfare depends on me.'

'Anybody else?' I demanded. 'Jimmo? The Batemans?
Jill?'

'Just me.' She dished breakfast out, smiling roguishly.

'You're going back. First boat.'

'No, Lovejoy,' she gave back calmly. 'You've to pay up.'

'Er,' I said uneasily. She must mean the sale. 'Well,'
I said slowly, working it out as I went, 'I had a lot of expenses.
I made about twenty per cent. Fifty-fifty?' I keep meaning to
get one of those electric calculators.

She was shaking her head. It was a pity we could see
ourselves in the mirror of the dressing-table opposite. She
watched me in the pale light. I looked away casually.

'A day. Remember?' Hard as nails, women are.

'Oh.' Of course. I owed her a day. I thought hard. Maybe
it wouldn't be too bad. I had a good dozen antiques dealers'
addresses on the Isle. Some were supposed to be pretty fair.
'Well, Janie love – '

'Before you say it, Lovejoy,' she told me. 'No. No antiques.
No dealers. No playing Bexon's silly game. One complete
day. And *I* say what we do.'

I groaned.

'My hands are hurting,' I said bravely. 'They're agony – '

'And you can stop that,' she interrupted. 'It won't work.'

'Look, love – '

'We're shopping, Lovejoy.' She ticked them off on fingers.
'And you're going to cook me a lovely supper. Then you're

going to sit with me in the evening, come for a walk and
then seduce me in bed. Here. Beneath these very sheets.'

'What if we pass an antique shop?' I yelped, aghast.
She'd gone demented.

'You will walk bravely past. With me.' She smiled, angelic.

I nodded, broken. Ever noticed how bossy women really
are, deep down?

'When?'

'Whenever I say.' She smiled, boss: 'I'll let you know.'

Day dawned grimly and relentlessly.

CHAPTER XVII

I PICKED up courage while we dressed. 'Is this your day?'

Janie thought for a couple of centuries. 'No, thank you.'

I cheered up at that.

'I have a car coming. Nine o'clock.'

'I've cancelled it,' she said innocently. 'We don't want
Lovejoy getting lost, do we?'

Of course we didn't, I assured her.

'Come on, then,' I said: 'Get your knickers on and we'll
look around.'

'Cheek.'

We walked down to the shore. The river runs into a
curved stony beach, only about a hundred yards across. The
stones are a lovely blue-grey colour. Steep jagged rocks rise
suddenly to form rather dour headlands. In the distance
towards Douglas we could see the gaggle of chalets forming a
holiday camp. I'd seen the sign for it during the drive along
the cliff road.

'How noisy.' It was a racket, stones clacking and shuffling
and the sea hissing between.

We gazed inland. The shale-floored inlet only ran about
two hundred yards back from the water before it narrowed.
into a dark mountainous cleft filled by forest. A wooden
bridge spanned the river there, presumably for us visitors to

stroll across and up the steep hillside. Well, whatever turns
you on, I thought. Then it occurred to me: what if it was
Bexon's favourite walk? After all, he had to have some reason
for coming this far out of town. Bushes and gorse everywhere. It would be a climb more than a stroll.

We walked over and explored the hillside. The footpath
divided about a hundred feet from the bridge, one branch
running inland along the glen floor to follow the river. The
other climbed precipitously on planked steps round the
headland. Janie chose left, so we followed that.

'Look. Palm trees.'

I was going to scoff, but they were. The valley bulged
soon into a level, densely wooded swamp for about a quarter
of a mile as far as I could tell. Somebody years ago had built
tall little islands among the marsh, creating lagoons complete
with palms. Here and there we could find pieces of rotten
trellis among the dense foliage. Once we came upon a large
ruined hut by the water. There were at least three decorative
wooden bridges.

'Betty Springer said they used to have dances along here.'

I wasn't interested. No engineering works, and I wanted
evidence. The valley narrowed again a little way on. The
trees crowded closer and the undergrowth closed in on our
riverside path. The water ran faster as the ground began to
rise. I didn't see any point going on. Ahead, an enormous
viaduct crossed the valley. The beck coursed swiftly beneath,
gurgling noisily. It looked deep and fast. We headed back
past the lagoons and took the ascending fork from the
bridge, talking about Bexon. The path was only wide enough
for one at a time. I told her over my shoulder how I'd got the
taxi-driver to find the place.

'Are you sure this is where he stayed?'

'Betty remembered him.'

Janie really found it first, a brick kiln set in the hillside.
Overgrown, like the rest, but reassuring.

'Look how flat the path is here.' She pointed out the iron
rails set in the ground. The path ran on the contour line
seawards from the kiln.

'That's odd. It looks dead level.' The flat path was wider now than any other on the hills.

'For hauling bricks?' she suggested.

'Maybe.'

It was a little railway. We traced it inland. It ended in a hillside glade. There we found a ruined station, wooden, collapsed into the forest down the steep slope. We walked back, almost hurrying now. A railway means an engineer. Maybe Bexon worked on it, probably a scenic run through the woods to view the sea from the headland or something. Of course, I thought. There'd be a junction further inland with the road. And on the road there was still a working steam railway. Hence Bexon's choice of Groundle Glen. It's where his railway ran.

I became excited. We followed the rails seawards. Some parts were quite overlain by small landfalls but at least you could see where the tracks ran from the shape of the incised hillside. We had difficulty getting past where sections had slid down into the valley but managed it by climbing up-wards round the gap – using gorse bushes to cling to. We eventually emerged round the cliff's shoulder in full view of the sea. Still the tracks ran on, high round the headland. A tiny brick hut lay in ruins at one point near the track. Curiously, a fractured water-tap still ran a trickle of its own down the cliff face. Over the years it had created its own little watercourse.

The railway finished abruptly at a precipitous inlet, narrow and frighteningly sheer.

'Dear God.'

At the bottom the sea had been dammed by a sort of stone barrier set with iron palings, now rusted. It was lapped heavily by the sea. I didn't like the look of it at all. Nor did Janie. I'm not a nervy sort but it was all a bit too Gothic.

'It's creepy,' she said, shuddering.

'Why dam it off?' I asked her. 'Look across.'

There seemed to be a sort of metal cage set in the rock face. It was easily big enough to contain a man. Anyone in it could scan the entire inlet. But why would anyone climb into it? A wave larger than before rushed in and lashed over the rusty barrier. If Bexon had anything to do with building that he really was round the bend. There seemed no sun down there though the day was bright elsewhere. Some places are best avoided. This was one.

'Come on.'

We hurried home, scrambling hurriedly along the railway track until we met the path. From there we took our time.

'It was *ugly*, Lovejoy,' Janie said.

She invited Betty Stringer over for coffee, a cunning move. We described our walk. I just happened to have the map out, quite casual.

'Your friend used to go over there,' she said brightly. 'Every day, practically. He used to get so tired. Always rested on the bridge.'

'Bexon?'

'Yes. He spent a lot of time walking along the glen.'

'Is it an old railway?'

'Yes. For people to see the seals.'

'Seals?' I put my cup down. 'Seals?'

'You didn't get that far, I suppose.' She traced our map with her finger. 'Follow the tracks and you come to where they kept the sea lions. You watched them being fed by their keeper. He threw them fish, things like that, but that was years ago. It's a sort of inlet.'

Both Janie and I were relieved. We avoided each other's eyes. We'd thought of all sorts.

'Did, er . . . Bexon say anything about it?' I asked, trying to smile in case the answer was not too happy.

'Oh yes. He kept on about it all the time. He used to help mend it years ago,' she said brightly.

He would. Not a happy answer at all. If that's where he spent his time, was it where he'd remember something best?

'Why the hell didn't he just stick to railways?' I asked Janie when Betty had gone. 'That seal pen's like something in a Dracula picture.'

'He mentioned other places.'

'So he did!' I said, brightening. 'So he did.'

'Good morrow, friends!' It was Algernon, wearing a deer-stalker and tweeds. 'All ready to go searching?'

'Let's go.'

CHAPTER XVIII

WE WENT to buy large-scale maps. I can't do without them in a new place, partly because I always have the addresses of antique shops and collectors about my person.

While Janie went to the grocer's I pulled Algernon aside on the pavement.

'When I tip the wink,' I said urgently, 'make some excuse to stop the car.'

'Why?'

'Because we'll be near an antique shop,' I explained.

He still looked puzzled. 'Lovejoy. Why is it always antiques?'

I recoiled, almost knocking an old lady down. There he stood in the cake-shop doorway, your actual neophyte antiques dealer. Typical. At that moment I really gave Algernon up.

'Never mind, Algernon,' I said, completely broken. 'It's just something that comes from breathing.'

'All ready?' Janie was back. We'd parked the car dead opposite Refuge Tower, now partly sinking its little island into the encroaching tide. 'Incidentally,' she warned, smiling prettily at us both, 'no sudden mysterious excuses to make stops near *unexpected* antique shops. Okay, chaps?'

'What do you take me for?' I said innocently.

I avoided Algernon's accusing gaze as we got in. Janie was rolling in the aisles so much at her really hilarious witticism she could hardly start the engine.

'What a lovely smile the lady has,' I said coldly. 'Are they your own teeth?' I only made her giggle worse. That's women for you.

'We're embarking to visualize entrancing spectacles of natural miracles!' Algernon cut in merrily, his idea of light chitchat. Cheerfulness from Algernon's enough to make people suicidal.

I'd the copies of Bexon's diary with me. We listed all the named sites, putting them in the same order Bexon had.

'It's less distance,' said He-of-the-Blurred-Vision, 'and more economical on petrol to proceed circumferentially round Castletown, with – '

'Hold it.' I was suddenly suspicious. 'You seem to know a lot about these place names.'

'So does everybody else, Lovejoy,' he said with maddening arrogance.

'Except me,' I pointed out. We were gliding upwards to the south of Douglas town.

'Motor-bikes,' he explained. 'The races.'

I'd heard of the TT races. Naturally, Algernon would know. I'd never seen him without a racing magazine. He started to tell me about engine classifications but I said to shut up.

'We'll do it Bexon's way,' I replied huffily. I saw Janie hiding a smile and explained, 'It's more logical.'

'Yes, darling,' she said, the way they do.

'Right, then.' We drove on in stony silence.

The Isle's a lovely place. The coolth gets into you quickly. You unwind and amble rather than sprint. Even the Lagonda began coasting, giving the feeling of a thoroughbred cantering on its home field.

We drove that day what seemed a million miles. After each place that Bexon had mentioned I took a vote. I had the veto, because of my detector bell, though Janie complained about being tired after only four hours or so.

We drove to the House of Keys at Castletown and from there hit the road to Cronk Ny Merriu's ancient fortwork. Algernon saw some sort of stupid swimming bird there, which led to a blazing row because I expected him to keep his

attention riveted on my quest, not bloody ducks. He got all
hurt, and Janie linked his arm till I cooled down. The
trouble is she thinks he's sweet.

We bowled into Port St Mary after that, then Port Erin for
fish and chips. Another tick, about one o'clock. They wanted
to rest but I said not likely. We walked from the folk museum
up Mull Hill to the six-chambered stone circle. I loved it,
but time drove us off. Janie thought it all rather dull.
Algernon saw another duck, so he was all right. The Calf of
Man, a little island, couldn't be reached, so we turned back
to the main road after Janie had flasks filled at the little café.
We climbed the mountainside north of Port Erin to the
Stacks, where the five primitive hut-circles were just being
themselves. Another tick, and varoom again.

Beckwith's Mines were rather gruesome, like any mine
with shale heaps and great shafts running into the earth
between two brooding mountains. I was relieved when
Bexon's lyrical comments led to nothing. After all, a mine is
nothing but a very, very deep hole. It was nearly as bad as
that seal pen.

'I don't dig mines,' I quipped merrily, snickering, but
Janie only raised her eyes and Algernon asked what did I
mean. No wonder I always feel lumbered.

The last thing of all was the great peak of South Barrule.
We left the car and climbed, walking with difficulty among
the dry crackly heather tufts. I was glad when Algernon
found something. We stopped. I almost collapsed, puffing.
He fell on his knees.

'It's *Melampyrum montanum*!' he breathed reverently,
pointing. 'What astonishing luck! The rare cow-wheat!
Glacial transfer, from Iceland with the Ice Age! How
positively stupendous! Oh, Lovejoy, Janie, look!'

He seems so bloody delighted at the oddest things. I
staggered closer and looked. He'd cupped his palms round
some grass.

'Isn't it breathtaking?' he crooned.

'It's lovely, Algernon,' Janie said. 'Isn't it beautiful,
Lovejoy?' She was glaring at me. Her eyes said, Just you

dare, Lovejoy, just you dare.

'It's great,' I said defiantly. I would have praised it anyway, because I'm really quite fond of grass. 'Really great, Algernon.'

'Nowhere else except this very hillside!' he cried. 'What a staggering thought!'

I gazed about. There were miles of the bloody stuff as far as the eye could see. And I knew for a fact that the rest of Britain was covered knee deep.

'Well, great,' I said again. 'Take it home,' I suggested, trying to add to the jollity. I should have kept my mouth shut. Algernon recoiled in horror.

'What about propagation, Lovejoy?' he exclaimed. 'That would be quite wrong!'

So we left the grass alone because of its sex life. Silly me.

And after all that, nothing. We rested at the top for a few minutes but I was worried about the daylight.

'You said we'd do it all in two hours,' Janie complained.

'I lied,' I said back. '*Avanti.*'

The rest of the search was enlivened by Algernon describing the spore capsules of the *Pellia epiphylla*, while I went over the Viking burials and tumuli we'd seen. Nothing. Still, I trusted my feelings about Bexon. He'd got on to something. Put me within spitting distance and I'd sense it. I knew I would.

I came to with us heading north on the metalled road and Algernon explaining the difference between a bogbean and a twayblade, whatever they were. I'd have given anything for a pastie. Not to eat, just to shut his cake-hole.

That day seemed months long. My mind was reeling with views of yachting basins, harbours, promontories, inlets, small towns huddled round wharves, castles, Celtic burial mounds, Neolithic monuments and encampments, tiny museums (musea? I never know the proper declension) and stylish period houses. We finished Bexon's list baffled and bushed. I was knackered. Only Algernon the Inexhaustible chattered on. Janie thinks he's marvellous. She likes talkers.

Whenever he seemed to slow up she'd actually ask a question
and start him off again in spite of frantic eyebrow signals
from me. I swear she likes riling people sometimes. He
seemed to know everything about everything except antiques.
He even tried telling me there were different kinds of sheep.

'Never mind, Lovejoy,' she said, all dimples, towards the
end of the day. 'We might have had to travel in your hired
Mini.'

I tried not to laugh but women get through to you and I
found myself grinning. Just shows how tired we were.

'Let's pull in,' I suggested.

'A mile further on, please, Janie,' Algernon asked. 'There's
a pull-in there.' Surprised, we all agreed. It wasn't far from
Douglas anyhow, and we'd reached the end of the list, so
what did it matter?

I saw why he'd suggested this when we arrived. Even
though it was quite late people were milling about. A café
stood back from the road on the exposed hillside. A mile
further along the hill a television transmitter's mast poked
up, its red light shining to warn aircraft. A large stand for
spectators had been built on a macadam apron beside the
road. Motor-bikes littered the ground.

'It's one of the TT checkpoints,' Algernon beamed with
delight. 'Look! An Alan Clews fourstroke! Good heavens!'

I went in and got some pasties. Three teas in cardboard.
When I emerged Janie was back in the car trying to keep
warm. A wind was getting up. Algernon was admiring a
cluster of bikes. Some were in pieces. Enthusiasts in overalls
and bulbous with bike gear compared spanners. What a life.

'Isn't it a positively stimulating scenario, Lovejoy?'
Algernon said, really moved. It looked a hell of a mess.

'Eat,' I said, thrusting a pastie into his mouth.

God help the Almighty when we all come bowling up to
heaven, each of us with a different definition of Paradise. I
wish Him luck. And if everything there's lovely and new I
for one won't go.

'Thank you, Lovejoy,' he said. 'Come and see this Villiers
engine.'

'No.' I'd rather his rotten grass than his rotten engines.
I gave the grub out.

'Oh, Lovejoy,' Janie complained. 'I hate this soya stuff.'

'I asked for it.' If you save only one cow a year it's a lot.
Indeed it's everything, if you're the cow concerned.

'We've finished, love,' Janie said, pausing. 'He didn't
mention any more places.'

'Don't nag.'

She gave me a searching look and then tried to cheer me
up with questions about Suetonius and Co. I was too
dejected to respond. The trouble is I tend to get a bit riled
when I'm down.

Wearily I leaned on the car. In an hour it would be dusk.
The motor-bike fiends were undeterred by mere changes in
the environment. Algernon was joining a group busy stirring
a heap of metal tubes on wheels with spanners. One oil-
daubed bloke even seemed to recognize him and shook
Algernon's hand.

'I'm so sorry, darling.' Janie put her hand on mine. 'I
wish I could help.'

I shook her off and looked about, simmering.

'Lovejoy,' she said warningly, but I was beyond talk. I'd
nothing against the bike fiends, but I had to sort somebody
out for light relief. I was suddenly breathing fast and angry,
all my hopes in ruins. Yet I *knew* we were close. One small
clue . . .

'Lovejoy. *Please.*'

Over in one corner was a little group clustered about a
couple of soap-boxers. One was a bird from the Militant
Feminist League. I ignored her, though I'm on their side. I
really do hope the suffragettes get the vote. I needed somebody worth a dust-up. And there he was, the inevitable
rabble-rouser, I saw with satisfaction. You get at least one
where there's a crowd. He had a soap-box near the café
steps. My blood warmed and I moved casually towards him.

'*Lovejoy.*'

I heard Janie come after me. I honestly wasn't spoiling
for a fight, but these political nerks do as well as any. You

can't go wrong because they're all stupid.

'You're all capitalist dupes and lackeys,' he was yelling, an unshaven political gospeller. He got a few catcalls and jeers back from the bike fiends but kept going, a game lad. 'Your bike races are personalized general crimes!'

I drifted past Algernon. He was asking the others about plugs.

'Joe Faulkner'll have a spare,' a voice replied from underneath a bike.

'Lives up near Big Izzie,' another explained. 'Anybody'll direct you to her.' The lads laughed along with Algernon. Some local joke.

Algernon tried to interest me in the bike's pipes but I strolled on to hear the politician. I'd give him five minutes' skilful heckling, then I'd cripple the bastard.

'It's the day of the Common Man!' he shouted. Nobody was listening. 'The day of equality is dawning! Share all! Possess all! Equality, the word of the age!' One of those.

He was really preaching against antiques. I hate jargoneers, as Florence Nightingale called folk like this twerp. It's today's trick, urge everybody else to be mediocre too. People everywhere talk too much about the Common Man, what a really terrific bloke he is and how anybody different's either a secret anarchist or fascist at heart. It's all balls. Let's not forget that the Average Man's really pretty average.

'Nobody's ever equal,' I pointed out loudly. 'It's a biological and social impossibility. Inequality's right,' I said pleasantly. 'Equality's ridiculous.'

I honestly believe this. I've been striving all my life in the glorious cause of inequality.

What can you say to stupid bums like this, that shut the Sèvres porcelain factory so we could all have none?

'Clever dick,' he sneered. 'Piss off. Go and piss Izzie round.'

A few of the bike fiends who overheard laughed at this crack from beneath their tangles. Probably that local joke. I began to move towards him happily, then stopped. Izzie?

Anybody'll direct you to her, they'd told Algernon as I'd passed him. To her. Female. Izzie. Isabel? Isabella? Piss Izzie round – like a wheel? It reminded me of something.

Janie came hurrying over. She'd collected Algernon.

'We really ought to be going,' she was saying as they arrived. I was watching them approach. 'We're all too tired to think. I can cook us a hot meal. It's been such a tiring day. We need a rest.' She looked at me, worried. 'Lovejoy?'

'Is anything the matter, Lovejoy?' Algernon asked.

'You're so pale,' I heard Janie say. 'Has he said something to offend you?' She spun angrily on the startled orator and snapped, 'You keep your stupid opinions to yourself, you silly old buffoon!'

'No, Janie. Please.' My mouth was dry. 'I'm so sorry,' I explained gently to the speaker. 'It's my first visit here. Where is Big Izzie, please, comrade?'

'I knew you were one of us deep down, comrade,' he said, smug with pride. 'It always shows through the capitalist-imperialist veneer. Comrade Marx's definition of class illustrates –'

'He never defined class,' I said. 'He promised to in that footnote to his first German edition, now very valuable, but never got round to it. Big Izzie, comrade. We've a, er, political meeting near there.'

'Laxey,' he said. 'We ought to get together, comrade, to discuss class fundamentalism –'

'It's a date,' I said. 'Laxey, you said?'

'Long live the revolution!' he called after us.

'Er, sure, sure.'

I rushed them to the Lagonda and had Janie hurtling us towards the road to cheers and waves of the surrounding multitudes of the bike people. She was screaming for instructions at the fork but I didn't know where Laxey was. We scrambled for maps, then two cars came by and we had to wait till they passed.

'Laxey?' Algernon said at this point. 'Go left.'

'Sound your horn!' I cried in anguish, but anyone who

beeps a horn in Britain is either on fire or psychotic. Janie's
upbringing held firm. We moved sedately out on to the
Laxey road.

'Who'll be there?' Algernon asked pleasantly.

'How the hell should I know who lives in Laxey?' I said,
baffled.

'He means the meeting,' Janie began to explain. 'There
isn't really any meeting, Algernon, you see. It was a . . . a
ruse.'

'There's an enormous waterwheel at Laxey,' Algernon
said brightly as Janie gave the car its head.

'Then why didn't you say so?' I hissed. If I'd not been in
the front I'd have thrown him out.

'Is it what we've been looking for all this time? Its picture's
on the coins.'

I fumbled in my pocket. It bloody well was, the imprint
of a great waterwheel. One day I'll do for Algernon.

'It's even got a name,' he continued cheerfully. 'Lady
Isabella. They say that when it was first made –'

'Algernon!' from Janie, tight-lipped. Algernon had known
all along, the stupid sod.

I closed my eyes. Sometimes things just get too much.

The wheel's beautiful. You know, the Victorians really had it.
If a thing is worth doing at all, they obviously thought,
then it's worth doing well. On the side of the supporting
structure was a plaque: 'Lady Isabella.' There she was,
gigantic and colourful, pivoted with such exquisite balance
that a narrow run of water aqueducted downhill was sufficient to power her round at some speed. She was breathtaking.

She was set in the hillside valley near a stone bridge. A
deep crevasse sliced into the hill, exposing a ruined mine-
shaft. Old discoloured mine buildings eroded slowly block
by block higher up. An enormous massive beam projected
skywards from the ruins, probably one arm of a pump of
some sort for the underground workings.

'How colossal!' Janie said it. Colossal was the word.

There were steps up from the path to its main axle. Algernon rushed up to see the giant waterwheel swinging its immense height skywards.

'Imagine the size of the bike engine you'd need to –'

'Algernon,' I interrupted. 'Don't. No more.'

Janie was watching me. Just then she tapped me firmly on the shoulder.

'Well, everybody!' she cut in brightly. 'Home time.'

'*What?*' I rounded on her.

'Home time, I said.' Janie put her hand on my arm like a constable.

'We've only just got here!'

'And now we're going. You owe me a day, Lovejoy.'

'But you said it wasn't today,' I yelped. 'And we've found her! My main clue!'

'No,' Janie said. 'It *wasn't* today, Lovejoy. But today's over. Look.'

I came to. The day had faded. Our car was the only one left in the car park beside the river down below. The little toffee shops had closed. In the distance lights showed where the seaside promenade of Laxey lay. Lights were coming on in the cottage windows. An old woollen mill blotted out the foreground. Mill owners of years ago had laid out the valley like a stone pleasure garden, now somewhat sunken and ill-kept. It was swiftly quietening into dusk.

'But, Janie, for God's sake –'

'It's dangerous, Lovejoy,' she said in that voice. 'Derelict mines, ruined mine buildings, horrid great pumps underground and a wheel this size. If you weren't so deranged by being near whatever the poor old man left, you'd realize how exhausted and frightened you really are.' She took my arm. 'Home.'

I tried appealing to Algernon but he backed down. Friends.

'I claim my day, starting from this instant,' Janie said. 'Twenty-four hours.'

Women make me mad. They're like the soap in your bath. You know it'd be good value if only you could find out what it's up to and where it is.

Algernon was nodding. 'True, Lovejoy. You're bushed.'

'There, then!' cheerfully from Janie. 'We're all agreed.'

I was defeated. I looked up at the Lady Isabella.

'Check the time, Algernon,' I said coldly.

'Twenty past eight.'

'Twenty-four hours, then.' I waited for orders. 'Well?'

'Home, chaps.' She fluttered her eyelashes and waggled seductively down the steps ahead of me. 'You'll thank me later, b'wana, when we're all cosy.'

Algernon joined in.

'Never mind, Lovejoy,' he said brightly. 'There's always another day.'

I didn't speak to either of them on the way home. People who know what's best for you give me a real pain.

CHAPTER XIX

'WHAT IF Edward Rink's come over after us?' I said. I'd got fed up sulking.

'Don't argue. You need the rest. You're a wreck.'

'And what if – ?'

'Rest.' Janie was painting her toenails reddish. 'A normal day's what you need, Lovejoy.' I was reading. 'Look how much good it'll do us. You get too involved in antiques.'

'I could have it by now.' I nearly dropped my drink just thinking of it.

'Rink's man's stupid. You said he couldn't follow a brass band. No sugar for me, please.'

I brewed up and carried her cup over. She was on the couch by the window. We could see Algernon stalking some innocent sparrow across the field. I sat watching her doing her nails. They blow on their fingers but not their toes. I suppose toes are too far down even with knees bent. She has a little enamelled case full of small tools for things like this.

French women used to have small cased sets of hooks and needles for unpicking gold-fringed decorations and embroidery. It's called drizzling, or parfilage. Women to the last, they'd collect the gold thread in a bag and sell it back to the goldsmith-embroiderer, who'd then make a lovely gold-fringed item, such as a bookcover, with an appropriate expression of devotion woven in. Then he'd sell it to a suitor, who'd give it to his ladylove, who'd take it to the theatre and unpick the gold thread and put it in a bag and sell it back ... Women may be very funny creatures but I never said they were daft. The unpicking sets are now valuable antiques and not uncommon. Gold fringe embroidery of the eighteenth century is, as you've guessed, very rarely found. Incidentally, this pernicious fashion was ended at a stroke and we actually know who stopped it. The writer Madame de Genlis condemned the habit in her novel *Adèle et Théodore* in 1782 and it vanished like snow off a duck. That saved a few rare pieces, now naturally worth a fortune. Light a candle for her, like I do occasionally.

'We go shopping.' Janie spoke emphatically.

'Er, great.' I tried to sound straining at the leash. 'Me too?'

'You especially.'

'Well, great.'

'Then we have a lovely quiet meal together.' She fanned her toes with her hand. 'Algernon can eat alone. Elsewhere.'

'Where do you cut your toenails?'

'In the bath.'

Funny that. We know the most intimate secrets about everyone throughout history except for toenail cutting. There's no really accepted etiquette. So you do it in the bath. Well, well.

'Couldn't we go past Isabella?'

'No.'

I gave in, but there'd be no half-measures. I decided I'd make the meal, a really posh one complete with garnish. I stood watching Algernon in the distance, thinking, what's garnish? It sounds some sort of mushroom.

*

In the town we had a great time shopping. I mean, really breathtaking.

It's great. You trudge along a row of shops, then trudge back. Then you trudge between two or three shops which all have the same stuff. Then you trudge about searching for a fourth, also identical. Then you trudge back and forth among all four. Then you find a fifth. You keep it up for hours. As I say, it's really trudging great. We got Janie some shoes. It only took a couple of months or so.

I cut loose and bought the stuff for our meal, following the advice of a booklet which told me about the teasing of my taste-buds by *tournedos bordelaise*. It sounded really gruesome but I persevered. It seemed to be some sort of meat with gravy. I met Janie under my mound of vegetables. She fell about laughing, but I replied coldly that I was working to a plan. We went shopping for a few more years before returning to the bungalow where I crippled myself cooking for the rest of the day. I learned my least favourite occupation. It's cooking. Janie sent Algernon out to eat.

By evening the kitchen looked like Iwo Jima. We started our meal elegantly, holding hands now and again over the tablecloth. Well, so far so good. But it'd be touch and go making love later on.

I was knackered.

That evening Algernon came in and said he'd have used a little more thyme and possibly a shade less garlic. Janie pulled me off before I could reach the cleaver. Then he made me feel quite fond of him by eating everything left over.

CHAPTER XX

I GOT RID of Janie and Algernon among the cottages where people park their cars. It's forbidden to drive right up to Lady Isabella. I was quivering with excitement.

'You'll miss me up there, Lovejoy.' Janie sat watching me go.

'No, I won't,' I called back. In an hour or so I'd own a wealth of genuine Roman golds. Mind you, I thought uneasily, I'd told myself that a couple of mornings ago and finished up bushed and poor as ever.

'Good luck,' from Algernon. He was geared for lunar orbit. A pal was lending him a motor-bike.

I climbed the steep road above the river. Where it turned right and humped upwards towards Lady Isabella I glanced down. Janie waved, small now on the flat stones by the water. I plodded on between the cottages. At the café I resisted the temptation to look. She ought to have gone by now because I'd said to, but I knew exactly what she was doing. She was noting the time. If I wasn't down in a couple of hours she'd come after me with the Army. They never do what you say. I heard the crackle of Algernon's bike maniacs arriving.

The wheel seemed even more huge in early daylight than it had in the dusk. One could stand on the paving and look upwards. From there the paddles were hurled swiftly towards the sky, dripping water where they thinned abruptly, then vanished, replaced by other swift soaring slats. I made myself giddy watching. Curious how a simple motion can be exhilarating and even beautiful. The clack-clack sound so close became almost numbing after a few minutes. I shook the feeling away and cast around.

The wheel was fed by a narrow stone aqueduct which ran from a hillside cleft to the left. One of the unpleasant facts was that the derelict mine shafts lay that way. The good bit was that the huge beam pump wasn't working, thank God. It looked gruesome enough as it was, still and silent. Like I'd thought at Beckwith's mines, a mine is a terrible intrusion into the earth, almost an offence against living rock. I could understand a mountain getting mad like when the volcano erupts in those old Maria Montez jungle adventure films. Anybody'd feel annoyed if a stranger suddenly barged in to root in the larder to see what was worth pinching.

A few early visitors arrived while I was gaping at the wheel. Judging from their knowing reactions I must have been the last person on earth to hear about Lady Isabella's existence. It was very annoying. They milled about exclaiming at the beautiful machine. Yet . . . no bell, no dingdong.

I walked round as far as I could go. Then back. A group of visitors climbed the steps down which Janie had wriggled so seductively to entice me home the evening before last. We saw the tremendous humming axle, the radiating struts seeming so gigantic they were like so many fairground complexes, stolen and cast into some skeletal giant. I touched and listened, touched and listened. Nothing. A rather matronly lady was giving me the eye. A month before I'd have had to, because I like older women, but being this close to my find gave me a greed-based willpower. There was no time to waste. I drifted away, leaving them gaping at the axle.

The road became a mere track up the incline, very stony and almost precipitous in parts. To the right the cleft below became practically a ravine, littered with fallen masonry and chimneyed mine vents. A narrow goyt spun water out of the rock and let it fall abruptly. God knows what cold deep subterranean chasm it squeezed up from. About halfway up the hillside the crashing noise of the water ended. I noticed the sound of Lady Isabella had faded.

I stopped to rest on the wall of a shallow stone cistern, wondering what Janie was doing. The great wheel turned silently down in the valley between me and the sea. Lovely.

It was about ten o'clock. The pale sun was catching the wheel's colours and flicking them about the mountainside. The main beams started out a silvery gold. By the time they flashed on to the dark browns and greens all about me they were a brilliant tangerine, a Thai enamel silver box's colour. They make these boxes now, real silver but cheap and modern. There are only about six modern designs knocking about so far, basically an opaque white or a translucent tangerine. Dishonest people are said to use deep-heat physiotherapy lamps and two hours' cooking at the back end of a good quality vacuum cleaner without its filter bag, to mimic the appearance of antique enamel. It works, but only if you look from a mile off. Look with a microscope. Uneven crazed surface=modern, faked. Even surface, with the occasional large deep 'bubbled' area, may be the real thing. Give me the first offer.

A motor-cycle skittered into view, way down below on the Laxey road, the rider anonymous in his bulbous helmet. Funny old place to be riding, I thought. I rose and began the climb again. Maybe he was training for a scramble race cross-country. Whatever it was, he was booming up the track behind me like the clappers.

I was only a hundred yards from the most ghoulish of the mine shafts when the bastard nearly ran me down. Now, it could have been an accident. I admit that. The track was only about four feet wide there. Like a fool, I had my eye on the mine ruins, not bothering to glance behind at the approaching rider. Maybe my apprehension was focused uneasily on the workings. Whatever distracted me, I was hellish slow, only managing to chuck myself to one side and not completely escaping. The maniac's handlebar slammed into my hip, spinning me like a top. There I was, clinging dazed to the stony bank while the dust shower settled. He didn't even stop.

My shirt and trousers were both torn. You could see the bruise swelling before your very eyes and blueing. Ugly. I was shaking so much it took me three goes to lift a stone and put it on the lump. I wetted it from a hillside ooze and sat there trembling, trying to press the damp cold stone on to my side to stop the swelling. The trouble is, once a person's inside motor-bike gear he becomes unrecognizable. He hadn't seemed heavily built. Quite slight, encased in leather crammed with insignia and no number plates that I could recall.

Three or four times I fancied I could hear a distant crackle but wasn't sure of the direction. My hip was murder when I pulled myself together and resumed walking. I

carried the stone to chuck at the swine if he came back. It's
funny what goes through your mind after a bit of a scare.
Algernon's thin. He's also a bike fiend. The rider was too
small for Beck. It was too crude a method for my friend
Edward Rink, and anyway he'd only to knock me off *after*
I'd found the stuff for him, not before. I wondered if the
rider could have been a woman. Not Janie, surely. Kate?
The question was, did he/she really attempt to do for me?
Or was it just a stray stupid rider showing off?

I was opposite the mine shaft. I stopped to listen. Nothing
again. Water welled from the rock and ran along the aqueduct
in a steady flow. I was out of sight of the wheel now. No
houses, no people. Only derelict buildings, the ungainly
beam engine projecting its huge arm, the trickling water
and the stone track.

From where I stood the cleft was only forty yards wide.
What had they mined in those days? It looked grim on a
pleasant sunny day like this, with holidaymakers trekking up
to the café and then down to the sea for dinner. On a rainy
winter's day it must have seemed to the miners like a freezing
hell.

Old Bexon must have been tough if he'd come all this way.
Could an elderly man, gradually sickening in his final illness,
climb down from the track, across the cleft and into the
mine? I limped back and forth for some time. There seemed
no way across. Maybe it would be wise to follow the path to
the crest. The miners had had to get over there somehow in
the old days, and I could make a quick check to see if that
bloody rider was lurking over the hill or not. I was starting
to hurt and had to rest a minute. I threw the stone away.
Seven long seconds to hit the bottom of the shaft with a faint
splash. A hell of a fall, even for a stone.

Bleak places have this effect on me. I get restless and
start working out how far's civilization. Not that countryside
isn't great on a postcard but it needs watching. I only want
Wuthering Heights not to spread about too much. A hundred
yards further on I found the causeway. A series of small
arches had supported it, but now only their stubs stuck

upwards from the little valley's floor. Some wise man had dismantled it. I'd have danced from relief if I hadn't just been injured. If there was no way across for me there'd been no way across for old Bexon. It couldn't be done. And lugging a leaden coffin over there would need a helicopter. I was saved. No dark deep hidey-holes for jubilant Lovejoy. Home again, still empty-handed. I turned back, relieved but disappointed.

I went over the possibilities on the way down. A list of named spots – nothing at any of them. The most likely spot was here, near Lady Isabella. But I'd got no vibes near the wheel herself. And in any case she was well-maintained, cleaned and painted. Obviously had plenty of vigilant engineers about and was, from what I'd seen, a popular tourist spectacle. The wheel seemed far too public. Yet some place near Lady Isabella was obviously the place a man like Bexon would remember best. *Wasn't it?*

Janie was sitting on a big flat rock near the car park chucking stones into the water. She'd taken her sandals off and her feet were wet. Her frock was up over her knees.

'Hussy,' I called down from the bank. I was still delighted about the mines. 'I can see all up your legs.'

'Cripple,' she said angrily. 'I heard you limping. I told you to be careful.' She was mad again. 'Did you fall?'

'Now, don't start, Janie lovie,' I said. Why do women keep getting so mad when they should be all worried? I honestly don't get it.

'Don't you lovie me, Lovejoy.'

'Where's Algernon?'

She looked up curiously. I'd tried to sound casual.

'Off on a bike. He told you.'

'Of course,' I said, easy still. 'So he did.'

She pulled herself up the river bank and stood inspecting me.

'Stop looking at me like that,' I complained. 'I feel for sale.'

'What happened up there, Lovejoy?'

'Nothing.'

'I'd better have a look at it.' She pulled my torn trouser away from my side. 'Dear God.' A family passing to their car exclaimed and tutted sympathetically. I moved away from Janie's fingers.

'Don't show my bum to everybody.'

'We'd better call at a chemist's for some ointment.'

Inside the car was hot. Janie put the air-conditioner on.

'Where to, b'wana?' she asked. I put my head on her.

'Love,' I said, 'I just don't know.'

That night I couldn't sleep. When that happens I always think, well, so what? Okay, so I'll be a bit tired next day. All the better rest you get the night after. There's no need to be so distressed as some people get. But Janie was tossing and turning too. Maybe it was the lingering effects of my grub.

Fitful patches came, blurred and then left me starkly conscious. I've heard that people mostly worry about work during the dark hours. With me it's faces. They came gliding into my mind like characters from a Kabuki play. Some just wouldn't go. Helen, for instance. Maybe I'd imagined her down at the shops yesterday, result of a subconscious longing, perhaps. We'd been very close but only briefly. The stress of competing for the same antiques had torn – well, snipped – us apart. What was she doing here? The antique shops, possibly. But 'possibly' also means possibly not. Then Kate the Wicked Sister, with her single-minded message not to help Nichole. Not surprising, really, because womankind occasionally has been known to be slightly tinged with the sin of jealousy, so it's said. But how could I possibly help Nichole, when she insisted on going about with that murdering pillock Rink, instead of a lovely hunk like me? Algernon's too thick to be anybody's ally, I told myself, isn't he? *Isn't he?* I got up at one point and padded in my pyjamas to peer through the back-door glass towards his bungalow. No lights. Well, three in the morning. But was he in there? Or maybe he was stealing back that very second to Big Izzie, having seen something I hadn't. I cancelled that possibility and slipped back into bed. The idea of Algernon stealing anywhere's an absurdity. Even when he brews up it's like a fife band. Janie stirred. I let my legs get warm before closing in on her.

Then there was Rink the Fink. No good wondering why a rich man like him wanted to bother with a possible find of possible valuables. Greed knows no rhyme or reason. I've actually seen a real live millionaire cover his face and weep uncontrollably in a famous Bond Street auction for carelessly missing a Penny Black – admittedly these stamps aren't all that common, but you can find them if you look carefully. I got up again.

There was no light from the hillside. I sat in an armchair after pulling the curtains back. Who was actually doing the watching? Or was there nobody there at all? I had this feeling again. Supposing Rink had two watchers, twelve-hour shifts. Possible, but how the hell would they contact Rink if I made a sudden dash anywhere? Some form of field transmitter? I gazed out into the darkness. Maybe the watcher and me were looking directly at each other, unseeing. Unless he had one of those night telescopes. Was he smoking out there? You can see a match at five thousand yards. That's what the sergeant used to say, on his belly in the mud, refusing to let the lads smoke two whole leech-ridden days before the ambush. I moved the armchair uneasily. There's something really rather nasty about being looked at when you don't suspect. It's a sick feeling.

Janie was trustworthy, though. I pondered a long time about Janie. Wealthy, lovely, attractive, and humorous. Exactly what the doctor ordered. You have to trust the woman you sleep with, don't you? I mean, if you can't trust the woman you sleep with, whom can you trust? I mean to say.

It was so dark outside. I could just see the skyline. There were some stars. The forecast said it might rain before dawn.

Yet Janie never trusts me. She keeps saying so. Still, that was easily accounted for – women aren't very trusting people by nature. They are a very unusual sex, when you think of it. I don't think they'll ever be the same as us, reasonable and even-tempered. What lingered unpleasantly in my mind about Janie was her husband. We'd never spoken about him, not properly. And she'd never mentioned him since that night except once to say, when I'd asked, 'Yes, that was my husband you heard. He only stayed a minute.' She goes back to him, though, most of the time. Whenever he returns from abroad she zooms home, the dutiful wife. And what was happening between them now was anybody's guess. I didn't even know where she was supposed to be this very moment, with a sick auntie at Broadstairs or what. I suspected she'd made him believe she was legitimately absent on some benevolent enterprise. But husbands get philanderers followed. They're known for it.

Lastly, Beck. Well, maybe the fact that I'd whittled him for the odd doubloon had filtered down through his cerebral cortex by now and he was doing his avenger thing. Most unlikely, really. Beck was a sort of positive Algernon, a mad bull compared to a gormless spaniel. He'd have crashed in here the minute the ferry docked: Lovejoy, you swine, did you whittle me?

Something moved out in the night. A patch of darkness suddenly became cohesive and shifted slightly. I knew it had been six feet or so to the right a minute before. Dark's solid where living things are. My hands groped about the arm-chair. Great. Caught without even a stone or a poker, in pyjamas. The black grew larger. Dear God, I thought, sweating, it's coming right up to the window. The window darkened to one side. I was so tightened up I couldn't even screech for Janie. A faint gleam on spectacles drenched me in a sweat of relief.

It was sodding Algernon, the stupid bastard.

I blundered to the window and scrabbled for the catch muttering I'd kill him, frightening me to death like that.

'Lovejoy.' A whisper.

'What?' I croaked back, third go.

'He's out there. Do you want my night glasses?' He was

whispering where the windows met. This was it. Dandy's killer had finally come.

I forced myself to push the window gently open. Cold air streamed blessedly in.

'Where?' Never mind *where*, Lovejoy, for God's sake, ask who. 'Who?'

'The badger.' He sounded surprised.

'*Eh?*'

'Shhh, Lovejoy!' he hissed in anguish. 'You'll distract him!'

A bloody badger.

He got a three-minute whispered torrent of invective. Once one person whispers everybody does it and nobody can stop. Ever noticed that? Contagious, like yawning.

I deliberately slammed the window and went back to bed. Once I'd got warm again and my terror had lessened a bit I began thinking. In spite of myself Algernon's stalking impressed me. How come that he was normally so clumsy? Maybe daylight did things to his co-ordination. I couldn't tell Janie about the incident. She'd only laugh and tell me what I should have done.

That's the trouble with hangers-on, I thought bitterly as I nodded off. I'm on a three-seat tandem. We all want to honk the horn but nobody wants to pedal.

It must have been in one of those semi-conscious states that my logic did its stuff. Tandems. My dopey dawn mind saw a tandem ridden by Kate and Nichole. Then it took them away and put the diaries there. Then it put the two sketches there.

I awoke at six stark with cold fear. *All Bexon's pointers were in twos*, everything from the Roman babes on the gold coins, Romulus and Remus suckling on the she-wolf. Everything. Except for one lonely horrid decayed nightmare place, one terrible exception. So obvious. Suddenly so clear.

Dear Jesus. The inlet.

It had to be the seal pen.

I rose, creeping out of bed and tiptoeing about.

CHAPTER XXI

I SHOULD have spotted it earlier.

His hiding-place'd had to be near Groundle Glen. Had to. Otherwise, why stay here? His diary said '. . . it's convenient.' There was only the old railway line and the seal pen. I'd walked the length of the tracks several times and seen nothing. There was one place I'd never inspected close to, though. And that was the seal pen. Courage, Lovejoy.

I was out at first light. No signs of life from Algernon's bungalow. Janie slept on. I hurried down towards the bridge and climbed up the path to the diminutive railway. There wasn't another soul awake among the bungalows. I was clear away. I trotted on.

In the dawn light the seal pen scared me more than ever before. The cleft seemed to run a thousand miles down to where the sea struggled over the stone barrier. Most of the palings on the narrow wall had rusted to jagged points with fallen pieces lying obliquely to trail nastily into the sea. I wondered if any seal had ever managed to escape. Surely they must have wanted to. It was like a bad stage set nicked from Wagner's Teutonic worst.

A concrete platform with a wonky railing was the only sign of civilization where the railway ended. I was frightened. The ledge was pretty dangerous even on a calm sunny day. What it looked like on a stormy night didn't bear thinking of. I edged my way cautiously on to the platform feeling like a figurehead on a ship. I'd never seen so much sky around.

The heather and the grass had created a bulge where the tiny rails ended. There were probably buffers under there, overgrown. A circular rim set in the concrete level looked oddly familiar, reminding me: a gun emplacement, probably anti-aircraft. They'd built the platform wider and stuck an ack-ack weapon on top, for the war. Which miserable gunner battery had snapped up this particular posting? Poor sods. They'd have had to struggle back along the railway in the dark even to fill a kettle from the leaky tap at the ruined brick hut. Well, at least they could have used the little train for hauling shells. To me they were heroes as brave as any fighter pilot. I looked down again. The nightmare cleft had deepened a few miles since my previous glance. Did it go up and down with the sea? Was its water connected underneath all that stone and rusted iron? There was a noise behind me. A sheep rolled its mandible at me over the wire fence.

'Bloody fool,' I said. 'Go away. I'm scared enough as it is.' It didn't shift. I've never been able to tell people off.

The cage on the other side of the inlet was set on a lower level than the platform where I stood. A dice-tumbler, I suddenly realized. That's what it reminded me of. Another Bexon joke? It had been constructed on a slight prominence, giving it for all the world the appearance of an iron pulpit projecting out over the seal pen. There was no way in except through the top, where the metal staves were curved towards their common centre. You could get in but you'd have a terrible time getting out.

I could see across into it. Some rubble. Double iron doors in the cage, one shut with a grille at eye level, the other ajar. Maybe it was a further wartime addition, which suggested there was another way in from the landward side, probably with steps cut down into a tunnel. That's how they made entrances to dug-outs in the trenches. Soldiers don't change much.

At one time there had been a catwalk across. I could hardly bear to look. Not that I'm scared of heights, but there's a limit. It had deteriorated over the years to a crumbling bar of weathered concrete, spanning the sixty or so feet across the gorge. Most of the iron struts and handrail were gone. The entire thing was rust-stained, giving it a horrid toothiness I found distinctly unnerving. The inlet must be like one great mouth if you looked from the sea.

The noise again behind me. The sheep hadn't gone.

'Can you see anywhere else it could be?' I asked. It said

nothing. You get no help.

Getting round to the other side would be bad enough, let alone climbing down to the iron pulpit.

'Shift,' I said. The sheep stepped away from the fence.

Intrepid ramblers obviously came along this way, along the overgrown railway track. It was only about as wide as a small path anyway. The only safe way round the inlet was to climb up the steep hillside into the sheepfold, walk over and descend from the hillside on to the cliff-top again. I did it, clinging to the barbed wire for all I was worth and not looking down.

I was quite calm and pleased until I glanced back at the old gun platform. Had I just stood on that? And looked *down*?

The platform was as thin as a match, a little white scar marking a rising mass of jagged rocks. Below, sea waves, pretty docile until they swept casually round the headland, rose into white claws and scrabbled viciously at the volcanic rock. It made my feet tingle. And Bexon's gang had somehow built a seal pen in this savage place. More annoying still, he'd come back to see it years later.

I found the entrance to the tunnel cut through to the pulpit, and the steps I predicted. The hillside had slid gently into it, simply folding the passageway in the rock. There was no way through. Worse, clearing it would take a million years. Two million, on my own.

My rope had some iron things on that the man in the ship chandler's yesterday had said would hold on to anything. A likely tale. I latched them mistrustfully to the tunnel upright, a beautiful thick post reinforced with a metal bar for a hinge. It was set solidly into concrete top and bottom, a lovely great piece. 'Stay there,' I told it, 'and don't budge. Please.' For extras I made a couple of knots (well, eight, actually) around the opposite post in case. I'd previously examined every inch of rope a few hundred times, peering for flaws and hidden gaps. Now I did it again, rubbing it through my hands and feeling for any old razor blades or chewing insects I'd overlooked. It seemed all right but

suddenly very thin. Had I put on weight? Thoughtlessly,
I'd had a glass of milk, which now made me mad. I'd have
been just as strong without, at least for a few hours, and I
was bound to be heavier. How stupid to eat like a horse. My
school science came rushing frantically to my aid. A pint of
water weighs a pound and a quarter. But it had only taken
one bloody light-weight straw to break that biblical camel
clean in two, and everybody knows how tough camels are. I
tried spitting out to make myself lighter but my mouth was
dry. I drew deep breaths to get rid of some water vapour from
my soggy fluid-crammed lungs but only made myself so
giddy I had to stop. I tried peeing, politely turning towards
the vacant sea away from the sheep, but couldn't wring out a
drop. I'd dried up. Maybe I was so dehydrated with fright
I'd faint and fall, turning over and over, towards the . . .

'Now, Lovejoy,' I said. 'Be reasonable.'

How reasonable is it, I heard myself begin to answer back
sharply, to dangle . . .? I moved quickly to the edge and
found the double bush of heather I'd picked out as a marker.
With luck I'd be directly over the iron pulpit. I slithered
untidily down, clinging to the rope and babbling incoherently
with fear. Not that I was really frightened, not too much.
It's daft to let yourself get too scared. I shrieked with terror
when the rock surface momentarily vanished underneath me.
I hung in space staring upwards. The crest was only a few
feet away. I seemed to have been going down for hours.

You mustn't look down. That's what they say. Then how
the hell can you see where you're going? I had to. I forced
my gaze along to my elbow, then made it leap the gap to the
wall of rock. It travelled down on its own from there. Down.
Down. My belly seemed to leave me and vanish, falling. My
legs prickled. The sea was green, so deep and green. Mad
white rims poked and swirled. The concrete gums and iron
teeth seemed actually to be moving, gnawing erratically at
the sea's body and running white blood back into the ocean.
But the most fearsome thing of all was the iron pulpit. It
was only twenty or so feet from where I swung but its very
oddness and its nearness set me moaning. The hole at the

top was smaller than I'd imagined. The rest of the cage was
disproportionately larger. Funny, that.

A lunatic wind whistled round the rocks from seaward,
making me dangle a few degrees from the vertical. I should
have looked to see how much rope I'd got. I tried to but
couldn't. How long I hung there I don't know. What finally
started me moving down again was a sudden spasm of fear.
My hands were sweating. They might slip and set me falling,
turning over and over, towards the . . . I edged down under
my own weight inch by inch, thinking suddenly, Dear God,
does sweat dissolve nylon? I might land down there in the
iron pulpit, find the stuff and finish up trapped with half a
ton of melted rope.

My moaning was interrupted by a scream. It was me. I
looked down. The top curled iron staves of the cage had
touched my foot. I found I'd curled up on the rope, my body
balled as tight as possible in a spasm of reflex clutching.
Stupid sod. I forced my reluctant leg out and crooked my
foot around one bar. It seemed staunch enough. I pulled
myself nearer. There was enough rope to reach. I could
trail the end into the cage with me. Even if it came undone
from inside the cage sooner or later it would flail within
reach under this huthery wind. Hanging for dear life on to
the line with my left hand, I grabbed at the pulpit with my
right hand and held on to the lovely strong iron. It's extraordinary how you want to keep curling up. I tried to bring
the rope and my left hand nearer but only succeeded in
clinging like a sloth to the cage's ironwork. Sweat poured
down my face yet I was grinning with delight at all this
success. Even the rope was miraculously behaving, having
somehow looped itself over my shoulder. I needn't look any
more. The worst part was straightening both legs and
dropping into the cage. I found I'd kept hold of the line,
probably not trusting the concrete floor of the cage. It may
sound daft but at least it's careful.

I examined the interior, avoiding the ghastly spectacle
of the seal pen barriers directly below and trying not to hear
the sea sounds sucking and gasping. Everything looked fairly

solid. The metal was rusted but mostly intact and hard. I couldn't bend it or shift any of the palings. Cast iron, the old Bessemer process. The concrete only reinforced living rock, I saw, so the chances of the base giving way under my weight were virtually nil. It was exactly five feet wide. That was where my luck ended. The stone, concrete and ironware hadn't been displaced or touched since the whole thing was first made. Bad news, Lovejoy.

Which left the recess. Presumably the tunnel ran to emerge somewhere back there. I examined the iron wartime doors first. Both were rusted in place. That's modern metal for you. Rubble had fallen from the walls and made it difficult for me to squeeze in. I could hear water trickling and dripping in the dank blackness. Would there be bats? Peat. It stank of peat. Did peat give off fumes like those that gassed you in coal mines? I had a pencil torch. But, I worried, are those little bulbs electrically insulated so they can't touch off an itchy explosive gas? Why the hell is all this never written on the bloody things? They always miss essential instructions off everything you buy nowadays. I was so angry I took the risk, cursing and swearing at manufacturers. No bang. The light showed me a brick-lined space about four feet wide. The start of the tunnel. The sea down below gave a louder shuffle which made my heart lurch. A few soldierly graffiti indicated the last time anyone had stood there. Dust covered the floor. The tunnel's infall began a couple of paces from the iron doors.

It had probably been deserted after the war. Weather, perhaps mostly rain and seeping water, had weakened the tunnel walls. Bexon could never have been here. I edged back into the daylight, still pressing the surface with my foot as I went. No sun seemed to strike into the sea-washed cleft. You'd think they would have built the seal pen to catch a lot of sun, if only for yesteryear's holidaying spectators. Lord, what a day out it must have been. I'd have paid not to come. I wasn't unduly perturbed when I didn't see the rope exactly where I'd left it. Ropes hanging free swing about, especially in winds. Actually I couldn't re-

member knotting it carefully on an iron upright but I'd
worked it out. I'd soon catch it as it flicked past.

I looked about from the cage. The sea had risen somewhat
but could never reach the pulpit. There was no sign of a
tidal mark this high. Safe as houses. The trouble was I
couldn't see the rope at all, flicking about or otherwise.

Oddly it didn't concern me much at first. It was probably
caught up somewhere, maybe on a clump of heather or on a
small scag of rock face. It had to get blown free sooner or
later, hadn't it? Hadn't it?

'Lovejoy.' Rink was waving from across the crevasse.

I didn't answer immediately. All I could think of was
rope.

'Yoo-hoo,' he called. Not a smile. That's the sort of
character you get in antiques nowadays. No soul. He'd
won hands down and not even the glimmer of a grin. He was
alone.

'What?' It took me two goes to croak it out. It suddenly
seemed a long way over there. And back up the cliff. And
down. It was a hell of a long way to everywhere. Bleeding
hell.

'Find it?'

'No.'

'Then good luck, Lovejoy. That's all I can say. Good
luck.'

'What do you mean?'

'You'll need it.'

He sat on the platform. The swine had a hamper. He took
out some sandwiches and a flask. He seemed prepared for a
long siege. It all seemed so exasperatingly strange at that
moment. There was Rink, in his smart suit, noshing an
elegant picnic breakfast. And there was me, stuck in an iron
pulpit like a caged fly in a gruesome grotto. His very appearance of normality was grotesque.

'I can climb out, Rink,' I managed to squeak after swallowing a few times.

'No, Lovejoy.' He was maddeningly calm. 'No. Look at
the cliff.'

I'd already done that. I didn't need to do it again.

'Where's the rope?' I called lamely.

'Quite safe.' He poured a hot drink for himself. 'Don't try.'

In a panic I jumped and caught on the incomplete roof of the pulpit. Better to try climbing out now while I was fresh than after being trapped a whole day – week? Something cracked sharply. The rocks nearby my left side spattered with ugly suddenness. My cheek ran warm. I dropped back. Rink was smiling now. He had a double-barrelled shot-gun.

'I won't run out of cartridges, Lovejoy,' he assured me.

'Bastard.'

'I'm only anxious to preserve your life.'

'Why?' I asked. Maybe Algernon had heard the gun and would come searching. But there were a lot of hunters after pigeons knocking about. I'd seen them about the middle of the island. One more shot wouldn't be noticed. Anyway I couldn't encourage Rink to keep on using that thing. It was a modern hammerless cartridge ejector, I saw with scorn, when you can still find brilliantly engraved antique hammer-locks of the early percussion period. They're even cheaper than good modern guns, the burke. He could have used a luscious Forsyth scent-bottle fulminate percussion weapon, damascus-barrelled and silver-engraved. What a slob. Honestly, some people, I thought. It really shows a typical low mentality.

'You'd better start, Lovejoy.'

'Start what?'

'Guessing.' He waved a sandwich at me. 'I can wait. Every guess you give will be painstakingly investigated, Lovejoy. If the box is where you say it is I'll return and drop your rope over.'

'And if not?'

'Oh, you'll be allowed as many guesses as you like. Take your time.'

'How do I know you'll come back?'

He smiled again then. What worried me was that he wasn't sincere. It should have tipped me off but I suppose I

was too scared right then. Oh, I know he'd been painstaking
and finding me had cost him a quid or two. And he'd risked
a hell of a lot, killing Dandy Jack like he did. But that spark
was missing. I should have known. Every single genuine
collector I've known is always on heat. Mention the Sutton
Hoo gold-and-garnet Suffolk cape-clasps to a collector and
his eyes glaze. He pants like a bulldog on bait. He quivers.
There's music in his ears and stars glitter in his bloodshot
eyes. Your actual collector's a hot-blooded animal. Not
Rink. I'll bet he did pure mathematics at school. I ought to
have realized. Unfortunately I wasn't in a thinking mood.

'I'll shout for help,' I threatened. Some threat.

'I dare you. Ever seen lead shot ricochet?' He was right.
One blast directly into my pulpit would mash me like a spud
in a grinder.

'Don't talk with your mouth full,' I said. He took no
notice, just sat noshing and gazing at the scenery. 'What if
I don't guess at all?' I shouted over.

'I can wait. Day after day, Lovejoy. You'll die there.'

'And the knowledge dies with me, Rink.'

'Don't be illogical, Lovejoy. If you know,' he said reasonably, 'it's a consequence of your visit to where you are now. Or
else, it stems from what's in the copy of Bexon's little books
which you carry on your person. As soon as you're dead I
shall come down and have access to both sources of information.'

'I don't have them any more.' Lying on principle.

'They're not at your bungalow,' he called. 'So you must
have.'

'My bloke'll come searching soon.' Get that, actually
threatening a maniac with Algernon. The cavalry.

'I've taken care of that.' He sounded as if he had, too.

'Er, you have?'

'I left them a note saying you'd gone home. Told them
both to follow you as soon as possible, urgently.'

'I'll do a deal,' I called. He said nothing. 'Rink?'

'You're in no position to do any dealing, Lovejoy.'

'All right,' I said at last. 'I know where the stuff is.'

'Tell me.'

'No. I want . . . a guarantee.' That's a laugh, I thought, an antique dealer *asking* for a guarantee. A record. It'd make a good headline. Antique Dealer Demands Guarantee As Typhoon Grips Ocean . . .

'You're inventing, Lovejoy.' He was looking intently at me.

'I'm not. I do know. It's true.'

And all of a sudden it was.

I yelped aloud as if I'd been kicked, actually screamed and brought Rink to his feet. I knew *exactly* where Bexon had put the gold. I could take anybody there. Now. A place I'd never seen, but the precise spot there and I knew it almost down to the bloody inch. I could see it in my mind's eye. The wheel. The water. The Roman coffin. Splashing water and the pompous lady of the sketch in her daft one-wheeled carriage. I was smiling, even, then chuckling, then laughing. What a lovely mind the old man must have had. How sad I'd never met him.

'I know!' I was laughing and applauding, actually clapping like a lunatic as if a great orchestra played. I laughed and cheered and jigged, banging my palms and taking bows. I bounced and shook my bars. 'The old bastard!' I bawled out ecstatically, laughing and letting the tears run down my face. I practically floated on air with joy. If I'd tried I could have flown up and landed running. 'The beautiful old bastard!' I roared louder still with delighted laughter. 'The old bugger's had us on all along!' And I was on the selfsame island, the very ground where the Roman Suetonius had landed, pouring his Gemini Legion on the Douglas strand. History was wrong. Bexon was right. The clever old sod.

'Where is it? Where?' Rink was on his feet, puce with rage.

'Get stuffed, Rink!' I screamed merrily, capering. 'It deserves *me*, not a frigging cold lizard like you, you – '

'I'll – ' He was raising the gun in a rage when he seemed to jerk his legs backwards. Perhaps he slipped. He gave a rather surprised but muted call, not even a shout, and tumbled forwards. The shotgun clattered on the platform. I

watched frozen as he moved out into the free air above the
yawning seal pen and started to turn downwards. It was a
kind of formal progression. I can see him yet, gravely pro-
gressing in a curve, arms out and legs splayed as if to catch
a wind. Only the scream told it wasn't as casual as all that. It
began an instant before the body dropped tidily on to the
iron stakes on the crumbling stone barrier. Rink seemed to
move silently once or twice as if wanting to settle the iron
more comfortably through his impaled trunk. An incoming
wave began its whooshing rush at the inlet's horrible mouth.
His limbs jerked once before the sea rushed over him. An
arm moved slowly as if reaching into the trapped lagoon of
the seal pen. The wave sighed back, stained dark. Oddly, it
only became a deeper green from his blood. There was no
red. I was staring at him some time. He must have been
dead on impact, I guessed. What a terrible, horrendous
word that is. Impact. There's nothing left once you've said a
word like that is there? Impact. I was shivering from head to
foot. Impact. I was violently sick inside the cage.

The worst of it was the sea kept moving him. It seemed
as if he was alive still, trying to rearrange matters so as to
make a slight improvement in the circumstances in which his
corpse now unfortunately found itself. The start of a
demented housekeeping in his new resting-place. I turned
away and retched and retched. Lighter now, I thought
wryly, maybe an easier climb.

'Lovejoy,' a pale shaky voice called. I could see nobody.

'Who is it?'

'It's Nichole. Are you safe?'

'Is there a rope up there?' A pause. Please don't let her
have fainted or anything. 'Nichole?'

'Yes.' Her voice carried distantly down the cliff. I strained
to see her. 'It's fastened to the wood.'

'Don't pull it off!' I howled in panic. 'Don't touch the
fastening. Just chuck the free end over. And keep back from
the edge.' I repeated the instructions time after time in a
demented yell until I saw the rope come. I tugged it,
swinging on it as a test. 'Does it look firm to you?' I shouted.

'Yes.' She didn't sound so sure. I swarmed up, holding the free rope between my feet like I'd seen circus climbers do to lessen the strain on my hands. It seemed an age but, knowing me, couldn't have been longer than a couple of millisecs.

I sprawled gasping on the rock at Nichole's feet. Why hadn't I noticed it had started raining? The poor lass was weeping but quite honestly my sympathy for others was a bit used up. I crawled away from the edge and rose shakily. We embraced, Nichole trembling and heartbroken and me quivering from relief and eagerness. It wasn't far to Bexon's hoard.

'I was so afraid,' Nichole said. 'You were so calm and brave. Edward was like a mad thing. He kept making me help.'

'Thanks for the rescue, love,' I said. I moved us further inland. Neither of us wanted to see the inlet and its seal pen ever again.

'Is . . . is Edward . . .?'

'Let's go straight home.' I comforted her as we walked towards the sheep. A group was watching. They looked so absolutely bloody calm. What right had they to be so unconcerned while I'd nearly snuffed it? I was furious and made them scatter with a sudden shout to teach them a lesson, the smug bastards. It was all right for them. They were safe in a field of their own.

'Don't we have to tell the authorities?' Nichole asked. 'Poor Edward.'

'In a minute,' I said. 'I'll show you my bungalow first. It's in Groundle Glen. Not far. You can rest there. I've got something to do. I'll only be a few minutes.'

Janie and Algernon would be gone, Rink had said.

We got through the wire into the fold. The sheep had assembled on the landward side. I avoided their accusing eyes as we made our way over the humped field and clambered down to the overgrown railway. Well, I thought defensively, they could at least have looked just a little bit anxious on my behalf. People are far too bloody complacent these days. Just let a sheep get into trouble and it expects shepherds, collie dogs, a wholesale search, the lot. Sheep have even got a parable to themselves, selfish swine.

'Look, love,' I said. 'About poor Edward.'

'He was obsessed with these fanciful stories,' she sniffed. 'He made me – '

'Yes, darling.' I explained how we'd better just go. People would assume it was some ghastly hunting accident. Nothing could be done for him now anyway. She took it really well. I said she was a brave lass.

Neither Nichole nor I looked back at the inlet, nor down into the water. We left the platform with Rink's gun and its open hamper. The seagulls would handle what was left.

I was still smouldering when we came within sight of the ruined terminus. I pointed out the bungalows across the valley from among the trees.

'See that one with the smoking chimney?' I said.

'Near the blue Lagonda?'

'Eh? Oh, er, yes.' Well, well. Janie was supposed to have gone chasing to the ferry. 'Anyhow, three roofs to your right. That's it.' I gave her the key. 'Wait there for me. I'll be back smartish.'

'Edward's car's there too,' she sniffed. 'We had the bungalow next to the shop place.' Cunning old Edward.

'I'll not be long.' I saw her off where the footpath wound down from the railway. She kissed me. Twice she turned to wave. I watched her go. I didn't move until I saw her slight figure appear on the valley floor below. She walked out upon the wooden bridge and turned to wave again, shading her eyes at me. I waved and stayed put. She stepped on to the metalled road, heading up to the cluster of bungalows.

I ducked behind foliage and raced along the railway track.

You can't blame me, really. The law of treasure trove says firmly that the person finding precious archaeological stuff is entitled to the treasure's value. No messing about. So if you find another priceless miraculous dump of 'old pewter', as it was called, like that pop singer did at Water

Newton – incidentally now the brilliant centrepiece of early
Christian silver exhibitions the world over – you claim its
market value. The coroner fixes the money for you with
independent assessors. Naturally, you can't keep the actual
trove itself. That usually gets stuck in the British Museum or
somewhere. But you get the market value. Fair's fair. The
trouble is that *two* equal finders are made to share equally
by the nasty old coroner, who cruelly wouldn't trust Lovejoy
to be reasonable. After what I'd been through I deserved
at least sixty per cent, I told myself as I hurtled through the
undergrowth along the steep hillside. If not seventy. In
fact, I was reasoning as I ran breathlessly by the ruined
terminus and started down the steep stepped path towards
the waterlogged forest floor and the clumps of palm trees, I
really deserved it all.

There must have been torrential rain somewhere on the
uplands. The river was in hectic spate. Even the lagoon
water was swirling. I noticed that several of the small
overgrown weed islands were partly submerged. The run
was taking it out of me, probably the after effects of the
climb and Edward Rink. I was astonished to realize blood
was running down my face. My own blood. Then I remembered, just before fainting with fright, that he'd taken a
shot at me. A rock chip had caught my face. It really had
been a hard day.

I slowed to a jog along the narrow river path, then a walk.
Finally I reached where the tributary beck trickled beneath
its elegant bridge. I had to sit on a wayside stone for breath.
Only now it was no trickle. It was a tumbling spouting
cascade which had dropped an octave from an innocent
lightweight chuckle to a deep threatening lusty boom. Spray
watered ferns high above and the ornate bridge was quivering with the sustained impact of the falling water. God help
fishes. I rested longer than I meant to.

I pushed on. It wouldn't be far. The steep valley narrowed
sharply at the next bridge. Despite the full daylight, now
the water noise and the steep forested rock sides made the
scene claustrophobic.

It was a real hiding-place for Druids on the run. Opposite the ruined wooden shelter that Betty Springer had said people used for parties I had to rest again. I panted and gazed at the vegetation. Algernon said the glen was famous for its celandines, bluebells and wind anemones, but like all flowers they're just basically different sorts of eccentric dandelions. Two days before he'd tried to show me a monstrosity called a bladderwort that ate insects, the maniac. I edged away from some long-stemmed red flowers and pressed on upstream. They looked full of appetite. The brick uprights of the causeway showed among the trees ahead. I crossed at the last bridge to keep to the main path.

The viaduct was gloomier and darker than ever. Janie and I had never gone all the way beneath. Now, the rush of the swollen river caused the path to be flooded by a nasty swark. The three races, parted for the giant columns of the overhead road, emitted as they ran a sustained bellow which echoed and intensified between the brick pillars. Thoughtful Victorians had cobbled the path but forgotten a handrail. People were made of sterner stuff in those days, probably. I pushed sideways along the path on to the cobbles and stepped into the flooded bit. It was only a few inches deep this high above the river but still rushed with disquieting force against my ankles.

Beyond, the glen couldn't really be called a glen any more. There was very little space from wall to wall. It was more of a dark crevasse whose walls were encrusted with polished tubers of igneous rock mortared by ferns and lichen. Trees soared upwards, practically meeting in a great knitted entombing arch two hundred feet high. The path stayed beside the hoarse river, now demented by the addition of grey-black honed rocks. I plodded on, occasionally having to take hold of a tree branch for my weight where the path was either too overgrown or vanished completely. Algernon had told me they were beech, fir, birch, alder, willow. Their names sound all garden and tea-on-the-terrace, don't they, but down in Groundle Glen they were having a hell of a time of it. They were twisted and scrabbling for toe-holds up the soaring valley walls. One had fallen here and there, slamming down into the river or lodging across the boulders. I was struggling breathlessly over a slain skinned trunk and thinking that some lunatics do this for fun and call it rambling, when I saw it, a few yards up ahead. I yelled out for joy, clawing up through the undergrowth towards the wheel.

If everything was twinned in Bexon's trail, what else for Big Izzie but a Little Izzie? And where else but long the very glen where he'd stayed? An old sick man just can't get far, especially with a digging job to do. I'm stupid, really slow.

Judging from the state of the old path nobody had been this far along for years at least. The river rose to a natural series of bouldered waterfalls. And that exact point was where years ago Bexon had sited his little ornamental waterwheel, a beautiful simple copy of the original Lady Isabella. Her twin. If I'd had any sense I should have guessed: two identical diaries, two sketches, two nieces, but the carriage in the picture he'd chosen to copy had only one wheel. Find the missing thing and you're there. Stupid Lovejoy. I'd stayed in the same glen and never worked it out.

A decorative wooden millhouse stood amid engulfing greenery, maybe thirty feet tall. It was painted a crumbling black and white, typical Tudor in style, to offset the faded yellow of the wheel itself. Trust old Bexon to get the colours right this time. Guessing now where the path probably went, I hauled myself towards the millhouse breathless with excitement. My chest was suddenly tightly constricted, clamouring and clanging. Warm and getting hotter. I stubbed my foot on a stone. Steps ran – lurched – upwards. A rusty old handrail showed in the foliage, curving along the rock wall towards the millhouse. Of course. In those days the people were families on a day out. For safety there would be no way to the actual waterwheel except maybe for a man to work it. I clambered up the steps. The handrail looked pretty precarious so I kept away and tried pushing myself along the rock face among the honeysuckle and

brambles. I smelled sweet but was gradually being shredded.
The steps curved narrowly up between the incised valley
wall and the millhouse planking, very similar to one bend of
fairground helter-skelter, with the millhouse representing
the tower and the steps the slide. It was about as steep.
Twenty steps and I was almost on level with the roof.

The path was rimmed by railing from there and ran level
but higher, perhaps to climb steadily along the glen to
emerge eventually on the main sea road, but I couldn't see
beyond a few feet because of the day-dusk of the over-
hanging rocks and the dense vegetation. The river was three
feet below me where it started its torrential dash to the
boulders. A wooden lock gate had once diverted the flow
from the millwheel's blades. Now the wood was rotten. The
river split on a big pile, spraying a race against the wheel in a
high bow wave. The wheel showed a gear on its millhouse
side, maybe half the full wheel's diameter.

Where else but in the millhouse?

The walls seemed fairly substantial. I tested by pushing
the planking carefully. Stable. I guessed the wheel to be
about ten feet tall. If that gearing was still in working order
the turning force of a millrace in this sort of spate would be
colossal. Decorative, but dangerous. I'd have to be careful.
There were no windows on this side but a diminutive
platform projected over the waterfalls. Entrance therefore
from below. I clambered down and peered up at the millhouse.

It's surprising how big things look when you're feeling
vulnerable. The millhouse seemed supernaturally tall and
thin. I could have sworn the wheel, clapped so firmly to its
side and spurting the rushing water aside into an aerial jet
to join the rest of the torrent, was no more than ten feet in
diameter. From below it had grown. I was standing level
with its lowermost blades. Only the merest trickle crept
out from beneath, a testimony to the builders' skills. Stray
trickles are wasted power, energy just chucked away. Even
in decoration craftsmanship tells. I splashed the few yards
through the muddied undergrowth. A wooden platform,

crumbling, about chest height.

The millhouse's downstream aspect showed four turreted windows, two and two, not large enough to enter. I hauled myself on to the planking, making two give away instantly. I tumbled through on to the fetid mud beneath the platform. I was in a hell of a state and cursing worse than usual. But if the platform was fixed and I was the first to plunge through, then nothing could have been hidden beneath, correct? I was grinning like an ape, sweating in the dank air and almost bemused by the percussions of the booming river. This close, the falls were indescribably ugly. I've heard people go over in coracles for fun. They're welcome.

The platform creaked and spat splinters as I crept over it on hands and knees to spread my weight. A hinge, smugly veiled by its grime, was a foot from my face. Part of the wooden wall was crosscut, just as you see in stable half-doors. I found the finger hole after groping, and pulled. Naturally I fell beneath it as it tumbled out, but that's what comes of slow mental processes. Doors open, rotten doors fall outwards. The interior was a revolting mess of bird droppings and feathers. A set of wooden steps and a platform on the riverward side seemed more trustworthy than the outside planks, perhaps because they were protected from weathering. I crept up, jogging cautiously and waiting for the creaks to subside before trying the next step. The wheel was visible through a slit. I pulled at the edges. Rotten pieces came away in my hands. The whole structure was dicey. Only the gears were intact and they were practically perfect.

The wheel was a working model, connected through its gear to an internal cogwheel about four feet across. Every single depression had been packed by grease, lovely thick grease, and the cogs were as clean as the day the gears had been cast. A solid locking lever held the teeth. Carelessly I unslipped the chain peg to see what happened. The wheel gave a great scream as its gears clanked round. I yelped and almost went through the crumbling floor. The outside rushing noise lessened instantly as the water pushed the wheel blades.

I looked out. The great bow wave had gone from the

waterfalls. Instead the millrace was busily turning the waterwheel, but nobody could get near the thing to examine it while it was heaving round. The great thing sounded alive, whining and groaning and sighing like that. It unnerved me. I leaned back. More wood came away. I judged the turning cogs exactly right and hauled the lever into place. The distressing human noises stopped and outside the bow wave spurted again. I'd rather have that going all the time than the horrid shrill whines from the wheel. I locked the lever firmly with its peg. It was rigid enough without it, but accidents happen. One kick and the wheel'd be off again, so careful. I'd had enough risks to last the day out.

The bird droppings below showed no disturbance for years. Every sign in the whole narrow millhouse indicated somnolence with nothing moved or replaced. I glanced upwards into the roof beams. You could see the entire recess, even to the odd feather stuck to the ties. Take away roof and walls and floor, and that leaves what? I couldn't reach any of the windows but they too looked as untouched as the rest. There was no real door. I stayed where I was for a minute to work it out.

Yet somebody, a devoted old engineer weary with years and illness, had carried a heavy tin of grease – not to mention a Roman lead coffin – along the glen and restored the simple machinery to pristine state. He'd greased axles, levers, every cog. That alone was a labour of love, because the wheel must have required stopping and starting a few dozen times. It had been a nervy business for me. For him less so but at least as exhausting. I pulled at the platform. A piece of wood came away near the gear wheel's axle. Nothing hung there. And a Roman casket's no matchbox. It's not the sort of thing you can tuck in a spare corner. No ledges, no shelves. A hollow millhouse. The gears themselves?

I felt in my pockets. A comb, a pencil, a few coins. I scraped at the inner gear with a milled edge. Whatever the metal, it was solid and not gold. That only left the outside. I stuck my head out through the slit. Seen from out there, the whole world seemed full of surging waterfalls. The waterwheel was inches from my face. Despite the wind and spray I could see the millrace's surface where the wheel blades deflected the torrent. I noticed the water-run for the wheel. How clean the stone slabs were down there. How very, very clean.

Now, why leave the wheel stopped? Engineers say machines are always better used. But it was locked. So the millrace channel obviously needed to be kept dry. Perhaps while somebody went down and removed a slab – one of those clean slabs – below? Or perhaps to show the way? If you risked a climb down the millrace while the wheel was turning you'd be squashed like a strawberry between two stones. Thoughtful old Bexon. I pulled back in, ecstatic. My bell was clanging delightedly. That old chest feeling was still there even when I heard her shout.

'Lovejoy!' She was below, but very close. 'Are you in there?'

'Yes. Stay there. I'm coming down.'

'I'll come in.'

'No need, love. The platform's unsafe.'

She came crawling in anyway. I reached the top of the wooden stair.

'Did you find them?' Nichole's eyes were shining unnaturally bright. She looked lovely.

'Why did you bring that bloody gun?' She must have been scared by the gloomy woods.

She was smiling impishly. One good thing, she was as out of breath as me. 'I came after you, Lovejoy. To help, in case you got hurt. Did you find them?'

'I've guessed. It's here. The millrace, behind the slabs.' I'd been first. The coroner would have to acknowledge that.

'Show me, darling.'

She hurried creaking up towards me. I yelped and tiptoed back. The struts couldn't take both our weights.

'For Gawd's *sake*!' I told her to go easy.

'Show me!'

'Not here, darling.' I smiled and reached a hand to her. She smiled up at me and pointed the twelve-bore.

'Yes. Here, darling.' There was something funny about
her smile. Her eyes were brighter still.

'Eh?'

'Show me, Lovejoy.' It was her eyes. She wasn't making
a polite request. I was being told.

'It isn't up here,' I said lamely. 'It's down *in* the millrace.'

'Where?'

'Have you loaded that?' I asked.

Her smile became a little less diseased. A trace of humour
showed. 'Certainly.'

'Look, Nichole, love.' I'd have to treat her gently, if only
for the wonky platform's sake. 'All this has upset you. Let's
get outside. This place isn't safe.' I edged towards her.

'I ran over Dandy Jack,' she said brightly, all confidence.
'So don't think I'm chicken, Lovejoy. I'll pull this.'

'That sod Rink.' I quite understood. He was one of those
sick cold people who impelled more normal people into
lunacy. 'He forced you to do it. Never mind, love. He's
gone. We – you and me – can manage without the others
now.' I pointed. 'It's hidden behind the pale slabs below the
waterwheel.'

'Is it really there?' She peered timidly out. So help me, I
actually steadied her by holding her elbow.

'For certain,' I told her, smiling. 'Can't you hear the
lovely radiance?'

'Why!' she exclaimed delightedly. 'So I can!'

She suddenly came back inside, staggering slightly as a
board cracked and gave way, straightened up and shot me.
What with the water noise, the sudden apocalyptic crack of
the gun, the bewildering realization what had happened and
being spun round by the force of the blow in my side, I was
disorientated. I heard somebody screaming, not me for once,
a high steady insane call. I was on the ground among the
bird droppings and bleeding like a pig. I wondered why it
didn't hurt. The rotten planking had given under the weight
of us both. We'd been tilted different ways, me inside and
Nichole out into the millrace. God Almighty, the millrace.
My arm was stiff and bloody as well. Most of the shot had

missed but I'd collected a hell of a lot of blast. She'd fallen
through the rotten boardwalk. My arm was stinging. That
smell was powder. Nichole. That was her screaming somewhere.

'Nichole!' I yelled, coming to. She screamed again.
'Hang on. I'm coming, love,' I shouted, coughing from the
acrid fumes of the gun's explosion.

I hauled myself back up the steps. She wasn't there, but
a great torn hole let the crazy view in, the still wheel, the
hurling water and the tumbling drenched rocks rising
abruptly above the falls.

'Please, Lovejoy!' she was screaming. 'Darling!'

'Hold on!' I called. 'Hold on!' The force of the gun and
the rotten platform giving under us had thrust her back
against the wall and it had simply fallen away. I spread
myself on the platform as quickly as I could and slid towards
the gap. She was lodged between the wheel and the stone
slabs, head mercifully out of the onrush.

I'd have to risk my arm and shoulder under the wheel. I
examined the locking lever, in case. It looked exactly as
I'd replaced it. One careless nudge against the peg could
edge the cogs into place and the entire bloody waterwheel
would turn, sweeping Nichole down and crushing her
against the sliprace stone slabs. And I'd go too.

'Please, Lovejoy!' She was moving, becoming frantic now,
in worse danger of slipping further under the wheel.

'Hold on!' I screeched. 'Hold on!'

'I can't!' she gasped. Water was pushing against her head.

'You must! One second!' I yelled into the roar. 'Drop
the bloody gun!' She was holding mechanically on to the
gun, for God's sake. As if it was any use. I turned aside to
see if there was anything for me to hang on to. Not a bloody
thing. Nichole must have feared I was going away because
she screamed.

'*Lovejoy!*'

'I'm still here, darling.' I turned back to reach into the
flood for her arm. I couldn't lose her now, not when I'd
everything in my grasp. As long as I kept my legs clear of

the gears and that huge ominous lever. 'Lift yourself,' I bawled, getting a mouthful of the water. '*Now.*'

'I – I didn't mean to.' She was babbling incoherently as our hands met. I pulled. Nichole started to come free of the water. I gasped at the exertion. My side was hurting now, but we were clinging firmer. I began to wriggle slowly back along the wooden platform. 'I didn't want to kill your birds, Lovejoy darling,' she gasped.

'*What?*' I yelled. Her relieved smiling face was an inch from mine. We were both practically submerged, me dangling upside down, hanging on, and her draped on the wheel in the funnelled mountain water. She still clutched the shotgun. As if I hadn't enough to lift.

'I knew you'd forgive me, darling,' she said breathlessly. I still held her in an embrace. 'And the bike was a silly joke.'

'*You?*' I shrieked.

'And I just *had* to push Edward . . .'

I was still pulling her up but now I stared in horror. She must have seen my eyes change. Her lips stripped back off her teeth. Even in that position she struggled to lift the gun at me, screeching hatred. Hatred at me, who practically loved her. And honest to God it was an accident but my hands slipped. Her fingers unlatched or slipped or something, I don't really know any more. I couldn't help it. Everything happened in a split-second blur. I swear it was beyond my control. My side suddenly gave out and my hand jerked away. It just happened. She slid back down screaming, wedging with a burbled shrill squeal into the millrace. She was howling dementedly with outrage. Her eyes glared up with pure hatred as she dragged the shotgun up against the force of the water. I removed my arm and edged frantically away from the wheel on to the crumbling platform. I swear my hand just slipped. Honest to God. And in the suddenness of her weight vanishing my flailing foot clanked the lever. Before I knew what was going on I heard the gears engage. It was a pure accident. Maybe I was trying to scrabble away from the coming blast of the shotgun. She gave one screech and the wheel lurched round. I heard it. Then there was only the moaning and whining sound of the big wheel's slow turning and turning. I lay there, gasping. The paddles had blood on, but only the first time round.

I'd *had* to roll over. She'd been lifting the gun at me again. You can see that. If she hadn't been trying to pull the trigger I'd have reached for her again. Accidents always happen when you're in a hurry. Everybody knows that.

I dón't know how long it was before I dared look out. She was crushed beneath the wheel, her corpse deformed and mangled on the rocks and washed quite free of blood. The recesses between the boulders were covered with dark brown discs. I edged along the planking. The turning wheel had used Nichole to scrape the slab covering off the bed of the millrace. There were hundreds down on the river bed. I'd been right. Bexon had walled the lead coffin, now lying crumpled and exposed in the water, behind the millrace.

I could see Nichole's waxen head in the clear water. It took me an age to work up courage to lock the wheel again. Honestly, hand on my heart, it was accidental.

But as I climbed painfully down pity was alien to me. At that instant it was utterly unknowable. Her arm swayed like the limb of some obscene reptile as I splashed into the water below the waterfall. My side oozed blood.

I stood knee-deep in the millrace, the onrush thrusting against my legs. Looking around it became obvious most of the fortune was in copper and the occasional silver coins. I didn't blame Bexon, picking out the golds like he had and putting them in the Castle for bait. It was exactly the sort of thing I would have done. Anyway, the Romans considered copper the mediocre twin of gold itself. There was a small crusted bronze statue, a she-wolf suckling two infants.

I caught a glimpse of one dulled yellow. Her palm was tilted in the water, exposing a Roman gold between two fingers. I took it carefully from her.

'Hold them by the edge,' I said. I keep telling people this but they take no notice.

I thought of saying something else to her submerged face through the rippling water layer, but finally didn't speak.

CHAPTER XXII

JANIE WAS telling me off again.

'We didn't leave,' she was saying angrily, 'because a *polite* note from you was just too good to be true. You'd have just gone.'

'Charming.'

We'd all but packed. The bungalow stood clean and aired ready for more, for all the world like a runner on starting blocks before another race. I knew Janie was working up to something. She attacked suddenly in the lounge, unfairly bonny and colourful with white net gloves and pastel shades.

'Lovejoy.'

You can tell it's trouble from the way they say things.

'Yes, love?'

'Look at me.'

I'd been staring admiringly at the hillside. St Lonan's chapel with the valuable engravings was only two miles off and nobody would be there as early as this. I'd visited briefly. Some scoundrel would nick them one day. He could slip up the hedgerow, turn left at the road and cut through the sheepfold. Nobody'd see him. People are rogues and can't be trusted.

'Yes, love?' I gazed innocently into her lovely eyes. They looked full of suspicion. Women get like this.

'Lovejoy. The Roman coins.'

'Don't,' I got out brokenly.

'You didn't mention them very much to the police, did you?' She waited.

'They almost slipped my mind. When I heard how Nichole had been . . . well, ill for so long, in close care and all that . . .' I paused bravely. 'Still, I did own up. Eventually.'

'Did you take any?'

'Me? Take – ?' I was outraged. 'Certainly not!'

'Look at me, Lovejoy.'

I'd accidentally turned away, honestly not because I wanted to avoid her eyes. I steadied up and gazed back.

'Did you,' she asked, grim all of a sudden, 'did you go back and steal some?'

I gasped, injured. Women have no sense of grief, not really. It takes a woman to be savage, even barbaric. Look at Nichole.

'Steal?' I demanded coldly. That hurt. 'I showed the police where they were and everything. I said how I'd been looking for Bexon's find. And how she'd followed me and tried to keep the Romans for herself. Shooting me as soon as I'd found them. And pushing poor Edward off the cliff . . .' I shuddered. No need to act for that.

'Steal,' she said, still suspicious as hell, very determined. 'Steal. As in nick, lift and thieve.'

'No,' I said, wounded to the quick.

'And,' she added unabashed, 'as in Lovejoy. There seemed very few coins. Only a dozen or so. Wouldn't a Roman army carry more than that?'

'How should I know?'

'Janie!' Algernon was suddenly there. I was very glad to see him. She never moved or took her eyes off me. 'How *dare* you!' He quivered with indignation.

'How dare I what, Algernon?' Janie kept judging and weighing me up. She's basically lacking in trust. It must be terrible to be that way.

'Make – ' he steeled himself – 'well, what can only be designated . . . *suggestions* about Lovejoy's character.'

'Go and see to the car, Algernon,' Janie said evenly. 'I've business with Lovejoy.'

'N – n – no, Janie.'

She stared at him then, astonished. Served her right for losing confidence in her fellow-man. She repeated her command but good old Algernon stood his ground quivering like a pointer.

'No, Janie. I can't allow these unpardonable insinuations against Lovejoy's character to go without demur.'

'Algernon,' Janie ground out, 'I think it's time you faced

the facts. Lovejoy's an unprincipled, greedy, lustful, selfish – '

Algernon scraped up some more demur and faced her, pale to the gills but still full of heroism.

'You're very – ' he swallowed and finally made it – 'wrong, Janie.'

I gasped in horror and turned aside, doing my strong-man-overcome. 'Algernon!' I exclaimed. 'Janie didn't mean – '

'The swine's acting, Algernon!' Janie cried. 'He's up to something. Can't you see?'

'If you only knew, Janie, what terrible events Lovejoy has been through,' Algernon continued icily. 'How absolutely courageous he was – '

'It was nothing,' I muttered, embarrassed.

'How calmly he explained to the police, despite a serious wound – '

'It's only a scratch,' I put in self-effacingly.

' – when he'd been in the very jaws of death!'

'Anyone would have done the same,' I whispered nobly.

'I want a minute alone with him,' Janie said angrily.

'I fully appreciate your . . . your relationship, Janie.' Algernon drew himself up for a last stand. 'Don't think I've failed to perceive your, well, your *weakness* where Lovejoy's concerned. I've turned a blind eye towards your . . . *goings-on* until now, perhaps even erroneously. But I must speak out.'

I listened, marvelling. How can somebody reach twenty-two and still talk like reading Bram Stoker? He darted a kindly glance at me. I hastily looked courageous.

'I'm going to search him,' Janie said sweetly. 'From balls to bootlaces.'

'I forbid it!' cried Bulldog Drummond.

'Then,' she said, smiling to show she wasn't smiling at all, 'I'm going to frogmarch him down to the Douglas police station and return the Roman things he's stolen.'

'He's not stolen a single item!' Algernon stood firmly between us, dauntless despite having lost his cutlass in the first wave of boarders swarming over his galleon. 'Your feelings are deforming your views. The very fact that your *obsessive desire* for Lovejoy is entirely *physical* – '

'Please,' I said, broken. 'I feel you are going too far.'

'Your fatal attraction continually upsets your judgement!' he cried.

Even Janie was speechless at that. I couldn't help thinking Algernon was making some real progress.

'Don't think, Janie,' he said with controlled calm, 'I'm entirely ignorant of your repeated *surrenderings* to . . . well, what can only be called . . . *temptations of the flesh.*'

'Excuse me, please,' I said quietly. 'I . . . I can't stay to hear this.'

'Stay here, Lovejoy!' Janie yelped.

The white-faced Algernon blocked her path as I trailed slowly and sadly to the door. 'It's time I remonstrated, Janie,' he was saying as I went, 'on Lovejoy's behalf as well as your own. Have you never thought of your husband? Have you never searched in your innermost heart to learn what value a woman must place upon her sense of loyalty . . .?'

Isn't education wonderful?

Outside I inspected the Lagonda's rear off tyre. You'd need a microscope to detect any change. It had taken me all bloody night. I scuffed the gravel in case there were telltale signs. Thank God, I offered up, for tubeless tyres. Hiding stuff in those old-fashioned inner tubes must have been almost impossible.

I stuck my ear near the door. They were still at it.

'I'm going to search every ounce of his stuff before we move an inch!'

'And I absolutely forbid – '

I looked again at the Lagonda. Anybody driving would have to take it slowly towards the main Liverpool ferry road. Especially on the bends, though the Romans were wedged thick and tight in layer after layer of unwaxed toffee paper and would be safe.

I'd left a lot of coins in the stream before climbing to the main road and phoning the police. Well, a dozen. I'd carried the main mass wrapped in my coat and stuffed it in an over-grown niche a hundred yards downstream for later. People

have to learn they can't always have everything. I've had to.
I would give several to the Castle's museum. Popplewell
would have kittens. I'd insist they were exhibited with gold-
lettered name cards, one blue, one green. They'd say: "These
Roman treasures discovered in the Roman Province of the
Isle of Man.' I'd make sure the donors' names got pride of
place, too: 'Donated by Messrs Dandy Jack, B. Manton and
B. Wilkinson.' '

And if he asked I'd tell him B for budgie.

'He's a selfish – ' Good old Janie, sticking at it.

Women can really get you down if you let them. What
disappoints me most is how suspicious they are for no
obvious reason. Even when you're being perfectly open they
can't stop imagining what you might be up to. No trust in
people. I'm glad I'm not like that.

It seemed a clear choice, Janie or the coins. Her, or a
Roman treasure. The trouble is I can't stand disagreements.
Women really like them. Ever noticed? Anyway, she probably
had enough for the fare home.

I got into the Lagonda and drove off.

THE GRAIL
TREE

TO
To the Chinese god Kuan Ti, guardian of antique dealers and pawnshops, this book is sincerely and respectfully dedicated.

He is also the god of war.   *Lovejoy*

FOR
A story for friends in Tripoli, for Tom in dock, Susan, and the Berwick lifeboat men.

It is naught: it is worthless, saith the buyer. Then having bought he goes laughing.   *Proverbs XX, verse 14*

CHAPTER I

Antiques and women are my only interests. It sounds
simple, but you just try putting them in the right order.

I was in this tent when somebody hissed my name. It was
Tinker Dill, unshaven and shabby as ever. Betty dived with
a muted shriek behind a trestle table, clutching at her
blouse. I couldn't blame her. I'd thought it was her husband
too for a second. Tinker wormed his way under the tent
flap. I almost went berserk. Trust Tinker to interrupt the
one chance Betty and I had, even if it was in the middle of
our village's annual fair.

'Can't you leave me alone when I'm – ?'

'Quick! Come and see, for Gawd's sake!' He looked
stupid, his head craned upwards among the grass.

'No,' I hissed back. 'Get out.' My heart was thumping.
This is typical of Tinker. Always around when you don't
want him. I could hear the band and chattering voices
nearby outside.

'There's an *antique* out here.'

I was just going after Betty again when the magic word
cleared the love fog from my mind and made me stop dead.
It has to. I'm an antiques dealer keen on survival.

'Eh?'

'Antique.' Tinker started to wriggle backwards, his job
done. 'One of the kids in the pageant's got it.'

'Who was that horrible little tramp?' Betty was ashen.
She started tidying herself mechanically.

'Tinker Dill,' I said, thinking hard. 'My barker. He finds
antiques for me.' I didn't add that he gets paid a fortune in
commissions from every antique I buy or sell. When I'm
not broke, that is.

'He won't tell on us, darling?'

I hoped not. Her husband's built like a shire horse.

'No. Er, look, love.' I began to edge away.

'But we haven't got long — ' She came to me smiling but I pushed her away and made for the flap. The huge marquee was full of spaced tables laden with food and jugs of orange. A million villagers would descend on it at four o'clock and clear the lot. Betty was in charge of the arrangements. Hence the solitude, if a love-tryst in a cathedral-sized tent in the middle of a village pageant can be called solitude, that is.

'You're not going?' She pulled at my arm, angry and disbelieving.

'Let go.' I got enough of the flap undone.

'Of all the — ' Betty tried a furious swipe at my head but I clouted her before her hand landed. She tumbled over a table and a trifle splashed nastily.

'See you Friday?' I thought she'd be pleased at that but it only seemed to make her more mad.

'You swine! I'll — ' She recovered and came for me again but I was through the flap and off. Safe and sound among the strolling hundreds, nodding and smiling as I went.

Sometimes women really nark me. No sense of priorities. Ever noticed that?

Things hadn't been too good recently for me. The few I'd seen lately were either rubbish or so highly priced it was heartbreaking. One gem had lit my life for an instant, a luscious porcelain Ting bowl from Hopei Province, about AD 1150. Some maniac had removed the bronze rim but the dazzling magnolia-ivory colour moved me to tears when I saw it. You'll have guessed by now I'm a full-time dedicated antiques dealer. I admit dealers are mostly lustful, greedy, savage, crude and vulgar — in fact, just like you. The difference is that I bet I'm a lot more honest about me than you are about you.

'Lovejoy.' A shout among the crowd. Tinker was waving across the field near the mediaeval pageant. I started over through the press of people. If you're going to belly-laugh at my name get it over and done with. I'm owner of Lovejoy Antiques, Inc. In fact, I'm the firm as well, the sole proprietor and its one miraculous asset. I add the 'Inc.' bit to make me sound a bit more like a huge American firm than otherwise might seem the case. Anything to help with the thousand-year mortgage on my cottage.

Pushing between rows of open air stalls on our village's fête days is like running the gauntlet. I'd only got a yard before a gushing voice cooed out:

'Lovejoy! You *naughty* man!' The vicar's wife playfully wagged a finger at me from the bottle stall. 'I've caught you at it! Red-handed!'

'Eh? Er . . . ' I dithered. Mrs Woking's a nice old dear in tweeds.

'Scrumping those cream cakes before teatime!' she trilled.

'Oh. Well . . . ' I broke into a sweat of relief. Of course. The nosh was crammed into Betty's marquee. The old dear thought I'd been after her meringues. Some hopes. I've still got my own teeth.

'Such an *appetite!*' The ladies with her tittered. Women love appetites, any old appetites. Ever wondered about that?

'I thought nobody noticed.' I shrugged with mock resignation, smiling.

'You're becoming known for it, Lovejoy.' Jean Evans gazed innocently at me as she put the barb in. Our village schoolmistress, addicted to young gentry with fast cars. She was running the bingo today. I grinned weakly and pushed on towards the silver band. I'd have to sort Jean Evans out sooner or later. Too cool by far. I hurried on. You can't help becoming excited at the sniff of an antique.

A good crowd had turned up to the pageant. Constable Jilks was in his element at the gate, flagging down the occasional car and pointing the way in to families walking over from our one crossroads.

'Hey, George,' I called as I trotted past. 'They all know the way to the village green. It's not shifted for three thousand years.'

His pompous smile faded as he blotted his helmet. 'What are you doing here, Lovejoy?' he asked suspiciously.

'Just enjoying the fresh country smog, George.' I gave him my blandest beam and left him to his useless job. Why people are so suspicious of me I honestly don't know.

'Here, Lovejoy.' Tinker was hopping about eagerly by the display field. People along the ropes had left a space round him, perhaps because he stinks of stale beer. He's not really completely horrible, as barkers go. But he usually looks dishevelled and half-sloshed, partly because he is and partly because of his tatty greatcoat. He's not taken it off since he was demobbed.

'You're always after the birds, Lovejoy,' he criticized.

'I was only helping her,' I said lamely. 'Where is it?'

'Aye,' he said, disbelieving old clown. Not even my own barker believes me. No trust these days. 'See that little kid dressed like Caesar?'

Tinker meant a little blond lad in tin. The Romans had dusted our local Iceni tribesmen over as soon as the pageant opened. They were now changing noisily behind the plywood castle façade while our band played manfully on. Parents and teachers ran about rounding up stray infants. There was bunting and flags, banners and coats-of-arms were everywhere. It was bedlam. What the hell we do it for God alone knows. I was knackered and blistered from helping Jean's assorted nine-year-old psychopaths to build a chariot in her school. I'd been really proud of it. It took me three days. Then they'd ridden it into the Boadicea scene for a couple of seconds and that was it. I tell you, never again.

'Behind him, Lovejoy.' Tinker had more sense than to point.

'The two serfs?'

'Between them.' Two little servants were carrying a long wooden board with something on it. I glanced at a neighbour's programme. They were probably up to King Arthur. A score of children, suddenly pious, were in procession across the grass towards a cardboard Camelot.

'See the sword, Lovejoy?' I edged away from the acrid fumes of Tinker's alcoholic breath and gazed.

The child was struggling but he managed to lift it above his head. A fanfare sounded. A dozen tinfoil knights on Shetland ponies trotted out of the painted castle's doors to welcome the new king. Applause rippled round. Suddenly I couldn't move. My breath froze and the world halted on its axis.

'Yes,' I croaked.

'Lovejoy.' Tinker was holding me back. I'd inadvertently started to climb the rope on to the field. I guessed Norman or late English. I broke into a sweat. A real find.

'Come on, Tinker,' I backed out of the press of spectators.

'Is it genuine, Lovejoy?' He trotted beside me as I started round towards the changing areas.

'Maybe.'

'Where'd the little basket get it?' The eternal wail of the barker.

'Where does anybody get anything?' I said — the eternal wail of the antiques dealer.

You can't help being bitter. Any collector will tell you why. You can spend your life searching for a particular antique and never get within a light year of the bloody thing. Then somebody will fall over it. Or buy it for a quid in a junk shop. Or decide to replace an old mantel piece, and it's eureka for somebody all over again. It happens a lot hereabouts. To damned near everyone else but me, that is. It really hurts.

In the past five years, I've seen valuable flintlock duelling pistols in old beam crannies. I've seen a Celtic gold torc hoed up by a farm labourer and brought in as a funny old bent horseshoe. I've seen a collector's Venetian veneered cabinet used as a mechanic's tool bench in a garage. And a beautifully preserved genuine 1751 Chelsea dish stuck under a penny plantpot out in a garden. It breaks your heart.

I tried not to run, Tinker Dill shambled alongside. The end of the green was roped off. A wooden scaffolding held a line of rickety façades in place. Various porchways were labelled to show where each group of children was to enter. Needless to say, many bits had blown off or been pinched by the little fiends.

'What are you doing here, Lovejoy?'

That's all people ever say to me, I thought furiously. 'Get back to your bingo,' I replied without looking at Jean. 'I've as much right on the village green as everybody else. I've got blisters to prove it.' That was a mean one.

'Shouldn't you be back in the tea tent?' she said sweetly,

shooing a cluster of wandering Druids back.

'That big sword.' I couldn't be sidetracked, not so near a precious find. 'Whose is it?'

'Why not ask Betty Marsham?' That sugary voice again. 'Perhaps she can . . . *satisfy* you.'

I gave her the bent eye and waited.

'Well . . . ' she said defiantly. There was a pause while Cromwell's Ironsides clanked tinnily past on ponies. Now two tiny Anglo-Saxons had got among the Druids.

'Are these in any sort of order?' I couldn't help asking. The milling children were giving me a headache. Jean laughed and shook her head.

'Supposed to be,' she said a bit helplessly. 'Actually, you'll have to see Mrs Cookson. She brought the sword.' She stared about. 'Over there. Flowered hat.'

I glanced from the plump elderly lady to Tinker Dill and back. The cultural shock would be too great for one of them. I gave Tinker a note.

'Meet me in the pub, Tinker,' I told him.

'Ta, Lovejoy.' He burned off through the crowd.

The Arthurian children were already streaming off through one of the gaps to scattered applause. I tried to cut past. King Arthur was flushed with triumph at having got his duty over with. He and one of his serfs were lugging the luscious sword along, trailing it on the grass because of its weight.

I reached the plump woman. 'Excuse me, please.'

'Yes?' She was pleasant, smiling, wide-eyed. 'Are you with the morris dancers?'

I repressed a shudder at the thought of all that energy. 'Well, not exactly.' I drew breath. 'My name's Lovejoy. I, er, helped Miss Evans with the chariot. It's the sword.'

A curious gleam of amusement flared for a split second. Then, oddly, when she spoke again it had gone and she was calmly shepherding children into the right pens. Some private joke, no doubt. 'Oh. Are you interested?' she said absently. Her accent was faintly transatlantic. 'It's very rare, I believe. Early English.'

'Is is yours?'

'A friend's,' she explained. 'Do examine it, if you wish.' King Arthur and his mob arrived. I practically fell on the sword, as politely as I could, gently brushed aside the two serfs and laid it reverently down on the grass. I could hardly breathe at first. Then I calmed and rose.

'Yes, well.' I stretched and cleared my throat, trying not to let my disappointment show.

'I don't suppose you've seen another antique like it?'

'No.' I couldn't bring myself to tell Mrs Cookson outright it was a forgery. A clever one, but a forgery. I fumed inwardly. There's only one really good metalwork forgery artist in our area. Bannon. I've a standing agreement with him to show me everything he makes before selling it. I decided to pop across and cripple him, in the interests of fair play.

'You don't sound very enthusiastic.' The gleam in her eye was one of genuine interest now.

'Er, no.' I moved off. There were signs Napoleon was on the move. I hadn't time to get conscripted into the Peninsular War.

'Wait a moment, please,' she called after me, but I was off.

I'd brought my car, a tiny derelict Austin Ruby. A black packing case with an engine. It stood near the hedge ready for a fast getaway. I only found it because I'd remembered where I'd left it among the tall grass. It no longer had its pram-top. Open air. I switched its ignition and stirred the insides vigorously with the handle. It'd win nothing at Silverstone but it will see the century out. 'I'll give you a lift, Lovejoy.' That familiar voice, so dear to all our hearts. He was sitting on one of the trestle tables. Two admiring women fawned nearby. The only person alive to wear an astrakhan coat on a bright summer's day, the goon.

'Get stuffed, Honkie.' Honksworth's as gruesome as his name. He's another antiques dealer, Edwardian furniture, late Georgian domestic silver, and ignorant. Like most antiques dealers, Honkie couldn't tell the Wartski collection of Fabergé jewels from frogspawn.

'You can put your toy car in my boot,' he said, cheerfully enough to give offence. He has a shop in Clacton for tourists. Some people you can trust. Some, like Honkie, you daren't ask the time.

My engine fired. I dashed round and flung myself behind

the wheel.

'This is ground control,' Honkie boomed into cupped hands. 'We have lift-off.' His adorers laughed adoringly. I clattered the Ruby across the grass and out on to the road. Tinker Dill waved from the beer tent as I passed. He hadn't even made it to the White Hart. I could understand that. It's almost two hundred yards farther on, and heat's so tiring.

Bannon was in his forge whistling happily until I pinned him by the throat.

'Now, Bannon,' I said. 'This sword.'

'For God's sake, Lovejoy.'

I stood off and let him rub his neck. His forge's furnace was fading because of our scuffle. I'd kicked the foot-bellows aside to reach him faster.

Blacksmiths are on the way back. Bannon does fancy metalwork now for East Anglia in general and the odd forgery for me – er, I mean for some unscrupulous local antiques dealers. Once he actually used to shoe horses. Now he couldn't tell Hyperion from a double bass. I examined the scrap of metal cold on the anvil.

'A Victorian interior balustrade decoration?'

'Torch-holder.' He coughed. 'What the hell's up, Lovejoy? I ain't done nothink.' He's a migrant Cockney.

'You've made a forgery of a late Saxon longsword, lad,' I explained gently. 'And before I break your two index fingers, explain why you didn't tell me.'

'Longsword?' He seemed honestly puzzled. Scared, but genuine. 'I never.'

'Bannon,' I said warningly. He tried to back through the wall.

'Honest, Lovejoy,' he said desperately. 'I don't know *how* to forge till you draw the bloody things for me and tell me what to do, do I?'

'Tea for you and Lovejoy?' his wife called cheerily from nearby. He lives in a cottage next to the forge.

'Yes, please, Mrs Bannon,' I called back merrily, a real bit of Merrie England.

'Two minutes, then,' she trilled.

'I can prove it,' Bannon urged in a low, frantic voice, still keeping out of reach. 'Just ask whoever has it.'

I paused. He had a point. 'Fair enough, Bannon. Know of any others besides yourself?'

'None any good.' He thought a bit more. 'That Southend geezer two years ago.' He'd been clinked by the magistrates and was still doing porridge. No remission. He'd used Britannia metal of 1897 vintage to solder a forgery of an eighteenth-century Florentine smallsword, so it served him right. I'm all for upholding law and order, I told myself piously. I'd have to find out from Mrs Cookson.

I stepped away, nodding. 'See you, Bannon.'

'See you, Lovejoy,' he called thankfully.

'Tell your missus I had an emergency.'

Luckily the Ruby's engine hadn't cut. I clattered round the pond in an erratic circle and headed for the pub half a mile away. The wind was behind me so I'd make it before dark. It's all downhill. Two kids overtook me on their bikes, pedalling and jeering like mad. If I'd the power I'd have caught them up and given them a thick ear.

So there was another expert forger living locally. But who the hell was he and why hadn't I heard of him? I was extremely peeved. The antiques game is difficult enough. If he was useless, like so many forgers of antiques, it wouldn't have mattered. But I'd seen the sword. It was good — too good by far.

The pub was crammed. I signalled ahead and Ted the barman waved acknowledgement. The crowd was mainly refugees from the pageant's shambles, plus the usual sprinkling of antiques dealers. Saturday evening is assembly night. We gather in pubs all over England and lie about how great things are in the antiques business.

Tinker was with a group of barkers near the fireplace chatting light-heartedly of happier and cheaper times, the way they do. During the fight through the saloon I had a word with Angela, a tiny flirtatious piece full of ceramics and pre-Victorian tapestries. She'd married a local landowner a year ago and ran her antiques business on the proceeds of hubby's colossal income. Every little helps, I always say.

'Bill's got a de Wint watercolour,' she told me.

'He says,' I shot back.

'And you still owe me for that Keppel.'

Today's tip: buy the best-condition first editions of the early scientific geographers you can lay your hands on. Like Keppel, Cooke, Darwin. Don't delay or you'll be sobbing into your beer too. My great fault is I don't let a little thing like my abject poverty get in the way of buying. It's a handicap. It's also why I'm always in debt, mainly to people like Angela.

'Ah,' I said. 'Er, will tomorrow do?'

'We might come to some arrangement,' Angela said, looking cool and straight at me. My eyes wavered first. You never know exactly what women mean, do you?

'I'll bring the money round,' I promised.

'Do,' she said precisely. 'Fancy a set of Windsor wheel-backs?' She was with John Laxton, her barker. He's a senile sour-faced rum drinker with a flair for porcelain. Not as good as Tinker Dill at sniffing antiques out but more knowledgeable.

'Thanks, love,' I said. 'But my warehouse is full.'

There was laughter at that. Ownership of a huge warehouse is the antiques dealer's favourite myth. Saying it's full is our slang for being broke.

'Tinker.' I got to the bar and Ted had it ready. He was going to exchange a word but saw my face. No chitchat.

'Here, Lovejoy,' Tinker began nervously. 'Don't blame me.'

I rounded on him. 'A bloody *forgery*, you stupid berk.'

'I wasn't to know, was I?' He slurped his beer fast to encourage me into buying another. Dealers have to provide their barkers with beer, and on very rare occasions food as well. 'Even old Sowerby said it was real.' Sowerby's been the village schoolmaster since Adam dressed. I wasn't mollified. Betty would be raging at me for days now, women being notoriously unreasonable. We might not get another chance to meet till the next Open Championship. Her husband's a golfer.

'Next time . . . ' I let the threat hang. Of course both of us were smiling affably, just being a dealer and his barker chatting in the pub. You don't advertise arguments in our game.

'I didn't know it was naughty,' he said defensively.

Naughty is also dealers' slang. Old pewterers' marks, if forged, were called 'naughty' hundreds of years ago. Now it means crooked, fake, wrong, in the sense of being deliberately falsified.

'Never mind,' I said, hoping some kind recording angel would note my forgiveness and somehow persuade Betty to say the same to me. 'What'll you have?'

'Ta, Lovejoy.' Tinker was relieved. 'Here.' He pulled out of the depths of his filthy old overcoat a piece of paper. 'That fat lady gave me this.' He meant Mrs Cookson.

I took in gingerly. A group of helpers gusted in from the pageant calling greetings and orders. It must be about finished. They had a lorry outside the pub's garden, laden with wood and scaffolding, obviously thirsty work.

Her letter asked me to call on her at my earliest convenience. An elegant little scribble on a page torn from a notebook, obviously done hurriedly on the spur of the moment. The address was in Buresford, a larger village about seven miles north.

'What the hell's she want?' I grumbled.

'You must have made an impression,' Tinker leered, nudging me suggestively.

'Shut your teeth.'

'It, er, looks a good tickle, Lovejoy,' he urged. I eyed him suspiciously.

You can always tell when a barker doesn't come clean. Barkers are a curious mob. They're never precisely honest on principle. This doesn't mean they're treacherous. On the contrary, it requires a very durable kind of morality to be a barker — you'll see why later on.

I decided I'd better go, even if it only turned out a commission job for a quid.

'Look, Tinker.' I spoke fast. 'When Lardie comes, tell him I'll have that Gujerat silver brooch, but his Whiff-Waff's too dear. Okay?' Lardie's a wealthy po-faced lanky dealer from Norfolk, in love with antique jewellery, old West African ethnology, a rich Clacton widow and himself, in reverse order. To him that hath shall be given.

'His what?'

'Whiff-Waff. Table tennis was called that years ago.' The

cased sets aren't worth much even now but they add colour
to any antiques shop which displays one. Our trade admires
touches like this.

I pushed to the exit, waving to Angela. Honkworth
barged into me at the door, arriving with sundry crawlers.
There are only two kinds of people who can't go about
without an entourage. One kind's the real leader of men,
like your actual Napoleon. The other kind's the born duckegg. Guess which category Honkworth's in.

'Why, it's Lovejoy!' he boomed. 'Let's see him off!' They
trailed me outside, to my embarrassment. We all park our
cars end-on towards the old inn's forecourt. Honkie had
cleverly placed his massive Rolls-Bentley tourer blocking
my little Ruby in, a typical touch of light humour. He made
a noisy exhibition of shifting it, revving and backing. I just
waited while this pantomime was going on, leaning on the
wall and saying nothing. A few people emerged from the
public bar to cheer him on. Honkworth attracts sightseers,
but so did Attila the Hun.

He had three adorers with him. One was a bleak unsmiling man, young and tall with a waistcoat like a flag day.
Hair slicked down, thin tash, early Gable. I'd seen him
before somewhere, a property agent if ever I saw one. Even
when he smiled it came out as a faint sneer. You know the
sort. The two women were sharp contrasts. The younger
was looking slightly uncomfortable at all this mullarky,
bonny and light. Good bones. I don't know quite what it
means when people say that, because all bones are good,
aren't they? But it sounded exactly right when I looked at
her. Somebody had chosen the wrong ear-rings for her,
pendants too long with a casual dress. The older woman
was florid and bouncy, given to sudden shrill burst of
laughter through teeth like a gold graveyard. She darted
excitedly malicious glances at me with every one of
Honkie's noisy witticisms.

'Milord, the carriage awaits,' Honkworth yelled. Only
Honkie can misquote a sentence that short.

I swung the handle. Naturally it didn't fire till third go,
to ironical jeers of all. By then I was red-faced and looking
at the ground.

'Remember the speed limit, Lovejoy,' Honkie yelled.

'Everybody pray for rain!'

And they say wit is dead.

I climbed in and clattered off. As the diminutive Ruby began to move I got in a wink at Honkworth's young blonde, just to set folks wondering. Passing between Honkie's massive tourer and the laden lorry made me feel I was pedalling a walnut. The swine reached out and patted me on the head as I passed.

I had to skirt the scene of the pageant to reach the main Buresford road, so I stopped to see if Betty was still about. The field was emptying now. Bunting was being rolled. A few stray coloured papers were blowing across the grass in the early evening breeze. Some village children called 'Hello, Lovejoy,' chasing rubbish into plastic bags. I waved. All the trestle tables were gone. Most of the stalls were dismantled. Some blokes from our victorious tug-o'-war team were getting the marquee down, Betty's husband with them. No sign of her. I've heard women take it out on their husbands when they're mad. I wonder if it's true. He'd soon find out.

No sign of Mrs Cookson either, so there was nothing for it. Throttle down to get the right feeble spluttering sound, and kerzoom. Off. I'd worked it out by the time I reached the road. Open country, seven miles. Say an hour, with a following wind.

CHAPTER II

The house was enormous, snootishly set back from the River Stour just in case any riverborne peasants disturbed the affluent class by nocturnal carousings. Some democratically minded leveller had parked a derelict old barge right against the private river walk. Even warped it to the balustrade with short ropes, I saw with amusement. A great mooring hawser was twined clumsily round an otherwise

graceful weeping willow. A drive curved among yews and
beech. There was a stylish ornamental pond and a fountain.
Thank heaven she'd avoided plastic gnomes. The mansion
itself was beautiful. Even the door furniture looked original. As I puttered up the gravel I examined the house.
Definitely Queen Anne, though some maniac had mucked
about with the gables. You always get some nutter wanting
to gild the gingerbread. The Ruby made it up the slight
slope, though it was touch and go.

'Lovejoy!' She was on the doorstep, smiling. 'How good
of you to come so soon.'

'I'll just point this downhill.' I coaxed one last effort from
the half-pint engine and turned the car round the fountain.
It wheezed thankfully into silence.

'So you got my message.' She hesitated. 'Hadn't you
better cover your motor up? It looks like rain.'

'I want air to get to it.' I don't like admitting it's not got
all its bits.

The hallway had its original panels, promising elegance
and style right through the house. To realize how grim
modern architecture is you have to visit a dwelling like this.
Once you're plonked down in a Sheraton chair gazing out
through hand-leaded windows set in a balanced oak-
panelled room you become aware what grotty hutches
builders chuck up nowadays. Even the walls had feelings in
this house. Beautiful.

She went ahead and we were welcomed by the drawing-
room. I'd have given my teeth for an engraved lead-glass
cordial glass, its luscious baluster stem done in the form of a
solid acorn. It stood, throbbing life, in a corner cabinet
among some Silesian-stemmed glassed and managed to
convey the appearance of having been there since it was
made in 1700. The cabinet and its contents were three times
as valuable as my cottage, with my tatty furniture chucked
in. I dragged my eyes away and paid attention.

'Do sit down.'

'Er . . . ' There was only the Sheraton. It was like being
told to sit on a kneeling bishop. I sank my bum reverently
on to it, trying hard to contract my muscles and minimize
the weight.

'You were very definite about the sword,' she began.

I hoped she wasn't the sulky kind. Some of the honest old public — a right swarm of barracudas — become very funny when their dreams are shattered.

'You obviously think it's a forgery.'

'A good one,' I said, anxious to please. 'Very good, in fact.'

'But still a forgery?' she said with careful insistence.

'Er, well.' There was no way out. 'Yes. A good guess.'

'I think not,' she said. We sat in silence digesting this.

She sat opposite, definitely in possession. Bright, too. A really resilient character who'd seen a few unheavals in her time. I began to wonder where all her wealth had come from. We were both being quite pleasant but wary with it.

'The point is, Lovejoy,' she resumed, 'the sword has deceived the most expert authorities in its time.'

'That means you know the faker.' I tried to turn it into a question at the last minute and didn't manage it.

'Yes.' More pause, with me wondering how to ask straight out. 'Your friend,' she continued. 'He told me you're one of those special people who just . . . know.'

Friend? She must mean Tinker Dill. Good old blabbermouth. 'He means well,' I said lamely.

'A . . . a divvie?' The word was unused to her.

Silence.

'Are you one, Lovejoy?' She seemed fascinated, full of interest. 'If there's a fee for revealing this . . .'

I drew in that lovely luscious aroma of money.

'All right. I'll tell you. No.' I stopped her reaching for her handbag. 'I only charge for work done.' I swallowed, nervous as a cat. 'Yes, I'm a divvie.'

She examined me as one does a specimen, head tilted, eyes everywhere. I felt uncomfortable. My shirt cuffs are always a bit frayed. If I'd known I was visiting posh I'd have hurried back to the cottage and pressed my one good pair of trousers.

'I'd heard there were such people but never expected to meet one. What actually happens?'

'I don't know. Honest.' I'm always nervous talking about myself. 'Saying you've a gift sounds like bragging, because it's so special. A divvie just . . . well, knows.'

'How?'

'I don't understand it myself.' I struggled to explain. 'Think of a woman who just knows when the colours in a redecorated room are exactly right. That's a sort of gift, too.'

'It's also common sense, Lovejoy.' A reprimand.

'No, it isn't,' I countered. 'It's a gift. Some have a gift for handling dogs, for designing clothes. Or take to the piano like — like Franz Liszt. Some have it for finding water with a bit of twisted stick — '

'Water-diviner!' she exclaimed. 'Divvie. I see.'

'Everybody's a divvie,' I added. 'Nobody's left absolutely without some special gift. For *knowing* the feel of a true diamond. For knowing straight away which horse will run fastest, which boat will balance right. There are divvies everywhere, for everything. For knowing next year's weather. Which bushes will grow. What musical notes will hold the imagination of millions. Even for knowing what'll happen.' I didn't mean to become so enthusiastic, but it's true. Nobody's left out. You as well, dear reader. You might be the world's greatest living divvie for antique Sumerian gold. Find out quickly what your special gift is, for heaven's sake, or you're being thrown to waste.

'And you're an *antiques* divvie.'

'Yes.' I wondered how to explain. 'It's like a bell. In my chest.'

She pointed to a picture, a small watercolour. It hung over a Pembroke table. 'Try that sketch.'

I crossed to look. A few dashes of the brush for a wash, a demented scar of Prussian blue, three fast smudges in Vandyke brown. All on a torn page. That was all. But it screamed of Dedham's church on a blustery autumnal evening, with the sea wind gusting up the Stour for all it was worth. Bells clamoured and rang. Beautiful, beautiful.

I could hardly manage the words. 'Original. Constable?'

'Good.' She'd followed me to watch. 'We have the provenance.'

Nowadays, with so many forgers about, provenance is vital. Innocent buyers should demand written proof of a painting's progress, right from the artist's lilywhites into your very own. That means evidence of the original sale, bills of purchase, auction dates and invoices. Don't say I didn't warn you. If you're going to become a regular collector you should make a secret list of the painters of whom forgers are especially fond. Just for a bonus I'll start you off with the first three: the brilliant David Cox, the elusive Samuel Palmer, the magic John Constable. Good luck.

'Even,' Mrs Cookson was saying, 'even the frame's original. Constable framed it himself.'

'Balls,' I said. 'Er, I mean, impossible.' I closed my eyes, touching the frame. No bell. No life. Phoney. I borrowed a tissue and rubbed gently. The frame gave up a light russet stain. 'Look, love. It'll stain a wet tissue for years yet. Modern crap.'

'But . . . it can't be.'

'Somebody's knocked it up recently.' You have to be patient. Women can be very possessive, worse than any bloke. I showed her the bright glistening creases, always a dead give-away. 'Easily done. Fresh beechwood. Varnish. Then sandpaper a spare piece of beechwood over the dried stain and rub it in with your finger. It'll age a hundred years in about ten minutes.'

'How dare you!' She rounded on me furiously.

I was half way to the door in a flash. 'I'll not stay for tea, love.' You get too many of these scenes in the antiques trade to waste time. Another end to a beautiful friendship. The trouble is that people love their illusions.

'He's right, Martha.'

I almost barged into the speaker. A thin wisp of a man blocked my way. Well, hardly blocked. A featherweight sixtyish. He looked as if he'd actually been born that tiny shape, slightly balding, in his waistcoat. And he hadn't grown much. If I hadn't spotted him in time I'd have stepped on him and driven him in like a tent peg.

'Henry!' Martha Cookson twisted anguished hands. 'Not you again!' *Again?*

'I'm afraid so.' He wore his cleric's dog-collar like a slipped halo.

'Er, excuse me please, Reverend.' I edged past. It was beginning to look like somebody's big scene. Rather private, but undoubtedly big.

'Don't go, Lovejoy.' I dithered uneasily. 'I apologize for having disbelieved you,' she added to me, wrenching the words out before lashing back at her frail old pal. 'But *why*, Henry?'

He shuffled like a caught child. 'Those wretched Council rates, Martha.' He tried to appeal to me but I wasn't having any. Definitely neutral, I began examining the Pembroke table's hinges. 'So tiresome,' he cried. 'Always more taxes, more charges.'

'You promised to ask me, Henry,' she said sternly, 'before making any more things.' My ears pricked. I'd found the forger, the cunning old devil. 'You *promised*.'

Hey-ho. The good old sexual stand-off. Woman versus man again. They said their lines a few more times while I moved gently to one side. Pembroke tables are among the most copied items of furniture on earth. Both of the natty little folding flaps must have three hinges. Each flap lifts up and rests on fly runners or rails. This luscious Pembroke was serpentined, double fly rails both sides. Glancing at Henry and Martha to check they were still at it, I stood on tiptoe and peered downwards. The inner aspects of the slender legs tapered elegantly, so maybe 1790. Definitely eighteenth-century, anyhow.

I came to, smiling. Henry and Martha were watching me. Silence.

'Oh, er . . . ' I cleared my throat and looked innocent. 'You rang?' Not a flicker of a smile from either. 'Er, just looking.'

'Henry. May I introduce Lovejoy.' We bowed. That's what a lovely old house like this does for you, puts back your manners a couple of hundred years. 'Lovejoy, may I introduce the Reverend Henry Swan.' We bowed again. No wonder people do nothing but slouch and yawn and scratch nowadays. There's no point in bothering with things like manners if everything all around you's plastic junk, is there? I even pulled out one of my cards and presented it with a flourish.

'Lovejoy Antiques, Inc.,' he read through lowered steel-rimmed specs. 'Sotheby's Authorized Expert, London.'

Christ! I'd given him the wrong card. A quick improvisation was called for. 'Ah,' I said casually, 'I'm no longer with — er — Sotheby's. Not right now.' You can have too much elegance. It'd made me forget which pocket held my legitimate cards.

'Were you ever, Lovejoy?' Martha Cookson was smiling now.

'Well, not really.' I shrugged at her but women get me really narked, always guessing more than is good for them. No wonder they get under your skin.

'Ahem.' Swan's eyes twinkled. 'A . . . freelance,' he brought out proudly.

'Yes,' I replied. And broke, but I didn't say that.

'Is this the young man of whom you have spoken, Martha?'

Of whom you have spoken, I thought. Dear God. I'd even have to get my tenses right. It was becoming one of those days.

'Yes, Henry.'

'Then why did he need to inspect the Pembroke?' he asked. A shrewd old nut.

'To find out *what* it was,' I explained. 'My bell only tells me *if*.'

They glanced at each other, signalling with looks. I watched with sudden interest. You can always tell when people are more than just good friends.

'Very well, Lovejoy.' Martha Cookson came to a decision. Henry nodded agreement as she spoke. 'We wish to commission you, Lovejoy, if that's the right expression.'

I sweated with relief. If things improved this quickly I'd be eating again soon.

'Fine by me.'

We all waited, some more patiently than others.

'Oh!' Henry Swan came to, a dusty little beam lighting his countenance. 'Oh. Quite, Lovejoy. We . . . *dig*, don't we, Martha?'

'Dig, dear?' She was lost.

'Yes,' he exclaimed impatiently. 'You know, Martha. To understand, comprehend, appreciate.' He gave a crumpled grin, unexpectedly toothy. 'We may live in deepest East Anglia, Lovejoy, but we do move with the times. The retainer, dear. Deposit.'

'Oh, the fee.' She did the handbag bit. I felt the blessed ecstasy of notes in my digits. After listening to Henry's dated slang I deserved every penny.

Suddenly, though, there was something wrong. They glanced at each other shiftily. We were waiting too long.

'Good, good,' Reverend Henry said, clearing his throat. 'Ahem.' He actually pronounced it A. . . *hem.* 'Good heavens! Is that the time?'

'Are you free for lunch tomorrow?' Martha Cookson asked affably.

'I'll be here.' Another nasty wait. 'Look,' I said at last. 'Sooner or later you'll have to tell me what you've commissioned me *for.*' I was beginning to lose patience. 'Or do I have to guess?'

'Goodness me,' old Henry said. 'How careless of us, Martha.'

'You'd better explain, Henry.'

'No. You, Martha.'

'Both together,' I suggested. A sudden thought. 'It isn't something you've half-inched?' They seemed quite blank. I translated. 'Pinched. Stolen.'

'Certainly not.' They were indignant enough to be truthful.

'Sorry. Well, funnier things have happened.' I tried to help. 'You want me to find some particular antique?' This is the commonest thing.

'Oh no,' said Henry earnestly. 'We already have it, you see.'

'And you want it examined? Dated?'

There were three Imari plates in the cabinet. The lovely precious colours were exactly right, but nowadays dealers will call any porcelain 'Imari ware' if it's got those delectable royal blues and mandarin reds even vaguely approximated. I'd known since I'd arrived they weren't legitimate. Oh, genuine antiques. But Dutch copies of the true Japanese. No Nippon potter ever drew bamboos in layers with a ruler like that. It's the really wooden feeling of the artistry that gives these copies away every time, so beware. I came back to earth.

'Your porcelains?' I nodded at the Imaris.

'Er, no.'

'But you want something authenticated?'

'That's correct.' More glances. I felt part of one of those music hall melodramas.

'Is it here?'

'Er, no. I'll bring it. We must explain about it first.'

'What is it?' I demanded. 'I might have to bring documents, references.'

Martha took a quick breath. 'It's — ' She smiled at me with something approaching defiance. 'It's — it's the Grail.'

'Grail?' For a moment the penny didn't drop.

'Yes.' They stood together, gazing at me.

'I only know of *one* Grail,' I jibed pleasantly, still stupid. 'And that's — ' I looked from Henry to Martha. Then back. Then from Henry to Martha again.

'Exactly, Lovejoy.' Henry let me in on it gently. 'I have it.'

I gaped back at the two lunatics for a second. Then turned on my heel and walked out, blazing.

I'd cripple Tinker. That was why he'd been evasive in the pub, the great Neanderthal buffoon. He's always doing this. Bloody barkers are all at it, hoping something will turn up without doing any proper bloody legwork. Supplying me with duds when I was on my uppers for proper worthwhile collectors. No wonder I'm always starving.

I swung the Ruby's starting handle viciously. It knows me too well to push its luck when I'm wild. An obedient first-time start.

'Lovejoy.'

Martha Cookson had followed me. As I clunked the handbrake down I saw old Henry peering anxiously from the doorstep behind her.

'You won't forget lunch tomorrow?' she said, rather pale. 'And he really has got it, you know, Lovejoy.'

'Missus,' I gave back like ice, 'you had Excalibur till this afternoon.'

She said something more but I was too upset to listen. I coaxed all ten ccs into throbbing power and spluttered the Ruby down the gravel drive. What a waste of a whole bloody day. First Betty. Then Jean Evans getting mad at me. Then Martha Cookson and her tame nutter. Tinker had better not be around for a day or two, that's all.

You get times when everything goes wrong all at once. And it's always women at the back of them, every blinking time. Ever noticed that?

CHAPTER III

I stormed angrily homewards down the Buresford road. The Ruby's G force even made me blink once or twice on the slope past St Margaret's Well. Who the hell makes up all these tales of Grails and tombs I don't know. Only I wish they'd pack it in.

Dusk fell when I still had about four miles more to go. I needed to borrow some matches so I called in at an antiques shop in Dragonsdale, a giant metropolis of seventeen houses, three shops, two pubs and a twelfth-century church. That's modern hereabouts. Liz Sandwell was just closing up. She came out to watch me do the twin oil-lamps on the Ruby. Well, you can't have everything. Liz is basically oil paintings and Georgian incidental household furnishings. She has a lovely set of pole-screens and swing dressing-mirrors.

'I love your little Noddy car, Lovejoy.' She's a great leg-puller. Twenty-five, shiny dun hair and style. She wears floral frocks. I know it sounds old-fashioned, but Liz never looks it somehow. 'Finished,' she asked blandly, 'your inspection?'

'Oh. Yes.' I must have been looking at her too hard and too long. I wiped the lamp glasses and set about trimming the wicks.

'Hard day at the pageant, I hear,' she said. She accepted my quick glance blithely, all sweet innocence.

'Not too bad.' I was very preoccupied.

'They say Betty Marsham's gunning for somebody.'

I said carefully, 'That's women all over, isn't it? No patience.'

She was laughing as I got both front lamps alight. The domes slid on with a comforting click.

'One day you'll get in real trouble, Lovejoy.' Her hand

paused, taking her matches back.

'Who, me?' I gave her my best angelic face.

'Time to come in for a sherry?'

The memory of her bloke floated across my mind. He's the one they wind the rope around at the back of our tug-o'-war line. Our anchor man on account of his size, muscle and weight.

'Er, another time, Liz. Thanks all the same.' I hesitated. 'Here, love. One thing.' I asked her about Martha Cookson and her tame priest.

'Henry Swan? Yes, I know him.' A couple of modern cars swished grandly past, their headlamps illuminating the houses and trees. 'He's a manorial lord, one of those ancient titles. Poor as a church mouse.'

'Poor? In a house like that?' I began describing the mansion but Liz gave one of those short laughs which show you've missed the point.

'It's hers. Not his. Not any more.'

'You mean . . . ?' I remembered their glances.

'They've lived together for years. His family went broke. Mrs Cookson bought it.' She shrugged prettily. 'It was a terrific scandal years ago.' Her dealer's antennae alerted. 'Why, Lovejoy? Are you buying from them?'

'Just wondering. Social call, really,' I lied easily. 'Look. Are they . . . well, reliable?'

'Never heard anyone ask that about them before, Lovejoy.' She paused. 'Pots of money, if that's what you're worried about.'

I nodded thanks, but I was getting one of those feelings. Maybe it was standing about in the evening cold after such a burning hot day. She told me about a couple of Jacobean pewters she'd salted away for me to see and said to come inside because it wouldn't take a minute. 'I've three lovely pieces of Irish cut glass as well, Lovejoy.' I wavered, sorely tempted, but that tough anchor man would be back soon and I was in enough trouble.'

'Tomorrow, if I can make it,' I promised, cranking away.

'I hope those lamps hold out, Lovejoy,' Liz called as the Ruby creaked into a rather drifting acceleration. 'Remember what happened to the Foolish Virgins and *their* lamps.'

'Promises, promises,' I yelled over my shoulder, but she'd gone in. Women always get the last word.

It was full dark by the time I reached home. This cottage where I live, occasionally without assistance, lies in a small village a few miles north of our nearest big town. It's one of those villages which people call sleepy, no street lights. Sleepy in East Anglia's moribund anywhere else. We only have two streets, a church as old as the hills and a few straggly lanes leading off into rather spooky low-lying mist-filled valleys. A fine evening drizzle began. Welcome home, Lovejoy.

'Good kid.' I patted the Ruby's stone-pocked radiator and blew its lamps out.

The door seemed intact. I always check because antiques dealers are forever being burgled. I found the key and switched off the key alarm to save old George Jilks having another infarct in his police hut. He's always on at me for being careless with it. That's our modern police for you. No dedication.

I washed and put the kettle on. There isn't much space in the cottage. I had it rebuilt after the original burned down, which is why I'm still broke. A minuscule hallway leads into the one main living room with a curtained kitchen alcove off. This divan I have extends into a double bed.

I made my tea: two pasties and beetroot, a pint of tea, five slices of bread and marge. You can get some of that sweet pickle but it costs the earth.

Normally, I turn on the telly to watch the politicians for a laugh. This evening I couldn't settle. You know the feeling. Books you'd normally leap at seem suddenly too familiar and the notes you desperately want to bring up to date are too irksome.

A few tickles had come in, letters replying to my newspaper adverts — I place two a week. My most successful gambit is always the innocent widow (as if there ever was such a thing) struggling to make an old groat from the sale of her pathetic belongings. This week I'd put:

> For sale: Pr. v. old & large Japanese vases, colourful embossed figures; Black Bess flintlock rifle; old silver tea

service with hallmark; box of old stamped envelopes. Late husband's effects. Please write with offers. Recently bereaved widow.

We call it breading, as in loaf. Just as anglers chuck bread into a river, so we dealers 'bread' the public pool. I'd no such articles, naturally, and of course I'd used terms just wrong enough to be convincing. Seven replies, five naturally from dealers taken in by my deceptive innocence. I read their ingenious scribbles with dry amusement, then chucked them away. The other two replies were from collectors. You can tell them a mile off. One, a stamps addict, babbled incoherent enthusiasm but the scent of money was missing. The second was a genuine collector, who wrote gravely that my Japanese vases sounded like Satsuma ware. We call them 'Second' Satsumas, in the trade, these gross and horrible pots decorated with too many colours and white-slip outlines. The Japanese made them in the nineteenth century to cater for the crazy European idea of current Japanese elegance. European collectors and Japanese potters finished up equally bemused in a lunatic situation, the former collecting the wrong stuff and the latter turning out hideous stuff they didn't like. Folk go on collecting it, thank heaven. 'First' Satsuma's beautiful delicate small stuff. I've yet to see a single real non-phoney piece anywhere in Europe, so beware. The collector, a Sunderland geezer, went on to ask did I not mean Brown rather than Black Bess? The former is the famous Land Pattern Musket, possession of which is the indelible mark of the flintlock collector. Black Bess, on the other hand, was a highwayman's horse. The collector offered to have my items priced by independent valuers at his own expense and even offered a deposit to guarantee his good faith. He would supply personal references from banks, *et cetera*. I filed his name and address reverently. I love a real collector.

Now, I thought, where the hell do I get a pair of Second Satsuma vases and a Land Pattern from?

Believe it or not, that was the high spot of my evening. I fidgeted some more.

*

I was worried. The point is that tales like the Holy Grail happen every day around here. I hear thirty a week. The commonest is King John's lost treasure, which gets itself found every few minutes. And next comes the poor tired Holy Grail which nobody will let rest in peace. A mere sniff of good old King Arthur's enough to set millions day-dreaming and digging in back yards from one end of these islands to the other. To a dealer whose next meal comes through finding real antiques these legends are a drag, an absolute pest.

I played a record of a Mozart flute piece. He hated composing for that instrument and used to write home to his dad moaning about it, but he'd get no sympathy from me tonight. I finally spent the rest of the evening ringing round my mates arranging things for the next day.

Angela was first, seeing I owed her a fortune. I swore an oath that I'd bring her bloody money in first thing. May I be forgiven. Jim Fleet, who is Japanese militaria and prints, came next. I promised to see him at the next antiques auction about a Kitagawa Utamaro print of 1800 or so which he said was original. Then I left a message at the White Hart with Ted the barman for Tinker Dill. I omitted the Yours Sincerely bit, seeing I sincerely intended to sincerely cripple him.

I gave in at last, got the divan ready and switched the light off. Outside it sounded as if it had started to rain quite hard. And I'd forgotten to cover the Ruby up with that ex-army tarpaulin. Great. It would be flooded in the morn-ing. The trouble with my cottage is that you can only see the lights of two other houses. Some nights it feels forlorn. That's the word. Forlorn.

I found myself listening for sounds. The odd bat, the odd hedgehog grunt. Nothing else. I don't care for countryside. There's too much of it knocking about by far. Anything could happen to me down in this crummy hollow and nobody would know for days. Great.

The phone rang, making me leap a mile. Betty apoplectic.

'Lovejoy! You absolute *pig*,' she blazed.

This is what I like, I thought bitterly. Compassionate understanding.

'Hello, Betty love.'

'Don't you Betty love me, Lovejoy.' She began wailing. 'How do you think I feel? I'm such a fool. I've had to say I'm going round to my mother's to come out and phone you.'

'Sorry, love. There was a chance of picking up an antique.'

'*Oh!* So you think more of an *antique* than you do of me, do you?' All frost.

I thought hard. Women always put you on the spot.

'Well, yes,' I admitted. 'It's antiques I'm always short of.'

'You absolute – '

'Swine,' I filled in for her and rang off. That's women. Very self-centred.

I was right when I said it looked like becoming one of those days. I climbed back into bed again, determined to erase the entire wasted day from my mind. Sleep didn't come immediately, though. I tossed and turned.

Holy Grail indeed.

CHAPTER IV

I'm not one of these people who let themselves be affected by the weather. Rain, sun, snow and gales are all the same to me. As long as there's an antiques shop or two around we could be in another stellar constellation for all I care, because then I'm as happy as a pig in muck. But next day dawned with a brilliance which dazzled the soul. The scores of our local artists, from Constable to Wilson on down, must have stirred in their graves with this dawn's invigoration and excitement. I just knew in my bones it would be a good day, full of profit and luscious antiques.

Mind you, you don't have to *like* all antiques. They're just like people. You get all sorts. Some can bring ecstasy the minute you clap your eyes on them. Others put the fear of God into you. Antiques are luscious or loathsome, but all are magical.

My breakfast was a barley cake made by my own lily-white hands, a couple of apples and a glass of milk, actually my crude copy of a Roman's breakfast. I do it because it's cheap as well as interesting. Of course, you need a pair of Campanian bronze *pateral* vessels in which our people and the Roman legions hereabouts used to heat their wines and food in the first and second centuries, rather like the Lancastrians used fire hobs right up to modern times. I believe you have to cook simple or sad, so to speak, to get anywhere near the historical man's grub.

Singing loudly, I locked up, fending off a strong temptation to make my bed and stoutly resisting the urge to wash up my breakfast things. Handling this sort of temptation's my strong suit. The Ruby was practically pawing the ground. 'No nonsense from you,' I told it pleasantly. The inside had mostly dried from last night's rain. I mopped the seat to get that extra mileage. Luckily the floor has more holes than a colander so drainage is adequate. I was full of beans, pretending to percuss its chest and chuckling. 'How's your middle lobe?' I asked it, leaping in. 'A bit chesty?' Wit. I throttled off down the drive, singing.

Stupid, innocent Lovejoy.

The biggest town hereabouts is on a hill above a curving river. It's only a handful of miles to the open sea. I always halt the Ruby at the middle bridge for a moment because that point was the limit of navigation for the Roman galleys arriving from Gaul. Our town council, a gaggle of real cack-handers, has tried ten billion river improvement schemes since Claudius limped off his Imperial trireme on to our wharf, with the result that boats can't even get this far nowadays. Politicians call it progress, but I do wish they'd stop trying. A huge shape purred alongside.

'Hi, Lovejoy!' Good old Honkworth with his admirers. The blonde bird again, that smarmy creep, and Diamond Lil doing her lipstick thing.

'Wotcher, Honkie.' I had to crane my neck to the vertical.

'Daydreaming? Race you up the North Hill.' A roar of
laughter at this witticism. He leaned over me, patting my
head again while the traffic behind hooted us to get going.
'Has your Bugatti Special recovered? It's got epilepsy, you
know,' he confided loudly to his mob. Two of them
laughed.

'So had Alexander the Great,' I said.

'Who?'

'Before your time, Honkie,' I told him, clacking the
handbrake free. You just have to be kind.

His giant motor wafted ahead in a second. From my
lowly position his nearside exhaust looked like the Mersey
Tunnel as his mobile castle dwindled grandly up the hill.
Now, what was he doing out so early?

I'd headed for the Arcade. Our local antiques dealers, a
merry band of siblings, have this covered alleyway with
stalls and booths. Our town planners stuck their oar in, so
the architectural style is neo-gothic catastrophic with a
smattering of postcard mosque. There's a cafe with its own
popular brand of travellers' enteric.

I parked the Ruby between two Fords and chatted up the
traffic warden, Brenda. She and I know each other from
the trainee snogging days of our shared golden youth.

'Have you noticed,' I asked her carefully, 'that my horse-
less carriage is illegally parked?'

Brenda examined the yellow lines and the parking
meters. 'No, Lovejoy. In fact,' she said, just as carefully
but smiling. 'I doubt if I ever would.'

I hesitated, but antiques called from nearby along the
narrow streets. She'd have to wait.

'One thing,' I said. 'Is your engagement ring illegally
parked too?' It's best to be certain.

'Get on with you,' she scolded, still smiling. Women
have all sorts of knacks we don't have, like two-way smiles.
Smiles should mean yes or no. Not both.

Temporarily immune to the laws of the highway, I
sprinted off, pleased. Well, the mayor parks free. In the
café Woody was in action, ash from his cigarette busily
spraying the edibles he'd carefully flung on the counter to
filter his coughed droplets.

'Wotcher, Woody.'

He swirled a couple of stale plaice into the frying-pan. I looked away.

'Watch your women, lads,' he croaked. 'Lovejoy's here.'

A muted chorus of jeers and greetings rose like an audible fog from the hunched dealers scattered thinly among the tables. It's not a sight for the squeamish. A plate of Woody's fried breakfast is enough to turn the strongest stomach. I waved to his survivors and called for tea. Every antique dealer in East Anglia comes through Woody's sooner or later. One or two, like Nick Maldon, came in for egg and chips the day Woody opened and never budged since. More deals are done in Woody's than on Wall Street and the Stock Exchange put together. Not all are carefully recorded for the Chancellor's tax accountants, however.

'Fry-up as well, Lovejoy?' Lisa's the only waitress in the known world with a Ph.D. in ancient history, between archaeological digs.

'And I call you friend,' I said theatrically. She slipped into the chair opposite and lit a cigarette. This always fascinates me. Women can flick a match and hold a cigarette and have you goggling at their elegance. 'Who's been in so far?'

'Too early yet.' Her gaze ranged the other tables through Woody's louring smoke. 'Most don't come till elevenish.'

I already knew that. 'Tinker?'

'No.'

I checked the tables as far as the bloodshot eye could see, about two yards. Fearless Fred was slogging his way through chips, sardines and toast. He earns his nickname every Tuesday from his bids at the local auction. He's silver tableware, Sheffield plate and a diehard gambler on the horses. Jimmo was there, another threadbare soul like me, though he now had a place across the way in the Arcade. He was going through a bad patch, and rumour was he'd have to sell up soon, poor bloke. I waved and we both beamed beams of derelict joviality to show how well off we were. That done, I cast around for more profitable contacts.

'Hey, Lovejoy.' Cask is one of those remarkable baby faces who never look as if they need a shave. He's always full of corny jokes. He'd be a good barker if only he'd stick to barking, but his delusions of grandeur make him deal in early scientific and navigational instruments. His long-suffering wife Has Faith In Him, which only makes his predicament worse because Cask can't tell a Persian astrolabe from a football.

'How do, Caskie,' I called. I like him, from sympathy.

'Lovejoy. Heard this one?' He fell about in his chair, spraying noshed egg as he laughed. 'Two savage man-eating lions in town shopping, and one says, "I thought you said it was crowded on Saturdays?" Get it?'

'Great, great, Caskie.' I laughed along to give him heart.

Marion laughed too, she of the aggressive manner and unplumbed appetite, delicately spooning yoghurt opposite her temporary escort Jed Radcliffe at an adjacent table. He's a quiet smart man like all print dealers. Curious how a prints man managed to pair up with a Regency furniture specialist like Marion. Perhaps he puts his engravings in her chest of drawers. A trio of barkers were in, one already moderately tipsy. They'd be clocking up commission for their wallies — a wallie's the dealer the barker finds antiques for — as soon as they could stand. Two flintlock pistol specialists were huddled over gruesome porridge, nodding and talking prices quite openly the way no other antiques dealers ever do. Why weapon people are like this I don't know. The shorter chap, Eric, has two wives. Every-body knows except them and the law, but one final day he'll need every loaded weapon he possesses, plus ten yards start. I wondered idly if he'd been at yesterday's pageant and seen the sword. Eric's good at his weaponry. But good enough?

'Lovejoy.' Lisa brought me back. 'Going to the fire-works?'

'Maybe,' I said cautiously. I'm sick of fêtes, fairs, pageants, displays. We have an epidemic of them every summer. Makes me wonder how we find the time for anything else.

'Take me.'

We looked at each other. I don't quite understand how they do it but women always seem to be one plot ahead.

'Castle Park. Saturday night.'

Middle of the town. That meant I wouldn't have to work

out how to fold Lisa's impressive length into the Ruby.
Even I have to adopt the foetal position to get behind the
wheel.

'Well, er . . . '

'I'm not a tart, Lovejoy,' Lisa said evenly. 'And too
many of those crummy popsies you choose to go about with
are.'

Since when does a man have any choice?

'Well,' I relented, 'I like fireworks.' When you think of
it, they're the only explosives you can make and not get
shelled at. Lisa smiled. Suddenly I realized I'd never seen
her smile before. It was this morning's sunrise all over
again.

'That's good,' she said. 'See you outside the Arcade.
Dusk.'

'Er . . . '

Margaret has a shop in the Arcade. Lisa swiftly understood.

'No,' I said suddenly. 'The Castle doorway.' It's a
common meeting place with no prying lights after dark. She
rose at Woody's emphysematous shout for her to get a
move on. I slurped my tea as a penance. Rising to go, I
crossed to Marion and Jed.

'German dolls?' I offered hopefully. We aren't ones for
formal greetings in the trade. Jed drew an eager breath but
Marion said no, too sharply.

'A Wellington chest, Lovejoy?' she countered. 'London
1830?'

I sighed, saying no. If only I had the money.

'I need Irish glass,' she said after a drink. 'And jade.'

My spirits rose. Irish glass? Liz Sandwell had offered me
some. Obviously the promised luck had just arrived.

'I've got two good buyers down from the North,' Marion
added.

'See you tonight at the pub,' I said. Well, if I had a chance
of earning a quid or two from Liz's cut glass, I could pop in
for a free nosh as well at Ma Cookson's and pick up the
Holy Grail. It should be worth a few pence, I thought
nastily, after all these years. And she had asked me to
lunch.

Mercifully I escaped without remembering to pay. Lisa

once said that my trouble is I always forget but sometimes remember, instead of it being the other way round. I hope I don't know what she means.

CHAPTER V

Liz Sandwell's three pieces of Irish cut glass were nearly what she'd told me. We agreed on prices, and by ten to twelve the Ruby was tottering up Martha Cookson's drive, obviously beginning to feel it had done its bit for the day. Naturally I hadn't the money to pay Liz, but a day or two's no problem in the antiques world where people who pay on the nail are regarded as imbeciles or eccentric.

Liz had been proudest of a 'real bluish antique Waterford flat-cut glass, Lovejoy'. That mysterious bluish tinge which is supposed to be characteristic of all Waterford glass is a myth. Hand on my heart. Antique Waterford glass is no more blue than you or I. Look at an authentic piece in a museum and see. If it *is* blue, it's a fake, manufactured by the skilful for the incredulous. Dutch imitators had flat-cut Liz's bluish polygonal glass bottle, using bluish-tinted glass. There's a lot of them about. I'm all for copying as long as I know what actually goes on. The Excise Acts from 1745 on messed about with English glass-making, so the free trade Ireland got after 1780 boomed Irish glass production, sales and reputation — you don't need to delve too far back in history to find out politicians making a balls-up. Hence the development of the sophisticated three-piece mould system for blown glass in America and Ireland before 1825 or so. Why the Yanks aren't proud as peacocks of their lovely glass beats me. Liz had one, a lovely barrelled spirit-bottle complete with stopper (remember the stopper — its presence doubles the price you pay. And if it's missing starts some hard bargaining). The last piece was a Cork Glass Co. decanter, quite attractive, but beware.

'Bainbridge,' I explained to Liz, 'says they made modern ones from the original moulds, and I think he's right.' Hers was genuinely old, though I didn't tell her that my bell was clamouring its lovely chime, so she said okay let's price it as modern. I didn't disagree. Well, all's fair in love, war and antiques.

So there I was, the Ruby crawling spluttering up Martha Cookson's drive. An ancient gnarled gardener rose from among some bushes to stare. I gave him a royal wave. He resumed work, shaking his head and grinning.

The river was running higher than last night from the rain we'd had. The old longboat seemed immovable, not rocking at its ropes like boats are supposed to do. Maybe it was stuck on the bottom by aeons of silt. If it wasn't, that thick hawser would keep it from accidentally winning any races.

No smoke rose from its black chimney. It was a fifty-footer, no longer neat but still embellished with carvings and painted floral and scenic decorations of the traditional bargee style. Curious how those gross reds, greens, yellows and light blues caught on with our itinerant workers, bargees, caravan-dwellers, tinkers and gypsies alike.

'I'm so very glad you came, Lovejoy.' I was brought back to earth. Martha Cookson came to say hello, both hands outstretched. I found her hands in mine. She was suddenly likeable, but I suppressed the fond feeling. I had to find a way to return the money she'd given me. 'Have you quite forgiven us?'

'Hello. Forgiven?'

'For offending you yesterday. Weren't we awful?' She drew me into the hall the way they do. I started to explain why I'd rushed off with such ill grace but she would have none of it. 'We quite understand. We're appropriately ashamed of our clumsiness, Lovejoy. Now, first names immediately. Absolutely the minimum of fuss.' She led the way into the same living-room. Sherry was ready on an occasional table. As we entered this bird turned to inspect us, smiling economically. Last seen this morning with Honkworth. This was all going to be rather a drag, her sour expression announced, so everybody keep illusions out of it and no hang-ups, okay? 'You must hear all sorts of ridiculous stories in your occupation, Lovejoy,' Martha Cookson said. 'We can't blame you in the least.'

'Er, well, Martha, I actually came to, er, say . . . ' I started a stumbling explanation that I wanted out.

'This is my niece, Dolly,' Martha Cookson introduced brightly. 'I made her come along in case you were still angry with us. Dolly, Lovejoy.'

'Er, I think we've met.' I gave Dolly a nod.

'So we have.' No change out of me, Lovejoy, her tone said loudly. She turned and poured sherry for us all.

'Really?' Martha was all agog. 'When and where?'

'He's a friend of Alvin's,' Dolly said. She held out a glass distantly, avoiding actually seeing me. I had to plod across a few million leagues of carpet to reach it. I felt like a passing pilgrim thrown a crumb. Alvin? Was poor old Honkworth actually called that?

'Not a friend,' I said. Let there be no fobbery, my tone said back. I saw Martha's quick glance but I don't go for all this coy stuff.

'You're both antiques experts,' Dolly said, innocent.

'No. *I* am.' I moved across to a de Wint watercolour, drawn by my clanging bell. Genuine, the boat reflected and the moonlight just right. I did my infallible watercolour trick. Always half-close your eyes and step back a few inches more than seems necessary. Then do the same from a yard to its right. Then ditto left. Do this and you're halfway to spotting the valuable genuine old master. It works even for painters as late as Braque. You need not know anything about the art itself. Forgeries and modern dross look unbalanced by this trick, full of uneven colours and displeasing lines. It's as simple as that.

Dolly was still bent on battle, woman all over. 'If you're an expert,' she was demanding sweetly, 'what does that make Alvin?'

I sighed. There's no hinting to some people. 'I'm an antiques dealer, love,' I told Dolly kindly. 'I'm the best I've ever seen, heard or come across. Alvin Honkworth is a nerk. Even other nerks think he's a nerk.'

'I'll tell him your opinion,' she threatened sweetly.

'Woe is me,' I said politely. I moved aside. The Imari

plates called. Dutch copies, as I'd thought. Lots of pretty famous porcelain is really artistically poor. Among the poorest (and somewhat 'overpriced' at provincial auctions nowadays) I rank these Continental Imaris, plus soft-paste Lowestoft, the enamel-painted hard-paste Bristol porcelain figures of 1775 vintage, and much of the underglaze-blue transfer-printed hard-paste porcelain garbage from Staffordshire's New Hall China Manufactory of the mid 1780s. Seriously underpriced, though, if you can currently believe that of anything, is the eerily glowing mother-of-pearl Belleek porcelain from Fermanagh, though it's more modern. (Incidentally, the mark 'Ireland' was only added to the harp and Irish hound mark after the McKinley Tariff Act took effect in America, 1891, so look before you leap.)

'Stop mauling Aunt Martha's porcelains,' Dolly snapped. I replaced the lovely Belleek jug with a wrench. 'Are you always so rude, Lovejoy?' Dolly was still bristling as old Henry entered our merry scene, floating discreetly in like a dandelion seed.

'Yes,' I answered to shut her up. 'Hello, Henry.'

'Ah, Lovejoy!' he beamed. 'The inherent benevolence of Man triumphs again over the onslaughts of the insensitive!'

'Before we begin,' Martha interposed firmly, 'let's be seated. Conversation over lunch is preferable to all this hovering with empty glasses.'

We hadn't been exactly stuck for words but clearly she was expert at scuppering Henry's theological chat. We trooped into the dining-room. I never know what to do with my glass. Other people usually manage to get rid of theirs somehow. Breeding, I suppose.

The meal was pleasant, served by two friendly women. I tried not to eat like a horse but you can't help being a born opportunist. Finally I threw elegance to the wind and ate anything they put in front of me. Old Henry and Martha spun their grub out to keep me company, talking of incidentals. Dolly sat determinedly trying to disconcert me, elbows on the table and pointedly glancing at her watch. I'd made a hit there, I thought. Henry prattled about his undergraduate days at Cambridge and Martha prompted him if he tended to ramble. I tried to feel along underneath the tablecloth's hem without anyone noticing what I was doing. It was obviously a two-pedestal table, but a genuine eighteenth-century pedestal-based dining table will have no inlays. Also, simply count the number of pedestals the table's got. Subtract one. That gives you the number of leaves the genuine table ought to have. I was quivering with eagerness to get underneath and see if the legs were reeded. I ate pressed hard against the table. If the table rim is reeded its four slender legs must be reeded. My bell was donging desperately, but the polite natter would have faltered if I'd dived underneath and fondled all available legs, so I ploughed on through the meal and kept my lust secret.

'Your visitor's a pleasure to feed,' Martha's principal serf said, all fond.

'Marvellous,' the other chipped in. 'Instead of your two wee appetites.'

'We do our best,' Henry said, pulling a face.

This really puzzles me. Why aren't women wild because all their work in making grub's gone up in smoke? I'd cleared the lot. Logically, you'd think they'd be annoyed.

'We shall have to make your visit a regular occasion,' Henry beamed. He looked like a happy pipe-cleaner. He'd only had a mouthful or two, without enthusiasm. No wonder he never filled out.

'Of course we shall,' Martha said. 'It's a standing invitation and you must ensure that it's frequently accepted, Lovejoy. See to it. But to work. I have a plan,' she announced. 'Henry and Lovejoy shall discuss our − er − business walking in the garden. Dolly and I shall keep out of your way.'

'How ridiculous!' Dolly snapped. 'That's . . . antiquated.'

'It's perfectly sensible, dear,' Martha corrected blandly. 'Seeing that I made a perfect mess of last night's discussion, and that you take after me on your mother's side. Besides,' she added, rising, 'you're always in such a temper these days. A quiet think will do you good.'

'Aunt Martha!'

'This is our signal,' Henry confided to me in a whisper, as

if Martha had given the obliquest of hints. 'I'll show you my barge.'

'Is that thing yours?'

'Yes.' He sounded so proud of it. 'Come down.'

We strolled down towards the river. A few serious anglers were spaced along the opposite river bank. Some sort of fishing competition, judging by the white wooden stakes driven into the bank to show limits. In the distance a pub and a bridge with a few Tudor houses and a thatched cottage or two. You've never seen such moribund boredom. Henry seemed amused at my reaction.

We reached the barge by balancing across the plank. Henry led down to the single log cabin. He had it arranged quite neatly, a folding bed, and a small unlit galley stove. He lit a candle stub, apologizing.

'I keep meaning to get one of those gas bottles,' he told me, 'but they always need filling. We must celebrate first.' He poured a drink for us in enormous tumblers, rum and orange. 'Martha understands my need for solitude.' We sat opposite each other and listened to the river sounds entering the cabin. I glanced out at the anglers but none had moved. They sat there like troglodytes, watching their strings and the still water, a real ball. Riveting.

'Er − look − Henry,' I began. Somebody had to get it over and done with. 'This Grail thing.' I launched into a summary of the endless rumours, the wasted searches, the endless time expended on red herrings. 'It isn't just the Grail,' I finished. 'It's a million other precious things.'

'I know all that, Lovejoy,' he said. He refilled our tumblers. 'And I'm grateful for your frankness.'

Funny, but the old chap didn't seem abashed.

'The chances of anybody ever finding an object like the Grail are . . . '

'About the same,' he put in, smiling, 'as finding the Cross?'

'Well, St Helena rather pushed her luck,' I said. That gave him one more grin.

'I know what you must be thinking, Lovejoy.' He leaned back reflectively. 'That age or mental instability has deranged me. But I do have it. The Grail, I mean. It is real. Actual. Material.'

'Oh for God's sake, Henry!' I rose and paced the narrow cabin. 'This relic game's overdone. All right – I give you there must have been some object, a pottery cup or glass –

'Pewter,' Henry corrected gravely. 'It looks like pewter.'

'Right. Pewter, then.' I rounded on him. 'Whatever. But relics were an industry. Do you know how many places have been founded on the faintest hints of hearsay? Even – '

'I know, Lovejoy.' He sat watching me and sipping his rum. 'Everything from Christ's milk teeth to hair and foreskin. The Centurion's spear, Magdalene's linen cloth, Peter's sandals – '

'Do you know,' I said rudely, 'that owning a relic – real or otherwise – was such an attraction that . . . that when Francis was dying at Assisi they even had to put an armed guard on the poor bugger so he wasn't torn to pieces of premature relic? It was a game, Henry,' I ended wearily. 'A sad demented game.' My glass was empty. 'And nowadays the game's over.'

He filled my glass to the brim, chirpy as ever. 'I've been looking for somebody like you for some years, merely to inspect the object. Confirm what it is.'

I thought about that. 'What if I say it's junk?'

'Supposing,' he said, 'an object, worthless in itself, was the focus of veneration for millions of people. Would that be – indeed, *could* it be – merely junk? Ever?' He shook his head with certainty. 'There is such a thing as sanctification by use, by belief. Loving,' he added, 'is the practice of love. Love is loving. There are no half measures, no staging-posts to love. It's not a noun, Lovejoy. It's an active participle.'

'Henry,' I said resignedly, 'you're beginning to sound like me. All right, I surrender. Where's your crummy old tin cup?'

He insisted on pouring still more for us both. I was having a hard time keeping up with the old blighter. 'I'll show you. Not today, but I promise.' He jerked his Adam's apple up and down under the tilted bottle.

I don't remember how long we stayed there. I vaguely recall some angler banging on the cabin roof shouting we were ruining the fishing match, but both Henry and I were sloshed and singing by then. We only yelled abuse back.

Eventually we ran out of rum.

'The swine have sold us an empty bottle,' the Reverend Henry accused. 'Let's report them.'

We fell about at his witticism and reeled back up the lawn to the house. Everything seemed hilarious. Martha had tea ready on the terrace. Such elegance. Two new visitors were there.

'Have you been hiding that foul concoction down in that dreadful boat?' she blazed. This made us laugh so much I had to pick Henry up.

'Shhh,' we both told her simultaneously.

'This is Lovejoy,' Martha was saying, which was odd because I already knew I was Lovejoy. I roared with laughter.

'I already know I'm Lovejoy,' I said. Henry fell about at this, because he knew it too.

'How do you do?' this woman said. 'I'm Sarah Devonish.' I noticed the specs, amber beads and aggressive handshake full of rings. 'Hello, Henry.'

'Ah, Sarah, my dear.' Henry gave an elegant bow and tumbled over.

'Have you been tippling again, Henry?' It sounded a threat the way she said it.

'Certainly not,' Henry said with dignity from the paving.

'That will do.' Sarah yanked him to his feet, full of anger and hating me, why I don't know. 'Thomas, give me a hand.'

Thomas turned out to be a pleasant embarrassed bloke about Henry's age, a bumbler. He made a mess of trying to introduce himself while struggling to prop old Henry into a chair. Somebody — Martha probably — called him Dr Haverro, but he's the sort who stumbles over your feet every second breath and never gets to his verbs.

'Wait!' our sloshed hero cried. 'I want to tell Lovejoy — '

'You've probably said far too much,' Sarah said severely. 'Martha. Try to sober him up somehow. Thomas and I don't want a totally wasted journey.'

It was interesting to see Martha subdued in the presence of this formidable younger woman. I tried to tell her that her amber beads, all opaque and neffie, badly needed cleaning. It's a fearsome risk to dip them in solvents or cleaning agents.

'Most people use rectified turps and alcohol,' I explained cheerfully, 'but for heaven's sake see that you *feed* amber afterwards. The beads will come lovely and deep, transparent as ever like a beautiful deep gold sea. Use dammar. Be careful to see that your beeswax – '

'*Please!*' Sarah snapped, so I shut up while they tried to bring Henry down through the superstrata. He crooned a light air from *The Mikado*. I could see she was a tough nut. Her amber beads deserved better.

'So sorry about this,' Thomas said to me apologetically in an undertone. 'First acquaintance and all that.'

'Not at all,' I said, thinking how reasonable he seemed compared to the bossy Sarah. She was an attractive middle age, but if you're savage and utterly merciless about amber, you can be as bad about people can't you?'

'Don't mind Thomas,' Henry said. 'We three are guardians of the most precious – '

'Do shut up, you old fool,' Sarah said furiously. Henry chuckled.

'Come, come, people,' Martha admonished. 'Let's all keep calm. It's just as well Dolly's companions came for her,' she went on reprovingly, 'or she would have disapproved even more than I about this, Henry.'

Henry and I sang a song about Dolly while they helped me into the Ruby. The gardener swung the starting handle, still grinning and shaking his head.

'I did my courting in one of these,' he told me. 'Before you were born.'

'Will you be all right, Lovejoy?' Martha asked anxiously. 'Perhaps it isn't really very wise for you to – '

'It knows the way,' I answered. Henry and I rolled in the aisles at that. His laugh sounded like a scratchy pen nib. 'Chocks away, mate.'

They stood aside as I rolled down the road. I thought I drove quite well. In fact I was still thinking that when I reached the outskirts of our village. Then George, our ever vigilant bobby, caught me up on his trusty bike and booked me for drunken driving.

I went in the tavern for a drink. Driving's thirsty work.

CHAPTER VI

I woke up a foul mood with a headache. My usual health-giving breakfast seemed even lousier than usual so I abandoned it and fried everything I could lay hands on. Tomatoes, celery chunks, carrots, cheese and two eggs. It was a grisly business but after that I tottered to the phone.

I had to get to town and catch Jed and Marion during this morning's summit conference in Woody's. If I couldn't unload Liz Sandwell's antique glass I'd be selling matches by the weekend. I dared not risk the Ruby now Constable Jilks had his teeth into me.

Margaret was frosty. I tried to put a cheerful grin in my voice. 'We must introduce ourselves some time,' she said.

'Er, look, love,' I croaked. 'Any chance of seeing you?'

'You haven't seen me for days, Lovejoy. And not a word of explanation.'

'Well, love, it was like this — '

'I know for a fact you were in the Arcade yesterday.' She has a booth there. I tried to cut in but she wouldn't let me. 'What do you want this time, Lovejoy?'

That really hurt. As if I'd only ring a fellow dealer — with whom I am on very friendly terms, I might add — when I wanted something. Women can be very cruel.

'Er, any chance of a lift?'

'If you think I'm going to leave my shop just to cart you about after the way you've ignored me lately — '

'But, sweetheart — '

Click. Burr. Another social triumph. There's a typical woman for you. Why they can't be calm and friendly all the time I just don't know. I phoned Marion's number, then everybody else I could think of. Jean Evans was in but just on her way to the day institute to teach sculpture. She sweetly suggested I ring Betty ('You could, shall we say, *ride* together, Lovejoy.') before banging the phone down. I even toyed with the idea of ringing Honkworth, but there's a limit. I was stuck, marooned. And I'd used up all my chances of rescue.

I stood up and shook the tablecloth for the robin. He cackled angrily for some cheese so I went and got the bit I'd saved. A right dogsbody.

'Don't you start,' I told him bitterly. 'That old couple really had me yesterday.'

The trouble is I'm too soft. If I'd just told Martha to get lost and kept her money as a deposit I'd not have got sloshed with old Henry in his crummy barge.

Nothing for it. I kicked the Ruby's tyres and went in. I dialled miserably.

'Well, well, *well!*' Sandy shrilled. 'Do I detect Lovejoy's dulcet tones?'

'Cut it, Sandy. Can you give me a lift today?'

'For you, dear,' Sandy gushed, 'no. Unless,' he added firmly. We listened to the silence. I gave in.

'Unless?'

'Wait, cherub.' His receiver clattered noisily. I heard Sandy call in the distance. Mel must be upstairs. They have an open-floored barn behind their house, which stands back from the road at the other end of our village. Mel is modern art, glass and porcelain as far forward as Art Deco. Sandy is Eastern items, and Continental household ware up to Edwardian days. They share Victoriana because Sandy says they have to meet somewhere. Despite their oddity they're a formidable pair of antiques dealers. 'Mel, dear. It's that hunk Lovejoy, positively *squirming* with embarrassment.'

'What's he want?' Mel's voice.

'A lift. What shall we do?'

'Exploit him to the uttermost.' There was some low-voiced — well, high-voiced — muttering.

'Hellow, Lovejoy dear?' Sandy cooed. 'Mel says he's all for charity, but it will cost you. Your peculiar little knack with some of the rubbish we've got here.'

Typical. Sandy and Mel were saying they'd reached their limit of knowledge with their supposed antiques and wanted me to divvie their stuff.

'No,' I told him. I get sick of wasting my time working for others.

'Then goodbye, sweetie.'

Click. Burr. I counted ten and milled about the garden a minute or two. I locked the cottage and strolled casually up the lane to the chapel. Maybe our supervigilant constable had forgotten.

'Morning, George.'

'Morning, Lovejoy.' As I'd guessed he was standing by the crossroads waiting for me to appear in the Ruby. 'Just let me see you in that old crate, Lovejoy, that's all.' He gets depressed if I smile so I smiled like a politician and strolled back, fuming. I rang Sandy again.

'I'll scan for you, Sandy, after you give me a lift.'

'You darling boy,' he gushed. 'Where to?'

'To Marion's. Then maybe Liz Sandwell's.'

'Oh, *pus* and *spit*.' He sounded even more resigned than I did. 'As long as you don't expect me to come in too and positively gape at La Sandwell's ghastly wallpaper.' I said I didn't. 'And no offering that whore Marion lifts in our beautiful motor. If she comes with us she comes running behind *chained* to the mudguard.' He tittered. 'Mel just can't stand her stinky perfumes.' I said okay. 'Promise,' he demanded. 'Say cross my heart.' I promised wearily. Even a phone call's a right pantomime with Mel and Sandy.

They couldn't come for me until five that afternoon, which was later than I wanted to be, but they were my only chance. I spent the day reading about Glastonbury and the various Grail legends. It was a wasted day. The whole story was as mystic and remote as ever. I was depressed by the numbers of experts who had broken their hearts trying to find the answer.

By the time they arrived I'd decided Henry was deranged. Their Rover had started out a royal blue saloon. It was now covered in a dazzling array of painted flowers, stripes, zigzags and twining greenery. A silvery fringe fibrillated all the way round the outside, above the windows. It was a mess. You can see why I'd left them till last.

Mel was sulking in the passenger seat.

'Mel's in a mood, Lovejoy,' Sandy called, reversing in.

'*Caveat emptor*. But don't worry, dear. I can sulk better than him.'

'Hello, Sandy. Mel.' I got in the back. It felt like a hovercraft after mine.

'I'd shake hands but I'm not to be trusted.' Sandy gave me a roguish wink.

'Marion's, please.'

'Mel and I had the most fearsome row,' Sandy said. We revved into the lane and took off.

'And for once, Lovejoy, it was *not* my fault,' Mel rounded in his seat. 'I've got this lovely clock by Tompion, *honestly* quite superbly divine, I *mean*. And this — this naughty little rascal here — '

'Oh, *language!*' from Sandy.

' — enters it into the next sale up in the Smoke. Honestly.'

'Well,' I said nervously. Some of their fights last weeks.

'Don't you dare agree with either of us, Lovejoy!' Sandy cried, 'or I'll smack your wrist. This conflict is only *apparently* about a clock. It's actually about sepia upholstery. We aren't speaking.'

'Like me and George,' I said. We halted at the chapel, Sandy happily grinding the gears.

'Yes, we heard all about your drunken el butcho spree.' He drew alongside George. 'Hello, sweetiepie.'

'Any of that and I'll do you — ' George tried threatening.

'Not here, love, surely?' Sandy reached out a languid hand. George backed away. 'Prosecute Lovejoy and I'll park outside your house all night.'

'And your mascara's just wrong, George.' Mel came alive long enough to add to George's discomfiture.

'Drive on, or I'll book you for obstruction.'

'No, George. Be serious.' Sandy fluttered his eyelids. 'Would *you* change our motor's fringe back to gold? Isn't silver on cerise and blue a *fearful* risk?'

George eyed the car with hatred. 'It's a bloody disgrace.'

'Fasten your flies, George — no advertising, dear.' Sandy adjusted the driving mirror to see himself better and accelerated away across the front of the arriving post van, causing an ugly squeal of rubber.

'Marion'll wear one of those maddening brown waistcoats that positively *drain* colours from every possible wall, Lovejoy,' Sandy predicted. 'The cow really is too much . . .'

I closed my eyes and leant back, thinking: this bloody antiques game. I sometimes wish I had a dull, easy job, somewhere peaceful like on an oil rig out in the North Sea.

Marion's place is past the Castle along South Hill. When she's absorbed all that Jed can teach her about prints he'll be shown the door. So far she's become quite expert in about eight branches of antiques. Hard work.

'Isn't it the female tarantula which eats its mate?' Sandy was saying innocently as we pulled in. 'Mel, dear,' he crooned, 'do we stay out here in the noisy, smelly traffic, or encounter dearest Marion?' Mel glowered silently. 'He means no, Lovejoy,' Sandy continued.

I shrugged and went inside. Marion was pricing two vinaigrettes, one a Willmore silver gilt fob-watch shape and the other an Empire-style gold oval of about 1810. Joseph Willmore loved the fob-watch style. Life in the good old days being sordid, dirty and full of the most obvious of human stenches, people wanted to disguise the terrible pongs of the cities. So you carried a bottle of perfumed vinegar, hence the name. Men carried them as well as women up to about 1840. You get them all shapes, even as 'vinegar sticks', where the container is cleverly made into the handle of a sword or walking-stick. Women tended to have them as lockets or on chatelaines. The commonest you find nowadays is a box shape.

I told Marion why I was late. We fenced quite casually, drawing blood over every groat the way friends will. The purchaser has of course only a few quid in hand and ten thousand starving children to support. The vendor has paid a fortune and wants at least a groat or two profit. You know the sort of thing. We settled finally, when our heartstrings could vibrate no more.

'I'll drop the stuff in tomorrow afternoon, Marion.'

'Great. Oh, Lovejoy. That creep Leyde was asking around after you this morning. Dealing with him nowadays?'

Bill Leyde. I'd heard the name. Of course. Honkworth's

pal, the sleek sourface who travelled about with Dolly and the blowsy blonde in Honkworth's car. Leyde, collector of antique gold — 'geltie' in our parlance.

'At Woody's. Got quite agitated.' She eyed me evenly. 'Jed and me got the feeling he was waiting for you.'

And me late into town because of George, the berk.

'Did he say why?'

'No. Jed had to shoot off to Gimbert's.' Our local auction warehouse near St Jude's derelict church.

'Thanks, love,' I said casually.

She waved to me from the doorway as I stepped into Sandy's car. I'd been over an hour.

'Marion, dearie,' Sandy called in syrupy tones. 'Don't stand about in the street. People are *so* quick to misunderstand.'

He drove off with a squeal of tyres into the traffic before she could reply.

'Did you see that absolutely fearful russet bolero she was *welded* into, the stupid hag?' Mel hissed malevolently.

'Couldn't look past those crocodile shoes, dearie,' Sandy said blithely. 'If only she had some friends willing to tell her, poor cow.'

'I thought she looked nice,' I offered.

'Lovejoy,' Mel said over his shoulder with feeling, 'you were so *brave.*'

'Liz Sandwell's, please, lads,' I said.

'That purulent green wallpaper!' Sandy shrieked.

They both groaned.

I had a lot to think about during the journey. Martha said Dolly had gone with 'her friends' when old Henry and I tottered up the garden yesterday, sloshed on his vitriolic rum. Presumably that included Leyde. Now here he was practically champing on his reins wanting to see me.

'Marion said Leyde was zipping about,' I said, too casually.

'A real el butcho,' Mel said. 'Consorts with your buddie Honkworth.' They tittered, knowing we didn't get on.

'Gelt man,' Sandy added. He gave a serene regal wave to a demented gate-keeper at the level-crossing towards the by-pass. I opened my eyes as the Norwich express thundered past inches from me. Sandy sounded his horn at it, irritated. 'Pestered the life out of us for some lovely Belgian niello and gold pendants, didn't he, Mel?'

I scraped my memory for details of Leyde but could find very little. I'd heard he seemed to deal mostly in London and the Midlands.

By the time we reached Liz Sandwell's place I was so uneasy I wasn't able to keep up with Sandy's racy comments on his side of the trade. Mel pretended I was lovelorn. Great jokes at my expense. The pubs were open as we pulled in to the kerb at Liz's shop.

'You will forgive us, Lovejoy,' Sandy said. 'But we need something to settle our little tummies. We'll come back for you elevenish.'

'She asked us to have a bite with her,' I said, but I know they sometimes go to this tavern for supper in Dragonsdale. They tittered, nudging.

'Bouillabaisse,' Sandy warned me. 'It's all she can do, poor cow. *Wrong* seasoning.'

'Do take care, dear boy,' Mel said. 'Avoid her horsehair sofa at all costs. Gallant lads have been known never to return.'

They blew extravagant kisses at Liz's window as they pulled away.

'They send their apologies,' I said apologetically to Liz.

She laughed. 'I quite understand, Lovejoy.'

'Leyde,' I found myself saying as we went inside. 'Any news of him lately?'

'Bill Leyde?' Liz sounded surprised. 'The geltie? Not for weeks. He got a gold-mounted George the Second scent flask from Margaret in the Arcade, last I heard. Why?'

'Nothing.' That sort of small purchase is a typical purchase for the dedicated geltie. 'Maybe a deal on, that's all.'

It lingered in my mind, but I chatted about this and that. It was bouillabaisse, Liz told me, whatever that is. I said fine and did the wine. I'm all thumbs at things like that but Liz only laughed at the shredded floating cork. She said we could spoon the bits out. We spent some moments on her horsehair sofa after supper.

It was a chance remark she made much later that connected oddly in my mind and fetched me back to earth.

'You've torn my blouse again, Lovejoy.'

'Oh, er, sorry.'

She smiled and said not to worry, rubbed her forehead on my face. The clock said eleven. 'Everything you touch gets changed, doesn't it?' she said, still smiling but looking into me. I pulled my eyes away and went for the antiques.

We settled faster than I should have done. Unease was settling on me. The air seemed thicker. For some inexplicable reason the Irish glass seemed suddenly of secondary importance. Everybody gets these feelings, don't they? By the end of our deal I was almost hurrying and trying not to. Eventually it was half past and the pair not back yet.

'I've suddenly remembered something, Liz.'

'Lovejoy.' She was looking at me. 'Are you all right?'

'Sure, sure.' I found myself at the door. 'I'll ring you about collecting the stuff, right?'

'Any time.' She followed me anxiously on to the step. A cold wet wind was blowing. 'See you at the White Hart tomorrow?'

'Sure.'

We waited, talking in brittle sentences, neither knowing quite what to say. Liz asked if it was something she'd said. I told her of course not.

They came at midnight, talking simultaneously, neither listening to the other's inane prattle. Beats me how they communicate. They had full glasses of wine.

'Goodness!' Sandy squeaked, pointing as I rushed in and slammed the door. 'What *did* she do to you, dear boy? You're so *pale.*'

'Er, could we go now, please?' I felt choked. 'Buresford,' I said.

'At *this* time?' Mel decided to sulk again. 'Sodding *hell.*' He gave me his glass to hold while he took the wheel.

Despite some bickering they did as I said. I was in an ugly sweat by now. Maybe I was sickening for something but I didn't think so.

'This is like going to London via Cape Horn, Lovejoy.' Even the tolerant Sandy was narked at me now. Great.

I began to wish I'd never heard of old Reverend Henry

Swan and Martha and their faked bloody sword. I didn't even wave to Liz.

Approaching Buresford a police car overtook us, flashing and wailing. I watched it, my heart heavy with foreboding. Mel drove one-handed, gave it a silent toast, his glass of port raised.

'They took no notice of us!' Sandy complained.

'It's their loss, dear,' from Mel.

We braked suddenly.

'Mel! You've spilled my drink!' Sandy squealed. 'Oh, it was *doomed* from the start.'

Ahead the road curved to enter Buresford near the church, the black-and-white cottages in headlights by the river bend. A constable flagged us slowly on. Two police cars at rest flashed impatient lights in Martha Cookson's gateway. An ambulance whirred out of the drive and tore past.

I racked the window down. My hand was shaking.

'Can we go in, Constable?'

'There's been an explosion. I've orders to admit no one.'

'Anybody hurt?' The feeling was gone now, only a certainty of tragedy remaining.

'Yes. One member of the family and two anglers.' He seemed worried and somewhat lost.

I told Mel to drive through the gateway. The policeman was relieved somebody else had made a decision and waved us in. I honestly don't know what the police are playing at these days, sending bobbies out the way they do. They all seem worried sick and green as grass. No wonder there are criminals about.

We couldn't reach the house because of two motor-cycles propped across the drive. It looked like a film set with lights and cables. Three policemen were talking and scribbling by the ornamental fountain. I made myself observe the lunatic scene yard by yard. A small cluster of people were down by the river. A few others were gathered around the ambulance parked incongruously in the centre of the lawn's edge. The ground everywhere was scored by tyre marks.

For some seconds the essentials failed to register in my

mind. Then I began picking them up more sensibly, one by one. It was as if my mind was checking off items accepted for recognition. The two white-coated figures. A nurse running the few steps in to the ambulance for something shiny. Tubes. An inverted bottle of yellow fluid. One doctor with shiny shoes, one doctor in white slipper things. Another constable being told to hold on to this for a moment, please, just like that thank you, and kneeling his creased trousers into the muddy ground carefully doing as he was asked. Sweat trickling from under his helmet. Smoke pouring up from the river and two fire vehicles blinking redly across the other side of the water. Hoses snaked down and pulsing in time with the throbs from the engine. One fireman in a yellow helmet shouting orders from among the bulrushes. Another ambulance over there, with doors flung wide and two white coats huddled down.

'My *God!*' I heard Sandy say faintly. 'Lovejoy . . . '

A policeman was holding me back on the drive. Somehow I was pushing past and saying get out of the bloody way. Then running to the little riverside terrace and the people there.

A long bundle on the ground. Anglers on the opposite bank in twos and threes talking and looking, one with his small son carefully folding a keepnet as black oily smoke rolled among the weeds. Everything was in half shadow, macabre.

Then the longboat. I never realized their hulls were so flat underneath, flat as a pavement. Rust showed and some weeds stuck along the sides. Smoke billowed. I mean that it *billowed* like smoke in famous poems and children's pirate stories, roll after roll from the barge. You only need to see a devastated boat for all the sea sagas ever written to become instantly understandable. Oh, I know a ruined house or a wrecked plane that can never fly again is utterly pathetic. But a crumpled boat is somehow so tragic that even to look is almost unbearable. The crackled windows, the ruptured cabin. The crumpled metal sides, sort of owning up that the gaunt sea-creature is actually a thing put together and made of iron plates and logs. The paint already blistering from an unseen fire at one end. Piteous.

It had been creased downwards, broken as if smashed

from above. Both ends were sticking out of the water, and as I stared a fireman clambered on to the front bit and ran nimbly through the smoke unwinding some trailing hose along its length. He managed it without falling into the river, jumping over the ruined sunken middle fold and hauling himself up into the smoke. Fishes floated white-bellied in the water.

I crossed to the ambulance, stepping over the steel hawser cut clean through on the grass and pathetically still warped to the angled bow. The weird medical ritual always looks the same, doesn't it? Whether it does any good or not nobody seems to know. I hope somebody is adding it up somewhere.

The long bundle was being stretchered into the slots. A nurse gave me the elbow to reach past. The constable was helped up, still holding the inverted bottle. One white coat was bloodstained to the sleeve elbow now, the other still spotless. Car tyres spun mud against my legs. A voice spoke from an intercom, horribly distorted. I realized I was coughing because the smoke was blowing over the lawn now. Whatever the firemen were doing was making the smoke worse.

A police sergeant was ordering the grounds cleared. Somebody else was taking names and addresses. Somebody spoke to me. I said sod off. The man put his hand on my arm and said, 'Cool down, friend. I'm Maslow, CID. We have to take a few details, that's all.'

Doors slammed and the ambulance rolled away towards the drive. A motor-cycle kicked into deep sound. A voice called to clear the gateway.

'He's a family friend,' Sandy said to somebody. He was ashen. 'We're with him.'

'The old chap,' I managed to get out.

'That was him in the blood wagon.' Maslow nodded at the drive.

I turned to see the ambulance leaving the garden. Mel was in difficulties. A constable was making him do a bad-tempered three-point turn. More sulks were on the way.

My mind registered again. The long blood-soaked bundle under the tattered old car blanket was therefore the Reverend Henry Swan. The person of, the expiring person of, or remains of?

'What are his chances?'

'None, I'm afraid.' The CID man was a benign elderly square-shaped man, neat and tidily arranged in a crisp suit. He had a clean handkerchief in his top pocket. I'd thought the non-uniformed branch were all fashionably sloppy and soiled. 'You know him, then?'

'A bit.' I walked back to the river. The smoke was as bad as ever. They'd got a punt from somewhere and two firemen were poling along the shattered boat. River water was shooting into the fire from three hoses. Why did the engines have to make that piercing whine? Probably something to do with pumping. How pathetic to bring such massive ladders for nothing. Then I apologized mentally when I saw the far tender's ladder was stretched sideways over the river, with a fireman stuck on the end of it spraying his jet into the split barge.

'There was an explosion.' Maslow had followed me. Sandy went back to rescue Mel.

I thought a bit. 'How can a boat burn when it's made of tin?'

'Steel,' Maslow pointed out. 'And wood. There's all its fuel.'

'It hadn't any.'

'Oil generator.'

'It had electricity from the house.' I nodded to the grass. 'There's a conduit cable under there to Mrs Cookson's.'

'Gas, then.'

'He'd none.'

There was a long pause. We both watched the oily smoke. Oily.

I decided he'd need prompting. 'Isn't this where you're supposed to tell me who did it?'

'What's your name?' Maslow asked. He seemed angry.

'Find out,' I said. 'You're the detective. Where's Mrs Cookson?'

'The hospital,' he answered evenly. 'And I would advise you not to adopt that tone with me, sir.'

I honestly pity them when they go all official. 'And I would advise you to use your frigging cerebral cortex,' I heard myself say. 'Try.'

'Are you impeding a police officer in the performance of his duty?' he intoned.

'Some performance.' Sometimes they're just pathetic.

I walked to the drive where Sandy and Mel were arguing. Mel rounded on me spitefully.

'If you think this is a *lift*, Lovejoy,' he spat, 'you can walk, because we're going straight home this instant.'

'Shut your face,' I said as patiently as I could manage. 'Look, lads. I'm going to the local hospital immediately. In this car. And if you've any other ideas, well, let's get the chat over with.'

They glanced at each other. I opened the driver's door.

'Into the back,' I told them. 'I'm driving.'

They looked at my face and obeyed while I asked the gate constable the way. I saw Maslow standing on the lawn watching us go. He didn't wave either.

It was the remains of, after all. The Reverend Henry Swan was dead on arrival. A shapely receptionist told us this, sounding really quite pleased everything had gone according to the book.

'DOA,' she explained, showing us the admissions list. 'Do you wish to see the deceased?'

'No.' I halted. 'Oh. Can you give a message to Inspector Maslow? He'll be along shortly, when he can be bothered.'

'Certainly,' she said with pencil poised, sixty-five inches of syrup between two pearl ear-rings.

'The message is that I want an explanation. And to be sharp about it.'

'And whom shall I say . . . ?'

'Tell him Lovejoy.' I walked out.

Martha Cookson was being accompanied to the police car. Her back had that brave look. No sign of Dolly. I watched her go. Sandy and Mel climbed silently in.

I can remember Sandy sobbing in the back. Just as well he wasn't driving. I can remember Mel saying with relish that anyway he'd told that awful bitch of a receptionist her nails were a *mess* and her twinset didn't *match*, so there. I had the feeling it was somehow supposed to be a compassionate gesture. I can remember George doing his night round grandly stepping forward and holding up his hand at the chapel, and I can remember driving past without a word.

I got out at my gate.

'I appreciate your help,' I told the silent couple. 'I'm sorry it was such a shambles. I'll, er, do your scan at the weekend. All right?' Mel drew breath to speak again but finally said nothing.

As Sandy, red-eyed and still catching his breath, turned the car I asked one last favour.

'Should you happen to see George pedalling this way,' I said kindly, 'persuade him to go home. If he comes knocking I'll break his legs. 'Night.'

I went inside and shut the door.

CHAPTER VII

I thought a lot next day. Now, antiques is a very rough game. Let me explain.

Once upon a foetid hot day in 1880 a daring young Captain rode out near Kabul and performed a heroic rescue of three merchants and certain important bits of their baggage from a fierce and marauding band of brigands. A brave lad. But the point is that he got nothing out of it, which is especially narking when you realize that inside those bags nestled part of the hitherto fabulous Oxus Treasure, almost priceless. Alas, the Captain never got a rupee. There's a lesson hidden in there, fans.

Don't you try telling me that virtue is or has its own reward because it's not and it hasn't. Virtue has a sickening habit of breeding poverty and oppression. Everybody else benefits except the virtuous.

I'm telling you all this because the Oxus Treasure — nowadays tantalizingly arrayed in the British Museum — is a typical instance of treasure-troving. Get the moral? Most treasure's in a minefield of one sort or another. And mines go bang. Old Henry Swan had learned that. And I'm no hero like that brave captain.

It was beginning to look as though the Martha and Henry saga of the Grail was not exactly Lovejoy's scene.

On the other hand, my mind went, you can think of a million examples of people finding treasure and living happily ever after. In dark old England people are at it all the time. Right from our sinister prehistory to the weird present day, mankind's precious works are scattered in the soil, under walls, on beams, in rafters, in chests and sunken galleys, in tombs and tumuli. You can't help thinking.

I got one of those Dutch cigars and sat on the grass to watch the sun reach the tall trees down in the copse. Nurse Patmore pedalled by, wobbling to wave. I waved back, feeling fond of her. Devotion to duty's a wonderful thing, isn't it?

The point is that you have a choice. You can reach for the apple or you can resist the temptation. I felt I'd been warned. All the other antiques dealers had been warned off as well. Message over and out. Some things just aren't my business.

'Sleep well, Henry,' I said. 'Sorry and all that.'

I fed the birds some diced bacon rind. I brewed up and got a pasty. There's a low decorative wall where the gravel drive starts. One day I'll finish it, but at the moment it's a convenient place to eat and watch the world turn.

On the *other* hand, I thought as I noshed, did you ever hear of anybody *not* reaching for a luscious dangling apple?

Even God guessed wrong on that.

I had a job to do that evening at the pub. Every year I accept a trainee. Usually they're ghastly. You've just no idea. The trouble is that doting parents can't accept that their offspring have the brains of a wooden rocking-horse. Even established antiques dealers make the same mistake and send me buffoons who can't tell a Rembrandt from a manhole cover. It's a laugh. They even expect me to turn them into divvies. I take a fee for teaching these psychopaths, which keeps me in calories and helps me to stay, undernourished and shoddy, in antiques. This is important, because antiques are everything. Everything.

By nightfall I reckoned the pub would be jumping and getting ready for Lovejoy. I'd recovered enough to wash and shave and think of facing the ordeal. Tinker Dill sent word there'd be six to choose from. My one good white linen shirt was specially cleaned for the ordeal. I'd ironed it early. The cuffs were fraying but it's better than those modern fibres which stick to your skin and never leave you alone.

I locked up and started for the pub.

Not every dealer has a trainee. Some don't trust them. Most dealers are so ignorant about antiques that everything they teach is unerring crap. I'm not being flippant. There was the case of the forger who wrote letters in *modern* French, signed them 'Plato' and 'Mary Magdalene' and sold them as genuine antique letters by those worthies. There was the famous case of Billie and Charlie who minted 'coins' with gibberish inscriptions dated in modern numerals — and did so well they had to start up really serious factory-scale production.

The saloon bar hushed for a split second as I pushed in. Then the talk quickly babbled up again, people just proving they weren't there to see me picking a pupil out.

Tinker Dill waved an arm. He'd got a drink for me on the bar. It's his day, really. Mostly people normally ignore him. An event like this is the only chance he has to show off. He'd even taken off one of his mittens to reveal the poshness of the occasion, otherwise he was as grubby as ever.

'Wotcher, Lovejoy!' He pushed the drink at me. I always wait for the chance to wipe the rim in secrecy. Luckily, the risk of Tinker buying a round is small so it doesn't happen often.

There was a bigger crowd than usual. Betty Marsham was being determinedly casual in stylish black with pearls and her husband. He looked on about his fifth pint. Liz Sandwell was there, bossing her bloke about near the dartboard. Then there was the inevitable good old Alvin Honkworth, Esq., showing his true wit by bellowing out, 'Hail! The Conquering Hero Comes!' while sleek Bill Leyde tapped time on his glass. Dolly gauged the performance and my arrival like a referee measuring distances by eye. The flirtatious Angela was in, giving me the thumbs-up sign of optimism, which I suppose is one way of putting it. Jean Evans was on pink gin chatting to them both. She was in midsentence but managed a disapproving frown in my direction. Marion and Jed were standing talking to a couple of barkers. Mel and Sandy were there, whispering cattily to one another.

Brad the flintlock dealer was eyeing up one of the new recruits, a plump young lass dressed plain and elderly with specs and a bun. He has an eye for hidden potential. She sat in an alcove table trying to smile at the other five who'd written in. Funny how some women do their damnedest to look offended before you even start.

'They're all here, Lovejoy,' Tinker told me, already partly sloshed. 'Three blokes, three birds.'

'Where've they come from, Tinker?' I sipped and turned to see them. They hastily pretended to talk, feeling my gaze.

'The quiet lassie dropped out of teaching college,' Tinker began. 'Her mum's not keen on the trade.' Sure enough, a frosty lady with a new Wedgwood cameo sat vigilantly by the saloon bar fire, knees tight together and clearly slumming in a bad cause. 'Those brothers,' Tinker growled on, 'belong in London, dad on the Belly.'

I sussed them in the mirrors. These two lads were cool and flashy, gold sovereigns mounted on tiepins and nineteenth-century Italian quartz intaglios mounted as rings, practically splashed down into scrambled gold by some berk. I hate to see antiques spoiled. You never add value by such fancy work. But having a father who traded on the Belly, London's Portobello Road, meant that I could ask practically any fee.

'My fame must be spreading,' I told Tinker sardonically. 'Tell those two to piss off.'

'*Eh?*'

'Get rid.'

The saloon quietened while Tinker did his stuff. It got quieter when my shoulder was tapped. I never turn round quickly because it doesn't do.

'Lovejoy?' The elder brother was looking me up and

down. 'I said,' he told me loudly, 'are you Lovejoy, the divvie?'

'Yes.' We were speaking through the bar mirror.

'Somebody's going to be narked,' he said. 'Somebody it doesn't do to push around. We're here to get taught, friend. By you.'

'Tell your pappy you're too flashy and too ignorant. I don't accept sham.' I gave them a look. They dithered uncertainly. 'Look, lads,' I said eventually, turning now, 'no hard feelings. But if you're going to take a swing, get it over with. You can see I'm busy.' They gazed about, unsure of the general feeling. They sussed me as a loner but hadn't the nerve.

'You'll be seeing us, Lovejoy,' the elder said, licking his lip nastily. They must have been raised on a diet of bad westerns. 'Sykes is the name.'

'What else?' I said affably. They went, glancing ominously back.

'In trouble, Lovejoy?' Honkworth yelled, to widespread relieved laughter.

I could see the remaining four in the mirror. Tinker slurped his pint glass to its echo. I signalled a refill.

'Jesus, Lovejoy,' Tinker worried. 'Sykes is a bad lad. His lot's a right tribe of tearaways.'

I let him panic for a minute, observing the alcove. The one lad now left was embarrassed and trying to chat to the prim miss but she'd enough trouble of her own. Her mother, somewhat pale about the gills, had shot across the room and was now whispering feverish instructions into her daughter's ear. She was getting only a determined head-shake in return. Quite a little drama. The two other women seemed capable and businesslike (not always good signs in the antiques trade) and were distantly engaged in light chitchat.

'Those two lassies have history degrees,' Tinker said. 'Both from shops. One's local, the other's from the Smoke.'

'Mummy's girl's also local.' Tinker's voice went wary. He cleared his throat carefully. 'The teacher sent her.'

'Which teacher?'

'The one you're after, with the big knockers.'

'Elegantly put, Tinker.' Luckily bar hubbub covered his flowery lingo. 'Jean Evans?'

'Yes.' Tinker nodded. That obviously explained Jean being here this late. There'd be trouble if I slung her protégée out. 'Margaret's sent that chap in.'

Hello, I thought, still more trouble.

'Let's get it over with.'

Their faces seemed so fresh and alive. The prim lass jumped a little as I slid along the bench. Traditionally spit-and-sawdust, the White Hart had upgraded its saloon to a feeble mock-Tudor plush but its alcoves stayed wholesome.

'This is Lovejoy,' Tinker told them. The bar hushed a moment. I'd glimpsed the CID man as I'd crossed over, his expression one of surprise at all this reverence. The goon was smoking a pipe, too, just like Sherlock Holmes, eyes everywhere. Some people make you sick.

'Hello.'

They said hello back. The prim girl started fumbling for references in her handbag but I stopped her.

'Tinker Dill's told me who you are,' I began. 'Let's get this straight. Whoever I take on gets no pay for six months' full-time slog. Okay?'

'In exchange for what?' asked the London lass, cool.

'Learning whether you're any bloody good,' I told her.

'How many university degrees have *you* got, exactly?' she cracked back, all eyebrows.

I gave her a second for the chuckles to die down. 'Bethnal Antiques Exchangery, right?' I leaned across the table, grinning. It's at times like this I'm at my most charming. 'Three weeks ago, Clever Clogs, you snapped up a lovely original Wedgwood jasper vase, right?'

'Yes,' she said, lighting a cigarette. I stopped to watch.

'Notice the spelling on it?' I said gently, still happy. 'Wedgewood never spelled his name like that, with a middle E.'

'So?'

'So Smith the forger couldn't spell, love. Always got Wedgwood's name wrong in 1840.' She was looking less cool now. 'Maybe spelling didn't matter in your university, love,' I commiserated gently, 'but it does out here.'

The other three were silent.

'Better now?' I asked the truculent lass. She nodded, grinding out her fag. I had to stop to watch that, too. 'Names, please.'

The tough nut was Olive. Her college pal claimed the name Angharad. The nervous lad said too quickly that people called him Col. With a name like Lovejoy you learn not to pry, so I just nodded. The prim lass was Lydia. And she looked as if she'd been striving to be a suppressed Lydia all her life.

'Mr Lovejoy,' a firm dulcetto cried. 'I want to protest at this perfectly preposterous form of interview in a public house – '

I turned. Good old Mummy steaming to protect young Lydia.

'Mummy! For heaven's *sake*,' from Lydia, mortified and scarlet-faced.

'Mummy,' I said wearily, 'shut your teeth.' Mummy stalked back to the fireplace to beam more hatred.

'You get a test tonight,' I said. I slid folded paper between the wet beermats to each of the four.

'A *test?*' Olive said. She was as scandalized as Lydia's Mum. 'You must be joking.'

'Just mark a few ticks with your eyebrow pencil.'

'Not a chance, Lovejoy.' She rose and patted my cheek in farewell. 'I didn't struggle through university to get grilled by a rough in a pub.

Some struggle, I thought, eyeing her shape to the saloon door. Three down, two to go. Good.

I said, 'Sitting comfortably?'

'Yes, thank you,' Lydia said, then reddened. I was almost beginning not to believe in Lydia.

'The test. Then do one other thing. Tomorrow, the Castle Museum. Have a wander. Spot which exhibit on Gallery Six is a cheap – ' I hesitated – 'an *expensive* forgery.'

'Gallery Six?' Angharad thought, wrinkled. 'Furniture.'

Lydia and Col drew breath simultaneously but stayed quiet. They too knew their galleries.

'And take your guess to Tinker.'

'Where do we find Mr Dill?'

I smiled kindly at Lydia's innocence. 'Try the George tavern,' I told her. 'He's thirsty about midday.'

Col hid a smile but Tinker sensed an opportunity.

'A little rum, love, when I can afford it,' he whined. 'For my bad chest, my dear.' He gave her his cadaverous gappy grin. 'The war.'

This charade was getting out of hand.

'Shut it, Tinker, you stupid berk.'

'*Lovejoy!*' from Lydia, offended. I got up. It had been a long day and Ted was glugging me another drink at the bar. I said good night and left them to it.

A few dealers moved casually to the alcove to see my questions, murmuring among themselves. I wondered how many of them could read. I also wondered who'd got my drink, and found the constabulary at my elbow, which solved that. Sherlock Mark Two, pipe on the go.

'Why are you so broke, Lovejoy?' he asked. 'Seeing as you're one of those magic divvies.'

'Antiques need money, and I've not got any.'

'Are you really that good?' He nodded at the alcove.

'One day I'll find another like me.'

He smiled the way bobbies do, meaning watch your step whatever you're up to.

'Not in as much trouble as you, Lovejoy, one hopes.'

'I'm not in any.'

'Oh, but you are.' He nodded at my glass. 'Drink up. You're coming down to the station.'

'Am I?' These goons really nark me. They'll do anything except use their cerebral cortex.

'Yes. Just a few questions.'

'Arrest?'

'Not exactly.' A pompous tap of pipe on an ashtray which the universe was clearly expected to admire. 'Just helping us with enquiries. I don't want any fuss.'

Suddenly it was all too much for me. Maybe it was the fug of the crowded saloon bar after a mad strange day. Maybe it was the indelible memory, suddenly brought back stark and horribly clear, of the pathetic bundle being pushed into the ambulance. Or maybe it was just the sight of Ted taking a glass of rum for somebody down the bar. Old Henry Swan had given me his rum in the hope that I'd stop being so bloody pompous and just bother to divvie some old pewter cup he'd got fond of. I had to fight back an abrupt nausea. I said, 'I'm sick of you. Get lost.'

'Look here − '

I reached for his drink and spat in it.

'People like you really make me spew.' I even dug a finger into his chest. 'Some old geezer got crisped and you haven't a frigging clue what to do.'

'Lovejoy. I could arrest you for − '

'Then get on with it, comrade. You think it's time you pushed somebody about and I'll do,' I said. There was an appalled silence all around. 'Well, you're wrong, mush. I'm narked. So I'll tell you something for free. Suss out the old geezer's finisher, fast. Or I'll do your job for you, you pathetic smug bastard.'

I told Ted I'd have another in the taproom and pushed through the swing door. I felt Old Bill go. He went quietly without a single further threat. A bit ominous, that. Still, owing to the hectic nature of our little chat Ted hadn't noticed I'd not paid.

I gave the CID five minutes to get clear, then slipped out. The evening had spoiled. Half way down the lane to our chapel near where my hedge starts a car pulled up, head-lights lighting the long trees.

'Get in Lovejoy.' A woman's watch-out-you're-for-it voice.

'Wotcher, Betty.' I felt a bit down so I got in and let her drive me to the cottage. She told me her husband had met up with some of his rugby coleagues and chased off on the razzdazz.

She waited in silence as I got out at my gate. I paused, thinking. She'd probably have to hang around a whole hour before her husband came reeling home after the pubs finally turfed him and his pals on to the High Street. I felt sympathetic. We could probably find something to talk about if she waited in the cottage with me. I cleared my throat.

'Er, want a cup of coffee, love?' I suggested.

She exhaled and gazed my way. 'I thought you'd never ask, Lovejoy.'

Well, forgiveness is my strong suit.

CHAPTER VIII

I'd better tell you here what the dark secret of Gallery Six is.

When you think of it, it's odd that the great furniture geniuses don't get the praise they deserve. Mayhew and Ince, Lock and a score of others are in the Sheraton-Chippendale class, but outside the antiques trade people are hardly interested. They'd rather take an outside chance on an escritoire being Chippendale than buy a genuine beautiful Mayhew cabinet. It honestly beats me. There's nowt as odd as folk.

Somebody once worked it out that the population in the George III period was about twelve million or so. Assuming there were 140,000 families wealthy enough to furnish their houses by purchasing from the great London makers, why, one might ask, are there so many pieces of this furniture still around in excess of the numbers you'd expect? The answer is, of course, that sinners abound still making 'old' furniture. Some are better than others, but all very, very busily plying their sinful trade. We have a saying that the Impressionists painted 1,000 pictures, of which 2,000 are genuine and 3,000 are in America. See what I mean?

Some years ago I was broke. Again. I made a lovely little slide-topped Davenport from new mahogany for a bloke who paid me well, in the days before money got funny. He wanted it aged, please, Lovejoy, to match this valuable antique bureau . . . Stained areas are easy to fake old. To do this I normally use copal varnish and a darking stain, repeatedly wiped gently with glasspaper between coats. The unstained areas are more difficult. Take a wet tea towel and stroke the mahogany vigorously till damp. Rush the piece into sunlight. Then take it, after maybe a good

half-day's exposure, indoors and repeat the wet-wiping.
Sun. Wet. Sun. If you live where I do and the weather's its
usual crummy self, use a sunray lamp. Other forgers use an
oven but risk damaging the wood, especially near the
dovetail joints. Result? One dark lovely mahogany
Davenport. My buyer sold it as an antique. I didn't know
whether to be proud or to sulk because he didn't share the
profit, but profit only ever belongs to one person in the
antiques game.

   The reason I'm telling you this is that my Davenport's
now in Gallery Six, Antique Furnishings, where I'd sent
Col, Angharad and Lydia. They label it as genuine, which
embarrasses me, but I don't feel heroic enough to own up.
Magistrates tend to get ideas.

I decided to have a quiet morning, richly deserved.

   Betty stayed until about one o'clock when all good
people are fast asleep. She'd put her car at the side of the
cottage so that our village's prowling spinsters couldn't
actually spot it from the lane because the hedge gets in the
way. By the time she went home we weren't mad at each
other at all, though we had a bit of an argument.

   'Aren't you going to- get up and see me off?' she
whispered, struggling to dress in the darkness.

   'No.'

   'You selfish – '

   'I want your warm patch,' I explained. You have to be
patient with them. 'Women always get a warmer part of the
bed than me.' Mistake, but sleep was on me.

   '*What* women, Lovejoy?' No whispering now.

   'You. I mean you. Honest.'

   We compromised. I dashed out once she'd dressed,
whisked her into the hall, gave her a quick peck and hurtled
back into bed, where I settled into a well-earned doze,
thinking that's the odd thing about being holy. It says Love
Thy Neighbour. That bit's easy. But sending a neighbour
on her way rejoicing's really a very difficult thing to do.

   Then the phone rang. At this ridiculous hour.

   'Lovejoy?'

   'I thought I told you to sod off, Sergeant.'

   'Inspector,' the voice said, but I wasn't having any.

'Do you know what the bloody hour is, Sergeant?'

'That's the point, Lovejoy.' We fell silent.

The only event had been Betty, pushing off in a rage. Hey-ho.

'If,' he said pleasantly, 'you're still refusing to help my enquiries, I shall pay a call on the Marshams and explain – '

' – how you just happened to be outside in the lane and saw Betty drive off?' I filled in uneasily.

'Precisely.'

'I might complain to the boss of the local CID,' I threatened, scraping the barrel.

'Do,' he said, still content. 'It's me.'

Well, I thought, wise trees bend in the gale.

'How about,' he suggested mildly, 'I meet you for a quiet co-operative chat? I'll stand you a brown ale.'

'Tomorrow dinner time.' I gave in. 'The George.'

'Great,' he agreed. 'Oh, Lovejoy. Sleep well.'

'Sod off,' I said, slamming the blower down.

When I climbed in the warm patch had cooled. There are times you can't rely on anything.

Quiet mornings are marvellous. This particular morning the sun was given to secret gleamings from a half-opaque white sky. A low mist hung between trees cooling their branches. Hedgehogs were stooging about the garden doing a final round on lifted pink feet. Some birds bummed about, mostly sorts of pointed sparrows. Till the dew's off the grass I go into my cellar to keep up the good work on antiques. I keep records.

Within an hour I'd found three Swans, curiously all collectors and all about Henry Swan's age. One, a born buccaneer, had written to me offering a miniature of Elizabeth I by the famous Nicholas Hilliard for a lowly price – as it should be, because the original's still in Berkeley Castle. Incidentally, Hilliard loved to paint these rarities (value: about eight times your annual wage, today's minimum) on playing cards, sometimes over-stretched with skin of chicks or aborted lambs. So forgeries are pretty easy to spot. The second Swan appeared three years back to win a lovely Georgian pole-screen (tip: all things being equal, shield-shaped ones are worth much more than rectangular or circular). The last Swan is well known around here and collects only 'friggers', small glass objects and figures made by the glass craftsmen from odd bits of glass left once the day's official glassworking had ended. Some friggers are worth a small fortune. But watch out for the cheap Czechoslovakian glass 'friggers' Woolworth's used to sell before the war — they were threepence then, and I think they should still be threepence now.

That accounted for all the Swans in my files. No record of the late Henry Swan, and the only other Cooksons I knew of were two sisters who collect Victorian manuscript diaries.

I telephoned a mate of mine who makes boat models, sea-going craft mainly. He knew a Mersea bloke in the same society who did waterways boats. It cost me the earth in phone calls during the next hour. After that I tidied away and got some bread for the birds. The garden hadn't changed, but now the morning seemed vaguely sour. The bus was due.

I used the journey to decide what to do.

Sentiment's a queer thing. It gets everywhere, seeps in and out of places you wouldn't normally expect. Old Henry had used that odd phrase of his twice or three times while we'd got sloshed on his barge. What was it — 'sanctification by use'? An interesting idea, but is it the sort that the Lovejoys of this world go to war about? It bloody well is not.

I can't remember much about our conversation except at one point when he'd said, rheumy old eyes atwinkle, 'It's an antique, Lovejoy. Maybe *the* antique.' Which at the time made me fall about laughing. Some claim. And yet . . .

Maybe old Henry had been telling me that his daft belief about his old pewter cup was exactly the same as mine about all antiques. Thinking, this quiet grey morning, he seemed close. After all, I reasoned uncomfortably, all antiques only start off a piece of wood, stone, marble or a few pigments mixed with oil and brushed on to rough old canvas, don't they? Henry was right in a sense. The love you work into a thing gives it life. On the bus I decided I'd help the CID with reluctance, but getting blown up like

Henry was not part of my plan.

I was in the George by opening time.

CHAPTER IX

Margaret Dainty had come from kindness. She is one of the slower age-drifters. She might be twenty-five or fifty, but that plump allure's still there. Hair deceptively casual, always looks a little dressy and over-groomed, but maybe that's because younger women have this crummy modern fashion of looking shop-soiled.

Margaret comes from an old army family, the sort that thinks drinking before dusk's unpatriotic, sinful and stirs up the natives. I don't, so I got some cheap white wine and started on the urgent job of restoring my nerves. We sat overlooking the crowded pavement through the leaded window. Elizabeth I seated herself precisely in the same spot once upon a time, gazing over the selfsame street. And fifteen centuries before that Claudius the God had ridden past in triumph. I love the human connection — was Bess tired, did she put her feet up? Did Claudius have difficulty keeping his laurel wreath on while his war elephants swayed ahead of his legions?

'Eh?'

Margaret was saying something. 'You shouldn't have risked trouble last night.'

'There was no trouble,' I said guardedly. Maybe she'd seen Betty follow me from the White Hart.

'The Sykes boys. And what did the CID want?'

'A football result,' I told her, avoiding her eyes.

'Be careful, Lovejoy.'

'You know me,' I said reassuringly.

We sipped and gazed out. Jimmo walked past carrying a long slender canvas bag and a basket.

'Jimmo's come up in the world,' Margaret smiled. 'A

new two-tone motor-car.'

I stared. He'd been broke a couple of days ago.

Margaret smiled happily, always pleased at the success of others. She's unique. 'That's his new craze.'

'The car?' It had been in a salesman's window yesterday.

'No. Fishing.' She was suddenly watching my face. 'What is it, Lovejoy? You're all on edge.'

Well, you can't help wondering, can you? Fishing equals a river, which equals Stour, which yesterday had been disturbed by a savage explosion in which an old dreamer got transmuted. And a couple of drunken bums laughing and getting sloshed in a barge on a quiet river reach tend to converse loudly. An angler who happened to be an eager antiques dealer might have heard . . . No. I shook the thought off. We'd known Jimmo for years.

Maybe it was a mistake but I found myself telling Margaret about old Henry, the explosion. Mel and Sandy giving me a lift and Henry's daft request. So she wouldn't assume I'd gone bananas I didn't admit he thought he'd actually got the Grail. I said nothing about Jimmo. She was commiserating when Tinker showed.

'How do, Lovejoy, Margaret.'

'Morning, Tinker. All ready?'

He came belching, still wiping his accumulated egg stains from his stubble with greasy mitten. I waved a pint over. First things first.

'Sure, Lovejoy.'

'One thing, Tinker. Just seen Jimmo, off fishing. Where's he go?'

'Oh, Stour, Layer Pits, down the estuary sometimes.' He gave me a theatrical nudge, winking. 'On the rebound. Broke off with that dollybird called Dolly.' He chuckled. 'Get it? Dolly, dollybird?' That was news. So Dolly and Jimmo . . .

'A superb play on words, Tinker.' I waited gravely for his creaks of laughter to subside. There's nothing you can do about some people. 'Sudden wealth, eh?'

'New car,' Tinker agreed, gazing soulfully into his empty glass. I got him another to prevent a relapse.

'How come? Jimmo done any buying lately?'

He thought hard — no mean task at this hour — and

shook his head. 'None I know of.'

'He sold a pair of Satsuma decoratives,' Margaret put in. 'A collector, out Ipswich way. I could be wrong.'

'Lovejoy?' Nan the barmaid was pointing. Lydia's interesting silhouette showed against the frosted glass. 'She won't come in,' Nan called.

'Why the hell not?' I growled. Margaret and Nan were smiling. Tinker went out. She came sidling in, frightened to touch the furniture and looking at the floor. She only managed to move her lips soundlessly when Nan called a good morning. With true grit she sat down on a pub chair without giving it a quick polish. Nerves of steel. Her fingernails were clean, just like Margaret's. I closed my hands in case mine weren't.

'What's up, love?' Tinker crashed in cheerfully. 'Never been in a pub on your own before?' He cackeld a burst of foul-stinking noisy breath, splitting his sides at his light banter.

'No,' Lydia whispered. That shut Tinker up. He'd assumed that's where people came from. 'Good morning, Mrs Lovejoy.'

'Er, Margaret Dainty, Lydia.' I got that in swiftly. These misunderstandings give people ideas.

'Oh dear.' Lydia half rose in panic but Margaret calmed her with a friendly word and sent Tinker for some more orange juice. He reeled giddily towards the bar, wondering what the world was coming to.

Actually I've been married, if that's the right word. It wasn't bad except that the aggro with Cissie got me down. I'd felt like a half-pint Tom pitted against a relentless armourplated Jerry. I scrutinized Lydia during the preliminary skirmishing between her and Margaret. They both seemed pleased. Despite Lydia's soft and shy appearance I was on my guard. I reckon women are a very, very tough-minded bunch, being gifted with all the advantages in life.

'I *was* married, once,' I chipped in, hoping to clarify matters. A mistake.

'Oh, do forgive me.' Lydia's eyes filled. 'When did it . . . ?'

'No, no.' This was all getting too much. Lydia was

obviously one of those birds whose conversation gets queerly deformed half way through. 'Divorce. Actually it was my fault . . . '

A woman usually likes this sort of modesty, knowing it can't possibly be true because each thinks all other women are basically undesirables even on a good day. My unblemished humility didn't work this time. Lydia froze.

'*Oh*' She switched instantly to outrage, lips thin as a bacon-slicer. '*I see.*'

'That reveals my base, carnal nature,' I said pleasantly, and saw from her expression that the million warnings she'd had were coming true.

'Miss Evans did furnish me with the advice that . . . *certain* antiques dealers were of a *certain* disposition.'

I couldn't help staring. She sat there indignantly, full of wholesome fruit, morals and wheatgerm. There's a lot of people about who actually talk like this, many more than there used to be. It's probably caught off the telly.

'Good old Jean,' I said. 'But about antiques, love.'

'It's only his way, Lydia,' Margaret said.

A familiar figure loomed in the doorway and waved. I didn't even gesture towards my wallet. Tinker, on his way back with a fistful of glasses, shied nervously.

'Morning, Tinker,' the Old Bill said.

'Why, hello, Mr Maslow.'

Lydia sat watching in horror as Tinker's filthy mittens distributed the glasses round the table. You could see that microbes were suddenly on her mind.

'Maslow, Lovejoy,' Tinker whispered. 'A right bast — er, a real grouser.' Street traders' slang for a bobby of serious and unpleasant disposition.

Maslow stood at the bar chatting to Nan, his back towards us. On the Continent he'd have been stymied, but you never get an English pub without six thousand mirrors on every wall. He could see in everybody's earhole.

I nodded for Lydia to start up. She drew breath.

'There's something wrong in Gallery Six. A Davenport in the central display.'

'But the Davenport's beautiful.' Margaret halted abruptly when I gave her the bent eye.

'It's an excellent piece of work,' Lydia said. 'Lovely. The

texture's almost right and the colour's exquisite.' Her eyes were glowing now behind her bottle lenses. 'Somebody has created it with such, well, feeling. But it is modern, not an antique.'

'Sure?' I said.

'Yes.' She examined her hands and said nothing.

'What tipped you off?' You have to be ruthless at this stage.

'I just don't know,' she admitted. 'The poor thing. So beautiful, yet basically a . . . well, just a trick, isn't it?'

I gazed at her in silence for a moment. Tinker gave me her answer paper, a lined sheet torn from a spring note-book. Eight out of twelve right. Only an average knowledge, but knowledge is only a small percentage of knowing after all.

'Have a look at this.' I gave her a dazzling little 1598 leatherbound copy of John Wylie's madrigals. Margaret had lent it. Lydia flipped it carefully, guessing it was special from my handling, but clearly bemused.

'An old book.' Quite lost. 'Is it genuine?'

'Yes. Rare. Superb. Brilliant.'

'Oh. I'm afraid I know so little – '

'He was inspired by an illicit love-affair. Lady Mary of St Osyth. They were always at it.' Lydia hastily dropped the book, reddening. 'You win,' I said. 'Look, love. If you come to learn from me you work like a dog as and when I say. I'll take you on for three months, then I might give you the push. No wages. A share in a non-existent profit. No expenses. No grumbling. And no comeback if I sling you out before time because I suddenly take umbrage.' She listened, still as a squirrel. 'Everything else comes second to antiques. And one last point. I don't like criticism.' I waited. 'Well?'

She nodded breathlessly. 'Am I . . . taken on?'

'Yes.'

'Col will be so disappointed,' she said sorrowfully, her eyes filling with tears. 'He was so thrilled, brimming with expectation.' Oh-ho, I thought. No tears for Angharad, only for Col.

'Tinker. Find Col and Angharad and tell them sorry.' Tinker nodded and started draining his pint glass.

'Margaret, would you explain basic survival? I want a word with Maslow.'

Lydia rose, figure meticulously tidy and handbag on guard. 'Thank you, Lovejoy,' she said politely. 'As your apprentice I shall endeavour to fulfil whatever promise you see in me, and perform — '

I got up and kissed her cheek and Margaret's.

'Welcome, love. Meet me on the gallery in thirty minutes.'

'Lovejoy!' she was starting up indignantly, but Margaret hastily whisked her out as Maslow came over.

'Wherever I go you're grilling young ladies in some tavern,' he quipped.

'A merry jest, Maslow.'

'Still in that public-spirited mood of co-operation, I see, Lovejoy.' He knew he was nettling me. 'Betty any good?'

I ignored that. We sat facing across the narrow table like gamblers. Nan was round in the other bar. It was too early for the regulars. Just me and this nerk.

I asked, 'Well? Who killed the old geezer in the boat?'

'Which is where we left off,' he prompted. 'What makes you think he was killed deliberately?'

'No fuel. No gas. No explosives.' These pedantic civil servants really get me. 'Does that add up to kerboom at the police college?'

'Boats have stoves, and petrol, oil. Old boozers drop matches.'

'Immovable boats don't.'

He shook his head and wagged his finger. It took all my self-control not to break it off. 'Engine-driven boats are always movable, Lovejoy,' he explained as if to an imbecile. 'A flick of a wrist to cast off. The North Sea,' he said, ramming it home, 'isn't all that far downstream.'

The bleeder actually sneered as he poked my collarbone with his pipestem. These pompous warts really chill me. I took his pipe away and dropped it into his beer with a succulent fizz. Second pint of his I'd ruined.

'Concentrate. The estuary,' I corrected, 'might as well be on Saturn. The barge had no engine.' Like I say, sometimes it feels like we're ruled by Neanderthals. I saw I'd have to explain. 'Engine number PDK oblique YOZ oblique

4331M oblique 299 was removed for scrap years ago.
Longhelp Mason's, bargeyarders, of Belchingham, Lancs.
They're on the telephone and everything, very willing
ordinary people keen to help with the most simple routine
enquiries. I phoned them. And one other thing, Sanders-
of-the-Trail.' I managed to stand up. I knew I was brewing
the wrong exit line but I was trembling with fury.

'Look here, Lovejoy – '

He tried to stand but I slammed him down. 'If your
shambolic gaggle of bumblers isn't going to bother, then I
am.'

'Are you sure about – ?'

'When you've done some thinking, Maslow,' I said, 'call
on me. Until then, leave us common folk to get on with
dishing out the justice.'

'Just you dare, Lovejoy.'

I was half way to the door but found I'd swung round.
'Oh, I dare all right, Maslow,' I said. 'I dare.' I even felt
pale. I went meekly out, not a little embarrassed at the
contumely. Notice that expression I just used, not a little
embarrassed at the contumely? That's what listening to
people like Lydia does for you. For some reason I was mad
at her as well as at Maslow.

It was high time I put my mind to trying to remember
what old Henry and I had talked about when we were
drinking ourselves paralytic. I always knew it would be left
to me. No wonder I'd been so on edge.

'Excuse me.' A traffic warden barred my way in the
alleyway. 'Is that your car? It's illegally parked – '

I kneed him and propped him gasping against the tavern
wall. 'Piss off,' I said. I nodded a breezy good day to two old
biddies gaping at the scene and stepped off feeling better
already, though I knew I'd worry all day in case he was a
friend of Brenda's, the only traffic warden friend I've got.

Having alienated practically everybody I could think of
– as usual, not my fault – I drifted into our town library to
suss out books on the Grail.

Lydia was waiting patiently on Gallery Six. I'd never seen
so many people in the museum. The galleries were crammed, at least a score of people and children to each.

'Can't you see?' she said, pointing excitedly. 'How . . . *guilty* the poor thing looks?'

'You're right,' I calmed her.

For the next hour I took her round the galleries, becoming more resigned every second. Lydia had the knack beating fervently inside her, but it was a furniture knack. I showed her the ancient Galileo pendulum hanging from the museum's glass ceiling to head height. It is really only a massive lead weight on a wire flex. Set swinging, it shows the rotation of the earth. Naturally our museum authorities forbid this because children are always playing 'chicken' at it. Lydia thought it stupid and ugly.

'How do they *clean* it?' she demanded. She also gazed blankly at a blindingly beautiful Thomas Tompion clock worth a fortune. She was merely puzzled by a rare collection of cased smoking pipes for a Georgian lady — ivory and gold decorations, silver-and-pearl-embellished tobacco pouch, of the kind occasionally put on sale as snuff-boxes — their greater size gives them away. She was bored stiff by a precious excavated set of Roman surgical instruments owned by the doctor of the famed — and doomed — Ninth Legion. She gazed, fingers tapping signals of boredom on her handbag, at a display I'd provided materials for in the English Civil War section.

'See,' I enthused. 'English doglocks are so very rare.'

'Mmmm.'

'Those two little heaps of powder I put there to show the ingredients of gunpowder,' I explained enthusiastically. 'I left out the charcoal because it might get wafted about on to those uniforms. The trouble is it all needs re-doing, really neffie.'

'Mmmm.'

A little kid pulled at my trouser leg and held up a bar of chocolate. I bent down and took a mouthful. It trotted off, pleased.

'The curator made me take out the flints because he said — '

'*Lovejoy!*' Lydia said, incensed, pointing after the infant.

' — it disturbed their line, made them look too much like weapons — '

'You ate that baby's chocolate!'

' — which is what they *are*. Eh?' I homed in on her outrage. 'I know. It insisted.'

'You — you insufferable, greedy — ' she stormed.

'Here endeth the first lesson,' I said wearily. 'See you.' And left.

I can't understand what women are on about half the time.

There are garden seats placed on an especially windy corner of the market square. I flicked through Ashe's book on the Grail for half an hour and finished up no wiser. Maybe I needed the close assistance of a desirable Ph.D. in ancient history.

I strolled off, deciding to chat up Lisa. But no silly obvious questions about the Grail, because a lot of other antiques dealers see Lisa very, very often.

CHAPTER X

But how does an entire civilization lose the Grail, for heaven's sake?

The whereabouts of all antiques isn't necessarily known, even if they are very, very important antiques indeed. In fact whole palaces full of them have even gone missing, like Nonsuch Palace, for example. The notorious Barbara Villiers was at the back of it all, otherwise Lady Castle-maine of glamorous reknown. This famous beauty, cold and grasping down to her very bones, was a profligate gambler. She acquired the lovely Nonsuch Palace by means best not gone into, and immediately considered the alternatives: to sell for hard cash, or to hang on to, this exquisite wonder of the Royal Tudors, crammed as it was with the breathtaking craftsmanship of the glittering age of Henry the Eighth and Queen Bess. It was money or beauty.

Needless to say money changed hands, and even the stones were savagely plundered. Finally the Palace was gone, vanished.

Well, if you can lose a palace you can lose a pewter cup, can't you?

I tried to calm down and forget my worries, wandering about the Arcade and chatting till Lisa finished serving. I saw Jason, a retired army man turned honest, and made him blush by telling him that the 'Linen-and-Calfskin Guinea-Pouch' he was advertising was an early contraceptive.

'They waterproofed them with linseed oil,' I told him affably. 'Sometimes even tar.'

'Is it *really?*' he said, awed, gaping at it.

'Making them impervious was the difficulty.' There were other more natural ways, if you follow. I gave Jason a few details. Bill Shakespeare's Dark Lady Emelia Bassano avoided, er the issue (so to speak) by diverse other skilful practices, about which I'd better not digress. But it's interesting that antique contraceptives, flea boxes and the like have to be called something else in order to sell them nowadays — we label them 'sovereign purses' or 'snuff-boxes', or some such, often unknowingly. Odd how our hang-ups still haunt us.

You have to laugh at some stuff, though. Every day you find a piece which sets you falling about. Today's gem was a plate of Spode type, priced high by Lennie. He hasn't a clue, but hope beats eternal in the human breast. He called me over. His mother-in-law Jessica was with him and glamorous as ever. She has him in thrall owing to the fact that he's penniless and she's aggressively rich. Jessica has somehow managed the older woman's perfect triumph — a kind of marriage by proxy, with every known practical, material and bodily gain. I've never even seen her daughter, Lennie's wife. I sometimes wonder if Lennie ever has, either.

'Lennie's found a superb piece, Lovejoy!' she breathed proudly. 'Spode. Believe it or not, 1732!'

She moved ahead of me into the shop wearing a ton of gold bangles.

'Hiyer, Lovejoy.' Lennie looked bushed. It had happened more and more frequently since Jessica took him in hand.

And Jessica was right, in that the blue-printed earthenware Spode plate was marked AD1732, which was a considerable achievement since Josiah Spode wasn't born till 1733. I explained this slight technical flaw. Jessica saw Lennie's face fall and pulled me quickly to one side. Lennie blundered eagerly towards two other customers.

'Look, Lovejoy,' Jessica said softly. 'I know Lennie's not too lucky at antiques.' She squeezed my hand gently. 'But couldn't you just see your way to . . . well, *suggesting* Lennie's successful for once? Made a really marvellous find?'

'If I could, I'd have done him that kindness years ago.'

'I quite understand.' We were suddenly eyeball to eyeball. It's a very disturbing sensation because Jessica's shapely and somewhat overpowering. 'Come in one day, say tomorrow. Use a lot of money to buy one of Lennie's pieces. Anything.'

'I've no money.'

'But,' she explained, looking carefully like they do, 'I have.'

'Look, Jessica, love . . . '

'You need clothes, Lovejoy,' she breathed softly. 'And other things. A woman always knows when a man's so clever he can't . . . fend for himself. And you need more than just money, sweetie.'

'Er, look Jessica.' My words stuck.

'Think it over, Lovejoy.'

I escaped thankfully, saying maybe. Which was a lie, because I would for certain.

For an hour I went round the town, looked in at the viewing-day at our local auction. Some good stuff, some utter dross. Liz Sandwell was casually inspecting the porcelain.

'Spending your ill-gotten profit, Liz?' I joked, meaning about the Irish glass.

'Precious little profit from you, Lovejoy.'

'Jimmo been in?'

'No.' She hesitated. 'Lovejoy – those vases.'

Genuine large Second Satsumas, big with ostentatious

white slip. I've already told you how little I think of them. They were nothing special, though honest Japanese nineteenth-century. Holland's full of them.

'Ordinary Satsumas,' I told her. 'Interested? When in doubt, Liz, buy.' Smiling, I quoted the antiques dealers' old maxim. It's good advice, but only sometimes.

'I could have sworn they're the ones I sold Jimmo a fortnight ago. I heard he'd sold them on the coast for a whacking profit.'

'Well, good for Jimmo. He's learning.'

'So why are they back?'

I shrugged. Double deals are common. You often handle things twice.

She was still doubtful, though. We chatted on about some French marionettes that were rumoured about town and then parted, both of us spicing the chat with cheerful falsehoods after the manner of our kind. I promised to see Liz for a drink on Saturday when I knew her bloke was splashing around a rugby field in Essex.

I tore myself away when I was sure Harry the attendant had popped out. Sure enough he was next door, where thoughtful brewers had guessed right six centuries back and built the Rose and Crown.

'How lucky to find you here, Harry,' I said, and persuaded Harry to a pint of beer. It took little time and less skill. He was busy at his newspaper with a pencil stub. 'The Satsumas,' I said. 'Left side of the Victorian bookcase.'

'Yeah?'

'Who sent them in?'

'Gawd knows.' He dragged his eyes from the list of runners. 'Want me to find out? I heard tell it was Caskie.'

I made a great show of thinking, finally shaking my head. 'No, thanks, Harry. Just thought I'd seen them before.'

'Cheers, Lovejoy.'

I walked back up East Hill and sat in St Peter's churchyard to watch the motor-cars go by on the distant London road. Some children were playing in the Castle Gardens across the way. Shoppers were streaking into town and trundling out again laden with bags. A really normal average scene, the sort I usually like to sit and enjoy for a minute or two. Happy and at ease.

But, folks. Old Henry dead *and* Jimmo suddenly well off?

Suddenly Jimmo has plenty of time to neglect his mediocre antiques business and go fishing, in a new two-tone motor-car. Second Satsumas are not worth much, and that seemed to be the only business Jimmo'd done. But again, so what? So Jimmo's made a few quid. That's the game, isn't it?

I rose and walked back through the alley towards the Arcade. Lisa saw me from the window of Woody's. I waved, signalling. I drew a deep breath so I'd enough oxygen and opened the glass door of Woody's Bar. She slipped out.

'Hello, Lovejoy.'

'Lisa. Do something for me?'

'Yes. Do hurry. Woody'll go spare. What is it?'

'Find time to go to Lennie's. Know where?'

'Yes. Him and Jessica.' She obviously disapproved.

'That's the one, love. Get Jessica alone, so Lennie doesn't hear you. Tell her from me the deal's on.'

'With her, or with Lennie?' I saw that anti-woman frown developing on Lisa's brow.

'It's to do with antiques. Honestly.'

'It had better be. She's a right vampire.'

'Shut up and listen. Tell her to buy the Satsumas at Gimbert's auction tomorrow, and that if she does I'll go through with it. Okay?'

'The Satsumas at Gimbert's, and you'll go through with it,' she repeated. 'You still all right for the fireworks?' She saw my blank expression. 'Our date. Castle Park.'

'Eh? Oh yes. I've not forgotten,' I said, having clean forgotten. Woody appeared at the window in a rage. 'Er, well, I'm a bit busy — ' I began but she had plunged back into the blue fumes. I should have scuppered that because the fewer complications the better. And young Lydia should be turning up for work. I'd glanced in at Margaret's as I passed. Lydia and Margaret were going through some Victorian tapestries, one of today's seriously underpriced antique items.

Getting Lisa to fix the arrangement with Jessica gave me half an hour to telephone Martha. It took a lot of nerve, but

it had to be done. Mercifully she was glad to hear me, and
said could I come over please as soon as possible and had I
heard the terrible news. We arranged to meet at a café on
the Buresford road in thirty minutes. She said get a taxi and
she would pay.

There'd been one whole day between my two visits at
Martha's house. It was high time I found out what Henry
had been up to in that time. Whatever it was, it got him
crisped. And one other realization came to me as the old
taxi trundled down the northside hill out of town past the
railway. If Henry had an old pewter cup which he thought
very special, well, it couldn't have vanished entirely, could
it? Henry might have gone, but his pewter cup was still
around somewhere.

CHAPTER XI

Gun Hill's summit now has a little walled garden, café,
roses and fountain with trellis to trip the unwary at every
step. It's a quiet place overlooking a valley and woods, with
sheep and barley fields adding local colour. Really average.
Martha was waiting.

'Henry and I used to come here.'

'I'm so sorry, Martha.' You never know what to say at
these times.

'You've just no idea, no idea.' She blotted her face a
minute while I gazed at the revolting rural scene below.
'We were so happy.'

'Martha,' I said carefully. 'I'm not after his pewter
thing – '

'Grail.'

Let her have her way. 'Grail, then. Honestly I'm not. But
one thing keeps nagging in my mind.' I weighed Martha
up. Maybe it wasn't the right moment to talk about killing.
'Is it possible that . . . well, that Henry had something

really valuable? I mean, did you ever see his, er, Grail?'

'No.' She shook her head.

'Didn't he show you a picture, draw it for you, anything?'

'No.' She was looking at me, though I tried to stare casually into the middle distance. 'Lovejoy, what is it?'

I shrugged, wondering how best to go on. For all I knew Martha herself might have . . . No. Impossible. Look at the woman, for heaven's sake, the state she was in. I decided to plunge.

'The boat. It was just a hull.'

'So?'

'So tin boats only explode when there's something to explode.'

I'll say this for Martha Cookson. She's pretty cool. She sat there a full five minutes, occasionally lifting her head as if to speak but saying nothing and letting her eyes wander about the garden. She was very pale.

'You believe . . . ?' she tried finally.

'Yes, love.'

'Have you told the Inspector?'

'I've tried to, the pompous sod. He takes no notice. I've had a go at him. Look.' I leant across our table earnestly. 'Henry said he'd fetch something back, right? A day passes. Then a . . . er, a tragedy. See what I mean, Martha? Henry said he was going to fetch something precious back. Well,' I ended lamely, 'maybe he did, see?'

'You mean — ?' Martha faced up bravely.

'You know what I mean, Martha. No need to say it.' We obviously had to go in stages or she'd be shattered. 'Where did Henry go that day?'

'I don't know. He took some money.' She wept a steady minute or so, remembering. 'Henry isn't — wasn't — a very worldly man. I always had a tobacco jar in the living-room with money in it, so he could take whatever he needed. It's empty. He was pleased that day, very quiet. Kept to himself.' Again the slight defiance. 'He prayed a lot. And before midday he went to church. They don't burn candles or anything hereabouts, so he does it in the stables.'

'He *what?*'

Martha fidgeted, obviously wondering if it was disloyal to reveal Henry's foibles. She decided I could take it.

'I was always having to buy candles. He had rather a thing about sanctification, you see. I can't say I quite understood entirely.' She sniffed again while I pondered the rum image of an elderly reject lighting candles in a stable. Some symbolism there, I supposed, if you bothered to look.

'Always in the stables?' I asked shrewdly.

'Not necessarily. The boat, the stables, the garden shed sometimes. On the little wharf, the river bank beneath the big willow trees there, if there were no anglers out.'

'Where would Henry actually *keep* it, though?'

'He only ever brought it once before, that he ever admitted.' She smiled, full of tears. 'About six years ago. Twenty pounds of candles, all in one week. You see, the church . . .'

I nodded. East Anglia's so Low Church you've to be careful blowing your nose in evensong — the merest flash of a white linen hankie's enough to set people worrying that papists are smuggling altarcloths in.

'Those two friends of his?' I asked. 'The ones I met at your house after lunch?'

'Sarah and Thomas?'

'How often did he see them?'

'Very rarely. They never stay, only maybe an hour or so. You know how old college relationships decay.'

'Show me the house?' I asked. She thought a bit, nodded and discreetly paid the bill.

She let me poke about on my own outside.

The stables were a short row of three but now they were connected. Henry or somebody had removed the intersecting walls. It was quite a large roomy building, single windows to each third and those daft half-doors horses like to gaze over, only there were no horses. Sure enough, you could see black smudges and opaque white droplets where his untidy candles had burnt on the sill. He had erected a trestle table for a crude work bench at the far end. I couldn't resist going across, though it seemed an intrusion.

A spindle, hand-drill and a few small saws. A power drill. A good piece of thickish mahogany. A lathe. Underneath a table was a chair, in pieces. I picked up a loose leg, lovely

African mahogany. Though you can't really tell without seeing it entire, it had the feel of a mid-1880 English withdrawing-room chair by a good maker. Its weight puzzled me until I found the plug. 'Whoops. Sorry, Henry.'

I'd intruded further than I wanted to. You fake old furniture by increasing its weight, making vigilant would-be purchasers think they're buying heavy and dense (and very rare) hardwoods. A really skilled faker will drill *down* the interior of a chair leg and insert a beaten lead cylinder, carefully plugging the hole up with filings glued in place by an epoxy resin, or plastic wood stained under a coat of hard polyurethane varnish. It isn't too easy to spot by naked eye alone if it's done really well, but I've never seen a 'reamer', as it's known in the antiques game, you can't detect with a reasonable hand lens.

'You sly old dog, Henry,' I said. He wouldn't want this wicked evidence found after his promise to Martha to go straight. I mentally asked Henry's permission to come up one day when Martha was out. I'd finish it for him. 'No good leaving a job half done, is it?' I asked the bare ceiling innocently.

There was also a drawing. An emigrant miner's brooch. It looked as though Henry was a regular contributor to the world of so-called antiques. These brooches are lovely small solid gold works of art. Cornish miners off to South Africa's gold-fields in late Victorian days made these precious brooches and pendants, often including a South African gold coin of the year in the design. Mostly though it is crossed shovels, picks, lamps, flags and suchlike. Naughty old Henry was obviously intending to fake one. I scanned around, but no gold.

The stable floor was beaten earth. Bare beams in clear view. No signs that one part of the whitewashed wall had been repainted lately. I went on to the cobbled courtyard to see the two loyal yokels duck back behind their kitchen curtains.

The shed was a blank. Hardly anything but garden tools. I meandered about to get the feel of the place. From the workshop bench in the stables you could see the shattered longboat and its huge tethering willow tree. I lit the stump of a candle and put it in a broken plantpot for safety before

heading back in. Martha would be wondering what I was up
to. I was careful to walk all round the house first. It took
some time.

'Did you see everything?' She'd made hot crumpets, for
heaven's sake. I like them but get covered in butter. Everybody else never does.

'Almost.'

'I suppose you have questions to ask, Lovejoy.'

I drew breath. 'There are two sets of stapled wires leading up to one of the windows.'

'That was Henry's idea.'

'An extra phone, aerials?'

'No.' She smiled, embarrassed again, but defiant.
'Henry's hobby was badgers, owls, wildlife. He had night
cameras and bleeps. They used to wake . . . us up.'

'And . . . ?'

'He'd sometimes photograph them.'

'At night? In the dark?'

'Oh yes. From our bedroom window. And night-glasses
by the bedside.'

She showed me Henry's elementary electronic centre
upstairs. One was a commercial warning device, an interrupted ray system. Anyone walking between an issue and
receptor outside activated an alarm by their bed. I'd found
three boxes concealed among low foliage and wires from
them dipping into the ground. The other was a battery-
operated bell for the outside tripwire, crude but good.
Benign old Henry had been pretty vigilant.

'Did Henry set them every night?'

'Without fail.'

I asked to see his books. They were theological, travel,
literary and biography. But who ever heard of a wildlife
enthusiast with no books about wildlife? Outside I walked
to and fro across the garden. Electronic cells were set in the
mortar of the balustrade. You couldn't reach the boat's
mooring without activating the alarm. The tripwire ran
from the river to the house. However you reached the boat
you'd create *some* sort of a racket. I had one crumpet for
the road, and said my thanks.

'Are you any nearer, Lovejoy?'

'Give me time, Martha, and I'll say yes.'

*

Martha gave me a lift back to the village. I waved at the lovable Constable Jilks to brighten his day and got Martha to drop me at the chapel to show the constabulary what posh friends I'd got.

Lydia was walking round the cottage. She jumped a mile when I bowled up.

'Admiring the view?' I joked. I momentarily wished I was in a Lagonda in which I could screech to a stop like Honkworth does in his massive roadster, but caught myself in time. Man's desire to impress a bird has a very bad record.

'Yes,' Lydia said, all misty, gazing at the obnoxious view. 'Isn't it just beautiful?'

'Eh?' I peered. She actually meant it. I cast a glance at the river below, the valley's green shoulder, the woods and fields and a few cows noshing grass. 'Do you mean the viaduct?'

A lovely railway still runs over the river a mile off, though trees obscure full sight of it. There are seven luscious brick arches soaring from the fields so the railway can straddle the obnoxious countryside and passengers need not notice it if they don't want.

'Of course not.' She smiled at me. 'The fields. The farms. How lucky you are.'

'Come inside,' I said, thinking: I've got another nutter here. I always seem to draw the short straw. 'None of that's man-made.'

'But it's still beautiful.'

'How can it be?' I decided to brew up for her. She was the sort who'd admire my domestic skills.

'Because it's alive, and pretty.' She shelled off her coat and was stuck for a place to hang it. I pretended not to notice because I've only one peg and that's snowed under. People should learn not to depend on me so much. 'You can't call a viaduct pretty, can you?'

'Yes.' I got the kettle on. She came into the main room carrying her coat on her arm. She'd brought a bag full of notebooks and learned tomes.

'That's absurd.'

I took her gently by the shoulders and sat her on the

divan, to her alarm. I saw Jean's dire warnings streak into her eyes.

'Listen,' I began savagely, more than a little narked. 'Once upon a time this valley was just as you see it, but without the wires, the bridges, the viaduct, the roads. Then a gang of hard tough men came hauling stones. They scrabbled in the fields and splashed in the water flinging up a beautiful arching roadway from hill to hill. The cholera came and they died in their ramshackle tents by the score. They drowned in the floods and some are still crushed under the landslides of that terrible winter. They froze in the snow and shattered their limbs under massive stones. Their women worked with them, carrying hods of bricks and iron rails. Their children were dosed with nepenthe so they didn't cry from their hunger gripes. They slogged twenty hours a day and died drunk and penniless.' I could see the fear of rape had dwindled. 'Now, love, don't you try telling me that a bit of dirt and a blade of grass is beautiful when there's an old viaduct to look at. If mankind made it there's beauty in every crack. Beauty's not a posh field or a bored cow.'

She said nothing. I let her go and rummaged about for books and catalogues to give her. She went all quiet making the tea. I gave her a summary of reading, starting with Savage on antique forgeries, Crawley on Furniture, Bainbridge on antique glass, J.N. George on short and long handguns, and a collection of catalogues on some famous antique auctions of the past decade.

'Read that lot fast. I want to teach you to buy later on this week.' I rather hurried her after that because I wanted to find out who'd been at Cambridge with old Henry. She said a friend was calling for her at the chapel crossroads and she'd get home all right. I had an idea it was Col. He was sure to be a fine clean-living lad. I watched her down the drive. She gave a half-glance towards the viaduct spanning the river valley.

'So long,' I called after her. She hesitated at the lane as if to wave, but her hand never quite made it. Ah, well.

There was nothing for it. A couple of minutes to lock up and I cranked up the Ruby. It notched a pacy fifteen up the lane. Your friend and mine stepped forward, hand raised, once more to enforce personal prejudice. I pulled in obligingly, smiling.

'Got you, Lovejoy!' George squawked delightedly, hauling out a notebook. Being already chained ostentatiously to a pencil, he was all prepared. I watched the little ceremony with interest. They're teaching absolutely everybody the alphabet these days. Education's wonderful.

'Doing what, Constable?' I asked innocently.

'Driving your car while – ' He paused.

I said, all patience, 'I know you've reported me for drunken driving, George, but my case isn't heard till next week.'

'Get out,' he growled, jerking his thumb to show he meant it.

'If I do, George,' I said gently, 'I'll kick you silly.' We waited. 'Well, George, what's it to be? Me resisting wrongful arrest and you with your leg in traction, or a general return to sweetness and light? Maslow will be very vexed.'

'Maslow?' They go all shifty when you've got them. He'd heard of Maslow, obviously a right bastard to everyone, police and all. It wasn't just me.

'You know him, surely?' I chatted. 'Burly bloke, about middle age, smokes – '

'One day,' our law-abiding constabulary threatened, uttering foul obscenities. 'One day, Lovejoy.'

'Any day, you like, George,' I offered back, 'but remember that I'll leave you seriously in need of an orthopaedic surgeon. Agreed? Mind your piggies.' I'd unlocked the handbrake while passing the time of day and zoomed off with a surge – well, a flick – of power towards the Cambridge road.

War, folks.

CHAPTER XII

East Anglian roads are a rum mixture of corkscrews and rulers. You're bumbling along a stretch running straight as a die over the low Hundreds, whistling and thinking how good it will be to reach the next antiques shop, when suddenly you're fighting to stay on the most macabre switchback roads on earth. The straight stretches we owe to the good old Romans. The crazy bits are legacies from the Ancient Britons or rearrangements carried out by the Early English, undoubtedly history's most forgetful organizers. They had an unenviable habit of losing parts of the Roman roads, or just simply deciding that too much straightness was a drag and that there were prettier views elsewhere. An artistic attitude, but death to sane travel.

My Ruby spluttered thankfully to a stop in Cambridge. We were knackered as each other by the journey. I streaked into the town library for an hour, then strolled to Selward College.

A hoary old philosopher led me through beautiful ancient doorways and across quadrangles to an office containing a choice of luscious bird undulating at one desk and a decrepit ancient crone withering away at another. He deposited me with unerring foresight at the crone. I explained the problem, my poor Uncle Henry dying. I wanted to get his obituary details right.

'Good heavens!' she squeaked. 'We were notified only yesterday! He was one of ours! How very sad! You must be so upset. May we express our sincerest condolences?'

'Er, thank you.'

'Same here,' said the luscious bird from the other desk. She didn't look sincerely condoling at all. She was doing things with a lipstick. I forgot to be downhearted.

'I'll get the records for you.' The crone wheezed off into

the middle distance. I sat on the luscious bird's desk.

'Look, Comrade,' I began. 'Old H.S. was no more my uncle than you.'

'So?' She pretended to be busy typing but I put a stop to all that by taking the paper out.

'So you have a golden opportunity to help me.'

'Cheek.' She wound some new paper in the machine but I could tell she didn't much care what went on it.

'Your reward will be a slender chance of making me, on some future nocturnal occasion,' I said, 'and the benefit of knowing that you've soared in my estimation of you — already very high.'

'Stop looking like that.'

She made a great show of buttoning her twinset.

'Send me a list of old Henry's class.'

'*She's* doing it for you,' she said, jerking her head. Women don't like each other. I've noticed that.

'Ah,' I added. 'I want their full addresses and other personal details, you see.'

'That's not allowed.'

'That's why I came to see you, love.'

She gave me a quizzical glance and typed a line in low spirits. 'What do you want it for?'

I could hardly tell her I was going to report one of the people on her list for complicity in murder.

'It's to do with a will,' I admitted reluctantly. 'The old man was a millionaire. He has these houses and big estates and that. His daughter's being done out of her inheritance by this old woman.' I thought of calling the old woman Mrs Blenkinsop, as that was the name on the crone's desk, but decided it was stretching the story too far. I shrugged, half-disclaiming. 'It's really none of my business, I suppose. But I was . . . well, friendly once with the old man's daughter, though we broke up, and . . . er, and . . . '

'And you still want to help her, don't you?' the little helpful darling finished for me, all misty. 'Despite having parted,' she prattled on, 'you can't let that grasping old bag do her down, and you've come here trying to protect her, though deep down — '

She rambled away adoringly while I looked cut to the quick but noble with it.

'I'll be outside the main gate, if you can do anything, love.'

I had a hard time tearing my eyes from her as the crone creaked back carrying a blue volume. We disengaged hands just in time.

Mrs Blenkinsop confirmed old Henry's dates. I quickly scanned the class photograph and the list of names, all casual. I thanked her, bowed gently towards Joyce's desirable shape and strode nobly from the room. It can be quite pleasant inventing the odd falsehood. The trouble is I start believing the bloody stuff. I was out into the college grounds before I could stop seeing myself as a broken-hearted lover and made my way to a pieshop opposite Selward's main gate.

She was almost an hour and arrived breathlessly, carrying a thick brown envelope. It took another hour prising it off her. Still, it was effort expended in a good cause.

There were maybe sixty names. Haverro was there, and Devonish, but no other I recognized. So Thomas Haverro and Sarah Devonish's late husband had been at Selward College as undergraduates when old Henry studied there. I drove south, angry at myself. I'm always like this when I'm worried sick about something, collecting facts that seem important but usually turn out no use at all. Thomas, Devonish and Henry Swan were old chums, but again so what? I tried to concentrate on the Satsuma-Jimmo problem but that only got me madder.

Some sleuth.

CHAPTER XIII

I rattled home, resisting the temptation to call in at Liz Sandwell's place at Dragonsdale. Every light her shop possessed was on. Gimlet-eyed and stoical, I drove noisily past.

Sooner or later, I'd have to see Liz made an honest man of me, as long as Margaret didn't find out. And Betty. And Lisa. And Jean. And their tough male hangers-on. Thinking what a rotten unfair world it was, I eventually chugged into my garden.

Once you try to put a thing out of your head it only returns with renewed vigour. Ever noticed that? As I hotted my frozen grub and washed up enough crockery to make noshing a respectable enterprise, people's faces kept haunting me.

Sarah Devonish is the sort of woman a man can't help going for. And J.H.C. Devonish was one of the names under the photograph of Henry's class, though I hadn't been able to locate which young smile had been his. Sarah must have been a lot younger than good old J.H.C. Yet for a forlorn widow she seemed particularly belligerent and nastily knowledgeable, which makes a bloke wonder why she'd been the main mouthpiece that day, telling old Henry to shut up and all.

I cleared a couple of square inches of table free of debris to eat on. Hardly worth laying the table just for me. The kettle boiled. I made some evil coffee and sat waiting for the oven to signal that my taste-buds were again about to be tantalized. Thomas seemed utterly benign and apologetic, for all that he was a medical scientist. Well, even that's still legal. The oven clicked but I telephoned Martha to ask about Dolly.

I cut through the chitchat. 'That day Henry and I were er, sloshed, Martha. You said something about Dolly's friends calling for her.'

'Well, yes.' Her voice levelled from the tremulous. 'It *was* rather shameful, Lovejoy — '

'Yeah, yeah. *Which* friends, Martha?'

'The one with the big car. I find them somewhat . . . well, showy isn't too strong a word, is it?' She thought a second. 'He has a funny name.'

Big car, showy, funny name. Couldn't be. 'Honkworth?'

'That's the one. Though he was so kind helping Henry that one often wonders if indeed one is somewhat prejudiced . . . '

'One does,' I agreed. 'Hang on.' I went and put the oven

back on to give myself time to think. The Dolly-Henry chain had suddenly lenghened by a few links it shouldn't have had. 'Er, helped? How?'

'Giving him a lift back from the station,' Martha explained. 'Didn't I tell you? He was so terribly late, and getting a taxi to meet the last train's absolute hell.'

'But you have a car, Martha.' I had a funny feeling even before she said it that I'd missed something terribly obvious.

'Oh yes. But Henry never learned to drive, you see.' Served me right for not checking.

We went round and round this same conversation a couple of times before ringing off because I wanted to drive the main facts into my thick skull. My pasties were practically radioactive from the heat by the time I settled down. Honkworth had not only seen Sarah, Thomas and me at Martha's house, but knew enough to be waiting in his flashy crate when Henry was stuck at the station. And give the old bloke a lift home, the crawler. Now supposing Henry had been carrying something precious, what then? A worm like the revolting Honkworth might be tempted . . .

It was midnight before I locked up and pulled the divan out for a bed. Some problems are better slept on, I told myself piously, wishing Margaret would happen by.

The police disagreed. Maslow rang at four in the morning and told me to get down to the Arcade fast. I never refuse an invitation, so I went.

You can smell malice. The stench of spite pervades the very air you breathe and stings your eyes. It's as horrible as that, something foul and stinking, exactly like the ancient mediaevalists sensed the corruption of evil. I nudged Tinker Dill awake at the High Street. He was already mad because I'd roused him from his drunken stupor and made him come with me.

'Nip down to the post office,' I told him. 'Keep an eye on me, for Christ's sake. If the Old Bill haul me off you know what to do.'

'Bloody four in the bloody morning,' he muttered. One thing, incredible to relate, he looks better in the daylight. He shuffled off into the darkness, merging with the gloom across the way. I parked the Ruby with flamboyant defiance on the main street. Just let Brenda or Jilks give me a ticket, I thought piously. Two police cars were parked by the Arcade, disturbing the peace with radios and blue lights irritating. Half a dozen bobbies stooged about wishing there were cameras on the go.

'Can't you manage without us civilians, Maslow?' Always start as you mean to go on, I thought, watching him pause at hearing my well-loved voice. I got a jolt by noticing that the activity seemed centred on Margaret's place. Lights blazed. They'd rigged up two spotlights to shine through Margaret's window on the antiques, what was left of them. A tired man photographed inside the shop, over and over. Lisa and Woody were there talking to Jimmo and Marion. The bobbies had called out everybody they could think of.

'Not really, Lovejoy.' Maslow gave me a bleak smile. 'We need you.'

'What did you let them do *this* time?' I asked, telling myself not to get talked under.

'You have a chance to shine, Lovejoy.'

'At . . . ?'

He pretended surprise. 'Why, at what you're good at, knowing exactly what went on.' His smile became more aggressive. 'When the rest of us don't know anything of the kind.' He tapped me with his pipe. One day I'll lose my wool and he'll go about left-handed. I can see it coming. 'Take a gander inside, friend.'

Margaret was speaking in a flat undertone to a scribbling constable. A policewoman was having difficulty with a portable tape-recorder whose microphone wouldn't fit. Typical. The place was wrecked.

Porcelain pieces crunched underfoot. Chairs and cabinets had been hacked to splinters. Margaret's collection of dolls were smashed and torn. I choked on fumes.

'Acid, Lovejoy.' Maslow actually sounded pleased. 'On the antique medallions. Ruined.'

The main window was broken, probably done last in case of the noise. A lovely Ince and Mayhew Pembroke table was fragmented. I found myself on my knees trying to fit pieces together.

'No use, Lovejoy. No use at all.' Maslow motioned me outside into the covered way. I gave Margaret a hopeless wave to show I'd stay around and followed.

'Which of these nerks,' I asked, 'was on the beat when it happened, Maslow?' I pointed to the lounging constabulary.

'None. We've withdrawn the beat constable.' He liked the question as much as I liked him. 'He can cover the ground in a car much quicker.'

'And in twice as much ignorance.'

'Look, Lovejoy.' He did the fire trick while I watched hopefully. They say it's bad for the health. 'Until now you and I haven't seen eye to eye.'

'Oh, but we have. You try to push me about. And I tell you to piss off because you're useless.' I could see him struggle for control. A constable within earshot started getting out of his mobile rest-room but Maslow gestured angrily and he retired into the car all hurt at not being allowed to play. 'Maslow,' I said. 'If I emerge with a few broken bones, a certain friendly barker watching eagle-eyed in the shadows will give my Member of Parliament a rude awakening.'

'I'm . . . I'm prepared to admit,' he tried to say evenly, 'we've made very little progress.'

'You checked the boatyard,' I said encouragingly. 'Quite bright.'

'How did you know?'

'I used the clever electric talking machine and asked the foreman.'

'Okay, Lovejoy. A truce.' We thought about it for a while. 'Whatever's going on seems to do with antiques. And you.'

'Not me, mate.'

'Oh yes.' He nodded. 'And you, mate. *Your* friend here gets her place done over. *Your* old pal Reverend Swan gets his boat blown up and goes early to heaven. And busy little Lovejoy's been sniffing around old colleges, hasn't he?' Oho, I thought. Cambridge.

'A casual call,' I said airily. 'My old alma mater.'

'Tomorrow − by which I mean early dawn, lad − you'll call casually on me.'

'Will I?'

'And enter into a partnership with us,' he went on, tough now. The uniformed man was out of the car and stayed out this time. 'You'll disclose all you know or suspect. If not, I'll arrest you by six this evening. Understood?'

'Marvellous man, your inspector,' I said to the constable. 'Useless as the rest of you, but goes after the innocent like a tiger.' I put my head round Margaret's shattered door. 'Coming, love?'

'She's needed here,' Maslow said curtly.

'I'd better stay, Lovejoy,' Margaret called, looking up from a list. Maybe something to do with insurance.

'Okay.' I meandered across to chat to the others. It took about ten minutes of muttered asides to vanish into the darkness with Lisa. The Ruby's oil lamps were still flickering when we reached it. Tinker emerged from the darkness abusing everything.

'What the bleeding hell's going on, Lovejoy? Wotcher, Lisa.'

'They've done Margaret's over.'

'Christ!' His groan was as much criticism of my extra passenger as sorrow at a dealer's plight. 'Did they break them two matching devs?' He meant the small devotional soft porcelain fonts, Continental, eighteenth-century and valuable.

'Yes.' They were the first things I'd noticed.

Lisa was furious.

'Charming,' she snapped. 'Is that all you two can think of, antiques? Neither of you so much as asked about Margaret.'

Tinker rolled his eyes heavenward.

'Er, how's Margaret, Lisa?' he tried courageously, but Lisa was mad and wouldn't reply. 'What about that little Ukrainian ikon?' he asked me in a hoarse undertone.

'Ruined. Some sort of acid. On her medallions, furniture, on the bloody walls.'

'Christ.'

We were finally crammed in somehow and zoomed off down the hill. The pong from Tinker's horrible gear was indescribable. I remembered to stop off and let him out on North Hill.

Which left Lisa and Lovejoy. Well, it's an ill wind and all that.

Lisa is trouble. That doesn't mean I don't like her. You can classify women only two ways: trouble, and very much trouble. The first kind's Lisa and Margaret. They're moderate trouble no matter what. Wherever you are they're in the background being vaguely irritatingly troublesome, like a gentle rain that trickles down your unsuspecting neck. The VMT model's the Betty, Jean Evans and Lydia kind. As soon as you clap eyes on them it's a shouting match and pistols at dawn. The first sort you never get free of and sets up immediately as a sort of chronic niggling part-time pest. The VMT is nonstop Typhoon Emma. Meet one at a vicarage teaparty and you finish up pinned in a corner like a baddie in *Zorro*. It can be very tiresome because you're knackered every single minute of every single day while one's about. I have difficulties with both kinds.

Next morning Lisa made the bed and swept up. She fried things and flung the doors and windows wide, then had us both breathing in time to a broadcast tune some maniac was tinkling on the piano before the eight o'clock news. By the time she'd taken the curtains down to soak I was in the garden, thinking. Lisa came out to bang a rug on my unfinished wall and pollute the lovely smog with dust. For a second I became quite interested.

'I didn't know I had that rug, Lisa.'

'I'm not surprised,' she said curtly, slamming back in. So much for the friendly approach.

The robin came on my arm for its cheese. It listens while I think aloud but has unnecessarily cynical views judging by the glances I get. I ran quickly over recent events starting with my Cambridge run and the vandals doing Margaret's place over.

'But suppose,' I said softly, 'it wasn't a casual mob, eh? Suppose it was done deliberately to get at *me* – I've no antiques, so they do over Margaret's place. Somebody in the antiques game, who knows that she and I were pretty close.' I thought a bit more and told it about the big bad London dealer who wanted his two Neanderthal brats educated. It gave me the bent eye, mistrustful little sod. But I obviously had to visit Sykes and have a brief word. I'd start politely with a gentle request and go on from there. Sykes and his merry men were a hard lot. I knew that. On the other hand, I can be very, very treacherous indeed.

One thing was worrying me. I'd have to call on Margaret. I needed an estimate of the damage the Sykes lads caused, otherwise I'd have no way of balancing up. It's called retribution.

Lisa called, 'Lovejoy, I need some help with this divan.'

'Coming, love,' I said, putting the robin down. I tiptoed away, quickly cranked my minuscule zoomster and rattled out into the lane towards town.

Lydia was already clearing up in the Arcade. She told me Margaret was asleep at home, having had a tiring night. There were barbs in them there undertones. A score of dealers and barkers were assembled to ogle Margaret's misery. They were concealing their heartfelt sorrow so effectively you couldn't tell they weren't actually delighted.

'I go to the Smoke tomorrow,' I informed Lydia. The mess was enough to make you weep. 'You've a job to do for me, love.'

'Very well.' That flinty voice again. She'd fetched a pinafore, dusters and polish, dustpan and a set of brushes.

'Er, sorry.' I'd been staring. She really was a lovely shape. God knows why it seemed to dismay her so much, but she did her utmost to hide it.

'I think you ought to know, Lovejoy,' she said, facing me bravely, 'that I called at your cottage earlier.'

'Er, great.' A significant pause. 'Why didn't you, er, knock and stay for coffee?'

'I could hear . . . two voices.' Lydia's face was scarlet.

'Er, *two* voices? The radio, probably.'

'Not the radio, Lovejoy. Lisa's.'

'*Now* I remember.' I laughed a light airy laugh. 'She'd called with a message from Tinker.'

'I told a *lie* for you, Lovejoy.' She was saving porcelain pieces in a cardboard box.

'Er, well, thanks, love.'

'Don't thank me! I should have done no such thing.'

''Course not, love. Er, what was it incidentally?' I had to ask. Truth can always wait a little, but lies can be very important. She avoided looking at me, busy.

'I advised Woody that Lisa was unable to come to work.'

'Bless you, Lydia.' Good old Lydia. Trust a woman to be devious and full of clever little falsehoods. I tried to show how pleased I was but she was all prim and disapproving and stepped back.

'I realize your . . . dispostion to carnality is not altogether your fault, Lovejoy,' she went on, getting more steamed up, 'but you really must acknowledge − '

The rest is lunacy of the sort only Lydia's ilk can invent, about being less reprehensible and suchlike jazz. I listened as long as I could stay meek and mild, then interrupted when I'd had enough.

'Love, go to Lennie's. A pair of Satsuma vases. He'll have bought them at yesterday's auction. Say we're interested, but tell him the price is too much − '

'How do you know without having seen − ?'

'It's *always* too much, love. Put a few quid deposit.'

'Why?' She was looking at me with that look.

'Well . . . ' I hesitated, exasperated. She was so charming. 'Why not?'

'Because they're cheap and nasty, Lovejoy,' she said with asperity. 'Those . . . the strange gentlemen said so.' She must mean Mel and Sandy, judging from her sudden bright pink face. She pointed to a volume resting on her handbag. 'And that.'

'You've been reading what I wrote!' I said indignantly. She'd got hold of my bloody book, the one I'd written on faults in antique collecting.

'If I'm your pupil − ' she began severely.

I slammed out in a temper. Lydia had the makings, I decided angrily, of a very treacherous woman. Women are never straight. That's their trouble. It's a terrible way to be.

I wanted to find Honkworth. Maybe if I rang Martha and asked where Dolly would be I'd scoop the pool and get Honkie and the slimy Leyde too, but I'd bothered Martha enough.

'How do, Lovejoy,' Woody yelled through the smoke. I

settled at a table, peering about for Tinker Dill. The place isn't big enough to swing a cat but I've never yet managed to see all the way across to the opposite wall.

'Tea, Woody,' I shouted through the hubbub. 'And a fresh table napkin. This one doesn't match your Nantwich lace cloth.'

Jason and Marion laughed. Hello, hello, I thought, where's Jed this sunny dawn?

'Morning, Lovejoy,' Marion said. 'Watch it. Woody's in one hell of a temper. Lisa's off.'

'Tut-tut,' I remarked. 'Nothing too serious, I trust?'

'You seen Lisa, Lovejoy?' Woody belligerently splashed a chipped cup of oily liquid down before me.

'Me? Not since this morning,' as true as I could get. He glowered suspiciously.

'That bird of yours came in full of excuses, and me with my hands full.'

'A thoughtful lassie, Lydia,' I said proudly, paying him.

No sign of Tinker or Honkworth, but in the next few minutes Liz showed up for a quick coffee.

Talk picked up about the week's luck. Finally just as I was losing hope the door creaked open and Tinker tottered in. Remember I said a bit ago that he looked better in daylight? I take it back. He looks horrible in daylight.

He shuffled across and practically fell into a chair. The smog instantly reeked of the habitual drinker's bitter breath.

'Chips, peas, sausages,' the apparition growled. 'And fried bread. Bacon. Fried egg. Tea.'

'Coming,' from Woody, blundering about in the smoke like a fiend from a Teutonic opera.

'You forgot the custard,' I joked. Tinker's bloodshot eyes wobbled.

'Hello, Lovejoy. You got me up at four o'bleeding clock,' he accused.

'I've not forgotten. I owe you. Look, Tinker.' I had to get out before the ghastly plateful arrived. 'Where will I find Honkie?'

'At that old pub, the Bellman, on the canal. His barkers meet him there, and his popsie, the one with the big – '

'Yeah, yeah.' I told him as a parting shot I was going up

to the Smoke street markets in the morning to have a harsh word with Sykes for letting his lads do Margaret's place over.

'You're a goner, Lovejoy.' He shook his head when I grinned. 'You never bleeding well listen.'

I was crossing to the Ruby when Mel and Sandy's multi-coloured motor streaked past, slowing a fraction for Mel to stick his head out of the window.

'Lovejoy, baby!'

I tried to dodge back among the crowd but Sandy braked to halt. Other cars screeched and swerved, a right hullabaloo.

'Did you see we've done the wings mauve and orange?' Mel cried, waving and pointing. 'Don't you just *adore* it?'

'Er, great.' I began to retreat into the Arcade. There's another way out across the pub yard at the back. It leads into the old market place where no dazzling motors may follow.

'About those poxy Satsuma vases,' Mel shrieked. 'Lovejoy! Come back!'

I hadn't time to listen to their fantasies. Lydia had already told me they'd given her the benefit of their advice.

I escaped thankfully past Margaret's wrecked shop. Lydia looked up as I passed. I blew her a demonstrative kiss. She stared at the floor but I definitely saw her hand flick upwards in the slightest shyest wave on record. Well, progress. Almost negligible, but very definitely progress.

Honkworth, Esq., was holding forth in the saloon bar. Note that phrase, please, holding forth. Only people as grotesque as Honkworth can hold forth. Other people have to manage simply with speaking. Bill Leyde's glittering waistcoat had clearly been woven by transalpine virgins among vine groves. The blonde popsie and Dolly were tittering at Honkworth's jollity. A few canal men were knocking pints back and smiling with quiet amusement.

'If it isn't my old pal Lovejoy!' Honkworth boomed. Leyde's piggy eyes took me in while the two birds fell silent in pleased anticipation. Under the glare of all this attention I made the best entrance I could manage.

'Can I have a word, Honkie?'

'For you, Lovejoy — anything! Well — ' he twinkled caution at the assembled multitude — 'almost anything!' Roars of merry laughter followed.

'Come over here, then.' I got a noggin from an intrigued barwoman. 'Sorry about Henry, Dolly.'

'I believe you've been filling Aunt Martha's head with silly ideas,' she said, frozen-faced.

'Your beliefs are beginning to get me down,' I said. She took a swipe at me as I turned. It caught me off balance and I went flying, the glass shattering on the wall. My head was ringing when I rose. The rest were still. I recovered and headed for the fireplace where Honkworth was waiting, hands on hips, belligerently. 'About the Reverend Henry Swan, lately deceased, of this parish, Honkie.'

'Who?' He was glancing from me to Dolly.

'You gave him a lift from the station. The last London train.'

His frown cleared. 'What about it? What's up?'

I was suddenly fed up with all the fencing.

'What did you talk about?' I asked. He stepped back, watching me carefully. 'Tell me now, Honkie, or I'll be cross.'

'He'd been to London.'

'Anywhere else?'

'Cambridge, I think he said.' He was still wary, though now Leyde was at my elbow.

'Did he say why?'

'No.' He thought further, shook his head. 'No.'

'Who'd he seen?'

'Why the hell should he tell me?' he demanded, working up to indignation.

'Was he carrying anything, Honkie?'

'What is this, Lovejoy? Get lost.' He tried to push past but accidentally stumbled and got my knee in his groin. It really was an accident. Honest, hand on my heart. He folded like they do and clutched at a bar table, gasping and whey-faced. It's very painful. Leyde moved in but he accidentally stumbled as well and got my elbow on the bridge of his nose. He fell back with his eyes streaming. Furniture clattered. I dropped a small table on him to keep him occupied.

'Any more for any more?' I asked gently, my back to the fireplace. People said nothing. The canal men weren't looking my way with anything like anger so I hauled Honkie up by his posh cravat. 'I asked you was he carrying anything?'

'A newspaper,' he gasped. I pulled his face close to peer into his eyes. 'Honest to God, Lovejoy. Not a bloody thing.' He seemed truthful and I believed him, the lucky lad.

I let go. He fell against a stool with a crash.

'Of all the – ' The southern indignity brought Dolly forward at a run, thinking perhaps to repeat her lone success of a moment ago. I gave her a clout to shut her up, spun her round and tore from the top of her dress down towards the hem. It split neatly along the zip stitches from the neck to the waist, which only goes to show the sort of rubbish people buy nowadays. You could never do that to a hand-stitched Victorian garment. The ice-bucket was only half-empty but I up-ended it inside her petticoat just the same. I handed the bucket back to the barmaid.

'Ice buckets that are only half full really get me,' I told her amid the shrieks and groans. 'There's no proper service these days.'

My spirits were dampened by Maslow, who rang joyfully the minute I got back to the cottage. Lisa told me he'd tried twice already.

'Who's been assaulting whom, Lovejoy?'

'Go on,' I said. 'Whom?'

'You, lad. I've a summons against you for common assault.'

'I'm delighted you're happy, Maslow.' Good old Honkworth had evidently done his duty. 'Giving pleasure to people's one of the joys in life, isn't it?'

'I gather he was today's suspect, Lovejoy. Well, cross him off.'

'Why?'

'He got a ticket for speeding that night he gave the Reverend Swan a lift.'

'So?' I said, sick to my soul.

'So he's on police records as the last person having been

seen with the deceased alone. No murderer's that dumb, to murder when he's the prime suspect.' He chuckled into my silence. 'If you'd asked, he'd have told you all that. And Reverend Swan spent all that day in the Guildhall Library, quite innocently. See you in the dock, Lovejoy, you stupid sod.'

He banged his end down before I could think of a witty ending. I thought only women could do that.

CHAPTER XIV

The inquest was held in Buresford village hall. Our coroner's a portly little man with fussy mannerisms. Glass partitions rolled back gave the hall a ludicrous gymnasium-like appearance. His secretary kept smiling meaningfully at the doctor giving evidence, but he wasn't having any and did his stuff without a falter. We had the indefatigable Maslow and a few uniformed bobbies, sundry fire officers and a secretary from the local angling club. And Martha and Dolly. And Sarah and Thomas, the latter falling over people's feet and apologizing.

We were called to order as if we threatened anarchy.

'What's that man doing, Officer?' the coroner demanded.

I became conscious of an atrocious yet familiar pong. A filthy mittened hand clutched my shoulder.

'Lovejoy,' Tinker's voice growled in my ear. A report of antique bargains he'd sussed out. 'Three Shunga prints by Utamaro, all showing people shagging like monkeys. Brad has them, for a swap. He'll accept porcelain or flintlocks, cash-jacked. Big Frank's got option on an eighteenth-century marquetry longcase – '

A belligerent bobby started tiptoeing through the throng.

' – clock by Scholtz of Amsterdam, nearly mint. He's asking the frigging earth for it and the whisper is Jenny and

Harry Bateman picked up — '

'Not a witness, sir,' the constable intoned. He had hold of Tinker now but there's no stopping a barker reporting in.

' — a host box, Irish silver, but I can never tell what the bleeding marks mean — '

'Evict that man, Constable.'

' — and an old lead cistern with a coat-of-arms is in Gimbert's auction for next week and a Pugin satinwood parcel-gilt table by Grace and that's about it — '

His voice receded and a door slammed. Sometimes I'm really proud of my friends. Devotion to duty is what makes a genius of Tinker. Whether he stinks to high heaven or gets evicted from every joint on earth makes no difference. Sometimes our shoddy human race warms your heart. I noticed Sarah Devonish trying to conceal her amusement with an elegantly gloved hand. Well, well, I thought, human after all.

'I will remind those in attendance,' the coroner said, 'that this is a court established under the Monarch's direct authority. Anyone creating interruptions will suffer immediate penalties.' You could tell he was peeved, but to me Tinker is an example to us all.

In the end I wasn't called as a witness. Maslow could feel my hate-filled gaze on his fat neck throughout the entire proceedings. I was gratified to see his ears redden. Everybody gave evidence about how good, kind and careless old Henry Swan had been.

The coroner had no alternative. The Reverend Henry Swan went down for all time as a slipshod drunken old bum. The coroner commiserated with the next of kin. The fire services and police were praised.

It was at this point that I found myself pulled at. Some force had me on my feet and people nearby were plucking at my jacket and whispering to sit down.

'Is that gentleman unwell?' the coroner called.

'No, thank you,' I heard my voice say. 'Is that the verdict, then?'

'The court is closed.' he said, puzzled. 'Did you have anything to contribute?'

I stared at Maslow for a long time.

'Not now, sir,' I said. 'Not any more.'

'I quite understand,' the coroner said sympathetically. 'All who knew the deceased are deserving of our condolences at this time.'

Outside cars were starting and people chatted in groups. Sarah was waiting. Thomas Haverro was having a word with Martha over in the school's playground. The scene had every appearance of Thomas clumsily saying the wrong thing and Martha weeping at the goodwill everywhere. I suppose as a doctor he has a collection of useful phrases for occasions like this.

'Good day, Lovejoy,' Sarah said. Well, at least it was better than her usual elbow. 'I gather from your display at the end you're unhappy with the verdict?'

Honkworth's motor breezed in just then. Martha was being given a lift. Dolly took her aunt in hand and was obviously urging Thomas to come along. He gestured at a car, probably his. Bill Leyde the geltie was with Honkworth but the blowsy woman had been left out of today's jaunt, poor thing. Maybe she'd have lowered the tone. The big car thundered off.

'There's something wrong, Sarah,' I searched for the easy words but they didn't improve with waiting.

'What else could it have been but accidental?'

'You tell me.'

Dr Haverro pulled alongside. 'Coming, Sarah?'

'This minute, Thomas?'

'I've to follow Martha back to her place.' He gave an embarrassed laugh. 'Somehow I always get myself into a quandary.'

'I'll give you a lift, Sarah,' I offered suddenly.

'Better come, Sarah,' Thomas said quickly. He opened the passenger door. I felt Maslow's deliberate advance from the right. The coroner's black limousine hissed placidly from the playground and on to the road. A constable saluted the royal coat-of-arms and relaxed as the car dwindled towards the motorway.

Sarah suddenly surprised me. 'No, thanks, Thomas. Maybe I'll come on later.'

'Are you sure?' He too could be determined.

'Yes. Give Martha my love.'

Thomas darted a smile at her, but the flash deep in his

expression was without humour or even hesitation. It got to
me for a split second. I put it down to being on edge. Surely
it couldn't have been a look of warning. How could benign
old Thomas be warning anyone as self-sufficient as Sarah
against innocent old Lovejoy? It didn't make sense. He
smiled, full of understanding, and was out of the way by the
time Maslow hove up. Maybe I'd imagined that gleam.

'Lovejoy.'

'What is it now, Maslow?'

He was very angry. I was glad about that, because I don't
like being angry on my own.

'What the hell did you mean by creating a disturbance?'

'We've an appointment to keep, Inspector.' Sarah linked
my arm. 'Would you excuse us, please?'

She whisked me towards my crate, leaving Maslow sizz-
ling. We hurried off, though the engine took six goes and a
push from two passing farm lads who were on their way to a
football match. They thought the car hilarious and made
jokes.

'Thanks,' I told Sarah. Then, on the principle that it's
safest to own up to what women are going to suss out
anyway, I added, 'I had this odd idea that we weren't
friends.'

'And you are correct, Lovejoy, so far.' She was smiling,
though. 'Hadn't you better explain?'

So I did, practically everything that had happened. Some
parts she guessed even as I spoke. Other bits she couldn't
see until I'd explained them over and over.

'Why are *you* so obsessed, Lovejoy? The antique cup?'

I found myself stumbling for words. 'It's Henry. Whatever it was he had, a ten-year-old kid could have nicked.
Henry couldn't have stopped a bus. Yet they killed him.'

'I see.'

'No, you don't, Sarah.' I pulled the crate to a tipsy stop in
a lay-by. 'He had these daft ideas about . . . about mankind being able to sanctify things. Any bloody thing at all,
just by using it right.' I saw her expression clear with
sudden understanding.

'Like antiques, Lovejoy?' she smiled.

'Well, yes.' Why do I always go on the defensive? I make
me mad sometimes. 'What about it?'

'I see.' She was staring at me full face. 'I do see, Lovejoy. How beautiful. How very beautiful.'

'Eh?' Women make me suspicious when they switch moods like this. I took my hand back from where she'd reached for it. There's no halfway house.

'I mean, so we're fighting for sanctified love?' I didn't like that plural. 'How can I help?'

I thought a minute or two, then decided to trust her. 'Tell me all you know about old Henry and this cup thing.'

'Have you somewhere we can go?'

'Martha's?' I suggested lamely.

'Possibly not,' she said, frowning. 'There are too many people there. Your cottage.'

'Are you sure?'

She fell about laughing. 'Yes I'm sure, Lovejoy. Even without a chaperone.'

When I have somebody like Sarah home I'm always embarrassed. Not that I'm uneasy fetching a woman in. In fact, trying to achieve this occupies a large part of my waking hours. It's just that women of Sarah's class will never complain about the state you've got yourself into, the way somebody like Lisa does, for example. But that only makes the general grubbiness seem worse. And the more you try to cover up, the worse things get. I said to look about if she wanted and started to brew up. She went out into the garden.

'I don't like to do much to it,' I explained to forestall her when I knocked on the window to call her in.

'So I see.' She was smiling again. 'No gardener.'

'Well, it's done nothing to me.' I carried a cup for her. She sank gracefully on the divan without giving it a glance.

'How wise you are, Lovejoy.' She didn't appear sardonic to my brief look. As I went into the alcove for mine I realized she'd caught my eye. 'It's time to make amends.'

'Eh?'

'Come and sit down.' She folded her legs under her. You can't help admiring the way their legs finish up in curves and sleek lines. I did as she said and stared gravely somewhere else. 'I must apologize. When first we met I supposed you were a . . . a chiseller.' She brought it out with a gratified smile.

'No need to apologize.'

'Yes, there is.' She pulled a face after a sip and moaned. 'How absolutely *terrible*.'

'It's the water,' I said defensively. 'They put chemicals in for our bones.'

'I was insufferable.'

'Forget it.'

'I think Thomas would have been kinder to you — if I'd not been so suspicious the day we all met.' She took off her hat and dropped it carelessly aside. I like how they loosen their hair. 'As I see it, Lovejoy, Henry's hitherto useless friends — Thomas, myself, Martha and her unsettled niece Dolly — ought to do what we can to help.'

'How?'

'Let's be practical.' She rose and wandered about the room. 'Your garden's unkempt, and your cottage. But that might be explained by your . . . ' She paused then added, 'Your — shall we say — solitary mode of life.' I knew she'd spotted some of Lisa's things. I thought I'd hidden most of them. 'You can afford a car, of sorts. You are therefore not destitute. On the other hand you are obviously less than affluent, despite your intuitive gift where antiques are concerned.'

'Maslow asked why I don't make a fortune.'

'That's because the man's an imbecile,' Sarah said. She sat down, doing the leg twist thing again, almost as if she hadn't noticed my difficulties when she attracted my attention this way. 'I'll pay you.'

I paused at that. She was smiling.

'An allowance, Lovejoy. Nothing sinister.'

'Antiques?' My mind began to race happily ahead into those meadows of buying and selling where antiques blossom like flowers in springtime, but she was shaking her head.

'While you find what actually happened to Henry.'

'And his Grail?'

'That too. But it comes second, a long way second. Agreed?'

I told her I agreed, though I had no right. Antiques naturally come first every time.

'I'll have my agent send you a weekly sum, payable from now.'

'Er, can I have some on account?' I asked, trying to be off-hand. 'I'm a bit strapped at the minute.'

She laughed and clapped her hands delightedly. This is an unusual response but women are odd.

'And tell me about this thing Henry lit candles for.'

She did, only getting into her stride after she'd rolled in the aisles some more while giving me a week's advance.

Henry Swan, Thomas Haverro and James H.C. Devonish had been undergraduates together at Selward College, Cambridge. Mainly for religious studies of the Established Church, it had tolerated Thomas when he had bumbled his way into the medical faculty across the way. In contrast, James and Henry went straight but only Henry served the Church. Devonish went to become adviser in the prison service and worked gallantly for malcontents till he died in a road accident. Sarah was the result of a chance meeting with an old friend. Though much younger than Devonish, she'd married him and they'd had a few years of happiness together before the accident.

'James told me about the Grail,' she told me reflectively. 'I remember it quite clearly, the odd story, even the words he used. An open, lovely man. But it was only in our last year he explained.'

As undergraduates the trio went on holiday to Berwick. A crumbling old church by the lovely Northumbrian shore captured their romantic imagination and they made quite a thing about trying to have the authorities restore it. Naturally, as with all such brave attempts, they failed. But it was there that they came across the Grail. With romance burning in their youthful souls they decided to adopt it there and then.

The church was obviously derelict. That particular bit of coastline is favoured by curious spells of beautiful pacific weather, dull gold sunshine and skies clear to the planets and back. The seas were clean and dark, the sea stones tumbled sharp in heaps on miles of crisp sands where birds fly flock after flock and distances from each inlet to the horizon seem infinite. I know the whereabouts of the ruined church but couldn't recall having seen it.

'South of Berwick?'

'James described it as a few miles from the Tweed estuary. He said you could see the sandbanks clearly from the churchyard. They used to cycle out and have picnics on the shore.'

An elderly man met up with them one day, the second holiday they took in those parts. He had heard of their attempts to rescue the old church and sought the trio out. He told the youngsters he had the Grail, passed down according to tradition from hand to hand. Listening to Sarah's second-hand account, I had more sense than to ask how it had got from ancient Jerusalem to modern Berwick.

'That's near Holy Island,' I remembered suddenly. 'Lindisfarne.'

This long promontory runs into the ocean from the coast, roughly south-east. At the end is a cluster of houses, a post office and an old monastery. It's where the magic and mysterious Lindisfarne Gospels hail from, those dazzling intricate pages made and embellished by the devout hands of saints themselves. I shifted uncomfortably. All of a sudden silly old drunken Henry seemed less daft.

'This old chap − ?'

'Was the last priest of that particular church.'

'Shouldn't he have given it in? Surrendered it to the local archbishop, something like that?'

'He distrusted the Church. He feared the Grail would be lost, derided − ' She shrugged. 'Henry felt the same. That's the reason James never took a parish.'

In a way I could sympathize with a tired over-stretched bishop, facing his millionth report of the Grail's finding, knowing as he wrote the report it was only the start of another epidemic of identical reports.

'And did this bloke just haul it out of his pocket and hand it over?'

'No. It took a year,' Sarah explained. 'He insisted on having them stay in his house and talk, explain their motives, beliefs. James used to joke about it, said it was worse than his Cambridge Finals.'

The elderly priest showed it them. From Sarah's description they were all chastened, Henry most of all. I suppose, reading between the lines, three young students can't really be blamed for a certain amount of cynicism. Maybe they'd even secretly joked about the mad old parson among themselves, in the same way as I'd thought how cracked Henry was.

'James was partly convinced,' Sarah said. 'Henry was utterly sold. I can imagine it. The very beauty of the idea *is* transfixing, after all.'

'And Thomas?'

'Well, scientist,' Sarah said defensively. It made me look at her. She laughed, embarrassed, for once caught out of her stride. 'He was bound to disbelieve, wasn't he? He went along with the other two, though. Paid his share.' I couldn't help thinking. Sarah and Thomas Haverro . . . ?

'Paid?' My voice must have sounded ugly because she cooled me with a brief chilling stare.

'Nothing like that, Lovejoy. It was a gift. In trust.'

She began to explain.

The cup was merely battered old pewter, 'shallow as an egg-cup', James Devonish had described to Sarah. It had come to light somewhere in the Great Civil War, about 1643. Unaccountably the legend stuck like glue to the little vessel. It apparently seized the religious admiration of the time throughout the district. It became a small focus of local miracles, was even worshipped. Pilgrimages were made. At the Restoration a Mercian prelate threw his conviction behind it and had a tiny silver casket constructed to contain it. The casket was tree-shaped, probably intended as a religious symbolism.

'It was sealed in,' Sarah said. 'You could only see through the crystal trunk. The cup was fixed.'

'Crystal windows, like an old lantern has?'

'Yes. That was how James explained it.' I switched the fire on to give us something to stare at. I was scared of interrupting Sarah's flow of reminiscences. Her face looked quite beautiful, lit by the red glow and smiling wistfully. 'Before then,' she went on, 'it had just been on a tiny gold plinth.'

'And after?'

'Oh, as it was handed on each generation seemed to have added to it.' I said I didn't follow. 'Well, made it more precious,' she said. 'Remember, I never saw it. But the old vicar had a list of the main things that had been done.'

'Are we still talking about a small pewter cup?'

'Why, yes, of course, but I suppose the value of the casket was extremely high.' I cleared my throat and blinked a few times. The fire was drying my eyes. 'Because of the additions, you see.'

I saw all right.

'*Who?*'

'I can't remember all the names James told me. Different jewellers and suchlike, down the ages.' She smiled reflectively. 'Thomas Tucker was one. Another was called Sweet. Those made me laugh.'

'And *they* did some work on the Grail?' My throat felt raw.

'Yes. It must have been beautiful.'

'Do you remember any other names?' Tom Tucker's about 1692. Sweet was one of many West Country silversmiths of that name spanning the period.

'Hester somebody.'

'Bateman?'

'That's it. And Fabergé, of course, in later years.'

I went giddy. She couldn't remember any more, but I'd been told enough.

The idea was almost infallible. Where a 'worthless' object needed to be preserved, impress succeeding generations by decorating it. A wealthy generation would expend enormous wealth on a religious relic, a poor lot much less. But for Hester Bateman, that extraordinary silversmith, to add a mystical silver decoration to the work of the other geniuses like Sweet and Tucker, and for that to culminate with the brilliant Russian designer Fabergé . . .

'He was the last,' Sarah said sadly. 'Before the Great War. The old vicar's father had taken it to St Petersburg.' I thought, Dear God. 'Henry had plans for us to put money together and add at least a token piece of art to the Grail. It came to nothing, though. Such a shame.'

I questioned her back and forth but got nothing more. The original crystal casket had become the trunk. Different workers had added branches, leaves, jewels for fruit. And inside the priceless tree the battered pewter cup which legend said was the Grail itself. It was in a small wooden box for carrying.

'James told me the order in which the various additions were made,' Sarah explained. 'But I can't possibly remember.'

'Jesus!'

We sat and watched the fire. Sarah's the sort that you never see putting lipstick or powder on. We held hands.

'Er, Sarah. You and Thomas . . . ?'

'Well.' That laugh again. 'After James died, Thomas asked me. I refused. We were close at one time. I decided to live alone.' She glanced across the firelight at me, smiling. 'I found the role of a viable widow at least as . . . worthwhile as the wife of a hard-working doctor.'

All my suspects were vanishing one by one. And now the commonplace myth was turned into a sober reality. Sanctification by use, Henry had called the process, I thought bitterly. But his precious Sanctification had taken place at the hands of several artistic geniuses over some three hundred years at least. The motive for sinking Henry's barge was no longer hidden. It was clearly and utterly greed. I felt ill. How bloody typical of our modern day. Absolutely bloody typcial. We can't even be wrong right.

'Are there no more people who might have known?'

'Well . . . no. Not really,' she said, hesitating. 'Thomas never married. I know for a fact James told no one but me. Martha's been the same, very much in the dark and reticent. Although . . . '

'Yes?'

'Well, I often wonder about Thomas's nephew.'

'Does he live locally?'

'Why, yes. Alvin. You know him, though of course he's perfectly trustworthy – '

'*Alvin?*' I suddenly didn't like this at all.

'Alvin Honkworth. An attractive sort, but – '

And Sarah went on to say how pleasant Honkie was . . . Now I had the missing motive, greed. And now maybe the killer as well. And a splitting headache, because didn't Maslow say that Honkie was the one suspect who had a cast-iron police-documented alibi?

As Sarah left we arranged for me to report in on my

progress. She was putting her hat on in the hall when I opened the cottage door. Betty Marsham's smile faded as she saw past me into the light.

'Good evening, Lovejoy.'

'Er, why, hello, Mrs Marsham!' I cried jovially, in an instant panic. 'I'm afraid your Regency floral-painted butler's tray hasn't arrived. Would tomorrow do?'

'Certainly,' Betty said, falling in. 'Would you please telephone me without delay?'

'I will,' I promised, and did a clumsy rotten introduction in the doorway.

Betty took one road at the chapel and I ran Sarah down to the railway station.

'I'm sorry about that, Lovejoy.' Sarah smiled as I dropped her off. 'How terribly disappointed Mrs Marsham was about her Regency serving tray!'

'A serious collector,' I lied casually.

'I could see that,' Sarah said sweetly. 'I'll endeavour to make it up to you. Good night.'

I watched her move into the station. She bought a ticket, had it clipped at the barrier and descended the steps. Still in sight, but without turning to look back, she raised a hand in an elegant slow wave while walking on down. I drove off. With idiots like me about, no wonder women are so confident.

That night I was so full of bitterness I hardly slept. Poor Henry's devotion had missed out, founded as it was on mere holiness. The murderer's love of the mysterious little pewter Grail wasn't holy. It was pure greed. This battle was my kind of war after all.

I finally dozed contentedly. I may not be much good at holiness, but I'm bloody good at greed. It's my subject.

CHAPTER XV

London has nearly as many street markets as it has streets, but the only ones which matter to me are the antique markets. Naturally, London being London and all, some of the most famous 'antique markets' aren't anything of the sort — like Petticoat Lane, which is mostly for new cheap goods. There's another slight difficulty: famous street markets with a name known the world over aren't on the map at all, being called something completely different — also like Petticoat Lane, which is officially Middlesex Street.

In case you ever go, take a tip: ask yourself the all important question, What am I going *for?* It's pretty vital. Supposing for example you are a diehard collector of antique silver or jewellery. Well, you'd turn off Houndsditch into Exchange Buildings Yard near Cutler Street, the world's grimiest, dingiest and most prolific antique silver market, about eight o'clock on a Sunday morning. And a real collector will be there long before that, when most of the deals are done. If you are only after second-hand modern furnishings, say, you'd go to Cheshire Street, also near Petticoat Lane, and romp there to your heart's content. A regular 'trade' dealer in antiques will do better going to Portobello Road — be there at eight-thirty on a Saturday morning to get the real flavour of the world's only antiques scrum. If on the other hand you've got a reliable alarm clock, breeze into the New Caledonian market in darkest Bermondsey, but five o'clock on a wet and windy Friday morning isn't too early because dealing starts long before that. But the 'ordinary' collector (pretending for the moment that there is such a thing) should go to Camden Passage for friendliness and merriment. Go on Saturdays, and arrive mid-mornings like I do, because it has its own nosh bars — all better than Woody's, you'll be astonished to learn. There are plenty of others.

I've left the Belly last. I'll set the scene first. Time: Saturday about six a.m. and Lovejoy rolling up exhausted in his crate after a nightmarish journey through the early London streets wondering if the engine was going to give out from fatigue. Place: Portobello Road, near Ladbroke Grove tube station and already people flocking there. Dealers are always on the site an hour before, but my zoomster wasn't up to it.

By the time I arrived the entire mile-long crush was alive. Seen from the Westway Flyover it looks like a tin of heaving maggots. No antiques market's pretty but they're all beautiful, and the Belly's most beautiful of all. There isn't a dealer who won't sweat blood to help anybody selling or buying. It isn't just a street market, either. Shops, galleries and antique arcades are there as well crammed into the entire glorious stretch, with alleys and crannies bulging with antiques of all periods — and I do mean all. Care is needed, because for every fixed stall or shop you get maybe ten wandering dealers with things to sell. Like I say, careful. A shop-bound dealer is likely to be reachable next morning, but strolling footloose dealers will tend to be very fleet of foot. Sykes is one of these.

I started at the south end because one's thirst is naturally terrible at the finish, when by sheer coincidence one arrives exhausted at the Duke.

Overcoated hard nuts were about, playing the 'casing game'. You do this by ambling, seeming to pay no real attention to anything except your pal's chat about Newmarket yet actually collecting details of valuable items. You decide which antiques dealer has most desirable stuff. Then you simply tell your minions to either (a) do over that particular dealer's home or shop, for the money therein, or (b) steal the main items and hold them for a ransom-price — commonly rumoured to be about a quarter to two-fifths of their retail price. Who pays the ransom, the trader or an insurance company, is largely irrelevant. Circuses have other endearing mannerisms, but 'going on the case' is their commonest trade. It does need a certain number of lackeys however. Sykes has plenty.

I passed a couple of hard lads and dropped word I was cross with Sykie. They knew my name and said he was about, while I went looking for pots.

That delectable puce colour on Derby porcelain is really rare, especially done with inset roses by William Billingsley. You find them with a blue and gilt border, with a landscape in the plate's centre by Boreman. I got an option on one, a perfect 1790 piece, all before I'd gone a hundred yards, though genuine chimes belled all around. I was almost in despair after another hundred. No cash, and a perfect 'banjo' barometer of West Indian satinwood by Broggi of London about 1787 was sounding sweetly across the crowded pavement. On I went, dropping a word about Sykie and sinking into gloom at the beauty all the way up the Road. Real — *genuine!* — Sheraton wine tables, Hepplewhite elbow chairs, Regency silverware to melt your heart, flintlock weapons by the immortal Nock and Manton, Meissen chocolate pots with the original handles, early blue and white of 'Worcester Tonquin Manufacture' — as the original article of June, 1751, termed it — enough apron-fanned serpentine English sideboards to line both pavements, and Islamic and Continental antiques by the boatload.

I was arguing about a piece of Iznik pottery which I craved when the Sykes brothers tapped me on the shoulder.

'Dad wants to see you, Lovejoy.'

'Comrades,' I said over my shoulder, not letting go of the shallow dish, 'you can wait, or we're going to hear the sound of shattered elbows.'

I returned the dish, confident that a responsibility problem will always thwart your stomp-happy Pilt-downer. 'Beautiful,' I told the dealer, and obediently followed the Sykes brothers. They were my rejects from that time at the pub when I'd picked Lydia. We passed out of the main concourse, walking steadily westwards until the hubbub of the market faded. Parked cars lined the roads. I chatted to these boyos about Iznik pottery as we went, quite instructively I thought.

'Can it, Lovejoy,' the elder one said sourly.

'I'm giving you free instruction,' I complained, and went

on doing so until he said, 'We're here, Lovejoy. Shut it.'

He meant my mouth, so I did. We three had come a long way from the Belly. We were under the flyover on one of those sudden desolate spots which modern town planners leave to prove that they too run out of ideas and finally can't be bothered. Sykes was leaning out of his car, casual as you please. No passers-by, no spectators. I noticed with amusement we had gathered three other minions.

'Morning, Lovejoy.'

'Hello, Sykie.'

He glanced behind me at his younger son, all knuckle-dusters. 'Put them bloody things away, you stupid berk.'

'Tell me, Sykie,' I said. 'Why?'

'How the hell do I know what the aggro is?' he asked, giving me a long quizzical glance. He looked honestly puzzled and sounded peeved. 'I thought I was doing you a favour, sending my two lads for teaching the divvie bit. First you sling them out. Then you're here on the Belly smoking cinders.'

'Maybe you got narked,' I said evenly.

''Course I did.' He gazed at the lads so hard I heard them shifting uneasily. 'Turned up dolled like a pair of ponces, I heard.'

'All rings and hair-oil,' I agreed, grinning. 'Quite pretty, really.'

I heard one of them move suddenly forward but he caught his shin on my heel and took a nasty tumble. It was quite accidental. Worse still, his hand got trodden on as I stepped to one side.

'All of you,' Sykes boomed. 'Stop it.' We stopped it. 'You two piss off. Get in, Lovejoy.'

The inside of his motor was like a small dance hall. He asked me where I'd left my car and drove me to the nearest surfaced road. He told me to cough up.

'A friend of mine got her antiques place done over,' I said.

'And you thought of me?' He tut-tutted. 'Bloody fool. I'd have done you over, not your bird.' He was right. He would have. 'And I'd have done it good and proper, not just broken a few pots.' He laughed. 'Hardly worth the journey.'

I should have stopped to think. Or maybe, I wondered, as Sykes swung us into Westbourne Grove, there was a serious flaw in my thinking.

'You can drop me at the end, Sykie,' I said, thanking him for a nice ride. 'I'm talking over an Iznik dish — '

'Not today you're not.' He pointed to my crate, still wheezing from its dawn rush. 'You're heading for the frigging fens, lad. I don't want you walking about unmarked after the way you thumbed around. My name'd be mud.'

'All right.' I slammed his door. He didn't drive away.

'Here, Lovejoy. My lads. Either of them got it?'

I thought a minute about how they'd marched me down a street full of the most beautiful antiques on earth and never glanced yearningly at a single one. I shook my head.

'Cold as a bloody frog, both of them.'

He sighed in weary resignation. 'I'll put them out book-making,' he decided. 'Go safe, Lovejoy.'

'Right, Sykie. And thanks.'

He drove to the intersection but I noticed his car stayed there until I'd reversed and turned towards Marble Arch. By the time I'd reached Brentwood reaction set in. I got out quickly and retched and retched on the grass verge. That'll teach me not to use my nut. I'd never been so terrified in my life.

So it wasn't Sykie. Therefore it was another possible contender. I drove wearily on trying to work out who the other contenders actually were.

Lydia was just leaving as I zoomed up.

'Lovejoy!' she lectured. 'I've waited two hours.'

'Read Lane, A., on *Later Islamic Pottery*,' I said.

'What's the matter? You're white as a sheet.'

'Travel sick,' I said. 'It's the speed.'

She faced me, suspicion emanating from her eyes. 'A child could run faster than that stupid thing.'

'You're beautiful when you're angry. Come in.' The cottage looked untouched, still suspiciously neat from Lisa's tidying. 'Brew up, love.'

'You aren't *organized*, Lovejoy.' She stepped gingerly towards the kitchen alcove.

'Go home,' I said, slumping on the divan. 'Or shut up.'

'What happened today?' She was standing there when I opened my eyes. I'd told her to go home or shut up and she'd done neither. That's typical too.

'I got frightened.' I closed my eyes. 'Don't bite your lip like that or I'll tell your mother.'

'I'm very cross with you, Lovejoy.' I felt her fingers loosen the zip at my throat. 'You need putting in some sort of order.'

'I'm *in* some sort of order,' I told her. You have to stamp on this sort of thing as soon as it raises its treacherous head. 'In fact I'm in a very orderly condition, though to the casual observer – '

'What help do you want?' Her weight sank the divan succulently to a tilt. I honestly believe women make this unsettling approach deliberately. You're expected to notice yet to take no notice, if you know what I mean. It's very subtle. And they're supposed to be moral. I concentrated, safe behind my closed eyelids. Relatively safe, that is.

'A barge blew up, killing a friend of mine.'

'I read about it. Go on.'

'I believe he was murdered.' She got up in the quiet. A tap gushed water. A lid. A click, the switch. The divan tilted. See what I mean, how insidious it all is?

'What had he done? Another woman?'

'No. Maybe for something he had. I don't know.'

'And you need help to . . . ?'

'To search the barge.' There. It was out. I felt clammy and trembling. I'm not scared of heights or depths, or water. And I can swim like a fish. No, honestly. It's just that a deep hull sunk at the bottom of a muddy river's a difficult place to get into, isn't it? And out of. I'm honestly not scared. I told Lydia this about eight times.

'And today?'

I explained my suspicions about Margaret's place and Sykes.

'Yet you were willing to risk thugs – ?'

'Antiques dealers, not thugs.' A silence. Pregnant, as they say.

'You must be very fond of Margaret.'

This too was dangerous ground. Still is.

'Well, compassionate,' I conceded. 'Old acquaintances, mutual help — '

The blessed kettle mercifully did its stuff. The untilt, nearly as seductive as the tilt. The cups, the click, pour, aroma, spoonish tinkle. Seductive tilt again. You have no real defence against it all.

'I dive,' Lydia said.

'So can I.' But that doesn't mean I want to, especially in deep dark waters where an entombed barge lurks in the murky depths.

'Not *into*. Under. Underwater diving. So does Col.'

'Col?'

'You . . . rejected him.' Years of criticism in the verb. 'We belong to the same underwater club.'

'You? And Col?' I sat up, recovering fast.

'Nothing like that.' She was red. I happened to open my eyes. 'We swim at the same place, that's all.'

'You'll search the barge?' I never look a gift horse and all that.

'Any time you want. Col will come with me.'

'An hour?' The untilt.

'I'll phone him.' She happened to have his number, not only a stroke of good fortune but an especailly interesting one.

'He's delighted,' she reported back. 'He'll come round.'

'Check there's no bloody fishing match,' I told her drowsily. 'I don't want you nibbling some hairy angler's bait.'

'You can just stop that sort of talk, Lovejoy,' She said. Her voice sounded smiley. Her shy fingers rubbed my forehead. I never thought fingers could be shy before, but they do funny things to skin. 'What are we to look for?'

'A pewter cup. In a miniature crystal, gold and silver tree. Boxed. Maybe, that is. I'm not really sure.'

'I'll tell Col. He's good in the sub-aqua club. He won last month's prize for . . . '

I dozed, dreaming of a sunken barge with its back broken over a small golden Grail.

Laughter is frighteningly close to terror. Time after time it comes to me that fright and giggling are nearer to each other than they really deserve. I mean, I almost rolled in the aisles seeing Col emerge from his estate car with his aqua gear on — flippers, mask, eyes goggling and a pole thing pointing heavenward from his mouth. And Lydia hauling a few tons of cylinders and tubes. One glance at the water cooled my merry chuckles. It was deep and black. The barge's front poked ominously up, still tied to the balustrade with one short rope but the steel hawser now trailing on to the grass. The rapidity with which Nature gets its own back scares me. The seeping willow was already encouraging long grass to cover the crescent of hawser about the foot of its trunk. The lawn was still muddied but starting to grass the denuded bits. It's the sides of a sunken thing which unnerve me, going down and down.

I looked towards the house on the opposite bank. No sign of visitors or inhabitants. A fairly warm afternoon but no tea on the lawn today. Maybe no tea on the lawn any more.

'Okay, team.' I sat nearby on the pile of stuff. Col sank back into the water with a wave. He wore cylinders and had left the black stick with the pingpong ball.

'I wish you wouldn't ogle me so, Lovejoy,' Lydia reprimanded, fastening her bathing cap. 'Think of Col's signals.'

'I can't even see him. How the hell can I see his signals?'

'You just aren't trying.'

'Anyway, I was only interested in your, er, valves and things.'

'Oh. Really?' She apologized for having misjudged me. I accepted with grace and listened attentively while she told me about air cylinders. Apparently the mouthpiece is sometimes difficult. 'There's Col.' The hull was being tapped. She stepped gracefully into the water and lowered slowly. For a few seconds she swam about the hull then dived. Once I glimpsed her orange cap, then nothing.

The bushes along the river bank had spider's webs shining in the dull sunlight. It's the moisture glistening which gives you the outline. Scientists call it the Tyndall effect, where oblique light allows you to see particles gleaming against an empty background which therefore remains dark. Like the sawn end of the hawser lying over there on Martha's lawn. The weak sun even picked up the severed end around the willow's base. Probably when the firemen cut it they'd had to step back sharpish in case it snapped and flailed across the grass, injuring somebody. What a risky job.

Col and Lydia had been gone a minute, maybe two. I walked about a bit, seeing if any spider's web was perfect enough to preserve. That may seem strange, if you've never seen one in a junk shop. Mostly people don't look when they come across this double square of glass sealed along the margins and possibly varnished. You may have to clean it free of thick brown copal varnish to see that, faintly refractile between the two small glass panes, glistens the outline of a spider's web. I always feel it's rather a gruesome hobby. They are made by waiting until the day's dried out the web thoroughly, and in windless air carefully and *slowly* clapping the web between the glasses. Make certain it's absolutely entire and not eccentrically placed. If it sticks to the glass skewed, give that one up and look elsewhere. You'll never rearrange it in a month of Sundays. For Christ's sake leave the spider to build again. Antique ones are mainly Victorian, about 1840 or so.

I screamed and scrabbled on my bum up the bank like a lunatic because a slimy hand shot out of the swirling water and grasped my ankle. Col was on the wrist end.

'You bloody idiot!' I screeched. My heart was thumping. 'You nearly frightened me to frigging death, you stupid – '

'About how big is this cup, Lovejoy?' He stood there like a weedy Neptune.

'How the hell should I know?' I could still feel my face prickling from fear, the moron.

'What's the matter?' Lydia streamed up beside him.

'Keep on looking,' I said disgustedly. 'I'm going for a country amble.'

I'd told them the general layout of the longboat as far as I could remember, where cupboards were and where Henry and I had sat when tippling that time. Pausing only to rifle Lydia's purse for small change, I hurried down the bank towards the village. It's the little things that worry you, isn't it?

There's a telephone kiosk near the tavern. I rang the fire station. The head man was an age coming to the blower.

'Are you the one who gave evidence at Reverend Swan's inquest?' He said yes, cautiously. 'My name's Lovejoy.'

'I see.' He'd obviously been warned by Bloodhound Maslow, but I'd had enough smarm to last a lifetime and cut in.

'Never mind what Maslow said about me, Chief,' I said in my most pleasant voice. 'Why the hell did you make your firemen saw through the barge's mooring hawser?'

'We released the stern rope only,' he said after a pause.

'And *then* sawed through that great steel hawser?' I heard a rustle of paper. Somebody had got the file out for him.

'It was already fractured when my men arrived.'

'You sure?'

'It's here in the report, Lovejoy. Now, one moment.' His voice went sterile again. 'State the exact purpose of these questions — '

'Ta.' I plonked the receiver down and hurried back along Martha's side of the river. They hadn't looked as carefully as I had. Not fractured. *Sawn.*

Bubbles were still rising in the water around the wreck when I climbed on to Martha's wharf. The hawser was thick enough to have moored a cruiser. An explosion tends to rip and fray the toughest steel 'rope' and blacken it. But a hacksaw cuts through a steel hawser leaving it shiny, with the serrated marks showing clean and gleaming. Now, why cut? Well, a hacksaw's silent.

I walked down to the balustrade and peered down into the river. The longboat's prow was about ten yards off. I kicked the hawser until Col's head emerged.

'I'm over here. On this side.'

He de-goggled, treading water. 'What are you doing over there? You gave the wrong signals.'

'Is Lydia all right?'

'Certainly.'

'Can you look at the front end where this hawser's tied?'

'I think we should finish — '

'No. Right away, Col. Both of you. See if there's a cupboard or a space where something could be hidden at the hawser's join.'

I was thinking, now supposing a longboat was securely

moored and can't move away. Why go to all the trouble of having a huge steel hawser between the bow and a nearby solid tree?

'Hey, Col,' I shouted.

'What?' He was climbing up the sloping deck, steadying himself by holding the gunwale.

'When I kick the hawser, what happens underwater?'

'I get the message you tap out. We use a variety —

'Great. But is it just a vibration or do you actually hear a sound?'

'Both.'

'And if it's a rope that somebody taps?'

'No use, Lovejoy. Ropes dissipate the vibration. We'd not hear anything.'

Metal carries sound. Ropes do not. I stumbled back up the bank, suddenly breathing hard. It had to be *in* the frigging tree. The reason you have a steel hawser wrapped round a tree is to keep safely locked a hollowed-out space in the trunk. And the slightest touch on the hawser quivered vibes into the world's largest sounding-box, Henry's old metal-sided barge. *It was all just one big receiver.*

I streaked over to the weeping willow. The hawser had been round the trunk so long that the bark had begun to grow over the outside of the metal, almost as if it was eating into the living wood. Quite high up, though, which explained why nobody had noticed the faint squared mark on the bark once the hawser was cut free. I scrambled up, clung to a low branch and dug my comb into a crack. A square section of bark fell out on to my face. The hollow had been very crudely dug out, maybe big enough to hold a small dinner plate. Empty.

I replaced the square tidily and signalled to Col and Lydia.

'We haven't finished looking underneath the front,' Lydia called. 'What are you doing to that tree?'

'There'll be nothing there. Dress up and collect me on the bridge.'

I waited a few minutes before Col's estate car drew up. Somebody had cut through the hawser to get Henry's precious Grail, which was hidden in the hollowed space in the tree, protected by the steel binding. Henry had been awakened by the vibes. Martha had said he was a light sleeper, always up and down in the night listening on his wires for animal sounds. A convenient covering hobby for somebody with the Holy Grail stuck in a tree.

So somebody had been sawing away, been caught by Henry. Maybe even been recognized. Henry was injured after a brief struggle or a sudden blow. He'd been lifted into the longboat. Then petrol or oil. A match, and run like hell to where a car was waiting, clutching . . . ? It fitted.

'Look, pals,' I said. 'We know now what we're looking for. We haven't quite obtained it, but I owe you both a favour.'

'What − ?' Col began, but I shut him up.

'Only please don't ask for your favour immediately, unless it's desperate. You're in a queue.'

'How sweet,' Lydia said, smiling.

I wish women wouldn't keep saying that. Col dropped Lydia and me at the cottage. She had a bath while I made some notes on people I'd met recently. Such as Honkworth, Leyde, Dolly, even Martha, Sarah and Thomas. Though sorely tempted, I didn't include Maslow. While Lydia trilled a trendy folk song in the bathroom there was a knock at the door.

'Hello, Lovejoy.' Jean Evans was smiling there. 'I called to make up,' she was saying when her smile froze. We listened attentively to splashes and singing. It was one of the Vaughan Williams adaptations of a Wessex melody, if I remember. Jean had a new book in her hand. It had every appearance of a peacemaking gift. 'I see,' she said witheringly. You can just see a corner of a rumpled divan from the doorway. I'd never realized that before.

I thought I might as well say it, if only for the record. 'I can explain, Jean,' I said.

'Typical!' she blazed. 'Absolutely typical.'

She stalked back to her car and roared off. Gravel in Lovejoy's face again.

'Who was that at the door?' Lydia emerged, wrapped voluminously in my dressing-gown. It's odd how their shape shows through.

'Only the postgirl,' I said. 'Tea?'

CHAPTER XVI

The range of possible murderers was getting smaller. I'd have to be more active. I went to town next day, counting suspects. Tinker said the massive Satsuma vases first arrived via Selly's shop.

Selly's antiques shop lies, symbolically enough, between the Cups tavern and a graveyard. It is remarkable in not being Selly's shop at all. He's the underdog of a team of three dealers but, as is often the case with underdogs, he's the only one that matters. The actual owners are two elegant enterpreneurs called Terence and Christine, who oscillate between Woody's and the Three Cups. The antiques game's full of this sort of person, good company but very low productivity.

'Rumour has it,' I said, putting my head round Selly's door, 'that Christine and Terence once visited here. Correct?'

'Wrong,' Selly answered without raising his head. 'A mirage.'

I've a lot of time for Selly, who's straight out of Dickens. He resembles the elderly benign desk clerk and wears those specs you have to peer over to see anything at all. He's no teeth, bald as a badger on top with tufts of white hair dangling over each ear. I went in and watched him sort a pile of old gloves. Selly always sits at an old-fashioned counter on a tall Victorian stool in bad lighting. I have a shrewd suspicion it's all a set-up, a really quaint scenario of bottle-glass windows, stained oak panelling and unsuspected nooks. What amazes me is that I've never yet called at Selly's shop and found him out, or even off his stool.

'Look at this lot, Lovejoy.'

He never seems to go out buying. His antiques come by a sort of osmosis. Either that or kindly hob fairies leave them by the fireside.

Ever thought how fascinating gloves are? People tend to forget gloves. Look for especially embellished Tudor pairs, but only at reliable auctions. They'll cost the earth. If you get your hands on − or indeed in − an authentic pair you can often locate the original owner from the insignia embroidered on the dorsum. The chances are it will probably be some important historical figure because gloves were a traditional gift to monarchs. Queen Bess got one measly pair for the cold Christmas of 1562 (when nobody needed to take much notice of her) but over two dozen lavishly jewelled pairs on New Year's Day in 1600 (when everybody had to).

This heap of gloves on Selly's counter was lovely. Colours are a reliable guide. Typical nineteenth-century colours are fawns, greens, buffs and creams, depending on what the gloves were for. Good Regency colours are sky blues and rose pinks.

'Any boxes?'

'One.' Selly fetched a paste-cardboard box decorated in panelled green with lacquered shells and lavender-backed lettering: GLOVES.

'Beautiful, Selly.' I let him open it, and held my breath. Sure enough there was a pair of ivory stretchers fastened to the purple satin lining of the lid. Imagine a pair of scissors without finger-holes or sharp blades. 'Flask?'

'Eh?'

That was disappointing, but you can't have everything. Needless to say, even gloves had accessories. You know what the Victorians were like. Button-hooks are the commonest for pearl or decorative buttons, and folding mother-of-pearl-handled button-hooks are especially collected nowadays.

'Sometimes they had a wooden flask with a metal plunger for pushing a sprinkle of powder down the fingers,' I explained.

Mind you, they're pretty rare. I quickly examined the rest of the gloves. Mainly Victorian outdoor ladies' walking gloves, but the boxed pair were a set of slate-coloured four button 'half mourning' short gloves from the London General Mourning Warehouse in 1891. Rare.

'Interested?' Selly asked. Yes, but broke.

'Let me think about it a week or so.'

'A day.' Selly only looks gentle. We're always like this, tugging for time. I nodded miserably and turned as casually as I could manage to what was niggling.

'Still got those Satsuma vases, Selly?'

'No. Sold them to Liz. Now Jimmo has them.' He beamed at me over his re-wired specs. 'Thank heavens.'

'I quite liked them,' I lied easily.

'Balls,' Selly said. 'What are you up to, Lovejoy?'

'Me, Selly? Nothing. See you.' And that was that.

Selly's opinion was the same as mine. The vases were the usual run-of-the-mill second period. He knew himself lucky to have got rid of them. I paused in the Cups for a gill, thinking what an odd old world it was. And it was becoming decidedly odder.

Mel and Sandy had shouted to me about the Satsumas. I realized how stupid I'd been to offend them by ducking back down the Arcade and not listening. Tinker was in the George, taking on fuel for the day.

'Sandy and Mel?' His expression veered into mischief. 'You'll love this.'

'Come on, Tinker. Where?' He gets me mad trying to be witty.

'Having their hair done.'

'Eh? You mean the barber's?'

'Not likely. Women's poxy hairdresser's. Evelyn's.'

'Oh.' I thought a second or two. 'Er, look, Tinker – '

'Sod off, Lovejoy.' He slurped from his glass and wiped his mouth on a stained mitten. 'You won't catch me going in one of them fancy places.'

I looked at him dispassionately. Tinker was right. An elegant ladies' hairdressing emporium just wasn't him. On the other hand it wasn't me, either.

'You're my barker,' I told him indignantly. 'You're supposed to – '

'I'm supposed to ferret the tickles out, Lovejoy, not ponce around – '

People who are in the right really irritate me sometimes. I gave him a bitter mouthful but only left him grinning and cackling into his beer. Friends.

I telephoned Lydia's home and got her mother, she of the elegant shape and frigid glare.

'Lovejoy,' I said. 'Where's Lydia, please?'

'She's upstairs, reading about *old chairs*.' She spat the words out to show whose side she was on.

'Tell her to get down here.'

'Don't you use that — '

'At Evelyn's hairdresser's. Forthwith, or she gets sacked, love. Okay?' I rang off.

I was waiting across the road when Lydia arrived, out of breath and curious. My face was smiling like a fool's when she came scampering along the pavement, dropping things and bumping into people. I hastily changed to a frown. There's no place for fondness in the game. I keep saying that to myself, for all the good it does.

'Why old chairs?' I demanded. 'I said read up Islamic pottery, Staffordshire, and Russian ikons.'

'Well, Lovejoy — ' she was instantly downcast — 'they aren't at all interesting. Not like furniture — '

I looked at her dear spectacled face, marvelling. I'd have to accept she was furniture. Yesterday she'd felt the precious Ming finger jade I'd shown her and asked if it was stone. I'd explained the chemical tests and the different appearances till I was blue in the face. 'Right, love. But do try not to miss an old master painting from ignorance.'

'Very well, Lovejoy.' She looked about. 'Why here?' A smile quirked her mouth. 'Are you going to get your hair done?' Suddenly everybody is a joker.

'Highly humorous,' I snapped, but she stayed smiling. She was less trouble icy. Not so human, but less trouble. 'Go and ask Sandy and Mel — '

'Are they in there?' She was all sudden interest. 'Tell them Percy's is cheaper for a shampoo and set — '

I took her shoulders and shook her to silence.

'Lydia, love. Just ask Sandy — ' I paused wearily. It was too complicated. 'No. Take me in. Just give me the chance of passing a quick word with Sandy.'

'I'll pretend to require an appointment. How exciting!' She pushed on the glass door, still smiling at my discomfiture. 'Stay close to me and you'll come to no harm.'

'Get in.'

It was half-gloom. A pong of chemicals mixed with perfumes stung my nostrils. There was a row of hoods, rather like beehives, with seated women beneath. Huge mirrors lined the walls. Machines hummed and water trickled. A plush carpet bounced underfoot. Acolytes swished about in shapely uniform. It was a right nightmare.

'There.' Lydia indicated a nearby hood. 'I'll talk to the appointments girl,' she whispered, 'but I'll attract his attention first. Is that all right?' She called hello to Sandy as she crossed the carpet. He fluttered his fingers in return.

'Yoo-hoo, Ldyia, sweetiepie!' he carolled. I stood by the door, one foot to another. Lydia pointed to me and Sandy screeched in delight. 'Why, it's Lovejoy, ladies!' he carolled. He couldn't turn his head much in the iron bonnet thing. Maybe it was fixed to his head. It should have covered his mouth.

'Wotcher, Sandy,' I said, embarrassed, shuffling over.

'Don't pay their prices here, Lovejoy! They're *extortionate*, dear! I'm going to Sweaty Bill's. Mel positively swears by him – '

'Shhh, you noisy berk,' I said in an undertone. The women were all smiling, pleased at the diversion. 'Those Satsuma vases. What did you and Mel want to tell me?'

'You *hated* our new silver fringe, Lovejoy,' he said sulkily. 'I could tell. We perspired *blood* doing that car.'

'No. It's great,' I hissed in a desperate undertone. 'Honest. About the vases – '

'Did you really like it?' He smiled at some recollection. 'Mel and I had a *terrible* fight – '

'Terrific, Sandy.' For Christ's sake, I thought. 'The vases – '

'Jimmo took them to Drabhanger.'

'Eh?' The words failed to connect. 'You saw him?'

A girl was sitting on a cushion by his knees doing his fingernails. You know, actually filing them like Nero. Sandy snatched his hand away.

'What are you doing, you silly bitch!' he screeched. 'Just look! She's marmalized my pinkie! Ooooh!' He broke into theatrical sobs. 'Maniacs. Maniacs on all sides.'

'*Please*, Sandy.'

He dropped the hysteria instantly, glancing hard at me.
'Ten per cent?'

'Anything.'

'A poxy slum on the seafront,' Sandy explained. 'Hal's.
Mel had this idea for a lobster-pot chandelier, but I said to
him just think of the *risk* with chiffon curtains – '

'Ta, Sandy.' I'd heard of Hal's.

'Toodle-oo, Lovejoy,' he trilled after me. I escaped and
stood breathing the fresh East Anglian smog with relief.

A hand gently touched my arm. Lydia, smiling, still.

'I'm going to Drabhanger, love,' I told her. 'Knock
around. Suss out whatever you can about Satsuma vases.
Tell Tinker what I said.'

'Where do I see you next?'

I hesitated. Her mother was tapping her foot and
drumming her fingers a few yards away. Lydia saw my
glance and flushed.

'I'm so sorry,' she said lamely. 'I keep telling her . . . '

'Well, the cottage. I've nowhere else.'

I waved to her mother and hurried off. Maybe Lydia's
parent was becoming keen on antiques, but I didn't think
so.

The North Sea coast has strings of small fishing villages.
Drabhanger's small even for one of these. The weather was
deteriorating into steady rain as I filled the Ruby with a
cupful of petrol and headed towards the sea.

Hal Asprey's Antiques Emporium in Drabhanger was
practically on the wharf of the fishing village, sandwiched
between an old church and a bakery. I'd never seen a shop
so small since my own place went bust. There was hardly
anyone about, just a shopper or two bending into the gale.
My old crate looked decidedly worried about its future. I
could swear its oil lamps were swivelled to keep an anxious
eye on the rushing seas. The wharf looked sound enough,
though it was already being engulfed by the biggest of the
waves at the southern end. The sky had lowered considerably since I'd set out. I stood in the worsening weather with
my back to the ugly sea.

'Yes,' Hal called from his doorway. 'The church tower
was used as a lighthouse beacon in the old days. Notice the

additional fenestrations?'

I dated it as maybe AD1100 and asked was that about right.

'Not far out,' he said, beaming. 'Of course the Romans had a beacon light here, but you know what the Saxons were like.' We agreed on the Saxons. 'Come in out of the rain. I'm just brewing up.'

I'd have to watch for the poison-ring bit.

'Thanks. I actually came to see you.'

'You did?' He had a little electric kettle and got busy, sounding pleased. 'Saw my advert in the local rag, eh? Thought there were only three of us read that thing every week. No, leave it open,' he said quickly. I'd shut the door because the wind was driving the rainstorm directly on-shore. The sea was rising in a white-flecked swell. I opened the door and perched miserably on a stool near the counter. Well, it was his Emporium and not mine, but the bloody weather inside was as bad as that outside on the sea wall. I replaced the cast-iron griffon doorstop, 1846 or so.

'Rough old day,' he said, happy as a sandboy while I looked about. He had a cram of Victorian tableware and household items.

'I'm here about those Satsuma vases.'

'That rubbish,' he said derisively, grinning.

'You didn't like them,' I observed.

'Would you? Fastest few quid I ever made, in fact, so I shouldn't complain, I suppose.'

I paused for breath, and it wasn't the gale whistling through on to my back that made my breath funny.

'Insurance?' he guessed, sitting at his counter. 'Mr Jamestown collected the envelope the same day. I didn't get a receipt for it, but it was all right . . . ?'

'Fine, fine,' I reassured him. The poor honest chap — if such he was — seemed so anxious. 'And the vases too, I suppose?'

'Yes. That afternoon.' A man ran by outside and a car's horn sounded in the distance, faintly submerged in the gathering sea roar. Hal Asprey became inattentive. 'It seemed an odd sort of deal, Mr Jamestown coming back for the Satsumas. I'd assumed he was selling them privately.'

'And the envelope arrived here on time?' I had to repeat

the question because he was suddenly on edge. A faint plop sounded in a lull of the whining wind. Something was going on outside. Still, it meant that we weren't all alone on this godforsaken coast. Hal was now restless and peering from the window.

'The envelope?' he said, in some secret fret. 'Oh, through the letter-box by hand, as Mr Jamestown said it would. *Dear God.*' He swung round. 'Have you a car?'

'Eh?'

'*Have you a car?*' he yelled, suddenly leaping the counter and ripping oilskins from behind the door.

'Er, yes, but it'll be hard to start in this. What's up?'

I was scared and on my feet. All hell seemed let loose. Three men ran past outside, one shouting towards us as he ran, but the words were wasted in the gale. A car's horn sounded in short blasts. Hal Asprey had dashed outside into the pouring rain, peering and struggling into his oilskins.

'Mind the place for me,' he yelled.

'But – '

'It's a bloody maroon,' he yelled and leapt into a passing car.

'A what?' I screamed. 'Maroon what? What the hell's – ?'

Another car tore by in a fog of spray, lights glaring. The church bell began a dull tolling as Hal's car vanished up the sea road. I tried asking another running man just as an almighty double crack sounded overhead. It was like the end of the world. A brilliant green glow lit the sky. Everything was tinged madly with a green sheen. Even the rain shone and flashed crazily with the colour in scary streaks.

'The maroon,' the man screeched against my ear, pointing down the coast, the bloody nutcase.

'It's green, you daft sod,' I howled, but he was already running after the cars.

A siren wailed nearby. What with the insane weather, the running people, the bells and the green sky I thought the world had gone mad.

I stood like a spare tool in Hal's doorway, wondering. You could hardly see a hundred yards for the rain and the gloomy sky. The hideous sea and lowering clouds seemed to meet a few yards offshore. Then I heard the distant sudden clanging, and got a glimpse of a faint blue light blipping near the shore. And I knew. The lifeboat. Hal must be one of the village's lifeboat men. I'd once seen our own estuary boat go out, angled crazily under the waves, the black waters lifting and pouring from her, a blue light bleeping on a stick thing above. I felt ill. They collect for new engines every May in our market.

I minded the place, selling a small lustreware jug to one miraculous customer for a good price. I was quite pleased with myself. If only it had been a so-called 'moonlight' lustre of 1805 Wedgwood type I'd have got Hal a small fortune. A tip: dull pink lustres, universally known as 'Sunderland' ware, don't always come from Sunderland. And some of the ones that don't are much more valuable than those that do — Staffordshire, for example.

'Hello.' Hal came in, grinning, two hours later.

I told him I'd just written him a note about the jug and put the money in a tin. He hauled off his wet oilskins.

'You okay?' I asked. He seemed so casual about being a hero.

'Not too bad.' He put his kettle on, dripping water everywhere. 'A Danish freighter on the Fasteners. Sandbanks. We got the crew off but the freighter's a write-off.'

I cleared my throat. 'A write-off? Sunk?'

'It'll stay up another day, then founder. Look,' he said, worried. 'Was that Satsuma trade okay? I mean, there's no insurance claim or anything? They were in perfect condition when I handed them over — '

'It was great,' I told him, rising. 'Exactly what I wanted. There's no fee for your information, but I'll try to put some antique business your way.'

'Who's put new price tickets on all this?' he asked suddenly, seeing his stuff slightly rearranged.

'Me,' I admitted. 'No good throwing money away, is it?'

He looked. 'You're no insurance man,' he said eventually.

'That's true, Hal,' I said. 'Cheers.'

I splashed over to the Ruby and lit the front lanterns with difficulty, using almost a whole box of matches in the devilish wind. All the while I was thinking how very odd of

Mr Jamestown, to bring out his pair of common vases to a dinky trader like Hal stuck on this remote stretch of coast. And receive payment in a big juicy envelope. And then, lo and behold, to collect the same vases he'd already sold.

Hal was still watching when I turned my motor round and came steaming past again towards the road inland. We waved politely, then the village lights faded in the storm's grey wash and I was chugging home. My lonely little cottage would feel like Piccadilly Circus after that lot back there. Mr Jamestown's nickname is Jimmo, who'd lately been fishing and bought a posh new car. In my innocence I sang happily as I drove. All I had to do now was knock hell out of Jimmo till he told me who he'd been blackmailing. I was still wet through and forty miles from my fireside, but in a sense I was home and dry. Within hours I'd do for the bastard who killed poor old Henry Swan. Downhill all the way. Or so I thought.

A note was on the mat, in a pink and slightly aromatic envelope. 'Lovejoy, Esq.' Only one person would give me an Esquire on an envelope. It had to be Lydia. I read the letter, a miracle testifying to decent standards and up-bringing.

> Dear Mr Lovejoy,
>   Mr Dill and I have ascertained that Mr Cask entered the Satsumas for Mr Jamestown in the auction. I think it quite possible that the arrangement was for the former to pay the money to the latter in secrecy.
>   With best wishes, I remain
>   Yours faithfully,
>   Lydia.

I'd never seen so many misters in all my life. Once deciphered, it meant that Jimmo had got Cask to slip the vases into Gimbert's auction anonymously for him. I'd hardly taken my jacket off before the phone was on the go.

'Lovejoy?' No Mister this time, I observed. Something was rankling.

'Thanks for the note, love. You did very well – '

'As instructed, I visited Lennie and that horrid Jessica,'

she told me icily. 'And put a deposit on the Satsumas.'

'Er, now, love,' I temporized.

'Don't now me,' she snapped. 'That horrible old vampire . . . '

'Lydia!' I gasped, quite overcome. 'How *could* you use such language!'

'Well. It was almost as if you and she were . . . party to some sordid agreement.'

I got myself all offended. 'Of course not. Anyway, why are you asking?'

'I'm . . . I'm only expressing a perfectly proper interest in your moral welfare, Lovejoy.'

'Thank you, Lydia,' I said, moved. 'I'll take care.'

'Please do.' We paused and listened. 'Very well,' she said at last. 'Right, then. Good night, Lovejoy.'

'See you, Lydia.' What a lot of pauses, I thought.

CHAPTER XVII

I was waiting outside Jessica's house. I'd knocked but she was probably oiling her face or whatever it is they do.

'Morning, Jessica.'

'This is an honour, Lovejoy. Sorry to take so long.'

I followed the Chinese floral dressing-gown into the living-room. She has this place overlooking the Colne estuary, with farms and ships and that being boring in the wide window.

'Don't you just adore the view?' She arranged her legs in an armchair opposite. She always has a lot of mascara and that green stuff round her enormous black lashes, and thick layers of lipstick. I gazed admiringly at her. Whatever they say about Jessica, she knows how to use cosmetics right.

'Yes.' My voice proved difficult.

'I *thought* you would. Cigarette?'

I shook my head. All this would have to wait till later.

'I've come for the Satsumas.'

'This very minute?'

I nodded. She shrugged, smiling at how the silk gown slipped about her shoulders with the action.

'I do appreciate your . . . gesture, Lovejoy, in this.' She was a long time getting up. 'It helps Lennie so much. Naturally I will settle your charges.' Our eyes still hadn't dawdled on the panoramic view.

'Jessica!' Lennie's drowsy voice murmured. 'Who is it?'

'Lovejoy,' she called back, eyes level on mine still. 'For his vases. Just going.'

'See you, Lennie,' I called.

'Lennie's staying a couple of days,' Jessica explained casually. 'He, er, has a touch of flu and needs looking after.'

'Wish him better,' I said.

We made it to her dining-room where the two Satsumas stood. I hefted them up, one in each arm. The white embossed overlaid outlines on them are so crude, but to keep up the façade I tried to look pleased.

'I'm sure my payments will give you every . . . satisfaction,' Jessica said without batting a single yardlong eyelash.

'I can't wait,' I told her in the doorway.

'Shall I ring to arrange an appointment?' she suggested, blowing a casual smoke-ring.

'Do.'

I stopped on the reservoir bridge to get my breath back and inspect the vases. I felt them, touched and stroked. Same old dross. Ah well. Nothing for it. I'd just have to go down the Arcade and strangle Jimmo to within an inch of his life.

I put the Ruby's engine up the hill at a giddy fifteen. Now that everything was inevitable I felt like singing from relief.

Jimmo's a born failure.

I sent word to Margaret and Brad to be on the look-out for Jimmo. Typically it was Tinker who found him, ringing and saying Jimmo was collecting stuff down at the Arcade.

'Keep him there, Tinker,' I said urgently. 'I'm on my way.'

'How the hell can I?' he quavered, peeved.

'Do as you're told.'

'Oh, Gawd. If you're in one of those, Lovejoy, I want nuffink to do – '

I tore into town. It was as if my old crate could sense the excitement and hurtled eagerly forward clattering and panting like a two-year-old. Even Tinker was surprised to see me so soon. There were very few people about. All but two of the Arcade's shops were shut. I could see the indefatigable Jason hard at it over his catalogues, and Margaret's always the last to leave anyway. Lydia was probably in there going over the year's local furniture sales. An occasional shopper cut through to the car park. The main street was emptying. Lovely. Hardly a witness in sight.

'Wotcher, Lovejoy.' Tinker was relieved to see me walk in. Invention's not his strong suit so he was having a hard time keeping Jimmo there. 'Just telling Jimmo here you're wanting a Sutherland table.'

'Ta.' I gave Tinker a note and the bent eye. He scarpered towards the George, leaving me and Jimmo.

'Could you drop by some other time, Lovejoy?' Jimmo was locking up but I accidentally nudged the key from his hands. I picked it up helpfully.

'Well, since you ask, Jimmo,' I said, smiling, 'no.'

'Eh?'

I went straight through. Jimmo has one of the smallest places in the Arcade, one room and a nook.

'Right heap of dross you got here, Jimmo.' It actually wasn't too bad. There was a perfect Coalbrookdale vase, for instance, but I felt in an offending mood.

'It's not so bad as some.'

'Tell me, Jimmo,' I said gently. 'All of it.' A pause, me smiling. 'About Satsuma vases. Start with them.'

I sometimes think we never really look at people until it's in a battle, and often by then the chance of looking and knowing others as they really are has evaporated. Jimmo's a burly bloke, neater now than ever I remembered him. There was an air of cockiness he had never shown before. I would change all that.

'Your good times are gone, Jimmo. Turned into slush and vanished down the gutters of time.'

'You're bleeding barmy.' The goon was grinning.

'Satsumas,' I said, between him and the door. We'd somehow changed positions.

'Them?' He cackled without an ounce of amusement in it. 'I sold them. I charged too little — '

'You know what I think?' I pushed when he tried to go past.

'I'm in a hurry — '

'I think they're the most crappy, ordinary Satsumas you could ever clap eyes on.' His sulks returned. He now looked the same old Jimmo, miserable and down on his luck, a scrubber through and through.

'Nowt to do with me, Lovejoy.'

'Oh, it is.' I prodded him, not too hard because there was his Sutherland table nearby. With those curved feet they tend to get kicked enough as it is. 'You went fishing on the Stour one dark night. You saw something odd happen on the other bank near the old barge. Like, say, somebody sawing a hawser. And an old bloke coming out and getting done. You put the screws on the murderer, didn't you, Jimmo? To make the handover look legit you said you'd sell him the Satsumas — the biggest, gaudiest things you had. So he's no antiques dealer, is he? To save him having to come here you took them to an out-of-the-way dealer down among the fishing villages. Drabhanger.'

'This is balls, Lovejoy.' He was pale to the gills.

'I had a long talk with Hal.'

'Hal?' He tried to bluster it out. 'He knows sod all.'

'The money came in an envelope, Jimmo. Hal passed it on to you.'

'It's legal, Lovejoy.' He was weighing his chances, glancing more and more at the Arcade outside. Where did he dream he might escape to, for heaven's sake?

'You stupid berk.'

'Stupid?' That stung.

'Why did you go back for the bloody vases?' You can't help wondering at people's mentality. 'Don't bother explaining, Jimmo. You actually began to wonder if they were *really* valuable, right? A kid of ten could tell you the world's kneedeep in Second Satsumas.'

'I didn't want to get robbed.' Sulks now, force five.

'Nobody does, Jimmo.'

'Anyway, there's no evidence. I sold the vases again.'
His unpleasing shifty look was there again. 'Anonymous
buyer, Continental. He's got them and only me knows – '

'No, Jimmo.' Some people are just wrong every time
they open their mouths. 'Me.'

'Eh?'

'Me. I own them, fingerprints and all. Yours. Hal's.
And . . . ?'

His expression cleared into horror as the penny dropped.
'You *bastard!*'

It was a yell, sustained and loud. He lunged at me. I just
had to take it because my bell had been going since I'd
arrived and I saw why the same instant Jimmo moved. The
beautiful Cuban mahogany chair was to my right in a space
near a phoney oak chest. If I hadn't been so worked up I'd
have known instantly. So there I was like a bloody fool
partly stunned by a swinger from Jimmo with my teeth
rattling in my head. A spray of blood sprang from my
mouth as he crashed savagely forward. In the cramped
shop the only way I could hit back would have been to kick
the luscious thing aside or leap up on to it to clobber the
advancing Jimmo. Naturally, retreating all the time, I had
to take three more vicious hooks from the stupid berk
before I was in the space near his open door. My right eye
got the last blow. By then my mind was clouded and he'd
kicked me in the belly but at least we were clear of the
lovely exquisite chair. I surprised him by bringing him
forward. That enabled me to hack his kneecap out of place
and while he screamed and doubled I fetched him one
under his ear. He fell heavily, still swinging. For a second
my heart nearly stopped because his foot flailed out and
almost scraped the ancient mahogany chair leg. Instinctively I stuck my own leg in the way, which brought me
down too. I had to twist to avoid the precious chair. My rib
cracked as I fell awkwardly.

Even as Jimmo kicked at me while we tumbled scrappily
among the furniture I knew it was a memorable piece. Only
the inside of the front legs tapered. Sabre-shaped curves
would have put it about 1810 instead of its true date of 1785.

Wheezing with the chest pain, I got to my knees a second
before Jimmo had managed to kick his damaged leg again.

There was one almighty crack. For a terrible instant I thought it was the chair but it was only Jimmo's bone, thank God.

'Lovejoy!' Women are always critical first and sympathetic eighth. I stepped over Jimmo and picked my way back to the chair, wheezing. Beautiful. 'What's happening?'

'Happened,' I corrected. Lydia was on her knees beside the rumpled Jimmo.

'It's my leg,' he whispered. 'I heard it go.'

'How much for this chair, Jimmo?'

'Lovejoy!' Lydia was up and pulling me round for a lecture, which hurt so much I groaned worse than Jimmo. 'Lovejoy! Have you set upon this poor man? How could you! Why – ?'

'Give you back the Satsumas for it, Jimmo?'

'Are you hurt?' Lydia was looking at me. 'You're a mess.'

'Call an ambulance for Jimmo, love. Go *on*.'

She rushed out after a short hesitation. I stood over Jimmo so he could look up and see if I was serious or jokey.

'Well, Jimmo?'

'For Christ's sake, Lovejoy – '

He screamed because I'd accidentally stood on his leg. It lay turned out in the usual position of a femoral fracture. I thoughtfully turned it inwards in case he'd misunderstood. He screamed again.

'Who was it, Jimmo?' He was sobbing and dribbling saliva. 'Who did you see at the barge that night?'

He finally yelled the name out but it took several seconds to register.

'Honest to God, Lovejoy,' he gasped, trying to palm my heel away from his leg. 'I took his car number from out in the lane. I only saw it again by luck the next day, or I'd not have found him. Please, Lovejoy. Leave me alone.'

'Where's the saw?' I needed evidence badly.

'How the hell should I know.'

'And the thing he took from inside the tree?'

'Some sort of box.' His voice rose again to a wail because I'd turned his foot again. 'For Christ's sake, Lovejoy. I'm frigging dying – '

'You got it?'

'No! No! Honest to God, Lovejoy — '

'Sell your car, Jimmo. And all other possessions you own. Understand?' I lowered his leg carefully. 'Give half to Margaret for her wrecked shop, and half to Hal towards a new boat engine. Understand?'

'Please, Lovejoy — '

He was finally persuaded by the unmistakable logic of my argument. I left him alone, satisfied now.

I examined the lovely chair. Mahogany was a delectable gift — one of many — from the New World to the Old. The most precious mahogany's Cuban. It's a dark, deep and heavy wood which furniture forgers have only recently learned to imitate with anything like accuracy. If you have the moving experience of handling old Cuban mahogany you'll see it doesn't plane into ordinary wood shavings like, say, pine. It *flakes*, as if you were trying to cut a bar of chocolate with a kitchen knife. Unjointed furniture made of Cuban mahogany over three foot widths is rarest. Nowadays original Cuban mahogany is practically impossible to get hold of.

This chair was practically black — the shade Cuban mahogany eventually takes up — but its eminences and edges shone brilliantly with a deep hot-toned russet that must be world's most exquisite colour ever seen on any antique. Sheraton preached that brick-dust in a linseed oil base was the way to get that final finish exactly right, and I won't argue.

Jimmo and I agreed to swap the Satsumas for the lovely antique chair, though he moaned a lot. When Lydia returned I was sitting proudly but gently on the beautiful object. I listed a bit but I'd stopped my face bleeding and made sure my teeth were still in place. My right orbit was bulbous and I couldn't see out of it. You can't have everything. I tell you it was bloody hard work just sitting.

A worried CID youngster came and took down the details — how I'd been strolling by when I'd seen my friend and colleague Jimmo struggling with two evil bandits, their faces hidden by scarves. Brave me, I'd gone to my friend's rescue and been injured. They'd finally taken flight on the arrival of Lydia from next door. He took it all down.

'She's a really game girl,' I praised, giving Jimmo the bent eye.

He glanced from me to Lydia and back again. He began to cerebrate. Slowly, but definitely.

'What is the, er, relationship,' he asked carefully, 'between yourself and this young lady, sir?'

'Apprentice,' I explained. Even the ambulance men paused at that. Jimmo was being put on to the stretcher. The CID man gazed at Lydia, who nodded.

I spelled helpfully, 'A-P-P-R-'

'Thank you, sir.' He wrote and turned to Lydia. 'Can you describe either of these assailants, miss?'

Decisions are funny things. I could feel Lydia's decision struggle with her training until it rose coherent and immutable. She avoided my eye, still full of conscience.

'In a way, Inspector,' she began earnestly. 'The tall one wore an old duffel coat and had brown gloves – '

I shrank back in a sweat of relief. No use phoning Maslow about the killer yet. He'd have us making statements and dithering till the Last Trumpet. I only wanted a bit of justice. And, make no mistake, justice includes reparation, punishment. In my book that doesn't mean two years in clink with ten months off for good behaviour. It means that one of us had to get finished when we met to settle the matter.

I came to with a tired houseman exaining me.

'You're not too bad. We'll sort you out in Casualty,' he said. 'Come with us.'

'No,' Lydia said suddenly, and added uncertainly when the doctor looked, 'if it's all right I'll bring him. We have a car.'

As Lydia drove I watched her face in the early street lights of the encroaching evening. She said nothing and I wasn't up to talking much. Anyway, I was thinking of what to do now I knew. Trust Jimmo. A precious, glowing, delectable antique throbbing and singing in his own back yard, and there's him trying to compete with an educated clever murderer like Dr Thomas Haverro. Don't people get on your nerves?

CHAPTER XVIII

That night Lydia made my divan bed up and went to fetch a hot meal in from town. We had it before the fire, by which time I'd made up my mind. You can't muck about with killers.

'Greed undid it, Lydia.' I told her what Sarah had said about the Grail. 'Only an antique pewter cup. A reputation as a local religious relic. Sarah's husband was loyal to the idea of preserving it by having generations of gold-and-silversmiths add to it. Old Henry protected it, too. Wires to the bedroom and everything.'

'It must have been a terrible temptation,' Lydia said. 'Almost as if it was a genuine Chippendale.' Her eyes glowed with relish.

'Er, quite.' I tried to distract her from furniture. 'Thomas Haverro just couldn't restrain himself. When he realized Henry was consulting a divvie – '

'You.'

' – it was too much. Maybe he worried about Henry selling it on the quiet.' I had to smile ruefully at the very idea of Lovejoy Antiques, Inc. offering enough to get it photographed, let alone buy it.

'Shouldn't you tell that nasty inspector?'

'Yes.' But I'd hesitated too long.

'I suppose that means you're not going to.'

'Yes.'

She slammed the dishes down and marched across to face me. 'Then you're wrong, you stupid man.'

'Am I?' I tried to speak gently, without rancour or anger but only succeeded in sounding tired.

'Have him arrested. They'll put him in prison.'

'For a week or two – '

'Life.' She walked about holding her elbows, the picture

of any woman wanting a serious issue avoided whatever the cost.

'If convicted, Lydia. Any lawyer will make our evidence look fraudulent. And the Grail. Think of that.'

'It won't vanish. It'll still be . . . well, *somewhere* around.'

'In the hands of Dr Thomas Haverro. He'll be out in a couple of years at most, and pick it up from where he's put it. And then?'

'Don't, Lovejoy. Please.'

'I want the Grail Tree off him.'

'Lovejoy.' She sat with me and almost made as if to take my hand for an instant. 'Don't. I know what you want to happen.'

'I don't want to kill anybody,' I said. 'Honest.'

'Then tell Maslow.'

'No.'

It was almost midnight when I phoned Haverro. He sounded as if I'd got him out of bed. I was nervous.

'Lovejoy here.'

'Oh, hello! How – '

'Cut it, Thomas, you bastard.' I let the hatred sink into his ear long enough. 'You killed Henry.'

'Killed – ? Don't be absurd! What an extraordinary – '

'The Satsumas were cover to pay Jimmo, Thomas. To keep him quiet. He saw you.' I added a bit more, about Hal in Drabhanger and the Grail Tree, to show him it was all up.

'A . . . a mad tale you crooked antiques dealers have cooked up, Lovejoy.'

'I knew you'd say that, Thomas. It's not a bad defence.'

'So why ring me?'

'Because I want the Grail Tree.'

A pause. 'I haven't got it.'

'Liar. You want me to call Maslow?'

'Very well,' he said, cool as you please.

'Okay, Thomas.' I was as smooth as him. 'And when Maslow gets a search warrant to see if you've anything hidden anywhere . . . ' We waited some more. 'This is killing my phone bill, Thomas.'

'Tomorrow, then.' He sounded strangled. 'We can leave it till tomorrow.'

'Tinker's already watching your place with three others,' I lied confidently. 'We don't want you sneaking off to hide it, do we?' A long, long think.

'What do you suggest, Lovejoy?'

'Give it to me, Thomas. Sarah told me about it in detail. It's too precious for the likes of you.'

'So Sarah's sided with you. The stupid bitch.'

It took another five minutes, round and round the same sentences. The threat of Tinker's mythical arrival at the nick to tell Maslow finally did it. He agreed.

'Call Tinker off, Lovejoy.'

'No. Just in case.'

He wouldn't dare taking any risks, in case I actually had Tinker's mob scattered in his bushes. I swear I heard his thoughts. Actually heard them, felt their very substance. He would agree to meet me, but it wouldn't be to give me any precious antique. He had a different intention in mind.

'I'll meet you, Lovejoy. Your cottage?'

'Not likely,' I said cockily. 'Too lonely out here, Thomas.'

'Then . . . in town?'

I'd already thought it out ahead of him. 'The Castle Park. Tomorrow. And no funny stuff. I'll have a bird for witness.' I was meeting Lisa there.

'You're off your head, Lovejoy. The fireworks. There'll be thousands there.'

'Not *in* the Castle there won't.'

'Inside? But the attendants — '

'At dusk, Thomas.'

'It'll be shut.'

'Try just the same,' I said cheerfully. 'There's only one way in. Across the old drawbridge to the main keep door.'

'Will it be guarded?'

I sighed with relief. He was beaten and I had him. In the palm of my hand. Him, and the Grail Tree.

'Let's hope, shall we?' I put the receiver down gently. 'Lydia, love. Call a taxi. Go and tell Martha Cookson all about it. That'll be one person less on our side to worry about.'

Needless to say Lydia's mother rang just after Lydia left. I put on my voice to say of course I wouldn't detain Lydia at the cottage on her own so late. I pleased myself by getting in a hint that anyway I preferred slightly older women. Only I said mature, not old. For once we parted friends.

Then, tired as hell, I turned in. It was going to be a hard day in the morning.

CHAPTER XIX

Fire day dawned clear and blue. I sang as I shaved, keyed up and wheezing from my scrap, but confident.

The Castle is not quite a ruin. It's a square, now covered in by a flat roof of ugly tarred concrete and lovely red pantiles capping the four corner towers. To save electricity they've put a central glass roof over the main bit. The stone is flint, like so much Norman building in East Anglia, with a crude mortar welding the stones. The Normans who were the builders of the keep — all that's really left of the original castle — were fairly useless architects. Bishop Odo (a nasty piece of work who got his just deserts at the hands of Rufus) built it on the ruins of the Roman temple to Jupiter and made his builders pinch Roman tiles and bricks for corners and reinforce the walls in clumsy lines. These flashes and columns of deep 'mandarin' red give a warmth and character to what would otherwise be a formidable and excessively grisly keep. It's a museum nowadays, with a main door reached by a fixed wooden bridge from a paved terrace mound constructed as a pleasant walk between rose-gardens and flower-beds. The rest of the ruins — Roman, Norman, practically everybody else you can think of — outcrops like a sea-washed cliff among the grass. Children and pigeons occasionally play there among the stone mounds, which pleases me.

Every year our town has a huge firework festival. Nowa-days we call it a 'gala' day, or seek some local or national jubilee to justify it. Last year it was the Anniversary Fire-work Festival, but after weeks of arguing none of us was quite sure which anniversary we were commemorating. Not that it matters. The point is that, like the rest of Merrie Olde England's festivals, it's entirely pagan and likely to remain so no matter what we pretend.

The Fire Night, as our locals call it, starts with a parade of torches and morris dancers into the plain below the Castle at dusk. There we build a great pile of wood and rubbish. The dancers and marchers as they arrive in turn sling their torches on to the heap, creating a massive bonfire which I've known búrn for three days sometimes. Anybody can make a torch and simply join the procession, which makes a lovely sight winding from across the river or down the slopes to whirl in a slow circle round the bonfire. All this is done to a crescendo of fireworks. By then we're all gathered on the Castle Keep's huge soaring mound, sitting on the grass and watching the exploding colours and gushing fire fountains marvellously reflected in the river's blackness. It's a major spectacle, as you can imagine. I hate to wonder how it all began.

It's more pretty than sinister now, of course. A little illuminated fairground brings roundabouts and catch-a-penny stalls near the bowling greens, which adds to the general gaiety and allows parents to come with the legiti-mate excuse that they're only taking children to the fes-tivities. Needless to say, Fire Night is always crowded. The town turns out *en masse*. Villages empty into Castle Park from as far as the Norfolk borders and the bigger fishing ports. Today they could have it all, from start to finish. I was only interested in one spectator. And he and I would have our own personal fireworks.

I have this system each morning. Up, radio to see who we're at war with, switch it off for sanity, bath, get mad because socks have gone missing again, breakfast from horrible powders and gruesome packets, and cut up some cheese for the robin. He's a tough nut, waiting by my unfinished wall scattering competitors. I feed him on my arm because I'm interested in how he manages to make so much noise. It's a really lovely sound, a thick mellow fluty singing made without effort. I mean, he never seems to breathe in or anything like that. Sounds just keep coming.

'The benign Dr Thomas Haverro,' I explained to his beady eye. 'He'll try to do for me tonight.'

He gave me a tilted stare and bounced up and down my arm to keep a couple of intrusive sparrows off. You never expect their feet to be so cold.

'The question is how. I'm younger than Haverro is, Rob. And fitter. And tougher.' He patrolled my arm, singing. 'He can't bring a howitzer and blow me to blazes, or good old Maslow will come sniffing. So what will he do? There'll be people everywhere. Picnics on the grass. And I've got to get into the Castle before he comes. Easy enough.' I'd done that before, to weigh and do specific gravity tests on various Bronze Age artefacts on the Prehistory Gallery. Our curator had said no, but true love will find a way. 'It's got to be an accident, Rob,' I explained. 'He could push me off a gallery. There's a Roman mosaic in the central area. I wouldn't bounce much. Maybe an old club or a sword from a display case.' But that would be useless. I'd hear him take it out, and then I'd be warned and could arm myself. He was stout, obviously slow. I could make rings round him. 'None of the bows is in working order. No strings in the cross-bows. The flintlocks are all in the barred case and can't be lifted out even if you break the glass.' It seemed just him and me. I said all this to the robin. He seemed un-convinced.

'Anyway, the Grail Tree will be worth it, whatever he has planned.' The point was, I told myself eagerly, he couldn't leave fingerprints or other sorts of evidence that he'd attacked me with some weapon from the display case because Maslow would trace him. Then Haverro would have lost just the same. Guns were out, because you can trace any modern gun by ballistics easy as that. And powder-burns on bodies. And minute flecks of powder on clothes and skin. Every kid who watched television knows these elementary facts.

'Rob.' I interrupted its effortless, windless song. "What weapons do we know which are neither prehistoric, Roman, Early English, Conquest, Renaissance, post-

Elizabethan or modern which will finish me, and let Dr Haverro get away unscathed and unrecognized? Well? Any offers?

He flew on to the grass to do battle with encroaching thrushes. An omen, I thought, pleased. Doing battle with only what he has. Like me and Thomas. A conquest with just ourselves. Still, I was certain I knew every inch of the museum. And Haverro didn't. That was my main asset. But I knew he was going to try to finish me. And I already knew he was capable of trying very, very hard.

Brenda was helping to shuffle the crowds into indescribable disorder when I arrived at the Park about two o'clock. Children ran about hoping to get themselves lost and dramatically re-found. Ice-cream sellers sounded their bells. The town's main streets were one gigantic concourse of people drifting towards the colours and sounds of bands from the show grounds. Teams of morris dancers tinkled to and fro or sprawled on the grass for a quick ale before the great procession.

'Still as big a shambles as ever,' I said.

'I don't want any criticism from you, Lovejoy.' She laughed, not a little distrait.

I paused. She looked attractive even in that grotty traffic warden's outfit. Why they don't pension these uniform designers off I just don't know. It would do us all a favour. 'Is there anything you do want, though?'

'Look. Don't bother me right now.' She waved out a small decorated lorry which was trying to enter the main gates. A jubilant group of dancers cheered and whistled, booing as their vehicle rumbled off down a side street towards North Hill. Brenda looked over her shoulder as I moved on. 'See you at the plinth, soon after dark, Lovejoy,' she said, smiling. 'Maybe.'

'I'll be there, Beautiful,' I said. 'Maybe.' And got away on to the moat walk as she was stung to a half-laughing retort I didn't quite catch. The plinth is on the opposite side of the Castle to the entrance, a small monument where two dubious heroes were executed by Cromwell's men. It's something of a lovers' trysting-place, lying as it does deep in the moated hollow. Her bloke would be around somewhere. I wondered who he was.

The Castle has this system of closing in the afternoon on weekdays. I checked on the wooden notice. There it was, three o'clock close. My heart was banging. I had an hour. I drifted casually into the Castle among a horde of children and their parents. The eagle-eyed museum guardian sits in a small booth placed back from the entrance. He was safely nodding off as usual, which meant my unlikely prepared story about having to go back in at closing time for a lost niece need never be tested.

The main central area was crowded. A Queen Anne coach stands to one side of a massive fireplace you could drive into, and a waxwork tableau had been arranged on the other side. It depicted the visit of Queen Bess to the town and showed how merrily she'd been received at the Castle on the selfsame spot. You have to smile. Not one of the notices mentioned the complaints Bess had made about how the Castle's primitive latrines stank to high heaven.

One of the children had ducked under the restraining rope and was trying to set the Galileo pendulum swinging. He got a cuff for his pains from the old uniformed attendant who creaked after him and returned him squawking to his indignant parents.

'You've no right — ' they started up angrily.

'Yes, he has,' I intervened, pushing among the throng. 'I'm Inspector Maslow, CID. Kindly keep your brat from damaging the exhibits.' I turned grandly to pat the old sweat on the shoulder. 'Well done, my man,' I said. 'Keep it up.' He looked bemused, because he knew I was Lovejoy Antiques, Inc. Wise in the sudden moods of the public, he said nothing but gave me a creaky salute. 'Carry on, Smith,' I said, hoping on statistical grounds the name wasn't far out. He'd remember I was in. With luck, he'd even be able to swear blind I left with all the others when closing time came.

I strolled on upstairs to the Roman Galleries and thought I'd have a look along the Georgian displays. Maybe they'd done something about them since my irate letter of complaint last month. The plan was to follow the main mob at closing time, ambling in stops and starts towards the main door where the attendants gather to check you out. They use a technique so as not to lose anyone. Rather like sheepdogs on the high fells, they move in crescents to and fro round the back of the crowd, sweeping us all towards the funnel which leads to the exit. If anyone shows a tendency to wait at an exhibit one attendant just stays politely by his side until he moves back into the crowd. That way you can't lose anyone, and the entire crowd gets winkled from the honeycomb galleries and poured outside. It's a well tried, almost foolproof system.

But.

There's one serious flaw in it. Think of the sheepdog. The one lamb he loses and has to go back for after lights-out is invariably the one which is too scared to move. For some reason it stays put. Maybe it has a foot trapped or something. Anyhow, it's immobile when it should be on the hoof. So the herd technique only works with those of the herd *who are moving*. Stay still and you're free. Next time you're in an art gallery or museum pay attention when the attendants call 'Time, Ladies and Gentlmen. Please proceed towards the exit!' *All* visitors will at least turn a head, take a step, glance at a watch, look about for a coat or reach for a child's hand prior to making their way. Get it? Movement. It's what the attendants look for. After all, the rest of the things in the museum are pretty well static, aren't they.

The Temple of Jupiter lies under the main area. An entrance, made into a descending spiral staircase of lovely Georgian wrought-iron, is situated to one side of the main area's bookstall. I'd chosen this because it's well-lit, and because most of the foundation arches of the underground temple are visible from the main level. Some five or six dungeons are down there, constructed for William Penn and similar subversives in early Quaker days. I've seen the attendants do their check a hundred times. They switch on all the lights, clatter down the iron staircase, glance along the arches and open the one – first – dungeon door which is unlocked. They lean in, holding the grille-and-stud door, peer about for strays, then come out and step upwards on to the main level. The one who does this stays there until the main door closes. Inference: nobody can get down again unnoticed once the ancient temple has been declared empty. But a cunning Lovejoy can hide behind an arch, casually stockstill so as not to create any moving shadows which could hint at an interloper getting himself left behind for possibly nefarious purposes.

I wandered round the main tier of galleries where the Roman and pre-Roman exhibits were on show. Glass cases lined the ancient walls, and in alcoves Roman funereal statues alternated with cased models of scenes – the wharves, galleys, household interiors, industries, clothes and military displays – constructed by local historical societies. I popped in to see my display of model Roman furniture for old time's sake. That was from the time when I actually made things to give away, which only goes to show how much sense I had. No change to the crummy Civil War section, I noticed in annoyance. The same two heaps of saltpetre and sulphur, the same single unmounted cannon and the dusty armour hanging askew. A breastplate had been added now, lodged unerringly on an old clock movement fixed to a wall. A bloody disgrace. I told an apologetic attendant so, but they haven't a clue and you might as well talk to the wall.

By the time three o'clock was approaching I'd made an estimate of the number of attendants the curator had put on duty this festival day. Eight. I hadn't forgotten to include the old lady at the bookstall, who was doing a roaring trade in reproductions and postcards. There is always a night-time caretaker, but he was lodged in a little office in a large house at the edge of the Park gardens, which the Castle had taken over as an art gallery and additional museum for household items of post-Georgian times. After an hour or so's concealment I reckoned I'd be safe.

The Civil War Gallery is on the second tier. As the Castle Keep is basically rectangular in shape each gallery is identical in area and has more or less the same margins and alcoves as all the rest. Four galleries to each of the two tiers, one gallery to a side. I only wished you couldn't see all the way across the central space. Still, I consoled myself, even Tarzan couldn't leap across a gap that size. I peered over into the central area below. The drop from the square glass ceiling to the floor I guessed was about a hundred feet. Without pacing it out, the galleries seemed maybe half as long again. A staircase split into symmetrical curves runs up to the first tier, too showy but essential for the crowds we get. My mouth was already drying when I noticed the Castle attendants beginning to signal across the space that time was getting on. My big moment.

Apart from the background blare of the distant bands and the murmur of the crowds outside, the chatter in the museum was deafening. That's the best of museums where antiques are placed in their original settings – the atmosphere, the antiques themselves, the customers, everything becomes so much more relaxed. In those brand new mausoleums the antiques know they're entombed for all eternity in unloved glass coffins made without a thought as to what a precious object, lived with for centuries and loved as it deserves, actually needs. It beats me why councils believe that a plate-glass cube glaringly badly lit is exactly right for displaying a Viking shield, a jewelled casket of Saxon design, Victorian spectacles, Georgian enamelled or gold toilet sets, and an array of Queen Anne ladies' shoes. They ought to remember that a glass box may look very swish and modern, but it's the only permanent home a precious antique will ever have once it gets stuck in there for us to gawp at.

The crowd was thinning noticeably as I reached the bookstall and bought a couple of postcards.

'Have you a postcard of Bishop Odo?' I asked Mrs Tyler across the counter. I'd seen the rack empty.

'All gone, Lovejoy,' she apologized. 'You're the third that's asked.' That was no good to me. I needed remembering, not to say remembrance, I thought uneasily.

'Er, then I'll have a reproduction Viking galley, love.'

'I'm so sorry. They've all gone too. We expected some more – '

'Er, then a copy of *History of the Local Bay Industry*, please.' I drove my demand home with a breezy grin.

'I'm out of those, too, dear,' she said helplessly.

'Pull your socks up, cock,' I remonstrated. 'Nil out of three.'

'Well – '

I pulled her leg some more till she was smiling and scolding, then said I'd see her in the car park if her husband wasn't around and melted swiftly back into the drifting tide of humanity certain she would remember my departure. I strolled round the postcard racks until I was near the spiral stairwell. A casual look about told me no attendant was in sight. I crouched down, quite offhand but seeming interested despite myself, to feel the surface of the Mithraic figure in the mosaic by the opening. One more casual glance and without rising I slipped my leg on to the lowest iron stair tread I could reach, drew in the other leg and slowly strolled down the narrow iron staircase with as little speed as my nerves would allow.

The lights in the underground temple were still on, naked bulbs placed every few feet to hang from the arches just above head height. The first dungeon's door was ajar. Nobody around. I trod the sloping sandy floor along the row of sealed dungeon doors, almost giving myself a heart attack when I peered in through the grille of one and came face to face with a wax image of a terrified dummy prisoner stuck at the bars, evidently rotting away in punishment for very little. My cry of alarm echoed along the subterranean vaults. Mercifully there was nobody there.

I'd cut it fine. They were calling closing just as I settled behind the arch's pillar second from the end. The very farthest would have been a mistake. I was near the Mithraic altar at this end. It was cold but I drew myself flat against the upright and checked the ground and walls for revealing shadows cast back to show my silhouette. None.

The calls on the main floor above were becoming more frequent. Families added to the racket. Children were being assembled and last-minute purchases made. Keys rattled as the single wooden bars were locked in place along the sections of each gallery. The attendants' calls and pleadings approached the head of the spiral stairs. If one came down and walked conscientiously along the length of the Temple I was done for. I'd a notebook and a black drawing stick with me just in case. My pose would be of an absent-minded artist drawing the altar if I got found out. Earlier, though from memory, I had drawn a rough sketch, partly completed, to lend more conviction.

'Thank you,' a voice called, too near. 'The museum is closing now.' A boot sounded on the iron stair. Steps and the same call. 'Three o'clock closing, please.' A pause. Scuffling steps on the floor. A door, chains going. My heart lurched again. Please God there wasn't an iron manhole cover or anything to go over the stairwell, was there? I'd be entombed in this bloody place. I almost cried out in fear but held myself back. Surely if there was I'd have noticed it on my way in. I told myself this a few times for encouragement, and was bathed in a sweat of relief when finally the steps receded up the staircase with no further sinister rattlings. I was clear. Still scared, I stayed rigidly behind the pillar until the main Castle door slammed with a dull booming echo overhead. Clear. And safe. A few boot-shod feet clashed on the paving above but my confidence returned. Naturally the attendants would make one last check for stray infants. They'd set alarms at the windows, switch on the central alarm. Then the round of the glass cases. Then lights off in the crypts, the Temple, the dungeons, the alcoves. Then the signatures to say they'd done the security check. Then the bookstall to be locked after signing the ledger. Then the phone call to the caretaker at the distant house.

Then, blissful silence as they departed and locked the main door with an utterly final boom. The echoes hummed and throbbed gently, and silence. I almost yelled with delight. I'd done it. The entire Castle was mine, the entire Keep crammed with precious antiques for which you could only feel reverence. The silence waited all about me, obedient and attentive.

CHAPTER XX

The trouble is there's silence and silence.

For the first couple of hours it was great. True to my original plan, I waited behind the pillar in the semi-gloom until the stiffness in my legs threatened to fix me irrevocably on the spot. My back, bum, knees, even my shoulders were cold. Down in the Temple the temperature was much below normal, a factor I had reckoned with. I'd thoughtfully put on a pullover and some socks Margaret once knitted for me, so I was frozen but movable.

In case I'd misheard the attendant's calls on the main level, when I eventually began to move I did so stealthily, working first one leg up and down, then the other. Arms, knee-bendings, rotations at the hips and touching my toes. I was scared at the coming attempt on my life, but not so stupid I would confront even a geriatric killer when I was stiff in every limb.

Sunshine was streaming obliquely from the windows, quite resembling the interior of a still, kindly cathedral, when I climbed at last from the vaults on to the main central floor. Curious what a sense of power being alone in a building gives you. When that building is a genuine castle's main keep and you are the only person on earth inside, the boost your ego gets is breathtaking. Nobody can come in unless you say so. We tend to forget these elementary but obvious points when reading history. No wonder the knights and their women wanted possession of these places. Once you're in there's no doubt who's boss.

The bands outside were still at it. I could hear the roundabouts and the organs piping away. Crowds were arriving still, pouring past in the late afternoon sunshine. Twice teams of morris men danced jingling by, fiddle and drums going. I danced whatever steps I could remember, skipping and trying to do the foot-waggle along with them, but it's never quite good enough without the bells on your legs and trailing hankies. The Queen Anne coach stopped me dead. The sounds, fife and drums, the delighted screams of the passing children as the team's Fool chased them with his painted bladder, the faint crash-crash of the bells and the cracks of sticks, all receded.

Then I noticed the hubbub was beginning to lessen. It was still considerable. The music, the fairground. It was all there, including the giant deep murmur of the crowd nearby, but not as nearby as all that. The silence inside had changed in character somewhat. Whereas before it was large and friendly, a personal sort of silence very much *belonging* to me, so to speak, now it seemed . . . well, not friendly. A moment ago I coughed gently, to clear my throat after dancing. The silence never went away at all. It stayed there, retired a step back and then shuffled back around me. Still protective. Of course it was still that, but not so much my own personal silence as it had been before. My control of it had gone, been lifted and folded away. Nothing sinister, but a bit disturbing because it went without asking.

After the crowd's all in they close the Castle Park gates so that folk can't wander out into the main street when it's dark and traffic becomes careless. In a way it's a good idea because wandering children can't suffer road accidents this way. I began to wish they weren't so careful. The Castle where I waited is situated close to the Park gates. Maybe, I hoped, they'd left somebody on duty there.

I climbed the stairs to the first, then second tier of galleries. A recess near the riverside corner, once used as a prison for religious offenders, leads to a few steps and a door set in the wall. It was easy to go round switching off all the peripheral alarms because there was a map of them by the bookstall in the porter's glass booth. The central one was just as easy. And by the recess door the key was hanging on a nail. Tut-tutting and shaking my head at their useless security I unlocked the door and stepped out on to the roof.

For some reason this action brought considerable relief. It wasn't that I was really very scared or anything, being alone in the Castle, because that would have been stupid. A grown man isn't that daft or that easily swayed. I'd checked every corner of the place as soon as I'd got going, and unlike the attendants I'd done it properly, inch by inch, until I became certain nobody else was inside but me. I'd even inspected the waxwork figures, palpating their arms and wagging a hand in front of their eyes. They were wax all right. I'd swung round a million times to surprise anybody tiptoeing along behind. Nobody. But the roof was pleasant. Slanting sunshine, birds, crowds below the ramparts and a perfect view to the north where the hills sloped up from the river and houses could be seen clearly — full of lovely normal people. The river plain below was ornamented by imitation decorated castle walls and scaffolding. Tiny figures moved along the pantomime ornaments, probably workmen responsible for the fireworks. They had a tableau for the big finish, as always. I could see the royal coat-of-arms in outline on the poles, and an immense crown and flags.

To one side the fairground glinted. Maybe fifty thousand people on the Castle mount's slope were facing the field. It was a lovely, cheering sight. Every one of them faced away, looking intently down into the plain. Well, they didn't want to stare at an empty castle, did they? And it would all happen down below. Marching regiments, bands, dances and then the bonfire. Fireworks. By contrast nothing was going on inside an old museum, so what's the point looking? I walked round the roof, carefully avoiding the central square, glassed over. The Park gates on the townward side were closed, as I'd suspected. Clinging tightly to the rampart railing, I peered over as far as I dared. Nobody on duty. Brenda had gone, the selfish woman. She could have stayed. Only she didn't know where I was. She'd assumed I was among the rest waiting for the spectacle to begin. Anyway, if any bobby was on duty at the gate he'd gone for a quiet smoke to one side among the trees. This sort of thing makes me bloody angry. I mean to say, no devotion to duty these days.

I went back inside. Stood there, thought a second, then locked the parapet door and replaced the key. How long had I been outside? I never carry a watch because they always stop, so I unlocked the door again and went out to look for the town hall clock. Five-thirty. How long till dark? I'd distinctly told him dusk, and I'd said *in* the Castle Keep. There could be no mistake.

Back inside. What time is dusk, actually? Absolute pitch black is too late for what people can call dusk, and late afternoon like now is too early. Anyhow, I'd told Lisa to see me at dusk as well. She'd be my witness. And I'd said on the drawbridge by the main door. Lisa's the sort who's never late. She'd be on time.

The interior really did seem dark now. It had somehow gathered up a dusk of its own while I'd consoled myself on the roof with the sight of so many thousands of people nearby. My steps echoed slightly, yet with a muffled echo I found distinctly unpleasing. The silence was developing an unnerving solidity I hadn't bargained for. It was just not mine any more. From being in possession I was now a mere visitor. If not an actual intruder. The feeling was hard to shake off.

Keep busy. That's the thing, people always say when you have an attack of nerves. I moved briskly about, putting up with the disturbing muffle my footsteps had developed. Inspection time again. It took me the best part of forty minutes to examine the entire museum again, inch by inch. I switched on the alarm circuits and descended to the Temple, but its vaults were still empty. Nobody doing a Lovejoy behind the arch's pillars. Nobody in the Queen Anne coach. Nobody except wax dummies in the clothes of Bess and her entourage. Nobody in the Egyptian mummy's case there shouldn't have been, and nobody in any of the huge earthenware granary pots lodged in the alcoves along the walls. Humming noisily, I poked the figures themselves to make doubly sure.

To make trebly sure I went downstairs and crossed the main central area to look again into the huge fireplace. Nobody. I peered upwards. The flue ascended, narrowing to about a third of its starting width, to open in the wall near the roof. The light was faint but convincing. When I turned in again the sudden contrast betwen the pale sky's reflected sunset inside the chimney flue and the darkening interior of the museum made me momentarily myopic. I walked back across the central mosaic straight into the Galileo pendulum, almost knocking myself silly. I picked myself up, staggering slightly. My nose was bleeding. No hankie, naturally. I dabbed my nose on my jacket sleeve, cursing inwardly at my stupidity. You'd think I'd have known about the pendulum. It's only been there a couple of centuries. I held the lead weight until it stopped swinging. The less movement the better when some bloke was coming to make an attempt on my life. At last I moved off, wondering what to do next.

Attempt on my life. The words have a final ring to them. Attempt's not so bad, but life is a finite and terribly temporary thing. I sat on the stairs leading to the first

gallery and thought what I would do if I were old Thomas.
Of course he had some advantages over me. A doctor.
Educated. Therefore poison was a natural weapon, I supposed, and you could stretch a point by assuming that you
could make a sinister kind of arrow from syringes. And a
surgeon's instruments start off pretty sharp and lethal. But
somehow all of these seemed unlikely. When the chips
were down and he stole the Grail Tree from old Henry it
had been with a crude and utterly devastating vulgarity. A
saw for the hawser. Petrol for the barge. Physical assault
for poor Henry. That was it. The message seemed to be that
Thomas, faced with the necessity of killing a fellow human
being, spurned anything which hinted of his profession. I
didn't like that word necessity, so tried desirability instead,
which was as bad. Wanting. He *wanted* to kill me. That was
more like it, because I wanted to kill him right back.

So it would be direct. Sudden. I glanced round the
museum. That bloody pendulum was swinging, almost imperceptibly it was true, but definitely swinging. Maybe half
an inch, side to side. I made myself smile. Try to stop it. A
chunk of lead on a string hung from the ceiling's centre will
carry on swinging however small its amplitude. Every small
breath sets it going. School kids are forever chucking toffee
papers at it to move it. Anyway, I had better things to do
than stand holding a plumbline. Count the weapons, for
example.

I set about searching on the first tier. Maybe I was stupid
not bringing at least a bread knife. A Great War French
bayonet would have made me a lot more cheerful, and I
had one of those back in the cottage. Like a fool, I'd been
too confident. Anyhow, I knew what I was up against. No
matter how uneasy I was becoming Thomas was still only
one man, and a lot older than me. And I'd already worked
out how little he could do, how restricted his choice of
weapons was. It would be straighforward. No matter what
mood I talked myself into, I'd have to keep my head and
remember that. Thomas Haverro was only one bloke,
unarmed, like me. We stood at least evens, and I had the
edge because he couldn't come in until he knocked and I let
him in. There was only the one door. I'd checked its one
key on the inside a million times. I switched the mains

electric off so we'd have to fight without lights. Better for Haverro to come into darkness from the lighter outside than to arrive in electric glare. I wasn't scared of him, but I was going to make sure any advantages going spare came to me.

The sun was slanted lower now, and fading. Across the central area the shadow of the Galileo pendulum had moved from the far corner, crept imperceptibly along the wall, and now was fading with the shadows by the staircase. Soon it would be gone. Anyhow, even without an electric torch there would be light from the big bonfire to illumine the night air. And fireworks. And the Park gates were surmounted by large spherical lamps, so there would be a background glow. And however keen Haverro was on the museum and its lovely antiques, I was damned sure he couldn't know it anything like as well as I. After all, ever since I'd come to live in the area I had been in two or three times a week. I've helped with the ancient coins, Celtic finds, tableaux, and paid several visits to guide the curator's special exhibitions of weapons because he's not strong in that speciality. And a doctor doesn't have all that much recreation, so I would be fitter. Every way you looked at it, I had a head start.

The Roman weapons were virtually crumbling. Best preserved were arrowheads and the blades from spears. Other than those there wasn't much, apart from a pair of hefty models of Roman siege implements, and I couldn't even lift the stones placed to show the size of the missiles used in the real thing. Good news, therefore. If I couldn't lift the bloody things, neither could Thomas.

Along on the other gallery were household items, pottery, querns used to grind wheat, even surgical instruments. Again, it seemed to me you were either tough enough to lift them and chuck them at an adversary or you fought barehanded. And the probes, scissors and lancets of the long-dead Roman doctor were too small and neat to be much use. For quite a while I tried working out whether any of them could be stuck into a stick as an arrow, or put into a blowpipe, but gave it up. There wasn't a usable bow in the museum, and the crossbows were too fragile on the cross to use without putting your own eye out, though their stocks were fine. The spear held by the Roman waxwork in the gallery's corner was, I knew, balsawood and easily snapped by a finger.

The Egyptian lot were useless. Two spears from the Ancient British were solid enough — firm and nasty sharp flints knapped in Suffolk by ancient hands in the prehistoric Grimes Graves. These two were set in roughly-hewn modern ash staves and looked pretty menacing, though they were drilled in the shaft and held in the case by a slender chain. I cheered up again. I'd hear the glass break, and while Thomas struggled to break the chain and get the spears out . . . The clubs were under lock and key, and the glass looked tougher than was used to make the rest of the cases. Good news again.

On the ground floor a few waxworks, the coach, sundry small cased models. Nothing. The Civil War Gallery was worth another visit, maybe. As I trudged upstairs to the second tier I began wishing I'd had the wit to come properly equipped. Sandals, or strong non-slip slippers to pad about unheard. That's what I needed. And, I realized, pausing at the top of the second flight, an electric torch. If the doctor brought one I'd be less well off by a hell of a long chalk. For some reason I was becoming uneasy, more so as the minutes ticked on. Had I forgotten something? I set off along the gallery, glancing down towards the main door, in case. But in case what? The swine would have to knock, and do as I said before I'd let him in. I could even search him at the door.

For a brief second I stopped to stare. I could no longer see the door. It was hidden in shadow. I peered across and failed to make out the shadow of the plumbline. That too was merged with the shadows on the far wall. And the shadows were shadows no longer. The whole museum was now not a pattern of sunshine and shadows. It was submerged in gloom. One faint gleam lit the glass ceiling, but even as I looked at it the shine died and the interior chilled further. The day had emptied from the Castle.

Come *on*, Lovejoy, I told myself. Dogs shake themselves, so I shook as best I could like I'd seen terriers do coming out of the Blackwater on the sands. It did me good, for a second. At least it got me moving again.

If you examine a museum there isn't a great deal of weaponry usable any more. Suits of armour: valuable in money but useless because a bullet or arrow can pierce almost any antique armour that can be worn. Shields: ditto. Swords: well, a couple of Civil War swords were in good nick − one an Ironside's Cromwellian basket sword, the other, with fine impartiality, a Cavalier's crosshilted heavy sword taken at Marston Moor. Both were open for inspection but chained, mercifully. There were three or four flintlock pistols but none had a flint in, so even if they were in working order they'd be useless and couldn't be fired. The cannon looked in good order, but of this date, 1645, they were still merely thick iron tubes without shells and working firing parts so I could rule it out. The local historians had obtained some cannon balls, probably wooden casts. Cromwell had to resort to round stones as often as not to keep going. I felt safer still.

Along the now dark furniture section of Gallery Six was my notorious piece. No weapons there. That left me back at the recess which led to the roof door, and now I was in accelerating gloom. In fact you really had to start thinking of it as dusk, if not actual darkness.

A bang startled me. A series of pops sounded overhead. The fireworks had begun. Successive whirrs and fizzes created light for me now. Cheers came in wafts, probably the breeze from the estuary carrying the sounds towards the town. A faint glow was established constantly as a kind of background. The processions were starting. There was my light, so I was back with all my advantages again. My heart was bumping and I could feel an ugly dampness trying hard to cool my forehead. Still, up here I could dimly see most of the central area as far as the fireplace and at least across to the opposite gallery, admittedly in outline. Well, better than nothing. And if I couldn't see the details of the main door I could make out the faint black limits of the entrance porchway leading into the museum's centre.

Red glows succeeded blues. Whites and greens and yellows came and faded. It was wiser to stay inside, I decided. Thomas might try to struggle if he somehow got to the roof. And it was a long way down to the dry stony spaces which once were the Castle's moats.

One thing was worrying me sick. *Why* was I cringing in a recess in a second-tier gallery, when the only way in Thomas possibly had was that single main doorway down below on the ground floor? Why was I so scared? I'd crouched down, stupidly believing that would help. Come on, Lovejoy, I lectured myself firmly. You are alone here. Be quiet, okay, but behave resolutely and with delibera- tion. I forced myself erect and, with the next swish of coloured glow from the ceiling, nonchalantly read the emergency notices hanging on a threaded card on the back of the roof door.

And there, in a wash of violet light crackling above me, I read the name Dr Thomas Haverro, MD. It puzzled me at first, like a simple arithmetic sum written down obviously wrong which you can't immediately decipher. With lunatic patience I waited for the next skyburst. It was a cluster of vivid screaming gold snakes exploded from a rocket salvo. The name was still there, on curling paper, among many others on a list. 'Contact in the event of an emergency,' it said in typed capitals. Still I stood there. Dr Thomas Haverro. It was his name and address all right. So what? So he was the doctor on call for the museum, for anybody taken suddenly ill. And a doctor needs access.

Like a key?

Suddenly I was prickling and sweating clammily down in the balcony recess. *The bastard could get in.* Last night I'd been too confident. Sure of myself, I'd agreed with his suggestion of the Castle. I had talked myself into believing it was my idea, whereas he had gently and cleverly nudged me into agreement. The bastard *meant* us to finish up here alone. He'd known I would come innocently to the slaughter. And as soon as dusk fell he would let himself in with his pass key. Of *course* there were other keys. Now it was too late I realized the obvious — no attendant leaving a museum *could* lock the door from the inside and leave himself outside to go home, could he? And I'd not realized the significance of that single key behind the main door. If it had been the only key, then how the hell could the attendants get back in tomorrow morning? Stupid, stupid sod. I moaned to myself and crouched lower, face tight with sudden fear.

Haverro could let himself in. *Had?* Already? I tried swallowing. Whatever state I'd landed myself in, I had to use my loaf. If he was here he'd come armed in some way. His cleverness in persuading me into this mess told me he wouldn't know if I would be armed or not, so he'd have to go carefully at first. That is until he realized. Then he'd walk up to me and . . . I tried swallowing again, failed again. Too dry.

And from now on I'd act as if he were here. Inside. With me. My legs were quivering uncomfortably in the confined space of the recess. At least the swine couldn't come through the roof door, could he? Not without a hang-glider or a lunar capsule. So he was inside, having come through the main entrance. I smeared my hair down over my forehead and peered over the ledge towards where the door was on the ground floor. The next bang lit the skies red and gold. No red glare from outside through the arched gloom down below. Therefore he had locked the door behind him. And, careful as ever, he would have taken the resident key for good measure. He wasn't the sort to forget details like that. It was only the accidental presence of Jimmo, silently fishing in the dark of a river bank, that had caught him out before.

Ducking back, movement caught my eye. I froze, frightened to ice and unable to breathe. The next glare was green, coming downwards in hideous washes which made gargoyles of every object down the long galleries. It was the pendulum, swinging gently. Well, I'd started that. My nose still throbbed. But hadn't I guessed its movement after stilling it to be minute, maybe less than an inch? Now it swung several gentle inches from the vertical, slowly to and fro. Somebody had moved it. A solid figure had brushed against the lead weight, gently nudging it into action. Somebody *else*, in here. Sweat trickled on my face.

I could get out on to the roof through the doorway behind me, maybe shout for help. But the distant bands, the morris music, the crowds' oohs and aahs at the fireworks and the fairground were creating a constant row. Who would hear me? Brenda *might* be immediately below, waiting for a quick snog by the martyrs' plinth. Immediately below. But Haverro would see the pale rectangle of the opened door. He'd been sickeningly confident so far. He wouldn't chuck it all away now.

My one hope was to get out or get help. My heart jumped suddenly. Lisa! She'd be waiting outside the main door this very second! Lisa! I stood up, practically lifted by elation, into the bathing light of a rocket salvo exploding white and gold directly above the glass roof.

'Lovejoy!'

A gun shot cracked below. Stone clattered on my face and I fell, stunned by the sudden action. I hadn't seen him but it was Haverro's voice.

'Stay where you are, Thomas!' I yelled in despair. 'I have a gun too, you bastard.'

'Liar!' The pig was deriding me. I gave a quick peer over the margin, but hadn't the nerve to stay looking until the next firework lit us up for each other.

'Try coming up, then,' I shouted.

'You're not that stupid, Lovejoy,' he yelled up. 'A gun can be traced.'

'So can yours, you frigging killer.' There was still something wrong.

'Mine?' He actually laughed. 'Have a look at the bullet.'

I fumbled and found the crushed lead sphere. The bastard was using a percussion muzzle-loader. You fire, not an elongated bullet, but a round lead one. No marks are ever left save those of the impact. Therefore they are utterly untraceable. Black gunpowder down the muzzle and a lead sphere. A box of percussion caps for a few pence, and you can murder with a hell of a lot of noise but nothing traceable back to you, no matter how clever the CID's ballistics lads became. I found myself on my feet screaming fear and hatred down into the main rectangle.

'Bastard! Murderer! And you call yourself a doctor, you — '

A pop overhead. In the scarlet glare I saw him lean out from behind the rear wheel of the coach, long arm raised and glinting. I flung myself backwards as he fired and felt the wind slice my arm along its length from wrist to shoulder before the wall snickered a shower of dusty spicules on to my upturned face.

Almost gibbering with pain from my arm and terror, I scrabbled back into the alcove. He was across the way. On the ground, two galleries below. I tore off my jacket as best I could, lying on my back and ripping the stupid thing. Underneath I had this woollen pullover but couldn't find a loose thread with my quivering fingers. When you want your clothes to stay mended they unravel and perforate in all directions. When you want one to fall to bits they're like chain bloody mail. I could hear the bastard scuffling below, probably loading as fast as he could. I was almost sobbing with fear. I hauled off a sock instead and bit the top end with my teeth. I caught a woollen end and began hauling, unravelling the useless malicious wool like a maniac.

'Lovejoy?'

'What?' I made my voice as even and confident as I could, while yanking and jerking the sock into its original thread in terror, cursing and blaspheming under my breath.

'Lovejoy.' His voice sounded modulated, carefully not needing to shout any more now we both knew. 'I don't believe you have a gun at all.'

'No?'

'No.'

'Why not risk it, then? Come on up, you murdering bastard.'

'Don't go on about Henry, Lovejoy.' He sounded full of reproach. 'I feel bad enough as it is.'

'You have no sympathy from me, pig.' I'd got a mound of wool unravelled beside me. The Pythagorean Theorem. What the hell was it? The square on the hypotenuse of a right-angled triangle was equal to some bloody thing. Why don't teachers take more care with our education, the useless buggers? I was sobbing, bleeding from my shoulder, pulling like a maniac at the wool until there was nothing left of the sock and thinking that if the maniac killed me it was my old teacher's fault for not drumming his idiotic algebra into my thick skull hard enough. He'd been a lazy old swine.

'I'm coming up, Lovejoy.'

'I'll shoot you, Haverro. I'm warning you.'

'If you have a gun why didn't you shoot earlier?'

'Trying to give you a chance.'

'Liar.'

'Anyway you've muffed it. I'll fire if you move an inch.'

I'd lost the sodding frigging bullets, found them after a lunatic grovel in the dark recess. I reached up and jerked the typelist card down and bit its string through. My arm was stiffening, the useless rotten thing. Just when you need a limb it goes and gets itself shot to blazes.

The bullets were heavy and deformed. Easy to tie the cord from the cardboard notice round each until they dangled like battered cherries from a single pliant string stalk. It was about a foot long. Small, but it would have to do.

'Then you'd better be ready, Lovejoy.'

'Take one step, Haverro, that's all.'

I tied one end of my wool to the middle point of the cord and desperately passed the wool's entire length through my hands. The bastard was coming.

'Very well. Ready?'

In a glow, a mad spurt of oranges and crimsons, I saw him step swiftly from concealment and then dart back.

'No shot, Lovejoy?' he chuckled. 'Too fast for you?'

'A little, Haverro. Do it slower and you'll regret it.'

I'd reached the wool's limit. Surely to God it was long enough to reach the penduleum's wire. It felt like miles, but my hands were wet with sweat and shaking. Maybe I'd over-estimated. Anyhow, there wasn't any more. A sustained glow came, silver and blue this time. He ducked out, back, then emerged finally to stand erect by the coach's rear wheel. The glow faded. A few seconds till the next firework salvo lit the sky.

I tied the free end of the wool to my ankle and swung the homemade bolus. As long as I kept out of the way of the wool cord as it followed the bolus in its flight — I threw. A pause. The bullets clattered on the mosaic floor below. Missed. A sky flash came. Haverro had darted back again. I hauled on the wool to recover the bullets on their string. They cracked glass, scraped exhibits, but I kept hauling dementedly until I had them in my hand again.

'Who's there?' Haverro said, puzzled by the clattering.

'Some friends,' I said in a hoarse quaver. I'd fixed the position of the pendulum's metal flex and threw again. No clatter. I pulled slowly on the wool. For Christ's sake it hadn't to break. Not now the bullets on their cord had wrapped themselves round the pendulum wire.

'Who?' he exulted confidently.

'Police,' I lied. Maybe he'd believe me.

'Liar, Lovejoy. They were the bullets. The ones I fired.' He laughed and I heard him step confidently out. I gave way to fear, pulling on the wool feverishly until the pendulum bob crashed a glass stand over on the gallery beneath. 'Panicking now, Lovejoy?' he purred, enjoying himself. 'No place to run to, I'm afraid. So sorry.'

I reached out, felt the swing and grasped the lovely life-saving metal cord of the Galileo pendulum in my hand.

'Okay, Thomas,' I said. 'Stay there. I give in.'

'Come down here.' He was suspicious.

'Let me go.'

'Not a chance, Lovejoy.'

'You can have the Grail Tree.'

'I've already got it.' He sighed, sounding like they do when telling you the needle won't really hurt. But then doctors are always on the blunt end. 'Come on. Here or there.'

I had the wire. The lead weight was hanging somewhere below. Please God. It couldn't be caught in anything, could it? Not after all this. I bit through the wool and waited.

'I'll come, Thomas. To talk.' He'd never believe I'd surrender so near the thing we both coveted.

'Very well. To talk.' He sounded full of smiles.

'Promise?'

'I promise, Lovejoy.'

His footsteps sounded clearly on the mosaic. He was crossing the central area.

'Coming, then. Stay there.' With a prayer I let go and stood up. The wire jerked away and outwards under the weight of the hanging lead. I took as long as I could, noisily stamping and cursing. What if he wasn't in the centre? The pendulum would miss him every swing. Please make him stand there, just where the lead would hit him. At least knock him over, daze him maybe. Give me a chance. 'You shot my arm, Haverro.'

'I was always quite good, but of course I'm more used to

a modern shotgun.' His voice changed. 'Hurry up, Lovejoy.'

'Coming.'

I started down the stairs. The pendulum would swing and return, swing and return. If he moved there was still a chance, a faint chance for each swing. As long as the fireworks didn't light it up at the wrong moment. Please, fireworks, I prayed. Don't light up the macabre scene in time for him to get out of the way.

'Jimmo's next, Lovejoy,' he was saying as I reached the top of the lowest flight. 'It's a bit hard on him, of course. Natually, I'm sorrier – '

The sudden thud coincided with a burst of violet sky and the skittering sound of aerial snakes from several rockets. By the time I'd reached ground level the light had died and I couldn't see a thing. I crouched shivering behind the staircase waiting for the next glare. If he was still on his feet and it was some trick I'd just have to try rushing him, even though it would be hopeless because he would be expecting it. Anyway I only had one arm any use. There was no sound from him, no footsteps. Had I heard a clatter, a gun falling? I couldn't focus my mind any more.

The glare came and I screamed. Haverro's head was inches from mine on the ground, only his was crushed to a bloodied mess. I retched on to my own feet, quivering and heaving. Sweat dripped from my chin. I leaned back, sitting under the staircase. I'd done it. Now all I had to do was find the Grail Tree and keep out of the way of that bloody lethal pendulum.

The next burst showed me the case, lying near Haverro's body. I lifted it reverently, feeling its beautiful weight. Even in my ruinous condition the chimes it emitted shook me to my marrow. Whatever it was, it sang and pulsed inside its case stronger and with more exquisite peals than anything I'd ever met before.

I crossed to the main door, carefully walking round the edges of the rectangular mosaic for safety and carrying the case. He'd left the key in the lock after turning it – a wise move. Then nobody from outside can possibly enter, key or not. I wished I'd have thought of that.

I turned the key. 'Come in, Lisa, love,' I called, and in

came Lydia, pushing and scolding.

'Lovejoy!' she cried furiously. 'Exactly what have you been up to? I've been knocking for over an hour − '

I looked beyond her into the reddish haze. Nobody.

'Where's Lisa? I told Lisa −'

'She's gone.'

We went inside. I was still carrying the case. Lydia saw it. We could see each other's faces in the rose-red sky sheen. Distant cheers sounded. They'd lit the bonfire. Soon the big finale with the firework tableau. Sparks would be tumbling into the night sky. The procession would be circling, chucking torches into the flames. Some would show their bravado by dashing tangentially at the fire and throwing from close to, so as to show singed eyelashes for bragging at the drinking in another hour.

Lydia left me recovering at the bookstall and went to where I pointed. 'Mind the pendulum.' That is, she didn't go all the way. Merely paused half way over to the huddled mess, took one further courageous step and halted.

'Is it . . . ? Is it . . . dead?'

'Thomas. Yes.'

She returned, spectacles glinting redly like a menacing figure's eyes on a Frazetta oil.

'The police.'

'No.'

'Whatever you say, I shall phone them.' She looked about. 'There's a caretaker's phone along the furniture gallery.' And by God there is. I'd forgotten. That explained why Thomas had come in so quietly. Despite all his confidence he couldn't afford to trap me on Gallery Six. Clever old sod. Lydia had gone. It was easy to see in the firelight. I trailed after her as fast as possible though I was badly shaken. My arm was leaking and dripping drops alongside all the way up the stairs to where Lydia was scolding the telephone for lack of co-operation. There were printed instructions but hard to read.

'No, love.' I put my hand over the buttons.

'We *must*, Lovejoy.'

It was precisely then that I knew we were going to die after all. A dull boom echoed through the museum. I signalled frantically for her not to speak.

'It's only the fireworks, Lovejoy.' I'd have crippled her if she hadn't whispered. 'What's the matter?'

'Shh.' I listened. Somebody had entered the Castle. Somebody who had no key, but who had followed Haverro or Lydia. And who now was here. They'd locked the door, because murderers always do. I heard the squeak and that horrible rumble of the ancient lock. Fireworks crack, zoosh, fazz and pop. They never, never boom. It takes a Castle door to boom. Or a gun. Jesus, a gun.

'Stay here.' My fright spread to her. 'Shhh!' I pointed to her necklace which gave a soft rattle with every movement she made. Of all things it was Whitby jet, a lovely old 1830s carved effort. Why the hell did she come dressed up like that? To a fireworks outing in a park it was bloody ridiculous, high heels and stylish suit. 'Stop that frigging racket,' I hissed. She nodded, frightened now. Lydia held my hand but I shook her off angrily and crept along the gallery to the Civil War section where you can see over.

A figure was crouching over Haverro. Hair glistening, shoes gleaming and watch sparkling. Two rings flashed dull gold. I crawled away from the edge just as he glanced up and around, but maybe he had seen me. I rolled over on my side to see where Lydia was and why the hell she was creaking and rustling so much. She'd got one of her stiletto heels stuck in the bloody planks on the gallery floor.

'For Christ's *sake*!' I mouthed at her, and mimed taking a foot out and leaving the stupid shoe where it was. While she was at it I pulled her down and clawed the other shoe off as well. If she fell about when balanced on two she'd be uncontrollable wobbling on one. We crept on hands and knees into the Civil War Gallery as far as we could go. That meant under the ancient silent clock and its lopsided breastplate. Lydia's jet necklace ticked a series of low rattles against the Cromwellian cannon, making me grab her and stuff the absurd beads into her clothes in a frightened rage.

A creak from below. A second while we stayed rigid. Breathless. He was coming upstairs. A third. Then a pause, with a faint tock of metal on metal. He was loading the muzzle-loader. A sudden loud rattle and a roll. He'd dropped one of the spherical bullets. It had rolled down the steps and across the floor a short distance, but from the silence he wasn't worried. Therefore he had plenty. Thomas had come really well equipped and here came the evil geltie to reap the rewards.

I caught a faint glisten on the ceiling of the vaulted gallery. Lydia's ring, picking up a gleam from a last single rocketburst. I clutched her hand. She clutched me back gratefully but I twisted away and dragged the ring off.

'Diamond?' I mouthed. She gazed modestly down.

'Yes.' She pulled my ear close. 'From Preston's in the High Street — '

I don't believe it, I thought, marvelling. She'd tell me where you get spuds on discount next. That's women, and me terrified by maniacal killers everywhere I bloody well go. I crawled one-handed to the flintlock case. No flints, but the ingredients were there, almost. I put the diamond down the glass in a horrid screaming squeak loud enough to waken the dead. A creak again. He was on the first tier now, was looking stealthily along the galleries and listening for the next giveaway sound. What the hell. I rocked the diamond ring down the window again and a third time, leant hard with my useless hand and kneed it through into the case. Too much noise now to worry. I reached and got the two little beakers. Sulphur in one, saltpetre under the belljar because it gets sticky from collecting air moisture. No time to check they were chemically okay. I mixed them swiftly in the inverted belljar, stirring the powders with a finger.

'Gunpowder,' I whispered in Lydia's ear. 'Sulphur, charcoal and saltpetre.' I had only guessed the proportions roughly when helping to arrange the display, but fat chance of weighing anything at this stage.

'Charcoal?'

'Carbon,' I whispered, pleased at my one stroke of luck, the artist's charcoal drawing stick I'd brought as cover in case I got caught in the Temple crypts. 'I've got some,' and felt in my jacket pocket. Only I'd no jacket pocket, because I'd ripped my jacket off when I'd tried to unravel my pullover. And no jacket pocket meant no artists's stick of lovely charcoal. 'I've no fucking charcoal!' I screamed in an insane whisper into her aghast face. '*We've no frigging charcoal!*' Gunpowder won't go off without it, not properly. You only get a faint hiss and smoke everywhere. Friar Bacon knew that centuries back.

I grabbed Lydia, thinking maybe to make a run for it, but paused. Her necklace was under my hand. Beads. And jet. Jet burns, being fossilized carbon. Light and lovely precious jet.

'Gimme a nail file.'

'I beg your – '

'Nail file. Quick!' I heard her fumble in her handbag. It only took a few months while those horrible creaks went on one by one. The second-level railings were creaking now under his weight. The cold nail file. I rummaged under Lydia's clothes and yanked at the necklace.

'*Lovejoy*! This is certainly no time to – '

'Shhh!'

'We should go down and discuss – '

Women. I snapped the string and began filing madly at the jet, working crazily to get it shredded into one of the beakers. He was near by our level, with maybe a few steps to go. No more time. I groped for a flat stone place and crushed five or six of the larger beads under my heel, scraped the crushings into the beaker with the finer filings and poured the lot into the belljar. I stirred the nail file frantically, even trying like a fool to hold the finished gunpowder against the practically non-existent light to see its colour.

'Hold this,' I hissed. 'Upright. For Christ's sake don't drop it.'

I pulled on the cannon. It rumbled round. Twice I darted in front of it to check the alignment. With those old cannons, which nowadays always look absurdly small, the elevation's always a problem. I'd just have to guess. The closer he came, the better. I didn't like the thought of that. I snatched the belljar and tipped it clumsily down the barrel. If the thing was spiked or blocked in some way we'd had it. The ramrod was no problem. I had scores of the bloody things, all too thin by a mile. Still it had to do. Frantically I tapped and tapped until that solid feel came. Then the ball. The fifth one fitted, but with too much windage. Anyhow, it hadn't far to go. I snatched Lydia's blouse. Another squeak, but a piece of flimsy cloth to go down the barrel on top of the ball. I rammed the lot in, breaking the thin ramrod in the process, silently swearing and abusing everything in sight, demented.

The last sprinkle of gunpowder I'd kept for the touch-hole. I made sure the hole was clear with the tip of the nail file and poured it in.

'Match.' I held out my hand.

'I beg your – '

'A frigging match,' I screeched in a mad whisper. 'I want a frigging match.'

'I'm afraid I don't carry – '

'*Lighter*,' I hissed.

'I'm so sorry. I don't smoke – '

'Oooh.' The moan came from my very soul. Now I could blow the Castle to blazes we had no matches. The nearby flintlocks had no flints. Furniture? We were near the furniture gallery. Adjacent to my forged piece was a Sutherland table. On it was a tinder lighter, a small gadget resembling a pistol but acting exactly like a modern flint lighter. A wheel and a flint. I was up and rushing before I knew what I was doing. I snatched up the attendant's chair and smashed it through the window-case. God knows what damage it did to my lovely piece, but to break fragments over the genuine stuff would have been criminal. I grabbed for the tinder lighter. A blessed flint. I raced back, ducking low. A flash and a spatter. The swine shot at me. Lydia screamed.

'There's two of us, Leyde,' I howled as I ran. 'We'll get you.' A second shot. Glass fractured all around.

Over the landing I flung myself down beside Lydia, ripped at her blouse again and threw it away. I wanted the string bunched up.

'The necklace string!' I thought for a second I'd lost it but she had it. I just don't believe women sometimes. Lydia was passing the gentle hours by rethreading the remains of her necklace on its original cord. Screaming again as quietly as I knew how, I scattered the beads with a grab and folded the string.

'Dear me,' Lydia whispered. I screamed silent abuse and

hatred at her to keep out of the way.

Three clicks to adjust the flint and I was off, clicking sparks on to a folded piece of Lydia's blouse. He'd have to reload. My hands were trembling so much I was practically useless. Clicks shed sparks but it seemed an age before the lovely aroma of smouldering cloth arose. I put the cord in, still clicking sparks down.

It caught. There was a red erosion starting in the cloth. I held the string to the spreading spark and blew and blew. That pure delicious scent of smouldering string came and I subsided in ecstasy. I had it all together, the touch-match, the cannon and now the time. For that split second I didn't care. Not a damn. Even if Leyde finished ahead, I felt overjoyed I'd created a weapon from nothing under impossible circumstances. I looked up to see Lydia thoughtfully spreading the smouldering remains of her torn blouse on the cannon's barrel to beat it out. That restored me to sheer screeching terror.

'You'll explode the frigging thing!' I hissed, pulling it away and flinging it aside.

'But it was a present from — '

I pulled her to me by the throat and thrust my face furiously at hers.

'Lydia. One more fucking word from you. That's all.'

'Well, really!'

'*Shut up!*'

My rage gave way to terror. The paces were loud and uncontrolled now. There was plenty of gloom about, and we had most of what there was. But the fireglow was constant. Even the alcoves caught reflections. You could see the statues and the cases lit from the sky's dull red light. He couldn't miss seeing us.

'Stay over there. When the bang sounds, run.'

'Where?' she whispered.

'How the hell do I know where?' I hissed. 'If I knew that I'd already be there, you stupid — *Any* sodding where. Just run.'

'I only wanted to do the right thing, Lovejoy,' she whispered, offended. 'There's no need to —'

'Shhh.'

We crouched on either side of the cannon, immobile. I'd

scraped the spare grains into the touch-hole by feel, and had the burning string concealed in my hand. I reached over and squeezed Lydia's shoulder hard to say stay put. A few more paces. The gallery darkened even more. He was there. He'd come. Leyde's silhouette.

The double-barrelled muzzle-loader was at the slant. Probably a Greener, or maybe a later retailed Birmingham-proved Forsyth. Certainly it was a high--quality antique. At least there was that. He loomed in the arch leading to our gallery, waiting for his eyes to adjust. One pace more. I needed one step forward. I reached across to Lydia and pushed. She fell from her crouching position with a cry of alarm. He heard, turned slightly, saw, stepped forward. My string dipped into the hole. I fidgeted it round and round. Nothing. He raised his gun as the cannon cracked a deafening double sound. My leg was smashed between it and the wall. I was screaming now and openly as loud as I could go. Lydia was tugging feverishly at the cannon, of course the wrong way but we finally got it off me. She looked a mess but I suppose I was worse.

It had caught the fleshy part of my calf, miraculously leaving the bone alone. The skin was ripped in five or six places under the trouser leg. The whole place was shrouded in smoke.

I leant back against the wall. There was no point in looking for Bill Leyde. I didn't even give the space where he'd last stood a single glance.

It was Lydia who rescued it all from the jaws of Maslow. She got us both assembled, found my jacket and note-pad, and incidentals like a million miles of wool. And her shoes, nail file and bits of blouse. There was no point in rubbing fingerprints off anything. I'd been putting them all over the museum for years, at the request of the curator. I remembered that luscious case.

We were outside in the lovely air before I spoke.

'I'm going down to the fireworks, Lydia,' I told her. 'I have to stand there and let Maslow see me. Can you find him, or bring at least one of his merry men?'

'Bring him to the fireworks?'

'Where they set them off. Soon as you can. Say I have

some news for him.'

'Will you be all right?'

She helped me across the bridge on the terrace walk. We'd left the Castle door ajar after a lot of careful thought.

'Yes. We can't be seen together, you helping me along like a bloody walking wounded. Tell him I've an urgent message, that Jimmo's a witness to old Henry's killing by Dr Haverro.'

'I understand.'

'And don't say anything about being in the Castle. We've not been anywhere near, see?'

'Will you wait there for me?'

'Yes.' I saw her look long and hard. 'Promise, love,' I said, which seemed to satisfy her honest little innocent soul. 'One thing, Lydia. You *did* explain to Martha?'

'Exactly as you said.' She glowed in the firelight with pride of a job well done. 'This morning.'

'And only to Martha?'

'Yes. Her niece Dolly was *so* interested — '

'*Dolly was there too?*'

'Oh yes. We had such a lovely chat . . . ' Her voice faded. 'Was that all right?' she asked anxiously.

Which explained how Bill Leyde had learned. It wasn't thick stupid old Honkworth who was monitoring the search for the Grail Tree. It was the geltie, clever, quiet and self-effacing. With Dolly to collect the essential details.

I looked into Lydia's face. After all, I'd ruined her lovely necklace. And I just hadn't the heart.

'Yes. You did fine, love. Exactly right.'

'I *knew* you'd be pleased,' she said brightly. 'Have you change for the phone, please?'

'Press the emergency button,' I said brokenly.

'Oh, how exciting! I've never done that before!'

I drew breath. 'Look, Lydia,' I got out. 'Sorry about losing my temper in there so much. It's just that . . . well, I don't really see the need of dying.'

'I quite understand, darling.'

'Eh?'

She checked me over once more and trotted eagerly off. I watched her go, marvelling.

That's what I like, I thought bitterly. Help. I limped

down towards the huge crowd and the fireworks. I needed to get round the back of the tableau where the reserve firework cases would be stored.

That Fire Night's big finish was marred only by an accident in which one of the many helpers at the fireworks lit the trailing blue fuse prematurely. It was reported that this caused a series of explosions in which the miscreant, one Lovejoy — a well-known local antiques dealer of Lovejoy Antiques, Inc. — received injuries inflicted as a result of standing too near to the main firework tableau. Reports were profuse and critical. Injuries sustained, the reporters said, were to his left arm and right leg, cuts in several places, and some facial injuries. He was allowed home after emergency treatment in the casualty department of the County Hospital. Doctors said no permanent defects were anticipated. Lovejoy has since apologized, a Festival spokesman informed reporters, to the display organizers and especially to the Silver Band who were not in position in time to play the required music appropriate for the final tableau which took place five minutes ahead of schedule. Lovejoy had inadvertently caused the tableau and six reserve cases of fireworks to ignite without adequate supervision.

    The miscreant when apologizing admitted his folly, but explained it had been the result of an over-enthusiastic desire to help. Lovejoy Antiques, Inc. had, it was reported, promised a donation to next year's firework festival. Festival organizers were preparing a report on existing safety precautions in the vicinity of the bonfire site. A report by the fire services was in preparation.

Nice touch that, I thought, being driven home by Lydia from the hospital, telling the reporters I'd see Lovejoy Antiques, Inc. would make a donation, though where the money would come from . . . I was covered in traces of firework powder which would nullify any sinister forensic investigation of my clothes for traces of gunpowder. My injuries accounted for, I waved to Maslow glowering at the hospital gates, but only to show him my bandages. He didn't wave back, the heartless slob. That's the modern copper for you, always losing sight of justice.

Fair's fair after all. It may not be legal and it may be miles away from proper justice, but fair's very definitely and unmistakably fair. Which is not too bad, as the antiques game goes.

CHAPTER XXI

Dawn was coming as we arrived at the cottage. I staggered out of the car and turned to thank Lydia, but she'd descended too.

'Er, well, Lydia . . . ' I began.

'Inside,' she said. I stared. She had my key. Somehow she'd nicked it from my coat. She scooped a letter from the doormat. No stamp, I noticed.

'If you'll just leave the case,' I suggested, limping after her.

'Sit there.' She dialled, leaving the door ajar so I could hear into the hall. 'Hello, Mother?' Pause. 'Yes. Cynthia and Mirabelle are here. Yes. Flight Five Nine.' Pause 'Oh, I expect a couple of hours. They haven't announced yet.' Pause. 'Of *course* I'll write. Don't fuss. Bye.' Click. Burr. I listened warily. Cynthia and who?

She came in and started taking my shoes off

'Er, look, Lydia . . . '

'I'm going to the Channel Isles,' she said happily.

'Oh, good. Er, have a good holiday – '

'*Stupid,*' she said scathingly. 'I'm not *really* going. That was only a . . . front for Mother's sake.'

'You're not?'

'I'm staying here.'

I thought this over while she felt for hot water in the alcove and complained in a mutter when everything ran cold.

'Er, Lydia.'

'Yes?'

'What happened to Lisa?'

Without turning, Lydia pointed. The unstamped letter lay on the divan. I opened it with one hand and my teeth. From Lisa, saying ah well maybe some other time but good luck and ending with three kisses. Somebody had given her the push. I wondered who that somebody could be, watching Lydia boil some water. The situation wore all the signs that Lovejoy Antiques, Inc. was going to be washed and darned to within an inch of his life. Amid the preparations I tottered to the clamouring phone for an unpleasant conversation.

'Lovejoy?' Lydia's mother. 'Sorry to ring so early.'

'Oh. Look — ' My anxious explanation was cut short.

'No need to account for Lydia's absence, Lovejoy,' she purred. 'Last evening she explained everything. I ought to say I've seriously misjudged you, Lovejoy. You were so *right* to suggest Lydia takes a holiday with her old schoolfriends, to give her time to . . . well, adjust to a new occupation.' I quickly realized I was being praised.

'Not at all,' I said, gently kicking the door to. 'I began to perceive signs of a certain . . . attachment, shall we say? It seemed wise to — '

'I do agree. So wise,' she breathed. I grew reckless, remembering my previous score with her.

'Anyway,' I cruised on. 'I find that maturity is something far too lacking these days — '

'I'm so pleased to hear you say that, Lovejoy. Youth is all very well, but — '

'Well,' I said happily. 'I'd better get on. Thank you for ringing.'

'Not at all.' She didn't ring off. 'I . . . I may be out your way later. Today or tomorrow. Only passing through to see a friend for coffee, that sort of thing. I may call in and thank you personally.' Then she rang off.

I watched the receiver in my hand but it just looked blank.

'Who was it?' Lydia asked, fetching a bowl to the table. 'Put your hands to soak in that. I'm going to wash your face and comb your thatch.'

'Er, Tinker,' I said. 'He's found an early penny-farthing

bicycle for sale.'

'How nice.' She put my hands in the water. 'Stay like that till I say take them out. I'm going to unpack.' I soaked as she instructed.

'Unpack?' I thought a bit. 'Clothes?'

'Of course, you silly,' she said briskly. 'Does it get very cold in the cottage at night? I've brought an extra blanket for us, till I get used to it.'

'Er, look, Lydia — '

'No.' She sat with me. That seductive lurch again. I was getting to know it. '*You* look for once, Lovejoy.' She faced me, serious and determined. 'I don't pretend to be Cleopatra. But lately I have been examining my, well, appearance. I have come to the conclusion that my figure is really quite presentable, even attractive. It pleases you to watch me. I've already observed that. Of course there's a problem.'

'Which is?'

'Inexperience,' she said gravely. 'I can't pretend my experience in . . . in *carnal* matters is very profound. But my willingness will, I anticipate, be equalled by your patience.'

'It will?' My head was spinning.

'Let's hope so, Lovejoy.' She rose but I pulled her back with a wet hand.

'Hang on. I usually have . . . other visitors.'

I'd been thinking of Jean Evans, if she ever cooled down. And Betty, who didn't need cooling at all. And Lydia's mother, who wanted to call for reasons as yet unspecified. And Jessica, who was keen to balance our respective books. And Sarah, whom I liked now I'd got used to all that high breeding. And . . . and Lydia had a scrap on her hands if she stayed. I sighed. Some days things are just too much. Lydia was smiling.

'I'm quite looking forward to those confrontations,' she informed me earnestly. 'In any arrangements between kindred souls, disputations appear an inevitable characteristic. Under your influence, Lovejoy, I am persuaded that attraction is inseparable from conflict — '

There was more of this junk.

'No,' I said finally. 'No, Lydia. I couldn't stand the

aggro. You're lovely, but – '

'Oh, but you can,' she said, all smiles. 'I'm going to be good for you, Lovejoy. In every way. You can't send me away. Or else.' I thought about that, but she had no cards left to play.

'Or else what?' I asked, narked.

She was smiling, absolutely confident.

I suddenly stood up, yelping at the pain. It had gone. 'The case.' The little box carrying the Grail Tree. I'd kept hold of it until I was taken into Casualty. Then I'd given it to Lydia for safety. 'Where is it?' I screamed. 'What have you done with it?'

'Safe, darling.' She put her arms around me happily. 'Perfectly safe. I'm keeping it for you.'

'*Where is it?*' I sank, groaning. 'Oh, hell fire.'

'In a month you'll be convinced of my . . . attributes, darling,' Lydia said calmly. 'If I haven't persuaded you that I am exactly what you need, Lovejoy, I will fully deserve to be banished. A month is a perfectly fair trial period. Do you agree, darling?'

I thought and thought while Lydia waited, smiling compassionately. There was no other way.

'And then you'll give it me, no matter what?'

'I promise,' she said seriously, placing her hands on her heart. I watched her hand and her heart. She did have a lovely heart. I swallowed. 'Agreed, Lovejoy?'

I managed to say it third go. 'Agreed, Lydia.'

'Lydia, *darling*,' she corrected.

'Lydia, darling,' I said at last. She clapped her hands delightedly. 'There's only one thing, love,' I asked. 'Will you, er, answer the door when people call? I don't feel up to many visitors just yet.'

Trapped, I listened helplessly to her singing as she brewed up, honestly not knowing whether to hate or admire her. You can't beat a woman for trickery.

I don't think they'll ever learn to be honest and fair-minded, like me.